All
GOD's
Children

CHRISTIAN

JEW

ROMAN

All God's Children

The tumultuous story of A.D. 31–71: how the first Christians challenged the Roman world and shaped the next 2000 years; by James D. Snyder.

© 1999 by James D. Snyder; Pharoscan, Inc. All rights reserved. Published 1999.
Published by Pharos Books / SAN: 253-0317
Pharoscan, Inc.
8657 SE Merritt Way
Jupiter, Florida 33458-1007
(561) 575-3430

Cover & interior design and production © Brian Taylor; Pneuma Books. For info, call: (410) 658-9497 or email: pneuma@eclipsetel.com Set in Adobe Spectrum $^{11}/_{13}$.

Copyediting by Janis Holmberg, Persuasive Pen.

Illustrations on pages 638–643 © Diana Nickels; Pear Design.
Maps on pages 644–650 © Brian Taylor; PneumaGraphics (except where indicated)

Printed in the United States of America by McNaughton & Gunn, Saline MI
05 04 03 02 01 00 99   7 6 5 4 3 2 1

Publisher's Cataloging-in-Publication
(Provided by Quality Books, Inc.)

Snyder, James D.
  All God's children : the tumultuous story of A.D. 31–71 : how the first Christians challenged the Roman world and shaped the next 2000 years : an historical novel by James D. Snyder. -- 1st ed.
  p. cm.
  Includes bibliographical references.
  LCCN: 99-96082
  ISBN: 0-9675200-0-2

  1. Church history--Primitive and early church, ca. 30-600-Fiction. 2. Christianity and other religions--Roman--Fiction. 3. Rome--Civilization--Christian influences--Fiction I. Title.

PS3569.N8915W44 1999   813'.54
                                 QBI99-1695

The tumultuous story of A.D. 31–71

CHRISTIAN
All
GOD's
Children
ROMAN
JEW

How the first Christians challenged the Roman
world and shaped the next 2000 years.

An historical novel by

JAMES D. SNYDER

Published by

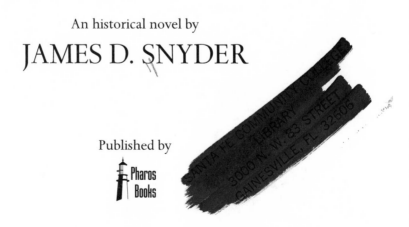

Pharos
Books

Lucky is he who can say he has been happily married for 42 years.
But what an added delight it is to find that your mate is also your most enthusiastic
travel companion, skilled photographer, discerning editor and honest critic.

To Sue, my wife and best friend.

ACKNOWLEDGEMENTS

BRIAN TAYLOR, Principal of Pneuma Books in Rising Sun, MD, is not only a conscientious book designer, but has been a valuable advisor throughout the process and a paragon of patience with an author who had a hard time learning that spending one's life publishing magazines has little to do with the world of book production. I thank him for coordinating this project from start to finish, as well as Diana Nickels of Lantana, FL, for her illustrations of Roman luminaries, and Jeanne Koepsell-Whirry of Green Lake, WI, for her assistance in the construction of ancient maps.

I would like to add my thanks to several clergymen who piqued my curiosity in church history at an early age and who have since furthered my education many times over many Sundays. They begin with my late uncle Ralph Hax, a Lutheran minister with callings in Detroit and Defiance, OH. Others include the Revs. Carl Cooper, Richard Grear and John W. Sonnenday of the Immanuel Presbyterian Church in McLean, VA; Rev. John Shaw of the First Congregational Church of Boca Raton, FL, and Dr. Patrick Shaffer of the First United Presbyterian Church of Tequesta, FL.

For reading the manuscript for historical accuracy, I offer my sincere thanks to Prof. John Freely of the University of the Bosphorus in Istanbul, Turkey, and to Gary J. Johnson, Associate Prof. of History at the University of Southern Maine in Portland.

BUT EQUALLY IMPORTANT in the process were my wife Sue and sister Christine Moats. Both read and critiqued the entire manuscript from the standpoint of an intelligent, curious book lover who simply wants to learn more about an important era in human history that impacts so largely on their own heritage. It is primarily for people like these that *All God's Children* was written.

CONTENTS

Senators: However ancient any institution seems,
once upon a time it was new!
— *Claudius*

The subject of this book began as a casual inquiry and led to a 20-year odyssey that took me to nearly all of the places you will read about. What made it so absorbing was the growing conviction at each step along the way that the years A.D. 31–71 were probably the most dramatic in the history of western civilization and without a doubt the most crucial years in understanding the underpinnings of its two major religions.

Obviously, no story of this magnitude simply "begins" precisely in a certain year – especially when it spans 3,000 miles, three cultures and a 40-year period 2,000 years ago. I will begin this one with Octavian Cæsar Augustus, who had already been dead for 17 years by A.D. 31, but whose legacy would affect everyone who lived throughout this story.

However, we can set the stage aptly enough in modern Rome. Just a mile or so northwest of the Forum ruins, where the stone walls lining the Tiber meet the Ponte Cavour and dozens of smelly buses take tourists across the river to the Vatican, squats a government-gray building with as much distinction as a traffic island.

Inside is a marble monument that was modest even by imperial standards when erected in Augustus' reign. But it may have symbolized his proudest achievement. Named the Ara Pacis, or Altar of Peace, it was built simply to celebrate having achieved what Augustus deemed to be lasting peace and stability. The intricate carvings around its marbled sides depict the happy members of the imperial family and their cheerful retainers from many lands all sacrificing to the gods of peace and plenty.

You'll need this reminder when you begin reading of the horrible acts and unspeakable cruelties that ensued at Rome's hands during A.D. 31–71, because things were not always so.

ix

Next, let us cross the street to a square block containing a circular ruin that might have been an arena or warehouse that was shelled in World War II and never rebuilt. A few evergreens remain around the fringes, but they are difficult to admire in a sea of empty bottles from idlers and litter from passing cars. A simple metal sign marks it as the Mausoleum of Augustus.

Let us imagine it just shortly after the emperor's death and deification in A.D. 14.

We stand in front of a perfectly round wall of white marble. At a second level atop the walls, as on the second layer of a wedding cake, stands a grove of slim evergreens. In its center is the mausoleum itself, with the circular roof topped by a gilt-bronze statue of the blond Augustus in his handsomest years.

At street level, we see the morning sun casting long shadows on the pink obelisks that stand at the entrance. And just inside we see the bronze tablets that describe the testimonial of Cæsar Augustus during a rule that encompassed 55 years:

> At the age of nineteen I raised an army which liberated the Republic...About 500,000 citizens were under military oath to me...I was acclaimed imperator twenty one times...I was ranking senator for 40 years...have been Pontifex Maximus, Augur, member of the College of Fifteen for performing sacrifices, member of the College of Seven for conducting religious banquets...

> I gave gladiatorial shows three times in my own name and five times in the names of my sons or grandsons...I extended the frontiers of all the provinces of the Roman people on whose boundaries were peoples not subject to our empire.

> In my sixth and seventh consulships, after I had put an end to the civil wars, having attained supreme power by universal consent, I transferred the state from my own power to the control of the Roman Senate and people. For this service I received the title of Augustus...When I held my thirteenth consulship, the Senate, the equestrian order and the entire Roman people gave me the title of "father of the country" and decreed that this title should be inscribed in the vestibule of my house...[1]

And so forth. Had the average Roman of that time been allowed to inscribe those bronze tablets, he probably would have added that Augustus, despite all the great wealth available to him, lived in a relatively modest home and governed graciously. His dress was as simple as the occasion would allow and his manner was calm and mild.

He governed with forbearance, as well, our common man would continue. He accepted criticism with patience. And no citizen – save perhaps some deserving members of his own household – lost a night's sleep worrying that he might be banished or flung into the Tiber for making a careless remark.

He was generous from the beginning, when he shared with citizens the spoils of the civil war that brought him power, to the end, when his estate bequeathed the million or so residents of Rome what was probably over $20 million in today's currency. During his reign, when leading citizens left him portions of their estates in the usual gesture of respect, he usually repaid the sums to their children with interest when they became of age. He also rendered an annual accounting of public finances, a practice that his successors, to the empire's detriment, saw fit to overlook.

Let's also visit the Mausoleum of Augustus as it would have looked at the end of our story in A.D. 71. We'll assume that the visitor's gate has been unlocked by a young Augustale, one of the priests of the cult of deified emperors who oversees sacred places like this. We now proceed up the entranceway to the upper level, through the grove of evergreens. We are now inside the mausoleum rotunda with the great statue of Augustus directly over us. All around us are the galleries containing the urns and ashes of the Julio-Claudian family:

- the emperor's wife, Livia, who outlived him by 15 years;
- his sister, Octavia, once wed to and shed by Marcus Antonius;
- his grandsons Marcellus, Gaius and Lucius, all heirs who died in the flower of their youth;
- Agrippa, his lifelong partner in building and soldiering, then ultimately his adopted son;
- Drusus, son of Livia;
- Germanicus, son of Drusus;
- Tiberius, younger brother of Drusus and adopted son of Augustus;
- the poor deranged Gaius Caligula;
- and Claudius, the lame, stammering family embarrassment until he, too, became emperor and managed to rule for 14 years.

This site symbolizes both the 55 years of peace under Augustus and the 40 years of awful turmoil that followed. While history can thank Octavian Cæsar Augustus for the strength and genius that produced his golden age, it can also indict him for creating an enterprise that required greater management skills than possessed by any of the lesser mortals who succeeded him.

All these, who so often schemed together and/or scorned one another and strew so many broken bodies and families and fortunes in their own tortured paths, now sleep quietly in the same house. And in its strange way, those in this "house" also symbolize both the strength and essence of the period. They enabled the world of Rome to endure. And the world somehow endured in spite of them.

Now let us complete the tour. Cross the Ponte Cavour to the other side of the Tiber and within a minute you are soon swept up in the immensity of St. Peter's Basilica, embodying the grandeur of today's Rome as it glistens after having been scrubbed and polished for the 2000th Jubilee Year of Christianity.

Finally, if you head south for a short distance and take the bridges across Tiber Island, you will be at the foot of an unpretentious gray synagogue housing an active congregation. This particular building was rebuilt in the 19th century, but on the same spot a synagogue has stood since even before the reign of Augustus when the neighborhood was a ghetto of Jewish leather workers and tradesmen. It stands as a living symbol of pride, independence and endurance through unimaginable adversity.

. . . .

AT THE BEGINNING of our 40-year period, the Roman empire encompassed about 54 million persons, including nearly 7 million Jews and probably fewer than 2,000 devout followers of Jesus. At the end of it one can guess the number of Christians at closer to 100,000. Why, in this well-ordered empire with its many gods, idols and temples to choose from, did the Jews cling so stubbornly to their nameless monotheistic deity and empty temple sanctuary despite obstacles that ranged from dietary inconveniences to certain death? And why did the even more radical Christians (in the eyes of Rome at least), make their choice at even greater personal peril?

Discovering those answers is what this book is all about. The only way to find them is to excavate through layers of centuries: back before there were popes, cathedrals, pogroms, reformations, inquisitions, crusades, schisms and saints — back even 200 years before the emperor Constantine declared himself a Christian and all but made Christianity the Roman Empire's official religion. Only by scraping away the patina of time can we appreciate that the reason why so many people wholeheartedly embraced a Jewish prophet whose path had led only to an ugly crucifixion was that they had personally seen him and/or knew others who had.

What keeps so many intelligent, otherwise curious people from discovering more about this period on their own is simply that it's such a daunting chore. One finds, for instance, that the 21 epistles of the New Testament aren't organized chronologically and that scholars still debate who wrote many of them. The works of Josephus, the indispensable Jewish historian of the time, consume over 1,000 pages of small print and archaic prose. Linking an event to a specific year is often difficult because first-century writers didn't assign numerals to years, instead identifying an event as happening "in the consulship of" one, two or three Roman senators who may or may not have left us something more than their names.

And those very names were often maddeningly similar. For example, many nobles took the name Agrippa (after Cæsar Augustus' illustrious deputy) while many wives and daughters of all nationalities were named Agrippina. Adding to the confusion is that the careers of great personages over this 40-year period can be explained only by parading on-stage countless sons, slaves, scribes, soldiers and other supporting actors.

Thus, I have seen my chief task as sorting and assembling this information so that you will be spurred along your route of discovery rather than feeling that you are alone digging through a 2,000-year-old archeological site with a teaspoon. To this end I have used the following tools:

1. The book is narrated by an ex-slave named Attalos, whose ancestors were from Pergamum in Asia Minor (now Turkey), and whose slave days were spent largely in Alexandria, Egypt. He writes from his adopted home of Rome during the years A.D. 79–81 as he looks back over 40 years that shook his world. Attalos lived at a time when the first eyewitness accounts of Jesus and letters of his apostles were being assembled in print. Attalos serves as your constant reminder that there was no perspective beyond that — no popes, cathedrals and all, as I have already noted.

2. The story is told chronologically in three books. By using numbered years for chapter headings, I have broken the "rules" for your convenience. Moreover, no one writing in this period actually thought in terms of B.C. and A.D.

    I believe that chronology is by far the most important determinant of historical events, and the most logical way to explain them. Should this seem like stating the obvious, consider that many histories are organized into chapters on economics, politics, sociology and the like. For example, most works on the apostle Paul tend to be analyses of his positions on various theological issues, all of which flit back and forth across timelines of his travels and writings. I believe the best way to understand the motives and actions of Paul or anyone is to realize where he was at the time and what events were apt to color his thinking as he peered into an uncertain future.

    Organizing that chronology was the most intricate and time-consuming task. Although this may be the most detailed chronology of A.D. 31–71 ever compiled, I readily acknowledge that conjecture and/or scholarly dispute loom large over these years — especially in the case of early Christian history. Thus, whenever the narrator, Attalos, is not on firm ground, he lets you know it.

In that regard, you should note in advance that the greatest of all uncertainties are those surrounding the final days and deaths of Peter and Paul. I have concluded that the oral traditions, which the Catholic Church has largely adopted, are the most likely scenario, and these are further explained in the *Epilogue*. To a lesser extent, debate continues over the year of Jesus' crucifixion. Most scholars have narrowed the probabilities to either Friday, April 7, A.D. 30 or Friday, April 3, A.D. 33. I have used the former.

3. I have done everything possible to spare you unnecessary "begats," characters with confusing names and rambling footnotes. Direct passages from ancient writers are presented in contrasting type, and you will find the sources listed in the *Endnotes* at the back of the book. Also in the appendix is a list of the places mentioned in the text and their present names.

You will also find several maps as well as liberal use of navigational directions and distances in miles. The intent is to help you appreciate, for example, how difficult it was for Paul to walk across Asia Minor or how relatively easily one could board a ship at Cæsarea and sail to a wide choice of Greek ports. Another purpose is to demonstrate how closely people of all nationalities interacted and passed on news.

The subject of money also looms large in the book, for the simple reason that people thought and talked about it just as much as they do today. Although many client states had their own coinage (for example, the Jewish *shekel*[2]) the prevailing monetary units were the Roman *as, sesterce* and *denarius*. In general, four *as* comprised a *sesterce* and four of these a *denarius*. It took roughly 6,000 *denarii* to make a silver *talent*.

For convenience sake, one might roughly equate a *sesterce* to today's U.S. quarter (25¢) and the denarius to $1. But precise comparisons are frustrating for several reasons. Cash was less crucial to ancient economies because most households produced more of their own goods and bartered for trade than today. Although the *as* (6.25¢ by the above reckoning) would buy six loaves of bread, it doesn't follow that an *as* should be valued at $6 just because we may pay a $1 for a loaf of bread today. The reason is that the value of human labor was more akin to that in today's least developed economies. A typical Roman soldier, for example, earned 900 *sesterces* a year. And to further complicate comparisons, the value of that pay would have been worth more in A.D. 31 and perhaps one-third less by A.D. 71. The reason: inflation took its toll then as it does now.

· · · · · · · · · ·

FINALLY, please keep in mind that there is nothing in these pages that did not actually happen according to someone who lived at the time or not long afterwards. Everything comes from the same primary sources that await all historians: The Bible (Revised Standard Version), the Jewish historians Josephus and Philo, and the Roman historians Tacitus, Suetonius and Dio Cassius. Among what one might label "supporting sources" are works by those such as the Roman philosopher-statesman Seneca, the early Christian bishop Eusebius, the biographer Philostratus (his two volumes on the philosopher Apollonius) and the Roman diarist Pliny the Younger. I have also drawn on several literary figures who wrote at the time, including Livy, Martial, Lucan and Seneca (the latter being listed twice because he was also a playwright).

The lone exceptions to the above statement are the "Letters from Rome" by the ex-slave Attalos, which appear at the beginning of each of the three books and following Book III. Attalos and the characters he addresses are fictitious. However, the events he describes (such as the eruption of Mount Vesuvius and the first attempts to develop the modern book, or "codex" format) actually happened in the times described.

You will soon read that the fictitious Attalos made his living as a book publisher. Scholars agree that Mark, the first of the gospels, was probably published sometime between A.D. 65 and 70. They agree that the letters of Paul were probably first assembled and published sometime during A.D. 80–90. Thus, if one were to speculate on who would have been the most logical person to compile and publish such works, why not an existing book publisher who realized a new market in the rapidly growing Christian community?

I give you Attalos.

~ JDS ~

LETTER FROM ROME — MAY, A.D. 79

To My cousin and partner Eumenes back home in Pergamum, my fondest greet-ings. And a warm embrace to your wife Polias and your enigmatic offspring Epi-darus, in whose hands the survival of our pimple of a dynasty would seem to rest.

I affirm that I am well and even allowing myself to feel a bit jubilant! But first I ask that you extend a family welcome to Diodoros, the young carrier of this letter and the heavy trunk he has sagged beneath and guarded for so long. Yes, this is the very Diodoros I mentioned to you three years ago when he became an apprentice at our fledgling bookstore and scriptorium in Rome. He has since become my trusted assistant and has the skills to do you much good in Pergamum. So I ask that you in-vite Diodoros into your home for supper, and then, as soon as you can, help him find decent lodgings.

Why spend all that money to send Diodoros in person when I could have shipped this "cargo?" What's in those bundles? A portion, I assure you, dear partner, is your share of the profits to date. As for the remaining contents, well, right now I know you are far more interested in my gossip from Rome than about some mere bundles that could make you the wealthiest book publisher in the Asian province and one of its leading citizens!

The business at my end of the partnership had been steady but unspectacular until recently. Just as you have proven that Asians and Greeks will buy books on the various temples and travel sites in Italy, I have justified our expectation that Roman families and libraries will pay for well-done guidebooks on similar sites along the Ægean. Our little shop in the Argiletum doesn't exactly compare to the emporia of Dorus or the Sosius Brothers on the Street of Booksellers, but we have our little niche and the scriptorium is keeping very busy.

I have now taken an apartment in the Subura, which is just a half-mile walk from the Argiletum and a joy to me for reasons that might escape you with your roomy villa and olive grove. The whole time I labored at the Tabularium during Nero's reign, I lived in one room or another in somebody's lodging house. And even when I became in charge of the Octavian library I slept in a converted storeroom in order to save the money for our little venture on the Street of Booksellers. Now, having four rooms is like being Nero in his Golden House. Oh, to be sure, I keep the doorway and the shutters unpainted and rough-looking so the neighbors in the courtyard won't be covetous. But inside, the light from the outer wall is ample and my third-story windows look out towards the new Baths of Titus and that interminable construction project, the Flavian Amphitheater. Moreover, I have haunted second-hand shops with a discerning-enough eye to have fetched a lovely old Minerva figurine and some other small statuary that, when impeccably arranged, casts beguiling reflections that play off the lamplight at night. Allow me to boast enough to relate that one recent dinner guest said she felt "as if I'm in a miniature palace on the Palatine."

Yes, yes, you say, but what about those bundles Diodoros brought? I'm getting there. I just told you that the scriptorium is "very busy," but in fact it's a confused jumble. Remember that small upstairs space, the one that we were renting out to the tailor when you first visited? Right now we have six copyists up there all bumping elbows and getting ink on each other. And the light is so bad that some of them prefer to sit outside at makeshift tables and risk some passerby spattering their scrolls with mud — or worse!

What I am trying to say is that we are at a crossroads in this business. One path leads to growth and opportunity. Admittedly, I myself brought this about in recent

2

weeks by deciding to try something different. Remember how many people devoured
The Civil War when Lucan first wrote it? Well, as you may know, Nero banned the
book and soon forced this young man of not quite 30 years to open his veins. I mention
all this because three months ago one of our frequent customers walked into the shop
and matter-of-factly asked if we'd make him three copies of The Civil War.

Now don't faint, Eumenes. This man is one of Rome's wealthiest merchants and
a patron of poets and publishers. His request was made so routinely that I said
without any hesitation, "Well, why not?" After all, the book was banned 14 years
ago and it wasn't because of the book or the subject. It was all because Nero
thought Lucan's poetry rivaled his own (what an insult!) and because this passionate young Spaniard got himself embroiled in that famous conspiracy plot with
Calpurnius Piso. And it wasn't as if I were being asked to publish a new and
untested commodity. If this leading citizen isn't afraid to own a copy, why should I
worry about manufacturing one?

So did we produce the three copies? Well, you'd be the first to say that would be
a waste of time when one reader can dictate to six copyists as easily as three. So, no,
we made 15, three for the customer and 12 for the store. And you'll probably be as
amazed as I was when I tell you that we sold them all within two weeks. What's
more, we got 200 sesterces apiece, which of course is like selling two dozen of our
Pilgrim's Guide to the Ephesian Temple of Artemis.

What I'm taking too long to tell you, dear cousin (who is more like a brother to
me), is that we now have the patron we have sought for so long! And, yes, he is that
same shopper, a man I will now refer to only as "Literato." He came back to the shop
a couple of weeks later and was amazed to learn about Lucan's good fortune to be reborn with our midwifery. Pretty soon we were in earnest conversation about the possibilities for publishing other luminaries and promising authors. I wish you could
meet him because he quickly sized up the way things are on the Street of Booksellers
and because he agrees with what you and I have been saying all these years. He and
other high-placed friends are sick of the high prices charged by the "Argiletum Oli-

3

garchy" and they are bored with the same old offerings. The Sosius Brothers sell Horace over and over; with Quintus Atticus it's Cicereo ad nauseum while Dorus continues scribbling his Seneca day after day, and so forth down the street. What Romans really want are new works written in this refreshing era of freedom. These old-time publishers merely cringe and roll their eyes and whisper about what happened to brave publishers under Tiberius and Caligula and Nero; but thanks to the sensible Vespasian (he becomes even better with age) we have now had almost a decade of civilized, common-sense government, and I truly believe that the young Titus will give us even more decades of the same when his time comes.

I'm now getting nearer to those bundles Diodoros brought. Each of the five sets of scrolls in the trunk that accompanied Diodoros includes specific instructions; but I want to prepare you for the fact that some of these works will be different from the tourist books we are accustomed to producing. For instance, Literato is also a patron of one Martial, a droll denizen of the taverns who has been penning epigrams around town for years, but who will soon become famous if Literato has his way and publishes them as an anthology for the private libraries of sophisticated, wealthy readers.

Epigrams, you ask? Yes: little verses for all occasions, such as this one for publishers like us:

> You blame my verse; to publish you decline;
> Show us your own, or cease to carp at mine.

Here's one from Martial for you and your copyists:

> A rumor says that you recite
> As yours the verses that I write.
> Friend, if you'll credit them to me
> I'll send you all my poems for free;
> But if as yours you'd have them known,
> Buy them, and they'll become your own.

Other publishing possibilities are all over Rome — and no doubt in a dozen Pergamums as well. For instance, how would you like to copy a manuscript that could yield 250 pages and maybe ten scrolls? That could happen because Literato knows of a certain Josephus, a Jewish priest and general who was brought back by Vespasian after the destruction of Jerusalem. Reportedly, he is finishing work on a history of the Jewish war for the consumption of Vespasian's court, the Senate and the multitude of veterans who sit around in the taverns telling how they single-handedly vaulted the temple walls in Jerusalem. Literato is going to write a friend of his in the imperial household to see if we can establish an introduction to this Josephus.

If that doesn't work out, then consider Quintilian. You may have gotten word out there in your provincial pastures last year when Vespasian appointed him the first official, state-paid Teacher of Rhetoric in Roman history. Literato has already collected several of Quintilian's speeches, which strike me as even windier than Cicero's. Now, cousin, I don't think the rabble of Rome is going to gobble up the rhetoric of Quintilian, but our new patron feels that a handsome anthology of such speeches will find its way into private libraries from Rome to Antioch to Ephesus.

At this point, my always-cautious, cynical partner, I can see your eyes blinking like hummingbird wings when you get anxious and flustered. In fact, I will now anticipate three matters that have you worried.

First, just who is this mysterious patron? Why do you call him Literato *and not by name? My reply: he is very reputable and trustworthy. If he has asked that we not use his name, I will not quibble. Frankly, I think he wants to shield his good rep-utation and find another publisher to invest in should you and I squander our good fortune and get tossed out of the Argiletum. And, yes, there's no reason he should suffer should some new book of ours incur the displeasure of someone in the palace. Now don't get excited. It's I who would be flayed and flung into the Tiber, not you or Literato.*

Next, are we giving up our books for pilgrims and vacationers? Why, not at all, good Eumenes! These will continue to provide our daily bread and wine. In fact, Diodoros has also brought you two short manuscripts to add to the collection: The Sacred House of the Vestal Virgins *and a new version of the* Jupiter Capitoline *that includes drawings of the impressive rebuilding work since the fire of ten years ago. I assume that you'll first supply our direct customers along the Ephesus-Miletus-Assos road before you reserve any copies for "outside" distributors. I still don't trust these people, what with their requests for credit and special discounts. Remember that so-called dealer from Crete who disappeared with half your inventory? (Well, it seemed like half to hear you wail about it!)*

I have a request from Rome as well. There is increasing interest here in The Asclepieum of Pergamum *as a spa and treatment center for the infirm (which seems to include me half the time). Yes, I know it is already part of the book on Pergamum, but there are many people who don't want to read all that stuff on the city's illustrious history.*

I would rather see you expand on The Asclepieum *as the separate entity it is. We need to entice people more with the background of the sacred healing waters, the hospital, the mud treatments, dream interpretation center, temples, theater and so forth. You can also fill up the scroll with the whole history of Asclepieus, his cult and the mystical rites going back 500 years. My experience is that sick people have the time to read and are looking earnestly for painless cures in pleasant surroundings. We can sell as many of these as we do of the Pergamum book, so get busy!*

Finally, you are asking: How on earth will we copy and sell all these new books?

Now I'll stop teasing you, dear brother, because here is another reason why I choose not to quibble with Literato's simple request for anonymity. In Diodoros' bundles are 100,000 sesterces and a bank draft for 150,000 more which our patron gave us in exchange for one-third of our future profits. Now do you feel better about him? I thought so!

You are the most important part of this arrangement — and for several reasons. The main one is that whereas we must indeed expand our scriptorium, Rome is not the place for it. Literato agrees that shipping books from Asia is inexpensive compared to the cost of expanding in the Argiletum, even if we could find the room. And even if we did find the space we would soon be conspicuous enough to arouse the suspicion of our dear neighbors, The Oligopoly. This, again, is why I have sent you Diodoros: to help you organize and operate a new scriptorium.

Now where should we put it? No, not where you are now in the Upper Citadel. This may be painful to read, but I am convinced that your present shop by the Great Library is not up to the challenge that lies ahead. You remain there, my loyal Eumenes, because our family name is identified with that of the great Pergamum Library and because this brings you respectability. But the fact is that our sales are limited to the library itself, the palaces of a few wealthy families and the tourists who trudge up that hill for the view when the weather is sunny enough.

Well, I have a way where you no longer have to climb up there every day at just the time when your 50-year-old legs are beginning to give out! I want you to take 150,000 of this money and use it to outfit a large shop and even larger scriptorium down in the city where the crowds are. Specifically, I would suggest it be right on the Via Tecta where you have the entrance to Pergamum on one side, and on the other, the beginning of the tourist shops that lead to the Asclepieum. There you'll have it all: crowds of locals, pilgrims to the Asclepieum and business travelers from all over the Mediterranean. And you won't be far from the street of parchment makers, either.

Parchment makers? O Yes! I know your old ditty about being able to smell them before you see them, but hear me out because this is important to our plan. Literato and I want you to take another 50,000 sesterces and start work on a new way of making books.

We want you to find at least one parchment maker who will help you produce a book in what is called "codex" form. Forget that you ever heard of a scroll. Under the concept Diodoros and I have come up with, the parchment vellum is stretched over a larger frame so that the sheets are nine or 12 inches high by perhaps 24 or 25 *inches wide (you'll have to experiment to find the exact size). Instead of gluing these sheets side by side for a scroll, you lay them out horizontally on top of one another and stitch them up the middle. Once you fold over the two sides of vellum you need a protective cover. Leather might be suitable. Or you might take two wooden writing tablets and bind them together by a thong. The exact method is up to you, the parchment house and Diodoros.*

But why, you say. Let us think first of the reader. A codex is easier to store and pick up. It can include much more reading material between the covers than a scroll, which means it's easier to store on a library shelf. It doesn't wrinkle like papyrus and can support better illustrations, which pleases rich people and makes them want to pay more. Finally, it will last longer, which is why some librarians I've talked to in Rome are interested in it. When many people handle a papyrus book, it doesn't last very long.

Let us think about cost as well. With a codex you don't need scroll knobs or roller wood. But the main thing is that I believe the cost difference between parchment and papyrus itself is continuing to narrow. It's because the Roman-owned estates that harvest most of the papyrus reeds along the Nile have grown fewer in number and larger in size. It is no surprise that this ever-cozier cabal has caused the price of all grades of papyrus to rise gradually with no end in sight. And all this is a big reason why all of us who work on the Street of Booksellers must charge so much for our scrolls.

Literato and Diodoros are convinced we can break this stronghold through wiser, more imaginative use of parchment. Indeed, Literato roared with laughter when I also told him that this is your chance to match your namesake, Eumenes II, who invented our famous Pergamum parchment nearly 300 years ago. And all because the Egyptians were so jealous that our library might surpass their wondrous library at Alexandria that they blocked the export of papyrus to Asia!

There's a sweet treat in this revenge for me, too, if you haven't guessed already. Around 120 years ago when Marcus Antonius looted our library so that Cleopatra could replace the books that burned in the great Alexandria fire, my great grand-father was one of the young scribes they carted off to look after the new supply in Egypt. Looking back, I would have to say that this event had more to do with mold-ing my own peripatetic fate than anything I've been able to effect on my own. So I should think you and I would derive a delicious little bonus from all this if it helped our little family phœnix rise over the pyramids of Egypt, if even for but a moment in history!

Now let me turn to the 50,000 sesterces remaining in your new "dowry." Once you get the new codex process perfected, we want you to use it to produce a few of the larger works we have discussed. Among them is the last of the bundles in Diodoros' baggage, which consists of a manuscript about one-third completed. All I ask of you at this point is that you keep the incomplete manuscript in a safe place until we decide when the time has come to publish it.

How's that? Well, of course I'll tell you what it's about! But before I do so, sum-mon Polias and allow her to read this, because I know she has had some contact with the people I am about to mention.

Literato and I want to produce a work on the history and beliefs of the Christians: how they sprang from the Jews and why their numbers continue to grow despite all the forces that seem to conspire against them. We are ideally suited for this because of the active Christian communities in Rome and — even more so — in the Ægean coastal region to be served by your expanded facility. Moreover, this might one day present a book market throughout the empire because there are already growing Christian communities as far-flung as Alexandria, Palestine, Tarsus, Cappadocia, Spain, Gaul and even Britain.

I hear you grumbling again. "What? Where are these Christian book buyers? How many have ever walked into my shop in the Citadel? I hear they give their possessions away, so how do they have money for books?"

I strongly suggest, Eumenes, that there are many more Christians than you think, if for no other reason than they don't necessarily go where you go. They sel-

dom frequent wine shops, the games or temples. Further, they have no special dress to mark them and have built no temples in which to congregate conspicuously. But if you look about, you will find many Christians — women, slaves, shopkeepers, even some prominent citizens. They meet mostly in private homes where they share readings, sing a lot and share meals together.

Take my word for it. I once took scant notice of them; but on my weekly strolls around Rome on my days of rest I have encountered numerous Christians along the city's southern outskirts. There the earth is laced underneath with tufa that has been hewn into corridors and grottos, and where Christians bury their dead.

I see the same to the west of Rome in the Vatican section. This district used to be dominated by the old Circus of Caligula and Nero, but it has fallen into idle disrepair for the last dozen years, and many lower-class opportunists have seized a chance to build family mausoleums on a hill just across from it. There you'll also find the tombs of many Christian leaders who fell at the hand of Nero. I mention this because there are constantly crowds around these Christian graves — people wearing the dress of all parts of the empire — and they have left hundreds of reverent inscriptions and votaries all around so that one might think it had been a busy day at the Temple of Artemis.

All this, of course, shows an intensity in their devotion to Jesus, the founder, and for us should mean an interest in having books that explain his teachings and the history of their religion. These are sorely lacking because most Christians — at least those in Rome — have lived in such fear ever since the Neronian persecutions that it's no wonder there are few books. Who would want to have his name on them? Or even be mentioned in them? Imagine that the authorities had just swooped down on your Asclepieum and carried off all the patients and physicians. Do you think you would want to admit you'd ever had so much as a mud bath there?

As you can see, I have developed a great interest in the subject and a concern that so few have written about it. Thus, you should not be surprised when I tell you that I am the author of the partially-completed manuscript that I am asking you to store.

And why not Attalos? Am I not addicted to reading? Do I not know every pigeon-hole and mousehole in the leading libraries of Rome? It is, I maintain, but a puddle jump from Attalos the librarian to Attalos the writer. Besides, I have acquired several letters and a diary or two that shed light on the story. With these and the histories already available to me in the libraries of Rome, I have the means to answer some intriguing questions, such as: Why did some people turn from religion that offered the most splendid temple in the world to a new one that had no temples or idols at all? What caused the Jews of Jerusalem to revolt? Why did Rome destroy all the Jews in Jerusalem but let Christians go free? Why do the Christians keep growing in numbers?

I can now hear you saying that we are beginning to sail in dangerous waters. Here I will not tease or trifle with you, cousin. Yes, there may well be some risk here, which is why you should put this manuscript in a safe place until we have a better opportunity to divine the omens. I admit that writing about dead and deified emperors is safer than about events that can be read by the living. Indeed, as a general, Vespasian had both feet in the Palestine that harvested the first Christians. But you, Eumenes, must admit that in his nine years as Emperor, Vespasian has proven to be a just and noble man, patient and lenient even with his severest critics. Recently a group of well-meaning Greek scholars went to great lengths to trace the origin of his family to Hercules. When they appeared with the "evidence" at one of the emperor's receptions, he simply waved them off, laughing that so much work could go into so ludicrous an exercise.

But worry not about the manuscript, Eumenes. You have a large and ambitious undertaking ahead and I urge you to concentrate on it for now. I hope that my absence in this endeavor will be compensated for by the presence of Diodoros, the money in his baggage and the assurance that we have a powerful patron on our side. I bid you and your family a fond farewell and hope you will write often with news of your progress.

—Attalos

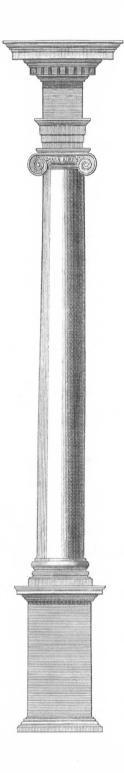

THE

SOWING

BOOK I

I begin this history in the 17th year after Augustus' death and deification. On the Isle of Capri, Tiberius was in his 72nd year and beyond embitterment at having had to govern the world for so long. In Judea, it was also the year in which the followers of Jesus faced a frightening new existence without him. And for the Jews of Jerusalem it was another year of tension and taxation under the unchecked Governor Pontius Pilate.

In Rome, what had begun as just another sultry summer day had burst into a fireball of repressed hate and rage. Sejanus was dead, and by nightfall the frenzied rabble had seen to it that not even enough body parts could be found in one place to effect a funeral. It should have been an equally jubilant time for what remained of the patrician and equestrian classes, but instead an eerie calm prevailed as people waited warily to see what the truculent old tyrant on Capri would do now that he had removed his upstart, once-presumed heir and "partner of my labors." For, since having removed himself and a small "court" of cronies, Prætorians, chamberlains and astrologers to this rocky outpost five years before, Tiberius Claudius Nero had not set foot in Rome. And his moods could be divined only from his occasional visitors or official correspondence with the Senate.

Oh what a contrast was Tiberius with his predecessor as he sat brooding atop his cliff-top villa. When Cæsar Augustus was 76 and in his last day of his life, he still had the grace and good nature to call some close friends to his bedside, and with a wan twinkle in his eye, recall the lines of a comedy actor at the end of his play:

> Since I've played well, with joy your voices raise
> And from the stage dismiss me with your praise. [1]

And then left alone, he passed away peacefully in the embrace of his wife, Livia.

Although an emperor can rule millions with a command, his ability to guarantee a wise and noble successor seems to be no better than his chances of turning up the "dog" with a throw of the dice. Augustus, who had a daughter by his first marriage and outlived two eligible grandsons, wound up having to choose between two stepsons Livia brought him when she became his second wife. When Drusus, the eldest and more outgoing, died in a far-off military camp, Augustus' realm was left at last to the candidate he least wanted and the candidate who probably least wanted it.

And that is one reason why I feel a mixture of pity and compassion for Tiberius the man, even though the spirits of many murdered patricians will no doubt curse me for saying so. Did he perhaps know instinctively that Cæsar Augustus simply created too large a persona and too large a responsibility for anyone but the equally gifted to inherit? And did Augustus himself not break the spirit of that successor even before he was called upon – yea, ordered – to rule?

Consider his case, O jury of readers. When Tiberius was but a small boy he was torn away from his real father when the young Octavian wooed away (some say abducted) his mother, Livia. From the age of 12 on, his only life was one of unquestioning and exhausting service to his stepfather. At various times he might be taking charge of the grain supply or leading a Senate investigation of slave prison conditions. He led an expeditionary force that restored Tigranes to the throne of Armenia. He journeyed to the easternmost borders of the empire to recover the Roman standards that the Parthians had snatched in battle. He was governor of southern Gaul. Tall, physically strong and the essence of the model Roman soldier, he led armies in Pannonia, in Dalmatia and throughout Germany. And at the proper times for his age and station, he served as quæstor, prætor and consul twice.

But honors always came at a cost and obligation. In his early manhood, Tiberius' burdens were lightened by his marriage to Agrippina (but not the Agrippina we will soon read much more about). He adored her and she bore him a son, Drusus, named in honor of his brother and fellow general. Then, when she was happily carrying his second child, he was forced to divorce her and to contract a hurried marriage with Julia, the unruly, unmanageable daughter of Augustus.

What a sad event indeed for all concerned! Julia was the daughter of Augustus' first marriage to Scribonia, whom he divorced in his twenties for "her shrewish disposition." But Julia remained his to contend with. Rebellious, flirtatious and all too fond of wine, she was given first to the son of Augustus' only sister. When he died, Augustus turned to a man his own age, his trusted confidant Marcus Agrippa, and prevailed on him to wed and tame the young widow.

Agrippa and Julia produced three sons before she was widowed again, but already tongues were wagging about her obvious infatuation with Tiberius. He, however, avoided her as though she were a leper – both because she was the emperor's daughter and because he was deeply in love with his own wife. But one day Tiberius got the greatest shock of his life when Augustus demanded the ultimate sacrifice: that he dissolve his happy marriage and marry Julia for the good of the empire.

Tiberius had been commonly described as stern and taciturn. Now the more accurate adjectives would become "sullen" and "morose." Although Julia's maudlin advances were now sanctioned by wedlock and Tiberius did his best to satisfy them, it soon became a hellish arrangement. First, the despondent Tiberius longed for his former wife to the point of following her in a crowd or staring like a sorrowful puppy whenever she turned around in his presence. Meanwhile, he had only succeeded in making Julia more repulsive. She was drinking more than ever, publicly mocking her husband as cold and callous. And the same flirtatious eyes that had beckoned Tiberius were already luring other men to her bed.

Augustus insisted that producing a child would rejuvenate the union, and the pair dutifully complied. But after the baby died in infancy, Tiberius and Julia were soon living apart for good. Augustus at first sided with his daughter. But soon the emperor became so outraged at her behavior that he banished her from the household, from his will and even from a place in the magnificent mausoleum that he had already built to glorify the imperial family after death.

Perhaps it was Julia. Perhaps it was the sudden death of his vigorous, able brother Drusus in Germany and the long and sad trip to retrieve his body. But shortly after his return Tiberius had made up his mind on a new course. In the prime of life and imperial service he announced his firm resolve to retire. Unofficially, he let it be known that he did not want to interfere with any succession plans Augustus might have for his grandsons (by Julia) Gaius and Lucius, both of whom were now strong and healthy boys about to embark on their official princely duties. But I think Tiberius simply didn't like his own life or the prospect of ruling. And had Augustus accepted it, how differently the times might have turned out!

Officially, Tiberius said he was weary of his offices and desired a rest. Neither the entreaties of his mother Livia nor his stepfather, the emperor, could change his mind. In fact, when they began scolding and insisting, he refused to take food for four days. And one day when Augustus ended yet another argument by throwing up his arms in despair, Tiberius chose to take it as a gesture of dismissal. He rushed away with his baggage and headed for the port of Ostia so quickly that he scarcely said a word of good-bye to anyone.

Tiberius sailed directly to Rhodes and spent the next eight years on this healthful island, living in a modest villa in the interior so as not to cause notice. He *was* noticed, of course, but always took pains to arrive at the gymnasium with a single lictor or to shun the attentions of the many generals and magistrates who sought to pay him homage during their travels to Greece. He even gave up his usual exercises with horses and arms and assumed the Greek dress.

However, the following incident shows how even the best of intentions can take a wrong turn when one happens to be a "royal" from Rome. During one of his first days on Rhodes, Tiberius announced his wish to visit whatever sick people there were in the city. Misunderstanding his intent, an attendant went to the village and ordered that all the sick should be taken to a public portico and arranged in groups according to their type of illness. When Tiberius came upon the shocking sight of so many feeble people tottering in the hot sun, he went to each person, apologizing profusely, no matter how humble their station.

It was another misunderstanding that ended his otherwise happy sabbatical after eight years. Upon learning that Gaius, his stepson by the marriage to Julia, was lodging on the nearby isle of Samos, Tiberius thought it proper to pay his respects. However, he was startled to find Gaius cold and distant. After returning to Rhodes, Tiberius learned that an overly protective aide of Gaius had spread rumors that he had designs on the young heir's life. So, too, came a report that a hot-headed young friend of Giaus had stood up at a dinner party and vowed that at his patron's command he would gladly set sail at once for Rhodes and bring back the head of "the exile," as Tiberius' detractors called him.

With just a few retainers and his modest villa offering no fortification, Tiberius actually began to fear for his own safety. This was probably the reason why he soon petitioned the emperor for a recall to Rome. Augustus, still bitter at being "abandoned" by his chief lieutenant in government, agreed to the return (mainly at Livia's urging), but only on condition that Tiberius not take part in public affairs.

No one, I suspect, would have been happier to comply than Tiberius. He soon moved to a modest (compared to the palace) suburban home and reappeared only when formal occasions dictated. But again, neither Augustus nor fate would leave Tiberius alone for long. When Augustus' two grandsons, Gaius and Lucius, both died within three years, he formally adopted Tiberius. In turn, the emperor compelled Tiberius to adopt Germanicus, the 30-year-old son of his late older brother Drusus. Succession would not come officially for many more years, but Tiberius was clearly back in the center of the arena and not enjoying it. When it did come, he reportedly told a friend just after Augustus' death, "I am holding a wolf by the ears."

In the first years afterward, Tiberius was regarded as diligent in his attention and fair in the way he administered taxes. But his prudence was matched by his austerity with the public purse. For two whole years after becoming Emperor he did not set foot outside the gates of Rome. Indeed, he sponsored few games, erected few public buildings and renovated disheveled ones at such a sluggish pace that many projects remained uncompleted at his death.

It is probably accurate to say that Tiberius thought of himself as a simple and modest man during those early years. He so loathed flattery that he would not allow any senator to approach his litter to pay his respects. If anyone in conversation or a speech referred to him in too flattering a manner he would not hesitate to interrupt and deflate the speaker on the spot.

The emperor's attitude was perhaps best reflected when a delegation from Asia requested permission to build a shrine to him. Noting that Augustus had allowed one temple to himself at Pergamum, he said that "one such acceptance may be pardonable. But to have my statue worshipped among the gods in every province would be presumptuous and arrogant." Looking up from the petition at his Senate colleagues, he added: "I emphasize that I am human, performing human tasks, and content to occupy first place among men. That is what I want future generations to remember. They will do more than justice to my memory if they judge me worthy of my ancestors, careful of your interests, steadfast in danger and fearless of animosities incurred in public service."

Of all the burdens on the new ruler, perhaps none was more omnipresent nor stifling than simply the presence and sincere loyalty of Germanicus. Where Tiberius was at best seen as austere and aloof and at worse morose, his brother's son — now his adoptive, presumed heir — was a ray of sunshine in the Forum. Athletic, admired by his troops, radiant of smile, he was also unswervingly loyal to Tiberius in two counsulships and endless military tasks. For example, when the army in Germany had been on the brink of mutiny over low pay and wretched conditions, it was Germanicus who came to quell them, invoking in his pleas the glorious past victories of these very brigades who served under the generalship of none other than Tiberius. And when some soldiers spontaneously shouted that they would support Germanicus if he wanted the throne, he leapt off the dais as if it had become polluted by their criminal intentions. Shouting that death was better than disloyalty, he pulled his sword from his belt. He lifted it as though to plunge it into his own chest, but the men around him clutched his arm and stopped him by force.

Agrippina, mother of his six children, was just as renowned and revered by soldiers and Romans alike. Acting almost as deputy commander in Germany, she took charge of dispensing clothes to needy soldiers and dressing the wounded. When the victorious but battle-weary legionaries returned across a bridge they had built across the Rhine, Agrippina was said to have stood at the bridgehead to thank and congratulate every soldier. Her children often visited the camp for long periods, and they warmed the hearts of men whose families had faded into distant memories. When her little Gaius tottered about the men in a German camp, someone made him a soldier suit, complete with boots, tin breast plate, sword, helmet and shield. Spoiled by everyone, he soon became camp mascot and was nicknamed Caligula, or "Little Boots."

To the common Roman, Germanicus and his family genuinely and effortlessly defined what they thought patricians should be – certainly more so than the solitary and suspicious Tiberius. As the grandson of Antonius and grandnephew of Augustus, Germanicus embodied to everyone who crossed his path the deeds and battles that were already joining the pantheon of Roman mythology. This, too, because Germanicus united the Claudian-Augustan household itself. He was not only son of the Emperor's brother Drusus, he had married Agrippina, one of the five children of Augustus' daughter Julia.

One man coveted the shadows, the other the sunlight. Yet their stations in life were reversed and neither could escape. How irritated the emperor Tiberius must have felt as his litter passed by buildings scrawled with graffiti that said, "Give us Germanicus!" Or by striding through the Senate house and overhearing a back bencher whisper "Ah, if only Germanicus held imperium."

Thus, the emperor must have had strikingly mixed emotions when he read a dispatch from Syria that Germanicus was severely ill. A week later he read another one announcing the death of his adopted son. All Rome knew that Germanicus had gone there to censure the rambunctious Syrian legate Cnæus Calpurnius Piso and that he had been met with a sulking insolence. But now came rumors that Piso and his ambitious wife had actually poisoned Germanicus. Some said Tiberius had put them up to it.

If the emperor had once feared Gaius's friends in Rhodes, how much more he must have shuddered when he witnessed the outpouring of grief for Germanicus, the widow and her beautiful but helpless children. The wailing had begun in Syrian Antioch, where the body was burned and eulogies offered by foreign kings and disconsolate members of his general staff. Some even likened him to Alexander the Great in that both were handsome, died soon after 30 and succumbed in a foreign land. But Germanicus, they added, was no less a warrior, yet also kind to his friends and modest in his pleasures.

In Rome, with the first news of Germanicus' death, businesses and courts had closed without awaiting any official edict. There was universal silence and sorrow, then a sudden soaring of hopes as some businessmen from Syria reported that Germanicus had actually revived and rallied. But public emotions plunged again a day later when the death was confirmed. With that came the decreeing of every honor which love or ingenuity could devise. Germanicus' statue was to lead the processions at the Circus Games. The Knights of Rome gave the name "Germanicus" to the group of seats at the theater which had been called the "junior block" and they decreed that their parade each July 15 would be led by his likeness. There were to be arches in Rome, on the Rhine bank and on Mt. Amanus in Syria with inscriptions recording his deeds.

The outpouring of mourning had scarcely begun to ebb a few weeks later when news came that a ship carrying the weary and miserable Agrippina, along with her two eldest children and the ashes of her husband, had crossed the rough wintry sea and had stopped at the island of Corcyra just off the Greek coast. At the news of her approach, it seemed that everyone on the Italian peninsula began flocking to Brundusium, the ship's expected destination.

When at last the squadron hove into sight, it was not with the usual vigorous rowing of men eager for home, but the deliberate rhythm of a funeral dirge. When at last Agrippina and her two children stepped off the ship, eyes lowered, they were already near collapse with the grieving and rough voyage. But as the throngs of soldiers, relatives and strangers filling the harbor and even lining the rooftops caught sight of Agrippina carrying the urn with her husband's ashes, their tortured hearts gave rise to a single universal groan of despair.

Where once the emperor's proximity restrained all such emotions in Rome, the sight of the funeral cortege now lumbering slowly inland from town to town was reason enough to cast aside all official decorum. Agrippina was soon joined by her remaining children from Rome and by two battalions of the Guard sent by Tiberius. A long procession of citizens, positioned according to their wealth, included both consuls, Tiberius' remaining son, Drusus, and Germanicus' only brother Claudius, who though a lame and stuttering embarrassment to the Julian clan, was always treated with official respect in his public appearances.

As crowds of common farmers and townspeople filed in behind the procession to Rome, questions arose among the marchers: Where was Tiberius himself? Where was his mother Livia? And where was her daughter-in-law Antonia, widow of Drusus and mother of Germanicus? Some said they remained in Rome to show that grieving was beneath them. Others suggested that Antonia was too ill, or so inconsolable that the emperor and his mother chose to remain by her side. But some said openly that Tiberius and Livia did not come because they would have been unable to contain the jubilation they felt at the passing of this comet from brilliance into darkness.

On the day when the remains were to be conducted to the Mausoleum of Augustus, the streets of Rome were full and the Field of Mars ablaze with torches. Everywhere people talked openly of a dim and dreary future without Germanicus. They exalted Agrippina as the "glory of her country" and "the only true descendent of Augustus." And they muttered openly that Germanicus was being denied the full state funeral that Augustus surely would have given him.

Tiberius heard it all. His only response was a rather terse public statement:

> Many famous Romans have died for their country. But none has ever
> been so ardently lamented before. That seems admirable to all, myself
> included – provided that moderation is observed. For the conduct of
> ordinary households or communities is not appropriate for rulers or
> an imperial people. Tearful mourning was a proper consolation in the
> first throes of grief. But now be calm again. Remember how Julius
> Cæsar, when he lost his only daughter, and Augustus, when he lost his
> grandsons, hid their sorrow – not to mention Rome's courageous en-
> durance of the loss of armies, the deaths of generals, and the total de-
> struction of great families. Rulers die; the country lives forever...[2]

All this again typified why the plight of Tiberius would never change. Had he
walked all the way to Brundusium, no doubt some of the same processionaires
would have claimed that he was there to silence the crowds or deflect the last
glory Agrippina would ever know. And so it continued. If Augustus was praised
as prudent for his frugality with public funds, Tiberius would be called mean
and miserly for attempting the same. When he asked senators not to accompany his litter, few attributed it to a modest man's loathing of vacuous flattery,
but to an insecure monarch's fear that the senator might be carrying a concealed knife. And when he urged senators to vote their conscience on a bill, the
reply from one leader was: "Yes, but will you please cast your own vote first?"
When Tiberius asked why, the senator replied, "I would not want to cast mine
before you and then learn that I had inadvertently voted wrongly."

Added to the weight on Tiberius' chest was the omnipresence of his mother.
Initially, Livia clearly expected to exercise an equal share of power with her son.
Already known as "The Augusta" upon her husband's death, she persuaded the
Senate early in the new reign to provide that "son of Livia" and "son of Augustus" be included whenever the name of Tiberius was used in public inscriptions.
Tiberius did, however, succeed in blocking a move to name Livia "parent of her
country" and thereafter saw to it that she was denied any conspicuous public
honor. Once when Tiberius learned that she had rushed to a fire at the Temple
of Vesta and had all but taken charge of the fire brigade, he warned her that it
was "unbecoming to a woman" to meddle in public affairs.

What led to an unhealable breach may have begun with a rather trivial spat.
In an upcoming trial, Livia repeatedly insisted that Tiberius select as a juror a
man who had only recently been made a citizen. An agitated Tiberius finally
said he would do so only on condition that the jury roster bear a notation that
one of the selections was forced on the emperor by his mother. With that Livia
flew into a rage and in the midst of it pulled out from her cloak some old letters

that Augustus had written her complaining of Tiberius' sullen and stubborn disposition. He in turn was so outraged that she had preserved the correspondence all those years that he seldom ever saw her again in person.

As Tiberius aged, his duties only seemed to multiply. His grandsons by Germanicus were too young to enter public service. His own son Drusus, when not carousing at night and sleeping late, seemed to dabble at brief and safe military commands, minor public tasks and raising a young family. But by then the void had already begun to be filled in the person of an ambitious knight named Lucius Ælius Sejanus. Having gotten a toehold on service to the imperial family through a friendship with Augustus' grandson Gaius, Sejanus soon gained Tiberius' attention as an able administrative assistant, and later as commander of the Prætorian Guard. Of strong and handsome physique, and concealing a burning ambition behind a modest exterior, he found no task too small in his proclaimed duty to relieve the weary emperor of his burdens. In time, they were seeing each other daily and Tiberius was proclaiming his young aide to the Senate as "the partner of my labors."

Yet, I think it was a matter of who was the more cunning: Sejanus in hurdling his way to power, or Tiberius because he had found – surely not in his high-living, indolent son, Drusus – the man who could (as we shall see) bring about his long-planned return to a life of tranquillity.

Of all the "innovations" Sejanus inspired, one would have an impact on the Empire and the succession for years to come. Until his arrival, command of the Prætorian Guard had been a position of slight importance. The Guard existed primarily to put down any civil turmoil or attacks on the imperial household. Guard battalions, scattered about Rome, were outnumbered even by local fire brigades. Sejanus approached the fiscally-practical Tiberius with the suggestion that the Guard be consolidated into one barracks just northeast of the city walls.

Well, why not? It would simplify supply logistics and help lighten city traffic. And their centralized numbers would boost the Guard's self-confidence as an emergency fighting force. Armed with the emperor's mandate, Sejanus soon had all subalterns reporting to him closely. He memorized the names of soldiers and bantered with them daily.

Within a few months statues of Sejanus were appearing in Pompey's Theater and other public places. Senators were bending his ear as to vacant governorships and public offices – all of which allowed his ambitions to soar to new heights. Now Sejanus even surveyed the imperial successorship. In his path were the emperor's son Drusus, and after him, the now adult sons of Germanicus, Nero Cæsar and Drusus Cæsar.

Of these, the emperor's Drusus was by far the most formidable. Hot-headed and resentful of his father's new confidant, Drusus had once struck Sejanus during a quarrel and never apologized. Moreover, Drusus never missed a chance to warn his father that the excessive ambitions of Sejanus would lead to no good.

So Sejanus, always continuing to probe for an opening he could penetrate, soon found one – the heir-apparent's wife. Livilla, a sister of Germanicus, was in the throes of pain over her brother's loss and the chronic emptiness in trying to co-exist with the less-than-attentive Drusus. Sejanus seems to have found seducing Livilla easy sport when accompanied by feigned compassion for her plight, promises of freedom from her husband and a "partnership" when the empire was theirs. That Sejanus was already married and had three children seemed inconsequential.

Let me step back a moment and relate that the wealth and reach of an emperor at this point were still limited compared to today. Levies of grain, indirect taxation and other revenues belonging to the state were managed by an association of Roman knights. Imperial properties were overseen by a cadre of professional clerks. They and the emperor saw to it that the provinces were not harassed by new levies and that the old impositions were not aggravated through acquisitiveness or brutality. Beatings and confiscations of estates did not exist. The emperor's own estates in Italy were few, his slaves unobtrusive and his household staff limited to a few freedmen. Any disputes he had with private citizens were settled in the law courts.

Tiberius, for all his taciturn and sometimes truculent demeanor, had continued to uphold these traditions. But now Sejanus, the outsider, deliberately began to break them down, beginning with the heir to the throne. He and Livilla chose a poison that she could administer to Drusus at mealtimes so as to cause gradual debilitating health. No one, of course, knew the cause at the time, but one could observe Drusus weakening daily, even as he and his father attended sessions of the Senate. When at last he wasted away, Tiberius continued to attend the Curia. "I know that I may be criticized for appearing before the Senate when my affliction is still fresh," he said from the rostra one day. "Most mourners can hardly bear even their families' condolences – can hardly look upon the light of day. And that need not be censured as weakness. I, however, have sought a sterner solace. The arms in which I have taken refuge are those of the state."

With that he declared that the sons of Germanicus were his only consolation in his grief, and asked that they be brought in. He then took them by the hand and said to the Senate: "When these boys lost their father, I entrusted them to their Uncle Drusus, begging him – though he had children of his own – to treat them as though they were his blood, and for posterity's sake, to fashion them after himself. Now Drusus is gone," he said, looking down on the boys. "My plea now is that these senators will take the place of your parents." With that the Curia was soon filled with the weeping of grown men and their prayers for the future.

The ensuing funeral, with more expensive adornments and more expansive oratory than even that of Germanicus, nonetheless left Tiberius with a bitter taste. First, he realized that Drusus himself was not sincerely missed. Second, the graffiti and overheard murmurs told him that people were actually joyful that the offspring of Germanicus were now next in line.

All this, of course, was reinforced by Sejanus in his daily advisories to the emperor. Privately, Sejanus reasoned that it was impractical to poison all three heirs because they were zealously guarded. Moreover, the reputation of their mother, Agrippina, was unassailable. But her constant outspoken criticism of Tiberius and his mother might be the chink in her armor that he sought.

Tiberius' solace at his son's loss soon became his preoccupation with legal cases and petitions from the provinces. But Sejanus used Livilla and other women close to the imperial household to spread talk about Agrippina's "seditious" designs. Rome, he declared, was split asunder as though by civil war, with some calling themselves "Agrippina's party." Sejanus insisted that this "deepening discord" could only be arrested if some of the ringleaders were removed.

And so a pair of scapegoats were carefully selected. Gaius Silius had headed one of Germanicus' German armies for seven years, and no one had shown greater sorrow at his passing. Silius' wife Sosia Galla was a close friend of Agrippina. Her husband had also incurred Tiberius' enmity by having boasted openly in Rome, "If the mutiny (in Germany) had spread to my brigades, Tiberius could not have kept his throne."

Well, services from clients are welcome as long as it is possible to repay them, but when they exceed that point they often produce hatred rather than gratitude. Charges of treason were filed against Silius and the Senate was summoned to judge them. So began what was to be a familiar pattern. Charges were hurled, not just by witnesses for the emperor, but by anyone who happened to be feuding at the time with the accused. Soon, just as the accursed one might feel himself suffocating under the weight of false testimony and with no rescuers in sight, a friendly senator might whisper to him that the conscript fathers might be much more lenient with the disposition of his estate and family were he to leave the world as soon as possible and spare them from further aggravation. If perhaps he would only put the greater good ahead of his own....

Silius obliged in this case by returning home and opening his veins. After deducting from the estate gifts that Augustus had given, one quarter of the estate was assigned to his accusers. Ordinarily, one-half of the remainder would have been confiscated by the state, but sympathy swayed the Senate to assign the remainder to the surviving children. However, their mother, Sosia, was banished.

Soon Drusus' widow Livilla was demanding that Sejanus make good on his promise of marriage. So Sejanus wrote a flowery memorandum to the Emperor stating that although he would be content to live the remainder of his life working, "like any soldier, for the emperor's safety...I have gained the greatest privilege – to be thought worthy of a marriage link with your house." Thus, he intoned, "please bear in mind, if you should seek a husband for Livilla, consider your friend, who would gain nothing but prestige from the relationship."

In time, Tiberius delivered a long reply. After extolling Sejanus' many contributions, he noted,"A ruler is compelled to consider public opinion." And in this case, he said, "Agrippina's feelings will be greatly intensified if Lavilla marries. This would virtually split the imperial house in two. Even now, the women's rivalry is irrepressible."

Tiberius added that Sejanus would be mistaken if he thought that Livilla, once married to an emperor's son, "would be content to grow old as the wife of a knight." However, he added, "What you and Livilla decide, I shall not oppose." And in closing he tantalized Sejanus by alluding to "additional ties by which I plan to link you with me. Of these I shall not speak now. I shall only say that for your merits and your devotion to me, no elevation would be too high."

The tepid reaction to his direct request caused Sejanus to write again urging the emperor "to eschew suspicions and ignore rumor and malignant envy." But it was clear that anything less than Tiberius' wholehearted endorsement made marriage too risky a venture at that point. So Sejanus altered course somewhat. He took every opportunity to sympathize with Tiberius over the crush of business before him. He began suggesting that the emperor might delegate more routine tasks and involve himself in far fewer tedious ceremonies if he were to move to a quieter, more idyllic location away from Rome. Left unsaid was the fact that such a move would also give Sejanus control over all access to the emperor and most of his correspondence.

But, again, one wonders who was the greater conniver. Undoubtedly Tiberius had already compiled a long list of other reasons for escaping Rome. The chance to put distance between himself and his nagging mother may have weighed heavily, but he had already done nearly that while in Rome. No, I would suggest other factors equally as compelling: the natural longings of an aging man for some peace; yes, the ghost of Germanicus and the annoying public affection for Agrippina; the overpowering dungheap of public problems dumped on his doorstep each day; the pitiful paucity of help from the Senate in sharing those burdens, the absence of any sign of appreciation from the Roman citizenry and no doubt the memory of a simple villa life in balmy Rhodes. Whatever the reason, the emperor decided to leave Rome for good.

And this time he had a place in mind far less accessible than Rhodes.

Tiberius took care never to announce his escape plan. Rather, he simply set off one day for Campania with a small entourage, presumably to dedicate some temples to Jupiter and Augustus at Capua and Nola. But after his official duties, the party soon headed south and across the Bay of Misineum to the Isle of Capri.

This was no popular, peopled Rhodes, accessible by many harbors and roads. Although only three miles at sea from the populous Surrentum promontory, Capri had only one beach, no natural harbors and a sea access that could be controlled by just a few sentries. The entire isle housed the summer villas of just 12 patrician families. The villa of Tiberius lay at the most isolated southernmost end. Reaching it first meant landing at the well-guarded harbor at the opposite end, climbing a steep hill to the island's spiny ridge, and then treking along a narrow, rocky roadway. As one approached the emperor's spacious villa, he could look down in three directions at thousand-foot cliffs of sheer rock surrounded by a sea that plunged to equally steep depths.

To this retreat Tiberius Claudius Nero repaired in the twelfth year of his reign. With him were a venerable senator and ex-consul, a knight, a few Greeks to entertain the emperor with their astrology and conversational skills, and several attendants. Foremost among them, of course, was Sejanus, now the carrier and interpreter of all official correspondence as he journeyed back and forth from Rome.

The astrologers had asserted that the conjunction of heavenly bodies when Tiberius left Rome precluded his safe return. Some even told the emperor that the signs indicated his end was near, which wasn't a bad wager given that their client was already 67. But Tiberius would live another 11 years on Capri, and many astrologers would pay dearly for their mistaken predictions.

Sejanus soon made the most of his new powers. Tiberius now had time on his hands, and the commander of the Guard used it to fill his mind with suspicions. At the same time he engaged agents to destabilize Nero Cæsar, the eldest son of Agrippina and first heir to the throne. Nero Cæsar's ex-slaves and dependents, impatient to enjoy the trappings of power, urged the youth to assert himself more in public affairs. Nero Cæsar tended to be uninformed and often made critical remarks that were, though harmless and immature, written down by Sejanus' agents and repeated wherever they might cause arouse suspicion. Soon, Nero Cæsar found others uneasy around him or making excuses to leave his company early. And whenever the family of Germanicus suggested new ways to increase his station, Livilla was usually on hand to report it back to Sejanus so that he could take counter measures.

By this time Sejanus was openly urging the emperor to take action against Agrippina and her Nero Cæsar. As incredulous as it might seem, Tiberius must have approved a scheme in which an ambitious ex-prætor, Lucanius Latiaris, was promised a consulship in exchange for treachery against a distinguished knight named Sabinus. Once among the closest friends of Germanicus, Sabinus continued to befriend and protect Agrippina and her family. Egged on by Sejanus, Latiaris made it a point to befriend Sabinus, praising him for his unshaken loyalty to the family. Sabinus, it seems, had been much alone and was soon complaining tearfully of the horrible treatment afforded the family of Germanicus by the cruel and domineering Sejanus. His accusations spared not even Tiberius.

Next, Latiaris and some allies were prevailed on to share these revelations with a few senators. This led to a shameful plot that illustrates how low the ethics of our conscript fathers had sagged. Latiaris now invited his new "friend" to another meeting in his home. This time three middle-aged senators had managed to stuff themselves into a space between his roof and ceiling with their ears straining at various chinks and holes. Encouraged by Latiaris at every opportunity, the unwary Sabinus expanded on the same theme, citing some fresh examples of imperial harassment as well.

Having climbed back down from their makeshift roost, the senatorial eavesdroppers wasted no time in writing Tiberius to disclose the shocking news. Somehow, most of Rome learned of the contents as well, and days passed while people avoided sharing confidences with their closest friends — even falling silent in their homes for fear that other ears were glued to walls.

On January 1 the Senate received a letter from Tiberius beginning with the usual new year's greetings. Then followed a list of charges against Sabinus, ranging from his "tampering" with certain ex-slaves of Tiberius and plotting against his life. And the letter demanded retribution. The condemned man was immediately dragged away with a noose around his neck. Thus, a day traditionally devoted to peace and sacrifices was now attended by manacles and nooses! This is why some whispered that Tiberius had done this deliberately to show that the newly-elected officials who opened the religious year could also open the death cells.

As the year wore on, the Senate sought relief in maudlin flattery. Thus, when it voted the erection of an altar to Mercy and Friendship, it was to be flanked by statues of Tiberius and Sejanus. This sycophancy could also be seen in the crowds that gathered in hopes of a moment or two with the imperial pair. Oh no, the senators were not allowed on Capri. Rather, they would huddle on shore in Campania in hopes of addressing the emperor's gate-keeper, who might or might not consent to see them.

All this became worse when the aged Augusta died. At her modest funeral the eulogy was delivered by her 16-year-old great-grandson, Gaius, already better known by his nickname of Caligula. Tiberius had excused himself owing to the press of business. And when the Senate decreed extensive honors in her memory — including deification — he approved only a few harmless platitudes.

Now it seemed as if the last moderating influence on Tiberius and Sejanus had been swept away. Soon after Augusta's death the Senate received a letter from Capri openly denouncing Agrippina and Nero Cæsar. It was harsh. The youth was accused, not of rebellion, but of homosexual indecency. Since no one would begin to believe a similar charge against his mother, she was attacked for "insubordinate language" and a "disobedient spirit." Both, he added, had plotted to flee to Germany, and there rally the troops in the name of Germanicus for a march on Rome.

Yet, left unsaid in the letter was what Tiberius wanted the Senate to do about it.

Knowing that at least one of their members had been appointed by Tiberius to take notes, members mostly sat in silence. Then a clever solon opined that surely the letter was a forgery because no emperor would favor plots to destroy his own family. And with that the Senate adjourned for the day.

But this only infuriated Sejanus and gave him more spears for battle. He informed Tiberius, who replied by dispatch that the Senate had shown disloyalty by scorning an emperor in his distress. Tiberius (as urged by Sejanus) was now requesting permission to act on his own by exiling Agrippina and her sons Nero Cæsar and Drusus Cæsar. The panic-stricken senators acquiesced.

When word of it began spreading, Sejanus saw to it that the Guards marched through the city's main thoroughfares with swords drawn and trumpets blowing, threatening to cut the free corn ration in half if any seditious demonstrations were held.

Very quickly, Agrippina was sent off to the isolated island of Pandataria and Nero to Ponza, an even tinier rocky islet halfway between Capri and the shores of Campania. It is said by some sources that on their road to exile Agrippina and Nero Cæsar were kept in fetters in a tightly closed litter while a guard of soldiers kept any who met them on the road from looking at them or even from stopping as they passed.

As for young Drusus Nero, he was accused of conspiring with the Rhine regiments to march on Rome. Tiberius had him confined to a remote attic of the palace under Sejanus' supervision. There, tradition says, orders of the emperor were to feed him just enough to keep from starving. Why? Because he just might be needed should the emperor's succession plans go awry.

It would be morbid and monotonous to report all the deaths and reputations ruined by the hand of Sejanus. As this year began, he was clearly in the ascendancy and was spending most of his time in Rome as his duties multiplied. The year before, Tiberius had elevated him to senatorial rank and made him joint consul. Now, as his consulship ended, the emperor wrote a letter to Sejanus in which he bestowed yet another laurel: he would soon be adopted as his grandson. As such, Sejanus was directed to marry – oh, to have been a mouse in the corner when he read that letter — not Livilla, but Livilla's teenage daughter, Helen!

Sejanus did not flinch, however. Outwardly he welcomed the betrothal with the same modest grace that covered his face whenever informed that another pubic statue had been erected in his honor.

Soon afterward a curious event occurred that again would have made me wish to be a mouse in a corner. This time it would be at the Temple of Apollo on the Palatine, which Augustus had built almost as an adjunct to his home. Tiberius had called for a special session of the Senate to meet there. Sejanus was approaching the temple that morning, surrounded by servants and Prætorians, when his chief aide, Macro, rode up with a small detachment and saluted. Sejanus was surprised to see them and asked why the Guards had left their barracks. Nævius Sertorius Macro (a name you will be reading more about), replied cheerfully that Tiberius had sent him a letter to deliver to the Senate.

"Why not ask *me*?" an unsettled Sejanus asked.

"Because the letter is *about* you," the smiling Macro confided with a wink. "My heartiest congratulations, General," he added. "I think you're about to be decreed Protector of the People and our next emperor."

With that, an elated Sejanus turned and strode beaming into the temple. As he went in to take his seat, Macro quietly ordered Sejanus' escort of Guards back to quarters to await further word. He then entered after Sejanus, handed the letter to the consuls and returned to his own small detachment of Guards.

By the time a consul began reading the letter, word of the "Protectorship" had already begun to spread, along with waves of titters and fawning nods of congratulations to the heir-apparent. Tiberius' letter began with the usual apologies for not coming to Rome due to press of business and ill health. Then, after mentioning some minor business matters, the letter swerved into a restrained criticism of Sejanus for having prosecuted the governor of Africa for bribery without preparing adequate evidence. Then began a litany of similar excesses and demands for prosecution of various friends of Sejanus who had profited from the ruination of others. So treacherous was Sejanus, read the letter, that its author could not even feel safe enough to travel to Rome. He had no choice but to ask the Senate to arrest him.

The only member privy to the drama was the consul, Memmius Regulus, whom Macro had visited the night before. By now, Sejanus sat slack-jawed. Many of the seats around him had been quickly vacated. The consul called his name twice from the rostra. Sejanus failed to answer at first, because he was so unaccustomed to anyone demanding anything of him. Finally he stammered lamely, "Me? You mean *me*?"

Now, one could hear the boos and hisses begin to spread like wind on wheat stalks as Sejanus' flattering friends suddenly turned to indignant defenders of

Roman morals. Macro's Guards were summoned and the dazed Sejanus was marched off to prison. The crowd that always loiters about and eavesdrops on the Senate had already picked up the scent, following the fallen Sejanus and pelting him with mud, vegetables and worse every step of the way. The Senate, now having assurances of the popular sentiment, soon reconvened and condemned Sejanus to death.

Sejanus was beheaded and the rest of his body thrown down the Weeping Stairs. For three days it was dismembered or otherwise abused by the rabble. When the time came for it to be dragged to the Tiber with the traditional hook through the throat, only half of the trunk remained and the skull was already being used as a ball in a public gymnasium. By nightfall the streets were littered with the broken limbs of his many statues.

Apicata, the poor wretched wife who Sejanus had already divorced as proof of his intentions to Livilla, was dragged off, too, along with her young son and 14-year-old daughter. The boy understood what awaited him, but the girl kept wailing, as if she had been caught committing some childish mischief. "Please, please, I won't do it again," she cried. "Where are you taking me?"

After the executioner had placed the noose around the girl's neck, he hesitated and sent word back to the Guard that it was illegal to commit capital punishment on a virgin. Within two hours this "advice" came back: She would no longer be a virgin if she were first violated — and the quicker the better. Under threat of death himself, the executioner laid aside his noose and raped the terrified girl. Then he strangled her to death.

I was probably her age at the time — and far removed from any knowledge of what was taking place — but my eyes blur even today as I dwell on how low Rome had sunk in such a few short years after the glorious Augustus had left it.

But, dear reader, you must know this as well: through all I have just reported, the process of governance throughout the empire had not been outwardly impaired. Although it is true that Tiberius expanded no boundaries nor erected any imposing public works, he kept the army and fleet up to strength, paid officials on time, maintained the corn supply, and stabilized food prices. And his frugality helped build a considerable surplus of public funds to meet any emergencies.

Finally, let me address a question you probably thought I had neglected. Why did Tiberius suddenly turn on Sejanus, the "partner of his labors," his joint-consul and heir apparent? The record is not clear, but I will tell you what I can.

Understand first that Tiberius never confined himself wholly to Capri. While it is true that he never entered Rome again, the emperor did travel in Campania from time to time. Once he went as far as a friend's villa just outside Rome. During those trips he was no doubt shocked to see statues of Sejanus in virtually every bath, theater and public place. Games were now given in Sejanus' honor and his birthday was a Roman holiday.

But Tiberius could blame only himself for all this. No, there was something else.

Just before his letter to the Senate, the emperor learned how his son Drusus had died.

Who told Tiberius? A strong tradition persists that one day a maid in the imperial household was routinely collecting trash from the various rooms. Part of it was a wastebasket from Livilla's suite. Having had standing orders to save papyrus by removing the ink and reusing the expensive papyrus where possible, the tradition goes, the maid began to do so but soon became engrossed in the contents. What she read were drafts of letters from Livilla to Sejanus protesting his sudden aloofness and demanding to know when he would marry her. The letters referred to the poisoning of Drusus.

The maid's ultimate superior was Antonia, the widow of Tiberius' brother Drusus, and, one might say, "empress" of the palace household in Rome. Exactly what happened next isn't clear, but the most common version is that Antonia dispatched Claudius to Capri clutching a copy of a history her son had just written on ancient Rome. Claudius also brought the emperor a note from Antonia suggesting that he would be especially interested in reading page so-and-so. Between those pages she had slipped another note explaining everything.

Other versions are told. But what counts is that Tiberius got the message. And his revenge would soon make itself felt far beyond Rome and even 1,000 miles away, where Judea was struggling to maintain a semblance of independence and where the yet-nameless followers of Jesus were struggling to stand on their own feet.

· · · · · · · · ·

JUST AS THE PERSONA OF CÆSAR AUGUSTUS lingered over Rome and Tiberius, Judea at this time was surrounded by the living legacy — in the form of massive buildings and a fragile political structure — left by a ruler who had died 35 years before.

Outwardly, no two more different men could be found on earth than Octavian Cæsar Augustus and Herod the Great. One was fair-haired, clean shaven and slight of build. With the patrician's calm and graceful exterior, his pleasant nod could charm a room while his icy stare could make a man wither. The other was a burly, bearded Semite whose moods could swing from outlandish generosity to fits of vile temper. He could be the most charming and obsequious of client kings or a ruthless ruler in his own right who would even kill his wife and sons.

Yet, Herod and Augustus had one bond in common that overrode all the others. Both had fought for their thrones. The king clung to his for 36 years and the emperor to his for 55.

Herod's rise may have been the more remarkable because he came from Idumea, an Arabic district south of Jerusalem that was a part of Judea in name only. Its central city was Hebron, perched on the southeastern slope of a mountain range that descends into a semi-arid desert. For an Arab from Idumea to become king of the Jews was an audacious feat in itself, not unlike the Athenians inviting a Persian prince to rule them. The reason is that most Jews identify the land of Idumea first as the successor to ancient Edom — the same kingdom that had rudely refused Moses and his wandering exiles permission to traverse on their way to Canaan. They were also the same treacherous jackals, who 500 years before had encouraged the Babylonians to destroy Jerusalem so they could join in the plunder.

Yet, Idumeans could be useful to the Jews because the Jewish kingdom needed cooperative clients to provide border protection against Egypt to the south. Herod's grandfather was a strong chieftain and willing ally for the right price.

But Rome, which ruled the Jews, had an even broader strategic need for such services. To the east lay Parthia, successor to the legendary Persian empire. Although still a loose confederation spread over vast treeless stretches, Parthia could, when aroused, muster the only fighting force that could rival Rome's. Long aware that the Roman client states along the eastern Mediterranean were both scattered and quarrelsome, Parthia had begun mustering armies for an invasion.

The Roman Senate responded by giving the general Pompey unprecedented powers over the eastern front. His first move was to gather all of the smaller client states into a new single province of Syria. Ranging from the coast to a hundred miles inland, the new province embraced all of Rome's protectorates from Antioch to the Egyptian border.

When Pompey favored the compliant Hycrannus II to rule the Jewish lands within the new province, it was too much for his brother Aristobulus. Rallying a mass of fiery nationalists, he seized the temple, uprooted Hycrannus, and, I would suppose, made ready to cast his lot with Parthia. But the rebels learned, as ever, that Roman political decisions are usually backed by the military power to enforce them. Pompey and a legion stormed the temple in Jerusalem, struck down priests as they officiated, massacred everyone they could find, captured Aristobulus and sent him back to Rome to be paraded as a showpiece in the triumph that followed.

All this happened in the year that Cicero was consul and in which Augustus and Agrippa were born. Herod was a ten-year-old boy living in the safety of the Idumean desert. In a few years he would come to know it only as a homeland in which to spend nostalgic vacations.

This time Pompey set out to "balance" — or minimize — the power of the quarrelsome and unruly Jews throughout the new province. To this end he carved out, or isolated from Jewish rule, most of the cities that consisted chiefly of Hellenistic populations. It meant denying Jewish rule over the already Hellenized cities along the Phœnician Mediterranean and Gaza strip. Because there were many Hellenistic cities in the central hinterland, Pompey created the state of Samaria, which had the effect of splitting the Jewish stronghold of Galilee in the north from its counterpart, Judea, in the south. Then in the arid lands that stretched up and down Syria west of the river Jordan, Pompey created the Decapolis, a loose league of ten Hellenistic city-states. Left in charge of the gutted but still-wealthy Jewish population centers was the newly-restored Hycrannus II. He returned, however, not as king, but as ethnarch — a term meaning "prince," but one which Roman provincial administrators have come to use as they see fit.

Herod's father Antipas had risen to become chief minister to Hycrannus. Now, although the ethnarch's powers receded, his Idumean advisor became increasingly active. Pompey, for instance, had wanted to invade and subdue Idumea. Antipas was the go-between who skillfully helped avoid it, then became the mediator of Roman and Arab interests. Several years later, Antipas — with the 25-year-old Herod at his side — rushed troops to reinforce Julius Cæsar during his march to Egypt. He also hunted down brigands in Galilee for the Roman governor of the new Syrian province. When Julius Cæsar was murdered in Rome, it was the 29-year-old Herod who raised money in Galilee for the armies of Brutus and Cassius. When these were defeated in battle by Marcus Antonius, Herod switched his support to the victors and did the same for them.

Now came the decision that defined the rest of his life. The Parthians at last decided to invade Judea, hoping again to exploit the chaos caused by Roman civil war. Much of the Jewish elite welcomed the prospect of a new form of servitude that might mean less tribute and taxes. But Herod was one of the a few leaders in the region to declare for Rome — and in so doing he bound himself forever to its fortunes.

To bolster his cause, Herod's immediate hope lay in Egypt where Cleopatra had cast her lot with Marcus Antonius and the Romans. In a daring dash to Egypt, he borrowed a ship from the queen and sailed off for Rome in dangerous late autumn seas in order to appeal personally for support. He needn't have worried about it, because Antonius and the young Octavian, with their pressing need for an energetic ally in Judea, greeted the young Herod like a lost cousin. With great ceremonial gusto, the joint consuls then escorted him arm in arm to the Senate, which was ready to award him troops and money .

Herod now needed a title to match his lofty new status. Because he was either all or part Idumean, he could not become Jewish high priest. The joint consuls quickly settled on a title that would soon lead to the reassembly of Judea's parceled domains into one political unit again.

The title was king.

What happened then must have raised the hair on the necks of Jews in Rome with their bans on "idol worship" and dining with Gentiles. As if to demonstrate that Jewish idiosyncrasies had been overlooked for a higher calling, Herod then departed with Antonius and Octavian to sacrifice at the Temple of Jupiter Capitoline. After that he gave the Roman leaders a lavish banquet.

Like the young Octavian, young Herod had to repel other contenders for his kingdom, for by now the Parthians had managed to install one Antigonus, an anti-Roman Jewish princeling, in the temple at Jerusalem. With 30,000 men of his own and 11 Roman legions, Herod reclaimed the Temple after a five-week siege and sent Antigonus to Syria, where he was beheaded in view of the governor and the visiting Antonius.

Like Octavian Cæsar, Herod was to reorganize the government gristmill and preside over more than 40 years of internal peace — or, to be more accurate, absence of open civil war. And again like Cæsar Augustus, he became the greatest builder his nation had ever known. Who in the reign of Tiberius could not have been dazzled by the man-made harbor at Cæsarea and the gleaming new Hellenistic city that surrounded Judea's first true commercial port? Who would not have gazed in awe at the steep fortresses that were carved by Herod's workers from the mountains at Masada and Herodium? What ruler anywhere would not envy the lavish Herodian palaces at Jericho and Ascalon and Sepphoris?

And was there a structure anywhere in the world more massive or marbled than the new temple at Jerusalem? There on the same highest hill in the city which the smaller temple of Solomon once graced, atop a platform of massive but perfectly-cut stone blocks, stood a huge complex of outer buildings, courts and cloisters. At the entrance were giant doors bedecked with golden vine and grape clusters. The inner walls were hung with the largest Babylonian tapestry ever made. Outside, the gold-plated, white-marbled walls were so striking that pilgrims and tourists could see them from miles away as they wound their way up to the historic city.

In the large colonnaded outer court one would see men buying lambs, rams, birds and bullocks for various purification or thanksgiving rites. Seated inside the long colonnades were money changers, ready to convert any of the world's currencies into Tyrian shekels, the only acceptable coins for temple offerings.

In the middle of this massive Court of the Gentiles, as most called it, stood a walled rectangular building, running east to west and containing the Inner Precincts. Inside these high walls, roughly one-half the space was occupied by the Court of Women which included 13 chests, each shaped like a ram's horn trumpet, to receive the various offerings. Several times a day the money in the rams' horns was transferred to one of the numerous treasury chambers built into the temple's inner forecourt. The Shekel Chamber, for instance, contained the half-shekel annual fee imposed on all Jewish men. The Chamber of Utensils housed the great store of gold and silver vessels for use in worship services. But there was also a Chamber of Secrets — so called because its function was to dispense money surreptitiously to those who were poor, but "of good family."

The remainder of the Inner Precinct contained the shielded Court of the Priests, so named because only priests could enter it. This enclosed the Sanctuary, and at the top of the T-shaped building, the Holy of Holies.

Perhaps because the Temple was the nerve center of Jewish life, it had also, by the time of Tiberius, come to symbolize its highly sensitive and easily inflamed nature. For in this nation barely 150 miles in length and half as wide dwelled Romans, Jews, Greeks, a Jewish royal family, a priesthood and three religious sects. Added to these were a constant influx of travelers. Hovering on its outskirts were gangs of outlaws that ranged from political rebels to highway bandits.

Of these forces, Rome was the most important, but this did not mean that the Jewish-Roman bond was strong or friendly. Yes, there were reasons why this should have been so. Rome and its Syrian province certainly needed the support of Judea as a borderland. The Armenians to the north were no less menacing than the Parthians to the east, and the Arabs to the south seldom offered more than a symbolic nod of vassalship.

Judea also needed to be embraced for its shrewd merchants and protected for its economic contributions to the empire. Who among us wouldn't agree that Judean linen makes for the whitest and softest of all garments? Would you want to go without the balsam we use for medicine and on funeral pyres? Would your life not be poorer without being able to serve Judean dates, wine and olive oil to your dinner guests?

Thirdly, Jews are different than, say, Celts or Scythians because the latter tend to live in one place. Jews, although often not at their own choosing, have formed strong communities in all corners of the empire and beyond. In the last census of Augustus there were some 4.6 million Roman citizens and an estimated 54 million persons of all kinds throughout the empire. Of the latter, roughly one in eight were Jews. The Jewish population of Alexandria alone was estimated to be a half-million. So if you step on the foot of a Gaul, his cry will be heard only in his courtyard. Step on the shoes of a Jew and an uncle in another land might be in a position to kick you back!

Because of all the above, Romans of all eras made concessions to Jews they wouldn't have considered for others. Thus, the military cohort was garrisoned in Cæsarea, some 60 miles from Jerusalem, so that the eagles atop our banners would not be seen by people who tolerate no images. And no pious Jew could be found among the troops because they are not subject to military service (due partly to their refusal to fight on the Sabbath).

Yet, I must add that these very concessions engendered the very enmity that plagues Jews to this day. Romans snickered at the male circumcision ritual. Many were affronted that Jews refused to attend games in the theater, that they cited their dietary laws as an excuse for declining a dinner invitation, and that they worshipped a god with no name or form yet would pay not even a passing nod to the shrines of other peoples. This, in turn, contributed in Tiberius' time to the uneasy suspicion that the Jews would again welcome the Parthians if an enticing opportunity arose.

Again, the temple symbolized this division just as it symbolized Jewish glory. To Romans nothing was more insolent than to observe a religious temple in the process of being rebuilt into an impregnable fortress. And nothing was more irritating than to observe the enormous Jewish wealth being amassed daily from the taxes and ritual fees imposed by Temple priests on millions of Jews around the world.

But the Jews had their own good reasons why the bonds to Rome were in such constant tatters. Nothing was more hatefully symbolic of the yoke they lived under than the Fortress of Antonius that loomed ominously over the temple. Built by Herod in honor of his Roman patron, this 375-foot-long colossus housed a fortress, a palace and a prison. Its three towers rose up from the massive building with porticos that looked out directly over the large Court of the Gentiles. It meant that a Roman detachment, up from Cæsarea to police a festival, could maintain constant surveillance on almost everything going on inside the temple complex.

One can almost hear the high priest seething: "I suppose next they'll be poking their spears into the Sanctuary!" Indeed, any Jew who lived in Jerusalem would have been told about the time nearly a hundred years before when Pompey had besieged the temple. Strolling into the sacred Holy of Holies just to satisfy his curiosity, he came out rather bemused, telling his soldiers, "There's nothing *in* there!"

The blasphemy was well remembered, so that when Pompey died a miserable death on the sands of Egypt 15 years later, Jews understood it to have been due to "the scourge of Yahweh."

The Jewish-Roman relationship alone might have made a cauldron boil, but there were many more ingredients to be added to the stewpot that was Jerusalem. The second is a truncated royal family and fragmented rule. The succession problems of Augustus were aggravated by having fathered too few children. Herod created precisely the opposite problem with ten wives and so many sons that one would need a census taker to count them. Added to this confusion was the fact that while Herod was mainly Idumean, his chief wife,

Mariamme, represented the Jewish royal Hasmonean line. Another wife was Samaritan. The leading Jewish families viewed Idumeans and Samaritans with equal disdain.

Herod had quelled his share of hatchling plots with relative ease, but as he reached his sixties and began to suffer from a mysterious, painful "gnawing" in his lower regions, his kingdom also become racked with agony. Already gone in executions were most of the Hasmonean line: his predecessor, the doddering patriarch Hycrannus, his daughter, and her handsome 17-year-old brother. And when his beloved wife Mariamme could stand no more of it and dogged her husband with venomous insults, he had her taken off as well.

Now, as the aging king's condition worsened, so did competition for the successorship among the royal family's Hasmonean and Idumean factions. And with that, Herod's fears and suspicions were again inflamed almost daily.

The hopes of the royal Hasmoneans rested on two sons, Alexander and Aristobulus. Both had become personal favorites of Augustus when living in his household as part of their "proper Roman upbringing." Now back in Jerusalem, they were openly arrogant and seized every chance to insult their Idumean kin as crude bumpkins. Not long afterwards they were summarily seized and strangled for plotting against the king and − almost as an afterthought, one would think − for seducing Herod's three favorite eunuchs.

This left the more cunning Antipater, the eldest son and leading Idumean hope. He wasn't content to wait for his certain succession, however, because a servant caught him preparing a poison for his father. So, Herod, raging that "no one shall escape who thirsts for my blood," had Antipater packed off to the governor's prison in Syria.

"It is safer to be Herod's pig than his son," lamented Augustus when he heard about it.

When Herod himself died 36 years after becoming king, in the 35th year of Augustus, his will was of little help to the Romans in picking a successor or knowing the old king's intentions. It acknowledged, in effect, that no one successor was deserving or capable of governing the whole kingdom. So back the Jews went into partition, with the exasperated emperor quite in agreement that none of the new royal custodians should be called king. Archelaus, whose mother was a Samaritan, was named ethnarch over Judea and Samaria. Next, Galilee to the north and Perea, an elongated strip of land on the east bank of the Jordan, went to another son, Antipas, along with the still-lower title of tetrarch. Thirdly, Gaulanitis and Trachonitis, two even smaller districts just south of the Syrian capital of Damascus, were given to another son, Philip.

At the time of Tiberius, both Philip and Antipas were still ruling − and competently, by all accounts. In fact, Antipas, known as a fair and peaceful man, had managed to keep the rambunctious Galileans in check by killing two birds with one stone. To show his devotion to the emperor, he built an entirely new city on the southern shores of Lake of Gennasaret and named it Tiberias. At the same time, he brought the Galileans under tighter control by coaxing them into residence in the new city by giving them land and building them fine houses at his own expense.

But Archelaus had not fared well in Judea and Samaria. The territory's revenue had been much diminished by its reduced domains and the new ethnarch had to curtail many of this father's public works programs, which in turn caused unemployment and unrest. And the fact that he was half Samaritan and half Idumean did not help Archelaus' standing with the Jewish populace. In the first Passover of his ethnarchy, crowds in Jerusalem rioted. Archelaus panicked, called to the Roman garrison for help, and some 3,000 people lost their lives either fleeing or fighting back. But soon the uprisings had spread to the entire region and the governor of Syria was forced to move in with a large Army. Order wasn't restored until part of the temple had been set afire and its treasury looted.

Looted? Or justifiably "appropriated" by the Romans to pay for the high cost of an unplanned police action? I would not know. However, it is clear that all this instability was too much for Augustus when he heard about it. The emperor ordered the hapless Archelaus to take up a new life of exile in southern Gaul and declared Judea and Samaria an official province of Rome. After a census to determine the proper tax base, the province would then be administered by a series of military prefects, or procurators.

Let us now add some more spices to the stewpot pot called Jerusalem. We have next the high priest of the temple, the symbol of the Jewish religion, protector of all temple rites and embodiment of the Jewish character. Among the traits that a good Jew should be known for were love of family, personal dignity, adherence to Mosaic law, tithing to the temple and — almost as important — avoidance of degenerate outside influences.

In its ancient and purest form, the priestly caste centered on a few families, such as the descendants of Zadok, who had been high priest a thousand years earlier under David and Solomon. Closely interwoven with these were the Levites, who were charged with maintenance of the temple, including the provision of music and moneychanging services as well as disposition of hides from all sacrificial animals. Together, members of these powerful, elite families traditionally made up the ruling council, or Sanhedrin.

But the rule of Herod had altered that pattern and created new tensions. By the time of Tiberius, the Hasmonean hold on the priesthood had been broken several times by Herod, his successors and now the Roman procurators so that the number of priestly families were more numerous and no longer united by the same ancient ties.

The Sanhedrin had also changed — or had been shattered. King Herod began his reign by murdering most of its members and reserving important decisions to his own circle of advisors. He then enticed the return of many of the wealthy families who had been carried off to Babylonia in the Diaspora more than 500 years before. Now accustomed to life in an eastern court, they were more amenable to Herod's hellenized way of life than the rigid traditionalists they replaced.

The Sanhedrin of Tiberius' day had expanded to 71 members, yet its responsibilities had been severely curtailed. Although the wealthy priestly families still dominated, they now formed what amounted to a party known as the Sadducees. Increasingly questioning their authority and rivaling their power was a newer school of thinkers called Pharisees. Many were sages and teachers. Few were wealthy and most, as one record shows, plied such common trades as stonemason, charcoal burner and public letter writer. Rather than focus their lives on temple ritual, the typical Pharisee adhered to a detailed set of religious laws governing his daily conduct. Of these, the most important were tithing and maintaining purity of dietary habits and personal cleanliness.

Another difference between the two chief sects is that Pharisees believed in life after death. A priest of the day wrote that Pharisees "believe that souls have an immortal vigor to them, and that under the earth there will be rewards or punishments, according as they have lived virtuously or viciously in this life; and the latter are to be detained in everlasting prison." In contrast, he added, Sadduccees believe "that souls die with the bodies." Nor, he said, "do they regard the the observation of anything besides what the law enjoins them; for they think it an instance of virtue to dispute with those teachers of philosophy whom they frequent."

Perhaps you have also heard of the Essenes, who made up still another force in Jewish life. These are men who renounced wealth and women to live apart in wilderness compounds for the most part. There they rejoiced in being free of all the travails and tensions I have been discussing. Suffice it to say that they shunned temple rites and tended to remain out of the center of the storm.

Our pot is now boiling, but we have still more herbs and spices to add. Let us now stir in the Greeks who inhabited either whole towns or enclaves in Jewish cities, who sneered at the strange superstitions of Jews and felt outraged that they were considered *am ha-aretz*, which means that a pious Jew who accidentally touched them would have to undergo a purification ritual!

Now add some Syrians, Egyptians, the endless stream of traders and a half million sullen slaves. Then assume it is Passover time in April or perhaps the Festival of Feasts 50 days later and we can add perhaps a million more persons to the city. With most of them either elbowing one another at the temple or fighting for attention at the taverns or standing in line for the latrines or listening to fiery speeches by rebels and would-be messiahs, the cauldron now begins to bubble and hiss.

Ah, but we have forgotten just one more ingredient. It is but a solitary man, but quite enough to ignite the whole potion as if it consisted of pure pitch. And this is the Roman procurator. Yes, Rome's objectives are his, too — order and taxes — but a procurator brings his own persona and agenda as well.

The first three procurators under Augustus and Tiberius were not necessarily cruel or violent, even though all did disrupt Jewish life by arbitrarily changing high priests as often as suited their own ends. But a sharply different era would unfold in the 12th year of Tiberius — about the time Sejanus' star began to rise — with the appointment of Pontius Pilate. Because Tiberius, unlike his predecessors, was known for keeping governors and procurators in office for extended terms, this ill-tempered and insensitive bully would hold his office for ten tumultuous years.

In Pilate's very first year he decided to test Jewish law by sending a large contingent of his troops from Cæsarea to Jerusalem for winter quartering. Moving by night, the column entered the city with Tiberius' effigies parading alongside the ensigns. Because Jewish law forbade even the making of images, other procurators had taken care to remove all such effigies before entering Jerusalem.

As dawn broke the next morning and as the Jews of Jerusalem yawned and looked out their windows, they were astounded to see Roman images poking out from atop the Fortress of Antonius. Their protests to the commanding officer went unheeded. Angered even more, a disheveled deputation of religious leaders and hangers-on walked the 60 miles to Cæsarea and beseeched Pilate himself for permission to remove them. For five days they persevered in their pleas and lamentations. Each day they were refused on grounds that removing the images would be an affront to Tiberius Cæsar.

By the sixth day the procurator was seething. When he heard the Jews from Jerusalem were at the barracks doors again, the procurator ordered his soldiers to have concealed weapons at the ready when he came to sit on his judgment seat to hear the day's cases. When the Jews came to petition him again, he signaled the soldiers to surround them and draw their swords. Now Pilate informed them that they faced immediate death if they didn't stop bothering him and go home.

But the procurator had not expected what came next. The Jews threw themselves on the ground. Laying their necks bare to the swords of Roman soldiers, they vowed that they would accept death willingly rather than have their laws transgressed. In a surprising decision, Pilate relented and commanded that the images be carried back to Cæsarea.

One historian states that the procurator was "deeply affected by their firm resolution." If so, he seems to have forgotten it a few months later. For Pilate had decided to build an aqueduct to bring a new current of water to Jerusalem, and he actually seized money from the temple treasury to pay for it. This time, many thousands of people gathered to plead that he abandon the idea and restore the money.

It was also a festival time, and some impassioned orators hurled insults at Pilate in the course of denouncing the aqueduct project. But, unlike the episode at Cæsarea, Pilate offered no warning this time. Soldiers in disguise had circulated among the crowd, and on Pilate's signal they unsheathed their swords and hacked a great many to pieces before the terrified Jews dispersed. Among them were many Galileans, who were often in the forefront of sedition in their homeland and rioting at festivals. And in this case, one account has it that the soldiers "mingled the blood (of the Galileans) with their sacrifices."

. . . .

CHAOS, HATE AND REVENGE were the emotions that dominated the city of Jerusalem in this eighteenth year of Tiberius. Not quite two years before, a man had entered its gates preaching love and forgiveness – a Galilean, no less.

To a Roman or Jewish authority, the first few months after the crucifixion of this unpredicatable messianic pretender would seem to have justified the means they employed to put down the rebellion he had been bent on fomenting. Many of those who had cheered Jesus on his entry to the city and had strewn his path with palm leaves had long since melted into the crowds and disappeared like water down a desert gully after the Passover festival. Even his closest followers had scattered immediately in fear.

Soon, around 120 adherents to The Way, as they called it then, had reappeared in Jerusalem. They slept in private houses and public inns. During the days they prayed together at the Portico of Solomon in the Temple. But as dusk came on they would meet in groups for a common meal. Some came to the same two-story house where Jesus and his disciples had bread and wine together during the fateful Passover.

Pilate had long since returned to Cæsarea, and none of this activity could have been enough to arouse temple authorities. For one thing, those of The Way were hardly wealthy or powerful or otherwise noteworthy as individuals. Almost all were small shopkeepers, craftsmen, women, unemployed laborers and even slaves. And they had to spend more time scraping together the means of survival than they could inciting rebellion.

Perhaps the city officials had also come to realize in the eerie calm following the Passover festival that the message of Jesus that these people prayed over was hardly seditious. After all, he had told the temple authorities himself that

Cæsar was entitled to his taxes and temporal allegiance. Nor had he encouraged slaves to rebel against their masters. Indeed, he had taught his followers to love their neighbors as themselves and to turn the other cheek should anyone strike them.

But Rome and Jerusalem were wrong. What began to take place was perhaps as imperceptible to them as a tide changing. When I was a boy we lived near a stream that flowed to the sea. Often I would spend what seemed like hours staring at the water, determined that I would remain there until I could see the exact moment when the low tide spent itself and the incoming flow began. I suppose those "hours" to a small lad were but a few minutes, because I would soon be distracted by a playful dog or go off hunting for crabs and forget my vow.

Just like that boy, most of us are too busy working, eating and sleeping to notice the tides of history changing. But I believe this is what began to happen in Jerusalem. What held all members of The Way together as the tide ebbed lowest was that they had heard a message they could not relinquish. No one else before had preached that there is but one creator of all people and that all are equal in his sight. No one had taught that all could gain salvation for their sins and eternal life if they would simply love that single, unseen god and their neighbors likewise. It meant hope and freedom of spirit to all those who had been raised since birth to believe that there was nothing after death but bones in an ossuary and that survival during life depended on obsequiousness to a master or sacrifices to amoral gods who might be indifferent, jealous or vindictive.

Of this I will report much more later; but we must search now for what made the tide change.

First, it seems evident that these early followers of The Way had no doubt that they had witnessed miracles. We have all been amazed by magicians; but still we went to our homes afterwards and went about our dull affairs. We have all been spellbound at hearing a great orator and vowed to enshrine his message in our memories; but in a week's time most of us are busy at our routine tasks with the Great Man's words reduced to a puddle in the corner of our minds.

The Galileans who joined Jesus at the beginning were not attracted by any evident riches or promises of conquest. They could have left him during any of the years that led up to this Passover, but always they remained devoted because of the healings and other miracles they saw almost daily. Those who had seen Jesus only at the Passover in Jerusalem had also witnessed miracles — from his healings to the disappearance of the sun as he expired on the cross.

Secondly, a great many people had seen Jesus reappear afterwards. Crowds had cheered as he had entered the holy city for Passover, and many thronged about as he taught in the temple. Just as many had seen him stagger with his heavy wooden cross through the busy streets and then witnessed the agonizing death of the crucified. One such eyewitness was a disciple of Jesus named John, who was last known to be still living near Ephesus, and whose word is already canon among the churches of Asia. He has sworn that when two of Jesus' chief disciples had come early to the limestone cave that served as his tomb, they had found it empty and had gone away in confusion and grief. Soon afterward, this John reported, two of Jesus' women followers had come to prepare his body according to the proper Jewish rites. Upon also finding the tomb empty, they had begun to weep with disconsolation, when suddenly standing before them was a man whom they at first mistook as a gardener. But they soon realized it was Jesus. After he consoled and reassured them, they ran back to the other followers to report what had happened.

John has said that on the evening of the same day the followers were hiding from the Jewish authorities in a locked room somewhere when suddenly they found Jesus standing amidst them. John says that Jesus calmed their fears, then gathered them closely and breathed on them in order to "receive the Holy Spirit" so that they could go out and forgive the sins of others.

It seems that another of the original 12 disciples – one Thomas – had not been there when Jesus appeared. When told about it, he said that he could not believe unless he actually saw the imprint of nails from the cross on Jesus' hands. So it was, said John, that eight days later, the faithful were again in the same place – only this time with Thomas present. Again Jesus appeared and bade Thomas to approach him just as he had requested. Thomas fell down in repentance, and Jesus then said something (again according to John) that bears heavily on how Christians of later years have been able to maintain their resolve in the face of adversity. Said Jesus: "Have you believed because you have seen me? Blessed are those who have not seen and yet believe!"

A strong tradition has it that at one point in their early flight from the Jewish authorities, the small band of Jesus' followers eventually reassembled at a place called Mount Olivet, about a day's journey from Jerusalem. There, many people testify, Jesus again appeared in their midst and charged them to return to Jerusalem. When asked if that meant he would restore the kingdom to Israel, Jesus said it was not for men to know what events and what dates God has fixed by his authority. But he said that they would receive power from the Holy Spirit to be his witnesses in Jerusalem, Judea and "to the end of the earth."

Jesus then vanished, it is said. But he reappeared to the band at various times over a 40-day period, sometimes after they had gone back to Jerusalem and sometimes when they were in Galilee. In any event, this group of faithful followers, almost all of them Galileans, soon took up residence in Jerusalem with a new and powerful resolve.

There is no record I can discover of any of them ever renouncing their mission or moving back to their former livelihood.

Indeed, it was only by returning to Jerusalem – as had Jesus – that The Way could appeal to the Jewish people and their leaders. Now that their witness to the resurrection had vindicated Jesus' claims, they felt authorized to urge it vigorously upon the leaders and people. The Way did not seek merely to win scattered individuals. In Jesus they now saw the fulfillment of God's promise to Israel.

Now I want to cite the third and final force that changed the tide. Some of these same fishermen, tradesmen, slaves and sinners began to display the power of healing.

How can a writer in Rome explain it? One can just report what reliable people say. When Jesus said, "Receive the Holy Spirit," how could anyone know what this would mean? Could they themselves not have been astonished at what would next unfold?

There, the Jews celebrated two major festivals in the spring. The first, where Jesus was crucified, was the Passover, which was followed immediately by the seven-day Feast of Unleavened Bread. Celebrated together, they marked the beginning of the grain harvest and the deliverance of the Jews from Egyptian bondage.

The second event occurred some 50 days later. Called the Feast of Weeks, or just as often Pentecost, it marked both the end of the grain harvest and the giving of the Jewish laws to Moses many centuries before. As we have seen, the followers of The Way had spent the first days in scattered confusion, then in reunited jubilation as they again saw Jesus, then in daily prayer at the Outer Court of the temple. But now this Feast of Weeks marked a new turn.

The followers were meeting in the same "upper room" as usual when tradition has it that a sound like a mighty wind rushed down on them and filled them with the Holy Spirit. Soon they were all speaking loudly in a cacophonous chorus of different tongues. Pilgrims and travelers began to gather on the street below to see what the commotion was all about. Some scoffed that it was a drunken rabble, but the morning hour was much too early to make that a logical reason. Others might have compared the noise to the hysteria that grips crowds during the rites of Bacchus or the frenzy some people work themselves up to when the goddess Cybele is paraded through the streets at her festivals. But just as many in the street below began to believe they were hearing a din of foreign tongues because the crowd now included Parthians, Mesopotamians, Egyptians, Romans and others there at Festival time. And many swore in amazement that these unlettered Galileans were shouting in their own native languages.

Before long one of the Galileans stood on the upstairs porch and began to address the people below. Peter, standing with the ten other disciples who had been with Jesus since the beginning, declared that what they were hearing had all been foretold by the Jewish prophet Joel when he said in part:

And in the last days it shall be that God declares,
that I will pour out my Spirit upon all flesh,
and your sons and your daughters shall prophesy,
and your young men shall see visions,
and your old men shall dream dreams;
yea, and on my menservants and maidservants in those days
I will pour out my Spirit and they shall prophesy. [3]

Peter until then had been a fisherman, untutored in rhetoric. But with a newly-discovered passion he boldly proclaimed that Jesus had worked God's wonders on earth, had been unjustly crucified and had been raised from the dead. "Let all the house of Isræl therefore know assuredly that God has made him both Lord and Christ, this Jesus whom you crucified."

Peter went on to urge people to repent and to "save yourselves from this crooked generation." And when he then beseeched them to repent and be baptized in the name of Jesus for forgiveness of their sins, it is said that more than 3,000 people did so that day.

From then on the numbers who prayed in the temple every day multiplied. So did miracles performed by the disciples. Many followers, believing that Jesus would return momentarily, sold all their possessions and distributed them to those in need. They invited others into their homes and gladly shared their meals with them.

Life would also change for leaders of The Way. As I had stated, the followers who remained in Jerusalem initially had numbered about 120, including the 11 remaining disciples, Mary, the mother of Jesus, and the brothers of Jesus, at the time seemed to have remained in Galilee. At or just before this time the disciples had brought their ranks back to 12, choosing one Matthias by lot to replace Judas, who had betrayed Jesus to the temple authorities. Moreover, there had also evolved a group of "elders" who were simply known as The Seventy, I suppose to carry out much the same duties as would the Jewish Sanhedrin.

Then when the number of followers suddenly multiplied, the 12 disciples soon found it too burdensome to preach as well as see to the tasks of distributing food, clothing and the like to their followers. So they met and formed a Council of Seven, headed by a young, energetic Hellene named Stephen, to administer their affairs so that they could devote all their time to spreading the word.

Now Peter and others were spending even more time each day preaching at the temple in the Portico of Solomon. Reports of their healings were so widespread that it is impossible to dismiss all of them as fabrications. I will relate just one that has come down in writing because it seems typical of the many. Peter and the disciple John (the same one living now in Ephesus) were going to the temple at the ninth hour when a man, lame from birth, was carried to the gates to take up his daily position as an alms seeker. Seeing Peter and John about to enter the gates, he asked for alms. As Peter fixed his gaze at him, John said, "Look at us." When the man fixed his attention on them, expecting to receive a coin, Peter said, "I have no silver or gold, but I give you what I have. In the name of Jesus Christ, walk."

Peter took him by the right hand and immediately his feet and ankles were strong. Leaping up, he walked and entered the temple with them, praising God all the way. Many people there knew him, for he was over 40 and had been a beggar there for many years. Many of these people followed the three to the Portico of Solomon, where Peter began urging them to repent and show the same faith that made the beggar well.

You may wonder why the disciples chose to preach at the temple when they might have chosen a place farther from the eyes of the authorities. One of many reasons would be that at the temple they would find people free from their daily cares and in a frame of mind more suitable for preaching and discussion. But I think a more powerful reason is that the disciples saw the risen Jesus as the rightful Lord of the Jews and one who would come soon to assume control of the temple. In short, the temple was the central place of Jewish religious life and they had every right to be there.

But, yes, these new preachers did draw unwelcome attention, for on the same day he healed the beggar I just told about, Peter's preachings were officially challenged. It was now early evening, and the crowd around the disciples had swelled to about 5,000 when the head of temple security, followed by several priests and Sadducees, abruptly scattered everyone and took Peter and John off to prison.

The next morning the disciples found themselves confronting Ananias the high priest and several members of the Sanhedrin. "By what power did you do this?" they wanted to know.

Peter answered firmly: "If we are being examined today concerning a good deed done a cripple, then let it be known that it has been done in the name of Jesus Christ of Nazareth, whom you crucified, whom God raised from the dead. By him this man is standing before you well." And he went on to preach that salvation of all could come only through Jesus.

Now on one hand the Jewish elders were taken aback by Peter's boldness and self-assurance. On the other hand, they quickly realized that he was uneducated and from some rustic backwater in Galilee. After leaving the defendants so they could confer in private, the elders agreed that it was impossible to deny the healing because it was witnessed by so many. So they agreed simply to chastise them against preaching again in the name of Jesus.

Summoned back and told this, Peter and John quickly retorted, "We cannot but speak of what we have seen and heard." By this time a crowd of Jesus' followers had begun to gather outside. So with another threat not to preach again, the elders let the disciples go.

Now the number of believers multiplied like never before, and many from surrounding cities would bring their sick to the Portico of Solomon to be healed by the disciples. Even those who feared the authorities too much to go there would carry their sick out into the streets in hopes that Peter would walk by and cast his shadow on them.

At seeing the crowds increase, the leaders of the Sadduccees grew more incensed than ever. So this time they had Peter and John thrown into the common prison. Late that night, the early writers say, an angel of God opened the prison doors, telling the two disciples, "Go to the temple and speak to the people all the words of this life."

They did so and were there by daybreak, teaching again. When the Sanhedrin gathered later that morning to decide the fate of the two men they thought were in jail, the temple security police astounded them by reporting that, although the prison doors were locked with guards standing outside, they found no one inside. Then someone rushed inside to report, "The men whom you put in prison are standing in the temple and teaching the people!"

When the two were at last brought before the Sanhedrin and asked why they persisted, Peter answered that "we are witnesses to these [deeds of Jesus] and so is the Holy Spirit whom God has given to those who obey him."

By this time the elders were on the verge of condemning the upstarts to death had they not been stopped by Gamaliel. As both head of the temple rabbinical college and one of the Sanhedrin's most respected members, Gamaliel asked that the defendants be removed so the council could again confer privately. Once they were alone, Gamaliel calmed his colleagues by citing similar threats in prior years and what had become of them given a little patience by the elders. He recalled a rebel named Theudas, who had once attracted some 400 brigands, all of whom had scattered eventually once Theudas was killed. Then he recalled another Galilean named Judas, who had led a brief rebellion at the time Augustus had ordered a census just after Herod's death. Again, said Gamaliel, "He also perished and all who followed him were scattered."

His advice was to "Leave these men alone." For, he said, "If this undertaking is of men it will fail; but if it is of God, you will not be able to overthrow them."

The perplexed Sanhedrin members could think of nothing better, so they took the advice of Gamaliel and let Peter and John go – but only after a severe beating. This, however, the disciples bore gladly, rejoicing that they had been deemed worthy enough to suffer in the name of Jesus. They continued preaching every day, and more people than ever came to hear them.

A. D.   3 3 — 3 4

The ghost of Sejanus still brooded over Rome. His single-minded rise to power had cost many leading Romans their lives and many more their self-respect. After his violent death the families of senators and knights waited for signs from Capri that Tiberius had been avenged and that he would free the many so-called "friends" of Sejanus who had been awaiting trial and liberate the minds of many others who awoke in their beds each day under suffocating clouds of suspicion. More than anything, they hoped for an end to that horrible era in which man had come to fear that a friend or neighbor or even a slave could be an informer eager to embroider a trivial comment into a tapestry of treasonous charges.

But it soon became evident that the real perpetrator of these threats was still alive and infuriatingly healthy in his seventy-fourth year. "Will Tiberius be rid of the ghost of Sejanus?" asked one knight rhetorically. "Hah! He is still grappling with the ghost of Germanicus!"

This was said after the eerie silence had been broken by a communiqué from Capri. It denounced as a "leading criminal" a former prætor who had once been on Germanicus' general staff and who later had become a friend of Sejanus (a double curse!).

When a senator had finished reciting the emperor's charges into the record, he was startled to see a note at the end ordering him to read aloud a second letter that had been enclosed. The second one, much to the emperor's mischievous delight, I'm sure, was the very letter that the same senator had first sent to Tiberius secretly denouncing his colleague. Then the embarrassed viper was ordered to press charges on his victim that very day. And to all this the senatorial sheep obliged.

It was as if the stage had been re-furnished with the same setting. Once again, senators became informers, both openly and secretly. A dinner party remark on any subject might be scribbled down by other guests later that night and used in a hastily-arranged trial a week later. Condemned men became informers, spreading the ring of persecution like the disease it was. Long neglected laws from the days of the Republic suddenly became instruments of condemnation. Thus, when a man was found removing the head from a statue of Augustus, he was examined by torture and condemned for treason. Soon it became a capital crime to beat a slave near a statue of Augustus, to carry his image (such as on a coin) inside a public privy or criticize any act he had ever done. One man was put to death because his native town had inadvertently voted him honors on the same day that honors had once been awarded Augustus.

Also returning was the arrogance of the Prætorian Guard, with its new captain, Macro, seeming to pick up where his onetime mentor left off. So sure was Macro of his imperial backing that he decided to take on Mamercus Æmilius Scaurus, the proud head of one of Rome's oldest and most prestigious families. The bone he picked first was Scaurus' friendship with Sejanus. Then he denounced a tragedy written by Scaurus as containing verses that reflected poorly on Tiberius. But by the time the charges had been formally brought before the Senate, they had been changed to practicing magic and adultery with Livilla, the emperor's disgraced and deceased daughter-in-law. However, the proud Scaurus denied Macro the pubic spectacle he had sought. At the urging of his wife of many years, the couple opened their veins and died.

Whenever the fires of suspicion and persecution seemed to subside, Tiberius reached out to stoke the embers. In one case the emperor arrested and executed two of his oldest and closet friends, men who had been his companions in both Rhodes and Capri. In another instance he had Sextus Marius, the richest man in Spain, seized and hurled from the Tarpeian Rock. The charge was incest with his daughter, but the real cause was his wealth. Although his property by law should have gone to the state, Tiberius personally appropriated his lucrative gold and copper mines.

Within a year, it seemed almost as if Tiberius had found the pace of individual persecutions too slow for his tastes. Suddenly, without warning, the emperor ordered the execution of all those who had been arrested for complicity with Sejanus and who were still awaiting trials. The massacre was without discrimination as to sex or age, eminence or obscurity. Soon corpses lay hacked up and strewn about or stacked here and there. Relatives and friends were forbidden to stand by them or even to show any signs of sorrow. Guards surrounded them, scrutinizing everyone for signs of bereavement. Then, at last, the rotting bodies were dragged into the Tiber where they simply floated away with no one to retrieve or cremate them. And still, all Rome lay gripped in the paralysis of fear and cowardice.

During the year that followed, the individual persecutions and deaths re-sumed unabated. One historian has written that not a day passed without at least one execution, including New Year's Day and other religious holidays. All victims, women and children included, were thrown upon the Stairs of Mourning and dragged into the Tiber with hooks – as many as 20 in a single day.

Many more chose other means of dying as their only means of revenge over Tiberius. The more ludicrous the charge, the more likely it was a signal that the emperor was bent upon the victim's death no matter what his defense. And so, upon learning of such a charge against them, such people might elect to retire behind closed doors, settle into a warm bath, open their veins and receive their grieving families before slipping into a drowsy death.

Besides the fear of execution, there were other reasons for this choice. People sentenced to death forfeited their property and were forbidden burial. Their children might be orphaned and left without a sesterce. But suicides were re-warded by the right to burial and recognition of their wills.

These might be considered fortunate when compared to the victims who were allowed to cling to life in the cruelest of conditions. Witness Germanicus' exiled widow and his imprisoned son, Drusus Cæsar. The latter, as you may re-call, had been locked in the upper reaches of the palace and kept on the edge of starvation. Why? Because it had been Tiberius' plan that had Sejanus caught wind of his arrest, the Prætorian Guard was to free the youth from his jail and proclaim him the emperor's true successor.

When that ploy was no longer needed, the same cruel routine continued. It was the job of a staff officer of the Guard and an ex-slave to peer into the cell and observe the prisoner's every groan, every private muttering. They also beat him regularly. Then food was withdrawn. For eight days Drusus Cæsar staved off death by eating the stuffing from his mattress. First, in either feigned or real madness, he shouted delirious maledictions upon Tiberius. Then, as his life began to slip, he uttered an elaborate and formal curse: that for deluging his family in blood Tiberius must pay the ultimate penalty to his house, his ances-tors and descendants.

The surprising thing is that after Drusus Cæsar finally succumbed, the Guardsman was summoned to the Senate and allowed to read his notes on the prisoner's last days into the record. When he began reading the curse against Tiberius, senators threw up their hands in what I can only imagine as mock horror, resulting in rounds of further denunciations of the dead man and his family.

All this was no sooner ended when news came that Agrippina had perished on her desolate isle not too far from Capri. It is not clear how. One account has it that she had sustained life on the hope that things might somehow change after Sejanus' death. When that hope dimmed, she gave up and starved to death. Another account is that Tiberius arranged to have her killed on the very same day that Sejanus met his fate. Either way, Tiberius must have been kept closely informed, because the announcement of her death came from Capri and was accompanied by a letter to the Senate full of the emperor's renewed slanders against her. Tiberius even congratulated himself for not having had Agrippina strangled years earlier and hurled from the Gemonian Steps. For this he was voted the thanks of the Senate.

Sometimes I think that one of Tiberius' greatest amusements was devising ever newer ways to test how much more humiliation the spineless senators would endure. And their sycophancy was only more grist for his mill. For example, one day the shameless flatterer Junius Gallio thought he would appease the emperor by moving that retired Prætorian Guardsmen be allowed to sit in the 14 theater rows traditionally reserved for knights. Back came a stinging rebuke from Capri. What had Gallio to do with soldiers? Were they not entitled to receive their rewards solely from the emperor? How clever of Gallio to discover something Augustus had overlooked! Or was he a secret agent of some foreign power, attempting subtly to subvert military discipline?

So Gallio's reward for kissing the emperor's feet was a boot in the face: instant expulsion from the Senate and exile from the mainland.

Not quite everyone chose to suffer in silence. Senate records show at least one member whose memory I revere without knowing any more about him than this: In the days right after Sejanus' death, when everyone in Rome was shearing themselves of all ties to him, a knight named Marcus Terentius was one of many facing charges of having been his friend. When asked to defend himself, Terentius faced the Senate and addressed the empty seat that was reserved for the absent Tiberius. "In my position it might do me more good to deny the accusation than to admit it," he said. "And yet, whatever the results, I will confess that I was Sejanus' friend. I sought his friendship and was glad to secure it. I had seen him as joint-commander of the Guard with his father. Then I saw him conducting the civil as well as the military administration. His kinsmen, his relations by marriage, gained office. Sejanus' ill-will meant danger and pleas for mercy. For we honored, not Sejanus of Vulsinii, but...your future son-in-law, Tiberius, your partner as counsel, your representative in state affairs."

Continued Terentius: "It is not for us to comment on the man whom you elevate above others, and on your reasons. The gods have given you supreme control. To us is left the supreme glory of obeying. Besides, we see only what is before our eye: the man to whom you have given wealth, power, the greatest responsibilities for good and evil — and nobody will deny that Sejanus had these. Research into the emperor's hidden thoughts and secret designs is forbidden, hazardous and not necessarily informative.

"Think, senators, not of Sejanus' last day, but of the previous 16 years. We thought it grand even if Sejanus' ex-slaves and doorkeepers knew us. You will ask if this defense is to be valid for all, without discrimination. Certainly not. But draw a fair dividing line! Punish plots against the state and the emperor's life. But as regards friendship and its obligations, if we sever them at the same time as you do, Tiberius, that should excuse us as it excuses you."

This crisp logic, no doubt reflecting everyone's private thoughts, resulted in the only act of senatorial courage I have been able to discover during these years. Terentius' accusers, a sorry bunch of petty informers who already had criminal records, were ordered to be banished or executed. But as for Terentius himself, there is no evidence of whatever became of him. Nor did his breath of fresh air bring any winds of change. The real feelings of Romans were scribbled on the walls of buildings in the dark or circulated in anonymous poems like this:

> No more the happy Golden Age we see;
> The Iron's come, and sure to last with thee.
> Instead of the wine he thirsted for before
> He wallows now in floods of human gore.[4]

Before leaving this scene for now, I must relate one thing more. The tensions and turmoil during the period that I have just described were overlain and aggravated by a financial crisis that enveloped Rome and spread to much of the empire. One might say that it happened because of Tiberius' miserly fiscal policies, but that it also was alleviated by the treasury reserves that those same policies had conserved.

To explain: Augustus had coined and spent money lavishly on the theory that its increased circulation, low interest rates and rising prices would stimulate business. They did so for many years, but the process could not go on forever, and in the last four years of his reign Augustus stopped the process of fresh minting.

Tiberius, perhaps thinking he had learned a lesson from his predecessor, jumped to the opposite theory — that a frugal government economy is the best guarantee of stability. Thus, in part by never sponsoring public games, by restoring only two public buildings during the whole of his reign, by keeping veterans waiting for their retirement bonuses until they died, by not paying provincial counselors salaries (so that they had to rely on bribes) and by confiscating numerous wealthy estates through political persecution, the state had built up a surplus exceeding 2.7 billion sesterces.

The other side of the coin was that all this resulted in a dearth of circulating currency, made worse by the flow of money eastward for everything from Egyptian wheat to Syrian linen. Prices fell. Interest rates rose. Debtors sued lenders after dusting off a centuries-old tribune's law that had capped legal interest rates at 5 percent. Financial houses, for fear of prosecution, practically ceased all lending activities, yet continued to call in overdue loans.

So many cases had piled up in the courts that the Senate was importuned to do something. Its response only worsened the situation. To check the flow of capital abroad, the Senate voted that two-thirds of every member's capital be invested in Italian land. But once again the sheep had managed to shear themselves. Senators found themselves calling in loans and foreclosing on mortgages in order to raise cash to buy Italian land. When the senator Publius Spinther notified the Bank of Balbus and Ollius that he must withdraw 30 million sesterces to comply with the law, the firm immediately announced its bankruptcy. With banks on the brink of ruin, so were businesses from Tyre to Alexandria that depended on them for credit. When rumors spread that the great Roman banking house of Maximus and Vibo would be broken by the great weight of its uncollectable loans, depositors began a run on the bank that forced it to close. Almost simultaneously came news that great banking establishments had failed in Lyons, Carthage and Corinth.

At this point Tiberius, to his credit, did come to the rescue. The emperor suspended the land investment act and distributed a hundred million sesterces among specially established banks in the form of interest-free three-year loans. In exchange, he received security of double that value in landed property. The rather rapid effect was to halt the upward pressure on interest rates. Soon, money came out of hiding and confidence slowly returned.

Yet, in all that process one people was left severely damaged. Jews, or more specifically Syrians, were so synonymous with banking and money lending throughout the empire that in some languages the name for "bank" was literally the same as "Syrian." When hard-pressed debtors began using the old usury laws as weapons against their creditors, Jews were often the target.

Only this prolonged tension can explain a decision made by Tiberius in the midst of the financial crisis. It seems that a certain Jew (the records do no confirm his name) was driven out of Judea for perpetrating various types of financial fraud. He wound up in Rome where he professed to instruct people in the laws of Moses. His converts, as has always been the case, were frequently women of high status who saw Judaism as a refuge of virtue and high principle in an otherwise corrupt world. But this rabbi had his own set of principles. At some point he enlisted three other unsavory characters in a plot against one Fulvia, a wealthy Roman woman of great dignity who had embraced the Jewish religion under his tutelage. It seems that the "rabbi" persuaded her to send a large amount of gold and purple to the temple at Jersusalem. The shipment, however, was intercepted and divvied up among the four conspirators for their own debaucheries.

When this became known, Fulvia's influential husband appealed directly to Tiberius for help. The emperor not only had the evildoers tracked down and arrested, but also ordered all Jews banished from Rome for good measure. As they were preparing to depart, the consuls had 4,000 men rounded up and sent off to Sardinia for hard labor on roadbuilding and other projects.

. . . .

JUDEA, AND INDEED, GREATER SYRIA, brewed its own forms of tension. In addition to the thankless job of controlling friction among religious and ethnic factions, the Jewish leadership faced an odd problem: an uncomfortable embarrassment of riches. The annual one-half shekel levy on some two million adult Jewish males throughout the empire continued to swell the temple treasury just as the financial crisis had rippled outward from Rome. And at a time when debt-besieged Greeks and others were cursing Jewish financiers, it struck some as ironic that a Roman military cohort of untested resolve was all that stood between them and instant financial recovery!

To this scene we can add the frequent absence of a Syrian governor. During much of his reign Tiberius maintained the strange practice of appointing men to this important post in Antioch, the empire's third largest city, but then forbidding them to take up residence there for years at a time. Perhaps it was simply due to the emperor's parsimony or that he felt any possible mischief on Syria's borders could be held in check by the numbers of hostages from Parthian and Armenian royal families who lived in Rome under the auspices of the imperial household.

Yet, once a provincial official did take his post, Tiberius tended to leave him there forever. The emperor once explained his reasoning with this little homily: "A man suffered an open wound and great number of flies flocked about the sore. A bystander pitied the man's misfortune and began to drive the flies away from him; but the wounded man bid him stop. When asked why, he replied: 'If you drive these flies away, you will hurt me worse. For as these are already full of my blood, they no longer crowd about or pain me as much as before. But the fresh ones that come in almost famished will be the cause of my destruction.'"

True to this policy, Tiberius saw to it that Pontius Pilate was only one of two Judean procurators during his entire reign. But Pilate himself did not prove true to form.

With the seat of government in Antioch vacant for prolonged periods, the Judean procurator was free to exercise his unsated greed and cruelty in his private "kingdom" more than 300 miles to the south. In fact, he must have taken new vigor at learning that Tiberius had banished Jews from Rome!

Added to the temple authorities' ordeal of co-existing with suspicious Gentiles was the delicate task of living with all the factions represented by the Jewish royal families and their shifting borders of jurisdiction. The latter was typified by the small Tetrarchy of Trachonitis-Gaulanitis that had been administered by Philip, one of the sons of Herod the Great. The territory was no more than 30 miles from north to south and not much wider, but still strategic because it bordered Galilee on the Lake of Gennesaret and was no more than 30 miles from Damascus. After 37 years in which he ruled quietly and efficiently, Philip died peacefully in the 20th year of Tiberius. Philip had been known most as a gentle man who was always accessible and who took his tribunal chair whenever he traveled. Thus, when approached on the road by anyone with a complaint or request, he would have the chair placed on the roadside and hear the case at once.

Although Philip had left no sons, it had been assumed that Tiberius would choose someone from the family to rule. But word soon came that the tetrarchy was to be added to the province of Syria and administered directly by its governor. However, I do not believe Tiberius did so from avarice or spite. Rather, it was the first open sign that Rome recognized the need for tighter control over the territory in the event a war broke out.

I relate the next events to show how the things a ruler does in his personal life can reverberate through his realm. This one involves Antipas, the son of Herod the Great who had been made tetrarch over the two states of Galilee and Perea, both separated north and south by the 30 miles that make up Samaria. Ostensibly, Antipas had governed rather well, keeping the hotheaded Galileans in check and pleasing Rome by building the new city of Tiberias on the Lake of Gennesaret. But Antipas got himself in trouble with a woman. He was married to the daughter of Aretus, whose Arabian kingdom of Nabatea ran along the eastern border of Perea (some 30 miles east of Jerusalem) and then stretched south and west over a great wilderness. Once when visiting his half-brother Herod, a minor princeling who lived in Rome, Antipas fell hopelessly in love with his host's wife, Herodias. He pursued this stealthy courtship until his sister-in-law finally agreed to marry him, but only on condition that he divorce his Arabian wife, the daughter of Aretus. And Herodias, quite contrary to Jewish law, agreed to divorce her own husband once Antipas upheld his end of the bargain.

Well, Antipas had been sailing toward home, no doubt still wondering how to accomplish this delicate deed, when the ever-efficient Roman system of spying and gossiping somehow overtook him and reached the ears of his Arabian wife in Perea. Soon she had packed up and was headed east with a small military escort to Macherus, a large town near the Perean-Nabatean border, under the guise of needing a rest or "vacation." Hardly had the dust settled from the hooves of the departing Jewish escort when riding into the border city came a much larger Nabatean contingent, ready to speed the aggrieved daughter to King Aretus.

The new escort included Aretus' leading vassals, all of them already alerted. The king, after tut-tutting his daughter and handing her off to the household women for more consoling, summoned the generals of her horse guard to what now constituted a war council. At that point I should think Aretus would have had difficulty concealing a grin. Aretus was already convinced that Tiberius was in his dotage and that the absence of a resident Syrian governor for so many years was ample proof. In fact, the Arab king had already been emboldened enough to assume control over part of the Decapolis, that loose collage of ten Hellenistic city states that spread out in the desert just beyond the eastern borders of Galilee and Samaria. Chief among the cities that Aretus occupied with no resistance from Rome was Damascus, a major East-West trade link since the most ancient of times.

Having just digested that large morsel, King Aretus had turned his attention to some choice pieces of Perean palm groves and other fertile lands long held by the Jewish tetrarch Antipas. And now his tearful daughter had brought him a perfect pretext for action!

Before long, nervous Jewish towns were hearing word of Nabatean troop buildups to the south and east. Then came the news that must have made them gasp in astonishment. "What?" I can hear them wailing. "Our lives and lands are to be endangered because a Jewish king wants to marry his *brother's* wife?"

But marry they did, just as soon as Herodias arrived from Rome.

At this point you should know about a man named John, who for several years lived in the desert on wild fruits and the like, emerging frequently to preach and prophesy. He was called John the Baptist because Jews would line up along the banks of a river such as the Jordan and he would submerse each one in a "baptism" that symbolically forgave their past sins and assured them of a new life. Jesus was known to have been so baptized, and after his crucifixion a few years later, the crowds that came out to greet John began to multiply. In fact, agents of Antipas told the tetrarch that the people would probably do whatever John told them.

On one of those occasions, a throng shouted in agreement when John saw fit to castigate Antipas and Herodias for breaking Jewish marital laws. He demanded that both seek the repentance of baptism for their sins. Instead, as one would expect from an insecure monarch, Antipas had this John clapped in the prison at Mecherus, at the outer reaches of his realm, so as to be as far as possible from his followers.

Not long afterwards, when Herodias had come from Rome to Perea along with her daughter Salome, she gave her new husband a sumptuous birthday banquet. When the meal was completed and the entertainment began, Antipas gazed at the fetching Salome and asked if she would dance for him on his birthday. When Salome demurred, her new stepfather, flushed with wine, I suppose, blurted out that he would honor any request if she would only take a little whirl about the floor.

At this point, tradition has it, Herodias leaned over to Salome and whispered something in her ear. I, for one, believe it, because what she then spoke could not have been conceived in the mind of such an innocent young thing: she would dance if her step-father would promise to produce the head of John the Baptist.

Salome — or rather, Herodias — soon got her wish that night, but the king would regret it in blood spilled many times over. The people became even more embittered against the tetrarch and his wife. And the Arab Aretus, as I shall describe later, soon exacted his revenge for the insult to his daughter.

But I must now return to the Roman procurator for the moment. Although he had refrained from provoking catastrophic episodes in Jerusalem, Pontius Pilate continued to make forays to the hinterland from his seaside military base in Cæsarea. This time his target was Samaria, just a few miles from his barracks.

Samaria, despite lying on a direct route between Jerusalem and Galilee, was such an odd and unfriendly place that many Jews chose to make the trip by a much longer detour to the east. The reasons are imbedded in Jewish history from the time of Moses. All scholars agree that the ancient prophet died before ever setting foot on the land of present Judea, to which he had led his people from Egypt. The Samaritans, with whom no one else seems to agree, cling like vines to an oral tradition that the sacred Ark of the Covenant (containing laws given by God to Moses) and other precious relics were stored on Mount Gerzzim in Samaria. Therefore, the Samaritans believe, theirs is the rightful homeland of the Jews and Mount Gerizzim its most sacred place.

One can therefore imagine the excitement in Samaria caused one day when a man (a charlatan, I assume), boldly announced that he would lead the people up Mount Gerzzim and show them where the sacred relics of Moses had been buried. Before long, a considerable crowd had gathered at a small town at the mountain base called Tirathaba. My guess is that the large and loud crowd was noted suspiciously by some Roman soldiers making their way to Cæsarea on the coast. In any case, the "pilgrims" were still congregating in the town when they could hear the sounds of horses charging up from Cæsarea.

When the troops arrived, Pilate himself was riding among them. Without asking questions, the Romans began flailing at the shocked and paralyzed Samaritans. When some drew their swords, even more were hacked down in the street. When the Samaritans scattered in all directions, they were either cut down from behind or rounded up and captured. Finally, Pilate had the exhausted survivors herded into a farmer's goat pen and ordered them all executed at once.

This massacre happened late in Pilate's eighth year as procurator. And although he would remain in Cæsarea to see his tenth year begin, he, for reasons I shall explain later, would never again be in a position to command without the close supervision of Rome.

As the last of these two years was closing, another new chapter was about to unfold for the Jews. The Parthians, whose western borders begin only some 500 miles from Syria, would agree with the Nabateans that Tiberius needed a test of strength. Lucius Vitellius, just completing his year's term as Roman consul, would become the first resident governor in years. Samaria would become a valuable resource for military recruits and supplies. Samaria would use its heightened importance to petition the new governor for relief from the cruelties of Pilate.

. . . .

ONE OF THE REASONS THAT HAD MOTIVATED the Apostles in Jerusalem to select the Council of Seven was that the Christians of Hellenized backgrounds claimed that their widows and poor were not being included in the regular distribution of food and other necessities. As such, the seven persons who administered affairs for the early Christians were mostly of Greek-speaking communities and backgrounds. Among them, their leader Stephen soon became more than a manager of affairs. He, too, became imbued with the Holy Spirit and began to preach The Way, healing and causing wonders as he went.

I mention this because there was something about young Stephen which aroused the ire of the Jewish authorities even more than had Peter and John. I think it was in part because he is said to have been strikingly handsome and naturally attracted attention. It was also partly that he may have preached in Greek and won many non-Jews as believers in Jesus.

And it was certainly because he preached in a tinderbox at that particular time. Temple officials, as I have said, had many reasons to fear the wrath of Romans and the invading armies of eastern powers. Doubtless they knew of the beheading of John the Baptist and took it as a signal that royal authority would condone harsh treatment of Jesus' followers. And that they may have considered John part of The Way could be easily understood. If John had baptized Jesus and recognized him as the son of God, they might reason, then John would have had to be a believer in the years that he remained on earth after Jesus.

All these factors were no doubt present one day when Stephen was preaching in one of the Hellenized temples that bore names such as Synagogue of the Freedmen and Synagogue of the Cilicians. He must have been fiery and abrasive in his youthful zeal, because he had already aroused the ire of these congregations before. On this particular day he soon had the elders on their feet contesting various claims about Jesus. They were especially aroused when Stephen referred to Jesus' prediction that the temple would soon be destroyed. They also interpreted his words to mean that the laws of Moses were no longer valid.

Shortly thereafter, a hostile group of elders from several synagogues had sought out Stephen and dragged him before the temple high priests. When asked to account for himself, Stephen was no less zealous amongst the temple elders than he had been to the elders of Jerusalem's synagogues. In a long dissertation that must have seemed patronizing, he traced the history of the earliest Jewish patriarchs through Moses to the days of Solomon and David, all things the priests knew by heart. Then he lashed out: "You stiff-necked people, uncircumcised in heart and ears, you always resist the Holy Spirit! As your fathers did, so do you. Which of the prophets did not your fathers persecute? And they killed those who announced beforehand the coming of the Righteous One, whom you have now betrayed and murdered, you who received the law as delivered by angels and did not keep it."

The more Stephen railed at them, the more rigidly irate his priestly interrogators became. He then gazed upward and said, "Behold, I see the heavens opened and the son of man standing at the right hand of God..."

But he was not allowed to finish. Crying out in a loud roar, they rushed as one upon Stephen. They dragged him outside the city gates and stoned him one by one. Stephen did not resist, but prayed to Jesus, "receive my spirit," just as he died.

On that same day, the Jewish authorities released all their pent-up frustration on the troublesome heretics of The Way. The temple police went from house to house of known adherents, dragging off men and women to prison. Many more were warned by friends and fled from anywhere there was Jewish authority, some even to Damascus far to the northeast.

One of the leaders of this repression was a temple worker named Saul, who I would judge to be in his early or mid-twenties. It was he who cleared the way for the angry priests when they brought Stephen outside the gates, and he who guarded the outer garments that had been flung at his feet by those who hurled the lethal rocks. Perhaps he cast one himself.

Once the Christians had fled, temple authorities grew concerned that they might have only succeeded in spreading a plague, that the exiles would simply infect other synagogues in major cities. Obviously, not many of the regular temple security guard could be spared: their job was tough enough keeping order in Jerusalem. So it is said that the Sanhedrin deputized several of its younger, hardier priests and administrative officials and dispatched them in small groups to the leading synagogues in the major cities.

Among them none would have been more zealous than the young, fiery Saul. He led a contingent to Damascus, armed with letters to its leading synagogues authorizing them to bind and bring back as many of the renegade leaders as they could find. Many years later a much older Saul would write (in a letter I have seen) of "how I persecuted the church of God violently and tried to destroy it...so extremely zealous was I for the traditions of my fathers."

From Jerusalem, Damascus required a dusty trek of some five days. As Saul would later confirm himself in letters, he was approaching Damascus on that hot, unshaded road when suddenly he was enveloped in such a stunning bright light that he felt himself knocked to the ground. At almost the same time he heard a voice saying to him, "Saul, Saul, why do you persecute me?"

And the terrified young man stammered, "Who are you, Lord?"

"I am Jesus, whom you are persecuting," came the voice. "But rise and enter the city and you will be told what to do."

The small group with Saul stood speechless. They heard the voice but saw no one else. Saul finally arose from the ground and opened his eyes. But he could see nothing.

Saul's companions led him by the hand into Damascus. There he sat dazed and without sight for three days, neither eating nor drinking.

All this is recorded by the earliest Christian historians. And they report as well that the voice of Jesus also came to a follower named Ananias at his home in Damascus. "Rise up," the voice told Ananias, "and go to the street called Straight and inquire in the house of Judas for a man from Tarsus named Saul; for he is praying there and has seen [a vision of] a man named Ananias come in and lay his hands on him so that he might regain his sight."

But Ananias answered, "Lord, I have heard from many about this man, how much evil he has done to your saints at Jerusalem and that he has authority from the chief priests to bind all who call upon thy name."

But Jesus said to him, "Go, for he is a chosen instrument of mine to carry my name before the Gentiles and kings and the sons of Isræl. For I will show him how much he must suffer for the sake of my name."

So Ananias found Saul just as Jesus had said. Laying his hands on the sightless young traveler, he said "Brother Saul, the Lord Jesus who appeared to you on the road by which you came has sent me that you may regain your sight and be filled with the Holy Spirit."

And immediately some opaque flakes resembling fish scales fell from Saul's eyes. He arose and could see again. And after he had taken nourishment, he was baptized.

Saul then spent several days in Damascus with followers of The Way. He appeared in the synagogues to exalt Jesus as the son of God. And all who heard him were astounded, saying, "Is this not the man who came here to bring those who called upon the name of Jesus bound before the chief priests?"

But this same enthusiasm for Jesus caused the leading Jews of Damascus to beseech King Aretus' governor to have Saul captured and killed. Because he was reported to be hidden away by his new friends, the governor's guards at the city gates were ordered to keep a steady eye on all strangers who came and went. One night, however, Saul was escorted to the home of a Jesus follower who lived in a tenement that formed part of the city's eastern wall. There, in the darkness of night, Saul was helped into a large basket and slowly lowered down the wall by a rope. And there he escaped by the back roads used by local farmers and herdsmen.

Meanwhile, the believers who had scattered from Jerusalem had indeed begun to do just as the temple authorities feared. They arrived in synagogues throughout Judea and Samaria and told of Jesus and The Way. One Philip, who had, I believe, been one of the Council of Seven with Stephen, took up in a Samaritan city and found himself with the Holy Spirit. The same written reports about Saul tell of Philip making "unclean spirits" come out of the possessed, "crying with a loud voice" as they did. It adds that "many who were paralyzed or lame were healed," and that Philip was soon followed by "joyous multitudes."

When the apostles heard that Samaria was accepting Jesus, Peter and John traveled there to pray that these people, too, might receive the Holy Spirit. Among the people was a man named Simon, who had become famous as a magician but who had joined the throngs who had accepted Jesus. When he saw Peter perform his first baptisms there and give people the Holy Spirit by laying his hands on them, Simon approached him with an offer of money if he, too, could receive these powers. But Peter turned to him and said, "Your silver perish with you because you thought you could obtain the gift of God with money!" Repent of this wickedness, he said, "and pray to the Lord that if possible, the intent of your heart may be forgiven you. For I see that you are in the gall of bitterness and in the bond of iniquity."

Soon afterward Peter and John headed back for Jerusalem, stopping at many Samaritan villages along the way to preach the gospel. Philip continued preaching up and down the coast from Gaza to the south and as far north as the towns just before Cæsarea. For Peter, John and the other disiples, new repressions by the Jewish authorities represented a threat and an inconvenience, but their basic mission had not really changed. A far greater force for change in their lives would come in the person of Saul.

. . . .

. . . .

Of all the men of public affairs I have studied, Tiberius is the most difficult to fathom. Typical of this enigma was the decision to move to Capri. Was everything that happened since then the result of being on this inaccessible outpost, cut off from routine discourse with those who could have offered beneficial advice? Or was Capri simply a natural setting for a man whose heart had already become an inaccessible outpost?

During the whole of his life on Capri, the emperor only twice approached Rome. Once he was rowed up the Tiber in a trireme. Although he never got more than 20 miles from the city, he posted a guard along the banks of the Tiber to turn away those who came out to meet him. The second time his entourage came up the Appian Way as far as the seventh milestone, but then returned after merely getting a glimpse of the distant city walls.

And yet, nearly every year there would be an announcement that Tiberius was to visit this province or that army. Preparations would be made by chartering carriages and arranging supplies in the surrounding towns and colonies. Tiberius would even allow vows to be put up for his safe voyage and return. But the visits would always be canceled at the last minute — to the point where people jokingly gave him the name of Callippides, who was proverbial among the Greeks for seeming to run without ever leaving the same spot.

Had the emperor gone mad? Was he overly cautious? Or did he simply get some strange pleasure from teasing his subjects and keeping them ill at ease? If one can't answer such basic questions, how can one judge his conduct as a ruler? Why, one wonders, was Tiberius loathed in Rome, yet generally respected in the provinces as a conservative, level-headed administrator? How could a man who was once an able general and tender husband turn into a morose tyrant? If Tiberius was astute enough to conserve the treasury surplus left by Augustus, why did he ruthlessly murder and confiscate the properties of so many wealthy families? If Sejanus was indeed a rat who deserved extermination, why did the emperor punish everyone who ever befriended him? If even the Senate was in his eyes a rotting tree in need of pruning, why did he chop at every bough and poison the roots? Even if the family of Germanicus required repression because it presented a threat to the emperor, why was it necessary to starve them cruelly and condemn even their memory after their pitiful deaths?

I will offer an answer, but I must again add a caution as to the tales and fantasies that have built up from Capri over the years. No doubt where you live there is a house that always keeps its windows shuttered or a person who behaves strangely and never speaks to neighbors. And you know as well that the less that is known about the person or place the more people enjoy embroidering stories about it to the point where some of the tales become outrageous. Well, Capri was that place and the taciturn, brooding Tiberius was just the person to evoke such stories. However, having warned you against such excesses, I will now say that the oral history that has come down from the villa atop those steep rocky cliffs has it that Tiberius had become both a misanthrope and a monster.

I have traveled to Capri, and one story was told to me by so many of the fisherfolk there that I, too, soon came to regard it as truth. It seems that not long after Tiberius had settled on Capri he was standing on his terrace overlooking the blue sea when he was startled to see a peasant man appear behind him. The scruffy old fellow proudly held out a large mullet, offering it to the emperor, I suppose, out of respect and friendship. But Tiberius was so alarmed that the man could have clambered up the rocky backside of the island and then eluded his guard that he had the man's face scrubbed with the sharp, scaly flank of the fish. In the midst of all this the man had enough wits about him to exclaim, "I certainly am glad that I didn't offer the emperor the enormous crab I caught!" With that Tiberius had the crab brought out and set it to tearing at the poor man's face.

But this was a mere child's spanking in comparison to what a guide told me. After we had walked some three miles from the nearest settlement, through brambles and olive groves, to the now crumbling villa, the townsman showed me a burnt clearing. There, he said solemnly, Tiberius had overseen long and exquisite tortures of his victims. Then he took me to the edge of a cliff where tradition has it that the condemned were cast headlong into the sea before the emperor's eyes while a band of sailors waited below in small boats. When the bodies crashed into the sea, the marines would row over and break their bones with boathooks and oars.

More widespread than the emperor's tortures were the consequences of his infatuation with astrology. Although Tiberius was never terribly diligent in performing his obligations to the gods of Rome, he had been addicted to astrology ever since his sojourn on Rhodes. Convinced that all events were in the hands of fate, the emperor now spent many hours interviewing prominent astrologers and hearing their prophesies. It is said that when seeking occult guidance Tiberius would retire to the uppermost room of his villa, which nearly overhung a cliff. An astrologer whose skills were about to be tested would be escorted up to the room by an illiterate, brutish ex-slave along a rough, precipitous path adjoining the house. As the interview ended, and if Tiberius by then suspected the seer of fraud or unreliability, he would give the ex-slave a silent signal with his eyes. Once the astrologer was inching his way back down the unsteady path, he would get a sudden violent shove from the emperor's "assistant" and tumble into the boulder-strewn sea below.

It seems that the hardiest of these contenders was one Thrasyllus, an old man who had first impressed Tiberius when they had met many years before on Rhodes. Now that they sat facing each other in that lofty perch with the ex-slave looking on, Tiberius surprised Thrasyllus by asking first if he had cast his own horoscope. And specifically, how did it appear for that particular day? Thrasyllus, after measuring the configuration of the planets among the stars, hesitated, then showed alarm. The more he pondered, the greater became his astonishment and fright. Then he cried out that he was about to encounter a critical — perhaps fatal — emergency.

Tiberius leaned over and clasped Thrasyllus warmly, commending his powers of divination and promising that he would escape the day's "emergency." The seer soon became one of Tiberius' closest confidants and his pronouncements were regarded as oracular. One can only speculate that "unfavorable omens" seen by Thrasyllus might have explained all those aborted trips to the provinces or even the beginnings of mass purges.

Stories also abound that the villa was a den of sexual iniquity. Some say that this demon in Tiberius had always been held in check when he was in Rome and when his mother's presence loomed over him. Without her and with the walls of Capri to shield him, they say, the place became a playground for perversity.

How can one know precisely some 50 years later? All I know first-hand is that common people on Capri insist that their families had children plucked from them to live at the villa where they became subject to what one writer describes as "criminal lusts...worthy of an oriental tyrant." I am loathe to elaborate, but will simply report this much from one more writer of that period:

> In his retreat at Capri there was a room devised by him dedicated to
> the most arcane lusts. Here he had assembled from all quarters girls

and perverts, whom he called *Spintriæ*, who invented monstrous feats of lubricity, and defiled one another before him, interlaced in series of threes, in order to inflame his feeble appetite.

He also had several other rooms variously adapted to his lusts, decorated with paintings and bas-reliefs depicting scenes of the most lascivious character, and supplied with the books of Elephantis (that lewd Greek poetess) that no one should lack a model for the execution of any lustful act he was ordered to perform. Different places in the groves and woods he also consecrated to venery, so that young people dressed like Pans and Nymphs lay strewn over hill and valley.

Still more flagrant and brazen was another sort of infamy which he practiced, one that may scarce be told, much less believed. He taught children of the most tender years, whom he called his "little fishes," to play between his legs while he was in his bath. Those which had not been weaned, but were strong and hearty, he set at fellatio, the sort of sport best adapted to his inclination and age. Once he was willed a painting in which Atalanta was represented as doing as much to Meleager. It arrived with a provision that the emperor would receive a million sesterces instead if he found the subject offensive. He not only chose the picture, but hung it in his bedroom as if it were a sacred object.

It is also said that one day during a sacrifice he was smitten by the beauty of a boy who swung a censer of incense. In fact, the old man was hardly able to wait until the rites were over before taking him aside and abusing him as well as his brother, who had been playing the flute. Afterwards, when Tiberius happened to hear both boys reproaching one another in their disgrace, he had their legs broken.[5]

It was into this den of soothsayers and Spintriæ that friends, senators and advisors were admitted from the mainland. How much of it they saw, one can't say, but those who stayed longest seemed to be kindred spirits.

At the height of Tiberius' military days he had been so well known for his excessive love of wine that he was nicknamed "Biberius." Now he continued his ways with a few old cronies, even announcing his support of an obscure lout for the quæstorship over other candidates from Rome's noblest families. Why? Allegedly because the emperor had lost a wager. He had promised the quæstorship at a banquet to the man who could drain an amphora of wine!

But many more offices went neglected as Tiberius paid less and less attention to affairs of state. I have said that important offices such as the governorships of Spain and Syria had gone unfilled for several years. In time the emperor had also failed to fill vacancies in the Decuries of the Knights and even neglected to change prefects or tribunes of the soldiers.

I regret to report that it was also Rome's fate that the only remaining son of Germanicus was being reared on Capri at that time. Caligula, who I will now call by his formal name, Gaius, had first come to Capri to live just before the fall of Sejanus. He was 19 at that time and was to live on and off the island for some six years.

It might be useful at this time to point out the sharp contrasts between how this very tall, thin-haired blond youth was perceived by common people throughout the empire and how he may have inwardly seen himself.

For the first viewpoint, one must begin with the fact that Gaius was born in the winter quarters of the legions to parents who were first in the hearts of all Rome. Overindulged by the soldiers, as an equally fawning poet would later write, he was

> Born in a camp, reared with soldiers, he;
> A sign assured he would a ruler be.[6]

When Germanicus met his death at age 34, so intense was the nation's grief that temples were stoned and the altars of gods thrown down. Some disconsolate people flung their household gods into the street and cast out their newly born children. Even barbarians who were waging war with Rome or with one another instantly agreed to a truce as if all had suffered the same family tragedy. All this outpouring of grief produced an overflow of love and indulgence that gushed upon the young son wherever he went.

But as Gaius approached manhood, there were other milestones in his life that he could look back upon.

His grandfather, a great general and the brother of Tiberius, had been poisoned. His father had, too. So had his uncle Drusus, the emperor's son.

Of Gaius' eight siblings, two had died in infancy and one as a small child. His brother, Nero Cæsar, had been exiled by Tiberius to the forlorn isle of Pontia and then strangled by a guard. His remaining brother, Drusus Cæsar, once paraded about as the emperor's likely successor, starved to death in a Roman jail while cursing the name of Tiberius and all his kin.

During his adolescence Gaius watched as his mother tried in vain to rally support for her cause, then watched as she pled with Tiberius merely to be left alone, and waited on Capri in silence as she faced her last painful days alone in humiliating exile. And during that banishment, the boy lived alone for several months with Livia, the very old mother of Tiberius, until her death.

With only two sisters remaining, Gaius watched as Tiberius married them off: Julia Livilla to a mild, mundane man from a family of knights; Drusilla to the dull descendant of a respected but plebeian family. Tiberius then dismissed them both from his life by sending a formal announcement to the Senate, along with perfunctory compliments to the grooms.

Gaius himself was wed at age 20. The emperor arranged his marriage to Junia Claudilla, daughter of Marcus Silanus, a man of noble rank and reputation. But just a year or two later she died in childbirth.

Through all these tragic events, the young man mostly watched—and acceded.

And what would you have done, dear reader? A wolf has dragged off your family, and now you are commanded to live with him in his lair. Soon it becomes clear that you are destined to succeed him as leader of the pack! The only other remaining contender is a mere cub named Tiberius, the offspring — and some say a bastard—of the emperor's poisoned son, Drusus.

There is even ample evidence that in Gaius the emperor had found a willing pupil. It is said that the gangly young man with the blotchy blond beard soon became adept at divining the emperor's mood each morning and pandering to his every whim. It is said, too, that he was a most eager witness of the tortures and executions by day and a reveler at night in gluttony and dancing — sometimes dressed in a woman's wig and long robe. Some wag summed up the "apprenticeship" by saying that there was never a better slave or a worse master. Tiberius himself had even remarked at a dinner party that "to allow Gaius to live would prove the ruin of himself and of all men." The emperor said to others that he was "rearing a viper for the Roman people and a python for the world."

Other Romans had already reached the same conclusion. Marcus Cocceius Nerva, a legal expert who had been Tiberius' most trusted friend on Capri, announced to the emperor one day that he had decided to die. And refusing ardent pleas of Tiberius, he simply refused all food until he had wasted away.

In Rome, Gaius Vibius Marsus, a senator from an ancient noble family, had been accused by Sejanus' usurper Macro of disloyalty to the emperor. Rather than waste time preparing a defense that would only be ignored, Marsus, too, decided that another resolution would be more honorable. "I have lived long enough," he said. "My only regret is that insults and perils have made my old age unhappy."

Implored by his friends to live and fight on, Marsus offered this reasoning: "Certainly I might survive the few days until Tiberius dies. But in that case, how can I avoid the young emperor ahead? If Tiberius, in spite of all his experience, has been transformed and deranged by absolute power, will Gaius do better? Almost a boy, wholly ignorant, with a criminal upbringing, guided by Macro—the man chosen to suppress Sejanus, though Macro is the worse man of the two and responsible for more terrible crimes and natural suffering. I foresee even grimmer slavery ahead. So, from evils past and evils to come I am escaping."

And with those prophetic words, Marsus opened his veins.

. . . .

ROME AND PARTHIA HAVE BEEN FOES for so long that we have forged closer bonds through generations of adversity than do most allies during a few years in common cause. Rome has remained dominant throughout most of the relationship, but it is still Parthia that can claim to have ruled the largest and most powerful kingdom in the world in the days when it was known as Persia. Then, great kings like Darius and Xerxes could march an army of 500,000 men to the edges of the Asian continent.

In the days of Tiberius, Parthian nobles were still sending their sons to live in Rome as proof of their fealty. But the thin fabric of friendship was showing tatters. The Parthian king had chafed under Roman suzerainty ever since Germanicus had shown up with two legions to persuade him against invading his westernmost neighbor, Armenia. Now this young, blustery king let it be known increasingly that he thought old Tiberius a toothless recluse. As always, threats made in Rome or the Parthian capital of Ctesiphon were felt first in the buffer states — in this case, Armenia and Syria to the north and west. The situation became even more serious when the young king decided he would at the very least have Armenia for himself.

Yet, as with Rome, Parthia was not in love with its ruler. King Artabanus III had been born of a Parthian monarch and his Scythian wife. Much of his youth had been spent in his mother's wild homeland north of the Black Sea with hard riding, harder drinking and a bullying bellicosity that was the antithesis of the refined court at Ctesiphon. Although Artabanus saw his calling as a warrior and conqueror, such notions were kept in check by Parthia's agreements with Rome.

The less Tiberius took note of his distant land, the more belligerent Artabanus became. First, he marshaled troops for minor successes in other parts of Parthia far removed from Roman provinces. Now, much to the discomfort of Parthia's noble families, he began lecturing Roman visitors that it was time to reestablish the frontiers that existed when Persia was ruled by Cyrus and Macedonia by Alexander. When word came that the aged king of Armenia had passed away, Artabanus decided it was time to act. He sent a delegation to the successor demanding return of a "treasure" that the Armenians had captured in battle so many years before that it was all but forgotten. And without waiting for a reply, he sent one of his sons, Arsaces, storming in with an army to claim the title of king.

Not long afterward, the consuls in Rome were visited by a secret delegation of Parthian noblemen. They complained that Artabanus was warlike, unpredictable and cruel even to his own people. And he had also killed off so many of his potential successors, they said, that it would be difficult to replace him with someone in Parthia of royal lineage. What they wanted was for Rome to approve one Prince Phraates, who had been living in Rome for many years. Once they had brought him to their boundary on the River Euphrates with Tiberius' blessing, all Parthia would rally to his support.

This was exactly what Tiberius wanted. Having been alarmed at Artabanus' hostility, the emperor had already tried without success to buy back his friendship with offers of bribes and gifts. Thus, monies were soon forthcoming to equip Phraates and send him off to Syria to muster an army.

With Phraates went the new governor of Syria, Lucius Vitellius. It was in the concluding days of his consulship that Vitellius had received the Parthian delegation. Now he was available for another high post – and just when Tiberius decided it was time that the Syrian governor resided in Antioch. Vitellius was known in Rome as a lazy administrator and the emperor's most sniveling sycophant; but at this time, as if leaving the shadow cast by the cliffs of Capri gave a man new vigor, Vitellius would soon earn a reputation as a wise administrator and competent provincial military commander.

Once again it was proven that confidential information spreads faster than horses can ride or ships can sail. Word of the "secret visit" to Rome soon reached the Parthian King, Artabanus. But instead of lashing out and purging his most influential families, he coolly used cunning – and luck – to turn the tide back in his favor. One of the "delegates" was invited to dinner, with the utmost show of friendliness, then slipped a poison that was to disable him slowly. Others were kept off guard with lavish presents and flattering words. Then came the luck I mentioned. Phraates, the new contender king, had no sooner arrived in Antioch than he became very sick and died. Those present attributed it to no more than the fate of a man who had adopted soft, Roman ways of living and could not adapt to the ways of a land that was now strange to him.

But with all these preparations already in place, Tiberius was not to be dissuaded. Another young princely hostage, Tiridates III, was dispatched from Rome to the Syrian capital. At the same time, the Roman client states of Albania and Iberia (both of the Caucasus region) mobilized a force that knifed directly into the capital of Armenia and killed its new Parthian king. The stage was now set for an escalation of the war. Artabanus quickly named another son, Orodes, king of Armenia (in exile, of course) and assigned him Parthian troops for an invasion. But before he did so, Orodes needed to enlist many more non-Parthians as auxiliaries and mercenaries. And none were more likely prospects than the Samaritans of Syria, whose chiefs were known for hiring out to the highest bidder.

This, I believe, explains why the Samaritans took courage in petitioning Governor Vitellius to redress the bloody massacre by Pontius Pilate that had taken place at the foot of Mount Gerizzim. And Vitellius welcomed their embassy. The result was that Pilate's days as procurator were now over. He was ordered to Rome, where the emperor would judge the Samaritans' charges.

Then Vitellius seized the moment to further win support of the Jews in repressing the Parthian challenge. He personally traveled to Jerusalem right at the time of the Passover. The governor was received amidst tumultuous cheers. One reason was that he decreed that the inhabitants would be released from all taxes on fruits bought and sold.

Perhaps more significant, Vitellius removed the high priest Caiaphas (who had sent Jesus to his death) and replaced him with the more politically-friendly Jonathan. And to assure Jonathan's instant popularity, he restored to the Jews the right to have permanent possession of the high priest's vestments.

This might seem to be a trivial concession, but only if you are not a Jew. They had been the ultimate symbol of priestly authority since the first temple appeared in Jerusalem. A Jewish scholar described them as follows:

> When [the high priest] officiated, he had on a pair of breeches that reached beneath his privy parts to his thighs, and had on an inner garment of linen, together with a blue garment, round without seam, with fringe work, and reaching to the feet. There were also golden bells that hung upon the fringes, and pomegranates intermixed among them. The bells signified thunder and the pomegrantes lightning.
>
> The girdle that tied the garment to the breast was embroidered with five rows of various colors, of gold, purple, scarlet...linen and blue, which...the veils of the temple were embroidered also. The like embroidery was upon the ephod, but the quantity of gold therein was greater. Its figure was that of a stomacher for the breast. There were upon it two golden buttons like small shields, which buttoned the ephod to the garment. In these buttons were enclosed two very large and excellent sardonyxes, having the tribes of the nation engraved upon them....
>
> A mitre of fine linen encompassed his head, which was tied by a blue ribband, about which there was another golden crown, in which was engraven the sacred name [of God] consisting of four vowels.[7]

These ornamented religious garments had been seized by Herod the Great some 50 years before and kept by his guards in the Tower of Antonia. Fearing that they might be used to rally the people to revolt, Herod had allowed the high priest access to the vestments only on three annual festivals. Later, when Rome had decided to remove Herod's hapless son Archelaus and govern directly, its procurators also kept custody of the garments. Seven days before a festival they were delivered to the high priest by a captain of the guard, only to be retrieved by the Roman guard the day afterwards.

Buoyed by a new wave of popular support in Samaria and Judea, Vitellius returned to Antioch as troops were mobilizing for war in Armenia. Orodes, Parthia's would-be king of Armenia, had garnered some recruits in Samaria, but even more Samaritan mercenaries had been enticed into joining the Roman-sponsored contingent of Armenians, Iberians and Albanians. And now they had nested in the rocky crags overlooking the rugged mountain passes that twisted into Armenia.

As Orodes, the would-be Parthian king of Armenia, led his troops through the passes, they were taunted and challenged by the heavily-fortified defenders, who knew that they had the vaunted Parthian archers and cavalry at a disadvantage. When the Parthians camped at night, the defenders would gallop close to their camp, plunder their sources of forage and block their desperate lunges to break out of their trap. Orodes' officers, incensed at such insolence, pressed him to make an attack.

At last the time came when battle lines were drawn. Orodes paraded before his men, contrasting the glory of the Parthian empire and the grandeur of his royal family with the rag-tag, rough-hewn men who glowered at them from up in the pass. Pharasmanes, brother of the Iberian king, headed the defenders. He reminded his troops that they had never submitted to Parthia. And, as he looked down at the Parthian generals in their splendid gold-embroidered robes, he said only this: "On our side, men. On their side, loot!"

The result was a confusing battle. It began as an orthodox cavalry engagement, with each force shooting their bows, then charging or withdrawing. But the Samaritan defenders, who found that their bows were inferior in range to those of the Parthians, began charging with pikes and swords. Soon riders were interlocked, shoving and hewing one another.

Then the Albanian and Iberian infantry struck, hacking at Parthian horses and trying to pull their riders from their saddles. Pharasmanes and Orodes were in the thick of it, supporting their staunchest fighters and rescuing those in trouble. Then they recognized each other and charged their horses. Pharasmanes rush was the more violent: he pierced the Parthian's helmet and wounded him. But because his horse had galloped well past his enemy before turning around, Orodes' bravest officers had time to rally around their stricken leader.

Still, rumors that Orodes had died spread like wildfire among his troops and the Parthians soon conceded the battle.

This time king Artabanus began marshaling Parthia's entire military might for another assault on Armenia. But now Lucius Vitellius made his presence felt. Gathering several of his divisions, the governor marched east toward Mesopotamia. The whole maneuver was but a feint, but Artabanus quickly realized that he couldn't face a war on two fronts. He evacuated Armenia.

Vitellius quickly followed up with a display of political skill. Parthian emissaries had already told him that they feared how their king, a violent man even in time of peace, might treat his subjects after a humiliating defeat. So Vitellius began by persuading the leading noble families, including Artabanus' own father, to abandon their king. Soon, all that Artabanus had left were a few mercenary bodyguards. With these he hastily fled to the remote borders of Scythia, where he hoped that friends of this mother might help him survive until his luck turned.

Immediately, Vitellius urged Tiridates III, the Roman-bred prince, to seize his opportunity. Marching to the bank of the Euphrates, which marks the western border of Parthia, Vitellius stopped to sacrifice to Mars the Roman boar, ram and bull. Tiridates appeased the river with a finely harnessed horse. Once they crossed, they were joined in increasing numbers by everyone of importance from the nobles who had made up the first "secret delegation" to Rome to royal officials who had brought him the imperial court treasure and its ceremonial ornaments.

At that point, Vitellius concluded that his display of Roman might had been sufficient. Exhorting Tiridates to honor the regal qualities of his forefathers and his new foster-father (Tiberius), the governor marched his army back to Antioch.

All Tiridates had to do was hasten to the capital of Ctesiphon and have himself enthroned. Instead, he languished in Mesopotamia, paying homage at various historic sites and banqueting in its finest homes. He thought it wise, perhaps, to display himself in public so as to show the contrast between his refined Roman ways and the uncouth, Scythian-bred Artabanus. When Tiridates' advisors urged him on to depart for Ctesiphon, he again delayed the coronation so that two far-flung satraps would have time to make the long journey back to the capital.

What Tiridates apparently couldn't see was a rapid erosion of support. The more he was on public display, the more observers began to conclude that the ruler they at first thought refined and mannerly was in fact a lazy and effeminate boy. Artabanus had once complained that "Parthians have always been inpatient with their kings." Now, in far-off Scythia those words would prove true enough, because he was soon tracked down by a delegation of Parthian dissidents. The man they finally encountered on a bleak, windy plain was a grimy, ragged refugee, reduced to eating whatever he could shoot with his bow. At first the astounded fugitive suspected a plot to lure him within someone else's bow. But when he heard the tirade of disaffection for Tiridates as well as the rivalries among those who were vying to displace him, Artabanus realized an all-important truth: however spurious his followers' affection, their *hatreds* were genuine.

With their enmity as his spear, Artabanus did not wait for second thoughts from his new allies. Gathering a large force of Scythian and Parthian supporters as he went, retaining his dirty beard and dress as his badges of revenge, Artabanus quickly marched to the large Mesopotamian city of Seleucia where Tiridates was last known to be lodged with his traveling banquet.

Should Tiridates fight now or delay? Again, he chose delay. By retreating across the Tigris River, he reasoned, he could await support from the Romans, Armenians and others. Besides, Tiridates had no taste for blood or danger. And as he sat awaiting word from various potential allies, those already in his camp began to melt away. Eventually he relieved the remaining ones from the dishonor of desertion by returning with a few followers to Syria. The campaign was over.

When word of it reached Tiberius, he acted predictably: he again ordered Vitellius to buy a Parthian truce. This time it worked. Artabanus, his nation every bit as exhausted as himself, was ready to extend his hand. Thus it was that Vitellius and an elite guard soon marched to the edge of the Euphrates, where the Artabanus contingent waited on the other side. A bridge was laid over the river and both men met on a platform in the middle. It seems that Herod Antipas had played the go-between, because it was the Jewish tetrarch who supplied an ornate tent to shield the parties and he who hosted a lavish banquet once they had come to terms.

And it was also Antipas who irked the governor considerably. As soon as Vitellius had completed the week-long march back to Antioch, he sent Tiberius a long dispatch explaining the details of the truce. But Antipas had upstaged his superior by penning a full account the day after the banquet and speeding it off to Capri. All Vitellius got for his efforts was a terse note to the effect that "I've already been acquainted with all this by Herod Antipas."

Hardly an incident of consequence, you might say; but it gnawed at Vitellius and may have cost Antipas dearly. The reason is that with Parthia safely back behind its borders and Vitellius presumably catching up on other business in Antioch, Aretes the Nabatean decided to seize the Jewish territories he had coveted for so long. Or I should say, he decided to retake lands — mainly Tachonitis — which had been Arab lands for hundreds of years before being given to the Jews. Because much of Tachonitis was still inhabited by Arabs, it wasn't difficult for

Aretus to recruit enough "traitors" from the tetrarchy of Philip to join his cause. In any event, the Nabateans totally destroyed the army of Herod Antipas. Desperate word went out to Vitellius for help, but there was not enough time to react, the governor replied.

Or so he said.

And among the Jewish common people, many openly insisted that the defeat of Herod Antipas was a mark of God's retribution on the tetrarch for having slain John the Baptist.

. . . .

ONE CAN PICTURE THE YOUNG SAUL WALKING along a rough desert road as the walls of Damascus receded in the distance. The night air was crisp and cold. The moon and stars loomed large over the mountains to the west. Except for the sounds of distant dogs or goats, Saul was alone in absolute silence.

No doubt he was frightened and uncertain of his destination. At the same time he probably found the stillness almost invigorating. After all, he had been at the center of a tempest in Jerusalem and had created another one when he entered Damascus. Now he was alone under the heavens to grapple with the brief experience that had transformed his life. What had happened? What did it mean? Where was he headed?

For us, it may be well to ask at the same time, who was this young man Saul *before* Damascus?

I must tell you here that the same attributes that have aided me in this work may in this case work to its hindrance. What I mean is that I am a man who has spent his life reading books, buying them, shelving them or publishing them. I tend to put my faith in the written word, I suppose mainly on grounds that anyone who would invest in expensive paper, take the trouble to assemble his thoughts and spend hours staining his hands with ink must be setting forth what he perceives as truth. Yes, yes, I know that brazen liars can write, too, but my heart tells me that the process attracts more honest and earnest people than the opposite.

At the same time, I also know that oral traditions deserve respect. The longer I live, the more I see what I thought was quaint folklore actually verified by the discovery of a diary in a cave or a scroll that fell behind a shelf in some home now unearthed by excavation for a new theater. The problem in this case is that there are as many stories about the early years of The Way as there are bees in a hive. I have sat beside an elderly Roman Christian in a grove outside the catacombs and asked what he knew of Saul, or Paul as we now call him. I hear that, yes, Paul was a Pharisee whose father bought his Roman citizenship with money made by selling large quantities of tents to various armies. The next week I befriend an old woman who once lived in Antioch. She knows for sure that Paul's father was one of thousands of Cilicians to be granted instant citizenship by Marcus Antonius (no doubt in a state of inebriation) when he and Cleopatra met there to consummate their lavish seduction of one another.

But there is next to nothing in writing. I would postulate that the experience Saul had on the road to Damascus so changed his very being that he soon came to regard his previous existence as hardly worth the effort to remember. Left to divine it for oneself, I am reduced to a few crumbs scattered by elderly people, often with scant education and suspect memories.

He was, all agree, born in the very last years of Augustus. And he was the child of a Jewish family in Tarsus, that cosmopolitan capital of Cilicia about 130 miles northwest of Antioch. Of this city I will write more later. Suffice it to say that Tarsus is a place that nature made beautiful and man made confoundedly complicated. Its position on a lake 12 miles up the River Cydnus is the reason why it is just as fine a seaport today as it was when Cleopatra sailed in with her gold-laden entourage some 50 years before Paul's birth. And because it straddles the road that cuts through the Taurus mountains, the city has been a well-traveled caravan stop since the days of the Hittites. Because of the road and the water, it should be no surprise that Tarsus has long been a jumble of Jews, Asians, Syrians, Persians, Phœnicians, Greeks, Romans and sailors from everywhere else.

Receiving his citizenship by birth, the child after being circumcised on his eighth day would be known by the usual two names: Saul to the Jews and Paul to his Hellenized neighbors. Paul (as I shall henceforth refer to him) was born into the tribe of Benjamin and named for Saul, the brave, impulsive and violent first king of Israel. The Benjamanites were known as fearless fighters who always stood in the forefront of the battle line. They had earned this honor because they were the first to cross the Red Sea when Moses led the Jews in their exodus from Egypt.

Paul himself has written that he plied a tentmaker's trade, and there is every reason that his father had, as well. And why not? As many know, the cilicium cloth used in so many tents, sails and the like derives its name from the word "Cilician." Cilicia is where they get the best goat hair for making cilicium. And since busy caravan routes are the best places to sell tents, I'm sure the successors to Paul's father are in Tarsus today doing the same thing.

As a child Paul no doubt played in streets full of Greek students, Stoics, Cynics, priests of Cybelle and even worshipers of Sandan, the god of vegetation. One can see Paul as a young boy, holding the hand of his mother, with her head covered and face veiled, as they passed by thickly made-up street women with their high-tiered hair, and their perfumed male counterparts, all gesturing obscenely as they traded raucous insults. But it seems evident that Paul's life as a young boy was centered on the synagogue. There he would have started his studies in the House of the Book, the Jewish center for instruction in reading, writing and The Law. This would have led to memorizing the whole of The Law and, I am presuming, to early training to become a rabbi.

And a Pharisaic rabbi as well. Pharisaism and its reputation as being preoccupied with the rule of Mosaic law can be better understood by a look at its genesis. Pharisaism sprang up in the years that preceded the revolt of the Maccabees against Rome around 100 years before Paul's birth. At the time, Hellenistic rulers in major cities were exerting growing pressure on Jews to forego circumcision, eat pork, renounce their sanitary laws and surrender copies of their Mosaic Law. But some rigidly refused, instead detaching themselves from the rest and devoting themselves to living and preserving The Law handed down by Moses. If The Law was an expression of God's will, they reasoned, then man might hope to carry it out so completely that God could ask no more of him.

In time, others would argue that Pharisaism had evolved into, not a fulfilling religious experience, but a slavishly meticulous routine. Nonetheless, it is logical that Paul's family found strength by clinging to this tradition in the profane and culturally cacophonous Tarsus, and that they would press this legacy on their son, Paul.

As such, it would best explain why Paul departed for Jerusalem, probably around age 20, and perhaps not many months after Jesus had been crucified. Because Paul later wrote to one of his churches that he had studied under Gamaliel, one must assume that he was enrolled in the House of Interpretation, or rabbinical college. Gamiliel was a grandson of Hillel, perhaps the most famous of all rabbis, and he led a busy life as a leader of both the college and the Sanhedrin. He represented the more liberal approach that his grandfather had espoused. Some years later it was even said that "When Rabban Gamaliel the Elder died, regard for the Torah ceased and purity and piety died."

To have "studied under" Gamaliel may have meant that Paul was merely one of a thousand or more students who were enrolled at the college. However, Paul was to write in another letter that he had, during the time The Way was gaining ground in Jerusalem, "advanced in Judaism beyond many of my own age among my people." Thus, I would surmise that Paul was just completing his studies or had recently done so and had been assigned to a position in temple administration reserved for young men of exceptional promise.

But so specialized and sophisticated was the organization of temple affairs that it would be impossible to speculate on the actual position Paul might have held. Temple administration was supervised by a permanent staff who specialized in such matters ranging from collection of tithes and management of private funds deposited for safekeeping to such chores as the offering of birds, shutting of gates, preparation of incense and baking of shewbread. Moreover, the supervision of daily ritual was an enormous task in itself. The temple day began with a procession of priests carrying a pitcher of water from the Pool of Siloam and pouring it on the altar. Animal sacrifices took place for eight-and-a-half hours each day. Priests were also needed constantly for the private offerings to pray for cure from illness, to mark a family reunion and the like. If an offering were made after confession of a civil wrong, a temple official was needed to collect the full restitution plus 20 percent.

During major festivals, the permanent staff was bolstered by the arrival of priests and Levites from surrounding cities. During Passover the high priest typically supervised some 200 chief priests, 7,200 ordinary priests and 9,600 Levites. Priests and Levites were each assigned to one of 24 "courses." Each priestly course, or clan, which was organized according to its region, drew lots to determine what tasks they would perform in assisting the regular temple priests with sacrifices and other aspects of worship. Levite clans were organized by skill, so that some within each group provided a service such as music or gatekeeping or cleaning of the temple mount. I'm told that 200 Levites were deployed each day just to open and shut the temple gates.

One story has it that Paul was employed by the temple guard, and another that he was a broker in hides of sacrificed animals. I doubt both tales simply because they don't seem like logical pursuits for a newly-graduated rabbinical scholar. It may well be that Paul received hides from time to time, just as the visiting priestly clans were given animal skins they could sell in order to defray their travel expenses. If so, it would be another good reason why Paul would take up his father's trade of tentmaking and leatherworking to sustain himself both as a student and as traveling missionary.

All that is known from Paul himself about the period immediately after his life-changing trip to Damascus is that he stayed in "Arabia" for three years, at least some of it spent in a return to Damascus, before he saw Jerusalem again.

Some say he stayed in the wilderness contemplating the events that had driven him there. Some say he preached his new faith throughout the Hellenistic towns of the Decapolis. Some say he plied a tentmaker's trade to keep body and soul together. The fact that we know so little would confirm that he was mostly alone.

It is logical that Paul did all of the above. In the beginning he may have gained work as a tentmaker in some quiet village. After all, he was — at least for many months — a fugitive sought by authorities in both Jerusalem and Damascus. And with the armies of Aretus constantly moving across the land to and from various maneuvers, it is unlikely that Paul would choose a conspicuous place.

Wherever it was, he would no doubt spend nights under the bright stars praying for guidance in sorting out the meaning of his experience on the road to Damascus. An impulsive, emotional person can change his life in an instant, but a thinker must have time to reconstruct the knowledge and values that are the foundation of his inner world. Paul had been swept away from his moorings and had nothing to cling to but a vision and a voice.

I have heard more afterthoughts about what happened on the road to Damascus than Paul probably had himself. A learned physician lectured me that Paul's experience was no doubt evidence of a person with epileptic seizures. "The light you mention was probably the bright aura that people with seizures usually experience before they are struck to the ground," he explained.

Yet, if Paul had such an affliction, why did he not attribute the experience to just another seizure? If it was his first such episode, why did not all the subsequent ones fill him with doubts about the veracity of his experience with Jesus?

And what about this Ananias, who was also visited? Did two men mistakenly hear the same voice? How were these strangers "accidentally" guided to meet at the same place?

Others have said that Paul's sense of guilt about Stephen was so overwhelming that it caused him to be "possessed" in the same way that initiates into the ecstatic Dionysian mysteries emerge with that glassy-eyed frenzy that makes one want to cross to the other side of the street when we see them coming.

Well, yes and no. Paul had not been "converted" to a cult or religion with rites and priests because The Way lacked both. But Paul had indeed become "possessed" in that he had surrendered his being and his destiny to a higher power. He was to write often that he had become "a slave of " and "a prisoner of" Jesus Christ." He said that God had been "infused in my weakness" and "when I am weak, then I am strong." He would write, too, that "God in foolishness is wiser than men" and "God in weakness is stronger than men."

The most convincing aspect of Paul is simply that, from the moment he saw the brilliant light and heard the voice on the road to Damascus, he never once expressed a doubt or looked back longingly on his previous life. Rather, Paul's early contemplation of his "reborn" status probably centered on three questions:

First, how did his revelation relate to The Law that he had been memorizing since boyhood? Suddenly, all the painstaking prescriptions for daily living that Paul had spent so many years acquiring and debating were dissolved into a few simple concepts. Repentance. Redemption. Salvation. Love. Faith. Forgiveness. Hope. Tolerance. Charity.

Second, was Jesus the messiah of Hebrew scripture? If so, was he the all-powerful, mighty warrior who would deliver the Jews from the yoke of the Romans? Or was he the "suffering lamb" of Isaiah in Jewish scripture who would bring eternal salvation to even the sickest and weakest person who believed in him?

Third, what was Paul's role in this to be? Should he preach his new belief? To whom?

Answering the last question was probably the easiest of all for Paul. He could still recite the words of Jesus some 26 years later when he stood on trial before a Jewish king:

> Rise and stand upon your feet, for I have appeared to you for this pur-
> pose: to appoint you to serve and bear witness to the things in which
> you have seen me and to those in which I will appear to you, delivering
> you from the people and from the Gentiles — to whom I send you to
> open their eyes, that they may turn from darkness to light and from
> the power of Satan to God, that they may receive forgiveness of sins
> and a place among those who are sanctified by faith in me.[8]

To answer the first two questions and to gird one's mind with the resources necessary to convey those answers to skeptical strangers could easily have taken a year or two. Whatever the duration, there is no doubt that Paul emerged believing that his spirit had been set free and that he was embarked on a great voyage to spread joyous news. One can see him now beginning to attract curious crowds in Petra, the Nabatean capital, and in cities of the Decapolis such as Philadelphia and Gerasa. Soon he would be approaching the familiar gates of Damascus, where he would build on the brief friendships with his courageous friends in The Way and deliver his new message without fear or compromise.

. . . .

. . . .

F orgive me for having thus far omitted a figure who loomed large throughout the period. I did so because he was not personally instrumental in the outcome of wars or affairs of state, and attempting to follow his many lives and travels would only have caused confusion.

I refer to Herod Agrippa I, grandson of Herod the Great and son of Aristobulus IV. Why this particular grandson of Herod? After all, the king had too many to count. In order to show you why, I must go back a century again to the beginning of Herod's reign.

In many respects, Herod owed his throne to the Parthians. That is, Augustus wanted a strong buffer state in Judea; his way of achieving it was to install a non-Jewish king who would build a secular state with many more Hellenistic cities and institutions. And thus began Herod's great building program. And to show his loyalty to Augustus, he sent two of his sons, Alexander and Aristobulus IV, to live in the household of a Roman knight known for his ostentatious wealth.

Despite the growing might of Herod's kingdom, his immediate household was a shambles. And what else might he have expected? Alexander and Aristobulus were the offspring of Mariamme, a wife chosen from the royal Jewish Hasmonean line. Two much younger sons, Archelaus and Antipas, he had sired of Malthace, a Samaritan woman he had wed to cement ties to that community. Complicating all this was the eldest son, Antipater, who would have been first in line for the throne except for the fact that Herod had divorced his Idumean mother some 20 years before.

Now you can imagine life inside the walls of Herod's palace in Jerusalem. Not a day expired without the Hasmoneans, their retainers, servants and slaves taunting their rough-hewn Samaritan relatives, retainers, servants and slaves in turn as comical bumpkins. Plots and schemes came and went, with each camp delighted to rush into the throne room to report the latest damaging news to an increasingly irritable king. Once a year or so the dangerous sport intensified when Alexander and Aristobulus, now married and with children of their own, would return from Rome on vacation. Indeed, they had become educated and erudite. They had also become suffocating snobs, with well-bred Roman wives who were even more insufferable. In fact, the brothers had a standing joke that when they reached the throne they would make their stepmothers work at the loom with the slaves and demote their half-brothers to village clerks.

Within ten years the jokes and taunts had flared into treachery. Herod had flown into a rage and killed his favorite wife, the Hasmonean Mariamme. Her sons Alexander and Aristobulus were both dead—executed by their own father for supposedly planning to take the old king on a hunting trip and kill him. Antipater, the eldest, was executed after being caught concocting a poison.

Each time a report went to Augustus with the latest news of the Herodian family war, it would come accompanied with a revised will naming yet another heir. Thus, when news came that the old man himself had died, the emperor had long since concluded that no one in Herod's family was capable of managing the entire Jewish nation. Herod must have agreed, because his fourth and last will asked that the kingdom be divided among the men I have named earlier: Antipas, Archelaus and Philip. And with this Augustus was all too willing to comply.

Now then, I am ready to introduce to you a young man whose life was destined to be even as colorful as that of his grandfather. Shortly before his death, Herod sent the widow of Aristobulus to Rome along with her offspring Herod Agrippa and his sister. Having executed their father, one might surmise that their presence in Jerusalem did nothing but fill his heart with tragic memories.

As Herod Agrippa matured, he was at one time or another a fixture in the households of, or had known intimately, no less than Cæsar Augustus, Tiberius, Antonia (the revered widow of the emperor's brother Drusus and mother of Germanicus), Drusus (the son of Tiberius), Claudius (the lame, stuttering brother of Germanicus), Gaius (the youngest son of Germanicus) and Herod Antipas (tetrarch of Perea-Galilee). And to this web we must add the high-strung Jewish princess Herodias, who also happened to be Herod Agrippa's sister.

This intricate spider web of so many princely nationalities amounted to a large family that traded on gossip as its most precious commodity. Thus, one could even surmise that the Romans were kept informed about detailed happenings in the Jewish world such as the beheading of John the Baptist. If so, I would also think they even knew something of the people of The Way, who were increasingly being called by the name "Christians."

Despite living amidst the lavish wealth to which they felt entitled, Agrippa and Herodias were still dependent on the whims of others to sustain them in such surroundings. For without patrons, the widow and children of Aristobulus faced uncertain futures.

Soon afterward, Herodias was betrothed to another descendant of Herod the Great, but in fact the "minor princeling" I described earlier. Thus, this granddaughter of the most powerful monarch in four thousand years of Jewish history smoldered at being consigned to a lesser station. And when her cousin, the tetrarch Antipas, came to Rome with a wandering eye, she was more than happy when it fixed on her. How sensitive — and incensed — she must have been when John the Baptist censured her. And the yarn about how Herodias had prevailed on her new husband to seek revenge must have been quite the conversation piece in Rome. It would have been so because her vagabond brother Agrippa traveled often between Judea and Rome. And Agrippa was often at the center of the liveliest conversation at gatherings of Rome's elite.

Had you taken aside any dozen of these Roman luminaries and asked them how they defined Agrippa, all would no doubt agree that he was handsome and engaging. But, depending on the person, you would also hear that Agrippa was a charming sophisticate or shameless flatterer, a magnanimous benefactor or habitual debtor, a man of honor or common thief, a loyal friend or dangerous conspirator.

In fact, Herod Agrippa was no doubt all of these things. He had gained a measure of self-esteem early when he became a favorite among the children in the greater Augustinian household. Agrippa was fortunate as well, when the death of Augustus brought about a new order, that he had also become a favorite of that great lady Antonia, the esteemed widow of Tiberius's brother Drusus. She in turn was a friend and patroness of Agrippa's mother, Bernice. Soon the lad was a fixture in their household, with Germanicus and Claudius as his boyhood chums.

From the time he was 10 to perhaps 18 Agrippa lived a happy family life, winning friends with his wit and charm. As did his playmates, the grandson of Herod the Great wore the purple of royalty and behaved as a kingly heir-apparent. At the same time, he developed the vexing habit of promising lavish gifts to his friends and patrons that only embarrassed his mother when merchants came asking for payment.

When Bernice died during his early manhood, the young prince seemed to cast off all pretense of moderation. Now wed to a devoted wife, Cypros, Agrippa lived on a royal scale and continued to lavish presents on friends. Always each new wave of fancy living was financed by an ever-larger loan from one of the emperor's freedmen or some wealthy chum to whom he'd recently given a racehorse or feted at a banquet. The pattern became so predictable — borrow so much to pay back the previous loan and have enough left to wine and dine the next prospect — that Agrippa's entire circle of friends was soon wise to his ways. Now creditors ceased their polite inquiries and rudely clamored for payment.

Desperate and dejected, Agrippa fled from Rome by ship for Judea, accompanied only by Cypros and Marsyas, their long-time freedman and servant of many talents. So destitute and ashamed of his condition was the wretched prince that he soon returned to the Idumean desert, deep in the heart of his grandfather's homeland. There he found a forlorn fortress outpost where he shut himself up for days on end and pondered killing himself while Cypros wailed outside his door. Her only hope was a plea to her sister-in-law Herodias, who now lived with Antipas not far away in Perea. In a tear-stained letter she begged for whatever help and hope Herodias and Antipas might offer her wretched husband.

The reply was the answer to her prayers. Antipas and Herodias had offered to make her ne'er-do-well brother magistrate of Tiberias, that newly-built Hellenistic city on the Lake of Gennesaret. There, he and Cypros would have a decent but fixed income while they sorted out their lives.

I doubt that Agrippa greeted this news with the same tearful relief as did his wife. He went stoically, I'm sure, as Cypros and Marsyas chattered cheerfully about a new beginning in their lives. Indeed, being chief magistrate of a major regional city might have been enough to satisfy many a man's ambitions, but to a prince who had entertained a dozen senators at a single banquet, Tiberias was a boring backwater. Soon he was grumbling openly about his niggardly income, and word soon reached Antipas and Herodias in Perea. The pot boiled over when both couples had journeyed to Tyre to attend the same feast. Despite the efforts of their wives to make light of the occasion, both Agrippa and Antipas managed to get drunk and wasted no time going head to head. Agrippa sneered that he hadn't enough money to befit his station. Antipas roared back that he damn well ought to be grateful for the food he was given. Agrippa stalked out. But instead of returning to his magistrate's home in Tiberias, he and his exasperated wife and servants were soon trudging up the road to Antioch, determined to test the hospitality of another patron.

Agrippa's new host was Flaccus, former consul of Rome and now governor of Syria (and the last to serve there until Vitellius arrived many years later). And why Flaccus? Perhaps because he was at the time also providing shelter to the prince's older brother, Aristobulus.

Like Agrippa, Aristobulus was a prince with neither realm nor revenue. Flaccus treated both with equal respect and generosity. The brothers Herod repaid him by bickering constantly. The cause, I am told, was that whereas Aristobulus was merely treated politely, the worldly, charming Agrippa soon became the governor's delightful companion and trusted advisor.

Thus, you won't be surprised to learn that one of the brothers was soon bound to depart. What prompted it was this: Flaccus had scheduled a hearing on a land dispute between the cities of Damascus and Sidon. The Damascenes had gotten word that Agrippa had gained great influence over the governor, so they promised the prince a great sum of money if he would aid their cause. However, Aristobulus must have had his ear to the wall, because he was only too happy to report the arrangement to the governor. When Agrippa confirmed the suspicions with a zealous appeal for the Damascenes, Flaccus angrily cut him off. Within a day Agrippa and family were out on the streets, more destitute than ever.

Can you stand any more of this, dear reader? Ah, but it gets far worse before it gets better!

Agrippa, Cypros and the freedman, Marsyas, had soon drifted to cheap lodgings in the seaport city of Ptolemais. Utterly without any prospect of further funds, Agrippa lamely beseeched Marsyas to do what he could to "go out and borrow something from some person or other." Well, Marsyas had once served in the household of the prince's mother Bernice. The master slave there had been one Peter. When Bernice died, Peter was bequeathed to Antonia, her patroness in Rome. It was now Peter to whom the desperate Marsyas appealed, asking for a loan secured by the wealthy and noble Antonia.

But when Marsyas did so, Peter retorted that Agrippa had already defrauded him in a previous loan. The result was that Agrippa signed a note for 25,000 Attic drachmæ, but received only 22,000 after paying Peter his arrears. Such is the web that the chronic debtor weaves for himself!

Soon Agrippa became entangled in that web again. The influx of funds enabled the tattered "family" to charter a small rig and sail several miles down the coast to Anthedon. Late one afternoon soon thereafter they were on the quay at Anthedon, preparing to set sail at sunset, when the prince was suddenly confronted by a band of Roman soldiers who announced that they had been sent by the prefect for the area. Agrippa must have felt the breath knocked out of him as the captain of the guard began to read a letter. The addressee (who had known of his exact whereabouts?) was ordered to repay at once 300,000 drachmæ of silver which had been borrowed from Cæsar's treasury when he was in Rome. His ship was to be detained until the amount was repaid.

Agrippa summoned up all his princely countenance and replied haughtily that the amount would of course be delivered the next day. But since it would soon grow dark, he asked permission for his party to remain on ship for the evening.

Permission granted. But that night, after pledging his honor to the departing guard, Agrippa cut the ship's mooring lines and slipped out of the harbor.

Down the coast they went again until they had glided into the busy harbor of the empire's second largest city, Alexandria. This time Agrippa avoided Roman authorities, who would no doubt be on his trail. Instead, he put on his finest remaining purple raiment and called on Alexander, the alabarch, or tax commissioner whose purview included the half million Jews who lived in the Egyptian metropolis.

But by now, even Alexander had heard of the prince's ways and quickly turned down Agrippa's request for a 200,000 drachmæ loan. But as the awkward silence grew tense, Cypros, who had stood calmly at her husband's side, broke down and shattered all pretense of royal dignity. She described her love for Agrippa and his misfortunes with such plaintive honesty that Alexander was touched – not by the prince's plight, but by the wife's fidelity. At last he said he would lend the money only to Cypros herself, and only thusly: he would pay her five talents in Alexandria and the rest once they reached Puteoli in Italy. Alexander's fear, of course, was that if he dispersed all of the funds at once, Agrippa would find a way to squander all of it even aboard a ship in the middle of the sea!

When they did land in Puteoli, Agrippa wasted no time in sending a letter to Tiberius saying that he would appreciate the opportunity to come to Capri and wait on him. As the prince feared, the emperor's delay was maddening. No doubt Agrippa recalled when, just after Drusus died, Tiberius asked that his son's old friends not appear before him because it saddened him so. But I offer another possible reason: the emperor once said he put off seeing deputations or answering letters for as long as possible because an early response only hastened the time when he would have to answer another letter or hear another round of pleas from the delegation.

However, when a letter from Tiberius did come, it was as obliging as Agrippa could have hoped for. He made for Capri immediately and was received cordially. Old memories were exchanged. Agrippa basked once again in imperial surroundings and went to bed happy that his fortunes were turning at last.

He awoke the next day to encounter a much different Tiberius. The emperor informed him icily that a letter had just arrived from the same prefect at Jamnia who governed the port city of Anthedon (from whence Agrippa had sailed to Alexandria). Again, the subject was the 300,000 drachmæ that Agrippa had borrowed from the Roman treasury. Only this time the prince was cited as a fugitive for having cut his slips at night and stealing away.

No doubt Tiberius had had men hurled from the cliffs of Capri for less. In this instance, he coldly informed Agrippa that he would not be welcomed on the island until the debt was repaid.

Now, Agrippa faced certain ruin – except for just one more possible oasis in his desert of disgrace. Employing either guile or guilt as his ploy, he went straight to Antonia, to whom he already owed the note for 125,000 drachmæ. As the most reliable record I can find states:

"[Agrippa] then entreated Antonia, the mother of Germanicus and Claudius...to lend him those 300,000 drachmæ, that he might not be deprived of Tiberius's friendship. So, out of regard to the memory of Bernice his mother (for those two women were very familiar with one another) and out of regard to his and Claudius's education together, she lent him the money; and upon the payment of his debt, there was nothing to hinder Tiberius's friendship to him." Indeed, Tiberius urged that Agrippa wait on his grandson Gaius and "that he should always accompany him when he went abroad."

Well, I suppose, dear reader, that we should leave this story with its happy ending. But Agrippa will simply not allow it. He did indeed meet and charm Gaius, and soon the wizened Jewish prince, now well into his forties, and the young Roman heir-apparent, probably 22 at the time, began to be seen everywhere together.

But Agrippa still had greater heights to scale when it came to his incorrigable borrowing. What I mean is that in the course of courting Gaius, Agrippa was also wooing one Thallus, a freedman who administered personal finances for both Cæsar and Gaius. The result was that he borrowed one million drachmæ from Thallus and repaid Antonia, thus regaining her confidence. Then he used much of the remainder to pay obeisance to Gaius, thereby becoming even more ensconced in his good graces.

Soon, Herod Agrippa the courtier and confidant had assembled a new retinue of retainers. They included a freedman named Eutychus, whose many odd jobs included driving Agrippa's carriage. One evening he was at the reins as Agrippa and Gaius made a leisurely tour around the villas of Capri. Agrippa, no doubt his flattery in fine form and escalating to new heights, said he was praying to the gods that Tiberius would soon "go offstage" and leave the matter of governance to the far more worthy Gaius. I suppose that similar asides were made often in Tiberius's old age and that the chariot driver thought little of Agrippa's remarks at the time.

But something happened that would make them loom much larger. A few days later Agrippa accused Eutychus of stealing some of his garments. Doubtless guilty as charged, the freedman fled Capri, only to be apprehended several days later in Rome. About to be punished as a petty thief, Eutychus cried out that he had something to say directly to Cæsar that involved the emperor's "security and preservation." Thus, the prefect of Rome had no choice but to have Eutychus bound and sent back to Capri.

Tiberius listened to the freedman, but kept him in confinement, I believe, for fear he would only bring about a scene that would embarrass Agrippa and his patroness. Meanwhile, the emperor made one of his rare journeys off the island, reaching Tusculanum, which is only 12 miles from Rome, and quite near a villa where his sister-in-law Antonia was residing. Hearing that Tiberius was headed her way, Agrippa huffed and blustered that he couldn't understand why his charges against his mischievous freeman had gone unheard. When he pestered Antonia to bring up the matter when Tiberius came calling, she agreed to do so that very day.

The emperor listened patiently, but added this comment: "If guilty, he (Eutychus) has suffered punishment enough by what I have done to him already. But if, upon examination, the accusation appears to be true, then let Agrippa have a care, lest out of desire of punishing a freedman, he rather brings punishment upon himself."

When Antonia reported this to Agrippa, he was like a peacock stalked by a wolf. To flutter to the nearest tree branch would be a signal of his own guilt. So Agrippa boldly puffed himself up, demanding that the charges be heard as soon as possible.

Not long afterwards, Tiberius, Antonia, and Agrippa were all part of a dinner party in Tusculanum on a hot summer's evening. It was just breaking up when it became known that Eutychus had been brought up from Capri and was being kept nearby amidst a cluster of prisoners and supplicants who stood ready for the emperor to hear their cases when he had the inclination. But Tiberius was tired. He had just eased into his sedan to depart for his lodgings when Antonia appeared again and asked that he have Eutychus brought out and examined.

Tiberius frowned, heaved a sigh and bid his attendants set him down. "Oh, Antonia," he said wearily, "the gods are my witnesses that I am induced to do what I am going to do, not by my own inclination, but because I am forced to it by your prayers." With that he ordered Macro, the chief guardsman, to summon Eutychus.

The freedman had by then many weeks in which to practice his delivery as to what Agrippa had said that night in the carriage. "Oh, my lord," Eutychus bewailed with arms gesturing as a Greek tragedy, "this Gaius and Agrippa with him were riding in a carriage when I sat at their feet. And among other discourses that passed, Agrippa said: 'Oh that the day would come when this old fellow would die and name thee governor of the habitable earth! For then this other Tiberius [the young grandson of Tiberius] would be taken off by thee and the earth would be happy, and I happy also!'"

The discourse was so literal that it had the ring of reality about it. When Eutychus finished, Tiberius turned to Macro and pointed toward Agrippa. "Bind this man," he said stonily.

But Macro, his mind perhaps dulled by the heat and the late hour, appeared not to comprehend. "Who?" he asked dumbly. Tiberius then impatiently led him right up to the stunned Agrippa and said plainly, "Macro, this is the man I mean to have bound."

Agrippa made a swooning supplication as if to posture himself as if the emperor's very own son were being wronged. But to no avail. Agrippa was led off in chains wearing his finest purple garments.

Soon the prince found himself, still stunned, leaning against a broad tree in the breathless evening. Standing and sitting around him were several wretches who had been languishing in jail, and who were now in bonds awaiting examinations or sentencing depending on whether they could gain the emperor's attention. According to what has been widely reported (of which I cannot vouchsafe but will nonetheless repeat), one of the prisoners was a gaunt old German who asked his guard to allow him to approach the Jewish prince. Said the German: "This sudden change in your condition, oh young man, is grievous to you; nor will you believe me when I foretell how you will get clear of this misery, and how divine providence will provide for you. Know, therefore, that all I am going to say about your concerns shall neither be said for favor nor bribery, nor out of an endeavor to make you cheerful without cause. Although I run the hazard of my own self, I think it fit to declare to you the prediction of the gods.

"It will not be that you should long continue in these bonds," said the old German. "But you will soon be delivered from them and will be promoted to the highest dignity and power, and you will be envied by all those who now pity your hard fortune. And you will be happy til your death and will leave your happiness to the children whom you shall have."

The story continues that the German then pointed to an owl that roosted in a branch high above them. "But do remember," he told Agrippa, "that when you see this bird again, you will live but five days longer. This event will be brought to pass by that God who had sent this bird to be a sign unto thee."

We will see later how this prophecy turned out. In the days immediately following, Antonia, no doubt seared by her role in hastening the prince's downfall, beseeched Tiberius often for leniency. At the same time, Rome's most revered patrician lady used all her sway to win assurance from Macro that Agrippa's guards would be gentle, that he would be allowed to bathe every day, and that his friends and freedmen would be able to attend him. Before long it seemed that everyone from Antonia to the centurion in charge of the guard to Agrippa's entire retinue were working hand in hand to ensure the prince's comfort and amusement.

Still, this confinement was to last six months, which, dear reader, now brings us to the beginning of the two years covered by this chapter.

The visit of Tiberius to Tusculanum may have coincided with his need to help Rome pull itself from the wreckage of a major fire that all but destroyed the homes and apartments in the Aventine section. It also devastated much of the Circus Maximus and nearly lapped itself up to the palaces that adorn the Palatine Hill. Since I have been quick to report the emperor's niggardly ways with the public purse, I should balance the scales by stating that in this case he donated 100 million sesterces towards restoration of the burned out neighborhoods. This was to be doled out by a special commission consisting of the husbands of his four granddaughters. For this — and perhaps because he had undertaken only two public building projects in all of his 22-year reign — the emperor was voted every compliment the sycophantic Senate could possibly imagine.

Not long after returning to Capri Tiberius came down with what appeared at first to be an ordinary cold. But, now at age 78, it began to get the better of him. The emperor did everything to make his regular appearances and shoo away physicians, for one of his favorite sayings had always been that no man who had survived his first 30 years should ever need a doctor. But as his visible signs weakened, his retainers began to grind their spokes like chariot drivers positioning themselves for the final furlong.

Macro, for one. It so happened that just about this time, the young wife of Gaius, Junia Claudilla, died in childbirth. Macro, now determined to forge bonds with Gaius like never before, encouraged his beautiful wife Ennia Nævia to seduce the youthful heir-apparent. Gaius, however, needed little encouragement. Perceiving that having an heir would further cement his succession, he not only gave an oath to marry her if he became emperor, but guaranteed it with a written contract.

By this time it may have been that a doctor or seer told Tiberius that the air or the omens on Capri were unfavorable. Or perhaps he knew the end was at hand and felt compelled to be nearer to his roots. Whatever the cause, Tiberius now had himself rowed across to the mainland where he settled into a villa on Cape Misenum belonging to a wealthy senator. Outwardly, he still tried to maintain a clear voice and firm expression. One reliable story involved the eminent physician, Charicles, who attended a small dinner party given by the emperor at Misenum. In the course of pretending to take his leave, Charicles grasped the emperor's hand and at the same time felt his pulse with an extended finger. Tiberius, fearing that others had noticed, prolonged the dinner and resumed his old custom of standing and personally bidding each guest farewell.

But soon the old man had surrendered himself to just two thoughts: death and succession. Despite all the years that he had to choose and groom a successor, Tiberius anguished about it to his last day. Tiberius Gemellus, the son of his brother Drusus, was closer to him in blood, but still a young, fragile boy. Claudius, the now-middle-aged brother of Germanicus, was considered intermittently, but his limping and stuttering exasperated even his own immediate family. Was this the Claudian strain that should wear the mantle of Augustus?

The fact was that even though Claudius haunted libraries and wrote histories himself, he was considered something of a simpleton in addition to all his physical shortcomings.

Gaius? Well, the dominant question was, why *not*? The son of Germanicus was well educated and popular among Romans; but Tiberius also knew well how Gaius Caligula was perceived by those who knew him closely. What was in the emperor's mind in his last days could be summed up by the recollection of his most trusted freedman, who reported being in the room a few weeks beforehand when both Gaius and the small boy, Tiberius Gamellus, were with the emperor in his salon. Then, the freedman related, Tiberius embraced his grandson and lashed out at Gaius. "You'll kill him," he said, weeping, "and then someone will kill *you!*"

In his final days Tiberius was reduced to resting upon his old crutch, superstition. One afternoon the emperor weakly beckoned his most trusted freedman, Euodus, and ordered that both Gaius and the young Tiberius be brought to him the next morning. At the same time, the old man prayed that the gods would send him a manifest signal as to which one should govern Rome. No sign came. So by evening Tiberius resolved that the first one who came to him the next morning would inherit the government. At the same time, he sent a message to his grandson's tutor, ordering him to bring the child to him early, hoping, I must presume, that his real choice would get the edge like the charioteer with the inside position at the Circus Maximus.

The next morning, at the time he had stipulated, Tiberius summoned Euodus and asked him to "call in the child who is there ready." Alas, Tiberius Gemellus was still at his breakfast. When the unwitting servant spied Gaius and said, "Thy father calls thee," it was Gaius who appeared at the emperor's door.

With that, Rome's foremost patron of diviners and astrologers succumbed to the fate that had befallen him. With an air of foreboding and dejection he informed the son of Germanicus that it was he who had been chosen to govern the inhabitable world.

Tiberius lived a few more days. And died. And lived. By this I mean that on March 14 the doctors grimly informed Gaius and Macro that the emperor could not last two more days. With that, dispatches went out to senators, generals and provincial governors. On March 16 Tiberius ceased to breathe, and was believed dead. Gaius, surrounded by a hushed but eager crowd, actually slipped the emperor's ring from his finger and prepared to assume imperium. But just then the "deceased" raised his head, blinked his eyes and asked for food. Immediately the crowd outside showed a flutter of panic, then, well trained by then, I suppose, instantly recomposed themselves as showing a single face of solemn prayer. Gaius simply stood there in stupefied silence, staring down at his new ring as if it were a serpent. It was then that Macro, perhaps realizing there was no way to return either ring or retrieve all those dispatches, calmly walked into the emperor's bed chamber and unceremoniously smothered with a pillow the wolf who had made the world cower for 22 years, five months and three days.

At last the small knot of notables and retainers at Misenum could erupt with relief and congratulations. But at first, this was not the effect on others as word spread across the continent. Romans were simply too wary to rejoice. Although they would have paid anything for guaranteed confirmation of the fact, they feared that it might be another wicked scheme by a man who had already ruined so many families to vent his wrath on those who remained.

All this may be why the case of Herod Agrippa may not have been unusual. When Marsyas, the tattered prince's long-suffering freedman, first heard the news (perhaps just after Tiberius's "resurrection") he rushed to where Agrippa was preparing to bathe and whispered breathlessly in Hebrew, "The Lion is dead." Now when the centurion guarding Agrippa saw with what haste the excited freedman had burst upon the scene, he asked what had been said. Agrippa tried to divert the conversation with a joke. But the centurion pressed him, and because the two had become fast friends, Agrippa relented and repeated what he had heard.

Well, the centurion soon became all smiles because he knew what it meant for his friend. Quickly he prepared Agrippa a feast and passed out cups. But in the midst of it the revelers were abruptly halted by another guard who reported that Tiberius was alive and was planning a return to Rome in a few days.

The centurion stiffened and his jaw squared. He knew that he had just committed a treasonous act, punishable by death. Turning on Agrippa, his anger flushed. "Do you think you can lie about the emperor without punishment?" he stormed. The centurion immediately ordered his prisoner clapped in chains again. And it was in a dank cell that the prince spent the night wondering what evil lay in store for him this time.

But the prophecy continued. The next morning all in town were shouting that Tiberius was indeed dead and that Gaius was on his way to Rome to take power. And yes, one of the new emperor's very first decrees at Misenum was that Agrippa should be removed from his prison and taken to the house in Rome where he had lived beforehand. Although officially still in custody, Agrippa was now free to resume his daily life.

Agrippa would have received much more from Gaius in those first days except for the intervention of Antonia. As soon as Gaius arrived in Rome, she cautioned the emperor that it would not be wise to set Agrippa free immediately lest people think that he received the death of Tiberius with pleasure by releasing someone who had been imprisoned for insulting him.

But Herod Agrippa did not have to wait long. Within a few more days, Gaius sent for the prince, had his beard shaved, and made him change his raiment back to royal purple. Gaius then put a diadem on his friend's head and appointed him king of the former tetrarchy of Philip (which ruled over Trachonitis and Gaulanitis northeast of Galilee). Then he gave him this present: a long chain of gold to symbolize his freedom from the chains he had worn as a prisoner of Tiberius.

With that the emperor also appointed one Marullus to be the new procurator of Judea. As for his deposed predecessor, Pontius Pilate was making his way slowly to Rome to face his charges when the news of Tiberius' death came. Henceforth he fades into history, presumably a relieved, happier and humbler man.

Such are the winds that blow with a new ruler. Gaius Caligula was just 25 and the winds were strong and cleansing. From the farthest foot soldier who had known him as a boy to the old comrades of his revered father to the senatorial families who had been ravished by Tiberius, word of Gaius' ascension caused dancing and weeping for joy. Even as he set out from Misenum in mourning garb and escorting the body of Tiberius, his path was lined with altars, blazing torches, sacrificial victims and a dense, joyful throng who shouted out such endearments as their "star," their "babe" and their "nursling."

Once Gaius had entered the gates of Rome, the Senate wasted no time in bestowing on him absolute power by unanimous consent – all to the shouting and prodding of a mob that had forced its way inside the Curia. Left almost unnoticed on the dais was the boy, Tiberius Gemellus, who had been named joint heir in his grandfather's will.

Soon thereafter, Gaius' every act only increased his support and popularity. After eulogizing Tiberius with many tears at a magnificent funeral, the emperor had himself transported to Pandateria and the Pontian Islands to retrieve the ashes of his mother and brothers. As if a dramatist had scored the scene, it was a stormy, windy day when a solemn Gaius approached the charred remains on a hillside and placed them in urns with his own hands. With no less theatrical effect, he brought them to Ostia in a birene with a banner set in the stern and sailed slowly up the Tiber to Rome. There, in the middle of the day, leaders of the Order of Knights carried the urns down crowded streets to the Mausoleum of Augustus. In a touching ceremony broken often by unrestrained cheering, Gaius decreed that games in the Circus were to be held in his mother's honor and that each year a carriage would carry Agrippina's image in a funeral procession. As for his father, he declared that the month of September would henceforth be named Germanicus.

The contrast between the meanness of Tiberius and the munificence of Gaius was everywhere to behold. The emperor's reticent Uncle Claudius, who at age 47 had never risen above knight or held government office, was made joint consul. His grandmother Antonia was voted every honor ever held by Augustus' wife, Livia. He decreed that his sisters be included in all official oaths and greet-ings, such as "Favor and good fortune attend Gaius Cæsar and his sisters."

Next, he adopted Tiberius Gemellus on the day he assumed the gown of manhood and gave him the title Chief of Youth. On that day in the Senate the emperor asked aloud, "What greater blessing could there be than that a single soul should cease to be laden with the heavy burden of sovereignty and should have one who would be able to relieve and lighten them? And I," he assured, "will be more than a guardian, a tutor and teacher. I will appoint myself to be his father and him to be my son."

The winds of change blew well beyond the imperial palace. Those who had been banished were recalled, and those being held for trial dismissed. All docu-ments relating to the trials of Gaius' mother and brothers were carried to the Forum and publicly burned as the emperor swore to the gods that he had read no documents that would have identified accusers or witnesses. And when a fawning senator tried to hand him a note warning of a threat to his safety, the emperor refused it, saying that he had done nothing to make anyone hate him and had no ears for informers.

As to matters of governance, Gaius gained even more good will by honor-ing every obligation called for in Tiberius' will and again publishing the finan-cial accounts of the empire, the Augustinian practice that his predecessor had ignored. He reinstituted some local elections, recalled banned books, ban-ished well-known bands of sexual perverts from the city, revised the lists of Roman knights judiciously and reinstituted imperial sponsorship of gladia-torial shows. He exhibited continuous stage plays in different areas − and those by night sometimes lit up the whole city. He completed the public works that had been left half-finished by Tiberius and began an aqueduct near the city of Tiber.

In an effort to symbolize a new era of generosity and fair play, Gaius twice be-stowed gifts of 300 sesterces each to the people of Rome and often tossed assort-ed gifts from his chariot to whomever he happened to be passing. He even made a show of giving 800,000 sesterces to a freedwoman because she had refused to make false charges against her patron despite being tortured severely. And twice he gave a lavish banquet for the entire families of senators and knights at which he distributed togas to the men and scarves of red to the women and children.

Because of these and many more actions during these six months, it was fur-ther decreed by the Senate that each anniversary of the day Gaius began his reign should be called the Parilia as a token meaning that the city had been founded a second time. He was also voted a golden shield, which was to be borne every year to the Capitol by the College of Priests, escorted by the Senate, while boys and girls of noble birth sang of his virtues in a choral ode.

But the emperor's praises rang far beyond Rome. So deliriously happy was the Jewish diarist Philo in far-off Alexandria that he penned the following:

> It was not now a matter of hoping that they [people everywhere] would have the possession and use of good things public and private; they considered that they had already the plenitude, as it were, with good fortune and happiness waiting in its train.
>
> Thus, nothing was to be seen throughout the cities but altars, oblations, sacrifices, men in white robes crowned with garlands, bright and smart, their cheery faces beaming with goodwill, feats, assemblages, musical contests, horse races, revels, nightlong frolics with harp and flutes, jollification, unrestrained, holiday-keeping, every kind of pleasure administered by every sense. In those days the rich had no precedence over the poor, nor the distinguished over the obscure. Creditors were not above debtors, nor masters above slaves, the times giving equality before the law.
>
> Indeed, the life under Saturn pictured by the poets no longer appeared to be a fabled story, so great was the prosperity and well-being, the freedom from grief and fear, the joy which pervaded households and people, night and day, and lasted continuously without a break for the first seven months.[9]

These same ecstatic people should have offered some of their praise to Macro as well. Although most surely one of the bloodthirsty accusers in the reign gone by, the General of the Prætorian Guard quickly found himself playing everything from father to tutor to nursemaid to the erratic young emperor. Having served Tiberius through the Sejanus mess and then promoting Gaius to his master at every opportunity, Macro felt he had earned the right to speak frankly and firmly to the new emperor. Thus, whenever he saw Gaius nod off at a banquet, he would awake him with the double objective of preserving propriety and public safety. Or if he saw the emperor frantic with lust for a nubile dancer or cheering a mime in a scandalous scene or making a loud youngster's guffaw at a joke, Macro would lean back at his side and nudge him to behave with more regal restraint. Or he might whisper, "It should not be perceived that the sovereign of earth and sea should be overcome by a song or dancing." On another occasion he might lecture: "When you are attending theatrical or gymnastic competitions or those of the chariot race, do not pay regard to what the performers actually do, but to the moral achievement shown in their doings. For remember that you have achieved the greatest art of all, the art of government, which causes the good deep soil in lowlands and highlands to be tilled and all the seas to be safely navigated."

And when Gaius would jump up to leave a desk full of unread dispatches to spend hours with a famous actor or chariot driver, Macro would be standing by with a stern admonishment. "The governance of everything to the ends of the earth had been entrusted to your single hand," he would observe solemnly. "Having under Nature's escort risen to the highest post in the stern, the tiller placed in your hand, you must steer in security the common ship of mankind, rejoicing and delighting in nothing so much as in benefiting your subjects."

In October of the first year, the hand went off the tiller and the ship ran aground. Gaius was struck down with a mysterious malady that left him unable to function as emperor. Many symptoms have been cited – crashing headaches, chills and nausea, but no one has ever identified the cause or the disease except that it might be related to his several bouts of epilepsy as a child. Since autumn had just begun and the north winds hadn't yet put a halt to water navigation, word spread faster than fire – and with equally devastating effects on public morale. Romans prostrated themselves at the palace gates, offering their own lives if the gods would spare Gaius. In the farthest reaches of the empire, every household was filled with anxiety, with their grief as intense as had been their joy just days before. People worried aloud of the famine, poverty, war, loss of property and chaos that would ensue if Rome were robbed of its leader.

A few weeks later, news of the emperor's recovery spread just as quickly, creating instant waves of exultation. Lest you believe this sheer exaggeration, I quote from the same writer from Alexandria:

> For no one remembers any single country or single nation feeling as much delight at the accession or preservation of a ruler as was felt by the whole world in the case of Gaius, both when he succeeded to his sovereignty and when he recovered from his malady.[10]

Did the illness scar the young emperor's mind? Or perhaps no one man can endure so much adulation without having an adverse reaction, as if from a slow poison. But it was not long afterward that a different Gaius began to manifest himself to the public. Those in the palace perhaps saw it first in the way that he treated Macro and his closest freedmen. Macro's fatherly admonitions were increasingly returned by surly retorts. Then one day when the emperor was standing with a group of men and saw Macro approaching, he remarked in a peevish but loud tone: "Here comes the teacher of one who no longer needs to learn, the tutor of one who is no longer in tutelage, the censor of his superior in wisdom, who holds that an emperor should obey his subjects, who rated himself as versed in the art of government and an instructor therein, though in what school he has learnt his principles I do not know."

Gaius had now warmed up to what may have been a rehearsed oration just awaiting the proper occasion. "For I from the cradle," he continued, "have had a host of teachers, father, brothers, uncles, cousins, grandparents, ancestors, right up to the founders of the House, all my kinsmen by blood on both the maternal and paternal sides, who attained to offices of independent authority, apart from the fact that in the original seeds of their begetting king-like potentialities for government were contained. For just as the seminal forces preserve similarities of the body in form and carriage, and of the soul in projects and actions, so we may suppose that to the governing faculty they contain a resemblance in outline. Thus, does anyone dare to teach me, who even while in the womb, that workshop of nature, was modeled as an emperor?"

Looking directly at Macro, now standing silently amidst them, Gaius asked, "How can they who were but now common citizens have a right to peer into the counsels of an imperial soul? Yet in their shameless effrontery they who would hardly be admitted to rank as learners dare to act as masters who initiate others into the mysteries of government."

Their relationship was never to be the same, as became evident by the conduct of government. Barely a year since he had assumed the throne, Gaius could not be dissuaded from a new fixation: that Tiberius Gemellus, his adopted son, was an oppressive nuisance. Only then did those who at first applauded the generosity of Gaius in adopting his cousin begin to realize his true intent: Roman law gives a father absolute power over his son.

At any rate, Gaius was soon heard complaining that the youth's breath smelled like an antidote taken to guard against being poisoned. In fact, Tiberius had been taking a medicine for a worsening cough. But Gaius would have none of it. He openly commissioned orders that the boy was to kill himself with his own hands under a centurion's supervision (this because it was unlawful for the descendants of emperors to be slain by others).

But the hapless lad lacked the skill to do the deed, for he had never seen anyone else killed and had not yet been trained in any of the martial exercises. At first he stretched out his neck to the emissaries of Gaius who had brought him his orders and bravely asked that they dispatch him. But when they could not bring themselves to do so, he took the sword himself and in his ignorance, asked them to point out the most vulnerable spot that he could strike and end his miserable life. They, shaken and weeping themselves by this time, gave instructions and showed him the part to which he should apply the sword. And having received his first and last lesson in martial arts, the poor boy became his own murderer.

Even then, the adulation of Gaius did not subside noticeably. People from

Antioch to Alexandria reasoned that it is dangerous to a monarch, and even a distraction from his need to concentrate on enlightened government, to be burdened with worrying about the whims and wiles of a possible competitor. "Sovereignty cannot be shared, this is an immutable law of nature," is one comment most heard by orators in taverns. Even if the co-emperor had remained a faithful supplicant, they added, he would have attracted partisans. And partisans, they nodded, usually grow into armed camps that mean war. So peace is better, they agreed. Yes, yes, it was a sad occasion indeed, but undoubtedly one best for the empire.

Thus encouraged, Gaius continued to address his list of imperial nuisances. An easier task was Macro, simply because it is not difficult to imagine an accuser being coaxed to confess having heard the general say something like this: "Yes, 'tis I, Macro, who made Gaius almost more than did his parents. Many times Tiberius would have had him violently removed had it not been for my intercessions. And even when Tiberius was dead, I had the military forces under my control, but I exhorted them to unite behind a single sovereign."

Well, as we saw with Tiberius and Sejanus, sometimes a man performs favors for another on such an epic scale that they can never be repaid. And that is unbearably threatening to those who must control all events. For his excessive zeal, Macro was forced to slay himself, but not before taking the life of his wife and thereby releasing the emperor from his "contract" to marry her.

When Macro and his entire household had been slaughtered, the emperor found the third task on his agenda even simpler. Although Gaius had lost his wife in childbirth during the last months of Tiberius, he soon found that he had not lost a family of in-laws. Its head was Marcus Silanus, a distinguished senator from a leading family who continued to take his duties as father-in-law seriously. Since Gaius had lost his natural father, Silanus showered him with attention and took it upon himself to act as unofficial guardian as well. The senior senator was forever offering stern advice on the art of governance and personal conduct. But whereas Macro posed a serious and dangerous obstacle to Gaius, the unsuspecting Silanus was but a tedious nag. Gaius seized on the flimsiest of excuses: he charged that his father-in-law had refused an order to join him when he sailed in stormy weather on the hope that he would take control of Rome should the emperor's ship go down. In truth, Silanus was prone to seasickness and had simply dreaded the voyage. The indiscretion caused him to slit his own throat with a razor on Gaius' orders. And when this Senate leader did so, the act also cut severely into whatever good will the emperor still retained among the patrician families.

Both Macro and Silanus fell on May 24, just a little more than 14 months after the death of Tiberius. It was also on the birthday of Germanicus, which I note only to show that the emperor's public display of honoring his father only a few months before was now forgotten symbolism as the young emperor became possessed by megalomania. Yet, no one wished to begin drawing parallels to those dark and increasingly distant years of Tiberius or allow themselves to think that Gaius was anything but kind and tolerant. So people labored at length to construct acceptable explanations. Macro, it was decided, had violated the Delphic motto: "know thyself." He had no business transferring the subject to rank of ruler and emperor to place of subject. As for Silanus, "He was ridiculous to assume that a father-in-law can have the same influence as a real father," went the common wisdom. "He did not understand that the death of his daughter carried with it the death of matrimonial affinity."

It is said that with these three murders, Gaius accomplished three objectives. He had brought the knights to heel by killing their leader, Macro. He subdued the Senate by eliminating a member who was second to none. And in his household, the departure of Tiberius Gemellus removed all threat of a family successor.

All true, but I think there was a more persuasive reason behind all of the killings. All of these victims had represented obstacles in the way of the emperor being thought of by the world as a god.

Ah, if only our foresight were as clear as our hindsight, what seers we all would be! In the case of Gaius, what became an all-consuming quest may well have been evident as early as his first month as emperor. Augustus, during his lifetime, had allowed only one city (Pergamum) to build a temple to him and sacrifice to its statue, and in this case only because it was jointly dedicated to the city of Rome. Tiberius showed equal restraint. But in August of his first year Gaius responded warmly when a deputation of Greeks sought to erect and worship statues all over the province. Gaius actually appeared modest by suggesting,"Confine yourselves to those to be set up at Olympia, Nemea, Dephi and the Isthmus so as...not to burden yourselves more heavily with expenses."

From that point forward other cities and provinces began to compete with one another to see which could erect the biggest temple and conduct the most lavish sacrifices. This in turn only gave credence to what was by now Gaius' most consuming enterprise: his deification while still in his "earthly" form. In fact, it was as if the names of Tiberius Gemellus, Macro and Silanus were but the first on a list that included each of the gods on Mount Olympus as well and that he could "eliminate" each of them as a competitor, if you will, by assuming their roles or exceeding their achievements.

Thus, Gaius began by pouring scorn on so-called demigods like Dionysus and Herakles, treating their oracles and celebrations as trifles compared to his own power. When at the theater, he assumed different costumes at different times, such as "becoming" Herakles by adorning himself with lion skin and club, overlain with gold. On another night he might appear as Dionysus, wearing ivy, thyrsus and fawn's skin. He would be jealous of any festivals and honors paid to various gods and demand their offerings and prizes for himself. In this way, he must have reasoned, he could demonstrate that he was more worthy than all the gods combined.

Once the people began to see their emperor riding in his carriage dressed as Apollo or standing in the Capitoline whispering in the ear of Jupiter's statue, they took pains to accommodate him. Soon Gaius had built an extension of the palace as far as the Forum so that the temple of Castor and Pollux became its vestibule. There he could parade down the raised walkway and into the temple, taking his place between the divine brethren so that he could exhibit himself and be worshipped among them. He also set up a special temple to his own god-head, with priests and sacrifices. Inside was a life-sized statue of the emperor in gold, which was dressed each day in the clothing that he was wearing himself. The richest citizens used all their influence to become priests of the cult and bid high for the honor. And each day they continued unbroken sacrifices of flamingoes, peacocks, guinea hens, pheasants and the like.

By this time, the people of Rome were probably well conditioned to absorb the shock when it became known that Gaius practiced incest with his sisters. Drusilla, his favorite, he even took openly from her husband and treated her like a wife. In fact, during his serious illness, Gaius made Drusilla heir to both his property and throne.

Nothing intrigues me more than the mechanism which supposedly educated people devised to explain all this. As to the incest, we hear that once a person has proclaimed himself a god, it follows that the only humans worthy of his sexual confidence should be those of his own earthly flesh (if only he had so confined himself!). As to the competition among provinces and potentates to erect temples of worship, it was agreed that because Orientals and other barbarians accept their rulers as divine, an emperor must be seen as equally so in order to command their respect in his conduct of diplomacy.

As far as explaining Gaius' own thought process, there is but one piece of information I can offer. Gaius is supposed to have said: "The shepherds who have charge of the herds of other animals are not themselves oxen, goats and lambs, but men to whom is given a higher destiny. In the same way I who am in charge of the best of herds, mankind, must be considered to be different from them and not of human nature, but to have a greater and diviner destiny."

. . . .

WHEN ARETUS THE NABATEAN ROUTED THE ARMY of Herod Antipas at the end of the previous period in which I wrote about the Jews, the tetrarch was incensed and frustrated.

Much of his ire was no doubt directed at Vitellius, the Syrian governor, who had failed to rush to his side. Yet, the ruler of Galilee and Perea also knew that it was only Vitellius who could restore his former borders. So Antipas took the only way out: he wrote his long-time patron, Tiberius, an impassioned letter, directing his indignation to the rebellious Aretus and the treacherous Jews from Philip's tetrarchy of Gaulanitis and Trachonitis who had aided the Arab leader.

Since Aretus had always ranked high on Tiberius's long list of untrustworthy clients, the emperor didn't need much persuading to order an all-out attack on Nabatea. It is also possible that the disloyalty reported in Gaulanitis and Trachonitis not long after Philip's death was one reason that Gaius gave Agrippa the tetrarchy to rule as king.

In any event, in the midst of winter, Vitellius was ordered to march towards the Nabatean capital of Petra with two legions and all the light armature and horsemen they could muster. This was no walk in a meadow. The Roman army first marched some 200 miles down the coast to Ptolemais, where it stopped briefly to reprovision. From there, still facing another 200-mile trek southward before reaching their walled objective of Petra, the hot, dusty and doubtless distempered legions had just crossed into Judean territory when they were beseeched to halt by a crowd of arm-waving men.

These proved to be the leading citizens of Judea and its chief city, Jerusalem. The leaders begged Vitellius not to march through their land – and especially through the capital city – because their laws would not allow the people to look upon the many images that were emblazoned on the Roman standards. And with throngs coming to attend another Passover festival, the leaders no doubt reminded Vitellius of the uprisings caused by similar displays in the procuratorship of Pilate.

Being cast by a people as an unwelcome liberator after being jostled on the back of a horse for over a week must have made Vitellius want to lead a cavalry charge right through their midst; but soon Herod Antipas himself rode up and joined in the entreaty. The result was that while the army would continue down the monotonous coastal plain, Vitellius, Antipas and a small entourage would go to Jerusalem to sacrifice to the Jewish god and attend the Passover festival.

Vitellius was already a hero in Jerusalem for his previous display of munificence, so one can assume that three days of rest, food, wine and adulation did much to improve his disposition. It had even more salubrious consequences for the Nabateans, because on the fourth day Vitellius received a dispatch that Tiberius was dead. Lacking any orders from Gaius to continue his objective, he returned north with his army and dispersed it for winter quarters.

King Aretus would say later that all this was not unexpected. The Nabatean had consulted his diviners about the expected military assault and had been told that it would be aborted by either the death of the Roman general or "the one who had sent him." Still, Aretus put to rest any more aggressive impulses for a reason that did not require divination to understand. Word soon came that the powerful Parthian King Artabanus, whose borders straddled Nabatea for hundreds of miles, had pledged allegiance to Gaius and paid homage to the statues of the Cæsars following the death of the man he had despised. Aretus could ill-afford to be squeezed by hostile forces on two sides.

Looking back, it could be said that the Jewish heartland, even with the interruptions caused by Aretus, enjoyed a fair measure of domestic peace and relief from being constantly trampled or traversed by armies in need of provisions. I would estimate this as lasting just over two years. This "interlude" more or less began with Vitellius' recall of Pilate and his granting the Jews greater control over their religious affairs. But it would begin to crumble after the reign of Gaius had passed only one year.

At that point, Herod Agrippa began to make himself felt in Jewish affairs. Despite receiving dominion over the deceased Philip's realm of Gaulanitis and Trachonitis, Agrippa waited in Rome for nearly a year before Gaius allowed him to go there and exercise it. This year, I might add, was time enough for his sister Herodias to hiss and sputter like a volcano about to burst. For while her husband Antipas remained a tetrarch, Gaius had made this irresponsible wastrel, the brother who had scorned a sister's charity, a king!

It's not known whether the aging Antipas himself really cared anymore about titles. But for Herodias, this would never do. She would remind her husband incessantly that *he* was a living son of Herod the Great, while Agrippa was but the rudderless offspring of one of several sons Herod had slain – until this stroke of ludicrous luck. Now, as her brother and the now regally bedecked Cypros returned to Palestine and marched with the ensigns of royal authority, it was too much for her to bear.

One day Herodias startled her placid husband by swearing that she would not continue living unless they went to Rome and pled for equal honors. "Why do you not seek the dignity which your kinsman has attained?" she fumed. "How can you bear this contempt – that a man who admired your riches should now have greater honor than yourself and be able to purchase greater things? Nor do you not esteem it a shameful thing to be inferior to one who, just the other day, lived on your charity? Let us go to Rome," she importuned. "And let us spare no pains nor expenses, either of silver or gold, since they cannot be used for anything better than obtaining a kingdom."

After days of bitter argument, Herodias eventually wore her husband down. After amassing gifts for Gaius and packing the most glittering finery possible, the would-be king of Perea and Galilee sailed for Rome with his resplendent wife and retinue.

But by this time Agrippa had learned what was up. As soon as he had heard they set sail, he equipped Fortunatus, one of his freedmen, with gifts and a letter to the emperor, dispatching him to Rome on the fastest ship he could find.

Antipas landed in Puteoli, then traced the steps of Gaius to Baiæ, a delightful spa in Campania with natural warm springs, where emperors have long maintained palaces with sumptuous apartments. So favored was Fortunatus by winds and weather that he came calling at the palace on the very day when Antipas was meeting with Gaius. Soon Gaius was holding letters given him by both parties while each remained uncomfortably in his presence.

Antipas was at a disadvantage because his entreaties merely sought an imperial favor, a new title. The letter from Agrippa was far more interesting because it was accusatory. The king charged that his brother-in-law, the tetrarch, had once plotted with Sejanus against Tiberius. Moreover, Antipas, he said, was now conspiring against Gaius with the wily Artabanus of Parthia. "Please ask him," Agrippa's letter urged Gaius, "to deny that he already has armor sufficient for 70,000 men stored in his armory at Jerusalem."

Well, it might have been that Antipas indeed had arms ready to fight against the Arabs, perhaps even with the blessing of the governor Vitellius, who had been ordered to march to his assistance. But the statement was intended to shock — and it did.

"Is this true?" asked the emperor, looking down with a frown. For an unwise moment, Antipas hesitated and began explaining tentatively — long enough for Gaius to take it as proof of his guilt. Not having all day for such matters anyway, he took away Antipas' tetrarchy on the spot and announced it would be given to Agrippa. Furthermore, he ordered Antipas banished to Lyons, a city being carved out of the forests of Gaul that was and still is deemed a special Hades for those who have lived soft and effeminate lives.

When a freedman whispered a reminder in the emperor's ear that Herodias was Agrippa's sister, Gaius turned and declared that she could keep her own money. But this leniency, he lectured her, was being granted only because she was Agrippa's sister.

Oh, what a dagger that final remark must have been, because it made Herodias rise up and enact the only noble gesture she had made since offering her brother a magistrate's position some years before. "Oh, thou acted in a magnificent manner," she said, supplicating herself to the emperor. "But the love I have for my husband hinders me from partaking of the favor of thy gift. For it is not just that I, who have been made a partner in his prosperity, should now forsake him in his misfortunes."

For some reason this only nettled Gaius further. So for good measure, he sent her with her husband into exile and awarded her estate to Agrippa. With that the couple disappeared into Gaul and into obscurity.

Agrippa arrived in the Jewish homeland at the beginning of a terrifying new era for Jews everywhere. Its cause was none other than Gaius' new preoccupation with being venerated as a god. As peoples around the world scurried to display their worshipful supplication, centers of Jewish population stood out because their laws prevented them from worshipping men or erecting idols. Jews would pray *for* an emperor – that is, pray to God that Gaius be granted safety and good fortune – but they would not pray *to* him.

This stubbornness served to magnify the differences between Jews and others. And it added to the irritations others felt about their clannishness, their prosperity, their strange customs – and above all – the special exemptions they enjoyed from military service, Roman festivals, certain taxes and the like.

At first, the outward manifestations of this ire crept up almost innocuously in what might have seemed at worst as loutish pranks. In this or that Hellenistic town, Jews would arrive at their local synagogue one morning to find that someone had placed a crude clay likeness of the emperor at its center.

This, however, escalated to monstrous proportions in the city of Alexandria. Before relating it, however, let me tell you why it happened in the empire's second largest city, which was the home of my youth. For over 60 years under Augustus and Tiberius, the Egyptians and other Hellenized denizens of Alexandria co-existed peacefully enough with what is the world's largest Jewish population outside of Jerusalem. But the rabble of Alexandria is flighty and capricious. Tensions were already flaring as the growing Jewish quarter expanded into the city's main business section and caused many disputes over choice property.

Now it happened that the Jewish community of Alexandria had either delayed or refused to send the customary greetings and gifts to Gaius upon becoming emperor. When nearly a year had passed, this had become an irritant to Gaius, one that was thrown up to the emperor often by his new chief freedman, Helcion, whom I will write more about soon. Why worry that one speck of the civilized world had not yet paid homage? Because all other Alexandrians had practically fought other cities to be the first to build statutes to Gaius. Of peoples everywhere, one would expect just this sort of behavior from a nation that has for centuries been building shrines to everything from the sun to cats, dogs, lions and crocodiles. Besides, as I can quote from a letter written by one of the city's Jewish elders: "For the Alexandrians are adept at flattery and imposture and hypocrisy, ready enough with fawning words, but causing universal disaster with their loose and unbridled lips."

To a man who wished to be worshipped as a god, Alexandria was the first place one would plan to visit on a triumphant tour to display one's deified self beyond Italy. Indeed, such a trip was already being promoted by Helcion. And can you guess the rest? Helcion was a native of Alexandria, to which he hoped to return almost as triumphant as his master.

The emperor's displeasure over the reticence of Alexandria's Jews was quickly divined by the rest of the population, which soon made the most of it. With a brutal rage, a mob overran the homes of Jews, expelling families and stealing whatever furniture and valuables they could lay their hands on. These they carried openly into the daylight and exhibited proudly to friends as though they'd been inherited. Within days, throngs of homeless, destitute Jewish families were subsisting in the streets without food. So the leaders of the rabble next herded them into a very small portion of the city so that they were penned up like so many cattle. It was now August, and there in the stifling makeshift enclosure they stood packed together for days, scarcely able to breathe, to move or to seek sustenance.

Unable to endure it any longer, the Jews at last broke loose and scrambled into the streets. Pelted by rocks as they went, they fled to the outskirts, where they clustered along beaches, among tombs and other deserted spots. Still, each day gangs of young ruffians would track them down and have their fun entrapping them in small groups and daring them to break loose. Those who tried, perhaps in need to search for food, would be beaten severely with branches or fists. Another gang became proficient at hanging around the harbor and robbing the ships of Jewish merchants that arrived with cargoes of trade goods. They would even carry off a ship's tillers, poles and planks for kitchen fuel.

A worse fate awaited those who were caught hiding in the ravaged Jewish neighborhoods. If any were caught inside the city, or if some unsuspecting Jewish traveler arrived at its gates, they were pelted with roof tiles or beaten with oak branches and left for dead. Sometimes the persecutors enjoyed heaping the injured with brushwood and setting it afire. Unlike wood, brushwood produces a feeble flame that extinguishes rather soon, but which creates so much smoke that it asphyxiates the victim.

But many, too, were tied with thongs and nooses by the ankles and dragged through the market streets, even on the wide, three-mile-long Canopic Way, the city's most splendid avenue. Then, more brutal than savage beasts, the assailants would sever them limb from limb and trample on them so that not even the last remnant was left for burial.

When the Roman governor showed no inclination to halt the atrocities, the mob became even bolder. Organized attacks were made on Jewish meeting houses. Some were looted, some burned and others demolished with their foundations as well. A few synagogues were allowed to stand, but only for the purpose of erecting icons and statues of Gaius therein. In one case, a gang of hooligans fetched a decrepit chariot from the gymnasium, a mass of rust and mutilated parts that had been dedicated to a great-great aunt or grandmother of Cleopatra, and dragged it to a synagogue where it was gaily dedicated to the emperor.

Now when the first news of these atrocities reached Gaius, it came by way of letters from Alexandrians in the Roman government. The correspondence was couched in such a way that any fair judge could conclude only that the violence was the result of insolent Jews who had stood in the way of the people's paying homage to their beloved emperor. The "gatekeeper" for such information was Helicon, whom I shall now introduce properly.

Reared a slave in Alexandria, he had once sold scrap for his master, yet managed to accumulate a smattering of liberal education. Much later, and now with a reputation as a clever rogue who could accommodate a master's every need, Helicon was sold to a prosperous trader who took him to Rome. There, the ambitious master had made him a present to Tiberius in hopes, I think, of establishing a personal conduit to imperial affairs that might improve his business prospects. But Helicon hadn't come close to gaining the imperial ear because the austere, taciturn Tiberius had no tolerance for the man's fawning and flowery pleasantries.

Now, with a new emperor who showed a fondness for dissipation and flattery, I am sure the ambitious slave said to himself, "Rouse yourself, Helicon, for now is your hour! You have an avid spectator of your exhibitions. You can scoff and jest more than others; you know how to amuse and play the fool with drolleries and quips. If you can also mix with your jestings the sting of malice so that you stir not only laughter but bitterness born of suspicion, you will have in your master a complete captive. His ears are always pricked up to listen to those who have studied to combine abuse with sycophancy. Now for your material you have the obloquy cast upon the Jews and their customs. In this you were reared, because right from your cradle you were taught it by the noisiest rabble in the city of the Alexandrians."

Soon, by using all his guile, Helicon was with Gaius in the gymnasium and at the bath. He stood behind his master at dinner and was the last to bid him good night. For Helicon by this time had been named the emperor's chamberlain and captain of the household guard, a post greater than ever given to any one man. And all during those times Helicon never spared a moment to toss a jest or a barb at the Jews of Alexandria. All the while, the now former slave was being plied by the Alexandrians with large fees and promises of honors that would be heaped upon him when Gaius visited their city.

It was several weeks, however, before the surviving Jewish elders were even able to determine what force in Rome was behind all of this, or at least supporting it. When they learned of Helcion, no one dared approach him because of the arrogance he showed to all. Nor did they know if his opposition to Jews stemmed from personal prejudice or some other reason.

Knowing of no other course, the elders decided to send to Rome a three-man delegation to present their case in a document they hoped to deliver directly to the emperor. The embassy was headed by Philo, a brother of the alabarch and one known to all as a learned man. Through the diary that he wrote, and which I have, it is possible to be "with" Philo and his companions when they were granted an audience.

One day Gaius was ambling about in some gardens by the Tiber that his mother had left him, while a gaggle of foreign ambassadors waited outside the walls for an audience to press their various causes. When several of them were allowed inside, they approached the emperor, only to be politely dismissed after a pleasantry or two. When the Jewish embassy was introduced by a court official, Gaius was disarmingly cordial and cheerful. After more of the same pleasantries, the emperor waved his right hand as if signifying good will and said only, "I will hear your statement of the case myself when I get a good opportunity."

When they had left, Philo's companions rejoiced almost as if they had already won their plea. They were, after all, the only ambassadors that day whose case Gaius had specifically promised to hear. But the older Philo felt otherwise. "Why would he hear us only?" the elder wrote in his diary. "For he must have known that we were Jews who would be contented merely to know that we were not treated worse than others. To suppose that we shall take precedence with a despot of an alien race, a young man possessing absolute power, surely borders on madness." Instead, Philo surmised that Gaius had probably attached himself to the other faction from Alexandria and that it was to them that he was giving precedence in promising to render quick judgment.

During the ensuing weeks, the Jewish embassy, like many foreign delegations, followed the emperor from Rome to Puteoli, where he had come down to the sea and was wending a leisurely way around the bay by visiting his numerous and lavishly furnished country houses. Throughout this time Philo tried to conceal his dark feelings for fear of filling his colleagues with a gloomy attitude that would somehow translate into disaster for thousands of Jews back home. For they never knew at what exact moment they might be summoned before the emperor and asked to make their case.

Soon summer had turned to autumn. One day the various ambassadors were waiting outside the thickly hedged garden wall of yet another imperial estate when an unnamed acquaintance rushed up to them, gasping for breath, and pulled the little band off to one side. The man was surely a Jew himself because he was literally apoplectic. "Have you heard the new tidings?" he gasped with eyes rolling. "When we shook our heads, he began to speak, but a flood of tears streamed from his eyes," Philo wrote. "He tried to begin a second and third time, until one of our party said, 'If you have facts that are worth so many tears, at least let us share your sorrow, for we have become inured to misfortune by now.'"

"Our temple is lost!" the man blurted out. "Gaius has ordered a colossal statue of himself to be set up within the inner sanctuary. It is to be dedicated to himself in the name of Zeus!"

As Philo put it, "We simply stood there, speechless and powerless in a state of collapse with our hearts turned to water. Soon others appeared bringing the same woeful tale. Then, gathered altogether in seclusion, we bewailed the disaster that was personal to each and common to all."

The Jewish delegation spent days discussing this course and that. But in the end they could reach only one conclusion: that while they could not predict what the emperor might do to them, they had no choice but to uphold their ancient laws. "Well, so be it," Philo said in ending the last meeting. "We will die and be no more, for the truly glorious death, met in defense of the laws, might be called life."

It was now very late autumn and the envoys managed to sail on one of the last ships bound for Egypt. The weather was stormy, but Philo feared that a worse storm might be awaiting on land. "For it is the work of nature that divides the annual seasons," he wrote, "but the other is the work of a man whose thoughts are not those of a man, but a youth with the recklessness of youth, invested with irresponsible dominion over all."

. . . .

FOR FOLLOWERS OF THE WAY IN JERUSALEM, this period began in a more relaxed, or at least non-threatening atmosphere than any they had known thus far. The only explanation is as follows. When the Roman governor Vitellius granted the Jewish authorities more dominion over their own religious affairs, and when King Aretus of Nabatea decided not to press his ambitions on Judea following the death of Tiberius, temple authorities felt their sacred institutions less threatened. Thus, they felt less need to observe or restrict the activities of those who might pose potential challenges.

And perhaps this is why one Paul, lately of Damascus and the Arabian desert, decided to march boldly back to the city that he had served just three years before as temple officer and persecutor of everyone associated with the prophet Jesus. One can imagine this energetic young man, emblazoned with the spirit of Christ, eager to enter the Holy City and use his newly reorganized zeal as a battering ram against the fortifications of disbelief. And naturally wanting to be at the heart of things, it is no surprise that he would offer his services directly to the leader of The Way.

Paul did so by first befriending one Barnabas, a Cypriot who was both gentle and respected among the followers as a man above reproach, one who could never be suspected of collusion with enemies of The Way. Soon Paul had been invited into the home of no less than Peter and his family, who had by now moved from Galilee to quarters in Jerusalem. It was in that home that Paul spent the next two weeks as a guest.

Nowhere is it written that Peter was instructed by Jesus or angels to accept this one-time persecutor of The Way; but if Paul was convinced by a voice to become a believer, one might surmise that Peter may have needed divine guidance to overcome his logical suspicions that the "new" Paul was but the "old" Paul up to some treachery. In any event, Paul must have spent these days mining from Peter's memory every event and word he had experienced with Jesus. He also spent time with James, the brother of Jesus, who had by now taken up residence in Jerusalem with the original apostles.

Paul accompanied Peter and James all over Jerusalem, "preaching boldly in the name of the Lord," as later letters describe it. And these sermons were no doubt crowned by relating Paul's astounding experience on the road to Damascus — to the point where he was accepted by Peter and most followers of The Way. And because Paul was fluent in Greek and they were not, Jewish leaders of The Way were no doubt eager to let Paul be their spokesman in spreading the word to Hellenistic audiences.

It also seems likely that the fire that burned within Paul ignited indignation among some of his audiences in both camps. Many of his Hellnized audiences were hearing about The Way for the first time, and it may be that Paul lashed out directly at their mysterious religious rites and idolatrous sacrifices. It also seems apparent that the sight of Paul still offended some of the Hellenic friends and followers of the slain Stephen. Thus, like his return to Damascus, it was only a few weeks before there again were plots against Paul's life.

So it was, then, that Barnabas and some of Paul's other new friends in The Way escorted Paul out of the holy city and over the 60-mile path to Cæsarea. Perhaps as they walked, they were able to reinforce the words that Paul himself had already heard on the road to Damascus: that his calling was not to be in Judea, but among the Greek-speaking pagans in cities quite beyond. They would have been able to cite the fact that some of Stephen's followers in The Way who had been scattered by the persecutions (of no less than Paul himself!) were now preaching in Phœnicia, Cyprus and Antioch. But perhaps they implied something else as well to Paul: that his colleagues would feel more comfortable about him with the passage of time — enough to produce evidence that he had indeed preached The Way and lived by his words.

One can picture a cloudy dark night at the man-made harbor in Herod's Cæsarea, when in another version of lowering Paul in a basket over the city walls, he was quietly put aboard a ship sailing for Tarsus on the high tide. Back he would go for the next two years. No doubt his feelings were tossed about like bilgewater in a storm as the ship lumbered its way 250 miles up the coast and finally into the mouth of the Cydnus River for its 12-mile entry into the busy harbor of Tarsus. Yes, the Cilician capital was the home he had left just a few years before, but it was as equally alien a place for his mission as had been the arid hills of Nabatea. Certainly Paul's father and family could not have been happy to know that the son they had sent off to become a rabbi was now returning full of zeal for a prophet he called the son of God, and who had actually spoken to him in some sort of vision. Nor could his father even be permitted to sulk in private. Oh, no! His strange son would have joined him at work on the Street of Tentmakers, sharing his new-found zeal with his father's long-time colleagues while they stole sideward glances at the mortified old man.

Still, the primary objective of Paul's mission soon became the many others who seldom came near the Street of Tentmakers. In this sense, Tarsus presented Paul with the most dramatic challenge possible because most of its people contrasted sharply with the clear, pure waters of the river that rushed through the center of town. Lined along its banks were the temples representing a polyglot of pagan religions and wooded groves given over to every form of perverted sensuality.

Neither Paul nor those who have written about him ever described his impressions of Tarsus. But it is interesting to note how it was described by Apollonius, the great philosopher and traveler. Apollonius was born about the same time as Paul, only in not-to-distant Tyana. Showing early signs of brilliance, he was taken to Tarsus at age 14 by his father to study with a famous teacher there, Euthydemus of Phœnicia. A book about Apollonius devotes only one passage to this city, but it is illuminating.

> Now Euthydemus was a good rhetor and began his education; but though he was attached to his teacher he found the atmosphere of the city harsh and strange and little conducive to philosophic life, for nowhere are men more addicted to luxury than here. Jesters and full of insolence are they all; and they care more about their fine linen than the Athenians do wisdom.[11]

The boy was soon sent to more tranquil environs to continue his studies. Paul came now, not to study, but to proclaim something he considered of momentous import. And nowhere would he find people so preoccupied with other religions and diversions. Let's wander a path down the riverbank and meet some of them. Just over there on the grassy knoll by the river's edge we can see the temple that serves as the center for the cult of Isis. This Egyptian mystery religion would have been gaining ascendancy in Tarsus at this time because Cleopatra had expanded and beautified the temple when she arrived there by barge to meet Anthony some 70 years before. Like peoples in many Roman cities, the citizens of Tarsus probably embraced this mother goddess because she, her husband Osiris and their son, Horus, formed a trinity that satisfied many yearnings of the human heart. Even today, many a young mother still recites a part of the famous hymn supposedly sang first by Isis:

> I brought together woman and man, I appointed to women to bring their infants to birth in the tenth month. I ordained that parents should be loved by children. I laid punishments on those without natural affection towards their parents.

To others Isis is the goddess of justice:

> I broke down the governments of tyrants. I made an end to murders. I compelled women to take the love of men. I made the Right stronger than gold and silver. I ordained that the True should be thought good... [12]

But as of course anyone initiated in the mysteries knows, Isis is also power.

> I am the queen of rivers and winds and the sea. I am the queen of war. I am the queen of the thunderbolt. I stir up the sea and I calm it. I am the rays of the sun. Whatever I please shall come to an end... [13]

And so, Paul had to contend with hundreds of daily Isis worshippers — and with thousands at festival times. As even today throughout the eastern provinces, he would see those who had been inducted into the mysteries parading through the streets, holding high the statue of Mother Isis, cradling in her arms the holy infant that she had borne her husband Osiris. And always, as part of the procession, Paul would hear the noise of sounding brass and the tinkling of the cymbals from the instruments initiates shook with their hands as they marched.

Further down the riverbank we see the temple of the manly cult of Mithras, still as well established in Tarsus today as it is from Parthia to Britain, no doubt because it is the religion of so many Roman soldiers. It is certainly a relief to the rest of us that these men call themselves Sons of Light and follow Ormazd, the "Lord of Life," rather than the God of Death (Ahriman) and his Sons of Darkness. Paul, the rabbi, perhaps appreciated the fact that its initiation requirements were difficult, being based on knowledge of ancient law (or Avesta) and seven levels of achievement. As a follower of Jesus, he might be expected to empathize with a mystic rite in which members eat bread and drink wine to remind themselves of the time when the god Mithras sacrificed a bull and created the first man and woman from its blood.

What of the other cults who seem to vie for governance of all matters of fertility — seeds of grain and grape, spawning fish, birthing cows and fecund girls? It's sometimes hard to tell them apart except for the stories of their origins. In Tarsus one could cite the temple that served the cult of Attis and Cybele. Why do we still give almonds, sugared blue and pink, to brides on their wedding days? To ensure their fertility, of course. But do you remember why? Aha! You can thank Attis, who was born of a virgin who had become pregnant by eating almonds from a sacred tree. Attis was so beautiful that the goddess Cybele fell in love with him. Well, he replied that he really had his heart set on a daughter of the king of Galatia.

The goddess was so infuriated that she decided to drive him mad, which she did indeed. He fled to the countryside in this crazed state where he emasculated himself at the foot of a big pine tree and bled to death. From those drops of blood sprang up the violets which we always associate with the name Attis in springtime. And it's why every March 22 we see the rites begin in which the cult priests attempt to "resurrect" the dead lad from his eternal sleep.

But nearly unrivaled are the temples of Aphrodite (or Astarte or Astaroth, depending on the name for her where you live). In fact, the most splendid of all was and is at Hierapolis, just 100 or so miles east of Tarsus. Wherever they may be, these temples to fertility are known best for the doves that fly constantly overhead, for the sacred fish that swim in their special pools inside the grounds, and for the young girls who frequent the place outside (on which I will comment in a moment).

Whatever the religion and their various rites, might they have evoked empathy in Paul? After all, they all struggled in their different ways to ease man's way through the pangs of birth, the ordeal of feeding one's family and the mysteries of death. Paul the Jew had known animal sacrifice. Paul the follower of Jesus could understand resurrection of a god. Some religions had even supplied leaders of The Way with customs to which their own adherents could relate.

But sympathy from Paul of Tarsus? A thousand times no! Oh, he knew enough of these practices to relate to them in furthering his own mission; but accept any part of them? Never! Collectively, they stood for exactly what Paul opposed with all his might. He was only saddened that these pitiful adherents had not been blessed to have heard the Word as he had; and sharing that Word filled him with energy and a sense of urgency. For who knew how long the world had to repent before Christ came again to take up the faithful?

Isis? A mere wooden statue whose mythical son had been pieced together from dismembered body parts! Mithras? The god was a myth. He never lived. Jesus had lived — created by a loving God and not by the blood of a sacrificed animal. The Mythraic communion service? I forgot to mention that the bread and wine are accompanied by a hallucinogenic drug, extracted from the Hellebore plant, which makes these people leave their senses during their "religious" ceremony!

Attis and Cybele? Since you would lose your life if you spied on one of these spring rites I mentioned, let me explain something of what happens. On March 22 a group of eunuch priests cuts down a pine tree and swaths this "corpse" of Attis with violet wreaths and buries it in a grave. After a couple of days of fruitlessly blowing trumpets to resurrect the dead tree, the priests conclude that the only way to do so is to shed the blood of worshipers. So, to the endless din of drums, cymbals, castanets and horns, the "worshippers" work themselves into a frenzy as they whirl about the "grave." All the while they gash their bodies with knives, splattering the altar with their blood to give Attis the strength to rise again. The climax comes when novices, who are waiting for the "right" to enter this priesthood, hack off their own male members and throw them into the lap of the goddess Cyble, who watches by the grave.

All becomes quiet until the early hours of the next morning. Then a priest cries out and everyone (rather, all those who haven't bled to death by then) runs out to the grave. There, amidst flares affixed to the branches of trees, they discover that the grave is empty. The tree is resurrected, and all the "worshippers" are "saved" as well.

Oh yes, I promised to say something more of the young girls who frequent the temple of Aphrodite. For years now, the fertility goddess has had her own ring of temple prostitutes! In some temples, and I think in Tarsus, too, it was even decreed that no virgin shall be married until she has first given herself to a stranger at the temple of Aphrodite. This is not the way the cult of Aphrodite began. It was legitimized and encouraged by the male priests who saw in it a way to compete with the brothels in harbor areas and to collect more temple taxes from all sorts of souvenir merchandise sold in their precincts.

Paul was no Essene monk. He was ready to confront all such religions and priests directly. There is no record of what he had to say at that time, but I do know what he later wrote to the Christian community in this very city of Rome. Regarding the nature of men, he said:

> Claiming to be wise, they became fools, and exchanged the glory of the immortal God for images made to look like mortal man or birds or animals or reptiles. Therefore, God gave them up in the lusts of their hearts to impurity, to the dishonoring of their bodies among themselves, because they exchanged the truth about God for a lie and worhiped and served the creature rather than the Creator, who is blessed forever! [14]

At this point, we do not know exactly where or how Paul started his mission in Tarsus. But I submit two facts as evidence that he did begin there and did succeed until called elsewhere. First, his later letters describe his having endured the lash — the full 39 strokes — on five occasions. Since later writings, which describe his life in much greater detail, do not mention any one specific instance of scourging, it is reasonable to conclude that some of these painful episodes happened during these first years in or near his native city.

Secondly, Paul adhered to The Way, because within two years Barnabas saw fit to come to Tarsus and ask him to undertake an important mission in Antioch. When they met, Barnabas no doubt encountered a man who, though always of slight and stooped stature, was toughened by scars and setbacks, yet emboldened by having reached into the souls of men when he preached of love, forgiveness and salvation only through God's grace.

. . . .

. . . .

A. D. 3 9 — 4 0

Did anything good happen in the reign of Gaius Caligula? Well, yes, in that a living god thinks grandly. Gaius was as lavish with the public purse as Tiberius was stingy. He completed the public works that had been half-finished under Tiberius, foremost among them the temple of Augustus and the theater of Pompey. He also repaired or rebuilt many aqueducts, amphitheaters, temples and palaces. And it was not long before the emperor also had his army architects busy on grandiose — many said unattainable — schemes such as the construction of a new city high in the Alps and a 50-mile canal through the Isthmus of Corinth in Greece.

But after two years, it was also clear to anyone who tended him daily or even observed him at the Circus or the games that Gaius was mentally unstable. Who knows why? Some say that one of his wives had once given him a love potion that drove him insane. More commonly agreed upon is that he suffered from crashing headaches that caused his moods to swing wildly from morosity to flights of wild fancy and hideous laughter. In any case, many will vouch for the fact that he could scarcely sleep at night, perhaps only two or three hours at most. When he did finally slumber he would often have terrifying dreams in which strange apparitions came to him. And when he could not sleep he would lurch among the colonnaded temples talking with statues or crying out in anguish for the light of dawn to come.

On one occasion three senators of consular rank were aroused from their homes at midnight by palace guardsmen. They were brought hastily to the small indoor palace theater where they trembled in suspense wondering what was to come next. After many minutes that seemed like hours, they were startled by a chorus of instruments from behind stage. Then out sprang the emperor of the Roman Empire, dressed in the long tunic and shoes of a woman. He danced before them to the din of flutes and clogs. Then, after singing an aria in a female falsetto, he tiptoed offstage and did not return.

The audience of three applauded wildly. Then they simply sat in agonizing silence, not daring to speak or move from their seats. Their eerie evening ended only when a servant came out and informed them matter-of-factly that it was time for them to go home.

During the daytime, Gaius seemed determined to react to any entreaty or any event he attended by creating the utmost shock possible. Were he not an emperor with the power of life and death, one could almost compare his demeanor to that of a petulant, prankish, undisciplined boy. He seemed to delight in reminding everyone in a room that he could have their heads lopped off at will; and when a crowd at the circus cheered for a horse that was racing against his favorite, he shouted, "I wish the rabble of Rome had but a single neck!"

Those in the theater never knew what to expect when Gaius attended. When the actor was his favorite, Mnester the mime, he would jump on stage and kiss him with passion. And if anyone made even the slightest sound when Mnester was dancing, Gaius had the offender dragged from his seat and scourged with his own hand. On another occasion, Gaius had the tragic actor Apelles meet him by a statue of Jupiter. Gaius then struck a similar pose and asked Apelles coyly which of the two seemed to him the greater. When Apelles hesitated, Gaius had him flogged.

When in a playful mood, Gaius might be guilty only of mischievous behavior. One night before the theater opened, he had his servants distribute tickets on the street entitling the bearers to sit free in the choice rows reserved for the equestrian order. When the knights arrived, they had no place to sit — much to the emperor's amusement. When he was attending the theater and a Roman knight created a disturbance, Gaius sent a centurion to bid him hasten to Ostia with an urgent message for King Ptolemy of Mauretania, who was lodging there at the time. When the breathless knight arrived, the puzzled king read the following: "Do neither good nor ill to the man whom I have sent you."

Did I tell you this man — I forgot — *god* would hide under his bed when lightning struck? Or that he fled in terror when he saw smoke coming from the crater of the volcano on Mt. Ætna in Sicily? Yet this same coward would enjoy having people tortured as he dined. Often, those who were brought before him from prisons would first have their hands cut off by a soldier who was known for his skill and efficiency with the blade. During a dinner, when a slave was brought to him for stealing silverware, Gaius ordered that the man's hands be cut off and hung about his neck while he was made to parade among the guests with a sign announcing what he had done. Indeed, the emperor seldom had anyone put to death except by numerous slight wounds. "Strike so that he may feel that he is dying," was his standing order. His favorite quote was from the tragic poet Atreus: "Let them hate me, so they but fear me."

Nowhere was the cruelty of Gaius more on display than in the many gladiatorial shows he staged. He often compelled leading citizens to fight against wild beasts just for his amusement. When someone told him how costly it was to feed these animals with cattle, he selected criminals for them to devour instead. When Gaius had fallen ill during his first October in office, and a senator had sworn that he would fight in the arena if only the gods spared the stricken emperor, Gaius remembered the solon's vow and made him honor it. The emperor even had the manager of his wild beast and gladiatorial shows beaten with chains in his presence for several consecutive days. He only agreed to killing the man when the stench of his pulverized and putrefied brain made him sick.

Gaius seemed to enjoy himself the most when his cruelty was combined with impudence. To wit: soon after succeeding Tiberius, he recalled a man from several years in exile. When asked how he had spent all that time on a rocky island, the man responded with well-rehearsed flattery: "I constantly prayed to the gods that Tiberius might die and you become emperor," he intoned. Caligula, however, concluded from this that all of the persons he had exiled must be praying for his death. So he sent emissaries from island to island to butcher them all.

One can only imagine the helpless plight of women before such a man. In addition to his sisters and Pyrallis, a renowned prostitute in Rome, there was scarcely any woman of rank whom Gaius Caligula did not approach if she struck his fancy. Typically, he would invite "candidates" to dinner with their husbands and inspect them, as he would a slave for sale, as they passed by the foot of his couch. Then as often as his fancy took him he would leave the room and send for the one who had pleased him the most. Returning afterward amidst obvious signs as to what had occurred, he would openly commend or criticize his partner.

It is difficult, actually, to determine how many wives the emperor officially had. If he particularly enjoyed one of his quick trysts during a dinner party, he might decide to send her husband a bill of divorce and have it listed in the public records. At the marriage of Livia Orestilla to a young man of the venerable Piso family, the emperor attended the ceremony himself and gave orders that the bride be taken to his own house. Within a few days he divorced her with instructions never to see her bridegroom again. When she was caught in his presence some two months later, the emperor had her banished.

If Gaius Caligula ever had a true wife, I suppose it was Cæsonia. Neither beautiful nor young, she was already the mother of three when the emperor professed himself to be passionately in love with her. The fact that she was also a woman of reckless extravagance and wantonness all the more endeared her to him. And so, the Prætorians soon got accustomed to her riding at the side of the emperor, decked with army helmet, cloak and shield. Or, he might enter a room with a nude Cæsonia at his side and urge everyone present to say how much they admired her. Cæsonia, however, only became a "wife" officially the day she bore Gaius a daughter. Named Julia Drusilla, he carried her to the temples of all the goddesses, finally placing her in the lap of Minerva, to which he commended the infant's "upbringing and education."

Meanwhile, Gaius continued to drain the surplus that Augustus and Tiberius had left the treasury – not so much by his public works, but by his private expenditures. Country villas? All emperors build them, and so did Gaius. But this emperor found new ways to spend that had not been dreamed up before. He would bathe in perfumed oils and drink precious pearls dissolved in vinegar. Frequently he would order that large sums of money be scattered to the common people from atop the Julian Basilica for several days in succession. So that he could coast along the shores of Campania, he built a new type of Liburnian galley, which traditionally had two banks of oars. Those of Gaius had ten banks of oars. Their sterns were embedded with gems, and inside were spacious baths, banquet halls and even vine and fruit trees.

You can perhaps begin to understand the magnitude of this extravagance if I tell you something of the emperor's favorite horse. Gaius was an avid follower of the Green Faction at the circus and his favorite horse was *Incitatus*, which means Flyer. On the day before a race, the emperor would send his guardsmen into the neighborhood around Flyer's stable to insure that his horse would have a peaceful night's sleep. Also insuring the animal's comfort was a stall of marble, a manger of ivory, purple blankets and a collar of precious stones. Amusing, you might say. But Flyer also had a house, fine furniture and a retinue of slaves in order to entertain guests invited in the horse's name. Gaius even cast it about that he intended to name Flyer consul.

But to me, the episode that best typifies what Rome was required to endure was what I will simply call "The Bridge." It has since been broken up and disappeared, but most of us have seen various paintings of it to know that it was as amazing as it was wasteful. Gaius decided that he wanted to bridge the gap in the Gulf of Baiæ in Campania that separates the promontory of Puteloi and the city of Baiæ, a distance of well over two miles. Before long, a corps of army engineers had commandeered every military and merchant ship in the area and tethered them all together in a straight double line across the Gulf. The most difficult part involved carting in tons and tons of earth, piling it over the ships and fashioning from this mound a replica of the Appian Way, complete with trees and monuments.

One morning, amidst calm waters and clear skies, Gaius appeared at the head of his Prætorians. Resplendent on a white horse, the emperor wore the actual breastplate of Alexander the Great (purloined from its vault in Egypt), a crown of oak leaves, a sword and a cloak of cloth and gold. As an assembled crowd of his court friends and ambassadors looked on, Gaius spent much of the day riding back and forth, shouting to anyone within earshot that the god Neptune must acknowledge his new master, because he, the emperor-god, had now tamed the seas.

The next day Gaius appeared in the dress of a charioteer in a cab drawn by a pair of famous race horses. With him as he drove was a young boy, one of the princely hostages from Parthia. This time the emperor was joined by his entourage of friends as they rode triumphantly back and forth across the new "Appian Way." That night the coastline around the beautiful blue bay blazed with torches placed every few feet. It also enabled Gaius to say that he had tamed the night, just as he had the sea.

Many have speculated as to why Gaius staged this stupendous spectacle. In one account I read that the emperor wanted to demonstrate his superiority as a commander to the legendary Xerxes, who had led his Persian armies into Greece some 500 years ago across a much shorter man-made bridge that spanned the Hellespont. Others say it was constructed as a show of Roman might to the envoys of the Britons and Germans, into whose lands he was planning a campaign.

Perhaps. But it is Neptune to whom the emperor's defiant shouts were directed. And I would support another reason as well. The story goes that when he first joined Tiberius on Capri, he once overheard the astrologer Thrasyllus telling the old man that "Gaius has no more chance of becoming emperor than of riding across the Gulf of Baiæ on horseback!"

Gaius did indeed embark on his first military expedition early in the winter of his third year. Britain was still unconquered at the time, and routing the expedition through Germany would allow the emperor a heroic return through garrisons and lands once commanded by his father, Germanicus. But these understandable objectives had almost become secondary by the time preparations began. The emperor's relationship with the Senate had been deteriorating badly since the previous spring when he had so thoughtlessly executed Marcus Silanus, his father-in-law and one of the Senate's senior statesmen. With his insistence on deification, his wild spending and part-time attention to governing an empire, at least one alleged plot against him had been quelled by the next summer. Now, with the military provisioning for the Britain-Germany campaign in full swing, he got wind of an even more ominous conspiracy.

Plans for the British campaign called for Gaius to use the Rhine garrison in Upper Germany as his staging ground. Now, as the emperor's guard prepared to leave Rome, word came that when he arrived at the staging camp in Germany he would be assassinated by Cnæus Cornelius Lentulus Gætulicus, the much-respected camp commander. The informants also speculated that Gætulicus then planned to give the throne to Marcus Æmilius Lepidus, a senator from one of Rome's most illustrious families and the nominal widower (because Gaius had snatched her away) of the emperor's deified sister Drusilla. Lepidus was now the lover of her younger sister Agrippina, and hence regarded as a logical successor should Gaius die childless.

One day in September, before his troops were actually ready to leave, Gaius and a cohort of Prætorian guardsmen left Rome for Germany, and with them by firm imperial invitation were Lepidus, Agrippina and the emperor's third sister, Julia Livilla. Immediately upon arriving in Germany both Gætulicus and Lepidus were seized and executed. Agrippina was forced by her brother to carry the ashes of Lepidus back to Rome. And when she arrived, both she and her younger sister were banished, Agrippina for having "improper relations" with Lepidus, and Julia Livilla probably for being no more than a confidant of her sister.

Gaius and his cohort spent the following winter and spring in Germany and Gaul, never venturing into Britain – perhaps because they couldn't trust the troops of Upper Germany to be at their rear. With no enemy force to challenge them locally, the emperor and his forces seemed to spend most of their time conducting various maneuvers designed to display Roman might and restore military discipline.

This "need for discipline" no doubt lingered in the emperor's memory from early childhood when the legions of Germany bristled with mutiny shortly after Augustus died. As I have written earlier, the troops deserved some sympathy because they were neglected, ragged and underpaid. But it had taken every ounce of personal courage that Germanicus could muster to "save" Germany for the new emperor, Tiberius – and at great peril to his wife and young son, Caligula, who had been in camp during the uprising.

Now the grown Caligula was determined to impose his own brand of discipline. After killing their commander, he dismissed in disgrace a few generals who had showed up late after recruiting auxiliaries in various regions. Once everyone was assembled, he reviewed his chief centurions and instantly dismissed those he deemed to be too old for service, even some who needed only a few more weeks to retire with honors and pay. Some say this was a subtle way of striking against those who had taken part in the near mutiny some 25 years before. Whatever the intent, it certainly destroyed morale. The emperor then added the finishing touches by announcing that he was reducing the bonus given on completion of full military service to around half the amount paid under Augustus.

The bigger problem he faced was the inability to find hostile forces ready to contribute to the military laurels of a young emperor who needed them for posterity. Thus, when a British prince named Adminius, who had been banished by his father, straggled into camp with a ragtag band of supporters, Gaius behaved as if the entire island had surrendered to him. He sent a grandiloquent letter to Rome by the fastest courier, demanding that the good news be read at a full meeting of the Senate.

In another display of his desperation, Gaius secretly ordered some of his German bodyguards to sneak across the river and conceal themselves in the woods. Shortly after the noon meal, scouts alerted the imperial party that the enemy had been spotted massing across the river. Immediately, Gaius sprang up and rushed off with some Prætorians, spending the rest of the day clopping about the woods and hacking limbs off trees. When they returned by torchlight that evening, the emperor proclaimed that he and his men had repelled an enemy attack. He presented his companions with ornamented crowns for their heroism and scorned those who had remained behind as cowards. He also dispatched a letter rebuking the people of Rome for frequenting theaters and banquets when Cæsar was exposing himself to the danger of battle.

After a few similar incidents, Gaius wrote his financial agents in Rome to prepare for a triumph, one that would be on a grander scale than had ever been known, but "at the smallest possible cost" to himself personally. Next, he pondered a prickly problem: having neither prisoners nor spoils of war to display in his victory parade. So the emperor enlisted the aid of the Gauls who had joined his armies as auxiliaries. He selected the tallest of them — those "worthy of a triumph" — compelling them to dye their hair red and let it grow long like Germans. They were also ordered to learn the German language and adopt German names.

Before departing Germany, however, Gaius was intent on settling an old score.

A moment ago I recalled how Germanicus, with his frightened young son peering out from a tent, had practically begged the legions of Upper Germany to accept Tiberius as their ruler. Now the emperor Caligula summoned his general staff and announced his determination to execute every man in his camp who had been a part of those legions.

A frantic hubbub ensued, with his leading commanders and centurions beseeching the emperor not to go through with it. The stubborn Gaius finally relented only on condition that the men be rounded up and their ranks decimated by the sword. Thus, the unsuspecting rank-and-file were summoned to an assembly. When they arrived unarmed to the exercise area, they were startled to find its outer perimeter rung with rows of fully-armed horsemen.

Within a few minutes the wary men were whispering to one another as they waited for the last of their comrades to assemble. Some, perhaps with a nod from their own centurions, began to sneak off and grab what arms they could find lying about. When Gaius saw what was happening, he jumped up, fled from the assembly and broke camp with his Prætorians. He was off to Rome in as great a rush as when he had left it.

By the time the men neared the city, all of the emperor's ferocity had been redirected to the Senate, against which he uttered repeated oaths and vowed never to frequent again. They, he somehow reasoned, had cheated him out of his well-deserved triumph (even though he had already sent a hasty letter canceling the triumph and promising death to anyone who should try to award him honors).

When a delegation of senators and knights rode out from Rome to greet the emperor and to escort him back, he merely glared back and slapped at the sword at his side. "I shall come," he said with clenched teeth, "but this shall come with me." He added that from then on, only the people and members of the equestrian order would be permitted in his presence. Never again, he vowed, would he enter the Senate chamber or meet with a senator.

In truth, the Senate already despised Gaius equally – and well before his "campaign" to Germany. If a date can be put on just when its adulation turned to loathing, it may have been as early as the spring of the emperor's second year when he executed Marcus Silanus, his father-in-law and one of the Senate's most respected leaders. The decisive break came early in the next year. Perhaps because his spies had told him of menacing discontent within the Senate, Gaius summoned the body one day to a special session at the Temple of Saturn, which he no doubt found a more neutral ground than the venerable Curia. In a rambling speech the emperor recalled how Tiberius had recommended that his successor continue the treason trials. They had, of course, been suspended for over two years. But now, said Gaius, "I realize that this was a very sensible recommendation, and I am introducing it straightaway."

The senators just sat there stunned as if all had suffered a stroke at once. Eventually they broke up without conducting further business. But the following day the old obsequiousness was back as sickly sweet as a tub of gardenias. The conscript fathers voted that annual sacrifices be offered to the emperor's clemency, and that at such times his golden statue should be carried to the Temple of Jupiter Capitoline while hymns were sung in his praise by boys from the noblest families.

Caligula, unsurprisingly, chose to put his own interpretation on this action. Back in the days of Julius Cæsar, he recalled, some senators who still yearned for the return of the Republic liked to maneuver the emperor into accepting extravagant honors in hopes of making him look so ridiculous that it strengthened their cause. So Gaius began doing everything he could to shower his contempt on individual senators. A favorite means was to have elderly solons accompany his carriage on foot for miles. Some he would order to wait on him at meals, standing at the end of his couch with a napkin. On August 31 of that year, when the consuls forgot to make a proclamation of his birthday, the emperor deposed them and left the empire for three days without its highest magistrates.

When Gaius returned from Germany, nothing could stop the stampede of savagery that the incensed emperor brought back with him. The purges flared anew, and in ways Tiberius may not have imagined. Some senators were disfigured with branding irons. Some were put in cages with wild beasts or sent to the mines or put to work building roads. One favorite amusement was to put a man to death secretly, then continue to send for him as though he were alive – only to remark days later with a comical shrug that the man "must have committed suicide."

As the purges worsened, so did Rome's financial condition. By now Gaius had already squandered nearly all of the 2.7 billion sesterces that Augustus and Tiberius had amassed in the treasury. By now the purges and the empire's deteriorating financial condition had become intertwined. The purges were enflamed in part because Gaius found he could collect revenues from the estates of fallen senators. And the more the Senate and equestrian ranks were ravaged, the fewer men of ability there remained to govern Rome's everyday affairs. But of the two maladies, the financial crisis was the worst because it affected everyone in the empire.

Certainly the emperor was no administrator, as I will now demonstrate.

Before journeying to Germany Gaius had, perhaps to leave on a wave of popularity, abolished a sales tax that had been in effect since the days of Augustus. But this proved to be such a miscalculated blow to the treasury that the Senate was thrust into the unpopular position of re-inventing taxes. And so Rome wound up with a patchwork of hated levies, the likes of which included one-fortieth of any awards in lawsuits, one-eighth of a porter's income and a prostitution tax based on (yes, so help me) the various types of acrobatics employed in each encounter.

Now came an almost frantic scouring for money from any source, even including the personal possessions the emperor's two younger sisters had brought with them to Germany. On the return trip through Gaul, Gaius decided to auction them off along the way, personally helping the auctioneer goad wealthy provincials into bidding on jewels, furniture, slaves and even freedmen. So joyous was he at the money raised that he sent soldiers back to Rome to retrieve virtually all of the possessions of the old palace, including carriages and animals.

Once back in Rome the emperor concentrated on new and better ways to raise revenues to fuel his lifestyle and new public works. I will relate but some of them here.

Gaius revoked Roman citizenship that extended beyond its passage from fathers to sons. All grants of citizenship or property by Augustus and Julius Cæsar were waived as being out of date. But all could be repurchased for a fee.

He served notice that chief centurions who had not named the emperor among their heirs would be accused of "ingratitude" and have their wills set aside. This aroused such widespread fear that people of all stations flocked to appoint Gaius joint heir with their family beneficiaries.

Everyone who had increased his property holdings since the previous census was at once charged with making out false tax returns. Gaius himself would sit in judgment of their trials, announcing in advance how much money he intended to raise from the confiscated property.

Auctions were set up to dispose of everything left over from games and shows, with the emperor himself ordering various onlookers to raise their bids — often beyond what they could afford. Have you ever heard the term "don't be an Aponius" at auctions? It refers to Aponius Saturnius, a Prætorian who nodded off so often during an auction after the games that Gaius nudged the auctioneer and said, "Don't overlook that man over there who bids with his head." When Aponius woke with a start it was to the laughter of the audience. He had bought no fewer than 13 gladiators for nine million sesterces!

When his daughter was born, Gaius complained that the burdens of parenthood had now been added to his already crushing burden as emperor. So he invited contributions for her maintenance and dowry. He did the same for New Year's gifts, standing at the entrance to the palace to collect offerings from people of all stations. But I daresay that coins from widows and tavern keepers scarcely matched what rolled in when he turned a wing of the palace into a brothel and gaming hall. Pages were dispatched to the Forum inviting men to come in and take their pleasure. When they arrived, clerks would take down their names as contributors to Cæsar's revenues.

Not the least of these contributors were the temples and other storehouses of wealth throughout the empire — especially Greece. The emperor sent out orders that engravings, statues and other local treasures should be brought to Rome on grounds that the best things ought to be set only in the best places — and that was the imperial capital. These he used to adorn his own houses and gardens. At the same time, he threw down the statues of famous Romans and forbade "for all time" the erection of a statue to any living man, anywhere, without his knowledge and consent.

Whether this represented competition to his godhead one can only surmise. But I *can* say that the one constant element throughout this period was Gaius' infatuation with his own deity. There were now two temples in Rome to his godhead, one erected at state expense and one at his own. And now, after his return from Germany, he sent to a crippled Senate a request that no other emperor had ever done. He asked for a decree officially authorizing what was already taking place at the two Roman temples and several others around the empire. He asked that he be deified while he was still alive, and that the decree take effect immediately.

The Senate complied.

. . . .

As PHILO AND HIS FELLOW ENVOYS SPENT the winter in Alexandria discussing how to dissuade Gaius from his calamitous designs on the temple in Jerusalem, they gained a piece of new information that further inflamed the situation. The cause was Capito, the tax collector for Judea, and a man who despised the Jews as much as they did him. Capito first came to Judea a poor man and quickly amassed a fortune through his rapacity and peculation. Then, fearing that he might be brought before the governor of Syria, or even the emperor, to face charges, he devised a scheme to turn the tables on those whom he had wronged.

Just by chance the coastal city of Jamnia, some 30 miles east of Jerusalem, proved an ideal setting for the tax collector's scheme. One of the largest Judean cities, Jamnia was a constant source of turmoil because the Jewish majority was endlessly taunted and tormented by a growing population of new immigrants from many lands. Hearing from travelers that Gaius had ordered his statue erected in the temple, some of these mischievous Jew-baiters slipped into a synagogue and hastily erected a crude altar to Gaius out of bricks they had fashioned from clay. The next day, the first Jewish elders to open the doors of the meeting house were shocked to see the monstrosity and threw it down.

All this was reported back to Capito, who had instigated the childish prank in the first place. Now the tax collector had all he needed for a letter to Gaius. With wild exaggeration, it described how the people of Jamnia had tried to worship their emperor and how they had been repulsed by these blasphemous ingrates — no less than the very elders of the synagogue!

First to read the letter was the freedman Helicon, whom Philo labels "that slave, scrap retailer and piece of riffraff." However, by this time Helicon had been joined in imperial favor by Apelles, that same tragic actor who had managed to get himself flogged by Gaius for not agreeing that the emperor was grander than Jupiter. Apelles had been raised in the Judean coastal city of Ascalon, a place, says Philo, known for its "truceless and irreconcilable hostility to the Jewish inhabitants." Now he had been named a councilor to the emperor on the promise of helping him improve his acting skills and gain a better rapport with audiences.

Apelles himself, says Philo, apparently acquired such talents after spending his youth "trafficking his charms" and then becoming an actor "when the bloom was passed." Of course, Philo notes sarcastically, "Performers on the stage whose trade is with theaters and theater-goers are lovers of modesty and sobriety, not of shamelessness and extreme indecency."

Thus, Philo adds, "Helicon, scorpion in the form of a slave, vented his Egyptian venom on the Jews and so too Apelles with the venom of Ascalon" by reporting Capito's letter to Gaius in an even more embellished form. And its timing was especially propitious for Helicon, because the emperor was beginning to take seriously the much-discussed plan for a triumphant tour of Alexandria. To do so, Gaius would need to travel in a convoy of warships. Rather than ply through rough open seas like merchantmen, the war vessels would have to circumvent the eastern rim of the Mediterranean to Egypt so that they could stop for provisions and enter safe, calm harbors at night for the emperor's comfort. All this would require help from a peaceful and friendly Syria.

This time the emperor's order to erect his statue was no mere petulant impulse. A lengthy formal letter was now drafted to the governor of Syria, setting forth careful, detailed instructions for what now amounted to a show of military might in Judea — and a war, if need be. Two Roman legions, with a full complement of auxiliaries, were to proceed south through Judea to escort a statue on its way to the temple. Once in Jerusalem, a large detachment was to be quartered along the Euphrates River on the Parthian border to guard against any forces that might be dispatched from Babylon or other Jewish population centers to prevent the statue from being placed inside the temple.

By now Vitellius had been replaced as governor of Syria by Petronius, a man known both for his even temper and sound administrative ability. He also seems to have taken time to study the culture of its inhabitants. But Petronius was also loyal to his emperor, and he wasted no time in gathering his two best legions, recruiting auxiliaries and marching them off to Ptolemais on the Phœnician coast. There they would winter and train for a march to Jerusalem in the spring.

Petronius was also a deliberate man who insisted on learning everything he could about the consequences of impending decisions. The more he remained in Ptolemais the more time he had to realize that the negative ramifications of this one would be considerable. He knew that opposing the emperor's order would almost surely mean his death. He knew, too, that many thousands would die before seeing the statue in the temple — regardless of whether they died by the hands of Romans or themselves.

When Petronius consulted his own advisors, they were unanimous against destroying anything the Jews held sacred, first from their feelings of justice and second from the fear they felt if the Jews retaliated. For the Jews were not just contained in one nation, but spread all over the world. If delegations could trek over mountains and risk robbery each year in order to bring annual tithes to the temple, would they not also rush from every quarter to defend it? And even if Roman reinforcements came from other provinces to crush them, might Petronius and his Syrian legions be wiped out before they arrived? Or what if the Jews of Judea simply refused to plant their spring crops? Worse, what if they burned their flax, wheat fields and forests? What kind of provisioning would this leave for Gaius in his "triumphant" tour? What kind of tribute would be available to pay Rome? And who would be killed for failing to provide it? Petronius first — *then* the Jews.

As the governor tortured himself with these unhappy options, only one ever so slight possibility offered him some escape, or at least temporary relief. Gaius had not said he was sending a statue from Rome. Nor did he order Petronius to remove and transport any of the many large statues of Gaius already existing in the eastern provinces. This implied that one should be made anew. If so, the emperor might also agree with a decision not to have it done in Jerusalem, which would only invite vandalism or worse. So the governor took the liberty of commissioning the most clever and conscientious craftsmen he could find in Phœnicia and then telling them to do the work up the coast at Sidon, where materials would be more plentiful. All this would buy a little time.

Next, Petronius decided to have a conversation with the Jewish leaders, not in Ptolemais, where they would be sure to be offended by a military camp full of bronze eagles and images, but in the more amicable setting of Tiberias, 30 miles to the east. When the leaders of Jerusalem arrived, the governor attempted to explain the emperor's intentions in calm, almost sympathetic tones. He asked them to accept the orders of their lord and master and to consider the dire consequences of doing otherwise. For, as he explained, the troops at Ptomelais were the finest he could muster and would have no choice but to strew the land with Jewish dead. He asked — almost begged — them to return and exhort their people not to show any opposition.

After the governor's entreaty, the air was numb with silence. As Philo says, "Besmitten by his first words, they stood riveted to the ground, incapable of speech. Then, as a flood of tears poured from their eyes as from fountains, they plucked the hair from their beards and heads" and wailed as if the dead were already being mourned.

As the Jewish leaders finally left for Jerusalem, Petronius still had no inkling as to whether his words would be heeded. And as his party traveled back to Ptolemais through the ripening wheat fields in late winter, he no doubt wondered if the crop would be harvested or torched.

Just a few days after his return, the governor's forward scouts reported a strange, incredible sight approaching in the plain from the south. What had at first seemed a large cloud of dust was instead a vast crowd of people. He learned soon that the elders had returned to Jerusalem and issued forth an appeal to Jews from every city to stream out and supplicate themselves to Petronius. Now, as they drew closer to the military camp, the Romans could see that they were totally unarmed, and they had been organized into groups – men in one, women in another, children in another. When Petronius beckoned their leaders to approach him he could see that they had been rolling in the dust. Their eyes were streaming with tears and their hands were set behind them as if pinioned.

At last the body of elders drew up to the governor and said: "We are unarmed, as you can see. Although some accuse us of having come as enemies, we present our bodies as easy targets for your missiles. We have brought our wives and children to you, leaving no one at home, and have prostrated ourselves before Gaius in doing so to you, so that you and he may either save us all from ruin or send us all to perish in utter destruction."

"Oh Petronius," one elder continued, "both by our nature and our principles we are peaceable. When Gaius succeeded to the sovereignty, we were the first of all the inhabitants of Syria to show our joy. For Vitellius, your predecessor, was staying in our city, and it was to him that the first message was addressed, and it was from there that messengers were sent to all other cities announcing the good tidings. Was our temple the first to accept sacrifices in behalf of Gaius' reign only that it should be the first or even the only one to be robbed of its ancestral tradition of worship?

"We are evacuating our cities, withdrawing from our houses and lands. Our furniture and money and cherished possessions we will willingly make over. But we would think ourselves gainers and not givers if we could receive but one thing in return – that no violent changes should be made to the temple and that it be kept as we received it from our ancestors. But if we cannot persuade you, we give ourselves up for destruction so that we may not live to see a calamity worse than death."

Throughout the elder's appeal, the people behind him continued to breathe spasmodically, the sweat streaming over every limb and their tears flowing ceaselessly.

Petronius and his advisors were almost driven to tears themselves at this point, but the elder continued: "Our final prayer, the justest of all, Petronius, will be this. We do not deny that you are not bound to do this as you are bidden, but we add to our supplications a request for a respite so that we may choose a body of envoys and send them to seek an interview with our lord. It may be that by this mission we shall persuade him, pleading in full either the honor due to God or the preservation of our laws undestroyed, or our right to be no worse treated than all the nations, even those in the uttermost regions, who have had their ancestral institutions maintained, or the decisions of his grandfather in which they ratified our customs with all respect for them. Perhaps when he hears this he will be softened. And should we fail to persuade him, what remains to hinder you from carrying out your present intention?"

Petronius rose slowly and retreated with his counselors to where they could talk privately. Most of them now believed in the cause of the Jews – even those who had been all for invasion in the beginning. After considerable discussion, Petronius returned to the crowd and announced his decision. He would not grant their request for an embassy. It was not safe for the ambassadors nor the person (himself) who would have to authorize their mission. However, the governor would not oppose any individuals who wanted to lay before the emperor their view of the matter. Moreover, Petronius said he would write a letter to Gaius that, while neither accusing the Jews nor reporting about their tearful entreaties, would merely inform the emperor about some delays that had taken place, mainly the need to construct a statue and the importance of gathering in the winter grain crops before any hostilities broke out.

In his letter, the governor dwelled on the latter, expressing fear that the Jews, in despair for their ancestral rites and not wishing to live any longer, might abandon or even lay waste their croplands. He cited the need for a military guard to insure more vigilance in gathering the fruits of the cornfields and orchards. Again, he cited the need to feed not only the imperial convoy as it made its way around the rim of the sea towards Egypt, but all of the throngs who would journey to the shore to worship him along the way.

Meanwhile, there was the matter of the statue itself. Instead of pressing the craftsmen, Petronius decided that, as worthy only of an emperor who was a living god, the statue must be absolutely perfect. The craftsmen would be encouraged to take all the time they needed. I might add that Petronius may have been encouraged in this ploy by having learned of a similar instance that happened some months before in Greece. It seems that in exercising his appetite for the artistic works of other lands, Gaius had even ordered that the ancient and famous statue of Jupiter Olympus, so named because it was commissioned for one of the earliest Olympic games, be removed from its base and brought to him. When the chief architect wrote with profuse apology that such a move would damage the ancient statue irreparably, he was told to get on with it or lose his life. So the Greeks and architects began to make plans for the project, but resolved to stretch out the planning process for as long as they could get away with it.

Petronius and his councilors also took the greatest care in constructing their letter to the emperor. But when it arrived, Gaius began fuming at its first words and never stopped. "Good Petronius, you have not learned to harken to an emperor," he exclaimed at last, pounding his fist on a table. "Your successive offices have puffed you with pride. Up until now you seem to have no knowledge of

Gaius, even by reputation. But you will soon know him by actual experience. You concern yourself with the institutions of the Jews, the nation which is my worst enemy; yet you disregard the imperial commands of your sovereign. You feared their great numbers. But had you not with you the forces that are feared by all nations of the east and their rulers, the Parthians? Did pity weigh more with you than Gaius?

"Go on," he stormed, "plead the harvest as your pretext – the harvest for which no pretext will avail you from what will soon be visited on your head. Yes, lay the blame on the ingathering of fruits and the preparations needed for our journey. Why, even if complete barrenness afflicted Judea, were not the neighboring countries so many and so prosperous as to compensate for the deficiency in one?"

Having vented his anger, Gaius composed himself and turned to his chamberlain, Helicon. "But why should he who is to reap this reward know my intentions in advance?" he said impishly. "I have stopped talking but I haven't stopped thinking."

After turning to other matters for several days, Gaius and his secretaries crafted a reply to Petronius. It was written carefully and civilly, because emperors always fear the power of provincial governors to create uprisings with their huge armies. The letter ignored the subject of the harvests and other concerns. Instead, Petronius was urged simply to concentrate on the completion of the statue and his mission to escort it to the temple.

When the emperor's reply arrived, winter had now turned to spring in Galilee as a reluctant Petronius summoned the Jewish leaders to another meeting in Tiberias. But unlike the first time, the elders were accompanied by tens of thousands of Jews of all ages who had again come out from all directions. So many were spread out over the hills overlooking Tiberias that Petronius remarked that he hadn't realized just how many people there were in Palestine. This time the governor was alarmed by reports that a great many Jews had left their spring crops unplanted. There were even intelligence reports that some groups of hotheaded youths were ready to defy the Romans to the death.

The meeting began with the Jews facing a sterner, stonier governor, his soldiers now ringing them in a formation that would enable them to attack at his command. Petronius rose from the judgment seat that always accompanied him when traveling and began, not by encouraging a dialogue, but with what sounded more like a decree. The emperor, he said, had reaffirmed his command and stated that his wrath would be executed immediately on anyone who disobeyed. "And it is fit that I, who have obtained so great a dominion by his grant, should not contradict him," Petronius added.

A mournful wail began to rise from the masses before him, but Petronius held up his hand and bade them listen. "Yet," said he, "I do not think it just to have such a regard for my own safety and honor as to refuse to sacrifice them for the preservation of you who are so many in number, nor for your law, which has come down to you from your forefathers. Nor will I, with the help of God, be so audacious as to suffer your temple to fall into contempt by means of the imperial authority."

By now the crowd was struck dumb with the import of this Roman's words. Not one of these occupiers had ever spoken thusly. "Therefore," the governor announced solemnly, "I will send another letter to Gaius to let him know what your resolutions are. I will assist in your case so far as I am able. May God be your assistant, for his authority is beyond all the contrivance and power of men. But if Gaius decides to turn the violence of his rage upon me, I will rather undergo all that danger and that affliction that may come to my body or soul rather than see so many of you perish."

After those words, the governor asked the subdued elders to urge everyone to go home and plant their crops and to be of good spirits. The elders could do no less, and my sources report that an amazing thing happened as the crowd began to disperse. Until then the land had been parched with drought and the skies on this day were cloudless. But now, as is recorded, "God showed his presence to Petronius" because the heavens opened up and a great shower of rain poured on the area. The Jews took it as a sign that Petronius would succeed in his petition. But the governor was equally impressed, observing to his counselors, "God takes care of the Jews."

. . . .

AT THIS POINT YOU MIGHT ASK, throughout all this, where was King Herod Agrippa, whose expanded dominions now included the very places where Petronius and the Jews met? All accounts I have seen agree that Agrippa was staying in Rome at the time, paying homage whenever he could to his master. What puzzles me is that these sources also agree that this wily ruler, whose strength depended on weaving webs of information, apparently knew nothing of the emperor's order to erect his statue in the temple.

All the more puzzling is that there are two accounts of what happened next — each one documented by sources deemed impeccable by historians. Rather than attempt to mix them into one version that represents a watery half-truth, I shall simply relate each one in turn.

The first is from Philo, who was at this time back in Alexandria waiting for Gaius to decide his appeal on behalf of the persecuted Jews of that city. Philo writes that very soon after the arrival of the second letter from Petronius, Agrippa was among several persons who were allowed into the emperor's presence to pay their respects. Immediately the Jewish king perceived that Gaius was staring straight at him, smoldering with anger. After searching his memory to recall anything he might have done to incur the emperor's displeasure, Agrippa concluded that Gaius had been upset by someone else and that he was about to be today's butt of imperial hostility.

But the emperor quickly observed his agitation and said, "I see you are perplexed, Agrippa, so allow me to release you from your perplexity. Have you sojourned with me all this time and not learned that I speak not only with my voice but quite as much with my eyes in every intimation I make? Well, here is why. Your excellent and worthy fellow citizens, who alone of every race do not acknowledge Gaius as a god, appear to be courting even death with their recalcitrance. When I ordered a statue to be set up in your temple, they marshaled their whole population and issued forth from the city and country nominally to make a petition, but actually to counteract my orders."

He was about to add further charges when Agrippa, gasping for breath, turned every kind of color—from blood red to deathly pale to livid again—all in a moment. Now every limb convulsed with trembling and palpitation. His nervous system seemed to shut down, and he would have fallen into utter collapse had not some bystanders caught him in the midst of swooning. After a brief commotion, a stretcher was summoned, and Agrippa was carried home, by this time in what could only be described as a comatose state. Gaius was no doubt dumbfounded by what he had just seen. Finally the emperor threw up his hands and shouted to no one in particular, "If Agrippa, who is my dearest friend and bound to me by so many benefactions, is so under the dominion of his nation's customs that he cannot even bear to hear a word against them and is prostrated almost to the point of death, what must we expect of others who are not under the influence of any counteracting force?"

Agrippa lay sunk in a deep coma for the rest of the day and most of the next as his physicians and family clustered about his bed. Then, as the sun began to sink on the second day, the king lifted his head slightly and opened his eyes. Obviously still unable to distinguish those around him, he asked, "Where am I? At Gaius's? Is my lord also present?"

"Cheer up," his relieved attendants replied. "You are staying in your own house. Gaius is not here. You have gotten a good rest. Now lift yourself up, lean on your elbow and recognize the company present. They are all your own people, your friends and freedmen who value you and are valued by you."

With that the physicians shooed everyone else out so they might further restore their patient and get him to take nourishment. But as Agrippa sized up the sober reality facing him, his mood remained morose. "The very idea of troubling yourselves to improve my diet," he wailed. "All it will do for me, illfated wretch that I am, is to assuage my hunger only so that I can live to surrender this miserable nation." Tearfully, he forced himself to swallow some food.

But he turned aside a mixture of water and wine and accepted only a glass of water. When that was done, Agrippa remarked sadly, "Now I have nothing left to do but make my petition to Gaius about our present situation."

With that he wearily picked up a tablet and began to write in a sycophantic style that no doubt flowed easily by then. "My opportunity, my master, of interceding with you face to face has been lost through fear and reverend shame — fear which could not confront the menace, and reverence which struck me dumb before the greatness of your dignity. But my handwriting will declare to you the petition which I put forward instead of the supplicant's olive branch."

What followed was a long and rambling appeal that spared no good deed the Jews had ever done the Romans, nor favors that Agrippa had done Gaius. He began by trying to explain and defend the ardor of the Jews for their traditions. "Every people is convinced of the excellence of their own institutions, even if they are not really so," he wrote. "For they judge them not so much by their reasoning as by the affection they feel for them." To show clemency in the matter of the temple statue would actually be a rare opportunity for you to demonstrate your clemency in a way that will magnify it, because there are Jews in every corner of the world and all will celebrate their love for their Cæsar with prayers, sacrifices and votive offerings that will "make the world resound with praise and thanksgiving."

Agrippa gave thanks for the privilege of being one of Gaius' closest companions — hoping, I presume, to make the emperor think back to the days on Capri when Agrippa was his constant champion to the point of being jailed for his exuberance. "Many a close friend might have sought Roman citizenship for all of his homeland, or at least remission of tribute." he wrote. "But, no, I have foregone all that and ask nothing more than a small favor that will cost you nothing. For what greater boon can subjects have than the goodwill of their ruler?"

And what people have shown greater love for their emperor, implored Agrippa. He recalled that it was when Vitellius was visiting Jerusalem that the notice of Gaius' succession had been received, and that it was from there that word was passed onto the eastern provinces. "For just as in families the oldest children hold primacy because they have been the first to give the name of father and mother to their parents, so, too, Jerusalem, since it was the first of the eastern cities to address you as emperor deserved to receive greater boons than they, or at least no less."

Agrippa next pressed his case for the sanctity of the temple, that its traditions had been honored by Augustus, "your grandfather Agrippa, and your other grandfather, Tiberius Cæsar." Livia Augusta and other women of the Roman royal family had furnished the temple with golden vials, libation bowls and other marks of their respect. "Thus," said Agrippa, "no one, Greek or non-Greek, no satrap, no king, no mortal enemy, no faction, no war, no storming or

sacking of the city, nor any existing thing ever brought about so great a viola-
tion of the temple as the setting up in it of any image or statue or any hand-
wrought object for worship." And without bothering to notice that he was
about to contradict himself, Agrippa pressed on by citing that when Pontius Pilate had attempted to place standards in the temple courtyard, Tiberius had
been "violent with anger" when told about it.

After a blunt appeal not to alter the "laws and traditions that have been
passed from emperor to emperor," Agrippa summed up his personal dilemma,
enveloped in more sycophancy. "You released me bound fast in iron fetters,
who does not know it?" he wrote. "But do not clamp me, my emperor, with still
more grievous fetters, for those which were then unbound encompassed but a
part of my body. Those which I see before me are of the soul and must press hard
on every part of my whole being. You thrust away the ever imminent terror of
death and kindled fresh life in me when I was dead with fear. You awakened me
as though I was born anew. Maintain your bounty, my emperor, that your
Agrippa may not bid farewell to life, for it will seem as though my release was
not given to save me only that I should become a victim to heavier misfortunes.

"The greatest gift of fortune that a man can possess, you granted to me – a
kingdom. Do not after granting me favors in super abundance... and after
restoring me to light of fullest radiance, cast me anew into deepest darkness. I
renounce all that brilliance. I do not beg to keep my short-lived good fortune. I
exchange all for one thing only, that the ancestral institutions of the Jews be not
disturbed. For what would be my reputation among either my compatriots or
all other men? Either I must seem a traitor to my people or no longer be counted your friend as I have been. There is no other alternative, and what ill could
befall me worse than these?" The only way out, concluded Agrippa, was
through the mercy of the emperor in canceling his order to erect the statue.

Now you would no doubt agree, dear reader, that Philo's story has merit if for
no other reason than that he claims to be furnishing the exact letter written by
Agrippa. Yet it is most intriguing that the Jews of Judea adhere to another version, which I will briefly relate.

Indeed, they say, Herod Agrippa had not known about the statue and was
shocked beyond measure when the news first reached him. After pondering his
dilemma at great length, he decided on a course that certainly seems in character with his past behavior. He arranged a banquet for Gaius that exceeded that
of all other imperial hosts to date for its expense. One Jewish-Roman historian
even claims that "it was so far from the ability of others that Gaius himself
could never equal, much less exceed it."

When this stupendous feast was in full swing and everyone was flush with
wine, a very merry and maudlin emperor reportedly staggered to his feet and
made the speech Agrippa had been hoping for. "I knew beforehand, of course,

what great respect you had for me, what great kindness you have shown me and what risks you undertook with Tiberius on my behalf," the emperor said, extending his hand in the direction of the resplendent King Agrippa. "Now you have gone even beyond your [financial] ability to display your affection for me. I am therefore desirous to make amends for everything in which I have been deficient. For I realize now that all the gifts I have given you are but little. Everything that might contribute to your happiness shall be at your service as far as my ability will reach."

Now it was Agrippa's turn. "It was out of no expectation for gain that I have paid my utmost respects to you," he replied to Gaius. "The gifts already bestowed upon me are already great and quite beyond the dreams of most men."

Gaius was astonished at this modesty and pressed again, asking if there wasn't but a wish he could grant.

Agrippa had pressed his luck far enough. "Since you, Oh my lord, have declared that I am worthy of thy gifts, I will ask nothing relating to my own felicity. For what you have given me already is sufficient. But I do desire somewhat which may make you glorious for piety and render the [Jewish] divinity an assistant to your designs. For my petition is simply this: that you will no longer think of the dedication of that statue which you have ordered to be set up in the Jewish temple by Petronius."

The die was cast. Once again, Agrippa's life briefly hung in the balance. For had not Gaius already issued his orders? Had not two legions already marched days to carry them out? Gaius was stunned, but quickly regained his composure, for he faced being guilty of a falsehood if he took back his offer in front of so many witnesses. So with a wave of his hand and a smile he granted Agrippa's wish.

You can choose which story you prefer, for I am tired of unraveling library scrolls and pestering old people about it. It may even be that Agrippa did write the letter and that he did hold the banquet later so that Gaius would be put in the position of publicly ratifying what he had already agreed to informally. But enough of my ruminations. Both accounts agree that Gaius soon wrote Petronius, saying, "If you have already erected my statue, let it stand. But if you have not yet dedicated it, do not trouble yourself further about it, but dismiss the army, go back and take care of other affairs, for I have no further occasion for erection of that statue. This I have granted as a favor to Agrippa, a man whom I honor so very greatly that I am not able to contradict what he would desire me to do for him."

But it may be that the slave Helicon and "councilor" Apellas were already whispering in his ear again, because Gaius added something else: if any persons outside of Jerusalem wished to honor him with altars, temples, statues and the like, Petronius was to punish anyone who opposed them. Thus, while relenting in one city, he had encouraged others throughout the eastern provinces to foment vandalism and violence against the Jews.

All this, alas, was written as the second letter from Petronius was still making its way by ship to Rome. In lodging his unprecedented second appeal to the emperor, Petronius no doubt exaggerated the situation by picturing barren fields and a people ready to revolt. In any case, his letter set Gaius to fuming again, this time with Helicon and Apellas at his side fanning the flames. The emperor eventually decided to exact his revenge as follows. He ordered that a colossal gold-coated bronze likeness of himself be constructed in Rome under great secrecy. The other statue in Sidon would remain unmoved so as not to disturb the populace. The newer monstrosity would be conveyed from Rome by ship during his planned voyage to Alexandria. When stopping in Judea, it would be transported up to Jerusalem. There, the emperor himself would lead a ceremony in which Herod the Great's colossal temple would be renamed "The Temple of Gaius, the New Zeus Made Manifest."

Next, the vindictive emperor sent off a letter to Petronius as follows: "Seeing as how you esteem the presents made to you by the Jews to be of greater value than my commands, and that you have grown insolent enough to be subservient to their pleasure, I charge you to become your own judge and to consider what you are to do now that you are under my displeasure. For I will make of you an example to present and all future ages that they may not dare to contradict the commands of their emperor."

In the meantime, Gaius resolved to maintain an outward calm as to his new plans for the Jews. Thus, in the fall when Philo and the embassy from Alexandria came calling again to press their case, the emperor seemed more in a mood simply to toy with them for the time being.

A year had passed since the first delegation visited. This time the issue at hand had become not only the redress from their previous persecutions and ongoing harassment, but whether the leading Jews of Alexandria were to be denied Roman citizenship. Moreover, the "delegation" from the city now included not just three Jewish elders, but five, accompanied by a like number of opposing representatives from the Hellenistic population.

One might have expected that such a case might be heard in a court with the emperor sitting as an impartial judge, Philo complains in his diary. "The actual proceedings showed a ruthless tyrant with a menacing frown on his despotic brow." For Gaius received them not in a court, but in some gardens at the edge of Rome where he had been staying in order to preside over the restoration of several villas within its walls. Ushered into the garden, the ambassadors bowed their heads to the ground with humility and saluted him as the "Emperor Augustus."

His greeting chilled the Jews. "Are you the god-haters who do not believe me to be a god — a god acknowledged among all the other nations but not to be named by you?" he snarled.

The opposing envoys squealed with delight, as if this first utterance had secured the success of their mission. They danced up and down and invoked blessings on Gaius in the names of too many gods to mention. "My lord," crowed one of their leaders, "you will hate still more these people and their nation if you understand their malevolence and impiety towards you. For when all men were offering sacrifices of thanksgiving for your preservation, they — and I mean *all* Jews — alone could not bear the thought of sacrificing."

Philo's party cried out in one accord. "Lord Gaius, we are slandered! We did sacrifice, not once but thrice — the first time at your succession, the second when you escaped your severe sickness and third as a prayer for victory in Germany. And we did not just pour the blood upon the altar and then take the flesh home to feast on, as many do. We gave the victims to the sacred fire to be entirely consumed!"

"All right, all right," said the emperor with continuing irritation, "you have sacrificed — but to another. Even if it was *for* me, what good was it if you did not sacrifice *to* me?

By now the Jewish party felt terror crawling in their flesh as it became increasingly evident that they could not win the emperor's good will — yea, not even his full attention. For as the conversation continued, Gaius was walking about taking his survey of the villas: the men's and women's chambers, ground floors, upper floors. Driven along with the flow, the Jews tried to continue, mocked and reviled all the way by their adversaries. "For indeed," recalls Philo, "the judge had taken on role of the accuser, and the accusers the role of a bad judge who had eyes only for his enmity and not for the actual truth."

After giving some servants more orders about making this or that room more magnificent, Gaius wheeled around to the Jews and asked impishly, "Why do you refuse to eat pork?" This was greeted by another outburst of laughter among the Hellenes. But a Jewish elder answered: "Different people have different customs and the use of some things is forbidden to us as they are to our opponents." And someone added, "Yes, just as many don't eat lamb, which is also easily obtainable."

"Quite right, too," said Gaius with a chortle, "for it's not right, either." Amidst more guffaws, the emperor suddenly changed the subject. "We want to hear what claims you have to make about your citizenship," he said.

A Jewish envoy began to recite the points of argument, but Gaius cut him off by striding briskly to a large room and ordering a servant to replace all the windows with transparent stones so as to keep off the wind and scorching sun. Then he was back asking the Jews idly, "What was that again?" After several more times of being interrupted to replace this painting or that piece of furniture, the Jews simply gave up and waited in silence for what they thought now was their impending death. Then, suddenly, Gaius was back and in a markedly softer mood. Addressing either God above or the ceiling, all he said was: "They seem to me to be people unfortunate rather than wicked. They were simply foolish in refusing to believe that I have got the nature of a god." And with that he waved off the ambassadors and left.

There had been no hearing, nor was there ever to be, for it was also late autumn in the life of Gaius Caligula.

. . . .

AT SOME POINT, which I judge to be at the beginning of the two-year period, Peter and a small group of disciples decided to venture from their homes in Jerusalem and preach in surrounding Judea, Samaria and Galilee. This may have been due, in part, to a formal decision among the apostles to go forth to many lands and spread the gospel. It may be, too, that their success in Jerusalem had again put the temple officials on edge. That the authorities were already tense and nervous was probably the result of a rippling across the Mediterranean that was caused by the emperor himself. By this I mean that the more Gaius became piqued at the refusal of Jews to recognize his godhead, the more trouble Hellenists stirred up against Jews up and down Palestine. And of course, such tensions always created the greatest shock waves in the temple in Jerusalem.

Of the people Peter encountered in the surrounding areas, more than ever were willing to listen. Farmers, shopkeepers, women and other common Jews felt more downtrodden than ever. The new emperor who would liberate them from dreary depression under Tiberius, the promising youth whose recovery they had prayed for so earnestly just two years before, had revealed himself as oppressive as his predecessor – and with a misguided hatred for their own people. Added to this was the fact that Roman taxes had been made onerous again under the unscrupulous Capito and increasing drought had made it more difficult to produce crops that could be converted into coins for tribute.

Thus, more people now cocked their heads and listened intently when Peter preached that God had revealed himself on earth not as a mighty, conquering messiah, but as a gentle, loving servant of man. Hope lept anew in their hearts when they heard that salvation and a blissful, worry-free eternal life were available to *all* believers – not just those who had the time and training to observe every jot and tittle of the Torah. And lo! Word spread that Peter had also worked miracles, just as some of them had witnessed Jesus performing them when they had been at the Passover feast some seven years before.

On one such occasion, Peter had come to Lydda, a town about 30 miles from

Jerusalem on the road to Cæsarea, to encourage a small group of believers that had already formed there. Upon arriving, he was asked to visit a man named Æneas, who had been paralyzed and bedridden for some eight years. When Peter entered his house, he gazed down on the man and said gently, "Æneas, Jesus Christ heals you. Rise and make your bed." Immediately the man rose — and word spread almost as quickly throughout Lydda and neighboring Sharon as to what had happened, and a great many gave themselves up to Jesus.

At the same time Peter was in Lydda, he was met by some followers who lived in Joppa, which is ten miles to the west on the seacoast. They had rushed the whole way, overcome with grief because one of the most esteemed disciples there had just died after being stricken with a sudden illness. Her name was Tabitha, and she was cherished among the people for her acts of charity.

When Peter hastened to Joppa, he found the body of Tabitha in an upper room where it had been washed and lain in a bed. All around stood women weeping. In their anxiety to pay Tabitha tribute and recall her many talents, they had displayed coats and other garments that she had made for her family and friends.

Peter stepped into the room and ushered everyone outside. He knelt down and prayed. Then turning to the body, he said, "Tabitha, rise." Her eyes opened, and when she saw Peter, she sat up in bed. He gave her his hand and lifted her up. Then Peter called out to the others waiting outside and they came in, astonished at seeing Peter and Tabitha standing together in the center of the room.

Many more came to the cause of Jesus that day in Joppa, so many that Peter remained there several days, staying at the home of a tanner named Simon. During this time, and throughout the first years of The Way, Jews weren't the only ones to hear the gospel or to witness the healings of the apostles. But great barriers remained to their understanding and acceptance of this message. Peter, for one thing, spoke only Hebrew and the native Aramaic of Galilee. Doubtless he had absorbed some Greek as well, being brought up among the Hellenistic towns of Galilee, but his smattering of words and phrases was probably far too rough and halting to use it in preaching to crowds. Secondly, common Jews simply didn't associate with Gentiles because their ancient dietary and sanitary laws proscribed too many restrictions to make it practical. Third, living apart bred ignorance, which, of course, only led to suspicion, rumor, enmity and the like between Jews and others. Thus, for all these reasons, it was not easy for most Gentiles to hear and accept the word of Jesus even if they might be so inclined. And if they did become believers, they could not share in common rituals, such as the taking of bread and wine. So, the preaching of the gospel to Gentiles had been left largely to disciples like Paul and the followers of Stephen.

I mention this here because it was during Peter's stay in the house of Simon that the apostle had a shattering experience. It was the sixth hour of the morning and Peter was hungry for breakfast. As the women were preparing the meal in the kitchen, he went to the housetop to pray as the glistening sea spread out to the west of him and the new sun rose to the east. It was then that the early writers say he soon fell into a trance. He saw the heavens open and something descending from the sky that resembled a great sailing sheet. Gathered up inside it were all kinds of animals, reptiles and birds. The sail was let down, its four corners touching the ground. Then a voice called out: "Rise, Peter! Kill and eat."

But Peter said, "No, Lord, for I have never eaten anything that is common or unclean." But the voice came to him again, saying, "What God has cleansed, you must not call common."

The voice repeated the same message three times. Then the huge sheet, or sail, was taken up again and disappeared.

Well after the breakfast that followed, Peter was still contemplating the meaning of this experience when three men stopped on the street outside Simon's house and called out to ask if a man named Peter was staying there. As Peter rose to look out, he again heard the voice that had accompanied the vision of the sail. "Behold, there are three men looking for you," it said. "Go down and accompany them without hesitation, for I have sent them."

When Peter did so and asked the men why they had come, they explained that they were servants of Cornelius, a centurion of the Italian Cohort who was posted at Cæsarea. Cornelius, they explained, had become a devout follower of The Way, along with his entire family. They added that the centurion was also known around Cæsarea as a man who always gave alms to the poor and who was just to the Jews who lived there.

"Cornelius," they explained, "was directed by a holy angel to send for you to come to his house and hear what you have to say."

Peter might have suspected a plot, but his vision gave him strength. So, perhaps, did Paul's account of how he was directed by a voice to go to the home of Ananias in Damascus. The next day, Peter, the servants and six of the brethren from Joppa departed on the 40-mile journey north to Cæsarea. When Peter arrived at the house of Cornelius, he saw a group of Romans and other Gentiles gathered outside. He soon learned that the centurion had called his kinsmen and close friends to witness what he believed would be a momentous encounter. When Peter came into his presence, Cornelius fell at the apostle's feet in a posture of worship. But the alarmed Peter quickly lifted him up, saying, "Stand up. I, too, am but a man."

When they were inside and the centurion's kinsmen had crowded in with them, Peter rose and said, "You undoubtedly know how unlawful it is for a Jew to associate with or visit anyone of another nation. But God has shown me that I should not call any man common or unclean. So when I was sent for, I came without objection. I ask, then, why you sent for me."

Cornelius explained. "Four days ago I was keeping the ninth hour of prayer in my house when, behold, a man stood before me in bright apparel. He told me, 'Cornelius, your prayer has been heard and your alms have been remembered before God. Send therefore to Joppa and ask for Simon, who is called Peter. He is lodging in the house of Simon, a tanner, by the seaside.' And then the angel departed."

Peter was next to speak. "Truly, I perceive that God shows no impartiality," he said. "Any nation and anyone who fears him and does what is right is acceptable to him. You know the word which was proclaimed throughout all Judea, beginning from Galilee, after the baptism which John preached, how God anointed Jesus of Nazareth with the Holy Spirit and with the power, how he went about doing good and healing all that were oppressed by the devil. For God was with him. And we are witnesses to all that he did both in the country of the Jews and Jerusalem. They put him to death by hanging him on a timber. But God raised him on the third day and made him manifest, not to all the people, but to us who were chosen by God as witnesses and who ate and drank with him after he rose from the dead.

"And he commanded us to preach to the people," Peter continued, "and to testify that he is the one ordained by God to be judge of the living and the dead. To him all prophets bear witness that every one who believes in him receives forgiveness of sins through his name."

Well before Peter had finished saying this, all those who were listening were seized with the Holy Spirit in the same way that the apostles had witnessed from their balcony in Jerusalem during the fourth Passover after the crucifixion. The circumcised disciples who had accompanied Peter were amazed that the gift had been poured out even on the Gentiles. For they were speaking in tongues and extolling God.

Then Peter declared, "Can anyone forbid water for baptizing these people who have received the Holy Spirit just as we have?" With that, he commanded them to be baptized, remaining in Cæsarea for several days to preach the word and baptize still others.

In time, Peter returned to Jerusalem. When he arrived, news of what had happened in Cæsarea had already reached the ears of what was now called "the circumcision party" among the Jewish brethren (in order to distinguish themselves from the Gentile converts). But when Peter gathered them together and patiently explained his vision in Joppa and that of Cornelius in Cæsarea, they sat in silence. Then, it is written, they rose as one and they gave praise to God, saying, "Then to the Gentiles also God has granted repentance!"

The following is not affirmed in the early writings, but some say that the ranks of believers swelled greatly in the months that followed. I say this because this was also around the time that the Jewish elders spread word in every direction that Petronius had been ordered by Gaius to erect a statue of himself in the temple. As the people despaired, as they abandoned even the planting of their crops, as they marched in sackcloth to Ptolemais and Tiberias, and as they lay in the dust before the army of Petronius extending their throats and not knowing if they would be slashed at any moment, disciples of Jesus were surely among them, urging them to repent now because the world was ending soon anyway and Jesus would call the faithful to be with him in eternity.

As for the Hellenists, disciples from Cyprus and Cyrene were so successful that they had made great numbers of believers even in cosmopolitan Antioch, the Syrian capital, the Roman empire's third largest city and the permanent headquarters of Petronius and his legions. A leader among those disciples was Barnabas, the Cypriot. So busy and demanding was his work that he needed assistance. Barnabas went to Paul in Tarsus and asked if he could join him as soon as possible. Paul did.

A new time had begun. Groups of believers were still meeting mostly in the homes of members, but they had in fact coalesced into "churches," or governing bodies for the selection of worship rituals, the collection of offerings and the distribution of alms to the poor and orphaned. And by now they had become easy in calling themselves by their new name... *Christians.*

. . . .

. . . .

LETTER FROM ROME — OCTOBER, A.D. 79

*Greetings to my dear cousin Eumenes, your family and all the workers of what will
soon become the biggest book publisher in Pergamum! Have I left anyone out? I
can't tell you how elated I am by your description of your move down to the busy,
bustling Via Tecta. I am amazed that in that crowded place you were able to find so
much space. My scribes in Rome will envy you. But more of business in a moment.*

*Your inquiry about my health makes me think of something in your own letter.
You mentioned experiencing monotonously gray skies over the Ægean coast and
wondered if it could have had anything to do with Mount Vesuvius. I think it could
indeed because I've heard similar comments by travelers from "downwind" countries even further away than Pergamum. The westerlies of fall can blow all the way
across to Syria; so as Vesuvius keeps sputtering, everyone downwind coughs.*

*In all, I suppose I'm doing as well as expected for a man approaching his sixti-
eth year, but I am indeed bothered by the aftermath of Vesuvius. It's now been two
months since the volcano erupted, and we've had but scant letup in the sooty skies
and fluttering "gray snow," as they call it here. It's even darker than usual inside
my apartment because everyone has to keep their shutters closed at all times or risk
having the fine ash in every crack and crevice. This morning I opened the shutters
long enough to check the skies and wondered at the same time if the stuff would also*

stick to a vertical wall. So I reached my arm around the shutter and found my finger poking through a half-inch of wet crust that clung to the outside wall.

The biggest problem is having to inhale this "snow" every day and feeling short of breath because of it. When I lived across the Tiber I used to make a fuss about the odors from all the foreigners around here cooking their strange dishes and burning so many different incenses to their household gods. Now I have something worse to grumble about.

Yet, being alive is reason enough to muffle one's complaints. It seems that everyone I talk to in Rome has a friend or relative who was in the midst of a peaceful seaside vacation when the mountain blew (which is why I'll soon discuss a manuscript on the subject). If you've heard that nearly the whole populations of Pompeii and Herculaneum perished, it is not an exaggeration. I would guess more than 20,000 in all. If you heard that whole families were "frozen" (suffocated) in the act of daily living as if turned into statues, this is also quite correct. One tale that I hope you will not fall for is that the eruption was caused by fiery giants. Some enterprising fellow with a big imagination has been collecting money from superstitious ignoramuses to stand in an assembly hall and describe how the whole thing started when giants sprang from the crater's top and ran down the sides holding huge torches. It seems that they are still prancing about the land at night, so if you have an earthquake in Pergamum it's because the giants are out stomping about near your home!

What news from Rome, you ask? Well, the emperor Titus (an exemplary ruler thus far, but I still miss his father!) is still in Campania overseeing the gruesome task of digging out Pompeii and Herculaneum and trying to restore bakeries, public latrines and other basics of life. Aside from Vesuvius, I would say the biggest topic of conversation is that the never-ending construction project at the eastern end of the Forum may be soon completed after what must be nine or ten years. If you get out our current tourist guidebook to Rome, follow the Sacred Way from the Forum to where the Subura begins. Right there a small stream flows down from where Nero's

Golden House stood before Titus began tearing some of it down and converting the rest to a public bath. This low flat area had been Nero's private lake. Now it's been drained (except for a stream that pops up from underground) and we have in its place a large piazza. Standing at one end is the nearly 100-foot high, gilt-bronze Colossus of Nero, which has been moved from its original position at the entrance of the Golden House. The big difference is that the head has been changed to some sort of sun god with golden spikes (sun rays, they say) protruding from his hair. Since no one seems to have any idea of what it is supposed to convey, we all just assume that the city prefect didn't know what else to do with so large a statue.

Occupying most of the former lake site is what you keep asking about. Yes, the new Flavian Amphitheater is every bit as awesome as I think my games-loving cousin would expect. The most arduous part of the construction is already completed. For four solid years 200 wagons and 400 oxen went back and forth from the quarries that lie along the Via Tiburtina hauling blocks of stone that weighed up to five tons each. All of the outside stonework is now up and sculptors have installed the first of what will be two tiers of statuary around the exterior. The construction statistics are the stuff that will sell many tourist books in places like Pergamum. The amphitheater is 590 feet around the exterior. The walls around the outer ring rise up over 150 feet. It will hold up to 70,000 people, which is double the Theater of Marcellus. They say that more than 300 tons of metal clamps were used just to hold the stone blocks in place.

I've heard, however, that the inside of this place has everyone talking. The workers have just finished an underground labyrinth of rooms and cages. An elaborate system of pulleys and weights will allow wild beasts to be raised up from the bottom so that they just suddenly spring into the arena above. The underground part will also have an extraordinarily large area for making and storing sets of all kinds. If they give hunting shows, for instance, they will be able put up, say, a jungle setting and then replace it quickly with perhaps a mountainside complete with caves and big boulders.

The part that hasn't begun yet is a thick wooden arena floor, around 225 feet by 150 feet, which will be covered with sand and raked after each event. What's to keep a lion from jumping up into the crowd? I asked one of the workers that question and he said they are going to install a series of ivory "rollers" all around the perimeter so that an animal can't get its footing. Even so, there will also be netting in front of the first rows. And just in case all this fails, archers will be posted all around in front row sections.

High overhead will be the largest canvas top anyone ever constructed. I haven't seen any sign of it yet, but they say this little shade awning will be held up by 240 enormous timber poles. Let's just hope it doesn't catch fire.

The best evidence I have that the project is drawing to completion is the fact that there are already two gladiatorial schools operating next to the amphitheater. I walked around the area last Sunday and actually heard the roar of a lion or tiger coming from inside the wall of one of these training schools. Frankly, I find the whole thing chilling, or foreboding, and the only reason I went over there was to be able to answer your questions.

I guess I also wanted to gather some tourist information as well, for, as I hope you'll agree, I aim to send your scriptorium an illustrated scroll on the Flavian Amphitheater as soon as possible (expect the length to be from 16 to 18 feet). I want to wait until after the opening because I hear it will consume several days and involve the greatest number of men and animals ever assembled. I will assign it to the same young man who is finishing up the Vesuvius book and expect to have a manuscript ready within three months.

It seems that I have already slipped into business matters. Regarding Mount Vesuvius, I sent this eager and nimble young fellow, Norbanus, off to the Pompeii area a few weeks ago to write us a first-hand account of what happened. You can take it from me that the only other information resulting from any imperial offices will be some clerk's turgid report about how many were killed and how many tons of this and that were displaced. But people from here to Ephesus and Antioch will pay to read about how the fiery lava raced down the hillsides, how a mother struggled to save her baby and so forth. I think we should produce several copies here, then have you do the same simultaneously so as to sell as many as we can before the "dust settles," if you'll allow a bad pun.

What else do I have in mind for you? I'll tell you what I don't have in mind. Do you recall my mentioning the Jewish general Josephus and that I hoped to send you a long manuscript about the Roman-Jewish war? Well, relax! I never got the introduction I had hoped for, but it was probably an unwise idea anyway. For one thing, Josephus apparently decided to include all of the Jews' troubles with Rome going back to the rule of Herod the Great more than a hundred years ago. The result was not just a book confined to the recent era, as I had expected, but one that takes up nine of the 26-foot scrolls. You'll be relieved to know that Sosius Brothers got the contract to produce it, because they've had to raise an army of copyists for their bulging scriptorium, including some apprentice secretaries from the Tabularium and temple of Saturn. The reason for the commotion is that the whole project, as I should have realized, is being underwritten by Titus. Now that the author's part is done, the emperor apparently can't understand why he suddenly shouldn't be able to hand out dozens of copies to various generals and senators. Our little boat of a business (at least the part in Rome!) would have been swamped. I'm told that this Josephus is now at work on a history of the Jewish people since the beginning of time! If he devotes as much ink to each period as he did to the one he just wrote about, whoever buys it is going to need a whole wall just to hold the scrolls.

As to your own projects, all one hundred copies of the Asclepieum at Pergamum and the revised Tourist's Guide to Troy arrived in decent enough shape, although I swear they must have made the voyage next to a cage of animals. We had to unroll all of them for an airing, which probably did little more than add a coating of volcano dust, but they're on the shelves and beginning to sell well enough. In time, more people will realize that your Asclepieum is much more extensive than the one on Tiber Island and probably the world's most splendid medical institution.

As for Troy, the battle sites and descriptions now conform more to what Homer described in The Iliad, *and are thus easier for people to read.*

Apart from all the above, I am glad you are turning your attention to the new way of producing books, but it certainly is disconcerting to learn of how the typical parchment purveyor reacts to a new concept! I'm sure the man who invented the two-horse chariot harness must have faced the same problem with everyone who made one-horse harnesses! If all this fails, aren't some of these people your fellow Mithraists? Tell them this is no way to treat a brother!

Seriously, I can understand their reluctance to cut hides to a larger size and construct different-sized stretch frames; and I can understand why they might not want to do this for one customer who could leave them at any time. But can't you get them to see the larger picture? This is a way for the Parchment Makers Guild of Pergamum to increase their business, reduce the production of papyrus and bring more honor to the city whose very name means parchment! But if they can only see the small picture, then find one of the humblest of these hideworkers and pay him a nice sum to produce a large amount of inventory that will justify his extra work. This is one reason Literato and I sent all that money!

Besides, this book I am writing is going to consume a lot of vellum. If you have unwrapped the bundle that came with this letter you have seen that Book II consists of nine scrolls (yes, I am rivaling Josephus). Perhaps it will also help you see why the new codex way of presenting books offers so many advantages.

Finally, I was surprised to learn from your letter that you took the trouble to read Book I of this history. I thought you were just going to store the scrolls in a safe place for now. Although I am flattered by your apparent interest in the subject, I am a bit concerned because I hadn't expected to be debating with anyone about it while the writing process was still going on.

I'm referring in particular about the part of your letter that seems to take umbrage at the manuscript's references to Mithraism. Please, Eumenes, when I described its places of devotion in Tarsus (or anywhere else for that matter) I did not mean to insult you personally or the brotherhood itself. Your beliefs stand for many good things and I know the cult attracts the noblest and most eminent people in the communities it serves, not to mention the best in the Roman legions around the world. The irony here is that these two movements share so many of the same beliefs that many Mithraists have also become Christians. At least in Rome they have.

Let me tell you something that I swear I am not making up. In Rome today there are at least ten and maybe 15 centers of Mithraism (one doesn't call them temples here because they aren't officially sanctioned right under the emperor's nose). Now then, right where the Subura meets the edge of the piazza in which stands the Fla-vian Amphitheater there is a very large insula that shelters many families of men who work on its construction. It also contains several Christian families. In the stone-walled basement of this building is a Mithræum with two long stone benches facing each other. At one end is an exquisite five foot-high statue of the god Mithras. His right hand is extended and holds the sacrificial knife. The left hand pulls upward on the snout of a young bull so as to extend its throat. When torches are lit the statue gives off an eerie green cast, almost luminous.

I am describing all this in detail so as to confirm to you that I have been inside the supposedly secret ritual "cave" of a Mithraist group. Indeed, on the very day I walked to the amphitheater I went to this apartment house across the piazza and saw Christians holding their own worship service in the Mithræum. You see, many of the poorer Christians don't have a large home at their disposal and they don't find it illogical or offensive to meet in the sight of Mithras because they find many of its beliefs admirable. Ormazd, the Lord of Life, certainly cannot be viewed as unwholesome by them, nor can your "mystical communion" of bread and wine or the seven stages of initiation, each dependent on achieving worthy attributes. It is undoubtedly because of rituals like these that many Mithraists have become Chris-tians as well. Just as they find the tenets of Mithraism valuable in achieving a vir-tuous life on earth, they find that through Jesus they have come to believe that there is only one true god of the universe and that he is not a statue but the creator of everyone and everything. They believe God's love and offer of salvation extends to everyone — quite beyond joining an elite, exclusive cult or trade guild. Observing rules for self-improvement and making close friends are admirable goals, but they just don't go far enough for these people.

I ask you to consider whether this is at the core of what you found offensive in my manuscript and whether your other comments are related to it. I'm sorry that it was a surprise to you that Diodoros is a Christian; I just hadn't thought it important to mention at the time. As for your complaint about Polias, what can I say? You have the right to order your wife as you see fit, but I would respectfully entreat you to let her continue going to the church at her friend's house. Has your wife become any less faithful to you because of it? Have her household responsibilities suffered? Does she not still prepare a fine table?

Could it be, dear cousin, that you are also thrown off stride by the fact that this congregation is so "mixed" — that people of high and low state, slave and free, rich and poor — are all meeting together as equals? I can well sympathize with how you might find this unsettling; it is not the customary order of things. But perhaps you will be able to persuade yourself to judge the group on the basis of the good they do here on earth. For do they not administer to each other's needs? Do they not take care of their widows and comfort the afflicted? Have you not seen them even reaching out to feed hungry strangers?

You are a good man, my cousin and only heir, and I know you will decide the right thing. Meanwhile, maybe it would be best if you did not read the remainder of this manuscript — at least not until well after I have sent you the last book. Until then, we have much to do together! By the way, what I really worship is the virgin olive oil you press from your own grove. The next time you ship some books, include a couple of jars to improve an old man's digestion! "Press on," Eumenes.

Farewell. Attalos

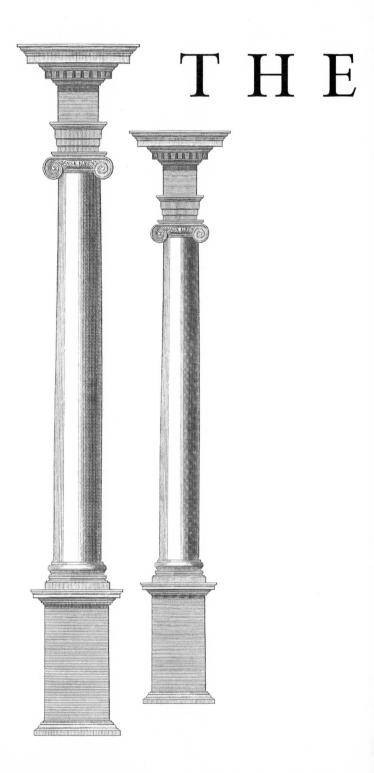

THE

GROWING

BOOK II

Many slaves and plebeians still cheered Gaius Caligula for his games and generosity. From the portico of the palace he had built onto the old domus of Tiberius on Palatine Hill, he could toss armfuls of gold and silver pieces down into the Forum and watch people scramble for them. But the rabble's delight could not be translated into power. The senatorial and equestrian classes, which any emperor must ultimately appease, had been nearly exhausted by unrelenting taxes, killings and confiscations of wealth. And so, as the year began, at least three plots were afoot to assure that Gaius would not live to see his thirtieth birthday.

The emperor certainly sensed the undercurrent of tension, because he regularly consulted seers and soothsayers about his safety. On one occasion when it was reported to him that the lots of Fortune at Antium warned him to beware of Cassius, he immediately ordered the death of Cassius Longinus, who had been proconsul of Asia. But the emperor did not seem to have noticed that Cassius was also the family name of Cherea, the military tribune who headed a cohort of the Prætorian Guard.

Cherea was probably in his early fifties at the time, a proud man with a toughness forged from years of field life in the provinces. No one would be thought less likely to be the butt of jokes all over Rome, but it happened to Cherea in the following way. One of his cohort's routine tasks was to call on citizens and enforce collection of overdue taxes. Because taxes had recently been doubled and because he felt their back-breaking burden on so many people, Cherea was often moved by pity to "forget" this man's debt or grant that one a delay. This in turn irritated Gaius, and when Cherea would come to receive the daily watchword, the emperor would often take the occasion to berate Cherea as "soft" or "effeminate" in enforcing the law.

In time, Gaius's reproaches grew into taunting Cherea in obscene ways that would bring guffaws from everyone around. Thus, when asked the watchword for the day, Gaius might give him "Priapus" (the god with the enormous penis) or another word for some part of the female anatomy. Sometimes the emperor would hold out his hand to be kissed, then wiggle his fingers obscenely just as the tribune was about to do so. Gaius might also greet the cohort dressed as a woman and tease Cherea in a way to make him look ridiculous.

Outwardly, this grizzled veteran bore his insults with stoic dignity, but inside he had become a wreck — yet more so from the atrocities he was ordered to perform than the insults of a warped bully. Early in the year when the horse races are inaugurated in the Circus Maximus, it has been traditional for the people to make various requests to the emperor, most of which are granted in the spirit of the new year. In this particular January they beseeched Gaius to relent on some of his more onerous new taxes. But the emperor would have none of it. He even ordered Cherea and other Prætorians to plunge into the crowd and kill those who persisted with their petitions.

The breaking point for Cherea probably came with the torture of Quintilia. It seems that a senator named Timidius reported to Gaius that an adversary of his named Pompedius had made some insulting comments about emperor. To strengthen his case, Timidius added that the offensive remarks had been made in the presence of Quintilia, Pompedius' lover and one of the most beautiful women in Rome.

Quintilia haughtily denied everything. Timidius implored Gaius to put her to torture. The emperor immediately assigned the task to Cherea, chiding him to go about it with as much fervor as he could in order to make up for his past "effeminacy." Quintilia gave him no room for compromise by declaring that he should "be of good courage" because she was prepared to bear up against anything he could inflict.

Cherea proceeded to put the poor woman through every cruel contrivance his prison offered. But when it was over he realized that he had tortured his own soul even more than her body. When Quintilia was reduced to a gasping, bleeding, grotesquely-contorted sack of broken bones, Cherea brought her before Gaius and asked in his most imperturbable manner what the emperor wished next.

Gaius looked up and was so visibly shaken to see this beauty reduced to such a state that he immediately freed both Quintilla and Pompedius of the charges. He even decreed on the spot that she should be awarded a large sum of money to make "honorable amends," as he said, for keeping her "glorious patience under such insufferable torments."

Cherea returned to the palace officer's quarters with his teeth clenched in hate. Until then no Prætorian had ever expressed his private feelings about the emperor for fear of informers within his own ranks. But this time the general Clement and tribune Papinius were in the room and Cherea could not contain himself. "There is no doubt that we have done our job in guarding the emperor against conspiracies against his government, because we have tortured some to such a degree that he himself pities them!" the old soldier seethed with sarcasm.

Clement and Papinius said nothing, but their faces were flushed and their eyes showed the shame they felt at having to obey Gaius' orders. Cherea could contain himself no more and out came a pent-up torrent. "It is we who bring these tortures on Rome and all mankind because it is done with our own consent," he lamented. "For whereas it is in our power to put an end to the life of this man, who has so terribly injured his subjects, we have become his guard in mischief and his executioners instead of his soldiers! We bear these weapons, not for the Roman government, but only for the preservation of a man who has enslaved both their bodies and their minds. And we are everyday polluted with the blood we shed. Yet this we do only until somebody else becomes Gaius' instrument in bringing like miseries on ourselves. For he scarcely employs us because he likes us. When many more have been killed, we shall ourselves be exposed to his cruelty!"

General Clement replied softly that he agreed with Cherea, but he urged the tribune to hold his tongue lest word of a plot get out "before it can be executed." Meanwhile, he urged waiting until "some fortunate event could come to our assistance."

But Cherea knew there was no turning back for him personally. Not really knowing the intentions of his first two confidants, Cherea gambled everything by approaching Sabinus, a fellow tribune and a man he knew as a lover of liberty. When Sabinus' declared his all-out support, the two officers decided to risk all by paying a visit to a man they considered the most eminent and virtuous senator in Rome. The senator was Minucianus, and they knew that he had been outraged ever since his good friend Lepidus had been murdered by Gaius in Germany for allegedly plotting against the emperor with the legion commander there. Minucianus reacted with almost tearful joy when the two tribunes described their intentions. Within days the number of senators or prætorians joining the secret confederation grew to more than a dozen.

Ah, but it's a giant leap from intent to action when it comes to doing in the ruler of the world. Days passed, some in which Gaius would appear unguarded in the Capitol sacrificing to his infant daughter or performing religious rites in front of a large crowd. On each occasion Cherea would flare up in anger at members of this "group" who let the opportunity pass without action, especially when some were strong enough to overpower Gaius even without drawn swords. His frustration grew as plans for the emperor's planned triumphant tour of Egypt drew nigh.

The Augustan games would have to be the occasion, Cherea at last informed his co-conspirators. Staged in late January, the games were then held at a theater on the Palatine that lay between the palace and the now-enshrined home of Cæsar Augustus. Attendees were chiefly Roman patricians along with their wives, children, freedmen and household slaves. Gaius would preside over the acts of singing, poetry readings and the like, and his personal guard of Thracians and German mercenaries could offer little protection in such a compact and crowded area.

All agreed that the deed would be dispatched on the first day. Yet, three days passed with conditions never being quite "just so," and on the night before the final day, Cherea assembled the conspirators.

"The more delay we effect, the more the chance of our exposure and the more cruel Gaius will be in his retribution," he hissed. "Do we not see how long we deprive all our friends of their liberty and give Gaius still leave to tyrannize over them? We should have procured them security for the future and by laying a foundation of happiness for all others, gain for ourselves great admiration and honor for all time to come."

No one contradicted Cherea, but neither did anyone speak. "Oh, my brave comrades," he wailed at last, "why do we make such delays? Do you not see that this is the last day of the shows and that Gaius is about to set sail for Alexandria? Is it therefore honorable to let a man who is the reproach of mankind go out of your hands and to a pompous triumph over land and sea? Shall we not be justly ashamed of ourselves if we leave it to some Egyptian or other to kill him? As for myself, I will no longer bear your slow proceedings but will expose myself to the dangers of the enterprise this very day and bear its consequences cheerfully."

The next morning Cherea was at the palace with his equestrian sword at his side, for it was the custom of the tribunes to ask for the watchword with their swords on. Outside in the theater a noisy crowd had already assembled. Rather than sitting in their usual assigned positions according to rank, this was more of a "family" affair for the emperor's court and the nobles who lived on the Palatine. Thus, people sat everywhere, with men and women together and freedmen sitting next to slaves. Gaius appeared on stage to their applause, and in a solemn manner offered sacrifice to the deified Cæsar Augustus. In the midst of it a priest holding a cup of sacrificial blood tripped and splattered some of it on the toga of a senator named Asprenas. Gaius pointed at the hapless senator with a derisive laugh, but for both it would prove to be an omen. At the outset, however, it was a relief to all that the unpredictable emperor seemed to be in a surprisingly jovial mood as he talked to those around him. The air of festivity was enlivened when some rare fruits were flung out to the audience. Many birds were released too, and there were shouts of laughter as some of the birds dove among the spectators to vie for the fruit they were eating.

Cherea took his seat to watch the shows, but was soon mulling all his possibilities. The theater had two doors. The one on the left led to the open street. The one on the right was a covered walkway leading to the palace cloisters. The latter walkway was divided into two partitions: one for actors to come and go from the stage without being seen, the other a place for the emperor and his guests to come and go as privately as possible.

As the ninth hour of the day approached, the audience's mood didn't seem to have been soured by the events onstage. The pantomimic actor Mnester, Gaius' own oft-time lover, danced a tragedy which had been enacted during the games at which King Philip of the Macedonians was assassinated. And in a farce called "Laureolus," the chief actor falls as he makes a climatic escape and vomits make-believe blood. After the play was over, so many understudies had been enticed to repeat the final scene that the stage by now seemed to be awash with this "blood."

It was still mid-morning when Gaius remarked to those around him that after three days, he didn't know if he could sit through another day's agenda. He might just retire for a bath and midday dinner, then return to the theater in late afternoon.

Minucianus sat just behind the emperor and heard this with alarm. He looked down towards the entrance and saw that Cherea had already slipped away. Fearful that the last opportunity might be lost, Minucianus stood up and prepared to go find the tribune and tell him of the unexpected change. Gaius turned around and grabbed Minucianus by the toga playfully. "Where are you going, my noble man?" he asked with a smile.

Minucianus sat down out of respect. But his fears overcame him and he got up again. This time Gaius didn't oppose his leaving, no doubt assuming that he simply had to answer nature's call. Just then Senator Asprenas persuaded Gaius to visit the baths as he first intended.

It was good that he did because Cherea had all but made up his mind to fall upon Gaius in his seat regardless of the carnage that would follow. By this time a few of the conspirators had managed to leave their seats and exit without much notice. Now Gaius also rose and trod down the aisle. At first he appeared headed for the left walkway that led to the street and some waiting servants. But then he turned right and disappeared into the private passage, which was closer to his baths. The emperor paused briefly just before the passageway partition and cocked his ear while some boys from Asia practiced hymns for the rites of the Augustan priesthood. Then he turned up the partition that led to the private walkway.

Within a few yards Gaius found himself confronted by a stern-faced Cherea.

The old tribune asked for the watchword. The emperor gave him another obscenity and stood giggling at his cleverness. Suddenly Cherea jerked his sword upward from its sheath and in almost the same motion hacked it down between the gape-jawed emperor's neck and shoulder. Gaius staggered back and groaned with pain. Gaius straightened up as if to flee, but Cornelius Sabinus rushed out from behind Cherea and threw him down on one knee. Then the narrow corridor was a hubbub of men taking their turns stabbing and slashing and shouting encouragement to each other.

Each man struck as if all of Rome had wielded his sword.

Then, suddenly all drew back as if each man were alone again as he realized the enormity of what he had done and what danger it meant to him. Gaius' attendants had been standing at the other end of the passageway and were already alerted by the commotion. Soon the wild, red-haired Germans and Thracians who served as Gaius' personal guard would be storming behind them. And who knew what the rabble of Rome would do when it found out?

The conspirators bulled their way through the passageway with swords drawn. With Cherea shouting impromptu commands, they managed to barricade themselves in the house of Germanicus, which is a wing of the palace that had been added for Gaius' father and his family in the early days of Tiberius. They were safe for at least the time being.

The emperor's guards knew nothing of Roman politics. Recruited for their daring and savage fighting skills, they knew only that they liked Gaius because he paid them more money than they had ever seen. Storming in from the theater, they came upon the bloodstained lump that had been their emperor and went wild with rage. They coursed through the passageway and the first person they encountered was the senator, Asprenas, who had arrived too late and who didn't know where his confederates had gone. It was this same man, you will recall, who had blood spilt on his toga during the sacrifice, and this was all the Germans saw. He was cut to pieces on the spot.

Next the marauders encountered Norbanus, one of Rome's finest nobles with a legion of generals among his ancestors. The Germans had no knowledge of or regard for his dignity. Norbanus, though old, drew his sword and dispatched two of them until he fell under a storm of flashing steel.

Another prominent senator, Anteius, had not been a part of the conspiracy but wished he had been when told what happened. Gaius had not only banished his father, but had sent out soldiers to slay him on his miserable rock. So Anteius was so flooded with emotion that he rushed from the theater and into the corridor to rejoice at the sight of the dead emperor. Now he, too, fell to the fury of the Germans.

Within 20 or so minutes everyone in the theater also knew what had happened, and their reaction was a miniature portrait of how all of Rome would react. First they sat babbling among themselves, which gave way to an eerie silence. For most could not believe that anyone would have the power to kill the already-deified ruler of the civilized world. And among the women, soldiers and slaves, many revered Gaius. Soldiers had taken his pay, lorded themselves over ordinary citizens and gained honors by being the handmaidens of tyranny. Women and children had been inveigled with shows, gladiators, coins tossed from balconies and free distributions of fresh meat.

Slaves, above all, had made Gaius their champion because they could count on his sympathy when they wanted to charge their masters with abuses. Why sympathy for the world's cruelest tyrant? Because Gaius rewarded slaves with one-eighth of his booty when they spied on their masters and disclosed unreported caches of wealth that could be taxed or confiscated.

Among the patricians and others who should have rejoiced, most remained mute for fear that the news might prove false or because they didn't know what their neighbor was thinking. For rumor was already circulating that Gaius was only wounded and under a physician's care. Fearing reprisals if they moved, they remained stuck to their seats.

In the next instant what seemed like an army of Germans streamed through the theater and surrounded the seats with swords drawn. People gasped as other Germans burst out of the passageway with the heads of Asprenas, Anteius and other victims on the tips of their swords. The spectators feared that they would be cut to pieces immediately and the theater reverberated with bellowing wails of people begging for their lives, praying to God and pleading ignorance of everything that had happened.

Courage can come from the strangest quarters. What brought the Germans to their senses and saved the crowd was the quick thinking of one Euaristus Arruntius, a public crier in the market and a wealthy man who had been severely pinched by Gaius' grab for taxes. Although no one hated the emperor more than Arruntius, he had the presence of mind to sneak backstage and don a costume that resembled mourning attire. Then he entered on-stage, and summoning up his loud crier's voice, sadly announced the death of Gaius as if he had been his own son. This dispelled the state of confusion that had existed about the emperor's condition and brought everyone a sense of finality and relief that comes with the possession of a common knowledge. Arruntius then went round the outer pillars of the theater, calling out to the Germans to put up their swords. And the latter, acknowledging that their master was dead, began to fear that they would be punished by the Senate if they slaughtered the theater goers.

With that the Germans hastened to their quarters and the crowd left the theater. It was just early afternoon by now, but many more dramas would be played out on separate stages long into the night.

Below the Palatine, in the Forum and in the surrounding neighborhoods, Valerius of Asia, a former consul, showed courage by going about and announcing the news. When asked who had done the deed, he would reply, "I wish I had been the man."

As restless and curious crowds surged toward the Forum, the Senate became center stage. Even as the rejuvenated conscript fathers assembled for an ad-hoc session, this was already their greatest day of independence and power in more than a century. Minucianus and his allies quickly asserted leadership. An edict was passed condemning Gaius. The Senate also emboldened itself by taking possession of the Forum and Capitol to prevent any looting of shops and temples. Soon the debate focused on how to restore the democracy permanently.

As afternoon turned to evening, another part of the drama was unfolding in the Prætorian barracks. To explain, I must return to that fateful morning. Claudius had been seated near his nephew. I think it likely that he was informed of the conspiracy, because he disappeared mysteriously from his place early on. In the first moments after Gaius' death, when the emperor's German guards were frantically searching for the killers, Claudius, it seems, had withdrawn to an apartment in the palace living quarters called the Hermæum. After learning of the murder and hearing the pandemonium caused by soldiers in their frantic search for the killer, he stole away to a balcony and hid among the curtains that hung before the door. As he cowered there, one of the Roman Prætorians, who was prowling about at random, saw two feet sticking out from the curtains, swept them aside and recognized the man who stood trembling before him. When Claudius fell at his feet in terror, the soldier called in some other comrades and said, "This is the brother of Germanicus; let's hail him as emperor!"

What happened next was a blur, as the soldiers took turns hauling the dead emperor's panic-stricken uncle in a makeshift litter to their barracks northeast of the city walls. There he spent the night, huddled between two sentries, perhaps no longer shaking with fear, but in no way expecting that the Senate would ever allow the despised monarchy to continue.

Ah, the republic! Nothing stirred men's hearts more than the dream of returning to the greatness that was Rome when it was a true democracy governed by the collective wills of free men. But it was *how* to reconstruct that golden heritage that consumed the minutes and hours as the senators debated into the night. As they did, soldiers milled in and outside the Curia. And the more they stood, leaning on one weary foot and then the other, the more they began to mutter. They recalled what errors the Senate had made in the days when it actually governed. Soon they were asking each other in louder, sarcastic tones how the world could be led by a spineless, babbling, bickering legislature that had already swooned before two tyrants, and they reminded one another just who had provided their wages.

At the Prætorian barracks, as the first rays of sunlight began to cut through the icy cold, other soldiers were of a similar disposition and quite oblivious to any senatorial rhetoric. Claudius himself was still too dazed and almost too limp of body to walk. At one point he looked up and saw himself being examined curiously by Gratus, the same soldier who had discovered him hiding among the curtains the day before. "Sir," said Gratus softly but firmly, "abandon these low thoughts of saving yourself. You ought to be having greater thoughts of obtaining the empire, which the gods have committed to your virtuous conduct by taking Gaius out of the way. Go and accept the throne of your ancestors!"

Indeed, Claudius' spirits warmed with the morning sun as the Prætorian camp became a magnet for soldiers and tribunes of the people filing in to declare their support for him. At various times Claudius would be hoisted back upon his sedan and paraded around the surrounding neighborhoods as his cluster of chairmen exhorted cheers from the people.

Down in the Forum, the Senate continued in deep division. Talk was of mustering military resistance to Claudius. Factions formed and melted like snowflakes. One that did not was the group supporting Marcus Minucianus, who had risked his neck to depose Gaius and who was loath to risk crowning another tyrant. And if there was to be another one, he himself was a prime candidate because he was married to Julia, the dead emperor's sister.

By midday, a delegation of senators entered the Prætorian camp and asked to address Claudius. In a firm manner bordering on insolence, they warned him against using violence to gain the government. He was but one man, they said, and ought to yield to the will of many and let the law take its course. Citing how tyrants had afflicted their city, they said how they would expect Claudius to "hate the heavy burden of tyranny." If he would but comply with the Senate and retire to a "quiet and virtuous life," they would vote him "the greatest honors decreed that a people can bestow." But if he insisted otherwise and "learned no wisdom from Gaius' death," they were prepared to gather a substantial army to thwart him — and even free slaves in order to swell its ranks.

Having made such a stern decree, the senatorial delegates must have had second thoughts upon seeing how large and enthusiastic a crowd of Claudius' supporters surrounded them, for they ended by falling on their knees and adding that if Claudius still insisted on assuming the throne, he should accept it only as given freely by the Senate.

The tide had begun to turn ever so slightly. Before I tell you Claudius' reply, you must know who was among those ambassadors and who had by then more to do with changing the tide than Neptune himself.

He was none other than Herod Agrippa.

After the frenzied German guards had run into the palace in search of revenge, it was the King of insignificant Trachonitis and Gaulanitis somewhere in far-off Syria who quietly stepped into the corridor and cradled the blood-soaked body of Gaius. It was he who laid the body on a bed, and I suppose in an effort to calm the guards' fury, told them to call a physician because Gaius was still alive. In the midst of that confusion, Agrippa saw the terrified Claudius being carried violently from the palace in a litter. He broke through the surrounding crowd just long enough to tell Claudius in a desperate whisper not to give up the government if the Senate demanded it.

When Agrippa returned home that first afternoon to wash and change clothes, he found a note summoning him to go to the Curia and offer the Senate his advice on the situation. When he arrived and was asked to speak on what he considered the sentiments of the people, Agrippa warned that the Senate would need arms if it was insistent on abolishing the monarchy. A senator replied that they were prepared "to bring money and weapons in abundance" and even give slaves their freedom if necessary to bolster the ranks of soldiers.

Agrippa stood again and solemnly raised his hand. He swore that he was prepared to lose his own life to defend the Senate's honor, but bade them think twice about military conflict. "The army that will fight for Claudius has long exercised in warlike affairs," he said. "Our army will be no better than a rude multitude of raw men, and perhaps made ungovernable by the addition of those who are unexpectedly released from slavery. Against men who are skillful at war we must use men who know not so much as how to draw their swords. Thus, my opinion is that we should send some persons to Claudius to persuade him to lay down the government. And I am ready to be one of your ambassadors."

Either before or during the delegation's arrival, Agrippa managed to pass a note to Claudius telling him of the Senate's state of disorder. He urged that Claudius reply in a conciliatory tone, but with dignity and authority.

And so he did. Claudius said he didn't wonder that they had no taste for another emperor. But under him, Claudius assured, they could expect equitable and moderate government. He would be ruler only in name, with authority common to them all. He had seen so much misery himself, he added, that they could well trust him to rule judiciously.

The ambassadors seemed mollified, and almost as soon as they had departed the army let up a great roar and swore an oath to Claudius. Another cheer went up when he decreed that every man in the Guards would be given 15,000 sesterces.

Night had fallen on the same day when the consuls called the Senate back into session, this time in the Temple of Jupiter the Conqueror. But the word of the delegation's meeting with Claudius had drifted out and many did not like the way the wind was blowing. Some senators stayed away because they simply

didn't know what to do. Others had already left for their country villas, resolved that it would be better to live a life of peaceful anonymity than to plunge
again into public affairs and set themselves up for censure — or worse. Minucianus and a few others were still in an obstinate mood, but they also knew that
the Prætorian camp had now been swelled by hundreds of gladiators, rowers of
ships and others who had left their posts to "protect" the city from chaos.

Not more than a hundred of the 600 senators showed up. They were easily
outnumbered and outflanked by soldiers and tribunes of the people shouting
for them to choose one ruler. It's not clear whether the shouting and bickering
continued through the night; but the Senate was still in session the following
morning when none other than Cherea strode in and attempted to address the
throng of soldiers milling about. But when he signaled with his hands for silence, the throng only raised a cacophonous din because they wanted no one
talking against the monarchy. Soon Cherea couldn't contain his anger. "Oh is it
an emperor you want?" he shouted above them. Well, he would give them one.
He would go ask the watchword from Eutuchus (whom everyone knew as
charioteer of the Green Band who had prevailed on his good friend Gaius to use
soldiers in building his stables). What idiots they were, he shouted, to endure all
the madness of Caligula only to turn their fate over to a stammering fool!

But this tactic failed. Cherea had pushed too hard and too far. His former
comrades were so incensed that they drew their swords and left for the Prætorian camp to swear allegiance to Claudius.

Suddenly the few senators who had remained that night found themselves
abandoned and strangely alone in the gigantic Temple of Jupiter. They knew
now that they had incurred Claudius' anger and they wondered what was
going to become of them. They were in the midst of reproaching one another
when a strong voice arose from the rear. It came from Sabinus, the second tribune to strike Gaius and perhaps the only soldier who had remained behind
with Cherea. Sabinus announced that he would rather kill himself than see
Claudius emperor and the "enslavement" continue. He even chided Cherea for
"loving life too much." Cherea responded that he, too, would kill himself if
necessary; but before doing so he merely wanted to sound out the intentions of
Claudius.

Some senators had tried to call on Claudius independently at the military
camp, but the soldiers had become so hostile (or at least exuberant) that some
had been roughed up and one of them even stabbed. So Claudius had himself
removed to the palace the next day and summoned his closest friends and what
was left of the Senate. There the chief topic was what to do with the slayers of
Gaius. None doubted that their deed had been "a glorious one," as one of them
put it, but the killers posed something of an embarrassment and a tricky question under Roman law. After all, Prætorian guardsmen swore an oath of fealty

to their emperor, and no one could maneuver around the fact that the conspirators had violated their pledge. Indeed, how could Cherea go free when he had so demonstrably opposed the monarchy and Claudius in particular? The only plausible accusation was that the old tribune had acted to avenge the personal insults of Gaius rather than from any concern for the nation's safety.

And so, Cherea was led to his execution and bore his lot courageously. When brought to the execution place, he calmly interviewed the young soldier assigned to do the deed, asked how skilled he was at it and offered a suggestion or two. Having satisfied himself, Cherea presented the young man with the very sword he had used to kill Gaius. He then stretched out his neck and was felled with one stroke.

What of Sabinus, who had first joined Cherea and who had struck the second blow on Gaius? For reasons that I can't explain, Claudius had pardoned the tribune and restored him to his former command. But after a few weeks Sabinus found he could no longer live with himself or the glares of his troops. He fell on his sword and drove it up to the hilt.

. . . .

WELL, DEAR READER, I am sure you have already anticipated what next greeted Herod Agrippa. Claudius, in order to make no uncertain show of his thanks, called a great assembly in the middle of the Forum and there proclaimed that Agrippa's small kingdom of Trachonitis and Gaulanitis would be expanded to include Judea, Samaria, Galilee and nearly all of the lands once ruled by his grandfather, Herod the Great. He also granted Agrippa's request that his younger brother, also named Herod, receive the small princedom of Chalcis (which lies not far from Antioch) and that he be given the privilege of nominating high priests. With these territories came a revenue of about 12 million drachmæ a year, which was said to be about three-quarters of what their grandfather took in.

All this was consummated by forming a league of mutual friendship and exchanging vows of fealty. This was even more important than the affairs of one kingdom, for it involved the question of respect and tolerance for Jews throughout the empire. I have already described the outbreaks of hatred against Jews by Hellenists and others in the Roman provincial cities. But these animosities extended even as far east as the Babylonian satrapy in Parthia, with its substantial Jewish population.

There is some irony in the case of Babylonia because it could be argued that Jews were the cause of it. Well before the reign of Gaius, the owner of a weaving business had whipped two young Jewish apprentices for being late to work. The incensed young men looted their employer's house and ran off to an island in

the Euphrates. Before long, they had made it into a bastion of refuge for a growing gang of brigands who thrived by stealing and exacting tribute from surrounding landowners. After defeating a small force sent by the governor of
Babylonia to root them out, it eventually took a major expedition by a general
of the Parthian King, Artabanus, before this Jewish state-within-a-state was
broken up. Once it happened, people from all over Babylonia joined in the revenge, slaying as many as 50,000 Jews. The tattered, terrified survivors fled to the
twin Parthian capitals of Ctesiphon and Seleucia in hopes of securing the king's
protection. But all this did was add to tensions with the large Greek and Syrian
populations there. Often at odds, they quickly united and drove the Jews out.
As Agrippa assumed reign over the Jewish homeland, thousands of Parthian
Jews had scurried to two smaller towns in Babylonia, uncertain of their fate. In
turn, Babylonians were uncertain of the new Roman emperor's intentions and
those of the newly-empowered king of the Jews.

As Jews were on the run in Parthia, those in the Roman provinces were wildly emboldened with the news of Gaius' demise. In Alexandria they had actually
taken up arms and inflicted so much damage on their oppressors that it was
now the Hellenist majority that sent ambassadors to petition the new emperor
for relief. The same petition attempted to smooth the way by requesting permission to erect various temples and inscriptions to Claudius in the same lavish
fashion they had been in the midst of doing for his predecessor.

So it provides us with instructive insight into Claudius' thinking at the time to
examine in detail how he responded to the leaders of Alexandria. I now quote in
large part from the emperor's reply, which has been preserved in the Tabularium.

> ...I gladly accept the honors given me by you, though I am not partial to
> such things. First, I permit you to keep my birthday as an Augustan
> day in the manner you have yourselves proposed. And I agree to the
> erection by you in their several places of the statues of myself and my
> family; for I see that you were zealous to establish on every side memo-
> rabilia of your reverence for my house. Of the two golden statues, the
> one made to represent the Claudian Augustan Peace, as my most hon-
> ored Barbillus [one of the Alexandrian ambassadors] suggested and
> persisted in when I wished to refuse for being thought too offensive,
> shall be erected at Rome, and the other according to your request
> shall be erected in procession on my name days in your city; and it
> shall be accompanied in the procession by a throne, adorned with
> whatever trappings you wish.

> It would perhaps be foolish, while accepting such great honors, to re-
> fuse the institution of a Claudian tribe and the establishment of sacred

groves after the manner of Egypt, wherefore I grant you these requests
as well. And if you wish you may also erect the equestrian statues given
by Vitrasius Pollio, my procurator. As for the erections of the statues in
four-horse chariots which you wish to set up to me at the entrances to
the country, I consent to let one be placed at the town called Taposiris
in Libya, another at Pharus in Alexandria and a third at Pelusium in
Egypt. But I deprecate the appointment of a high priest for me and the
building of temples, as my opinion is that temples and the like have by
all ages been granted as special honors to the gods alone.[1]

Turning to the subject of Jewish persecutions, which Gaius had so readily encouraged, the new emperor tried his best to declare a new era without enraging
the Hellenistic majority.

As for which party was responsible for the riot and feud (or, rather,
if the truth must be told, the war) with the Jews, although your envoys...put your case with great zeal, nevertheless I was unwilling to
make a strict inquiry, though guarding within me a store of immutable indignation against any who renewed the conflict; and I
can tell you once and for all that unless you put a stop to this ru-
inous and obstinate enmity against each other, I shall be driven to
show what a benevolent emperor can be when turned to righteous
indignation.

Wherefore once again I conjure you that, on the one hand, the
Alexandrians show themselves forbearing and kindly toward the
Jews, who for many years have dwelt in the same city, and dishonor
none of the rights observed by them in the worship of their god but
allow them to observe their customs as in the time of the deified Augustus, which customs I also, after hearing both sides, have confirmed. And, on the other hand, I explicitly order the Jews not to agi-
tate for more privileges than they formerly possessed, and in the
future not to send out a separate embassy as if they lived in a separate
city – a thing unprecedented – and not to force their way into gym-
nasiarchic or cosmetic games, while enjoying their own privileges and
sharing a great abundance of advantages in a city not their own, and
not to bring or admit Jews from Syria or those who sail down from
Egypt, a proceeding which will compel me to conceive serious suspicions. Otherwise, I will by all means proceed against them as fo-
menters of what is a general plague on the whole world.

If, desisting from these courses, you both consent to live with mutual
forbearance and kindness, I on my side will exercise a solicitude of very
long standing for the city, as one bound to us by ancestral friendship. I
bear witness to my friend Barbillus of the solicitude which he has always shown for you in my presence and of the extreme zeal with
which he has advanced your cause... Farewell.[2]

Armed with this as his precedent, Herod Agrippa pressed his good fortune
even further: he persuaded the much obliged Claudius to restore the same
privileges to Jews throughout the empire. An edict soon went out that read:

Upon the petition of King Agrippa and [his brother] King Herod, who
are persons very dear to me, that I would grant the same rights and
privileges to the Jews which are in all the Roman empire that I have
granted to those of Alexandria, I very willingly comply therewith.

This grant I make not only for the sake of the petitioners, but as judging those Jews for whom I have been petitioned worthy of such a favor,
on account of their fidelity and friendship to the Romans. I think it
also very just that no Grecian city should be deprived of such rights
and privileges, since they were preserved to them under the great Augustus. It will therefore be fit to permit the Jews, who are in all the
world under us, to keep their ancient customs without being hindered so to do. And I charge them also to use my kindness to them
with moderation, and not to show a contempt of the superstitious ob-
servances of other nations, but to keep their laws only. And I will that
this decree of mine be engraven on tables by the magistrates of the
cities, colonies and municipal places, both those within Italy and those
without it, both kings and governors, by the means of the ambassadors, and to have it exposed to the public for a full thirty days, in such a
place where it may plainly be read from the ground.[3]

Having demonstrated that he was a good Roman, Herod Agrippa was eager
to show that he was a good Jew as well. After spending a few months to help
Claudius settle into his throne, the anxious king landed in Cæsarea and was
soon in Jerusalem offering all the proper temple sacrifices. Having been able at
last to repay his many debts, Agrippa embellished his old habit of winning
friends with great flourishes of generosity. In one such instance he abolished
the tax on houses, which endeared him to just about every head of household.
And like his grandfather, Agrippa began undertaking large building projects,
such as an elegant new theater, baths and porticos for the people of Berytus on

the Phœnician coast. When the complex in Berytus was dedicated, Agrippa assembled more musicians and gladiators than had ever been seen in those parts. On one day at the new theater, 700 condemned criminals were pitted against a like number. Virtually all were killed in hand-to-hand combat as the frenzied crowd roared without letup.

For his first year or so in Palestine Agrippa showed remarkable skill in dealing with his many constituencies. His position was bolstered early when the edict of Claudius was put to the test. It seems that a group of young rabble rousers in the Hellenistic city of Doris carried a statue of Claudius into an empty synagogue and conducted a mock ceremony erecting it. Agrippa immediately reported the event to Petronius, the very popular governor of Syria, who came down swiftly on the city's magistrates for allowing it to happen. After sending a letter of stern rebuke, Petronius ordered the city fathers to round up the culprits and send them under a centurion's guard to Antioch for punishment.

Soon afterward, Petronius was recalled to Rome and Marcus went to Antioch to replace him as governor (or president, as some call it) of Syria. Marcus had been selected because he was a friend of Agrippa's, but there soon became no question as to the governor's first loyalty.

Soon after arriving, Marcus sent Agrippa a letter announcing that he was coming to Jerusalem for a visit. The governor was doubtless unaware that Agrippa was in the midst of hosting and entertaining kings from five nearby countries, including his brother Herod of Chalcis. Like Chalcis, none of these kingdoms came close to Agrippa's in size and power, but all of the six monarchs present decided that it would be properly respectful to journey out some seven furlongs from Jerusalem to greet Marcus and escort him into the city. How surprised they must have been to see Marcus approaching with an almost hostile look in his eyes. "What was the meaning of so many kings acting so friendly and familiar?" he had wondered to his aides. "How could this cohesion be good for Rome?" And so, he sent various assistants to the other kings with orders to go their separate ways without delay.

Agrippa simply gritted his teeth while attempting to appear hospitable. But another encounter took place in Jersusalem that would make Marcus his enemy. The Syrian president soon found himself looking out of the palace on one of Agrippa's most massive construction projects, the reinforcement of the walls of Jerusalem. So high and thick were these giant blocks of stone that the alarmed governor quickly wrote Claudius asking what he should do about it. When a letter arrived from the emperor asking him to "leave off" the project, Agrippa hoisted no more blocks out of respect to Claudius. But neither did he dismantle what had been done.

Agrippa's most perplexing problems came from Jews who charged that he was too Roman or too Hellenized or not pious enough. But the king was able to deflect such complaints with his gifts, his careful observance of Jewish laws and his good humor. As a Jewish historian wrote at the time: "He was not at all like that Herod who reigned before him; for that Herod was ill-natured and severe in his punishments. But Agrippa's temper was mild and equally liberal to all men. He was humane to foreigners and made them sensible of his liberality. He was in like manner of gentle and compassionate temper. Accordingly, he loved to live continually in Jerusalem and was precise in observing the laws of his country. He therefore kept himself entirely pure; nor did a day ever pass over his head without its appointed sacrifice."

At the same time the king gave public testimony to a lifetime of changing fortune. The golden chain that Gaius had given him — the one with weight equal to the iron chain that had bound his hands under Tiberius — the king had hung up over the entrance to the temple treasury chamber for all to see as an inspiration as to how one fallen so low can regain the heights of dignity.

But the chain was also an omen as if hung there by an old German prisoner — the one who found a dazed, deposed Jewish prince leaning on a tree one hot summer's night on Capri. Do you remember what the old man said to him?

· · · · · · · · ·

AT SOME EARLY POINT, I believe it was the beginning of his second year in Jerusalem, Herod Agrippa decided to purge the Jewish leaders of The Way. And by choosing to do so at the Passover festival, he intended to make his action as public as possible.

Why would this good-natured ruler single out this group at a time when he was trying so hard to consolidate support from all quarters? One simple answer is that this particular "sect" was not large enough to warrant any concessions from the king. At the same time, these Christians, as they were coming to be called, posed an increasing threat to his three most important interests: himself, the temple leadership and the Romans.

Regarding the temple leaders, Agrippa already had seen fit to change high priests three times in his first two years. I have not been able to discern the precise reasons, but certainly it indicated unhappiness with their performance; and the latest appointment, one Simon, may have felt his duties impeded by failure of the Christian sect to observe proper worship procedures at the temple or or assist in its administration. If so, their constant growth in numbers would certainly aggravate the priesthood's difficulties.

The perceived threat to the Romans and Agrippa himself were one and the same. A movement preaching the return of a messiah as king of the Jews was no great source of joy to an incumbent king. As for the Romans, the prospect of a growing religion that united Jews and Gentiles alike carried the seeds of sedition. At the very least, every Gentile who became a Jew might feel entitled to special privileges such as exemption from military service and various taxes. They might even build an empire within an empire!

On a more practical level, Agrippa by this time was seeking ways to demonstrate his loyalty to a new governor already suspicious of his re-fortification effort and cozy relations with neighboring kings. Thus, the Christians offered a convenient way to advance all three goals. And no one stood in his way, because thanks to the Claudian edict, all Roman troops had been withdrawn, leaving Agrippa free to "manage" local affairs with his own army.

Once having concluded that the Christians were undesirables, it is not difficult to see why a king known as gentle and just could justify dispatching troops to arrest people in the midst of preaching love and mercy. Indeed, had he hesitated to see 1,400 convicted criminals destroy themselves in a theatrical spectacle?

Peter, who had already survived one arrest, was an obvious target. Why Agrippa chose James, the son of Zebedee, as his first example seems unclear at first – but perhaps not after closer inspection.

According to a tract by John Mark, one of the earliest Christians, James and his younger brother John were raised on the shores of Lake Galilee very near where Jesus grew up. Their mother, Mary Salome, may have been a relative, perhaps even a sister, of Jesus' own mother, Mary. The boys' father, Zebedee, was both a pious Jew and prosperous fisherman. He had a home, servants, and a second home in Jerusalem that he visited frequently. In fact, I would guess that Zebedee was more than a mere fisherman because he seems to have been a partner in a larger enterprise with one Jona, another lakeshore fisherman. Jona had two sons named Andrew and Peter.

It appears that all four young men grew up knowing Jesus. At least some of them had also become believers in John the Baptist. One cannot know exactly when and why all four decided to drop everything they held dear and join Jesus in his wanderings, but one of many stories will suffice to explain why they *remained* with him. Jesus, who had already acquired his band of disciples by this time, was preaching at the edge of the Lake of Gennesaret one early morning and was being pressed hard by a crowd that had grown so large that the farthest from him could neither see nor hear him. So Jesus commandeered Peter's fishing boat and asked the crew to keep it steady in the shallow shore waters as he spoke to the people from a short distance away.

Peter and his partners had already been out all night rowing, casting nets and having nothing to show for it. No doubt very fatigued and hungry when the sermon was over, the crew was about to wash their nets and head home for a meal. But then Jesus turned to Peter with what must have seemed like an irritating request. "Launch out into the deep and let down your nets for a draught," he said.

One can see Peter replying wearily, "Master, we've already worked all night — and for nothing." Besides, anyone in these lake towns knows that fish are active at night and not when the hot sun shines on the waters. "Nonetheless," sighed Peter perhaps with a trace of sarcasm, "at *your* word I will let down the net."

What happened then must have been momentous for a disciple who was also a fisherman. When they pulled the net back up they had taken in such a load of fish that the crew could scarcely haul it in. I wonder if that event alone didn't sustain Peter more in his dark, lonesome trials than any of the many miracles that he was to witness.

I mention this because James and John, the sons of Zebedee, were part of that experience. While there is no mention of their father's reaction to joining Jesus, their mother, Mary Salome, became a devout follower as well. She followed the disciples on their last trip to Jerusalem and was one of the women who anointed the body of Jesus after it was removed from the cross.

Mary Salome's two sons were among Jesus' most zealous followers and among the three who appeared to be brought in to share his most intimate experiences. The three were Peter, James and John, all fishermen from Galilee. In what Mark records as the first time Jesus raised anyone from the dead, he took only these three with him across the lake and into a city of the Decapolis where the 12-year-old daughter of a synagogue leader had just died. There, in the leader's house with the family and three disciples looking on, Jesus took the girl's hand and said, "*Talitha cumi*," which means "Arise, little girl," which Mark says she did. In another instance, Peter, James and John were the only disciples to accompany Jesus when he was transfigured on a mount as he met with Moses and the Jewish prophet Elijah.

At one point in his ministry Jesus began calling James and John the "Sons of Thunder." One assumes it was because they were zealous in their cause and preached in a strong, demonstrative manner or spoke in a way that caused thunderous torment in the souls of those who heard him.

At one point in his ministry, the prideful mother of James and John actually petitioned Jesus to decree that her sons would sit on his right and left when he came into his "kingdom." Jesus refrained from rebuking her, but on the road to Jerusalem when James and John raised the matter again, he shook his head and said simply: "You know not what you ask."

Then said Jesus, "Are you able to drink from the cup I am about to drink, and to be baptized with the baptism I am about to be baptized with?' And instantly they replied "We are able!"

Not long afterwards, Jesus chose only Peter, James and John to be with him when he agonized in the garden of Gethsemane on his final night on earth. But those who had proclaimed themselves "able" to share in his "baptism," according to Mark, spent the night dozing and sleeping as Jesus confronted "the hour and power of darkness."

All this may have made James resolve never again to weaken should his own trial come. If so, it would explain why this "Son of Thunder" stood out among the apostles in Jerusalem and why he went with calm resignation when the soldiers of Agrippa took him away one night and killed him with the sword.

Peter, as if to confirm that he was more widely known, was seized and thrown into prison. It was, as I said, during the Feast of the Unleavened Bread, and it was Agrippa's intent to bring Peter out to the people the next day. It was the practice then for an oriental monarch to present a few imprisoned persons to the festive crowd and allow them to select one or two for freedom on the strength of their shouts — all, of course, to demonstrate the ruler's generosity. It would appear that Peter was to face the same fate as Jesus had, for no fewer than four squads of soldiers were rotated around the clock to make sure no one would try to free him.

All night long the Christians prayed to God for Peter's safe delivery. That he was *delivered* — and certainly with no help from Agrippa — is indisputable. To explain how, I have heard no account but the following: In the dead of night Peter was sleeping between two soldiers, bound with two chains. Sentries outside were guarding the door of the prison cell. Suddenly a light shone all around and an angel of God appeared. He nudged the sleeping Peter in the side and said, "Get up quickly."

With that the chains fell off Peter's hands. "Dress yourself and put on your sandals," said the angel. As Peter did so, the angel said: "Wrap your mantle around you and follow me."

Peter still thought he was dreaming. But when the two had passed the first and second guard outside the cell, they came to an iron gate that separated the prison from the city. The gate opened of its own accord. They went out into the street and immediately the angel left him.

Peter stood open-mouthed in the dimly-lit street before he began walking. He wound up in front of the house of Mary, mother of John Mark, whose home was undoubtedly used for Christian worship services. In any case, many people were inside, all in the midst of praying for Peter's safety.

Peter knocked. A maid named Rhoda came and listened to a voice begging to be let in. Recognizing it instantly as Peter's, she forgot to open the door, but ran joyously to tell everyone that Peter was standing outside.

"Either you are mad or it's his angel," someone said.

But when the knocks continued and they opened the door, they fell back in amazement to see it was indeed Peter. Motioning with his hand for them to remain silent, he quietly described how an angel of the Lord had brought him out of prison. Then, deciding that the house of Mary was a place that would be searched first, Peter stole away to another hiding place.

The sentries did indeed come calling. And when they could not find Peter anywhere, Herod Agrippa had the soldiers examined by torture to determine if they had aided Peter. Then apparently finding no evidence there, either, he had them all put to death.

. . . .

WRITINGS OF THE FIRST CHRISTIANS SAY only that Peter "went to another place" at this time. Indeed, no one seems to know for sure where Peter did go for the next three or four years. However, it does suggest to me that Peter and at least some of the original disciples (whom I will now call apostles) left Jerusalem during the persecution of Agrippa. The fact that the 12 apostles did not replenish their number this time (as they had upon the suicide of Judas Iscariot, who betrayed Jesus) further suggests that the group fanned out at this time to begin preaching beyond Jerusalem.

It is also reasonable to assume that the apostles had to travel farther than they had done before. This is because all of Judea, Samaria and Galilee were again under control of one king – and one with friendly rulers in many neighboring lands who would gladly return any fugitives he requested.

Beyond that, I can offer only conjecture and oral "tradition" (some say hearsay), handicapped as I am in being confined by circumstances to one city. Not that I wouldn't choose Rome if forced to select one place for scholarly research; but even my "command" of the libraries here (I say this without blushing) is of no use if they yield up nothing on the subject of one's inquiry. Except for having some colleagues in Alexandria and the province of Asia who might help track down answers to this or that question, I am reduced to walking up to elderly foreign-looking strangers in the Subura and asking if they are Christians. Some think me a lunatic. Some will show fear in their eyes and ask why I want to know. Some empty out their memories. Of these, some are undoubtedly accurate. Ah, but which ones?

My inquiry goes on even as I write this book. What I can suggest, at least for some of the original twelve, is the following:

Peter may have spent time in Babylonia preaching to the Jews of the Dispersion, for no city except Alexandria had a larger Jewish population. Some say he was in Rome during this time, but I think that the many friends of Agrippa would have prevented him from preaching openly if not actually delivering him back to the king.

Thomas is reported to have gone to Parthia, and then as far as India.

Bartholomew is also said to have journeyed to India and Parthia, later settling in Armenia.

Andrew also reportedly journeyed to the Black Sea region and preached among several cities along the coast.

Philip preached among several Greek cities, and I will mention later a legend that comes from Hierapolis.

Simon the Zealot went to Gaul and the British Isles. I will report soon on what I know.

Thaddeus reportedly returned to settle in Edessa, a small state approaching Armenia some 600 miles north of Jerusalem. I say "returned" because there is a widely-circulated story that during his ministry, Jesus had received a letter from Abgar, the king of Edessa, stating that he was dying of a seemingly incurable disease, and imploring Jesus to come heal him. Jesus, the story goes, sent Thaddeus to cure the king, who gratefully became a Christian along with all his nobles. That there is a strong Christian community there today would seem to confirm the story.

Despite the lack of details about the early whereabouts of the apostles, there is also absence of an equally important piece of information. That is, there is no written source nor oral tradition nor even hearsay that any of the original apostles ever rejected Jesus or retreated from his mission. Equally noteworthy is that The Way, a term falling into disuse by now, did not shrink or shrivel when Agrippa tried to slice its heart out in Jerusalem. In fact, new disciples came forth to fill the roles played by the dispersed original apostles. And not the least of them was another James, the elder brother of Jesus. A conservative orthodox Jew, he had at first chosen to refuse Jesus' invitation to join his ministry, or perhaps even to oppose it. Now he came forward in Jerusalem to become the leader and spokesman for the Christians. And perhaps because he was pious in observing traditional Jewish worship, he was a tolerable substitute to the authorities for the unpredictable Peter and James.

. . . .

. . . .

Just who was Tiberius Claudius Cæsar Augustus Germanicus? When his first volumes of ancient Roman history were published during the time of Tiberius, there were nods of praise among the literary noblesse and even gasps of bemused surprise within the Julio-Claudian family. But they weren't enough to keep his mother and her household from scolding Claudius for his stammering and twitching. Claudius scarcely helped his own cause when he gave the first reading of his works to a large audience. No sooner had he begun when a fat man's bench broke beneath him and sent him sprawling on the floor. The house erupted with laughter — including Claudius. In fact, he would scarcely resume his reading when he would spot the rearranged fat man out of the corner of his eye and lose himself in a wave of giggles.

But as emperor, a much different man soon emerged for all to see.

Claudius was born in the twentieth year of Augustus' reign. As I have already said, his mother was Antonia, the daughter of Marcus Antonius. His father was the great general Drusus, who was six months in the womb of his mother Livia when the young emperor Augustus prevailed on her to leave her first husband. Born in Lugdunum in a military camp, Claudius lost his father while still an infant. Raised by his mother in the household of Augustus, it was clear from a very early age that Claudius was not the physical equal of his handsome brother Germanicus or his sister Livilla. People have described all sorts of maladies that plagued him all through his life: stammering, a wobbly head, a nervous twitching of the face, drooling, bloodshot eyes, a lame gait and so forth. However, based on what I have heard from those who have personally observed Claudius, I would venture that all these things were caused by some sort of weakness or paralysis that infested some of the muscles in his body at a very early age.

His mother doesn't seem to have been very sympathetic to his plight, however. She would deride his stammering and refer to him among friends as a "human that nature had begun to create but failed to complete." Augustus seems to have borne this family embarrassment with good grace, but remained perplexed as to what tasks or career the lad might be fit for. As Claudius approached the age where a young man of the emperor's household could be expected to dedicate his first games or otherwise be introduced to patrician society, Augustus penned a long note to his wife Livia after having conferred with Tiberius (then his chief advisor). The games of Mars were coming up and it would have been logical for the young Claudius to have played a role in their dedication ceremonies.

Now we are both agreed that we must decide once and for all what plan we are to adopt in his case. For if he is sound and, to say, complete, what reason have we for doubting that he ought to be advanced through the same grades and steps as his brother? But if we realize that he is wanting and defective in soundness of body and mind, we must not furnish the means of ridiculing both him and us to a public which is wont to scoff at and deride such things. Surely we will always be in a stew if we deliberate about each separate occasion and do not make up our minds in advance as to whether we think he can hold public offices or not.

However, as to the matters about which you ask my present advice, I do not object to his having charge of the banquet of the priests at the games of Mars if he will allow himself to be advised by his kinsman, the son of Silvanus, so as not to do anything to make himself conspicuous or ridiculous. That he should view the games in the Circus from the Imperial box does not meet with my approval, for he will be conspicuous if exposed to full view in the front of the auditorium.

I am also opposed to his going to the Alban Mount or being in Rome during the days of the Latin festival. For, why should he not be made prefect of the city if he is able to attend his brother to the Mount? You have my views, my dear Livia, to wit that I desire that something be decided once and for all the whole matter to save us from constantly wavering between hope and fear...[4]

There is no doubt how Augustus eventually decided, because Claudius gained no more than the sacerdotal duty of Augur during his reign and was included only among many lesser and non-family heirs in the emperor's will. But Augustus had not forgotten him completely. I am sure it was at the emperor's urging that the famous historian Livy took a special interest in the bookish, introverted youth and encouraged him to pursue a life of learning.

When Tiberius took the throne, Claudius, then 24, pleaded with him for a Senate appointment. All he received in reply was 40 gold pieces and a note expressing the emperor's best wishes that he enjoy himself at the upcoming Saturnalia.

With that, Claudius abandoned all hope of a public career and retreated to a life of obscurity, much of it spent at his small, plain villa in Campania. But was it bad luck or providence? For it was largely there that Claudius began to take the advice of Livy seriously and demonstrate to anyone who was not himself a fool that his infirmities were merely physical. Claudius composed a history of the reign of Augustus, 20 volumes of Etruscan history and eight of Carthaginian history — all in Greek. His other works ranged widely, as for example, a pamphlet in defense of Cicero, a treatise on gambling with dice and an essay on why three new letters should be added to the Latin language.

When his "quiet" years ended, Claudius probably wished by then that they hadn't, because from the moment Gaius summoned him back as consul, his life was made miserable by the emperor's cruel practical jokes. And it was frequently endangered by the ruler's wrath. In just one of many precarious occasions, Claudius had accompanied the entourage of senators that journeyed out of Rome to greet the emperor on his return from Germany. Having already made up his mind that he loathed the sight of all senators, Gaius unleashed a torrent of abuse on his uncle for having accompanied them — as if he, the emperor, "were a child in need of a guardian." With that he reportedly had Claudius tossed roughly into a rocky riverbed, clothes and all.

But Claudius also had a taste of public adulation as well. Having accompanied Caligula frequently or hosted games in his absence, Claudius had also grown accustomed to hearing crowds roar "Success to the Emperor's uncle" or "All hail to the brother of Germanicus!" Thus, buttressed by knowing every corner of the imperial household and by having acquired his deep knowledge of Roman history and decorum, Claudius at age 51 was as well prepared to assume the role of world ruler as could be expected of anyone.

Just as anything about an emperor becomes magnified, so were the other good qualities of Claudius as he settled into his throne. He was tall of stature and full of frame, with a lively countenance and handsome grey hair. He had a certain imperial majesty about him, and would always rise to a dignified attention when approached by an official visitor. His health, despite the infirmities just discussed, remained excellent throughout his adulthood.

I might add that the infirmities — or perhaps "unappealing mannerisms" would be a better way to put it — didn't seem to slow down his lifelong chase of women. Nor apparently their interest in him. Before he became emperor,

Claudius had been married and divorced twice (and this doesn't count a be-trothal in which the bride had taken ill and died on the eve of the wedding). In the year before he became emperor, Claudius had already been married again for a year to a woman of only 20. Valeria Messalina was the fetching daughter of a cousin and the grand-niece of Augustus. For the first time in memory, Rome had an empress. When she wasn't vying to be the most admired and bejeweled woman in Rome, Messalina found time to bear the emperor two children: a daughter Octavia and son named Germanicus.

At the same time, Rome also began to know some unexpected shortcomings in their new emperor. One of them was an ever-present appetite and a pre-dictable penchant for imbibing too much at banquets and falling asleep. Unex-plainedly, he who had been bullied by a madman soon acquired a taste for the bloodshed and tortures inflicted on others in games and gladiatorial shows. And he often exhibited a temper that certainly had been dormant or well-concealed during his "previous life."

Over the years I have learned to pay special attention to the first official acts of an emperor because they usually provide great insight into his character and the nature of government to follow. They also serve as indicators of his special interests or problems he feels passionate about solving. Claudius began by de-creeing that the events of the two days when the Senate vacillated between ac-cepting or fighting him would be "forever forgotten." Next, he had the Senate bestow divine honors on his grandmother Livia (Gaius had impishly refused) so that a chariot drawn by elephants would lead a procession into the Circus as had been done for Augustus. And carriages carrying images of his mother and father were to be led into the Circus on their respective birthdays. But as to his own dignity, Claudius quickly dismissed any notions of emperor worship as lu-dicrous. And he refrained from taking excessive honors, even refusing the title of Imperator.

As one might have predicted from his interest in history, Claudius reinstitut-ed many ancient religious rites that had been allowed to lapse from disuse, and he soon showed that his main day-to-day interests lay not so much in the Sen-ate or foreign affairs, but in presiding over imperial court cases. Whereas Caligula had found his judicial duties so boring as to all but abandon them, Claudius showed a zeal for both hearing cases and reforming the administra-tion of justice. Instead of having the traditional winter and summer seasons for courts, he made them continuous. He then took steps to speed up proceedings, to protect the weak and assure that every man had his say. This compassion ex-tended to the most lowly, as when Claudius learned that some landowners were abandoning their sick or decrepit slaves at the gate of the Asclepieum on Tiber Island. The emperor put an end to it by decreeing that all such slaves were to have their freedom instantly whether or not they got well.

In these early years Claudius would often be seen sitting well into the night judging an endless parade of cases, even to the point of neglecting an anniversary or dinner invitation. His attitude was probably best described by the word on the coins that were struck in his early years and which still circulate. Coins are wonderful mirrors of an emperor's philosophy because he is reduced to describing it in a single word or short phrase. In this case the coins read simply: *Perseverance*.

In short, Claudius was such a pleasant surprise in his first year that he had gone well beyond calming a fearful populace to earning its affection and respect. Thus, when rumors circulated that the emperor had been ambushed and killed on the way to Ostia, so many people rushed to the Senate with charges of "Murderers!" that the magistrates were forced to mount the rostra and pledge their lives that Claudius was alive and on his way to the city.

But Claudius also got an early taste or two of real danger, as I suppose stalks every ruler who ever lived. On one occasion a lone assassin was caught near his bed chamber in the middle of the night with a dagger in hand. On another night two members of the equestrian order were found lying in wait for the emperor as he prepared to exit the theater. And, worse by far, a brief civil war erupted when the governor of Dalmatia declared a rebellion. It was put down in five days, but the effect was to draw a cloak of security around a man who had begun his reign vowing to go about in public places as a man of the people. Soon, in what I suppose must invariably take place to shield the ruler of the world, people were routinely searched before entering the emperor's presence and only his personal staff was allowed to attend him at a dinner party.

Throughout his reign, the bedrock foundation of Claudius' strength and support was always the Prætorians and the army, the former because he paid them well and the latter because he was the son of the great Drusus and brother of the revered Germanicus. So it was natural that early on, Claudius sought to strengthen his bonds with the army by presiding over a successful military action. And looking around for a likely opportunity, none presented itself more clearly than the isles of Britain. Although its denizens were as elusive as they were savage, the paramount reason they had never been formally subjugated by Rome was that it hadn't been able to summon the resolve and resources to order a Roman army to cross an unruly sea and endure the discomfort of subduing a strange, shaggy lot who might prove unworthy subjects in the final analysis. Yet, Britain had been on the Roman agenda for quite awhile; Gaius had botched the job and it was time to get on with it. It was an especially apt venue for Claudius because he could look forward to marching through Germany and hearing the cheers of men who paid allegiance to his father and brother.

The expedition got off to a shaky start with a wind-battered sea crossing from

Ostia to Massilia in the southern shore of Gaul. But after that Claudius and the young Messalina enjoyed a flawless march through Europe and a smooth crossing to the rainy isle. His legions had already knifed into its southern and central parts. Now Claudius arrived for the decisive capture of the northern-most advance point, the town of Camulodunum, and his formal annexation of the new province of Britannia. Within four months the emperor and empress were back in Rome to receive a triumph of great splendor that no doubt would have provoked his predecessor to ungodly fits of jealousy.

. . . .

AFTER THE PREVIOUS PASSOVER, Herod Agrippa and his court decided to spend some time in Cæsarea. And it was while there that the king received news of Claudius' conquest of Britain and subsequent triumph. To show his respect and celebrate the occasion, Agrippa organized a festival of shows and games lasting several days.

The chief magistrates of the Phœnician cities of Sidon and Tyre no doubt thought that the happy event would be a good time to send a delegation to Agrippa to patch up some long-standing dispute. I don't know what it was except that it was said that the year's grain harvest was looking scanty and the two maritime cities depended on Agrippa's granaries for their bread and corn.

In any event, Agrippa was scheduled to address a crowd about the matter in the theater at the beginning of the festival's second day. As the royal entourage filed in to take their seats early that morning, the spectators were soon abuzz. They had seen that the king wore a resplendent garment made entirely of silver. As he moved through the aisles, the low angle of the sun sent ripples of reflected light through the theater while the points of the king's crown seemed to shoot out sparks of fire. When Agrippa stood to speak, people began to shout, "Oh look, it is not a man but a god." And orthodox Jews joined in with impious flattery. "Oh be merciful to us," one of them mocked. "For although we have but revered thee only as a man, we shall henceforth know thee as superior to mortal nature."

A strong tradition has it that as Agrippa stood waiting for the shouts to quiet down, an owl swooped in and settled on one of the ropes above his head that was used to pull an awning of shade over the royal box when the sun got over-head. In a sickening instant, the grandson of Herod the Great recalled the old German's prophesy that night when he was in chains and knew this was the bird he had nervously scanned the skies for ever since.

How can one hope to verify such stories? What history does confirm, at any rate, is that a severe pain began to stab at the king's stomach or chest. Instead of addressing the crowd, Herod clutched at his middle and turned to those in his party. "I, whom you are calling a god, am now commanded to be hurried away by death," he said, grimacing. "But I am bound to accept what Providence allots as it pleases God; for I have by no means lived ill, but in a splendid and happy manner."

With that the pain became more violent and the king was carried to the palace. Soon, those who had dressed in their finest for a celebration spectacle were wearing sackcloth and beseeching God for the king's recovery.

Inside the palace, as the stricken Agrippa lay in an upper chamber and looked down on people lying prostrate on the ground in prayer, he began weeping softly. After five days of no longer being able to bear the pain in his stomach and the foreboding he felt for the future of his people, Herod Agrippa gave up the ghost in the fifty-fourth year of his life.

The government decreed days of public lamentations, and I would like to tell you that this complex-yet-compassionate man was universally mourned. The truth is that it took but a few hours for the fragile coalition of support he had built to begin crumbling. The orthodox Jews who had taunted him as a pompous, walking idol were just as jubilant as the Hellenists who resented Jewish rule over their cities. Even in Cæsarea itself and nearby Sebaste, people put garlands on their heads and engaged in wild drinking and dancing to celebrate Agrippa's passing. Despite the fact that five Roman regiments were stationed in Cæsarea, many of their ranks joined a frenzied mob that stormed into the palace and carted off everything from statues to furniture. I believe that even the king's daughters were abused in the rampage.

But the price for a few days of wild abandon in some cities would be extracted from all of Palestine a millionfold in the years to come.

. . . .

ANTIOCH, 350 MILES NORTH OF JERUSALEM, was large and nonchalant enough to absorb whatever disputes erupted within its many ethnic enclaves. And if any group threatened to disrupt the usual busy hum of life in the Syrian capital, two Roman legions were on hand to change their minds. All this worked to the advantage of Paul and Barnabas in the more than two years they spent there.

Some think that because Antioch has become the empire's third largest city, it is also one of the oldest; but the Syrian capital is still 20 years short of marking its four hundredth anniversary. Founded by Seleucus, one of Alexander's generals, and named for his father Antiochus, the city became the western capital of the Seleucid empire for some 250 years. When Pompey conquered the region 20 years before the joint consulship of Antonius and Octavian, Syria became a province with Antioch as its capital. And it has been governed by a Roman legate since that time.

Thanks to Seleucus, Rome found itself in possession of a well-fortified city to mark its key line of defense against Parthia to the east. Seleucus first built a naval base in one of the Great Sea's finest harbors. Located near the mouth of the river Orontes, it was protected to the north by Mount Pierus, which rises 4,000 feet and offers impregnable fortifications.

Having secured the sea, Seleucus next built the city itself some 20 miles inland on a bend where the Orontes breaks out of the valley and begins to race down-hill to the sea. The city, which straddles the land trade route, was laid out as a square between the left bank of the river and the slopes of Mount Silpius to the east. To the north, the river valley, a lake and a plain assured a generous supply of grapes, olives, grain, fish and vegetables. Deep springs in a sacred grove five miles to the south provided much of the city's water supply.

To the west, the commercial and military highway led through Cilicia and across the province of Asia. To the east it reached all the way into Mesopotamia. And to the south lay granaries of Syria and Palestine.

Seleucus divided his new city into two parts: one for native Syrians and the other for his retired soldiers. Later Seleucidian emperors built other sections, including one on an island in the river connected to the mainland by several bridges. Rome in turn continued the expansion. Julius Cæsar added several public buildings, a theater, an amphitheater and an extraordinary aqueduct that brought water from a source 45 miles to the southeast. Owing to the gen-erosity of Herod the Great, the broad, colonnaded main market road was paved with marble. Augustus and Tiberius added more public buildings and statues, and Tiberius had been honored with a bronze statue that dominated the public square until just a few years ago.

It was to this vibrant, cosmopolitan city that the Jewish Christian leadership in Jerusalem had sent Barnabas. His apparent mission was to verify word that the fleeing followers of the martyred Stephen had coalesced there and had es-tablished a growing, enthusiastic group of Hellenistic adherents to Jesus. But no doubt Barnabas, the Jewish Cypriot, found himself somewhat flustered in try-ing to communicate effectively with persons who were attempting to fit into a movement rooted in Jewish customs and law.

So it was natural that Barnabas should think of Paul in nearby Tarsus. After all, Antioch was but a larger, more crowded version of Paul's native city and an even frothier stew pot of races and religions. Paul, almost as if in an apprentice-ship, had been living among and speaking Greek to a polyglot of people, yet all without abandoning his Pharisee's moral code or sharpness in debate. So when Barnabas sailed the brief trip to Tarsus and found Paul, no doubt hunched over while stitching some goatskins, I can imagine that there was no question in the mind of either man that the time had come for both to engage in an important new mission.

One can also envision the sites that Paul and Barnabas saw as they pulled into the commercial harbor and walked to the great city along the fast-flowing Orontes. Clustered about the center city, to be sure, were tenements as dense and dark as any in Rome. But the original core that had been laid out by Alexander's army engineers was splendidly spacious. Built much like the town plan of Alexandria in Egypt, Antioch employed the popular Hippodamian system of broad streets cutting one another at right angles. The two main colonnaded thoroughfares intersected at the town center. There stood the baths and theaters, which were no doubt the center of life for a people known for their enjoyment of music and stage plays. The baths alone would tell you this because inside were statues and reliefs of Apollo, Olympos, Scythes and other deities all playing the Antiochenes' favorite instrument, the flute.

Throughout the city the most frequent adornments were statues to Zeus, who had gradually absorbed the various local gods and who had been acclaimed with many titles. But set in profusion among them were temples and statues to Apollo, Isis, Demeter, Aphrodite, Artemis, Athena, Hermes and a dozen more. In fact, the most dominant single statue was one of Tyche, who represented the good fortune of Antioch. Seated on a rock representing Mount Silpius, the robed goddess wore a turreted crown representing the walls and gates of the city. At her feet was a youth representing the river Orontes.

Still, the one sight Barnabas would have observed more than other as they passed along the Orontes was the sacred Grove of Daphne. This large riverfront oasis of grass, tall trees and temple buildings commemorated the nymph whom Apollo had attempted to rape – unsuccessfully because Mother Earth had heard Daphne's pleas for help and had changed her at once into a laurel tree in order to protect her. From its leaves Apollo made a wreath for his head, thus originating our tradition of the laurel crown.

The Grove of Daphne began as both a public park and a sanctuary in which criminals, escaped slaves, debtors and others could not be seized within ten miles of its borders. But by the time Paul and Barnabas arrived, this "sanctuary" was known more for being dedicated to the pleasures of the flesh. Male and female prostitutes from all over the East thronged through the woods, paying a fixed portion of their earnings towards the upkeep of the temple and supporting buildings. It is much the same even today, judging from the way authors and playwrights use the term "Grove of Daphne" as a symbol for wicked places.

In many ways, Antioch represents all that raised hackles on the backs of conservative Romans like Cato the Elder. Whereas it's been said that Alexandria combined the vanity of the Greeks with the superstition of the Egyptians, the Antiochenes combined every vanity, every superstition and every sensual excess from all over the eastern world. And as Cato himself said, it wasn't the military might of the East that threatened to destroy Rome, but rather the exportation of its "luxury, languor and vice."

When Barnabas had first arrived alone for his one-man "inquiry" the year before he summoned Paul, he found that the Christians there already were led by dedicated disciples from places as diverse as his own native Cyprus. The records mention Lucius, a Cyrene, and Nicholaus, who was a native of Antioch and one of the seven who had served in Jerusalem with the martyred Stephen.

But there were others without Greek backgrounds. The early writings also mention Manæn (derived from the Hebrew name Menahem) who had been a childhood companion of Herod Antipas and probably came from a Jewish family of wealth. And there was Simeon Niger, who seems to have been a black immigrant from the western section of North Africa. In fact, there is a strong tradition that Simeon Niger was the same Simeon whom the Roman soldiers had pulled out of the crowd in Jerusalem a dozen years before and made to carry the cross of Jesus. The experience had caused him to become a believer, and now he had become a leader among the Christians.

An equally diverse group were in Antioch calling themselves Christians and growing in numbers. Surely the primary cause was the persecution of Stephen and the dispersion of his Hellenistic comrades. But since then some Jewish Christians had found themselves more comfortable in Antioch after the persecutions of Agrippa. And non-Jewish Christians felt the same because they no longer felt the watchful eye of temple authorities and smothering effects of Jewish temple ritual in their daily lives. And for much of this they could thank Peter, who, through his encounter with the family of the centurion Cornelius had affirmed that salvation through Jesus definitely included Gentiles.

But defining precisely *how* Gentiles were to behave was the question left to the Antioch church to sort out for itself. By the time Barnabas and Paul arrived, a dozen years after the crucifixion, the young church at Antioch was a mirror of roughly four schools of thought that had already evolved in Christian centers of population.

The first group was Jewish Christians who insisted on total adherence to Mosaic law. In fact, they came to be known as the "circumcision party." Providing them a reservoir of potential believers was the fact that Antioch at the time had the largest Jewish community in northern Syria, with as many as 40,000 people occupying the city's southwestern quarter. Thus, Jewish Christians could count on receiving at least a polite hearing in most synagogues because their message was steeped in Jewish tradition: the God of Abraham, Isaac and Jacob had fulfilled his promises to his chosen people by sending them a messiah, a fellow Jew, whom he had also raised from the dead.

A second group was comprised of Jewish Christians who did not insist on the painful circumcision ritual but who required non-Jewish converts to observe many of their traditional dietary and hygienic practices. Peter was best identified with this group, and so was James, the brother of Jesus, when he assumed leadership of the church in Jerusalem.

The third group was best represented by Paul of Tarsus. It spared Gentile converts from both circumcision and the observance of Jewish food laws. But neither did they require Jewish Christians to abandon any of their traditional practices.

The fourth and perhaps smallest group was the most radical. Identified with Hellenists such as Stephen, Philip and others of The Seven, these zealots for Christ saw no significance in observing any of the Jewish traditions. They regarded Judaism and Christianity as two distinct religions. Indeed, they believed that Christians could not breathe free in their new life unless liberated entirely from the beliefs and rites of those whose leaders had persecuted Jesus.

This is not to say that these groups formed altogether different sects and worshipped as separate entities. Although a house church in the Jewish quarter no doubt had a different complexion than one elsewhere, it would be more typical to find persons of all persuasions within one congregation as well as persons whose opinions were changing or still forming. After all, Christians everywhere were facing questions not always addressed by Jesus. How were they to provide for the poor? How much should they allot for widows? How much of their personal wealth should they share among the Christian community? Should one punish a Christian caught stealing? How long might it be before Christ returned to earth for the Judgment? In the meantime, should they postpone pending marriages or delay having children?

It was in this atmosphere that Paul labored for longer than two years. And I might add that in these years the writings always mention his name after that of the gentle Barnabas. For by now the fiery preacher of Damascus and Jerusalem had learned to become a teacher and reconciler as well. And soon he would be called upon to employ all of these qualities at once.

. . . .

A. D.   (J U L Y)   4 4 — 4 6

Whether Claudius ever experienced true contentment, I cannot say; but if there were such a time, it was probably in these early years of his reign. Certainly it was then that his energy and zeal for the task of governance was at their zenith. And because he spent so much of his time hearing court cases in full public view, lawyers, jurors and other Romans developed an easy familiarity with the emperor that hadn't existed with his predecessors.

Thus, a typical day might find Claudius holding forth at the tribunal while nibbling on an apple or chicken leg. Once when holding court in the Forum of Augustus his nose followed the aroma of a meal the priests were preparing in the Temple of Mars nearby. Soon the emperor had left the bench and joined the priests at their table while plaintiffs and defendants paced and muttered. When the emperor returned, he gazed down on the glowering barristers, then blurted out: "Well, now I ask you: who can do without a good snack now and then?"

Unsurprisingly, one might also find the chief magistrate dozing off at the bench during midday. So, the more Claudius nodded off in the early afternoon, the louder the clerks and lawyers would raise their voices to keep his attention.

Judicial observers also grew accustomed to imperial decisions that defied precedent or common wisdom. Although Claudius would not hesitate to condemn anyone convicted of deliberate murder or other heinous crimes to face wild beasts in the arena, the same man was adamant at protecting the unfortunate and usually willing to hear the appeals of those who had lost their cases before private judges. When a woman refused to recognize a young man as her son and heir despite convincing testimony, he ordered her to marry him, thus forcing her to admit the truth.

Familiarity often allowed contempt to flare up as well. When the emperor berated a lawyer for failing to produce a witness he had summoned, the barrister spat back: "He's dead! I think that's a lawful excuse, is it not?" One Roman knight, flabbergasted that Claudius would allow several well-known prostitutes to testify against him, hurled his stylus and tablets into the emperor's face and cut his cheek badly. Other lawyers would take such advantage of his good nature that they would grab onto the fringe of his robes as he left, begging him to stay for one more case.

The rest of the government was well run at this time. Although at the same time paying meticulous respect to the Senate in his rhetoric, Claudius tended to take things into his own hands or else recruit senators for various tasks as though they were his personal aides. At one point a leading senator declared acidly that Claudius had "taken the whole race of men under his personal care." And one might indeed think so, given the steady stream of edicts that poured forth. Once when I was perusing some of them in the Tabularium, I noted no fewer than 21 decrees in a single day. Among them was the following proclamation: "This year's vintage is unusually abundant, so everyone must [apply pitch to] his wine jars well." If that wasn't imperial enough for you, consider this manifesto, that the emperor finds, "Yew-juice is sovereign against snake-bite."

That Claudius could spend most of his days at court and even take four months off for a major military excursion was the result of the growing use of skilled freedmen in the conduct of government. Augustus had employed a few Greek or Hellenized ex-slaves to help with his correspondence. With Tiberius and his long stay on Capri, some of these freedmen assumed expanded duties, but their numbers were still limited. With the next emperor too engrossed in attaining deification to worry much about earthly affairs, more freedmen rose up to fill the breech of responsibility (but just as many were pruned by constant purges). Under Claudius, educated freedmen would eventually receive official titles and duties in the financial and foreign affairs areas. They would also amass great wealth and exercise, collectively, as much power as the Senate itself.

In the very first years of Claudius these administrative assistants were clearly organized and controlled by the emperor. And they were kept in check because Claudius also relied heavily on a few friends from the Senate to help him govern. Chief among them was none other than Lucius Vittelius, the same man who had served Tiberius ably as governor of Syria and whose experience in Jewish affairs would soon prove especially valuable.

All in all, I would surmise that Claudius at this time had good reason to feel confident and even content in the way he governed during these first years. But if he felt the same way with regard to his wife, he should not have. Sadly, the same 23-year-old empress who by day looked so regal in her husband's presence turned into an alleycat by night. Apparently Messalina couldn't wait for her husband to snore off in his bed before she would be up and prowling about for anyone else's. It's possible Claudius didn't know about any of this or that he was shielded from it, but sometimes cuckolds make themselves blind by their own hand. All I know is that before long, everyone else in Rome knew of Messalina's exploits to the point where even today her name is synonymous with the word *strumpet*. In fact, here is what the young satirist Juvenal had to say about her in a satire written this very year:

> Hear what Claudius had to put up with.
> The minute she heard him snoring,
> His wife — that whore empress — who dared to prefer the mattress
> Of a stews to her couch in the Palace, called for her hooded
> Night-cloak and hastened forth, alone or with a single
> Maid to attend her. Then, her black hair hidden
> Under an ash-blonde wig, she would make straight for her brothel
> With its odor of stale, warm bedclothes, its empty reserved cell.
> Here she would strip off, showing her golded nipples and the belly
> that once housed a prince of the blood.[5]

It was just about this time that word of Herod Agrippa's sudden death came from Cæsarea. Any worries that Claudius retained about Herod's growing military power must have been erased by a floodtide of memories: the two playing as boys in the household of Augustus, suffering together the torments of Tiberius and Gaius, and mustering all their wits to secure Claudius the grand prize when it could have been denied at any moment by a Prætorian's sword.

The same dispatch from Judea informed the emperor as to the infamous conduct of the people of Cæsarea and Sebaste. Now, with both grief and anger contending inside him, Claudius had to report both events to Herod Agrippa II. The king's 17-year-old son was living at the palace while completing his education. Out of loyalty and a sense of revenge, the emperor's first impulse was to send Agrippa the junior to Judea at once as successor to all his father's lands. But Vitellius, the former Syrian governor, and all of the emperor's freedmen urged against it on grounds that the people were far too quarrelsome and divided for an inexperienced lad to hold together in one nation. At last it was decided to send one Cuspius Fadus, a freedman and experienced administrator, as procurator over Agrippa's entire kingdom until the son reached maturity.

So Fadus departed by early fall with three primary orders. The first was to punish the citizens of Cæsarea and Sebaste for dishonoring the king's family and household. The second was that the five disobedient regiments in Cæsarea were to be transferred to bleak Pontus on the Black Sea and replaced with a like number from Antioch. Thirdly, Fadus was to remove the high priest's control over the vestments used in temple sacrifices. Once again, as in the dark days of Pontius Pilate, the ritual garments would be stored in the Roman Fortress of Antonia and the high priest would have to endure the humiliation of asking a garrison commander for permission to use them.

Claudius took a separate action as well. In previous weeks he had received several letters from Agrippa complaining about the icy, suspicious demeanor of Marcus and asking the emperor to send a new president of Syria. So out of respect for his companion's memory, he did just that, replacing Marcus with Cassius Longinus, whom the king had befriended in Rome.

Beyond that the emperor could only watch and wait.

. . . .

Extracting meek apologies from the magistrates of Cæsarea and Sebaste was perhaps the easiest of Fadus' tasks, for upon arrival in Palestine he encountered many tempests and troubles that had not been anticipated by any of his orders from the emperor. Virtually every town of any size again seethed with the old Hellenist-Jewish tensions, only this time with an added ingredient to stir in. The spring grain crop had been skimpy. Now, with no letup in sight to the drought, prophets and diviners were crossing the countryside predicting a great famine. This, of course, caused the wealthy to hoard and the poor to loot. It also gave impetus to brigands of common criminals, who hid themselves along the trade routes and preyed on travelers without discrimination.

If that wasn't enough, new crises flared up where Fadus hadn't even expected them. To the east, Parthia was again in a state of internal agitation as its grandees rose up against the durable but difficult king Artabanas. If the long-time king were permanently dislodged, who knows where else his emboldened successor might strike? Yet, the Jewish state hardly presented itself as a united and stable Roman buffer state. Fadus had scarcely arrived when the Jews of Perea, just east of Jerusalem, decided to make war on the chiefly Arabian city of Philadelphia, which lies on Perea's eastern border. Fadus, incensed that no one had bothered to consult the procurator about any disputes, arrested the leaders and had one of them executed.

No sooner was that trouble quelled when along came some "magician" named Theudas, persuading a horde of people from around Jerusalem to pack all their possessions and follow him to the river Jordan. It seems that Theudas had promised to part the river so they could walk across and into a new "promised land," which unfortunately, was already quite well settled by people who didn't think much of his plan. So just as the throng had departed toward the river, Fadus ordered a cavalry unit to ride into their midst, cutting down everyone within range of their flailing swords. Then they cut off the head of Theudas, brought it back to Jerusalem and displayed it on a spear tip to prevent any rumors that he had escaped and was leading another exodus.

Now one might not think that requiring some pieces of cloth to be given up would compare with the above challenges, but it was the one order Fadus worried most about carrying out. When it came time to receive the temple vestments from the high priest — for the Jews a most unpleasant ceremony in itself — the many other tensions afoot threatened to make this an explosive encounter.

To these I will add one more element. Shortly after Agrippa's death, Claudius had received and granted a petition from Agrippa's brother Herod, the one who ruled over the tiny state of Chalcis (near Antioch) that he be given authority over the temple — including its treasury and the right to name high priests.

Thus, when Fadus confronted the temple priests, he had behind him what the official records call a "great army" led by Longinus, the new governor. Arduous as their long march must have been, the show of Roman strength was clearly a wise move because it stifled any notions of armed rebellion. It also put the procurator in a position of strength to appear gracious in responding to what came next: a plea from the temple priests to let them send ambassadors to beg Cæsar that they be allowed to retain the vestments. To this Fadus acquiesced — but only when the ambassadors promised to leave their sons with him as hostages.

The embassy afforded Claudius two opportunities: displaying his mercy at absolutely no cost and strengthening the position of the young Agrippa II, who still lived in his household. After the ambassadors had stated their case (but after a year in all had passed), the emperor issued this decree:

> Upon the presentation of your ambassadors to me by Agrippa, my friend, whom I have brought up, and have now with me, and who is a person of very great piety, who are come to give me thanks for the care I have taken of your nation, and to entreat me, in an earnest and obliging manner, that they may have the holy vestments....I grant their request, as that excellent person Vitellius, who is very dear to me, has done before me [when he was governor of Syria]. And I have complied with your desire...because I would have everyone worship God according to the laws of their own country; and this I do because I shall highly gratify king Herod [of Chalcis] and Agrippa junior, whose sacred regards to me, and earnest good-will to you, I am well-acquainted with, and with whom I have the greatest friendship, and whom I highly esteem, and look on as persons of the best character.

> Now I have written of these affairs to Cuspius Fadus, my procurator... [6]

With some relief on the political front, Fadus and the Jews alike now found another kind of relief – an unexpected delivery of grain and money that helped feed the poor just as the famine reached its severest point. This good fortune came from Helena, the queen mother of Adiabene, a small but prosperous kingdom on the Parthian border. It is still known in the region as the place where one can see the remains of a great ark that delivered the Jewish prophet Noah from a great flood that was said to have enveloped the world in ancient days.

At any rate, Helena had become a Jewess many years before – not because of any ark relic but because she admired the Jewish religion – and her son, Izates, had declared himself as well upon becoming king. When Helena realized that Izates had been able to achieve a peaceful reign (she had feared his subjects might rebel against a Jewish king), she decided to go see the great temple in Jersusalem for the first time and offer thanks.

When Helena arrived and saw the desperate straits the people were in for wont of food, she sent some of her servants to Alexandria with money to buy a great quantity of corn. Others she sent to Cyprus to bring back cargoes of dried figs. When they had returned, she distributed all of this largesse to the poor. A few years later Helena had three large pillars erected some two miles outside Jerusalem to commemorate her activities there. But well before that she had already left a far greater memorial to herself through her life-saving generosity.

. . . .

WHEN THE CHRISTIAN COMMUNITY IN ANTIOCH learned of the worsening famine, they made great efforts to collect food and money for their brethren in Jerusalem. It would also be a chance to display their respect for the church headed by James (the Just, as he was now called) and perhaps demonstrate that their bonds in Jesus were stronger than the differences between Hellenistic and Jewish ways of worship.

It testifies to their growing respect in the Antiochene community that Barnabas and Paul were chosen to lead the delegation. There is no official record of who they met with in Jerusalem or what took place, but Paul makes an illuminating statement about it in a letter he wrote much later. Referring to the meeting with James the Just and the Jerusalem elders, he says "they shook hands with Barnabas and myself and agreed that as partners we would work among the Gentiles and they among the Jews. All they asked was that we should remember the needy in their group – the very thing I have worked to do."

Since no reference was made to Peter's presence, I'm sure he was still a fugitive from the temple authorities, yet at the same time probably the most active apostle to Jews outside of Judea.

Another symbol of the new accord is that Barnabas and Paul returned to Antioch with a new companion, John Mark, the young son of Mary, whose house Peter had gone to the night he escaped prison. Mark's presence was surely a symbol of the Jerusalem church's support and participation in what was unfolding in Antioch. And it may be that he was sent because he could offer vivid first-hand impressions of Jesus' life and death. It is said that when he was a boy he had followed Jesus and a few of his disciples into the Garden of Gethsemane on the night before the crucifixion. The story goes that when the soldiers rushed into the garden to grab the whole lot, the willowy lad left one of them clutching his cloak as he ran off clad only in his loincloth.

It would also seem that both churches were in agreement that it was time for the Antioch apostles to preach the gospel (or "good news") in communities quite beyond their present confines. Early writings state that "after much praying and fasting," it was decided to send Barnabas, Paul and Mark to begin that mission in Cyprus once winter had yielded to the spring sailing season. Having already collected money from members for the famine relief, they demonstrated the depths of their conviction by again reaching into their purses to provide the missionaries enough of a stipend to meet their travel expenses.

Cyprus was a logical choice for a first missionary effort. Its closest point lay just 70 miles east of Seleucia, the port city of Antioch. Measuring 140 by 160 miles, it was the largest island in the Mediterranean, and located equidistant between the busy Roman provinces of Asia and Syria. A Roman province itself, administered directly by the Senate, fertile Cyprus was valuable both for its agricultural and mining exports. In fact, it was the latter that spawned the rise of a large Jewish community there when Augustus leased the highly-productive copper mines of Cyprus to Herod the Great.

Barnabas was an equally logical choice as mission leader. Born in Cyprus, he surely had family and friends there ready to help the three travelers. Having lived in Jerusalem, he was personally acquainted with followers of the martyred Stephen who had fled to Cyprus and formed the beginnings of a Christian community there. Barnabas was known for his great heart and ideal temperament (his name means "Son of Encouragement") and must have been witness to Jesus' ministry. Indeed, many say that Barnabas was one of the candidates who were put forth when Matthias was elected to replace Judas Iscariot. Finally, he seems to have been the uncle of his new companion, John Mark.

And so, one spring morning one can picture elders of the Antioch churches escorting Barnabas, Paul and Mark in a barge down the Orontes to where it met the port city of Seleucia. There the three would have no trouble finding passage on one of the many 100-ton merchantmen that carried manufactured goods to Cyprus. Twice a week they would make the overnight run, returning to Syria with salt, fruit, wine, copper and other raw commodities.

The first stop in their overseas missionary career was the port of Salamis, the island's largest eastern city and a center for salt mining. There, one record says, "they proclaimed the word of God in the synagogues of the Jews," then worked their way southwestward along the coast toward Paphos, apparently without encountering any hostility. It would have been difficult not to have a cheery outlook during the Cypriot spring; the snow-capped mountains of the Troodos range loomed to the northeast and their slopes of pine forests radiated with the brilliant colors of wildflowers.

But cities are seldom tranquil, and such was the case when the three reached the population center of western Cyprus. Paphos is home to a cult of Aphrodite who worships a crude phallic cone rather than a sculpted statue. Then as now, I presume, the sanctuary was served by a priesthood that compelled young virgins to prostitute themselves to strangers after being persuaded that it is better to suffer the pain of defloration with a stranger than with one's bridegroom. Whatever the reason, the practice produced a fine income for priests and fine sport for the sailors and traders who called at the busy port. And shopkeepers did a brisk trade in silver amulets shaped like the Aphrodite phallus because they were said to ward off shipwrecks and other bad luck.

It was in this setting that the three missionaries were preaching when word came that Sergius Paulus would like to hear this message personally. Now Paphos was also the home of the Roman Senate's proconsul, and Sergius Paulus was known as a man of keen and curious intellect. He was anxious to test the wisdom of these Jewish travelers before his own resident intellectual, a seer and magician named Bar-Jesus. Known also in Greek as Elymas (or simply "Sage"), this member of the proconsul's court seemed to perform everything from interpreting the stars to performing magic tricks.

By now, it seems that Paul had assumed the role of preaching before large audiences. Not long after he had begun proclaiming the "good news" to this important Roman official and his entourage, Bar-Jesus could no longer stand either what he heard or the looming threat to his "dominion" — or both. He interrupted with a question, then again and again with this and that counterpoint. Paul's temper was never far from the surface anyway, and he soon had enough of this sleight-of-hand-and-mouth scoundrel who made his living doing tricks and whispering tips to those who sought the proconsul's favor.

"You son of the devil!" Paul shouted, wheeling on the surprised Bar-Jesus with a pointed finger. "You enemy of all righteousness, full of deceit and villainy, will you not stop making crooked the straight paths of the Lord?"

Looking squarely at the "Sage," he railed, "Now, behold, the hand of the Lord is upon you, and you shall be blind and unable to see the sun for a time." Immediately Bar-Jesus staggered about and cried out for someone to lead him by the hand, for he could no longer see.

Some say Paul made a believer of the proconsul right then — and perhaps many in his court. I wonder why Bar-Jesus himself wouldn't have become one, too, just as temporary blindness had convinced a young Jewish temple official while traveling to Damascus.

Whatever the case, the three seem to have concluded a successful stay in Paphos. It was now early summer when they decided to use the prevailing and pleasant "beam winds," as mariners call them, to sail 170 miles northwest to the mainland province of Pisidia. Passing by the main port of Antalya, the merchantman sailed on to the smaller harbor of Perga eight miles inland, where it probably had a load of timber to collect.

At a time of year when the heat in the lowlands was becoming stultifying and the marshes malarial, the three missionaries faced an arduous 95-mile climb up the Taurus mountains to their destination, the major commercial center of Pisidian Antioch. Moreover, they now traveled among people who were neither as Greek nor cosmopolitan nor friendly as the Cypriots. In this, the Pamphyian region of the province, the people were more indigenous than Greek, and their begrudging use of Greek for commerce was corrupted with barbarian slang. All too many of them roamed the mountains in bands, preying on travelers. Thus, I don't doubt that the missionaries would have done like most of us and joined a trade caravan. In return for greater protection, they would be required to take their turn standing watch at night with their swords at their sides and listening to camels groan, horses snort and men snore.

However, when this leg of the trip set out, it included only two missionaries. Early writings say simply that John Mark departed at Perga and took a ship back to his home in Jerusalem. I can't seem to find out why. Some say the young man became sick, or maybe just homesick. Some say he resented the fact that Paul had emerged as the leader and behaved in an overbearing way. I really can't say for certain except that Mark did not stop being an active Christian, as we will see later.

Several days later Paul and Barnabas emerged from their climb through mountain gorges and on to the high plains of central Anatolia. There they must have felt exhilaration at the cooler air, fertile fields and blue lakes that spread before them in the fullness of summer. Soon visible on a hill beyond was a town with the literal name "Antioch towards Pisidia." Founded by a Seleucid general (probably Antiochos 1) for his pensioned veterans, it became a Roman colony around 150 years later when Augustus offered it to settle his own legionary veterans. Situated on the East-West military highway, Pisidian Antioch was now a frontier town of more than 100,000 Romans, Greeks, nomads, Jews and native barbarians, guarded by mounted troops who rode out from its walls regularly to skirmish with the bandits who menaced the countryside.

As ever, Paul and Barnabas headed first to a synagogue. As a matter of fact, I think it would be useful to Gentile readers to describe the Jewish meeting house and what takes place therein, especially because the early writings describe in detail the first sermon Paul gave at Pisidian Antioch.

Synagogues are usually rectangular stone basilicas, with a row of columns running along each of three sides of the interior. Seats are ranged along the walls, with front rows for men and rear ones for women, or with a separate gallery for women. Against one of the shorter walls is an ark, or cabinet, containing sacred scrolls. At the opposite wall is a lectern. But worship isn't the synagogue's only purpose, for many such buildings are used for education of the young and community meetings. Some even have rooms for travelers like Paul and Barnabas.

The religious ceremony begins with the congregation reciting together a creed, commonly called the Shema, as set forth in their sacred books. The first sentence begins:

> Hear, O Israel: The Lord our God is one Lord; and you shall love the Lord your God with all your heart, and with all your soul, and with all your might.

Next, the ruler of the synagogue appoints someone to be the leader in a prayer consisting of 18 invocations and petitions. This being done, an attendant takes a scroll of the Law out of the ark and a few men from the congregation read in Hebrew the passages that were selected for the particular day. After the readings comes the sermon, which usually expands upon the passages that have just been read. However, it is also possible for any member to address the assembly upon the ruler's invitation.

On this Sabbath in Pisidian Antioch, the ruler of the synagogue turned to Paul and Barnabas and said, "Brethren, if you have any word of exhortation for the people, say it." Paul began with the same approach that he would use everywhere. He would quote ancient scripture by heart and relate how the word of the prophets had been fulfilled in the life and resurrection of Jesus Christ. After beginning thusly in Pisidian Antioch, he said:

> ...Before his [Jesus'] coming John had preached a baptism of repentance to all the people of Israel. And as John finished his course, he said, "What do you suppose that I am? I am not he. No, but after me one is coming, the sandals of whose feet I am not worthy to untie."
> Brethren, sons of the family of Abraham and those among you that fear God, to us has been sent the message of this salvation. For those who live in Jerusalem and their rulers, because they did not recognize him nor understand the utterances of the prophets which are read

every Sabbath, fulfilled those by condemning him. Though they could charge him with nothing deserving death, yet they asked Pilate to have him killed. And when they had fulfilled all that was written of him, they took him down from the tree and laid him in a tomb.

But God raised him from the dead; and for many days he appeared to those who came up with him from Galilee to Jerusalem, who are now witness to the people. And we bring you the good news that God promised to the fathers; this he has fulfilled to us their children by raising Jesus; as also it is written in the second psalm, "Thou art my Son, today I have begotten thee."

And as for the fact that he raised him from the dead, no more to return to corruption, he spoke in this way: "I will give you the holy and sure blessings of David."

Therefore, he says also in another psalm, "thou wilt not let thy Holy One see corruption."

For David, after he had saved the counsel of God in his own generation, fell asleep, and was laid with his fathers, and saw corruption; but he whom God raised up saw no corruption. Let it be known to you, therefore, brethren, that through this man forgiveness of sins is proclaimed to you, and by him everyone that believes is freed from everything from which you could not be freed by the law of Moses. Beware, therefore, lest there come upon you what is said in the prophets: "Behold, you scoffers, and wonder, and perish; for I do a deed in your days, a deed you will never believe, if one declares it unto you."[6]

This was an astonishing message indeed. This visitor was declaring that a new Law had been established and that it had freed not just Jews, but everyone who believed in the resurrection of Jesus, from the imprisonment of their sins.

People left the synagogue in a hubbub. A great many were already asking the elders to invite the newcomers back the following week. But some were so caught up by the message that they followed Paul and Barnabas right out of the building and declared themselves believers in this gospel.

When the two missionaries returned to the synagogue the next week it seemed as if the whole city had crowded inside to hear them — including Gentiles, women, children and slaves — because Paul and Barnabas had spent the previous days with everyone who would listen. To the synagogue elders, this kind of turnout was unprecedented, disruptive to their accustomed routine and even menacing in a way. But Paul did nothing to calm the consternation he saw in their eyes. Rather, he spoke out boldly to them, saying, "It was necessary that the word of God should be spoken first to you. But since you thrust it from you and judge yourselves unworthy of eternal life, behold, we turn to the Gentiles. For so the Lord has commanded us, saying 'I have set you to be a light for the Gentiles, that you may bring salvation to the uttermost parts of the earth.'"

When the Gentiles in the audience heard this, they cheered and some gave thanks to God. Afterwards, a great many followed Paul and Barnabas all over town, and as an early historian states: "The word of the Lord spread all over the region." The missionaries probably stayed on for several weeks to instruct their new followers. But by then the elders of the synagogue had been able to meet often and digest what all this would mean to themselves, the synagogue and the families it served. After all, Paul had offered scant advice on how this "new order" would be administered. Besides, the elders feared that accepting all these outsiders into the Jewish community would overwhelm their resources and shatter their sacred traditions. And for *them* to join a brand new "religion" would not just corrupt the law of their forefathers but pitch it into the trash heap altogether. So they stirred up opposition to the apostles and prevailed on the city magistrates to send them away.

It is written that the missionaries symbolically "shook off the dust from their feet" at the scolding elders as they departed the city walls. Yet, at the same time they were "filled with the Holy Spirit."

It was now autumn, I would judge, and the two walked another 110 miles to the east and the smaller city of Iconium. Although the chief city of the Lycaonian province, Iconium was still within the influence of the march larger Pisidian Antioch. Again, Paul and Barnabas began by addressing the synagogue, then stayed several weeks preaching to Jew and Gentile alike. But this time the opposition grew even more intense. A delegation of Jewish elders from Pisidian Antioch eventually arrived and were actually in the midst of inciting the local Jewish leaders to stone the two apostles when they were warned in time to pack their few things and move on.

This time, with the first winter winds now swirling, the undaunted itinerant preachers walked south along the military highway and stopped only 30 miles away at Lystra. Known only as a town where big city merchants came to buy grain for the winter, Lystra was still smaller than Iconium and had no Jewish community to speak of. Worse for two Greek-speaking preachers, its people spoke an even more fractured dialect than anywhere they'd been in Pisidia or Lycaonia.

One might think Paul and Barnabas quite justified if they had intended to hole up in this peaceful, out-of-the way place until winter passed, but all evidence points to the contrary. Lacking a synagogue, they seem to have gone straight to the local forum (or agora to these people) and began to proclaim the gospel to everyone within earshot.

Gradually, they became a familiar albeit curious sight in the marketplace. But one event changed all that. It seems that Paul was addressing a fairly skeptical crowd one day when he took note of a crippled man in their midst. This fellow had been unable to walk since birth and was well known to the locals because his family carried him about town. I imagine Paul had seen him often as well, because on that day he turned to the man in the middle of his sermon and said in a loud voice: "Stand up on your feet."

And with that the man sprang up and walked. The crowd was flabbergasted because they knew this was no fakery by some itinerant magician. Word spread all over town and people even began chanting, "The gods have come down to us in the likeness of men!" Soon they were calling Barnabas "Zeus" (because of the likeness, I suppose) and Paul "Hermes" because he had delivered the words that cured their townsman. Before long some people rushed up to where the missionaries were staying and announced that the priest from the old temple of Zeus that stands in front of the town was bringing oxen and garlands to the city gate and was about to sacrifice to them. Could they come quickly?

Well now, I rather think what was on the priest's mind was an ancient legend. It seems that one day Zeus and Hermes decided to visit Lycaonia disguised as humble travelers. After being scorned and turned away from the doors of rich and poor alike, they had come to the cottage of a poor elderly couple where they were gladly given some country wine and bread. The gods were grateful. But before they left they turned the old couple's hovel into a splendid temple of marble and gold. The husband and wife were turned into two immortal cypress trees that even today stand guard in front of the temple.

All the other Lycaonians who had spurned the gods were turned into frogs.

Perhaps if Paul and Barnabas had known the tale they would have had a good laugh over the whole thing. Instead the two rent their garments in anguish and rushed out to the city gate where a crowd had assembled. "Men, why are you doing this?" shouted the one they knew as Hermes. "We are also men like you. And we have brought you good news that you should turn from these vain practices to a living God who made the heaven and earth and the sea and all that is within them!"

Soon Paul was delivering a sermon on the temple steps. "In past generations God allowed all the nations to walk in their own ways," he said to the crowd. "Yet he did not leave himself without witness, for he did good and gave you from the heavens rains and fruitful seasons, satisfying your hearts with food and gladness."

Words like these gradually deflated their fervor, and the people went back to their homes. But not long after this affair another angry group of Jewish elders arrived in town from Pisidian Antioch and Iconium. This time, without asking permission from any authorities, they rushed to Paul in the marketplace and began pelting him with a hail of rocks, stones and curses. When he finally collapsed, bruised and bleeding, they thought him near death. So, since it was illegal to leave a corpse within the city walls, they dragged Paul outside the main gate and left him there. Then they fled because they feared that the civil authorities would arrest them.

Barnabas and the new disciples weren't far away. As soon as the persecutors had left, they rushed out and managed to pull Paul to his feet. As it was growing dark, they had no choice but to half-carry him back into the city where they spent the night putting salve on his wounds and praying for his recovery. The next day, though Paul was still badly bruised, they were fearful of staying any longer, so Barnabas got him upright and they made their way east. In what must have been the 50 most painful miles of Paul's life, they finally arrived at the even smaller town of Derbe. It was no more than a dull frontier village, but Derbe may have been an ideal place for a sick man to recuperate and spend the winter.

One might ask why Paul wouldn't have continued his journey as soon as possible. Just another 125 miles away was his home town of Tarsus, where he could have spent the winter snug in his parent's home or in the care of his many Christian brethren. But there is no evidence of it. And the only reason for that must be that Paul was determined to head right back where he came from as soon as winter ebbed and the icy roads were passable.

. . . .

. . . .

Having already imposed several striking judicial changes in his first two years, Claudius continued to press for measures against what he saw as the unbridled power of trial lawyers.

"The most readily purchasable commodity on the market is an advocate's treachery," was a common saying. An oft-cited victim was the distinguished knight, Samius, who had paid a leading advocate 400,000 sesterces to defend him against malicious charges. He fell on his sword after learning that his lawyer was in collusion with the other side.

Instances like this prompted cries for enforcement of a 250-year-old law forbidding the acceptance of money or gifts for legal services. Gaius Silius, the consul-designate (whom we will meet later in another context), recalled the ancient orators who had wanted no rewards for their eloquence other than fame. "What would otherwise be the finest of talents," he said, "is defiled by mercenary hire. If no one paid a fee for lawsuits, there would be less of them! As it is, feuds, charges, malevolence and slander are encouraged. For just as physical illness brings revenue to doctors, so a diseased legal system enriches advocates."

No sooner had the Senate applauded the speech when the lawyers came to Claudius in a body. Led by one Suillius, the same advocate who had double-crossed his client for 400,000 sesterces, they pleaded that attorneys, like anyone else, must earn a living, and that a wrongfully-injured person should not be deprived of finding the best advocate possible. More arguments flew at Claudius:

"Eloquence is not acquired for nothing."

"Other senators can make a living by military service or agriculture."

"No calling attracts candidates unless they can reckon its rewards in advance."

"Remove a profession's incentives and the profession perishes."

"It's easy for some senators, whose families were gorged by the spoils of previous wars, to act so high-minded today, but we are people of modest means who seek only peacetime incomes."

And on they went. Claudius did agree with some of their points but still decreed a limit on fees of 10,000 sesterces per case. Anyone charging more would be guilty of extortion, which could mean banishment or death. For good measure, the emperor added one edict easing the harsh treatment of debtors and another one forbidding minors to receive loans that were to be repaid after their fathers' deaths. The latter was an attempt to curb the nastiest of practices in which a shameless son could pay an equally despicable advocate to bring serious charges against his own father in hopes of plundering his assets.

Many other things embroiled Claudius in this very busy year. Much effort was expended to contain a flare-up in Parthia where the throne was contested by two brothers at the same time they were trying to conduct a war with Armenia. A German tribe, divided by civil war, petitioned Claudius to name them a king. Claudius himself prevailed on the Senate to establish a Board of Soothsayers so that "the oldest Italian art," as he called it, "will not die out through neglect" (and because many Romans were embracing foreign cults). Rome hosted the Secular Games to mark the eight hundredth year since its foundation. Claudius revived construction of an aqueduct that was to take 30,000 men 11 years of steady work, including tunneling a mountain. He began construction of a completely new harbor at Ostia so as to speed the off-loading of grain ships. He finished building the Vatican Circus (begun by Caligula) and gave games there featuring a wild beast baiting between every five races. He presided over a census of the empire, which counted 5,984,072 Roman citizens and their immediate families (with non-citizens numbering ten times that many, I would judge).

In the midst of all this activity, Claudius was carrying on what amounted to his most delicate and dangerous innovation: he assumed the long-vacated post of censor of the Senate and equestrian order. Many years ago the Senate itself had appointed one of its senior members to this position, who in turn assembled a panel of leading citizens to review the qualifications of the conscript fathers and knights. In the case of the 600 senators, it meant determining that each had property exceeding one million sesterces, was not engaged in merchant trades, was not "celibate" (had at least one son) and was of acceptable moral character. Knights were subjected to a lower standard for wealth (400,000 sesterces) and were not barred from engaging in business trades (because, I should add, they provided important financial support for many a senatorial family).

Claudius announced that he alone would conduct the lengthy review, and in the process opened himself to widespread charges that his judgments were inconsistent. In the case of one senator known widely for corruption and adultery, he merely admonished the man, adding, "Why should I want to know what mistress you keep?" Yet, in another case he censured (and even took away citizenship from) a high-born knight from Greece on grounds that he hadn't learned Latin. Another saw his name erased on the novel charge that he had left Italy without obtaining a leave of absence from the emperor.

Yet, I think cases like these were well in the minority. In fact, his critics fail to credit Claudius for devising a clever face-saving gesture for all who were "purged" for lack of qualification. He simply issued a single list for both those who resigned (for reasons of health or old age) and the others. Thus, the way was open for anyone to avoid humiliation by saying simply that he had decided to resign for whatever reason he wanted to give.

Why, you might ask, would Claudius, in the midst of so many other enterprises, take on the task of probing into the lives of some 3,000 leading men and harvesting only unpopularity in return? The lesser of two answers is that, after all the years without a censor, the rolls were indeed laden with the names of those who no longer qualified for their positions. The larger reason is the emperor's strong belief that the empire would be strengthened if certain non-Romans were chosen to replace those who were "erased" (from the rolls), as the proper term for it goes. Indeed, everyone from cultured Spaniards to long-haired tribesmen of northern Gaul could produce treaties showing that they were citizens of Rome and had the right to hold public office.

Well, the stream of rhetoric this prompted among the incumbent senators consumed an all-night debate no less intense than the one about restoring the republic after Gaius' death. I'll just give you some of the flavor from opponents (you can glean more if you wish from a weighty scroll on a shelf in the Tabularium):

> Italy is not so decayed that she cannot provide her own capital with a senate. In former times even peoples akin to us were content with a Roman senate of native Romans only; and the government of those days is a glorious memory.

> Is it not enough that Venetian and Insubrian Gauls have found their way into the Senate? Do we have to import foreigners in hordes, like gangs of prisoners, and leave no careers for our own surviving aristocracy?

> Every post will be absorbed by rich men whose grandfathers [ancestors] commanded hostile tribes, assailed our armies in battle and besieged the divine Julius Cæsar at Alesia.

Claudius calmly and politely let it all play out, then he rose with an oratory of his own that may be as important for succeeding generations as any he uttered. (I have paraphrased some of it, but not much):

> The experience of my own ancestors, notably of my family's Sabine founder Clausus, who was simultaneously made a Roman citizen and a patrician, encourages me to adopt the same national policy [of] bringing excellence to Rome from whatever source. For I do not forget that the Julii came from Alba Longa, the Coruncanii from Camerium, the Porcii from Tusculum. And, leaving antiquity aside, the men from Etruria, Lucania and all Italy have been admitted into the Senate; and that finally Italy herself has been extended to the Alps, uniting not merely individuals but whole territories and peoples under the name of Rome.

> Moreover, after the enfranchisement of Italy across the Po, our next step was to make citizens of the finest provincials, too. We added them to our ex-soldiers in settlements throughout the world, and by their means reinvigorated the exhausted empire. This helped to establish peace within the frontiers and successful relations with foreign powers. Their descendants are with us, and they love Rome as much as we do. What proved fatal to Sparta and Athens, for all their military strength, was their segregation of conquered subjects as aliens. Our founder Romulus, on the other hand, had the wisdom – more than once – to transform whole enemy peoples into Roman citizens within the course of a single day. Even some of our kings were foreign. Similarly, the admission to former office of the sons of slaves is not the novelty it is alleged to be. In early times it happened frequently.

> "The Senonian Gauls fought against us," it is objected. But did not Italians, Vulsci and Acqui as well? "The Gauls captured Rome," you say. But we also lost battles to our neighbors. Actually, a review of all these wars shows that the Gallic war took the shortest time of all. Since then, peace and loyalty have reigned unbroken. Now that they have assimilated our customs and culture and married into our families, let them bring in their gold and wealth rather than keep it to themselves.

> Senators, however ancient any institution seems, once upon a time it was new! First, plebeians joined patricians in office. Next, the Latins were added. Then came men from other Italian peoples. The innovation now proposed will, in its turn, one day be old. What we seek to justify today by precedents will itself become a precedent. [7]

This speech by Claudius stopped the opponents in their tracks. His proposals were approved, and before long the Ædui in Gaul were the first to be made eligible to enter the Senate.

Now then, one reason I have described in such detail so many matters of governance is that the sheer weight of them on Claudius may be the only way to explain how he could have been so naively oblivious to the outrageous events that happened under his nose in his own household.

Yes, Messalina again. At first, the nocturnal adventures of an over-sexed adolescent (for this is how she behaved) had no particular effect on governance. But soon, she was using freedmen and influential lovers to punish a rival or (as in one instance) force the suicide of a senator because she coveted his lavish gardens. In my opinion, the sexual adventures were no longer enough, so she found ways to combine them with the thrill of doing something dangerous.

Well, she certainly found it, because Messalina had soon snared none other than Gaius Silius in her web. Silius, the dynamic consul-designate who had campaigned against overzealous lawyers, was young, ambitious and conveniently with no wife or children. In fact, the intensity of his ambition may have been more than even Messalina bargained for. One day when the two were discussing the possibility of getting caught by Claudius, Silius mused aloud that perhaps impending peril can be met only by perilous action.

"Let's simply drop all pretense of concealment," he told the young empress. "Why do we have to wait until the emperor dies of old age? Besides, only innocent people can afford long-term plans. Flagrant guilt requires audacity. We already have accomplices who share our danger. I am without wife or child. I'm ready to marry and adopt Britannicus (whose name had been changed from Germanicus after the British campaign). Your power will remain undiminished."

What fired such zeal? It may have been that Gaius Silius already knew how brief life can be under emperors whose power is unchecked and behavior erratic. His own father had been forced to commit suicide by Tiberius and Sejanus merely because he had been one of Germanicus' most loyal generals. His mother had been banished and all but a small part of the family's property carved up by the government and the accusers. One might think Silius would have been able to lean on the loyalty of the emperor to one of his brother's closest friends, but perhaps he feared the power of Messalina more than her husband. It was as if Silius knew he was already snared in the spider's web and had found a way to bring his death before the spider could do it at her own pleasure.

Messalina, the daring and deceitful, had clearly met her match, for her lover's scheme filled her with both fear and excitement at once. It wasn't out of any love for Claudius, but from fear that a victorious Silius might discard her once he assumed the throne. Yet, the more she thought about it, the more inclined she was to accept the dare—if only for the exhilaration brought by its sheer audacity.

I have difficulty picturing what happened next, but it did, I assure you. Silius and Messalina waited until Claudius left for a brief trip to Ostia to supervise construction of its new harbor. He was especially interested in a bold project in which an "island" lighthouse would be formed in the middle of new harbor by sinking an enormous grain ship (one which had been used to bring a colossal obelisk from Egypt) and then filling it with a rock foundation for the pharos.

Once the emperor had gone, the oh-so-witty and pretty coterie that revolved about Messalina received invitations to witness her wedding to the consul-designate Gaius Silius at the palace of Claudius. I have no idea how they felt the affair could be secure amid the greatest gossip factory on earth, but on this autumn day Messalina donned the wedding veil and sacrificed to the gods. Then she and Silius were joined in formal marriage, blessed by a priest "for the purpose of bearing children." After that the happy couple hosted an obscenely lavish banquet, embraced on a couch in full view of all and spent the night as husband and wife.

It seems that the only ones outraged by all this were the emperor's household staff. They had turned their heads enough times when everyone from senators to mimes and dancers would slink in and out of Messalina's bedroom, but this was too much. Their worst fear was that the uxorious Claudius might rationalize it as an ill-advised but harmless caper because it had not affected government affairs. But from their perspective, they saw Messalina as a schemer who was capable of assassination – of the emperor *and* themselves.

They also knew that Claudius was pliable and that he was terrified of assassination rumors. If they could convince him of the enormity of the outrage, Messalina might be condemned and eliminated without trial. But would she then turn Claudius away from it by employing her well-known "little girl" act of fluttering eyelashes and trembling chin?

Soon a formal meeting was convened among the emperor's chef advisors in the palace. And here it is interesting to note that they all were freedmen: Callistus, once the secretary to Gaius Caligula and one of the confederates in his assassination; Pallas, who served as financial secretary, and Narcissus, now secretary-general and probably the man most relied upon by Claudius. Might they simply feign ignorance of the whole thing and secretly persuade Messalina to abandon Silius? No, this was too risky to themselves. Narcissus insisted in taking immediate action with no forewarning to Messalina, and eventually the others agreed that this was their only hope.

When Claudius sent word he was prolonging his stay in Ostia, Narcissus knew there was no other choice but to go there himself. Curiously, he sent the emperor's two favorite mistresses ahead to break the news – probably, I think, because their tearful descriptions would confirm to Claudius that everyone in the palace had witnessed the shameful spectacle.

Narcissus waited just long enough to expect that the emperor would have recovered from the news and be ready to take action. What he found was a man
still dazed and uncomprehending. Narcissus became blunt and unyielding. "I
am not prepared at this point to complain of Messalina's adulteries," he said,
"but are you aware that you have been *divorced*? Her wedding to Silius has been
witnessed by members of the Senate and army. The whole nation knows. Act
promptly or her new husband controls Rome!"

Claudius summoned what friends and advisors he could at Ostia, men such
as the commander of the Prætorian Guard, the prefect of the corn supply, and
his inseparable companion Vitellius. Gaius Turranius, the guard commander,
urged that Claudius first hasten to the Prætorian camp and secure the garrison
there. "Safety comes before vengeance," he cautioned.

"But, but, am I still emperor?" Claudius kept on stammering. "Is Silius still a
private citizen?"

The next day Messalina and Silius were still entertaining their friends in
what seems to have become a marathon marriage festival. The autumn
weather was mild and the "bride" was hosting a mock grape harvest on her
grounds. Presses were working and vats overflowing, surrounded by women
capering and sacrificing. Messalina, with hair flowing, was brandishing a Bac-
chic wand. Silius stood beside her dressed in ivy wreath and buskins. Around
them were besotted revelers. One of the guests heard something outside the
walls and climbed a tree. He peered to the west and called down that he saw "a
fearful storm over Ostia."

Whether it was simply a weather forecast or an ominous prophecy, I can't say.
But very soon after, messengers began rushing up to say that Claudius knew all
and was on his way back, bent on cruel revenge. With that everyone scurried in
all directions. Messalina took refuge in the Gardens of Luccullus, the same ones
she had contrived to wrest away from their former owner by treachery. Silius
retreated to the Forum, where he pretended to go about his business as though
nothing had happened.

Within hours, the Prætorians had rounded up nearly all of the participants save
Messalina. It seems that her only "contingency plan" was to flee into the house of
the Vestal Virgins for sanctuary. There she begged Vibidia, the senior priestess, to
seek the emperor's ear as Pontifix Maximus and beg his pardon. Failing that,
would she beg Claudius to see his wife face to face? At the very least, would she
prevail on Claudius to receive young Octavia and Britannicus in his embrace?

The chief priestess must have hesitated, or said only that she would consider
it, because the frantic Messalina now fled from the house, determined to intercept Claudius herself on his way from Ostia. Accompanied by just two female
attendants, she darted from villa to villa along the Ostian Way begging for a carriage and driver to take her. She was refused by all, both because they feared for

their own skins and because Messalina was universally detested for her monstrous misdeeds. Finally she was reduced to hoisting herself on the back of a cart used to haul garden refuse.

All was not going smoothly with Claudius, either. As his carriage with Vitellius and Narcissus lumbered along on the 25-mile journey, the occupants decided that the tribune in charge of the palace guard probably couldn't be trusted because the "festivities" had, after all, taken place under his nose. Thus, Narcissus prevailed on Claudius to make *him* commander for one day as the only way to save the emperor's life. More vexing to the freedman was how Claudius spent the whole return trip in his carriage with his emotions veering from outrage ("How wicked of her! How sinful!") to tearful reminisces of happier times and worries about raising motherless young children.

As they neared Rome, Claudius was startled to see a woman jump down from an approaching mule cart and come scampering towards his carriage. It was Messalina herself. Now she was running alongside and shouting his name between sobs. The carriage stopped and Messalina was on her knees weeping uncontrollably. "Oh please just listen to the mother of Octavia and Brittanicus," she begged. But she was quickly shouted down by Narcissus. Every time the tearful empress would gasp for breath to speak, the freedman would denounce her by spouting a lurid detail of the "wedding" feast and brandishing a document he had brought Claudius summarizing her evils. Angrily, he commanded the driver to push on.

As they neared the city, Claudius saw some servants holding his children's hands along the roadside, but Narcissus again ordered the driver to keep going. Then they spotted Vibidia, the senior Vestal Virgin, shouting sternly from the roadside that a wife should not be executed without being heard. Shouting back that Messalina would have a chance to clear herself, Narcissus waved her off with an admonition to "go and attend to your religious duties!"

Claudius merely sat in his carriage as if in shock. Next to him, the usually resourceful Vitellius, skillful and clever advisor to three emperors, slumped limply in his seat. Narcissus the freedman was clearly in charge.

As the carriage ascended to the Palatine neighborhood, Narcissus thought of a way to stiffen the emperor's spine. On one of the side streets leading to the palace, he ordered the carriage to stop in front of a villa with high, vine-covered walls. Narcissus commanded the servants inside to open the gates. As they drove through, the freedman announced to Claudius that this was none other than a house Messalina had bought and furnished for Gaius Silius. In this corner he pointed out a large statue of Silius' father, placed there in defiance of a Senate decree when he was condemned for treason. Then Narcissus led the emperor around the atrium where they saw statuary and heirlooms — even things Claudius had given Messalina — that had been taken there from his own palace.

Now Claudius had come to life again, sputtering and spouting threats. With that, Narcissus ordered the carriage hasten directly to the Prætorian camp. Once inside its gates Narcissus quickly assembled whatever men he could find there at attention. As to the reason for it, Claudius could only muster a short, stammering speech; he was both too angry and too embarrassed at not being able to prevent his own wife from causing the mess the guards were now having to clean up.

But Claudius didn't need much of a speech. His voice was drowned out by soldiers chanting that the offenders should be punished. All they wanted was his permission. Claudius gave it. And he didn't have too long to wait thereafter. The next commotion in the camp was that of Prætorians dragging Silius himself and some of his fellow revellers inside the gates and up onto a platform. Without asking for a trial or saying a word in his own defense, the handsome senator, now bound in chains, simply asked for a quick death. Now his supporters and wedding revelers were herded out in chains as well and pushed onto the platform. The last to be thrust among them was the palace tribune under whose auspices the festivities had been allowed to take place.

All remained silent except one. He was Mnester, the famous mime and ballet dancer, once the favorite partner in Gaius Caligula's perversions and now the playmate of Messalina. Tearing his clothes, he entreated Claudius by displaying lash marks on his back. The others, he pleaded, had defied the emperor for money or ambition. But surely Claudius would remember that it was *he* who had ordered him to attend Messalina — even having him flogged for refusing the first request!

What's this you say? Floggings? Let me explain, dear reader, because it illustrates the emperor's infernal naivety and/or absent-mindedness. Because of the young actor's seemingly inexhaustible supply of bedroom energy, Messalina had become obsessed with making Mnester her household pet. When he declined her offers, she actually went to Claudius with fluttering eyelashes and pleaded that the emperor command him to be her dancing coach (or something equally innocuous). Claudius complied, and when Mnester still dallied about it, she ordered him flogged and said it was on the emperor's orders.

In subsequent weeks when dinner party talk turned to the theater, someone invariably would ask Claudius why Mnester was not dancing. The emperor would always give a surprised double-take, wondering why *he* was being asked about Mnester. Eventually, his friends came to believe that Claudius really was ignorant of what was going on in the palace — behavior so salacious that it was even circulating among foreign kings and generals as evidence of Rome's vulnerability.

Now, at the Prætorian camp, Mnester displayed his scars to Claudius and shouted that he had been *compelled* to feed Messalina's passions in order to remain faithful to the emperor! And if Gaius Silius had become emperor, he — Mnester — would have been the first to die.

Claudius hesitated briefly — but all too long for Narcissus. The freedman took it as a sign the emperor was about to grant clemency, so he and the other advisors were at his ear again, whispering hotly that Claudius couldn't spare a ballet dancer after executing so many men of distinguished reputation. Besides, they said, the rogue had already committed so many perversities and crimes, who should care about having to prove that the latest ones were deliberate or not?

So Mnester's appeal was rejected, but his outburst emboldened others. A good-looking young knight asked for his life because he had never really made love to Messalina. He had been summoned to her bedroom one night, he said, but her wiles were so capricious that he was sent away for reasons he knew not. Appeal rejected.

Another knight begged that he should be spared because at the wedding night festivities (which must have been quite an orgy) he had only played the role of a female. Appeal rejected.

Now when Messalina had been left at the roadside, she returned to her Gardens of Luccullus and composed an appeal. Her letter alternated between fond reminisces, indignation at the charges leveled against her, and hope for the future of their "loving family." But it never had a chance to be sent. Claudius, back at the palace by evening and soothed by his dinner, ordered that "the poor woman" (as he phrased it) be brought to him the next day to defend herself. Clearly, thought Narcissus, the emperor's anger was cooling and his love returning. No doubt his memories of Messalina's considerable conjugal gifts would soon fill his mind as well. But now the stakes were too high. If Messalina were allowed to live, Narcissus clearly wouldn't — not after the way he had denounced the empress from the carriage that day.

With the dinner party in full swing and Claudius distracted by lively conversation, Narcissus quietly slipped away. He was still commander of the Guard for the day, after all. Ostensibly on the emperor's orders, Narcissus ordered a tribune and some staff officers to go to the Gardens of Lucullus. Meanwhile, he dispatched Euodus, an ex-slave, to run there quickly to prevent Messalina from escaping and to remain until the soldiers had carried out his command.

When Euodus arrived at the villa beside the gardens, he was apparently admitted easily on the thought that he might have a message from Claudius. There, Euodus was surprised to see Messalina weeping, her head in the lap of her mother, Domitia Lepida, one of Rome's foremost noblewomen. During the whole of her marriage to Claudius, Messalina had belittled and quarreled with her mother, but now the woman had been filled with pity and was, in fact, the only person to come to her daughter's comfort.

"Your life is finished," Domitia Lepida said softly, stroking her distraught daughter's hair. "All that remains is to make a decent end."

But Messalina still hadn't accepted her fate. She was still writhing about, churning over this and that possible way of appeal or escape when she heard the heavy knocks. Then she felt the force of the door breaking down and saw the soldiers storming in.

Only then did Messalina truly understand her position. Without further word, the mother calmly opened a drawer and offered her daughter a dagger. Messalina looked at it as though it were a serpent. She put it to her throat, but could not strike. Then she moved it to her breast, but her hand was as if frozen.

The soldiers watched her for a few silent seconds. In the next instant an officer ran her through.

Claudius was still at his dinner table when news came that Messalina had died. He did not even ask whether it was by her own hand or by whose. After an eerie pause, Claudius called for more wine and the conversation went on.

In the days that followed, the emperor exhibited no human feeling about the matter. No hatred. No remorse. No satisfaction. No distress. Not even a murmur when he saw little Octavia and Brittanicus dressed in mourning. Once at dinner he absent-mindedly asked where Messalina was, then caught himself and went on eating.

The Senate helped erase her memory from his by decreeing that Messalina's name and statues should be removed from all public and private sites. Narcissus was awarded an honorary quæstorship.

Claudius did say often that he had been unlucky in marriage and that he certainly didn't intend to fall into that trap again.

But he did. This time it *would* affect the course of government—and the world.

. . . .

WHEN PAUL AND BARNABAS finally left Derbe in early spring, they had managed to win believers and form a church even at this small junction on the Roman military highway. Healthy again, Paul no doubt was filled with renewed vigor and optimism.

And so, the two apostles decided to retrace their steps. They walked back along the same road to Lystra, Iconium and Pisidian Antioch. Incidentally, it is on the return trip to Iconium that someone penned the only written description of Paul I have ever encountered. It seems that a certain man named Onesiphorus, when he heard that the apostle was on his way, rushed out to the military highway with his wife and children in hopes of enticing him to stay with them.

For Titus had told him what manner of man Paul was in appearance; for he had not seen him in the flesh, but only in the spirit. And they went by the king's highway that leads from Lystra and stood expecting him, and looked upon them that came, according to the description of Titus. And they saw Paul coming, a man of little stature, thin-haired upon his head, crooked in the legs, of good state of body, with eyebrows joining, and nose somewhat hooked, full of grace; for sometimes he appeared like a man and sometimes he had the face of an angel.[8]

There is little doubt that Paul and Barnabas did accept the hospitality of their brethren, because it was their purpose to spend most of their time on these visits fortifying the congregations they had already established. This they did by leading worship services, appointing elders and attempting to answer the dozens of questions that believers would raise about how to conduct their daily affairs.

Why didn't the same opponents mobilize to drive out Paul and Barnabas as they had done before? One answer is that the number of believers in each city was not in the hundreds, but perhaps in the dozens. Yet, they could not have numbered much less than this because each church had elders, and elders usually corresponded to the 12 that had served Jesus. Absent any historical text to explain it, one might only surmise that the apostles stayed away from the synagogues this time and the Jewish elders no longer felt in danger of losing their flocks. This would indicate that the great majority of the new church members were Gentiles (or "God Fearers," as the Jews called them).

By the time the missionaries had finished nurturing their new churches in the highlands, it may have been early autumn when they made the twisting, arduous trek down to the low plains of Pisidia. To retrace their steps completely, they would have sailed again to Cyprus, but they decided to break new ground in Perga and Attalia, the principal cities on the Pisidian coastal plain.

Then it was time to leave. Again, Paul could have walked aboard a merchantman in Attalia and used the northwest winds of the season to cruise some 250 miles to Tarsus. Instead, the missionaries sailed some 60 miles past Paul's home city and into the Syrian port of Seleucia, which they had left a year-and-a-half before.

Once in nearby Antioch, one wonders who reported with the greater enthusiasm, the two missionaries or the Christian leaders at the Syrian capital. The latter could cite great progress in the numbers of believers and they were thrilled to know that their "investment" in the mission had planted churches in Asia Minor.

This euphoria, however, was broken not long afterward when a small delegation of Jewish Christians arrived from Jerusalem, all Pharisees, it would seem. Now I should say here that correspondence was continuous between the Christian communities at Jerusalem and Antioch, and I would surmise that it was a glowing report of Paul and Barnabas' success that had unnerved many of the brethren in the cradle of Christianity. The problem was the impression they had gained that most of the missionaries' converts in Cyprus, Pisidia and Lycaonia were not Jews, but Gentiles, and that scarcely any were circumcised or trained in Mosaic law. Worse, they continued to eat anything at all – and often in the company of Jews.

This will never do, said the Jewish Christians. It certainly will not, Paul retorted. Had it not been understood during his earlier visit to Jerusalem that *his* mission was to the Gentiles – that Peter and others would preach to the Jews? Did they not understand that being one in Christ left both groups free to practice their traditional customs when it came to temporal life?

All agreed civilly enough that another meeting of the church leadership was needed to settle the matter. Understandably, Paul and Barnabas were elected by the Antioch elders to state their case in Jerusalem, and off they went. I find it interesting that whereas the Antiochenes might have considered breaking relations with Jerusalem and forming their own branch of Christianity, they gave no thought to it. They, too, regarded Jerusalem as the "mother church." Many knew and loved James, Peter and the other Jewish apostles.

Jerusalem wasn't the only stop on this trip. The first writings show that Paul and Barnabas wound their way south through many towns of Phœnicia and Samaria, "reporting the conversion of the Gentiles and giving great joy to all the brethren." Nor was their greeting by the Jerusalem church in any way cool. The writings say that "they were welcomed by the church and the apostles and the elders, and they declared all that God had done with them."

But the purpose of the visit was, after all, a confrontation, and it was indeed the faction of Jewish Pharisees, these devout practitioners of Mosaic law, who began by expressing their surprise and serious concern at learning of all the untutored Gentiles who were now calling themselves Christians. I should point out that the Christian Pharisees were not necessarily a majority. Nor, it turns out, had they actually been sent to Antioch as official ambassadors of the Jerusalem church. But they were a group large enough to be named the circumcision party, and James the Just, who presided, apparently thought their concerns certainly justified the meeting.

The concerns of the Pharisees were not frivolous, either. Focusing first on the subject of circumcision, they could point to the fact that the custom had not begun on the order of a king or prophet; they could show that the Book of Genesis, the first of the ancient Torah, quotes the very words of God himself as demanding that every descendant of Abraham – including foreigners who become members of his household – practice circumcision "throughout your generations" as "an everlasting covenant."

Beyond this was the fact that circumcision was the Jewish mark of identity – a sign of Israel's election as God's people. Throughout history, pious Jews had faced death bravely rather than deny the necessity of circumcision. Moreover, Jesus was a Jew and any true follower should be glad to bear the same identification in order to signify his faith. To be sure, Gentiles were welcome in the church, but they must be circumcised and observe the Mosaic law.

Next to speak was none other than Peter. When I first read this I was astonished because there had been absolutely no word of him after escaping Agrippa's jail and disappearing that night to "another place." Well, I suppose one shouldn't be all that surprised, because it was now some six years later, Agrippa was dead, and the renewed presence of a Roman procurator could provide some protection against the impulses of Jewish kings and temple priests.

"Brethren," said Peter, rising,

> ...you know that in the early days God made choice among you, that by my mouth the Gentile should hear word of the gospel and believe. And God, who knows the heart, bore witness to them, giving them the holy spirit just as he did to us; and he made no distinction between us and them, but cleansed their hearts by faith.

> Now therefore, why do you make trial of God by putting a yoke on the neck of the disciples which neither our fathers nor we have been able to bear?

> But we believe that we shall be saved through the grace of the Lord Jesus, just as they will. [9]

Next it was the turn of Paul and Barnabas, and it was Paul, of course, who rose. Just as circumcision was a bedrock belief of the Pharisees, it was an enormous boulder in the path of missionaries to the Gentiles. When an eight-day-old infant undergoes this rite, we can only hope that his brief cries are the only pain he bears; but stop to consider what this procedure means to an adult male. In the first part, called *milah*, the rabbi uses a metal knife and cuts away the outer part of the foreskin. Next is the *periah*, in which the *mohel*, or expert circumciser, uses his thumb nail and index finger to tear the inner lining of the foreskin that has been left adhering to the gland. In the final step, the *mohel* takes the penis into his mouth and cleans the wound by sucking away the blood.

In an adult male the bleeding can be considerable, the pain intense and prolonged. Indeed, just as devout Jews believed that anyone who was not circumcised would delay the arrival of the messiah, Paul went as far as to say (no doubt only in moments of exasperation) that circumcision might well "cut you...off from Christ."

Nonetheless, there is no indication that Paul mentioned any of this in addressing the conference of church leaders. Trained as a Pharisee himself, he knew that his only hope of overcoming his antagonists lay in citing the Law as well. Nor would he want to sever the church's tie with the Judaism of Abraham and Moses.

In part, Paul's answer was that God's promise to Abraham preceded by centuries the giving of the Law to Moses. Therefore, the Law, which came later, could not annul that promise or replace *faith* as the basis of God's acceptance of men. The Pharisee Christians could point out that it was to Abraham whom God first gave the explicit command to circumcise both Jews and any foreigners who became members of their household. But Paul could counter that God, first of all, gave Abraham the *promise* and thus justified him on the basis of faith. Therefore, faith is more important than observing any particular rite.

Paul then turned to his second tenet. The coming of Christ had signaled the beginning of a new day in God's dealings with men. Yes, before this, all God's people were required to keep the Mosaic law. Now, with the messiah's arrival, the period for God's people to live under the law was at an end. The first and central requirement is faith in Christ. And where that is found, through this "new covenant," the believer is acceptable to God and will be forgiven and blessed by him.

But the Scripture, Paul argued, is not to be discarded. Indeed, it is full of promise and points to the day when the prophecies will be fulfilled and men will live under a new covenant.

When all had finished, they looked to James for the last word. Who would have thought that it was only in Jesus' final year that James began to accept the true nature of his brother? Now he had long since given up his home in Galilee and become the center or ballast of the young church in Jerusalem — all without giving up his rigid adherence to Mosaic Law or his allegiance to the temple. More than any others, his piety and personality bound together all the believers.

James rose. "Brethren, listen to me," he said. "Simeon [Peter] had related how God first visited the Gentiles, to take out of them a people for his name. And with this the words of the prophets agree, as it is written:

> After that I will return,
> And I will rebuild the dwelling of David, which has fallen;
> I will rebuild its ruins,
> And I will set it up,
> that the rest of men may seek the Lord,
> and all the Gentiles who are called by my name,
> says the Lord, who has made these things known from of old.[10]

"Therefore," continued James, "my judgment is that we should not trouble those of the Gentiles who turn to God, but should write to them to abstain from the pollutions of idols and from unchastity and from [eating] what is strangled, and from blood." For these are the words of Moses, he added, and have been read every Sabbath in the synogogues for many generations.

It would seem that all those present agreed with this course. To reinforce what had been said, a letter was composed and two "leading men." Judas called Barsabbas and Silas, were chosen to accompany Paul and Barnabas back to Antioch to read its contents aloud. Here is the letter they read upon arriving:

> The brethren, both the apostles and the elders, to the brethren of the Gentiles in Antioch and Syria and Cilicia, greeting.

> Since we have heard that some persons from us have troubled you with words, unsettling your minds, although we gave them no in-structions, it has seemed good to us in assembly to choose men and send them to you with our beloved Barnabas and Paul, men who have risked their lives for the sake of our Lord, Jesus Christ. We have there-fore sent Judas and Silas, who themselves will tell you the same things by word of mouth.

> For it has seemed good to the Holy Spirit and to us to lay upon you no greater burden than these necessary things: that you abstain from what has been sacrificed to idols and from blood and what is strangled, and from unchastity. If you keep yourselves from these, you will do well. Farewell.[11]

The Antiochenes were clearly jubilant, and Judas and Silas stayed there sever-al days to help reinforce this new spirit of unity. Now, for once, Jewish and Gen-tile Christians felt at much greater ease in each other's company.

In time, however, the Jerusalem accord inevitably produced more questions. Interestingly, maintaining "chastity" seems not to have been among them. One might have asked whether the phrase was intended to restrict sexual inter-course to marriage, whether it proscribed close relatives from marrying, or whether it simply meant for Christians to avoid the orgies that so often accom-pany cult rituals.

Most of the questions concerned dietary customs. Should Jewish Christians share in Gentile Christian foods such as pork? Should they even sit at the same table in which it is served? How could one be sure that the meat in a Gentile Christian's house church had not been sacrificed or strangled? Did James and the elders really intend for Christians to dine at the same table? Or were they to eat separately, each observing their own laws and customs?

In truth, I have no doubt that most Christians in Antioch managed to circumvent such indelicacies easily enough, just as we do today. If you are invited to someone's house for dinner and find a something you don't like on the table, you just do your best to overlook it (and the host is usually considerate enough not to rub your nose in it). But if the host knows in advance that custom bars you from certain foods, he usually has the courtesy not to offer it at all. Yet, such questions did linger in Antioch, and the most serious of these was whether Gentile and Jewish Christians should eat together in the first place. And what brought the matter to a head was no less than a visit by Peter.

I'm sure he had not planned it that way at all when he arrived in Antioch one day not too long after the Jerusalem meeting. It would seem that his intent was purely to promote well-being and reconciliation among Christians. But Peter was put to the test soon enough. He must have felt pressure from James (who continued his strict observance of Mosaic Law), because he declined to eat at the same table with his Gentile brethren. Paul was astonished at this — from the very man who had visited the family of Cornelius, the Roman centurion, and who had defended the Gentile cause in the meeting of church leaders. He was all the more incredulous when Barnabas voiced his agreement with Peter.

Paul overlooked his traveling companion for the moment: Peter had a higher ranking in the Jerusalem church. Paul, who writes that he rebuked Peter "to his face," did not cite the letter that had been read at Antioch, but stabbed right to the heart of the matter. If both Jew and Gentile can find salvation only in the grace of God through Christ, then Mosaic Law has no saving power for either party. Thus, it was not right for Peter to begin observing the Law again as though it was necessary to salvation. What is not necessary, said Paul, should not be made compulsory.

There is no record of what Peter said. In time, he probably relented, as we shall see later; but for the moment there was tension again in Antioch. And it hovered over the leaders there as they prepared to sponsor a second and more ambitious mission to the west. Paul was ready to go, of course. He would be expected to take Barnabas. Barnabas was willing and wanted to take John Mark again. But it was undoubtedly two points of friction — the "defection" of Mark from the last trip and the apparent unwillingness of Barnabas to share meals with Gentiles — that proved unreconcilable. Soon, Paul departed with Silas (the "ambassador" from Jerusalem) to visit his new churches in Pisidia and to cultivate new ground in cities further west. Barnabas took Mark with him and headed back to his native Cyprus.

· · · · · · · · ·

HERE IS AN IRONY: Rome, with its Tabularium and 26 public libraries, has an astoundingly sparse record of the formation of the Christian community in Rome itself. Yet, it is safe to say that in the Claudian years of which I now write, a body of God Fearers had already been here for perhaps ten years or so.

For their beginnings, one again must look for roots planted in Judaism. Jews were long settled in Babylonia and Alexandria before they ever arrived in Rome, except perhaps as traveling merchants. In fact, one of the earliest confirmations of their presence is a notice of their expulsion. Not quite 200 years before Claudius, a Senate transcript records a decree banning all Jews from Rome "because they were converting too many Italians to their customs."

Their ranks were thinned when Tiberius ordered another expulsion, but soon thereafter an estimated 20,000 to 40,000 Jews lived again in Rome. During the time of Claudius, their numbers continued to increase with immigrations of everyone from traders to storekeepers to craftsmen such as linen weavers and perfume makers. And as always, nearly all of the Jews lived in Trastevere, the crowded neighborhood where foreigners were confined on the other side of the river from the Forum and major public buildings.

The first Christians who weren't Roman citizens also lived in Trastevere. What made them become Christians? I can only offer the reasons that prevail today. They yearned for simpler truths. They were tired of and confused by having to pray to gods that were angry, capricious, demanding and served by greedy priesthoods. They were pulled toward a loving, forgiving God of all peoples who promised eternal life to all who simply believed in his goodness and asked for his grace. And nowhere on earth did the simple, understandable Christian code for daily living seem more refreshing than in this city of deceit, divorce, and depravity.

Yes, you ask, but who brought The Way to the gates of Rome? Maybe the centurion who met Paul later re-settled in Rome. Maybe some followers of Stephen came this far. Maybe some of the 500 who had seen the resurrected Jesus were Roman visitors. I haven't been able to discover just who, but I would be the first to agree that it would be logical to assume that it would take one of the great church leaders to win an audience in a city as cacophonous as this one.

Therefore I will repeat for you a legend that is believed by many, but which I cannot document. Do you remember my telling you of Simon the Magician, and how he encountered Peter laying his hands on the sick in Samaria, and how he offered Peter money to bestow on him the Holy Spirit? Peter rebuked him, but this Simon later did go to Rome. He performed many feats of magic here, and these must have included the curing of some illnesses, because some Romans declared him a god. Those who believe this point to a statue on Tiber Island which stands by the Asclepieum there. It is inscribed *Simoni Deo Sancto* and is said to be of Simon's likeness. (Others scoff that it is of a Sabine god, but let me finish the story.) When Peter learned that Simon had gone to Rome and was deified, he became concerned that he had done his wonders in the name of Jesus, so he came to Rome to expose the magician. While he was there, he preached the new gospel to the Jews and formed the first church.

In any event, Peter's first stay in Rome could not have been nearly as long as his second visit many years later. As to the veracity of this story, I ask simply: if Peter indeed perceived himself as the chief apostle to the Jews, why would he not have included Rome along with such other major Jewish population centers as Babylon and Alexandria?

Regardless of who was leading the first Christians in Rome, there is little doubt that their numbers were growing. As they did, they produced a two-fold effect on those around them. First, orthodox Jews felt threatened. They had no temple or strong priesthood as a source of strength. It was enough to attend their meeting houses in peace, retain their special privileges under Roman law and keep suspicious Gentile troublemakers at bay. Seeing some of their flock become Christians not only diluted their own ranks, but might threaten to make them a minority within their own religion.

Second, Romans were confused — that is, whenever they stopped to think about what was going on in Trastevere. To the average citizen, whatever happened in these synagogues or house churches was all part of a single religion that had its many sects and strange customs. What was one more sect? The chief concern of Roman leaders would be that any one "private" religion might experience great growth and become seditious to Rome or a threat to its state religions. Indeed, in Claudius, Rome had a scrupulous guardian of traditional rites. He was determined that Rome's heritage would not be allowed to be replaced by the beguiling ways of imported mystery cults.

To the delicate coalition of Jews, Jewish-Christians and Gentile Christians came word of the Jerusalem agreement about circumcision and dietary observance. It foretold of a new era ahead. Would the Christian sect now swell with Gentiles? Would Roman Jews lose their identity?

The Roman Jews looked to Jerusalem for guidance.

The Jews in Jersusalem looked back to Rome for the emperor's guidance.

The emperor would look to his new wife and freedmen for guidance.

. . . .

. . . .

T his was the period in which Claudius expelled the Jewish population from Rome. In the official histories of that year it does not even rank as one of the major events. And I personally doubt that Claudius himself, friend and protector of Judaism, had much to do with issuing the decree. In fact, its most lasting significance may be that it stands out as a milestone along Claudius' transition from active and sole emperor to collegial and passive ruler.

There is nothing to indicate that Claudius was ever again personally in charge of Rome from the day his freedman, Narcissus, took the reins of his carriage on the road from Ostia. For, after Messalina's death, Claudius would always seem dispirited and distracted, and his trio of chief freedmen would from then on appear uninhibited in their exercise of imperial power, as if they had seized it by necessity.

The death of Messalina, however, was not a sudden event in the growth of power among Narcissus, Pallas, Callistus and other palace freedmen. Although Claudius certainly dictated and controlled their actions in the early years, it seems inevitable that royal advisors, be they Egyptian viziers, Parthian satraps or Roman secretaries, tend to grow in importance because they sit so close to the center of power. Thus, while they may only "advise" the decision maker, they soon gain influence over who sees him and what advice he hears. In the case of Claudius, they eventually read his mail, summarize what was said according to their own perspective, compose answers for his approval or even simply go ahead and issue a directive in his name because they "just know" it is what he would wish.

People who want an imperial favor are willing to pay the messenger who delivers it – and even reward him with a portion of their earnings should their request result in, say, a shipbuilding contract or military command. Thus, Pallas, the financial secretary, was already known to have amassed a personal fortune of more than 400 million sesterces after just seven years of service to his emperor.

Proof of their power was that these freedmen could even choose another "emperor" – and with the approval of Claudius himself.

I will begin to explain this outrageous statement by recalling the emperor's vow never to marry again. Britannicus, now eight years old, was the only heir to the throne. His father was eating and drinking to the point of having to be carried off to bed almost every night. And so, it was not unreasonable for the emperor's advisors to ask themselves how long he would last. If Britannicus came to the throne, how would he deal with those who had been responsible for killing his mother? The solution lay in finding Claudius a new wife, a strong helpmate who could assist with the burdensome duties of governing the world, and, of course, someone who would retain the current corps of advisors.

Before long, the chief dinner conversation, after Claudius had been plied with enough wine, centered on the emperor's impoverished love life. Wasn't his majesty getting lonesome? Would he not welcome a beautiful companion? Certainly all Rome deserved it. Yea, the people were clamoring for it because they loved seeing their ruler in the company of a lovely empress!

Claudius, never one to see any virtue in an empty bed, backed down from his vow without much persuasion. Soon word was circulating that a "contest" of sorts was being held to find the most beautiful, well-bred woman in Rome to wed the emperor. After much political skirmishing, the finalists seemed to be three, each one of them, you will not be surprised to learn, championed by one of the three chief advisors.

Callistus, once Gaius' freedman, supported the middle-aged but still ravishing Lollia Paulina, who had once been wed to his former master. Being childless, argued Callistus, she would be an enthusiastic stepmother with no other children to impede her.

Narcissus supported Ælia Pætina, who had been married to Claudius a long time before, and who had already borne him a daughter. This, said Narcissus, would create no family disruptions because Pætina would cherish Britannicus and Octavia as though they were her very own.

Pallas championed the cause of Agrippina II, the daughter of Germanicus. She embodied the Julian-Claudian strain, and like Claudius, the prestige of the idolized Germanicus. Having first seen her mother and brothers exiled by Tiberius, and then having herself surviving exile by her brother Gaius, Agrippina was steeled to the harsh realities of governance. Indeed, you may remember that it was she whom Gaius had carted off to Germany with her lover Lepidus, then ordered to carry the murdered senator's bones back to Rome.

Agrippina was also as beautiful as any of the contenders. And having easy access to Claudius, it is said she had already given him opportunities to sample her favors. Finally, she was the widowed mother of a not unattractive 12-year-old son. His name was Lucius Domitius Ahenobarbus. He was known simply as Nero.

The big problem for Agrippina was one of public perception: she was Claudius' niece.

As the palace debate went on (with Claudius invariably agreeing with the last party to entreat him), the scales were gradually being tipped by a fourth influence. Lucius Vitellius, that venerable Claudian confidant, thought he saw a future emperor in Nero and enlisted himself in Agrippina's cause. Among her goals was to marry her son to Octavia, the daughter of Claudius, thus strengthening his succession chances over the young, shy and altogether flaccid Brittanicus.

Alas, Claudius had already promised his daughter to an outstanding young man, Lucius Junius Silanus Torquatus. What to do? Well, Vitellius now shared the position of censor with his friend Claudius. One day Silanus learned that his name had been erased from the Senate rolls. Something about a plot against the emperor, it was whispered. Well, an emperor can't have a plotter or disgraced senator marrying his daughter, so the engagement was broken off.

Next, the designing Vitellius asked Claudius if he would yield to a decree of the Senate regarding the subject of marriage. The emperor replied that he was a citizen himself and would bow to unanimity. Vitellius, bidding Claudius wait at the palace, hurried off to the Senate house, where he entered asking permission to speak "on a matter of highest national importance."

I rather think the assembled Senate had already been well-rehearsed for what was to come. Intoned the venerable Vitellius: "In his exceedingly arduous duties, which cover the whole world, the emperor needs support to enable him to provide for the public good without domestic worries. Could there be a more respectable comfort to our Censor – a stranger to dissipation or self-indulgence, law-abiding since earliest youth – than a wife, a partner in good and bad fortune alike, to whom he can confide his inmost thoughts, and his little children?"

Having heard a chorus of unanimous agreement, Vitellius then refined his request.

"We agree that the chosen lady must be aristocratic, capable of child-bearing, and virtuous," he intoned. "Such a person is Agrippina. She has demonstrated her fertility. Her morals are equally outstanding. For the emperor, who knows no man's wives but his own, her widowhood is welcome and providential. You have heard from your parents, indeed you yourselves have known of the abduction of men's wives at an emperor's whim. The respectable arrangement which I propose is strikingly different. We can create a precedent: the nation presents the emperor with a wife!

"Now marriage to a niece, it may be objected, is unfamiliar to us," Vitellius conceded. "Yet in other countries it is regular and lawful. Here, also, unions between cousins, long unknown, have become frequent in the course of time. Customs change as circumstances change, and this innovation, too, will take root."

Thus, Vitellius not only emerged with a Senate "edict" beseeching Claudius to marry, but a decree legalizing future marriages with a brother's daughter. A delegation of senators left for the palace to inform the emperor of their wishes, and a great effort was made along the way to whip up such huzzahs of support among the crowds in the Forum so that Claudius would be able to hear them from his portico on Palatine Hill.

It was not long after the wedding that Agrippina took charge of Claudius and the government. Lest this seem like a forceful one-woman cabal, I should say that there was immediate relief at having a decisive, sober, energetic person at the side of a man who had become as enigmatic as he was pliable. Before long virtually all of the freedmen and household staff had united behind her. Pallas, however, had the most to gain because at some point during the "empress contest" he had become her lover as well.

Agrippina moved quickly in three ways to consolidate her power. The first and easiest was to betroth her 12-year-old son to Octavia. The rejected Silanus made this easier by committing suicide on the wedding day of Claudius and Agrippina. Now a leading senator was persuaded by lavish promises of future office to propose a petition beseeching Claudius to betroth Octavia to Nero. Thus, her son became Claudius' son-in-law.

Now came a longer and more intricate project, the adoption of Nero as Claudius' eldest son, and of course, heir as well. First, to confirm the seriousness of her intent to groom Nero for rulership, Agrippina had recalled the philosopher Seneca from exile to take charge of his education. Because he was truly one of the most remarkable men in Roman history, and because you will read so much more about him in the pages to come, allow me to interrupt this account of Agrippina and Nero to introduce him properly.

Lucius Annauus Seneca, about 50 when recalled from banishment, was by birth a Spaniard of Cordova. His father, a knight, known as "The Orator," brought his wife and three infant sons to live in Rome during the time of Augustus. Seneca's father trained him in rhetoric and insisted he pursue a law career, but by age 20 the young man was already absorbed in philosophy. Although pushed by his father into the practice of advocacy and having also advanced in public service from quæstor to prætor, Seneca was devoted to the investigation of morality and virtue, and his essays on such subjects became well known in Rome. In the process, he became an admirer of Cynics and then an adherent of Stoicism.

In the first year of Claudius, Seneca's life took an abrupt change that presumably ended his public career, but which turned out to enhance his standing as philosopher, poet and playwright. The cause was Julia, another of Germanicus' daughters. It wasn't enough that Tiberius had murdered their mother, nor that Gaius banished the two remaining sisters to the bleak isle of Pontus. Julia, the sister of Agrippina, had scarcely been brought back under Claudius when Messalina perceived her as a rival and prevailed on the emperor to banish her again. The charge, by the reigning adulteress of all time, was adultery — all the stranger because Julia was recently widowed. Equally bizarre was that Seneca was named as her paramour. How can one know for sure? But the record also shows that Seneca was known to be devoted to Paulina, his wife of many years.

So off he went to the island of Corsica for eight years, with the faithful Paulina at his side. In a way it was like sentencing a rabbit to live in a cabbage patch. Living a simple, uncluttered life, Seneca contentedly devoted himself to scholarship and writing. In several essays later gathered into a book, *On Morals*, he elaborated the Stoic's view on such subjects as "Life and Death," "The Happy Life," "Clemency" and "Gratitude." Seneca also wrote some Greek-like tragedies reflecting his bitter view of politics and the man who would drive him to exile on such a flimsy excuse; but it was the well-reasoned treatises on living a virtuous life that seemed just right to Agrippina for nurturing a boy who was already beginning to demonstrate a vain and selfish nature.

In the beginning of the next year Nero's formal adoption was now hurried forward, with Pallas leading the charge. He urged Claudius to consider the national interest and furnish the boy Brittanicus with a protector and helpmate just as Agrippina had become the emperor's. After all, he pointed out, "the divine Augustus had advanced his stepsons at the same time he had grandsons; Tiberius adopted Germanicus, alhough he had children of his own. So Claudius should provide himself with a young future partner in his labors."

Thus, Claudius was prevailed on to go to the Senate and propose a formal adoption of the grandly-renamed Tiberius Claudius Nero Drusus Germanicus Cæsar — even though he would, in effect, be superseding the younger Brittanicus in rank. The Senate voted thanks to the emperor and historians noted that this was the first instance of an adoption in the patrician branch of the ancient Claudian family. And lest it appear to outsiders that Claudius had betrothed Octavia to her brother, he had his daughter adopted by another patrician family!

Now Agrippina was free to complete her third objective: the assurance that the new "proctorship" of Nero would reduce Brittanicus to a neglected nobody. She even went further, removing or putting to death all those who had been devoted to the boy's upbringing. Sosibus, who had been entrusted with his education, she slew on the pretext that he was plotting against Nero. After that she handed Brittanicus over to her staff in what one might call imprisonment without bonds. She would allow him neither to be with his father nor appear in public. As one observer wrote some years later, "No one was hard-hearted enough not to feel distressed at Brittanicus' fate. Gradually deprived of even his slaves' services, he saw through his stepmother's hypocrisy and treated her untimely intentions cynically. He is said to have been intelligent. This may be true, but it is a reputation which was never tested..."

With power thus consolidated, the combination of Agrippina and the freedmen were uncontested. Callistus had died that year of natural causes. But the secretary Narcissus and treasurer Pallas were given the insignia of quæstor and prætor. They had already amassed such wealth through their official positions that when Claudius once complained of the low state of his funds, one wag suggested that he would have enough and some to spare if he went into partnership with his two chief freedmen.

Still, it was Agrippina who now ruled above all. Shortly after the Senate approved the adoption of Nero, it bestowed on her the title of Augusta, which had been given only to Livia and Messalina. From then on hers became what one contemporary called a "rigorous, almost masculine despotism." In public, Agrippina was seen as austere and often arrogant. Her proper life was described as chaste, unless power was to be gained. For her all-consuming passion was to acquire money – the last remaining barrier to her sustained supremacy. She overlooked no possible source of revenue, either by paying court to wealthy persons in a position to help her or having executed those who stood in her way. Indeed, she even destroyed some of the foremost women out of jealousy.

Thus exited Lollia Paulina, one of her rivals in the "marriage contest" (and not to be confused with Seneca's wife) because she had been married to Gaius and was seen as the next candidate for Claudius should Agrippina falter. However, the formal charges against Lollia were quite different: association with Chaldean astrologers (who had been banned from Italy) and having consulted the statue of Apollo concerning Claudius' marriage. The emperor spoke often about Lollia's noble connections, but was persuaded that her designs constituted a national danger and said that her "potentialities for mischief must be eliminated."

Lollia was ordered to leave Italy after being shorn of all but 5 million sesterces of her vast property. But shortly after she left, a tribune of the Guard was sent to her new quarters and forced her to commit suicide. So icily efficient had Agrippina become in the execution of her perceived duties that she had Lollia Paulina's head brought to her to inspect. Not recognizing it at first, she wasn't convinced until she had calmly opened the mouth with her own hand and inspected the teeth, which, I suppose, had certain unique features.

Now then, why did I mention the expulsion of the Jews from Rome at the beginning and fail to explain it? The reason is my hope that the cause would become self-evident as I told of the transition from Claudius the emperor to Agrippina and the freedmen as de-facto joint rulers.

Beyond the brief decree itself, there is scant mention of the Jewish expulsion in the public records, which I take to mean that those in power wanted it to happen as quietly as possible (as if some 30,000 persons can be expected to tiptoe away). The records say simply that the decree was occasioned by "continuous disturbance at the instigation of Chrestus." Since the Christians were still perceived as a sect of Judaism, it suggests that they were made scapegoats in the conflict that was growing between Roman Jews and Roman Christians of Jewish and Gentile origin.

That they could be made convenient scapegoats there is certainly no doubt. One problem of the Christians' own making was that those who discussed the resurrection of Jesus in Greek used the term "Anastasis Christou." To most Greeks, *Anastasis* carries the connotation of "insurrection" as well as "resurrection." This suggested a Messianic uprising by revolutionaries, a concept difficult for Christians to explain away considering that they also used the term "Christ the King." Add to this their prophesy that all but Christians would be swept away in a final judgment, and one might not expect to be viewed with favor by a rival king who believes himself to be ruling in "The Eternal City."

Still, I believe that practical considerations were the greater reason for ousting the Jews and their "sects." That is, Agrippina and her allies saw an excellent opportunity to confiscate wealth and property. Their agents would make the rounds offering to buy up what they could cheaply from the majority of Jews who departed quickly. For those who stayed and tried to melt into Trastevere or the Subura (for neither Roman nor foreigner is required to carry official identification papers), rooting them out would depend on a cadre of professional informers who lived on their rewards.

And most knew they could garner the quickest payments from Agrippina and her freedmen.

. . . .

NEWS OF THE EXPULSION MUST HAVE puzzled the Jews in Palestine. Herod Agrippa II was still an honored guest in the household of Claudius – no doubt even learning at the hand of Seneca from time to time – and had just been favored with an extension of his future kingdom. As you may recall, Herod, the brother of Agrippa, had been granted the tiny kingdom of Chalcis and the right to nominate high priests. He had also married Agrippa's daughter Bernice and had two children by her. Now Herod departed this life and Claudius quickly awarded Chalcis to Agrippa II. His sister Bernice would in time become his consort and partner in ruling over the Jews.

The obvious explanation for the above is that the rulers of Rome (i.e., advisors to Claudius) saw the Jews of their city through one pair of eyes and the Jews of Palestine through another. The former was one of many convenient tools in helping a new regime establish a financial base. The latter were needed as a stable border ally against new commotions on their eastern flank.

Again, the Parthian succession was at stake. It seems that the reigning Gotarzes II was such a cruel despot that a delegation of desperate nobles came to Rome asking for help. Specifically, they wanted their young kinsman Meherdates, a hostage being educated in the imperial household with Agrippa, to lead them against the hated Gotarzes.

I find it ironic that the Parthians would come to the land of Tiberius, Sejanus, Gaius and Agrippina to seek relief from royal treachery. But there they were, appearing before a special session of the Senate, with Claudius presiding. Gotarzes "has exterminated his brothers and other near relations," their spokesman pled. "Now he is turning even upon pregnant women and small children. A slovenly administrator and unsuccessful commander, he plunges into brutality to disguise his inertia."

Every senator must have thought of Gaius and muffled a laugh in his toga.

"You and we have an old, officially inaugurated friendship," continued the delegation leader. "We, your allies, rival you in power but take second place out of respect. Now we need your help. That is why Parthian kings' sons are given you as hostages, so that if our rulers become distasteful, we can apply to the emperor and to the Senate and receive a monarch trained in your culture."

Claudius, assuming his most imperious posture, spoke of Roman might, recalling that both Augustus and Tiberius also had been asked to name a Parthian king. Turning to young Meherdates, who was at his side, the emperor urged the Romanized Parthian not to think of himself as an autocrat among slaves but as a guide of free men. After reminding everyone that kings must be endured however they behave (because continual changes are undesirable), he ordered Gaius Cassius Longinus, the governor of Syria, to conduct the prince to the bank of the Euphrates with sufficient troops to challenge for the throne.

Longinus, never a soldier, but a superb administrator, mobilized an escort that in a few weeks brought Meherdates and the Parthian dignitaries to the most convenient river crossing. There they met two allies in King Abgar v of Edessa (the son of the king who reportedly had been cured by the apostle Thaddeus) and King Izates of Asiabene (whose mother had rescued Jerusalem from famine). Longinus urged them on to Mesopotamia for a speedy showdown with Gotarzes.

But a familiar scene played again. Just as Vitellius, when Syrian governor, had left another would-be king at the Euphrates nearly 20 years before, this soft and self-indulgent young man allowed himself to parade through the countryside and be entertained by various nobles throughout Mesopotamia. At the time, Gotarzes' army was seriously undermanned; but the longer Metherdates dallied, the more his allies succumbed to bribery offers and joined the incumbent king. Then, just before the desertions became a floodtide, Meherdates decided he had to risk everything on one battle. The struggle was furious and undecisive until one of Meherdates' own vassal commanders treacherously captured him and delivered him in chains to Gotarzes.

When the king first saw the youth, he walked around him disdainfully and proclaimed that he was no Parthian royalty but an alien Roman. He allowed Meherdates to live as a demonstration of his clemency, but cut off his ears to remind everyone of Rome's humiliation.

Alas, all of this was of little avail to anyone because Gotarzes II fell ill and died not long afterward. His successor lived only a few months as well. The new ruler of Parthia was Vologeses I, who seemed to view Rome with rancor and his neighbors with a restless eye. We shall see more of him soon enough.

Meanwhile, Palestine itself was not exactly the rock of stability Rome and its governor of Syria had hoped. After the brief and fairly peaceful procuratorship of Tiberius Alexander, son of the well-known alabarch of Alexandria, it befell the lot of one Cumanus to become procurator just as passions were flaring again. No I won't bore you with the cause, because they were the same flash points as always: stifling taxes, absentee "Romanized" Jewish rulers, too many requisitions to feed the latest military excursion and too little left over to feed a family.

And as ever, a predictable setting was the Passover Feast in Jerusalem. Cumanus, newly arrived and forewarned of possible trouble, perhaps overreacted by ordering a Roman regiment to stand at attention in the temple cloisters ready to put down any sign of insurrection. All was going peacefully enough when, on the fourth day of the festival, someone in the crowd – or maybe boredom itself – must have provoked one of the young soldiers standing watch on the portico of the Fortress Antonia to the point where he lowered his breeches and waved his privy member at the multitude below.

Now those who saw it went into a furious rage, shouting that the Roman had insulted God in his own sanctuary. When reported to Cumanus, the procurator tried to calm their ardor and ask that they treat the incident as an isolated aberration. But when the vast crowd grew all the more agitated, the procurator abruptly changed his stance, ordering the whole army to don full armor and hasten to the Fortress of Antonia.

When the huge Passover throng, already more than the city was ever built to hold, saw the soldiers running in formation and in battle armor, they scattered in panic. But the exit passages were only so big, and as panic set in people began to trample and suffocate each other in the narrow passageways. It is said that some 20,000 perished, turning a supposedly glorious occasion into a mournful time of lamentation and weeping – and all because of a single soldier.

As (bad) luck would have it, a distinctly different calamity was unfolding at the same time. Stephanus, a servant of Claudius, was journeying to the Passover (perhaps with an imperial greeting to the high priest or a directive to Cumanus) when he was beaten and robbed by thugs as he traveled within view of the city gates. When word of this reached the procurator he ordered soldiers to ride out immediately and plunder the neighboring villages, presumably in search of booty from the robbery, and to bring the most eminent persons there-in to him in bonds.

Well, in the midst of their searching, which may have been more like pillaging, one of the soldiers seized a scroll of the Torah (the Law of Moses), and while shouting an invective of curses and insults, tore it to pieces in front of an astounded crowd. Thus, soon after the Passover was done and Cumanus had returned to Cæsarea, he was visited by a group of elders from the afflicted village. They wailed that they could not go on living knowing that he had not avenged the affront they had witnessed to God and his law. Knowing that word of the incident was spreading throughout Judea and that sedition was in the wind, the procurator ordered the offending soldier to appear before the delegation and had him beheaded on the spot. This quenched the flames for the moment, but not for long, as we shall see.

. . . .

PAUL'S ZEAL FOR HIS SECOND MISSION burned brighter than ever. As he set out with Silas on foot from Antioch, there is little doubt that he had already determined to spread the gospel across Asia Minor, Achaia, Italy, and then to Rome itself. For whatever his trials and setbacks, Paul could always visualize success.

The first stop, however, was a very familiar one. Paul finally had a chance to spend some time in his native Tarsus, giving encouragement to the very first churches he had created and doubtless reacquainting himself with his family as well. Then, just as soon as the melting snows of spring would allow, he and his new companion from Jerusalem would make the climb through the beautiful but treacherous Cilician Gates and down into the high Anatolian plains of Galatia.

Traversing this narrow pass through the 4,000-foot-high Taurus Mountains was no routine feat for well-equipped armies, let alone two middle-aged hikers. The same steep rocky north-south wagon road, in some places no more than 30 feet wide, had been the only way for the Hittites to conquer Syria a thousand years before. And some 700 years later Alexander the Great had skillfully led an army of more than 100,000 from the west on his way to defeating the Persians at Issus. Even in spring, if the snows had fully melted, Paul and Silas would have been constantly wet and cold, chilled to the bone by the darkness of the cliffs towering above them. Once they emerged onto the Anatolian plains, they still faced a 90-mile trek to their first destination in Pisidia.

Derbe again! How reassuring it must have been for Paul to be greeted so warmly by the Christians he had left behind just a year before in this small wayside. They, too, must have been reassured when Paul and Silas, as would be their custom when reaching all the new churches of Asia Minor, read the letter of accommodation about circumcision and dietary rules that had been circulated by James the Just after the meeting of Christian elders in Jerusalem.

Then it was on to Lystra. In the same town where Paul had been stoned and left for dead, they now found a thriving Christian community. There they stayed in the home of a Jewish-Christian widow and must have been extremely impressed with her son, Timothy, because they decided to take him on the rest of their journey. The only problem was that the young man's father was Greek and hadn't circumcised his son. Paul insisted that it be done; and when Timothy agreed he performed the procedure himself as a Jewish rabbi.

Circumcised? Wasn't it the right *not* to circumcise Gentiles that Paul had campaigned for so arduously? True, but Paul was also practical. Timothy's late father was apparently well-known enough as a Greek in Lystra and surrounding towns that having the lad at the apostles' side would have ruffled Jewish elders every time the missionaries appeared in a synagogue. Moreover, it may be that Timothy (who perhaps witnessed Paul's healing of the cripple the year before) himself insisted on circumcision to persuade Paul of his zeal as a Christian and worth as a traveling companion. Then one must also consider the nature of Paul himself. Having won the ideological struggle over circumcision, he could now afford to be magnanimous to the most stubborn of Jewish Christians.

The next logical path in the journey would have been through Asia and on to the populous regional capital of Ephesus, but the early histories say that the apostle found himself "forbidden by the Holy Spirit to speak the word in Asia." Some add that Paul had at one time suffered from malaria and was deterred by the prospect of being in that hot, coastal area during summertime.

Nor would the Spirit, Paul said, permit them to enter the cooler but more primitive and sparsely-settled Bithynia on the Black Sea coast. Thus, they traveled on steadily westward towards Mysia until they reached the port city of Alexander Troas.

Many Roman travelers know this place well because it lies near the ancient city of Troy, whose ruins so many of us visit and in whose agora we sit reciting Homer and his tales of the Trojan War. Founded by Alexander the Great, it was given the added name Troas (for the large plain that led up from the sea) to distinguish it from the Alexandria in Egypt. The city also sits in the shadow of Mount Ida, whose northwestern spur runs almost to the coast.

There in Alexandria the three Christians would have found themselves in the midst of tourists and their guides as they left to spend the day in Troy or a night on the sacred mountain. On its peak, where Homer says Zeus sat watching the war's changing fortunes, stood an enormous 200-foot pine on which names of tourists are carved going back a couple of centuries, I'm told.

Paul, who probably never made it through *The Iliad* with all its idols and conniving gods, was to find Alexander Troas important for another reason. It was there that a vision appeared to him at night. The writings say that "a man from Macedonia was standing beseeching him saying, 'Come over to Macedonia and help us.'"

Paul had no doubt of his destination from that point on. Macedonia, lying northwest across the Ægean Sea from Alexander Troas, was, of course, the home of Alexander and the hardy mountaineers who had conquered Greece before felling nearly every other empire to the east and south. But in midsummer, Paul's impatience to get started may have been tested by the forces of nature. The *Meltemis*, those fearsome hot winds from the north, were blowing as usual at this time and were not to be ignored by any ship captain contemplating a northwest passage. Their destination was Neapolis, a Macedonian port lying 100 miles dead into the eye of the prevailing winds. It meant tacking among some offshore islands for 160 miles in all. It also meant waiting until the winds abated somewhat.

I mention the above chiefly because it was probably at this point that the three Christian travelers linked up with a Macedonian physician named Luke. Alexander Troas was home to many Macedonians and a maritime crossroads for many more. Was Luke the Macedonian in Paul's vision? Did Paul, who suffered from his unknown chronic malady, welcome Luke also because he could help sustain his health by medicines or massages? Who can say? All that can be supposed is that Luke was converted by Paul in Alexander Troas and agreed to escort the missionaries to his native city and beyond. The reason for this conjecture is that Luke is the chief recorder of Paul's travels and it is from this point on that his reports stop referring to the missionaries as "they" and begin writing of "we." The writings also become more detailed, as if events were taken from a personal diary.

One can picture the ship passengers draining their last draughts of Trojan wine at their quayside inns and scurrying upstairs to get their belongings as their captain sent word that he was finally ready to sail. Once their ship was towed out of the harbor by a longboat, they would soon find themselves hunched over and holding fast on the tilted deck as the vessel hove up and down to the music of the *Meltemis* and salt water sprayed their faces. The captain would first make for the lee of Tenedos, a small island in which the Greek fleet once hid before surprising the Trojans with their invasion. From there it was on to Samothrace, where they most likely stopped to let some passengers off alongside its 5,000-foot mountain. For it would soon be August when Samothrace is host to the great festival of the Cabeiri, those mysterious fertility gods whose rites were secret to all but their initiates. Because seafarers also worshipped the Cabeiri as their protectors, the missionaries would have seen some of the sailors wearing purple sashes or amulets as their marks of initiation. And they probably found something else to do when the crew and many passengers kneeled in worship and burned incense in the Cabeiri shrine that was mounted on the ship's stern. Those who disembarked would journey to the deep valley where the Samothracian gods live and where incense fumes in front of the stone phalli that are their symbols.

After spending the night moored in the mountain's shadow, the ship passed by the lovely isle of Thasos, which marked the northernmost extent of the Ægean and which is famous for its marble, wine and nuts. Then it was on to the Macedonian coastline, with the sailors trimming the sail as gusts of wind came rolling off the nearby mountains. Soon the port of Neapolis was dead ahead, and directly south was the peak of Acte, which jutted into the sea and soared 6,000 feet.

The missionaries' destination was Philippi, eight miles from the port city and involving another of their many steep climbs. As the sweltering Neopolis receded behind them, they could see the foam of breaking waves below, and above, their first view of the ancient acropolis of Philippi with its fortified barracks. Founded nearly 500 years before by Philip of Macedon, Alexander's father, Philippi was certainly the regional capital and perhaps even "the first city of Macedonia," as it still calls itself. It was nearby that Octavian Augustus had met Brutus and Cassius and avenged the murder of his uncle Julius Cæsar. Although some would point out that Augustus was too ill for battle at the time and that the glory belongs to Antonius, my intent is not to rekindle an old argument among Romans but to explain the massive triumphal arch that adorns the main gate and through which the wide Via Egnatia begins winding all the way to Rome. It also explains the fortified barracks on the acropolis. Philippi's identity had been remade when Augustus chose it as a place to settle retired veterans and administer Roman provincial affairs. Roman in outlook and not too rooted in any provincial religions, Philippians are still noted as people who get along well with strangers and listen to new ideas.

As part of this different complexion from most Greek cities, Philippi had no synagogue. Since it takes ten Jewish men to form a *minyan,* or quorum to from a synagogue, one may assume there were not many Jews as well. Thus, the missionaries found themselves starting a prayer meeting of God-fearers by the side of the river Gangites. There, on the Sabbath, this small band of Jewish and Gentile converts would gather for the ritual washing of their hands before prayer and a reading of the Law and the prophets.

One of the members of this group was a widow named Lydia, who seems to have been a woman of some means. She came from the town of Thyatira, known for the quality of the purple dye it makes from the murex shellfish. We know it as the most luxurious of dyes, being used in everything from priestly vestments to senatorial togas. Thanks perhaps to the liberal views of this city towards the role of women, Lydia seems to have been the owner of both a prosperous business and a large home.

She was also a devout God-fearer, perhaps from an association with the active Jewish community of her hometown. Certainly she must have been one of the first to receive Paul's message unconditionally, because soon after having been baptized with her whole household she came to the four missionaries and said: "If you have judged me to be faithful to the Lord, come to my house and stay."

Thus, Lydia's home may have become the first house church in Achaia. All indications are that it was growing and prospering when Paul ("as usual," one could add) found himself in trouble with the authorities. This time he certainly did not instigate the trouble. One day he and his followers were going to their place of worship when they found themselves being followed by a slave girl, who kept chanting: "These men are servants of the Most High God, who proclaim to you the way of salvation." Following the girl at some distance and urging her on were two men.

Upon closer inspection, the missionaries determined that the men were the girl's owners and that they made their living promoting her powers of divination and charging people for her soothsayings. Obviously, divination's most respected ancestry is in Greece, where it dates back centuries to the first oracles of Delphi. Also obvious was that the girl's "keepers" had watched the Christians at worship and hoped that they would pay to hear some prophesies about their leaders.

Paul put up with harassment for several days, but enough was enough. Suddenly turning about-face, he addressed the spirit that ruled her. "I charge you in the name of Jesus Christ to come out of her," he commanded.

"And it came out that very hour," the diary records.

When Paul had walked on and the girl's owners finally recovered from the shock at what they'd witnessed, they realized that all they had left in place of their commercial asset was an ordinary housemaid. Now sputtering with anger, they rounded up a gang of sympathizers and went out to the riverside in search of the two foreign troublemakers. Later that day the local magistrates were already in the midst of hearing some routine cases in the city marketplace when suddenly there arrived a mob kicking along a pair of strangers. "These men are Jews and they are disturbing the city," charged one of the slave owners. Amidst much shouting and confusion, no doubt too noisy for anyone to hear Paul and Silas claiming their Roman citizenship, the magistrates had the apostles stripped to the waist and gave orders to beat them with rods.

"And when they had inflicted many blows upon them," Luke recorded, "they threw them into prison, charging the jailer to keep them safely." Taking this to mean that he might be flogged himself or even lose his life if they got away, the jailer put them in the inner prison and fastened their feet in stocks.

This was one of the three times Paul wrote about having been beaten with rods. Delivered to a man who still might not have fully healed from the previous year's stoning in Lystra, the pain and damage were doubtless even more intense than the usual punishment. Then having to sit upright in the stocks when his body begged to be stretched out and soothed must have been almost unbearable. Yet the history records that "about midnight Paul and Silas were praying and singing hymns to God, and the prisoners were listening to them..."

No doubt being in a thickly-walled stone building they had not felt the first tremors. Singing, they would not have heard what had already reached the ears of cats, dogs and birds in Philippi. Then the first wave of the earthquake hit the city. Soon the vibrations were shaking the building every few seconds. Then the whole jail rocked. Wood-beamed doorways groaned and many bars securing the cell doors from the outside tumbled to the ground. In the innermost cell, the two prisoners even found that the bolts holding their common chain had pulled out of the wall.

The jailer just outside the cell had been sleeping; and when he scrambled to his feet with a start, all was dark. He must have assumed the noise and trembling were the result of a mass escape. The prisoners were still probably too stunned to do or say anything; but hearing only silence and knowing the penalty for an escape, the jailer drew his sword and shouted that he was about to kill himself. Then came a voice from out of the darkness: "Don't harm yourself, for we are all here!" It was Paul.

The jailer called out for lamps to be lit. Then he entered the cell, and trembling with fear, fell down before Paul and Silas and asked, "Men, what must I do to be saved?"

I suspect the poor shaken wretch associated the earthquake with divine powers of his prisoners, just as some in town would explain it by insisting that the sea god, Poseidon, who dwelled on the sea bottom near Macedonia, would sometimes shatter rocks with his trident just to remind men of his power. But Paul talked to him of another God instead. "Believe in the Lord Jesus, and you will be saved, you and your household," he said. The jailer then took Paul and

Silas to his home in the middle of the night where he treated their wounds and gave them food. Then they preached the gospel to his family and baptized them all, probably with the same well water that was used to treat their sores. "And he rejoiced with all his household that he had believed in God," Luke recorded.

The next morning, as all of Philippi was staggering to its feet after the night's calamity, Lydia and other Christians probably went to the chief magistrates and told them they were about to be in big trouble for flogging and jailing two Roman citizens without trial. Paul and Silas apparently had been brought back to jail and bolted up again when some lictors arrived with an order. "The magistrates have sent us to let you go," they announced with official airs. "Now therefore come out and go in peace."

It would not be that easy. Paul, sensing he now had the upper hand, sent them back with a message of his own. "They have beaten us publicly, uncondemned men who are Roman citizens, and have thrown us into prison," he said. "And so now they cast us out secretly? No! Let them come themselves and take us out."

The subdued magistrates soon came in person to apologize and to free them. But they also begged the missionaries to leave town quickly because their safety couldn't be guaranteed if the mob got stirred up again. So the two went back to Lydia's house and called in the small congregation for a final meeting. Some say they left Luke behind for a good while to practice his profession in his home city and to help lead the small church, but I cannot verify it.

Autumn was coming on quickly as Paul, Silas and Timothy set out for the southwest on the Via Egnatia for what would be a 100-mile trip. They passed through Amphidpolis, once a bone of contention between Athens and Sparta, then Apollonia on the waters of Lake Bolhe. There seems to have been little missionary activity along the way, for their destination was a city that could influence the whole region. Thessalonica, named for the daughter of Philip, had become arguably the paramount city of Macedonia because the Via Egnitia crossed it and because it was the chief port for the northern inlets of the Ægean Sea. Southwest across its sheltered gulf lay the awe-inspiring peak of Mt. Olympus, nearly 10,000 feet high and covered with eternal snow. In that midst were the palaces of the gods, from which they maintained a dispassionate, bemused watch on the activities of the mortals below.

Thessalonica also had a large Jewish population, and Paul entered knowing, I'm sure, that a familiar scene would probably be played out again.

Why did Paul seek out such large cities? Why did he not head for the countryside, where people tend to hold simpler values and not make weapons out of their wit and cynicism as they do in big cities? First, Paul felt the power of his message and his ability to deliver it would withstand assault by anyone. Second, he felt an urgency to preach the gospel to as many as he could in the shortest possible time. It would appear that Paul went to smaller places only when ill, injured or fatigued — as if he felt the need to reach out to at least some people even when in need of rest or recuperation. As his later letters indicated, Jesus had fulfilled all of the ancient prophecies and had risen from the dead. His second coming was imminent and everyone should be forewarned to live each day as if it were the last before the final judgment.

Indeed, Paul had not relaxed or modified his message in any way when he again approached a synagogue in Thessalonica and asked to speak. This time he found the congregation receptive, and for three consecutive Sabbaths "he argued with them from the scriptures, explaining and proving that it was necessary for the Christ to suffer and to rise from the dead, and saying, 'This Jesus whom I proclaim to you is the Christ!'"

Some were persuaded and joined the missionaries immediately. They included "a great many of the devout Greeks and not a few of the leading women."

In the markets, Gentiles appeared receptive, too, although often not for the right reasons. That Thessalonica was a stronghold of Orphism serves to explain what could happen to Christian leaders in many cities with special cults. Orpheus, whose origins are shrouded in the distance of centuries, was the son of a Thracian king and one of the Muses. After sailing on the Argonaut he married the nymph Eurydice, who soon died from a snakebite. Orpheus took a lyre to Hades and so enchanted the underworld gods with his music that they allowed Eurydice to return to the world above. The only condition on Orpheus was that he not look back on his wife, who followed behind as they made their way up to the sunlight.

Naturally, he couldn't resist one look over his shoulder, so immediately Eurydice became a ghost and disappeared. Again devastated, Orpheus thereafter treated all women of Thrace with cruel contempt. Thus, at one of the Bacchanalian orgies held in Thrace, the women got their revenge: they tore Orpheus to pieces and flung them into the sea, whereupon they were collected by the Muses and buried at the foot of Mt. Olympus.

Today those who practice Orphism have a mystic ceremony in which they eat raw flesh and drink blood to symbolize the tearing of the young man to pieces. Somehow all this has evolved into a spring rite in which sin is expelled and the soul purified by the symbolic suffering and death of a god-man. During the year, believers lead an ascetic life, which includes wearing white garments, abstaining from all animal foods and avoiding attendance at births and deaths.

One can see why neither Jewish customs nor the story of the ressurection would be strange or uncomfortable to such persons. But this would only have dismayed Paul and Silas. Against these traditions they had to preach that Christianity was more than a club created to ensure the salvation of members who have been admitted by secret rites. Yes, they promised salvation, but none of them enjoined love and kindness towards one's neighbors. Only Christianity extended God's love and kindness to all!

And this takes us back to the synagogue where Paul was preaching. Once again, the elders of a Jewish meeting house could not live with the concept of an invitation open to just anyone. Now the missionaries were staying at a home of a man named Jason, who lived near the synagogue. The elders, "taking some of the wicked fellows of the rabble," as Luke reports, "gathered a crowd, set the city in an uproar, and attacked the house of Jason, seeking to bring them out to the people. And when they could not find them, they dragged Jason and some of the brethren before the city authorities, crying, 'These men who have turned the world upside down have come here, also, and Jason has received them. And they are acting against the decrees of Cæsar, saying that there is another king, this Jesus.'"

The rest isn't clear, but it seems that the authorities extracted some sort of stiff fine or security deposit from poor Jason that would be handed back only if the strangers were made to leave town. Thus, in another nighttime exit, the young Christian community in Thessalonica bid Paul and Silas farewell on the Via Egnatia. Timothy stayed behind for several days to offer the new church what assistance he could.

Walking another 70 miles to the west, the missionaries reached Berœa, a much smaller place in the foothills of Mt. Olympus. Twenty miles upland from the sun-baked seacoast, it was cooled by winds and streams rushing down from the mountain. Berœa also seemed a more temperate place in which to introduce the Christian message because the members of its synagogue were known to be friendly and open-minded. As Luke, the travel diarist, puts it, "These Jews were more noble than those in Thessalonica, for they received the word with all eagerness, examining the scriptures daily to see if these things were so. Many of them therefore believed, [including] not a few Greek women of high standing as well as men."

Well, somebody from the Jewish congregation must have made a business trip to Thessalonica. No doubt he went to the meeting house on the Sabbath. Perhaps after the service he was catching up on the news with some old friends and innocently mentioned the two visitors to his synagogue in Berœa and their compelling message. One can envision an elder overhearing and exclaiming, wide-eyed, "What? These same troublemakers who defiled our house of prayer are now polluting yours? Don't you understand that they preach the establishment of a new kingdom that flies in the face of both Roman and Mosaic law? Don't you realize that these are the same kind of meddlers who got all Jews expelled from Rome? Is that what you want for the whole province of Achaia?"

After that, it was only a matter of time before the Jewish elders came to Berœa from Thessolonica and threatened to incite another mob scene. The only "victory" for the missionaries was that the indignant delegation seemed to be pacified by removing Paul alone. Silas and Timothy could remain to teach the new brethren for awhile.

They conducted Paul down to the nearest seaport and soon Paul found himself on a ship for Athens. There is no indication that Paul had ever intended to invade this ancient citadel of philosophy and idol worship, but there he was, perhaps because it was the only place where ships from that small port were headed. Thus, he would have found himself on one of the combination sail-and-oared "coasters" that ply the strong tidal currents that surge in the narrow channel that runs between the long island of Euboea and the coast of Attica.

Being alone, and supposedly just waiting for Silas, Timothy and Luke to catch up with him, Paul had ample time on his hands to survey this dazzling city. Long impotent as a political power, Athens then as now remained the symbol of everything that was noble about Greece. As the center of its learning and culture, it was here that Roman emperors went to find the best teachers, orators, physicians, sculptors and musicians to grace their households. And it was to this beehive of ideas and commerce that wealthy Romans visited to polish their culture.

What Paul seemed to notice most in his strolls around Athens was not the glittering Acropolis 180 feet above the plain, nor the marbled, much-emulated public buildings, but the hundreds of idols and statues that lined street after colonnaded street. Yes, Paul had seen enough of them in Tarsus and Antioch, but perhaps not so many kinds in one place as this. Here it almost seemed that the owners or priests of various idols competed to paint each one in the most vivid colors possible. Altars smoked with burning sacrifices, incense billowed out of temples, people stood with their backs turned on the street as they proffered some small gift to one of the many small shrines erected in almost every recess. Statues of naked women vied for attention with Priapic statues whose erect penises people stopped to rub for good luck or a laugh.

Silas or no Silas, Timothy or no Timothy, Paul couldn't stand watching all this misdirected devotion and expense. "His spirit provoked," as Luke records, the apostle went to the synagogue and argued there on the Sabbath "with the Jews and devout persons." On other days he was "in the market place every day with those who chanced to be there." Eventually, word of this man with a bold new message reached some leaders of learning, who invited him to the Areopagus to speak to a group of scholars and other luminaries.

This was no streetcorner lyceum. The Areopagus, on the Hill of Ares, is where major criminal cases are held. But when not in use for that purpose it is also open for noteworthy public debates and readings. It is in constant use, for as Luke's diary notes, "all the Atheneans and the foreigners who lived there spent their time in nothing except telling or hearing something new."

In any event, the invitation was made in a genuine spirit of hospitality and honest inquiry. Paul quickly accepted. It is likely that Luke and the other missionaries had arrived in Athens by the time the apostle spoke, because the diary has captured its most important passages:

> Men of Athens, I perceive that in every way you are very religious. For as I passed along and observed the objects of your worship, I found also an altar with the inscription, "To an unknown god." What therefore you worship as unknown, this I proclaim to you. The God who made the world and everything in it, being Lord of heaven and earth, does not live in shrines made by man, nor is he served by human hands, as though he needed anything, since he himself gives to all men life and breath and everything.
>
> And he made from one every nation of men to live on all the face of the earth, having determined allotted periods and the boundaries of their habitation, that they should seek God in the hope that they might feel after him and find him. Yet he is not far from each one of us, for "in him we live and move and have our being." Even some of your own poets have said, "for we are indeed his offspring."
>
> Being then God's offspring, we ought not to think that the Deity is like gold or silver or stone, a representation by the art and imagination of man. The times of ignorance God overlooked. But now he commands all men everywhere to repent, because he has fixed a day on which he will judge the world in righteousness by a man whom he has appointed, and of this he has given assurance to all men by raising him from the dead. [12]

It is safe to say that this unvarnished, direct message was not met with either the jubiliation or intense questioning that had characterized audiences in, say, Lystra and Philippi. One answer may be that while people professed their eagerness to hear new ideas, most already championed a religion or philosophy. Chief among those who hold sway in Athens are still the Stoics and Epicurians. Stoics, their name derived from the very Painted Hall in Athens (called Stoa), believe in virtue as man's highest calling. This is achieved by performing one's duty according to rigid ethics – chief among them, mastery over desire, control of soul over pain, and absolute justice.

And what is the soul? Remember that I am generalizing becuse there are many shades of Stoicism. The soul is seen as man's invisible quantity. Its true home is in the great universe, perhaps in the light of the sun or the silence of the stars. Man must not fear death, say the Stoics, because it is no more than an absorption of the soul and its consciousness into the universe.

Describing Epicureanism is more difficult because it has been twisted often since Epicurus came to Athens from his native Samos nearly 400 years ago. The highest good, he taught his followers, is happiness, and this comes by cultivating virtue. Many, of course, have embellished these basic tenets to the point of rationalizing that if happiness is indeed the desired end, then it is perfectly proper to achieve it through such short cuts as an amphora of fine wine and heaps of succulent morsels.

Overlaid upon these barriers to Paul's message was one common to all Athenean scholars. I would call it "polite indifference." If you view an orator's performance strictly as entertainment, you aren't likely to bring a mob upon him as the offended Jewish elders did on Paul. Thus, Luke states simply that "when they heard of the ressurection of the dead, some mocked; but others said, 'We will hear you again about this.'" And so, they just slipped away, no doubt chatting amicably in clusters about the next play or poetry reading. It was as if Paul had gone to the arena prepared to fight a gladiator and instead found himself facing a greased pig.

Some Athenians did thirst for more — including a member of the council that governed the Areopagite where Paul spoke — but there is no record of a church being established there. The missionaries soon departed, and their lack of success may not have filled them with confidence, because as they headed west for Corinth, a larger, tougher, bawdier commercial seaport, Paul described himself as approaching "with fear and trembling."

. . . .

Tiberius Claudius Nero Drusus Germanicus Cæsar was now all of 13. He was already entitled to wear the adult dress, and the Senate had voted that he would become consul on his 19th birthday. So perhaps it is time you knew more about him.

So ancient and prominent is the Domitian family that its founder was said to have been blessed personally by the gods Castor and Pollux. It seems that nearly 500 years ago, one Lucius Domitius was returning on a road to Rome from the countryside when the twin deities suddenly appeared in his path and implored him to rush to the Senate house with news of a great battle victory. As if to confirm their divinity, the two stroked Lucius' cheeks and turned his black beard into a ruddy hue like that of bronze. Since then Domitians have been known for their red beards. Through the years they attained seven consulships, a triumph and two censorships. They all used the same surname and confined their forenames to Gnæus and Lucius.

Nero's immediate forefathers were always in the thick of Roman affairs, though not always illustrious. His great grandfather had commanded a fleet for Brutus and Cassius, but surrendered it to Antonius when it became plain he would be on the losing side. His grandfather was as well known for his chariot driving as for the triumph he earned in Germany. But he was also haughty, extravagant and cruel. When holding the consulship under Augustus, he gave wild beast baitings both in the Circus and in all regions of the city. He also gave gladiatorial shows, but with such inhuman cruelty that Augustus, after his private warnings were ignored, was forced to restrain him by edict.

Nero's father, Domitius, has been described by one historian as "a man hateful in every walk of life." For,

When he had gone to the East on the staff of the young Gaius Cæsar, he slew one of his own freedmen for refusing to drink as much as he was ordered. And when he was in consequence dismissed from the number of Gaius' friends, he lived not a whit less lawlessly. On the contrary, in a village on the Appian Way, suddenly whipping up his team, he purposely ran over and killed a boy. And in Rome, right in the Forum, he gouged out the eye of a Roman knight for being too outspoken in chiding him.

He was so dishonest that he not only cheated some bankers of the prices of wares which he had bought, but in his prætorship he even defrauded the victors in the chariot races of the amount of their prizes.

Just before the death of Tiberius he was also charged with treason, as well as with acts of adultery and with incest with his sister Lepida, but escaped owing to the change in rulers. He died of dropsy at Pyrgi after acknowledging [that he had fathered Nero with] Agrippina, the daughter of Germanicus.[13]

Nero was born at Antium nine months after the death of Tiberius. I have read many doleful predictions that various seers and astrologers were supposed to have given upon his birth (all of them no doubt composed long afterward with the aid of hindsight), but I find a comment by his own father the more prophetic. When congratulated by his friends on the event, Domitius retorted that only something abominable and a public bane could be born of Agrippina and himself.

Another early recorded event seems to have been the infant's naming day. When Agrippina asked her brother, the emperor Gaius, to give her child whatever name he liked, he just gave an impish giggle and pointed to his Uncle Claudius across the room. It was meant in jest, and Agrippina scorned the proposal, because Claudius at the time was the laughingstock of the imperial court.

When Nero lost his father at the age of three, he would have been heir to a third of the estate, but Gaius seized the whole thing for himself in his insatiable appetite for other people's property. When the emperor later banished Agrippina, Nero was brought up in the house of an aunt in conditions so plain that his tutors were a dancer and a barber.

When Claudius became emperor and Agrippina was brought back, her station, of course, rose like the tide in a British bay. Before long Agrippina had pushed the boy so aggressively onto the public stage that the empress Messalina began seeing him as a rival to her Brittanicus. One day, according to a widely-accepted story, she sent some hirelings to strangle Nero as he was taking his noonday nap. Much to her chagrin, the would-be assassins were frightened away by a snake that darted out from under his pillow. A more likely version is that a serpent had shed its skin near the boy's bed. In any event, when Agrippina asked her favorite seer to explain what a snakeskin might have had to do with her son's survival, the reply was this: "Just as serpents slough off their old age by discarding their old skin, your son will receive great power from an old man." Armed with that knowledge, Agrippina had the skin enclosed in a golden bracelet, which Nero wore on his right arm for many years.

At age 13, with his promised consulship still six years off, Nero was already designated Prince of Youth, a title Augustus had bestowed on his grandsons Gaius and Lucius Cæsar. Gifts were made to the troops in Nero's name and at games held in the Circus he attracted much attention by wearing triumphal robes. Brittanicus appeared wearing boy's clothing, which made their contrasting destinies obvious to everyone. So precarious was little Brittanicus' position that when he once addressed Nero as "Domitius," Agrippina complained sternly to her husband that this was a contemptuous refusal to recognize his adoption and the new name that had been voted by the Senate.

Indeed, it would seem that the most conspicuous undertaking at the palace during these two years was the building of a foundation for the succession of Agrippina and Nero. The Augusta, as she was now called, was granted the privilege of driving about Rome in the Carpentum, the ceremonial carriage that had been allowed Livia, and then Messalina. She now attended the emperor frequently in pubic, sitting on a separate tribunal when he was transacting ordinary business or receiving ambassadors.

And at every opportunity, Agrippina drew the palace machinery more tightly under her control. Thus, her attentions focused on the commanders of the Guard, Lucius Geta and Rufrius Crispinus. Convinced that they were loyal to the memory of Messalina and to the cause of her children, Agrippina went to Claudius and protested that the two commanders were in a dangerous rivalry that would only endanger the royal family. In this way she got them replaced by a distinguished soldier who was well aware to whom he owed the promotion. His name was Sextus Afranius Burrus, and he would soon become one of the major forces in the fortunes of Rome after Claudius.

Meanwhile, Pallas, the financial secretary and apparently Agrippina's only other love object, continued to gather fame and fortune. Just how far it went can be illustrated by the fact that the Senate voted this ex-slave an honorary prætorship and 15 million sesterces for his stellar services. One of the consuls added the suggestion that Pallas be voted the nation's thanks, because although he had been descended from Arcadian kings, he preferred to be regarded as one of the emperor's servants rather than exploit his royal lineage. Claudius was present at this session and confirmed that Pallas was content with this distinction and preferred not to exceed his modest means. On and on they praised Pallas for his service and "old world frugality," at last agreeing to engrave in bronze their thanks to a man who had already amassed 300 million sesterces in "public service"!

Now where, you ask, was Claudius as his powers were being gnawed away? One answer was that this emperor, a lifelong practitioner of the art of survival, was well-conditioned to recognize and acquiesce to powers greater than his own. He had also acquired a fine-tuned sensitivity to conspiracy – or even the slightest hint thereof – to the point of dodging his own shadow. Remember that this was a man who never anticipated being emperor and who had to be dragged from behind a curtain to accept it. Once in his early years when an ambitious senator sent him an impudent letter demanding that he give up the throne and retire to a life of privacy, Claudius called together some leading patricians and offered to abdicate if they wished. By now he had come to the point of having his soldiers serve him in a host's home and even having the pens taken from men who called on him. When a man with a dagger was caught near him when he was sacrificing in a public rite, he summoned the Senate and bewailed that there was no safety for him anywhere. He refused to appear in public for a long time afterwards.

I mention all this simply to portray a man who was unlikely to challenge his wife and freedmen, and whose first instinct was to accommodate what he saw unfolding around him. But I said I had a second answer, and this was that Claudius was still extremely busy and preoccupied with endless ceremonial duties and other issues that no one else wants to confront.

Among the latter were earthquake and famine. During these years some sections of Rome were flattened by sporadic earthquakes; and as terror spread, people were often trampled to death as they scurried about the streets in mass confusion. As luck would have it, these were also years of sparse grain crops in Egypt and Africa. At one point word got out that Rome's corn supply had dwindled to no more than 15 days, and Claudius, as he was holding court in the Forum, suddenly found himself surrounded by a frenzied mob. When he made the mistake of fleeing, the panicky emperor was driven into a corner between two buildings and might have been crushed had not a detachment of Guards broken through and forced a corridor through which he could exit. After that lesson in what the people expected most of their emperor – above beast baitings or being an effective censor – Claudius personally guaranteed ship owners that he would bear the expense of any losses incurred in storms. He also offered special subsidies or bounties to encourage the building of more merchant ships.

Claudius was kept busy with foreign affairs as well. Aside from placing their own agents as tax commissioners throughout the provinces, Agrippina and Pallas seemed willing enough to let the emperor suffer the thankless task of sorting out disputes among vassal kings and deciding what prince should wed whose daughter. And in this period there were enough such crises to bedevil the most enlightened of rulers. In the east, a feud among the Iberians and Armenians threatened to draw in neighboring Parthia and once again threaten the latter's fragile alliance with Rome. In Upper Germany, the Chatti tribe battled constantly with their perpetual enemies, the Cherusci, often requiring the intervention of Roman legions at great risk and cost. Even more persistent and intense was the situation in Britain. Despite the hasty "conquest" and subsequent triumph celebrated by Claudius some nine years before, the tribes of this rainy, rocky island were never truly subdued. In the years that followed I have spared you from reading of an endless array of insurrections by these ferocious primitives against one Roman settlement after another.

Public works and games constantly occupied the emperor as well. I have already mentioned many of them — new aqueducts, harbors, temples and the like — but I would like to mention one here that was both public work and games. This period marked the completion of the massive, II-year tunneling project that would drain the Fucine Lake (just north of Rome) into the Liris River, thereby leaving many square miles of fertile land for new agriculture. But before the water was drained, Claudius saw an opportunity to stage a naval battle on a scale that would have even impressed the spendthrift Gaius.

The freedman Narcissus was put in charge of building a ring of portable grandstands around the lake's perimeter. On the appointed day it appeared as if all of Rome and its surrounding towns had turned out on the expectation of seeing a few thousand condemned criminals fight to the death. To effect this they had been organized into two sides, the "Rhodians" and the "Sicilians," each with 12 triremes.

The stands were overflowing, with thousands more peering from various hilltops adjoining the lake. Claudius and Nero were dressed in resplendent military garb. Agrippina wore a chlamys woven with threads of gold. Surrounding the stands around the entire lake were rafts manned by companies of the Guards to make sure that no combatant could escape. Strategically placed in various positions were ramparts holding stone throwers and catapults just in case they were needed to defend the crowd from an escape or enliven the performance with a bombardment from shore.

All that were needed were willing combatants. As the ships made a ceremonial pass by the emperor's box, the men on one ship shouted "Hail, Emperor. We who are about to die salute thee."

"Or not!" Claudius retorted, a feeble attempt at humor, I suppose. But word quickly spread from ship to ship that the emperor intended to spare them all.

So now the "battle" was on, signaled by the sound of a horn from a silver triton that arose from the middle of the lake by a mechanical device. The crowd arched forward as the two sets of triremes converged for battle. But the ships simply glided by one another as the surprised crowd hooted and groaned. Outraged, Claudius considered having all the "marines" blown out of the water by the catapults, then hacked up by the Guards as they swam to the rafts. But at last he thought better of it, jumping from his throne instead and lumbering along the edge of the lake with his ridiculous tottering gait and waving his arms in an effort to make them fight. His exhortations must have included some promises, too, because the criminals gradually began clashing in earnest and eventually shed so much blood that Claudius spared the survivors from extermination.

Lake Fucine was also the site of another deadly skirmish, albeit more subtle. Just after the naval games had ended, the engineers tried to open the channel that would begin draining the lake into the river that ran below it. But they realized that the tunneling had not reached more than halfway through the lake bottom. So, while the project dragged on, Claudius decided to sponsor a second evening's festivities, this time an infantry battle fought by gladiators on pontoons. Well, the crowd had just gathered, some already banqueting in their portable wooden stands, when the tunnel must have broken through from the sheer force of the water above it. Like a bathtub whose plug was pulled out, the water began to course towards the end that contained the tunnel. As it gathered momentum, the current swept along pontoons, stands, people and everything else in its way. The result was sheer panic and many serious injuries.

When everyone began to sort out the mess, the name of Narcissus was invoked and cursed more than any other. The freedman had been given a budget to direct the whole project and now he found fingers pointed at him from all directions. But none more consequential than from Agrippina. Narcissus — wholly the client of Claudius — was one of the few remaining barriers to the impatient new order of Agrippina, Nero, Pallas, Burrus and the like. So the Augusta now led the chorus of critics who accused Narcissus of building cheap and unsteady stands in order to pocket the difference and swell his already staggering personal fortune. Narcissus could do little but bite his tongue and hope that his days weren't numbered.

But they were.

. . . .

CUMANUS, THE NEW PROCURATOR OF JUDEA, never quite had a chance to settle in or to get the knack of governing the Jews. Nor did they ever conduct "business" in the way he expected.

As you may know by now, Galileans, the most exuberant or rebellious of festival attendees (depending on their point of view at the time) always had to make their way southward to Jerusalem through the suspicious and often hostile region of Samaria. On one of these occasions following the Passover a band of them arrived in a village called Ginæ, no doubt tired and thirsty and seeking service at some hostelry. They must have been too raucous or demanding, because they were refused. One can picture a tavernkeeper facing a hot, thirsty, defiant gang of strange men while his servant scurries out the back door to find some local young toughs to help defend the honor of Samaria. The result was an ugly skirmish that left several dead on both sides. Before long, Cumanus was confronted in Cæsarea by a delegation of Galilean elders and parents, all demanding that he avenge the deaths.

But it seems that their counterparts from Samaria had anticipated the appeal and had already plied the procurator with enough money to do nothing about the matter. When the exasperated Galilean elders returned home and reported that they were helpless to obtain retribution, their young hotheads became all the more inflamed. Declaring that anything was better than the "slavery" they were subjected to, they took their case to Eleazar, an infamous robber who abided with his brigands in the mountains. Off Eleazar and his new allies soon went, plundering many villages of Samaria in the name of revenge.

Now it was Cumanus' turn to fan the fires. Borrowing four regiments of footmen from Sebaste and arming many more Samaritans, he ordered the tribune Celer to lead them all against the Galileans. The Roman-Samaritan forces soon surprised Eleazer and his new recruits in the middle of some mischief. Many Galileans were killed, but many were also taken alive.

This settled nothing. For many weeks, bands of armed adventurers from Galilee would strike into Samaria, pillaging and destroying. As they did, rival brigands from Samaria would be doing exactly the same thing in Galilean towns. Soon there was talk of civil war. It was at that juncture that the leading families of Jerusalem took it upon themselves to douse the flames. They put on sackcloth, heaped ashes on their heads and approached their seditious countrymen with warnings that they would utterly subvert their entire country and its temple if they did not cast aside their weapons and return to calm.

The Galileans finally desisted and retreated to their local strongholds, but it was more like a temporary truce. Already, robbers and brigands crawled over the land as never before, and their favorite targets were Samaritans. No sooner had Cassius Longius been recalled as governor of Syria when his replacement, Ummidius Quadratus, was confronted by a group of Samaritan principals demanding retribution for the plundering and firing of several villages by the same Galilean marauders who had supposedly broken their pledge to desist. Moreover, the Samaritans were downright insolent to Quadratus, charging that they would have settled the score swiftly if they didn't have to await permission from Roman rulers. Summoned later to reply, the leading Jews of Galilee insisted that the Samaritans had started the fighting and that Cumanus had been bribed to look the other way.

Quadratus, determined to make his new administration a fair one, sent everyone away so that he could begin a more thorough investigation. After a trip to Samaria, he had all but convinced himself the Samaritans were the guilty instigators of the affair when he learned that Galilean adventurers again were out in the hillsides fomenting trouble. He ordered that all the Jews that Cumanus had captured now be crucified as a warning against further trouble. Then he came to the Samaritan village of Lydda and heard their case a second time. There he learned that a Jew named Dortus and four collaborators had incited a crowd to revolt against Rome. After having them all executed, and convinced that the high priest Ananias was a part of the plot, the governor had him sent in bonds to Rome to give an account to the emperor. He also ordered the chief Samaritans, the leading Galileans, Cumanus the procurator and Celer the tribune all sent to Rome for the same reason.

When the court date appointed them drew nigh, Cæsar's freedman became very concerned about the fate of the Samaritans and of Cumanus, whose appointment they had brought about. But here Claudius rose to the occasion. When the young Agrippa II beseeched him to hear the case personally, he agreed to it. The upshot was that Claudius determined that the Samaritan delegation should be slain and that Cumanus should be banished for taking illegal bribes. The tribune Celer was brought back to Jerusalem and dragged by horses through the city so that all people would see that retribution had been carried out by a just emperor.

Yes, Claudius was still active in hearing judicial cases, but he still exercised little control of governmental appointments and administration. Proof enough of that was the next procurator. Felix was none other than the brother of the imperial financial secretary, Pallas, whose deeds you have just read about. It seems evident that this connection gave the new procurator confidence that he could do anything he wished to build up his personal fortune. And this assumption, I daresay, led to a new level of friction in Roman-Jewish relations that would one day escalate out of control.

Felix began with an "acquisition" that will take more than a few words to explain. To begin, this was a time when several alliances in the region were being formed or strengthened. Rome, more fearful than ever of all-out war with Parthia, decided to exercise direct rule over Chalcis, the small-but-strategic kingdom just to the south of Antioch. To appease the young Agrippa II, Claudius awarded him the region of Trachonitis (formerly known as the tetrarchy of Philip) and the city-state of Abila to the north.

As part of assuring that the Syrian client kingdoms were united, Agrippa himself strengthened his royal connections by marrying his two eligible sisters to rulers of some small states in the region. One of them, Drusilla, was given to Azizus, the king of Emesa, which lay along the Orantes south of Antioch. Many said Drusilla was the fairest beauty in all Syria. She was also quiet and modest, fearing the jealousy of her older sister Bernice.

Now enter the new procurator. On his first glimpse of Drusilla, Felix resolved that he must have her for his own even though she was newly-married. At first he showered her with promises of great wealth and happiness. When Drusilla refused, even feigning illness so as to avoid this unwanted suitor, Felix sent a Cypriot Jew named Simon to beseech her on his behalf. This Simon was a famous magician (not the Simon who had the statue to him in Rome) and I haven't the faintest idea what sort of magic he plied, but the next thing anyone knew was that Drusilla had agreed to annul her wedding and marry Felix.

Transgressing the laws of her forefathers did not endear Drusilla to her sister Bernice, nor to their brother. Rather than presiding over one happy family, Agrippa II would soon assume governing a kingdom that was at odds with an aggressively ambitious Roman procurator for more reasons than ever.

· · · · · · · · ·

PAUL WENT ON BY HIMSELF TO CORINTH, having sent Timothy and Silas back to Macedonia to buttress the young churches of Philippi and Thessalonica. If Paul went west by sea, it would have been but an easy day's sail from the Athenian port of Piræus across the Gulf of Corinth to its own port of Cenchreæ. Or, he might have walked 60 miles, probably breaking the trip with a stay at Megara. Always in view towards him as he approached Corinth would be the 1,800-foot mountain known as The Arcocorinth and its citadel overlooking the whole region.

So short a distance, but what contrast from Athens! Although both were founded in ancient times, Corinth was not even a hundred years old when Paul arrived. How can I explain that? Because Corinth, the center of Greek resistance during the Roman Republic, was reduced to rubble at the same time Rome destroyed Carthage. Despoiled and desolate, its people having been sold into slavery and its treasures shipped off to Rome, it was not until Julius Cæsar — in the year of his assassination — decided to rebuild and resettle the city as the new capital of Achaia that Corinth was reborn.

Given the city's natural location, it wasn't long before it became the commercial center as well. Set on the narrow isthmus, it not only divides north and south Greece but also is the closest city on the mainland to both the Ægean and Adriatic seas. The city might even see more shipping traffic if someone would complete the coast-to-coast canal that ancients first began to scour from the rocky isthmus, but no one has ever mustered the money and manpower and resources to do so. As it is, some ships are transported from sea to sea overland by a cumbersome series of rollers, which is a fascinating tourist attraction in itself. So regardless of what happens to the isthmus, Corinth will always be a naval center because the trireme was invented there and the city still leads the world in building them.

This of course suggests a sailor's city, and you are right. But it is just as much the favorite destination of traders and tourists. There, both can find any goods by day, and after business hours, diversions that run from the finest sporting facilities in Greece to old wine and young women. Indeed, a man on the prowl might find himself among a thousand available "priestesses" (actually slaves) atop the mountain at the flourishing temple of Aphrodite. As proof of its infamy we have only to cite our Greek slang word *korinthiazesthai*, the very name for fornication!

When it comes to religion, it's been said that an Athenian enjoys arguing the finer points of its philosophy or rituals. In Paul's Corinth religion had already been captured by the commercial prophetess, the temple priest and the seller of amulets, trinkets and incense. But the striking exception, of course, was Judaism. There were many pious, hardworking Jews in Corinth who observed The Law, and, as ever, Paul made straight for them.

How fortunate it was for Paul that in the very first days of his visit he befriended Aquila and Priscilla while attending their synagogue. Aquila (and perhaps his wife as well) was a Jew from Pontus, that same land by the Black Sea to which the Roman Agrippina – now the Augusta – had been exiled. This couple was in the tentmaking trade and had most recently lived in Rome, from which they had just been forced to move when the emperor banished all Jews from the city. What a wonderful source of support they must have been to Paul. He arrived short on funds, required lodgings, needed a way to make a living and sought his first converts to Christianity. Aquila and Priscilla offered him a home and a place in their business operation. Perhaps they had already been baptized as Jewish Christians in Rome, because they became the cornerstones of the first church in Corinth from almost the time Paul set foot there. And if Paul still lacked intimate knowledge of Jewish-Christian affairs in Rome, these new allies could certainly provide it.

Although Paul argued his case in the synagogues as usual, I believe his stay in Corinth got off to a more successful start than elsewhere because he was also introduced to many people who belonged to the same trade guild as Aquila and Priscilla. Assuming that the tentmakers and leathermakers of Corinth joined the same kind of clubs as they do in Rome today, they probably also belonged to the Freemasons' lodge, which gave them opportunities to meet their fellow workers on a social basis. I would suggest, then, that this added opportunity for Paul to meet people provided the basis for the first church of Corinth, just as Lydia's group of clothworkers may have in Philippi. I would further assert that Aquila and Priscilla offered their home as the first Christian meeting place.

On the Sabbath, however, Paul could always be found in a synagogue, and not always the same one. According to Luke's account, the apostle first converted Crispus, the chief elder of one synagogue and all of his family. He then did the same later to one Sesthoges, who was also described as the "ruler" of a synagogue, and a different one from Crispus, I assume.

The only thing that must have marred Paul's elation with his efforts in Corinth was his constant worry about the fate of young, fragile churches of Macedonia. After all, he hadn't spent much time at either one and was forced to depart suddenly, which is why he had sent Silas and Timothy back to them. Beyond his concerns for the churches themselves was the fact that his whole mission — his ability to spread the gospel all the way to Rome — would be severely impeded if the light dimmed in Macedonia. For Paul believed that the time left before the Messiah's return to judgment was growing short.

Then one day there they were in front of him, Silas and Timothy, reporting the joyous news that the churches in Philippi and Thessalonica had endured! They had never doubted his message. They had personally experienced the same harsh ostracism that Jewish and Gentile Christians faced from the synagogue establishment. But their faith was strong and they had even grown in numbers! They missed Paul just as much as he missed them, and as evidence of their love and respect for him the churches had taken up a collection so that he could spent less time earning a living and more of it preaching the gospel in Corinth.

Now able to pay his own rent, I suspect that Paul felt he had imposed long enough on Aquila and Priscilla. He now took a room in the house of one Titus Justus, a "worshipper of God" who lived right next door to a synagogue that Paul often attended. I have the urge to say that being so close to the synagogue was a mistake and was the reason why relations between Paul and the elders grew tense, but it's also important to note that Paul's entire stay in Corinth lasted 18 months. Much of this time must have been spent living in the home of Titus, which indicates that Paul continued to have many more weeks of success in converting both synagogue members and Gentiles.

In fact, it was probably these gains in numbers that disrupted the synagogue congregation and prompted the elders to try ousting Paul from Corinth altogether. Paul certainly saw it coming because he later recalled wrestling with his conscience one night when God spoke to him. "Do not be afraid," said the inner voice, "but speak and do not be silent, for I am with you and no man shall attack you to harm you, for I have many people in this city."

With that, Paul seemed to worry no more about the consequences of confronting the Jewish elders. One day when testifying in a synagogue that the Christ was Jesus, the members "opposed and reviled him," according to Luke. With that he "shook out his garments" and said to them, "Your blood be upon your heads! I am innocent. From now on I will go to the Gentiles."

Whether this served as a rallying cry for the elders I cannot say, but it was shortly thereafter that an embassy of leading Jews hauled Paul before the Roman proconsul in Corinth.

Let me catch a breath at this point and tell you something about the man who sat on the judgment seat. The proconsul (Achaia is ruled by the Roman Senate rather than the emperor) was a man whose connections may have figured later in Paul's destiny. Junius Gallio was born one of three brothers in the household of the Spanish knight Lucius Annæus Seneca. His brother of the same name was Nero's tutor and a growing force in Roman affairs. One proof of Seneca's rising ascendancy was the appointment of his younger brother, Gallio, as proconsul to the biggest, busiest city in Greece.

Gallio, as well-bred and erudite as his brother in Rome, had been proconsul but a few weeks when he sat in his seat of judgment in the southern part of the immense open market square in Corinth. On these regularly appointed days anyone could come forth to lodge a complaint, and on this occasion Gallio faced a smoldering group of men in official robes and long black beards. In their apparent custody was a small older man who certainly seemed like one of their own kind, given the proper clothing.

After identifying his colleagues as the eminent leaders of several synagogues, the spokesman got down to business. "This man," he said, pointing to Paul, "is persuading men to worship God contrary to the Law."

Just then there was a hubbub as the spokesman tried to continue and the defiant Paul began to interrupt, but Gallio calmly raised his hand and shushed both parties. "If this were a matter of wrongdoing or a viscious crime, I should have reason to bear with you, O Jews," he said. "But since this is a matter of questions about words and names and your own law, I refuse to be the judge of these things."

Paul continued to preach in Corinth for some time thereafter. But he also had continuing responsibilities to the new churches in Macedonia and Asia Minor. In particular, Timothy and Silas had brought with them several questions that were being asked by the believers in Thessalonica. Although the questions and concerns that reached Paul are not preserved, they must have dwelled on the end of time: when it would come and how one should live in the meantime. Paul's reply, which is the earliest of his writings to the churches he established, begins with lavish expressions of his love for the Thessalonians, then attempts to answer these concerns:

...For the Lord himself will descend from heaven with a cry of command, with the archangel's call, and with the sound of the trumpet of God. And the dead in Christ will rise first; then we who are alive, who are left, shall be caught up together with them in the clouds to meet the Lord in the air; and so we shall always be with the Lord. Therefore, comfort one another with these words.

But as to the times and the seasons, brethren, you have no need to have anything written to you. For you yourselves know well that the day of the Lord will come like a thief in the night. When people say, "There is peace and security," then sudden destruction will come upon them as travail comes upon a woman with child, and there will be no escape. But you are not in the darkness, brethren, for that to surprise you like a thief. For you are all sons of light and sons of the day; we are not of the night or of darkness. So then let us not sleep, as others do, but let us keep awake and be sober. For those who sleep sleep at night, and those who get drunk get drunk at night. But since we belong to the day, let us be sober, and put on the breastplate of faith and love, and for a helmet the hope of salvation. For God has not destined us for wrath, but to obtain salvation through our Lord Jesus Christ, who died for us so that whether we wake or sleep we might live with him. Therefore, encourage one another and build one another up, just as you are doing.

But we beseech you, brethren, to respect those who labor among you and are over you in the Lord and admonish you, and to esteem them very highly in love because of their work. Be at peace among yourselves. And we exhort you, brethren, to admonish the idle, encourage the faint-hearted, help the weak, be patient with them all. See that none of you repays evil for evil, but always seek to do good to one another and to all. Rejoice always, pray constantly, give thanks in all circumstances, for this is the will of God in Christ Jesus for you. Do not quench the Spirit, do not despise prophesying, but test everything; hold fast what is good, abstain from every form of evil...[14]

This was not the letter of men trying to establish a new religion or a complex theology. Paul and Silas, and perhaps Timothy, made no effort to mask their Jewish identity and heritage. They simply believed that the promises of Judaism had been fulfilled by Jesus, who had established a new covenant between the one God and all his children.

Paul now felt his stay in Corinth at an end. Leaving Silas and Timothy behind again to cultivate the seeds the three had planted in Macedonia, Paul's destinations this time were Cæsarea and Antioch. His confidence in the abilities of Silas and Timothy was illustrated by the fact that Aquila and Priscilla packed up and left with him.

Luke writes that they stopped at the Corinthian seaport of Cenchreæ, where Paul "cut his hair, for he had a vow." Most sea travelers to Cenchreæ make it a point to stop at its temple of Poseidon and make an offering to the god in hopes of good luck at sea. Since that would hardly be the case with Paul, the head shaving may provide a clue as to his mysterious ailment. I say this because it was an ancient custom among Jews who were seriously ill or distressed to shave their heads and vow to go to the temple in Jerusalem. They would keep the shorn hair, then have it ceremoniously burned at the temple altar. The marshy Corinthian lowlands were especially known as a place where people caught malaria, and it may be that Paul was afflicted. In one of his later letters Paul mentions a woman named Phœbe, a deaconess in the small church at Cenchreæ, who "has nursed myself and many others." If this was in fact Paul's affliction, he would have had something in common with the proconsul Gallio, who came down with malaria in Corinth and had to take an extended sea voyage in hopes of improving his health.

From Cenchreæ, Paul, Aquila and Priscilla boarded a coaster headed across the Ægean 250 miles due east to Ephesus, the largest city in the province of Asia. There, the diarist says that Paul "went into the synagogue and argued with the Jews." They even asked him to stay on and preach again, but Paul declined. They, I believe, were not the primary objective of his first visit to this busy commercial center. There were already a few Christians living in Ephesus and Aquila and Priscilla would serve as Paul's "advance guard." Here they would set up their tentmaking business, join the local trade guild, acquire ample quarters and use it as perhaps the first Christian house church in Ephesus.

Ultimately, Ephesus would be the site of Paul's longest visit and largest Christian congregation — a sturdy bridge between the growing churches of Asia and Macedonia. But first he needed time to rest and gain new resources.

This meant returning to Cæsarea and Antioch. It was mid-summer by now and instead of bounding into the salt spray kicked up by the northerly *Meltemi*, he could use the strength of these ocean winds to shorten the 620-mile southeastern passage straight into the calm harbor of Cæsarea. In all, the second missionary journey would traverse 2,800 miles.

. . . .

A. D. 5 3 — 5 5

Ominous periods are invariably introduced by historians with a flourish of
prophetic hindsight. Thus, the new year
in Rome was described by one chronicler of this time as "a series of prodigies
indicating changes for the worse":

Standards and soldiers' tents were set on fire from the sky. A swarm of
bees settled on the pediment of the Capitoline temple. Half-bestial
children were born, and a pig with a hawk's claws. A portent, too, was
discerned in the losses suffered by every official post: a quæstor, ædile,
tribune, prætor and consul had all died within a few months.[15]

Agrippina was especially frightened by such signs because it was only recently that Claudius had been in his cups again muttering that it was his destiny first
to endure his wives' misdeeds, and then to punish them.

One might question the Augusta's anxiety. Nero, now 17, had been wed to
Octavia for nearly a year. The path to the throne was all but clear, with only a
few potholes in the way. Even Claudius himself did not seem to be one of them.
It was now becoming difficult to distinguish his tottering as owing to his physical malformities or too much wine. Certainly no bold edicts issued forth from
him during this period. Still, Agrippina remembered that Claudius had seemed
equally benign and befuddled just before Messalina met her fate. So the new
empress decided to get on with her designs without further delay. First, she
went about destroying the only other woman who could claim to be her equal.
Domitia Lepida was a grand-niece of Augustus, divorced wife of Nero's father
and mother of the late Messalina. Equally as wealthy and beautiful as Agrip-

pina, she was more Claudius' age and might appear just as imposing at his side should ill-fortune overtake the present Augusta. Moreover, she had the annoying habit of babying Nero with kind words and presents in sharp contrast to his mother's own practice of rearing by threats and scoldings.

But petty jealousies don't make compelling court cases. So, one day Lepida found herself charged with attempting the life of the empress by magic. A totally different and novel charge was that some slave work gangs she owned in Calabria had repeatedly disturbed the peace. In truth, Lepida was no less immoral or opportunistic than Agrippina, but these particular accusations were purely manufactured. Narcissus, still the emperor's chief freedman, tried vigorously to defend Lepida, but she was sentenced to death. Some shrugged and recalled a line from Virgil: "If you find two queen bees in a hive, it's best to kill the weaker one."

Narcissus seemed to know that there was little room in the hive for himself anymore. "Whether Britannicus or Nero comes to the throne, my destruction is inevitable," he told his closest friends. "But Claudius has been so good to me that I would give my life to help him. The criminal intentions for which Messalina was condemned with Gaius Silius have re-emerged in Agrippina." Better that he had done nothing about Messalina and her "marriage" festival, Narcissus lamented. "Once more there is unfaithfulness [because] Agrippina's lover is Pallas. *That* is the final proof that there is nothing she will not sacrifice to imperial ambition — neither decency nor honor nor chastity."

The freedman's anxieties soon eroded his health, the one thing his 400 million sesterces couldn't buy. He talked within earshot of the emperor and Agrippina about taking a long sojourn to Sinuessa, where he hoped the mild climate and health-giving waters might restore his strength. To his surprise, Agrippina obligingly pointed out that it would also be good for his gout, from which he suffered increasingly.

So off went Narcissus. In so doing, the person most faithful to Claudius unwittingly stripped the emperor of his last shield and armor. Agrippina now sought expert advice on how to choose just the right poison. One with a sudden, dramatic effect would give her away. A gradual wasting potion might make Claudius, slipping into death, summon his son and restore his powers in a burst of tearful repentance. No, better to have a recipe that would create a physical disturbance — vomiting, fainting, whatever — where the victim would be carried off his couch with apparent food poisoning, then lapse into a deathly coma somewhere behind the scenes.

Agrippina's agents searched the records of criminal convictions and found the name of a woman, Locusta, who had recently been sentenced for poisoning. Pressed into imperial service, she prepared a potion that was sprinkled on a particularly succulent mushroom. When it appeared on a tray with several untainted mushrooms, Agrippina was counting on the habit of everyone present to reserve the largest or most luscious morsel for the emperor.

With diners all helping themselves from the same plate, Claudius' food taster, the eunuch Halotus, was apparently caught off guard. The emperor reached out and down went the mushroom. Now Claudius had but one defense remaining: he was drunk. If there was an immediate effect upon him, his wife couldn't discern it. In time, the emperor staggered to his feet and lumbered off.

Agrippina waited in agony. Soon an attendant whispered in her ear that the emperor had evacuated his bowels – and apparently the poisoned mushroom in the process. Now the empress was beside herself. Had he realized? She waited, trying to make conversation and look composed. Then, a bearded man appeared in the back of the room and, with one arched eyebrow, gave her a look of reassurance.

The bearded man, and one of her few confederates in this unseemly business, was none other than Xenophon, the emperor's physician, and I assume, already a much wealthier man for a briefly forgetting his Hippocratic Oath. Xenophon soon confided to Agrippina that while pretending to help the discomfited Claudius to vomit, the physician had put a feather down his throat as he frequently did after one of the emperor's drinking bouts. But this time the feather was dipped in quick poison.

And so, on the night of October 12, the man who had never expected to be emperor but who managed to endure the office with reasonable aplomb, succumbed to unnatural causes after ruling Rome for 13 years, eight months and 20 days. He had lived 63 years, two months and 13 days.

The rest of Rome, however, would not know about it until Agrippina was quite ready. The Senate was summoned and told of the emperor's serious illness. Consuls and priests offered prayers for his safety. But upstairs in the palace the lifeless body of Claudius Tiberius Nero Germanicus Cæsar had already been wrapped in blankets and poultices.

Agrippina's whole being was now focused on negotiating that last remaining step. First she went to the room of Britannicus and held him in her heartbroken embrace as she prayed for the recovery of his father. At the same time she had troops positioned throughout the palace, with orders that Britannicus and his sister were to be detained in their rooms until further notice. Meanwhile, she issued periodic announcements as to the emperor's "condition," all the while awaiting the word from her astrologers for the most propitious time to bring Nero onto the scene.

Finally at midday on October 13, the palace gates were suddenly thrown open. Nero, attended by Guard Commander Burrus, approached the battalion that was on duty for the day. After the briefest of introductions from their commander, the new emperor was cheered, put into a litter and carried off to the Guards' camp. There, after reading a brief speech (written by Seneca) in which he promised them all gifts as generous as Claudius had bestowed 13 years before, Nero was hailed as Imperator. After that, Senate approval was a mere formality. The only one of the many honors and titles conferred on him that day that Nero turned down was that of "Father of His Country." The new emperor, aged 17, had decided it might be a bit pretentious.

The same Senate also voted Claudius divine honors and named Agrippina as chief of its priesthood. The funeral was as grand as that of Augustus. Agrippina imitated the grandeur of her great grandmother, Livia, the first Augusta. Nero, reading Seneca's carefully prepared speech, evoked the solemn respect of all assembled when he cited the deified emperor's illustrious ancestors, his great literary accomplishments and the absence of military disasters during his reign. But when he went on to hail his predecessor's great wisdom and foresight, one could hear muffled snickers. Soon the crowd was awash in a wave of unrestrained laughter.

In just a short time, people were also laughing at the demise of a man whom they now remembered more for his stammer of speech and lame left leg than anything else. Nero was now given to calling mushrooms the "food of the gods" because "my father was made a god by eating one."

Indeed, Seneca himself, the author of that fawning funeral speech, had already circulated "backstage" copies of a biting satire that reflected his true feelings about the emperor. Seneca had never forgiven Claudius for exiling him for eight years on a trumped up adultery charge. Now, in his "*Pumpkinification of Claudius*" [a play on the Latin word for deification], he opens with a scene in which the ghost of the newly-departed stands enraptured as his funeral train passes by and the mourners chant:

> Pour forth your lament, your sorrow declare,
> Let the sounds of grief rise loud in the square:
> For he that is dead had a wit most keen,
> Was bravest of all that on earth have been.
> Racehorses are nothing to his swift feet:
> Rebellious Parthians he did defeat;
> Swift after the Persians his light shafts go:
> For he well knew how to fit arrow to bow.
> Swiftly the intrepid barbarians fled:
> With one little wound he shot them dead.
> And the Britons beyond the seashores which one sees,
> Blue-shielded Brigantines, too — all these
> He chained by the neck as Roman slaves.

He spake and the Ocean with trembling waves
Accepted the axe of Roman law.
O weep for the man! This world never saw
One quicker a troublesome suit to decide,
When only one part of the case had been tried.
(He could do it indeed and not hear either side!)
Who'll now sit in judgment the whole year round?
Now he that is judge of the shades underground,
Once ruler of fivescore cities in Crete,
Must yield to his better and take a back seat.
Mourn, mourn, pettifoggers, ye venal crew,
And you, newer poets, woe is to you!
And you above all, who get rich quick,
By the rattle of dice and the three card trick.[16]

As Claudius stands transfixed before the mourners, he is unaware that the gods on Mount Olympus are in the process of discussing his admission into their company. They had been favorably inclined until their newest member, Augustus, breaks the respectful silence of a novitiate and reveals his outrage at welcoming a personage who had nonchalantly taken off 35 senators, 221 Roman knights and all too many members of his immediate family. Oh, it wasn't that emperors weren't compelled to do such things from time to time, but scarcely had a ruler done it so many times without a proper hearing or at the insistence of a jealous wife or because some aide asked him to sign a paper that he was too lazy or cowed to read.

So the Claudius in Seneca's *Pumkinification* is consigned instead to the underworld. As he is escorted below, he can hear the clapping of hands and singing: "Claudius is coming! The lost is found! O let us rejoice together!" As he enters he sees all the condemned senators, knights, old friends, Mnester the dancer and the like. Then come his many deposed relatives – "the whole family, in fact," says Seneca. Claudius is befuddled. "Friends everywhere," he exclaims. "How came you all here?"

To this one of them answered: "What, cruel man? You ask how came we here? Who but you sent us here – you, who murdered all the friends that you ever had!"

A trial is immediately ordered. Claudius is denied a delay and the right to counsel. The prosecutor has a field day amidst loud applause. Someone ventures a comment in favor of the defendant, but the judge will hear none of it. He declares the defendant guilty as charged.

Now a long debate ensues as to the proper punishment. It must, they agree, be something unprecedented lest Claudius find some loophole in existing law.

At last they have it! Claudius, once the author of a treatise on the art of dice playing, should be consigned to rattling the dice forever in a box with holes in the bottom. Thus,

> ...when he rattled with the box, and thought he now had got 'em,
> Both little cubes would vanish thro' the perforated bottom.
> Then he would pick 'em up again, and once more set a-trying:
> The dice but served him the same trick: away they went a-flying.
> So still he tries and still he fails; still searching long he lingers;
> And every time the tricksy things go slipping thro' his fingers.
> Just as when Sisyphus the hilltop touches with his boulder,
> He finds his labor all in vain — it rolls down off his shoulder. [17]

Everyone seems pleased with this novel punishment when all of a sudden in walks Gaius Caligula. He claims Claudius for his slave, reminding all that he is already used to flogging and caning him. The mob turns Claudius over to him, but the fickle Gaius gives him to a freedman, who consigns him to be his law clerk for eternity.

· · · · · · · · ·

THE REMAINDER OF THE YEAR belonged to Agrippina. At first she managed virtually all the business of the empire on her son's behalf. Indeed, one can still find gold and silver coins in circulation that show the profiles of Agrippina and Nero facing one another (with hers the more prominent, I might add). When the Senate met on the Palatine, a door was built in the back of the hall so that Agrippina could stand behind a curtain unseen and listen. She and her son often went forth together, usually reclining in the same litter. But equally often, she would be carried while Nero walked beside her. When the Guard commander would request the password of the day, Nero would often give, "The best of mothers."

Agrippina's dirty work was not done, however. Apparently she had some poison left over, because an agent used it on Junius Silanus, the governor of Asia. Known as an untalented and lazy administrator, Silanus had been nicknamed the "Golden Sheep," which is what Diogenes the Cynic had called rich fools. No, Silanus had not provoked anyone. His "crime" was that he was a great-great grandson of Augustus and might be perceived as an adult alternative to Nero.

Now came the turn of Narcissus. The freedman had banked all his allegiance on one client, and now he was odd man out. Imprisoned and harshly treated, he chose to commit suicide rather than face the execution Agrippina had planned for him. Interestingly, Nero seemed genuinely sorry to learn of the freedman's demise. Narcissus had been second to none in his greed and extravagance, but the young emperor found him more tolerable than the increasingly arrogant Pallas.

The death of their colleague alarmed Burrus, the Guard commander, and Seneca, the emperor's tutor and speech writer. Knowing what might await them as well, they resolved to oppose other executions Agrippina was planning and blunt her growing administrative power. It didn't happen overnight, but through many steps. If any one episode symbolized it, however, it may have been the time an Armenian delegation was pleading before Nero. Agrippina entered the reception room and was walking up to take her place on the dais just beside Nero. "Everyone was stupefied," recalled one witness. "But Seneca quickly whispered for the young emperor to descend and meet his mother before she could get there, as if to extend some special greeting to her." Having done so, the emperor did not return to the tribunal chair, but made some excuse for them both to leave "so that the weakness in the empire should not become apparent to the foreigners." Thereafter, Seneca and Burrus resolved between them to prevent her from conducting any public business.

One such way was to make the 17-year-old ruler appear informed and enlightened beyond his years. "No civil war, no family quarrels, clouded my early years," he noted in his first speech to the Senate (by way of Seneca). Vowing to reverse some of Claudius' most unpopular practices, "I will not judge every kind of case myself," he said, nor "give too free rein to the influence of a few individuals by hearing prosecutors and defendants behind my closed doors. From my house, bribery and favoritism will be excluded. I will keep personal and state affairs separate. The Senate is to preserve its ancient functions. By applying to the consuls, people from Italy and the senatorial provinces may have access to its tribunals. I myself will look after the armies under my control."

And most of his promises were kept, to the increasing delight of the people. They also applauded when he abolished fees for advocates and put an end to the practice in which provincial governors extorted enormous sums from their local populations in order to stage gladiatorial shows.

Meanwhile, the young man was receiving a daily diet of instruction from Seneca on how to rule wisely. One can picture him nodding, but fidgeting, as the tutor read sternly from his own work, *On Clemency*:

> Clemency does well with all, but best with princes; for it makes their power comfortable and beneficial, which would otherwise be the pest of mankind. It establishes their greatness, when they make the good of the public their particular care, and employ their power for the safety of the people.

The prince is, in effect, the soul of the community, as the community is only the body of the prince; so that being merciful to others, he is tender of himself. Nor is any man so mean but his master feels the loss of him, as a part of his empire. And he takes care not only of the lives of his people, but also of their reputation.

When a gracious prince shows himself to his people, they do not fly from him as from a tiger that rouses himself out of his den, but they worship him as a benevolent influence; they secure him against all conspiracies, and interpose their bodies betwixt him and danger. They guard him when he sleeps and defend him in their field against his enemies. Nor is it without reason, this unanimous agreement in love and loyalty, and this heroic zeal of abandoning themselves for the safety of their prince; but it is well in the interest of the people.

In the breath of a prince there is life and death, and his sentence stands firm, right or wrong. If he is angry, nobody dares advise him. If he goes amiss, who shall call him into account? Now, for him who has so much mischief in his power and yet who applies that power to the common utility and comfort of the people...what can be a greater blessing to mankind than such a prince? Any man may kill another against the law, but only a prince can save him so. Let him so deal with his own subjects as he desires God should deal with him...[18]

How many of these words were absorbed you may judge for yourself as we continue. For the moment it was almost providential for Seneca and Burrus that the young emperor, who had only recently shaved for the first time, cared scarcely a fig for the intricacies of government administration. During this period the government that *they* administered in his name was efficient and above reproach. As for Nero, his mentors tried to bide their time until he could reach a more mature and noble sense of the office he held. If this meant occupying his time and energy with race horses, slave girls and seeing how much he could drink, well, they were harmless enough for now and would be outgrown soon enough.

In time, this "policy" began to work against all involved – mentors, mother and Nero himself. With no one to reprove him for his drinking and amours, Nero concluded that his conduct was quite acceptable. When his elders urged restraint, the emperor's young friends would pander to him by asking, "Do you *fear* these people? You *submit* to them? Do you not know that you are Cæsar and that you have authority over them rather than they over *you*?"

Before long Nero's exploits had become a battle of wills with his mother and mentors, as I will show by just one of many episodes. Nero, without consulting anyone else, ordered that a gift of 10 million sesterces be given to one Doryphorus, who was in charge of receiving petitions from all over the empire. This shocked his mother. In an attempt to make him understand the value of money and hopefully rescind his irresponsible impulse, she had the sum in coins brought in and piled before him. Nero sneered at the heap defiantly. "Double the amount," he said. "I didn't realize I had given him so little."

Next, as if to one-up his mother, Nero fell madly in love with a slave girl named Acte, who had been bought in Asia and later adopted into a Roman family. Agrippina flew into a rage and the idea of having an ex-slave as her rival and a possible daughter-in-law (Octavia, by the way, was but a mouse in the corner, as Agrippina had trained her.) The more Nero's mother railed and threatened — which included having some of Nero's friends beaten for encouraging him — the more the fires of adolescent passion burned even brighter.

Then one day Agrippina was suddenly a different mother. As if transformed by a metamorphosis, she was calm and sweet. She admitted to her son that her conduct had been rather "untimely." She offered him the privacy of her own bedroom in which to indulge himself. Her financial resources would also be at his disposal, she added.

This behavior puzzled Nero. His young friends were alarmed and told him to be on guard. But it didn't last long. One day Nero was looking at the resplendent robes worn by the wives and mothers of former emperors. Picking out a jeweled garment, he sent it to his mother's quarters as a present — a spontaneous, generous gift of something she had greatly admired. But Agrippina quickly lost her composure. She stormed into her son's quarters and let it be known that he had doled out but a small fraction of what he owed her for making him emperor and ruling while he dallied. The rest, she added, was being unfairly kept from her!

Perhaps it was that episode that broke whatever bonds that remained between mother and son. Nero, I suspect with Seneca's tacit approval, suddenly deposed Pallas from the position of financial secretary that had allowed him (along with being Agrippina's lover) to control most of the empire. As many know, a senatorial official is required to swear an oath upon retirement that he has done nothing illegal. Pallas had wrested from the Senate a stipulation that there should be no investigation of his past conduct and that all accounts were to be regarded as settled upon his departure. So, as Nero saw the ex-slave leaving the palace with his retinue of sycophants, he remarked that Pallas "is going to swear himself out of all his state functions."

Soon Agrippina was on the rampage again. This time she would let Nero and anyone else within range hear her snarling that Britannicus was now grown up (just going on 14, to be exact) and fully worthy of his father's supreme position —

now held, she added, by an adopted intruder who used his office to maltreat his mother. Next would come a diatribe against the Domitian family and all of its infamous deeds she could dredge up from the past. She spared not even mentioning her own hand in poisoning Claudius. "But thanks be to heaven that my stepson is alive!" she would add. "I'll take him to the Guard's camp. Let them listen when Germanicus' daughter is pitted against the men who now claim to rule the human race – old Burrus with his crippled hand, and Seneca, that deportee with the professorial voice and fancy words."

Until then Nero hadn't thought much lately about Brittanicus. Now, just as Agrippina should have realized that once absolute power is conferred there is no retrieving it, there was no way to save the lad once that imperial power was trained on his demise. The emperor now saw Britannicus as a threat. And there was no doubt more to it than the ravings of Agrippina. Britannicus, to all, was a mild, pleasant lad who inspired friendship and sympathy. For instance, during the amusements of the previous Saturnalia, the young men of the palace had thrown dice to see who should be king and Nero had won. The "king" issued some harmlessly amusing orders to the rest of the lads; but he had hoped to cause Britannicus some embarrassment by commanding him to come into the middle of the room and sing a song.

Well, the wine was flowing and the young pack growing more boisterous, but there was something that shut them up when this composed boy, who had yet to take part in a drinking bout, stood up and strode to the center. Then Britannicus sang a poem that he had written about his feelings of loneliness at being separated from his father and the throne. When he had finished, everyone remained silent for an all-too-awkward time, and Nero could sense the affection and sympathy that his friends felt for Britannicus.

Now, how to make him disappear? Nero, it would seem, had no more imagination than to follow his mother's example: the increasingly popular Locusta was again pressed into imperial service. When her first potion was given Britannicus and it only made him fly to the toilet, Nero had the woman brought to him and flogged her with his own hand for giving him "medicine" instead of what he ordered. When she admitted that she had prescribed a smaller dose to shield Nero from the odium of crime, he brought her to a room adjoining his own bedroom and forced her to mix her swiftest and most potent poison as he stood before her.

It is the custom for young imperial princes, from Parthian hostages to the sons of Roman noblemen. to eat with one another within earshot of the more luxurious tables of their parents and mentors. This is where Britannicus dined, although a servant was on hand to taste his fare. In this case the youth was handed a harmless drink. The taster did his part, but Britannicus found it too hot (as anticipated) and sent it back. At that point another server in the hire of

Nero added cold water containing the poison. With Britannicus' first gulp his whole body convulsed and he instantly ceased breathing.

His companions jumped back from their seats horrified. Some panicked and fled. Others, understanding better the ways of high stakes palace politics, remained rooted to their seats looking at Nero. The emperor remarked idly that this sort of thing often happened to epileptics and that Britannicus had been one since infancy. Carry him off, said Nero, and surely his sight and consciousness will return. With that he continued his dinner conversation.

Agrippina struggled to control her emotions, for she knew well that her last lever of control over her son had been removed. What shocked her more was that he had already learned to murder.

Octavia, seated beside Nero, was less transparent. As if trained at her father's hand, she hid all sorrow, all affection, every feeling behind a mask of imperturbableness.

Nero announced the boy's death later the same night. It was accompanied by a short speech at the palace recalling the traditional custom of withdrawing untimely deaths from the public gaze and not dwelling on them with long eulogies and processions. This event, however sad, Nero added, would allow all his future energies to be centered on the welfare of his country.

Now let me tell you just why everything was done so hastily that night. The reason is that Locusta had warned Nero that the reaction of this particular poison makes the victim's skin a tell-tale reddish, opaque color. Thus, after his brief announcement, the emperor arranged a hasty procession through the Forum and on to the Field of Mars, where a funeral pyre had already been prepared. The need for a fire that would burn quickly gave Nero a convenient reason to have the boy's body and limbs smeared in advance with gypsum. But that night there was a driving downpour, and as the body was carried through the Forum, the still-moist gypsum washed off. People there had already caught wind of rumors of poisoning. Now they saw the strange colored skin and knew they were true.

In the next few days, Nero tried to dampen the effects of his deed by distributing lavish gifts to those who had been at the table that night. Eyebrows were raised when even political opinion makers suddenly received — and accepted — gifts of country mansions as if they were so much loot from a pirate's raid. And I almost forgot Locusta. She was rewarded with a full pardon and a large country estate. It is said that she opened a "school" there and that Nero actually sent her some pupils.

Now for Agrippina. Her first reaction was to cling to Octavia, and as one of the only two remaining Claudian offspring, to build her up as a more prominent member of the royal household. At the same time, the empress became outwardly solicitous of everyone from tribunes of the Guard to leading patricians.

All this seemed to be part of some embryonic, yet inarticulated plan to form a conspiracy against Nero. But whatever it was, it was enough to alarm the young emperor.

Suddenly, Agrippina found her military bodyguard withdrawn. Then her own "inner guard" of German mercenaries disappeared. Next, the Augusta (by now in name only) learned that she was no longer entitled to hold morning receptions nor evening soirees. Instead of living in the main part of the palace, she was assigned quarters in a wing once occupied by Antonia, her great grandmother. Nero kept up the formality of calling upon his mother from time to time, but he was always accompanied by guards, and after a quick embrace and a few words, he departed. By then all these omens had driven away Agrippina's crowd of courtesans, leaving only a few faithful relatives and servants who probably had nowhere else to light.

And what of Seneca and Burrus? Surely Agrippina's downfall did not displease them. Yet, they had seen their now 18-year-old year protégé shed himself of a powerful freedman, murder a supposed rival and threaten the existence of an empress. I will merely quote one historian's assessment: "After the death of Britannicus, Seneca and Burrus no longer gave any careful attention to the public business, but were satisfied if they might manage it with moderation and still preserve their lives."

. . . .

WHENEVER ROME APPEARED WEAK or its leadership in precarious transition, Parthia was always ready to test its strength. Once again Armenia provided the arena.

Radamistus the Iberian had given up his ambitions there. Armenia supposedly remained a Roman protectorate, but its throne was still contested. Thus, it wasn't a total surprise when reports reached Rome that King Vologeses had led his Parthian armies into Armenia and was pillaging at will.

This happened very soon after Nero had become emperor. The central question might have been: "Will Rome make good on its commitment to guarantee peace in its client states?" But in the gossip capital of the world, conversation centered more on whether an emperor barely past his boyhood was capable of directing a major military campaign. Some said that a youth under feminine control was not reassuring. Nor could tutors manage battles and sieges. Nor had Nero himself shown the slightest interest in military affairs at this point. But these views were countered by those who observed that Pompey had conducted a civil war at 17 and the future Augustus at 19. "At the top," they added, "command and planning count more than physique and weapon-wielding." A good test of the emperor, they agreed, would be whether he appoints the best man as commander or favors some adventurer who wants to fatten his purse.

But Burrus and Seneca were up to their responsibilities. Under their direction, Nero commanded the eastern divisions to be increased to full strength by drafts from adjacent provinces. Agrippa II, now back in Jerusalem, was ordered to raise an army, again mostly from Samaria and Galilee, and join the king of nearby Commagene at the Euphrates for an all-out invasion into Parthia. Quadratus, the Syrian governor, was to remain on watch in Antioch with two brigades (down from the usual four). And as commander to coordinate the whole affair, Nero chose an experienced general, Cnæus Domitius Corbulo. A former consul under Gaius and a rigid disciplinarian under Claudius as commander of Lower Germany, Corbulo's appointment quickly quelled any doubts as to whether promotions were to be made on merit.

Corbulo was barely getting underway when Vologeses and his troops suddenly left Armenia. The reason, unknown at the time, was the king's need to put down a revolt by yet another contentious royal brother back home. Vologeses fully intended to return to Armenia. But when word of his departure reached Rome, you would have thought that all Parthia had swooned at its feet. Senators performed lavish celebrations, decreeing days of thanksgiving on which the emperor would wear the triumphal robe, enter the city in ovation and have his statue erected in the temple of Mars the Avenger.

Some of this, I suspect, was an excuse to portray Nero to the Parthians (and any other wobbly client states) as a brilliant and fearsome foe. But as it was, the lull probably proved to be a lucky circumstance for Corbulo. Officers from an advance guard reported back that the main bulk of the eastern armies weren't exactly the precision-drilled troops of Germany. Softened and dulled by years of peace, some lacked even breastplates and many had never dug a ditch or manned a rampart. So Corbulo tried to bide time by sending Vologeses a message: choose peace over war and present to Rome the traditional royal hostages as a sign of your continued obeisance.

Corbulo had marched as far as Cilicia at the time. Obviously, the lines of authority hadn't been worked out because Quadratus, in Antioch, had the same idea on his own and Vologeses soon found himself with two identical messages. Either way, they offered a convenient course for the Parthian king. He needed time to regroup before invading Armenia again and wanted to select his own time and place for battle. The demand for hostages afforded an opportunity to dump on the Romans all of his most menacing rivals in the royal household.

A quarrel soon erupted between the commander and the Syrian governor over who would have the honor of presenting the hostages in Rome, but Nero's astute advisors smoothed things over by having the emperor declare that the fasces and other emblems of imperial authority be wreathed with laurel "owing to the successes of Quadratus and Corbulo."

. . . .

THERE IS NO RECORD of what Paul did in Cæsarea or Jerusalem upon his return from Greece and there is no use speculating. But after visiting the temple and descending the 2,400-foot mount on which sprawled the Jewish capital, he undoubtedly would have stopped often in Samaria and Phœnecia to re-energize the many Christian communities that now flourished along the Roman road. By winter the apostle would be in Antioch, from where he had departed, to give an account of himself to the churches that had in part financed his second mission.

A long rest must have been on his mind, too, before setting out on his next mission to establish a bastion of Christianity in Ephesus that could equal the one at Antioch. But as a shepherd's flock increases, he can also expect that more sheep will wander off or fall to predators. So it was with the small, fragile churches of Galatia in the northeast corner of Asia Minor. Drawn mainly from the Jewish members of synagogues where Paul had preached in his first visits, these Jewish Christians were being swayed once again by the Pharisaic "circumcision party," which insisted that man was not freed from observance of the Law just because he believed Jesus to be the Messiah.

Paul had assumed that he had already surmounted this hurdle some 14 years before when the Christian elders met in Jerusalem. Now he was simply too weary of the whole business to resort again to friendly persuasion. In a letter to all the churches of Galatia, dictated to an amanuensis as he paced and gestured, Paul let his famous temper "out of the pen," as they say. After a few restrained words of greeting, Paul plunged right into his reason for writing:

> I am astonished that you are so quickly deserting him who called you in the grace of Christ and turning to a different gospel — not that there is a different gospel — not that there is another gospel, but there are some who trouble you and want to pervert the gospel of Christ. But even if we, or an angel from heaven, should preach to you a gospel contrary to that which we have preached to you, let him be anathema. As we have said before, so now I say again, if anyone is preaching a gospel contrary to that which you received, let him be accursed.[19]

This rather surprises me, because the language Paul used implies no less than the curses that priests of so many mystery religions will (for the right fee) put on someone's intended victim. I'm thinking also of the wax figurines into which people put the hair or nail cuttings of enemies, as well as the lead tablets on which they inscribe curses and bury in the ground in hopes it will endure "as long as lead," as the saying goes. And for good measure, Paul adds his wish "that those who are shaking your faith by insistence on circumcision would go all the way and mutilate [castrate] themselves as well!"

> O foolish Galatians! Who has bewitched you, before whose eyes Jesus Christ was publicly portrayed as crucified? Let me ask you only this: Did you receive the Spirit by works of the law, or by hearing with faith? Are you so foolish? Having begun with the Spirit, are you now ending with the flesh? Did you experience so many things in vain? — if it really is in vain. Does he who supplies the Spirit to you and works miracles among you do so by works of the Law or by hearing with faith?

> Thus Abraham "believed God, and it was reckoned to him as righteousness." So you see that it is men of faith who are the sons of Abraham. And the scripture, foreseeing that God would justify the Gentiles by faith, preached the gospel to Abraham, saying, "In thee shall all nations be blessed." So then, those who are men of faith are blessed with Abraham who had faith.[20]

The Law, though of ancient derivation, continued Paul, was only meant to be subordinate and temporary, almost like the attendant who looked after the boy on his way to school and saw him safely into his teacher's hands. Thus, the Law has now guided man into the presence of his true teacher, Jesus Christ. In Christ, all are children of God through their faith.

> There is no longer Jew nor Greek, there is no longer slave or free, there is no longer male or female; for all of you are one in Christ Jesus. And if you belong to Christ, then you are Abraham's offspring [and] heirs according to the promise.[21]

The Galatians joyfully accepted this new freedom when Paul first preached to them. Why, he asked, would they now want to turn back from it to such material matters as having to observe a rigid litany of rules about how they lived and dressed and ate? The men who have been undermining him in Galatia have their own ends in mind, said Paul. They mean to make the Galatians dependent on them for admission to the church. They want to claim as *their* prerogative the right to fix the price and terms of a person's salvation. If only Paul could see them in person and talk to them now!

In a short while, his anger spent, Paul became the loving shepherd again. Neither circumcision nor uncircumcision "is of any avail" in the eyes of God compared to "faith working through love."

> For the whole law is fulfilled in one word, "You shall love thy neighbor as yourself." But if you bite and devour one another, take heed that you are not consumed by one another.

> But I say, walk by the Spirit, and do not gratify the desires of the flesh. For the desires of the flesh are against the Spirit, and the desires of the Spirit are against the flesh. For these are opposed to each other to prevent you from doing what you would. But if you are led by the Spirit you are not under the Law.

> Now the works of the flesh are plain: immorality, impurity, licentiousness, idolatry, sorcery, enmity, strife, jealousy, anger, selfishness, dissension, party spirit, envy, drunkenness, carousing and the like. I warn you, as I warned you before, that those who do such things shall not inherit the kingdom of God. But the fruits of the Spirit are love, joy, peace, patience, kindness, goodness, faithfulness, gentleness, self-control, Against such there is no law. And those who belong to Jesus Christ have crucified the flesh with its passions and desires.[22]

As soon as the next spring made the Cilician Gates passable, Paul was off again on the road to the churches of Galatia, Phrygia and Pisidia to restate this message himself with the same power and vigor he had used in the letter. Timothy and probably others must have been with him through the dangerous climb onto the Anatolian plain, but I believe they went on to visit the churches of Greece. Paul's destination was Ephesus, and he entered it alone one autumn day for what would be a stay of some two years.

As Corinth was the hub of east-west communications for Greece, this city of 300,000 is the same for Asia Minor. Yes, Ephesus serves the sea trade (by means of a narrow bay from the Ægean); and trade routes intersect there from all directions; and it is the home of the Roman proconsul of Asia. But the city is known first as *neucorus*, "the servant of the goddess." Tradition has it that over 700 years ago peasants saw a rock of some sort fall from the sky and land by a mountain stream that ran below a hill. They deemed it a sign from the fertility goddess and erected a small Achaic shrine over it. In time the modest shrine was replaced by successive temples. Earthquakes took their toll, but each rebuilt temple was more splendid than the one before. The one today, which had taken over 100 years to build when Paul arrived, is one of the Seven Wonders of the World. It measures 305 feet long by 180 feet wide, surrounded by Ionic pillars 60 feet high — many of them erected by Croesus the wealthy king of Lydia before he was captured and enslaved by the invading Persian, Cyrus.

The temple's object of veneration, however, has always been Artemis, or "Diana of the Ephesians." Today, embracing the features of the Egyptian goddess Isis as well, she is the female embodiment of fecundity and the eternal rebirth of all living things. And so she is called The Mother of All Things. She has many breasts to embody her fertility. She bears the triple-tiered model of the temple on her head in the form of a crown to identify herself as the protectress of cities. A crescent on her forehead shows that she is also the moon goddess.

At first the city was built around the temple, where winemakers and tailors worked amidst its hubbub of eunuch priests, prostitute-"priestesses" and souvenir shops. But Ephesus has always had a serious silting problem where the mouth of the Caystrus empties into the bay, so it seems that whenever an earthquake caused major damage (the most recent one in the early reign of Tiberius), it was a good excuse to move the center of commerce nearer to the receding waterfront to the southwest. Today the famous temple is no less visited, but sits apart from the central city on the eastern side of the Caystrus.

In the shadows of the great temple are many practitioners of magic and the occult. Ephesus is still known as "The Magic City," and therein flourish the followers of Dionysus, of Isis and Cybele with their frenzied whirling and incoherent babbling in the grip of strong drugs or too much wine. In time, Paul would meet them all head-on, but at first he had to contend with a disturbing surprise.

As expected, Aquila and Priscilla were on hand to offer Paul shelter and their tentmaking shop should he need to support himself. As usual, the synagogue they attended had shown few signs of receptivity to The Way, but the couple had managed to preserve and nurture a core group of a at least a dozen Christians. The "surprise" I mentioned was that not long before Paul's arrival, their synagogue at Ephesus had offered its rostrum to one Apollos, a Jew from Alexandria who preached a message that seemed more centered on John the Baptist than Jesus. Eloquent, persuasive and probably impressive of stature as well, he came from a refined center of Jewish learning that had produced men like the historian Philo — in sharp contrast to the increasingly divisive and disruptive Jerusalem. With great fervor and effect, Apollos preached to the synagogue about repentance and of John's preparation of the One to come. And in John's name, he had baptized several people.

One night Aquila and Priscilla took Apollos home and patiently told him of the ministry of Jesus and all that had followed. To their relief, he accepted the gospel willingly. He left soon thereafter with their letter of introduction to the church at Corinth, and since then word had already come back that Apollos was not only becoming a formidable Christian preacher in Greece, but was also "powerfully confuting the Jews in public."

Paul was puzzled at first on hearing his friends' report. As various members of the small church came calling at the house of Aquila and Priscilla, Paul would interview them. "Did you receive the Holy Spirit when you declared your belief?" he would ask. "No," was the usual reply. "We never even heard there is a Holy Spirit."

"Well then, into what were you baptized?"

"Into John's baptism," they answered.

"John," said Paul, "baptized with the baptism of repentance, telling people to believe in the one who was to come after him – that is, Jesus."

Soon Paul gathered 12 of these church members together, took them down to the banks of the Caystrus, and baptized them in the name of Jesus. "And when Paul laid his hands on them," Luke reports, "the Holy Spirit came on them; and they spoke with tongues and prophesied."

Having reclaimed his small flock, Paul spent the next three months trying to increase it by preaching in the synagogue. I suspect that the influence and friendship of Aquila and Priscilla helped restrain the congregation from the uprising that usually confronted Paul after just a few weeks, but eventually too many were "stubborn" or "disbelieved," and some were "speaking evil of The Way before the congregation." So Paul withdrew from the synagogue and instead found daily access to a lecture hall owned and/or used by a private teacher named Tyrannus (his students must have had fun with his name, which means "Tyrant").

Now this was an altogether different setting. If the small lyceum was just off the busy Street of Curettes, as some say, it would be in the midst of shops and travelers. For some two years, Tyrannus would finish his classes by late morning and Paul would take over during the long afternoon siesta period, that is from around eleven until four. At his feet would be some of his Christian disciples, but invited to join them would be anyone who wandered by and felt like dropping in – from nappers to curiosity seekers to serious scholars to drunken hecklers. But they were both Gentile and Jew, and before long "all the residents of Asia heard the word of the Lord," Luke's diary proclaims.

Part of the spreading word had to do with miracles. Or magic. In this "City of Magic" the two were bound to get mixed up in the minds of the people – with both good and bad results for Paul. Luke's narrative states that "God did extraordinary miracles by the hand of Paul" during this time – chiefly by healing the physically sick and casting evil spirits from the mentally afflicted. Paul won people to Christianity who had witnessed him healing, but as word spread, the apostle's true purpose was garbled. Soon people begged for bits of his clothing – perhaps a handkerchief or a rope he had used while tentmaking – because they, too, were bound to have healing powers. And in this city of wizards, witches, seers, sorcerers, astrologers, diviners and palm readers word spread among those who hadn't even seen him that a man named Paul was exercising an extraordinarily powerful brand of magic over at the Hall of Tyannus.

Some even tried to practice it in his name. At one point an iterinent "rabbi" named Sceva and his seven sons came to Ephesus — I suppose them to be pseudo-mystics of some sort who hawked their curative powers or sold papyri describing "secret" prescriptions for medicines in an Aramaic script that no one could read. Walking about the streets to get the feel of the city, and seeing or hearing about Paul, they decided to incorporate the popular preacher's "Lord Jesus" in their mystic rites for curing a violent lunatic. No doubt after first pocketing their "fee" from the young man's family, Sceva the rabbi addressed the evil spirit inside him and said, "I command you in the name of Jesus, whom Paul preaches" to come out of him.

With that the evil spirit (perhaps the young man himself?) answered: "I know Jesus, and I know Paul. But who are *you*?" With that, the story goes, the lunatic flew into a frenzy and began clawing at their clothes until the "healer" and all seven sons all ran off yelping.

Paul knew that his healings came only to those who believed in the word. At the same time, his natural reaction was to lash out at all magicians in an attempt to clarify the difference between acts of the loving God and flimsy fakery. Now I can't say that these charlatans at last grasped the gospel or that they were cowed by their awe of a more dominating power, but the fact is that there was a wave of repentance by astrologers and magicians throughout the city. "Many of those who were now believers came, confessing and divulging their practices," Luke reports. "And a number of those who practiced magic arts brought their books together and burned them in the sight of all; and they counted the value of them and found it came to 50,000 pieces of silver [drachmas, I presume]. So the word of the Lord grew and prevailed mightily."

Its impact, in fact, even reached the mighty temple of Artemis on the outskirts of the city. Everyone from the shopkeepers in prime rental locations to the lone waif who proffers a cheap trinket in a tourist's way began to see their daily sales fall off. Yet the weather was fine and the city as crowded as ever. What could be the reason? Without too much head-scratching, they were able to pin the cause on the man preaching about Jesus down in some schoolmaster's assembly hall. But the people who became the most alarmed were the few dozen metalworkers and silversmiths who manufactured the amulets, replicas of the temple and thousands of miniature Artemis statuettes that tourists bought to take back for their little household shrines.

Before long, one Demetrius, who seems to have been the head of the silver-smith's guild, called a general meeting of his fellow tradesmen. "Men," he said, "You know that from this business we gain our wealth. And you see and hear that not only at Ephesus but almost throughout Asia this Paul has persuaded and turned away a considerable company of people, saying that gods made with hands are not gods. And there is danger not only that this trade of ours may come into disrepute, but also that the temple of the great goddess Artemis may count for nothing, and that she, whom all Asia and the world worships, may even be deposed from her magnificence."

By the time the meeting had ended, the tradesmen had whipped themselves into a lather, chanting, "Great is Artemis of the Ephesians." Before long rumors were flying across town that these Christians, Jewish-Christians or whatever they were had determined to take away the freedom of people to worship the gods of their choice. They might even try to bring down the temple itself!

The crowd was so riled up by now that during the same day they marched down through the center of town and massed at the main theater with the intent of getting a magistrate to try Paul on the spot. Paul probably would have welcomed the chance to address an entire theater of Ephesians, but friends were able to hide him from the angry guildsmen. However, the protesters did manage to get their hands on two of Paul's young Christian co-workers, Gaius and Aristarchus, and strong-armed them into the theater. Also dragged in was a man named Alexander, presumably the ruling elder of a synagogue and perhaps even a member of the metalworking guild.

While one of the guild chieftains scurried about to find an appropriate city official, the crowd continued to roil and boil in the theater. The gathering had now developed into a general display of trade guild strength. Some had brought the banners, drums and cymbals usually reserved for their official processions and now, to the beat of their thumping and clanging, the crowd chanted, "Great is Artemis of the Ephesians!" at the top of their lungs for over an hour. At last the Jew Alexander asked to speak, probably to tell the crowd that this had nothing to do with the Jews of Ephesus, but with some splinter sect led by a foreigner. But every time Alexander tried to speak he would be drowned out by the shouts of "Great is Artemis of the Ephesians!"

At last onto the stage strode an official everyone seemed to recognize and respect. The chanting wound down as he raised his hand. "Men of Ephesus," he said in deep, soothing tones, "what man is there who does not know that the city of the Ephesians is temple keeper of the great Artemis and of the sacred stone that fell from the sky? Seeing then that these things cannot be contradicted, you ought to be quiet and do nothing rash. For you have brought these men here who are neither sacrilegious nor blasphemers of our goddess." If Demetrius and his craftsmen have a complaint against anyone, the courts are open, and there are proconsuls, he said. "For we are in danger of being charged with rioting today, there being no cause that we can give to justify this commotion."

From "rioting" he probably inferred sedition, which might just send a company of sword-wielding Roman soldiers into the theater. In any case, the official dismissed the assembly and people departed orderly enough, much to the relief of the trembling Gaius and Aristarchus, I'm sure.

All this happened in the midst of Paul's greatest success as a missionary. He clearly had many friends in Ephesus, no doubt some in official positions, and probably could have endured there if he had insisted upon it. But when his friends and followers strongly advised him to depart, the apostle did not refuse. For one thing, he had already made up his mind to go to Greece and take up a collection from the churches there for the impoverished Jewish Christians in Jerusalem. After delivering it personally, he was determined to go to Rome — and from there to Spain.

But there was another reason for going to Greece as well. Throughout most of his stay in Ephesus, the joy Paul must have felt at spreading the gospel successfully in the Asian capital had been offset by letters and travelers with depressing news. They described dissension and even immorality in the church he had founded in Corinth. Paul had even taken a brief side trip there from Ephesus at one point and found himself rudely treated. It hurt him deeply, but he felt compelled to go back.

. . . .

A. D. 5 6 — 5 7

Wickedness, it is true, may escape the law, but not the conscience. For a private conviction is the first and the greatest punishment of offenders; so that sin plagues itself; and the fear of vengeance pursues even those who escape the stroke of it. It would be ill for good men that iniquity may so easily evade the law, the judge and the execution if nature had not set up torments and gibbets in the consciences of transgressors. He who is guilty lives in perpetual terror. And while he expects to be punished, he punishes himself; and whoever deserves it expects it.

What if he be not detected? He is still in apprehension that he may be. His sleeps are painful, and never secure, and he cannot speak of another man's wickedness without thinking of his own. Whereas a good conscience is a continual feast.   —Seneca [23]

It is a dangerous office to give good advice to intemperate princes.
                                                    —Seneca [24]

NERO WAS NOW 19 and spending less of his time in tutoring. Seneca was spending more of his governing Rome, which may have functioned more smoothly in this brief span than at any time since Augustus. But the emperor, seeming to show interest only in the display of pomp and circumstance at ceremonies requiring an imperial presence, reserved his most ardent energies for living the life of an idle rich youth with no restrictions on his appetites.

The latter became more excessive and turbulent with each passing day, as if the only lesson the youthful debaucheries of Gaius had taught Nero was a desire to compete so as to exceed them. All this was unknown to the public until the restless young emperor, having no restraints upon him inside the palace, began rampaging the streets of Rome at night with a gang of young rowdies. No sooner was twilight ended when he would slip on a wig or slave's dress and go out to the taverns with his friends. After tearing up a public house or getting tossed out by the unsuspecting keeper, the aroused pack would prowl the darkened streets, breaking shop windows, grabbing whatever merchandise they wished and then auctioning it off to strangers on the street. Then they would go off and lay in wait to attack some innocent stroller, stabbing him to death and casting his body into the sewers.

Before long the desire for greater and more dangerous thrills led Nero and his band to scale walls and rob homes and manhandle the women inside them. Sometimes the invaders themselves were punched or beaten by men who knew not whom they were resisting. In one instance a junior senator, Julius Montanus, ran into his dark atrium one night to find a stocky masked intruder groping indecently at his wife. The man wheeled on him with a blow to the head, but Montanus bulled him to the ground and fought for his life. The young senator had grabbed the man's hair with one hand and was bashing his head with his other fist when he felt the hair strangely slipping from his grasp. Just then some more hooligans rushed in and pried their confederate loose. They were carrying him off when they crossed a patch of lamplight and Montanus realized that the man had been wearing a wig, and that it was askew across his face.

Could it be *him*?

The more the dazed Montanus recovered and recalled that frenzied night, the less he could deny the fact that he had been wrestling in mortal combat with the emperor of the Roman Empire. He waited in agony for a word, a reprisal – anything – from the palace on Palatine Hill. The irony is that Nero thought himself unrecognized and was not about to do anything that might interrupt his nocturnal adventures. Indeed, no one at all heard much from the emperor for the next several days because he had two black eyes and several bruises. He was equally apprehensive of being found out.

But Montanus did not know this. At last, unable to endure the suspense any longer, he sent Nero a note apologizing for his unintended attack on the imperial personage. "So," fumed the emperor after reading it, "he knew that he was striking Nero." A message was sent back to the young patrician. A few days later, Montanus, who had not even begun to serve his first day in the Senate, paid for his slur by committing suicide.

As you might expect, word of the emperor and his midnight marauders was soon all over Rome. Their impact on the city was thus magnified in two ways.

First, Nero was now always accompanied by a few gladiators or soldiers. They would remain hidden in the background when the roving hooligans would get into a brawl, but would storm to the rescue if the tide turned against their "clients." Second, other young street gangs emerged, led by psuedo-Neros, and behaved with impunity as if it were the fashionable thing to do. As one historian recorded: "Attacks on distinguished men and women multiplied. Rome by night came to resemble a conquered city."

Before long, the end of the night no longer brought down the curtain on the emperor's excesses. Nero's true identity was now public and he displayed it all day long. Lest I seem to be the persecutor of a noble young man, I will quote another writer of the times:

> He prolonged his revels from midday to midnight, often livening himself by a warm plunge, or, if it were summer, into water cooled by snow. Sometimes, too, he closed the Naumachia [the huge enclosed basin, used for mock naval battles] and banqueted there in public, or in the Campus Martius, or in the Circus Maximus, waited on by harlots and dancing girls from all over the city. When he drifted down the Tiber to Ostia or sailed about the gulf of Baiæ, booths were set up at intervals along the banks and shores, fitted out as brothels and eating-houses, before which were matrons who played the part of bawds and hostesses, soliciting him from every side to come ashore. He also coerced his friends to give him banquets, one of whom spent 4,000,000 sesterces on a dinner at which turbans were the favor, and another spent a considerably larger sum on one at which thousands of roses were distributed.[25]

Not surprisingly, theater and games also began to occupy Nero's interests increasingly. Whereas bodyguards accompanied the emperor on his nighttime violence, he dismissed the Prætorians who usually stood guard in the theaters to prevent public disturbances. His given reason was that they should be confined to military duties. The real reason was that he wanted nothing to impede riotous behavior in the theaters. He incited performing mimes to fight like warring gangs on stage by offering large prizes for the victors, then would have himself brought up to the rear of the theater in a covered sedan to watch in secret. One time when these "actors" were pelting each other with stones and pieces of broken glass, Nero himself was hurling stones from his balcony and actually cracked the skull of one of them.

Offstage, these "mimes" and "dancers," if they could really be called such at this point, caroused about town at night behaving no differently than the other gangs of young toughs. Eventually, the Senate behaved as though the emperor was not involved and would be equally insulted by this behavior. Citing concern for public safety, it voted to expel the actors from Italy and re-station troops in the theaters.

Nero's attitude towards games and gladiatorial shows leaves me a bit baffled. At first glance, he would have seemed to be a moderating influence on them because he forbade anyone to fight to the death. He also ordered that no provincial official could give shows of wild beasts or gladiators (this, mostly because governors would soak their subjects for the cost and then rake off a portion for themselves). But in Rome games were promoted and everything short of death encouraged. Within one year Nero began and completed a wooden amphitheater on the Campus Martius. At its opening, the arena was flooded and a naval battle took place between rival "Persian" and "Athenian" forces while various sea monsters swam in their midst. The next day the water was let out, and when the ground had dried, a mock battle between land forces was staged. On another occasion men on horses chased down running bulls and tried to wrestle them to the ground. In another scene, Nero's bodyguards brought down 400 bears and 300 lions with their javelins. Tiring of this sport, the emperor compelled 400 senators and 600 Roman knights to fight in the arena — even those of old age and the highest dignity.

But what was beginning to enchant the emperor the most was the sound of his own voice reciting a poem or singing an air. He had now begun singing and acting lessons. The reason why he now delivered all judicial opinions only in writing was not so much a desire to craft them carefully, but not to strain a voice that his confidants told him had "magical qualities."

Where was his tutor and voice of reason at this time? Was Seneca among these sycophants?

> Some place their happiness in wealth, some in the liberty of the body, and others in the pleasures of the sense and palate. But what are metals, tastes, sounds and colors to the mind of a reasonable creature? He who sets his heart upon riches, the very fear of poverty will be grievous to him, He who is ambitious shall be galled with envy at any man who gets before him, for in that case he who is not first is last.
>
> —Seneca[26]

> Our ancestors, when they were free, lived either in caves or in arbors; but slavery came with gilding and marble. I would have him who comes into my house take more notice of the master than the furniture.
>
> —Seneca[27]

It is said that Seneca declined to eat at the same table with his royal pupil because he preferred to spend as much time as possible in quiet philosophical studies. But at one point in his imperial service the Stoic tutor owned 500 identical tables of citrus wood, with legs of ivory, on which he served banquets to those who doted on him.

I have never encountered a man whose public and private personas are so sharply debated. On one hand, there is no doubt that in his youth and during his exile on Corsica he had lived the stoic, æsthetic life he preached in his nobly-written works. Nor does anyone seem to question that the tutor Seneca made an attempt to instill these principles in his pupil. And finally, they agree that he, with the help of Burrus, governed as moderately in the name of Nero as could be expected.

On the other hand, his detractors are too numerous to ignore. They point to the fact that this man of moderation quickly amassed a fortune of over 300 million sesterces, much of it by charging usurious lending rates in outlying provinces. They say that this proponent of sexual restraint succumbed to improper relations with Agrippina, who tried to enlist him in designs against her son. They charge as well that the same tutor who declined to kiss the emperor upon entering or leaving his presence enjoyed the sexual favors of young boys. Even those who admire his books or heard him bemoan the unfairness of Claudius for banishing him to Corsica are quick to cite his work, *Consolatio and Polybium*, which contains maudlin praise of the emperor and his chief freedmen at the time. If Seneca was content with the simple life on Corsica, they ask, why did he take such pains to have the book sent to Claudius and his household?

I wish you and I, dear reader, could ask Seneca himself. I can only guess that most of his largess, homes, slaves and the like, came at the insistence of his grateful student, who was in the habit of bestowing such things on many people who caught his fancy. If that were the case, Seneca might have referred us again to his essay *Of a Happy Life:*

> The virtuous man is content with his lot, whatever it be, without
> wishing that he was not,
> Though of the two, he had rather abound than want.[28]

. . . .

JERUSALEM HAD AGAIN BECOME a boiling cauldron, and the procurator Felix drew most of the blame for it. One might think that with a Jewish wife he would have gained great insight into the customs and a certain empathy for the people. Instead, no less than a Roman commentator of the times described him as a man who "practiced every kind of cruelty and lust," one who "wielded the power of a king with all the instincts of a slave."

However, this observer, at least, will proffer a measure of sympathy for Felix: He was beset by so many colors and shades of dissension that it was all but futile to sort them all out and deal with them differently. Thus, whether the apprehended were robbers or political activists or violent overthrowers of Rome or religious visionaries, his clumsy sense of even-handed justice doomed all alike to the sword or the cross.

In his early years as procurator, Felix had concentrated on rooting out brigands in the name of assuring public safety. He was fortunate in capturing alive one Eleazer, the most brazen among them, who had ravaged Judea for over 20 years. But when Eleazer was sent to Rome for trial, it was as if multitudes took his place. Hundreds were caught and crucified, but always there were more.

The reason there was no end to their numbers, I would surmise, is that the ranks of what Rome defined as "robbers" included political opponents of Rome as well. For many years before, both Jerusalem and the Galilee region had their share of "Zealots," although they had never had enough numbers to be considered sects as had the Pharisees, Sadducees and Essenes. Who was a Zealot? Typically, he was an impatient, risk-taking young man who saw Rome as an excessive tax levier and oppressor of Jewish customs and pride. And he was ready to forgo family life and live apart in the hills, associating even with criminal marauders if the end result was the same – disruption of civil authority and eventual expulsion of Rome from the region.

And so, when a "prophet" from Egypt arrived in Judea and called for a religious revolt, he attracted some 30,000 followers in rather short order. I can't find a record of his name, but the histories state that this "prophet" led these rag-tag troops some five furlongs away from the city to the Mount of Olives, which overlooked one of its walls. He promised them that at his command the city walls would fall down and that he would then lead them through the breech and on to victory over the small Roman garrison that happened to be guarding the Fortress of Antonia at the time. Before he had a chance to make good on his promise, Felix rode out with a great number of horsemen, who had raced up from Cæsarea. Splintering and splattering the poorly armed commoners in all directions, his men cut down 400 of them and took another 200 as prisoners. The ringleader got away, but in his retreat he raced through neighboring villages, exhorting the people to take up arms against Rome. When they refused – as all did – they had their homes burned and plundered, and the band of survivors took up camp in the surrounding wilderness where they fomented trouble for many months to come.

Meanwhile, in Jerusalem, some Zealots for Jewish liberty decided that stealth would serve them better than open rebellion – a course that proved far worse to Roman and Jewish leaders alike For it was at this time that Jerusalem became infested with the more menacing and undetectable *Sicarii*.

Picture yourself completing a long journey to the temple. You could be a Jewish elder from Babylon on your way to deliver tribute from your synagogue, or perhaps a Syrian merchant on your way to buy hides from a temple official. It's the eve of a festival and the streets are full of loud noises and fast-moving strangers. Suddenly – you don't even know from where – you see the flash of a short blade in a glint of light and feel a sliver of steel slice into your midriff. As the blood begins to spurt, you look for just a split second into the burning eyes of a young man whose face is hidden in the folds of a robe supposedly drawn over his face to protect against the desert winds.

Enter the Sicarii. The name is taken from the short, upturned Roman sword, the *Sicæ*. A political movement? Nothing that well-articulated. An emerging religious sect? No, because few of its "practitioners" ever met in one place or long enough to effect a philosophy. Rather, carrying a concealed dagger and puncturing a target in a crowd at lightning speed was, in my view, a quick and efficient way that the wronged or downtrodden or impatient – but invariably infuriated – young rebel could exact a stealthy revenge upon whomever he deemed to be his oppressor.

The first man who was slain by Sacarii was Jonathan, the high priest. After his death many were slain near the temple every day. However, the impact was worse than the actual number of deaths that resulted. For one thing, a man feared to walk the streets, and would look suspiciously on the approach of another man who had been his friendly acquaintance just the day before. For another, the stealthy manner in which such deaths were afflicted sowed the seeds of fear and suspicion into organizations that were once seen as pillars of their community, including the temple priesthood itself. When Jonathan was stabbed, none of the priesthood knew by whom or why it happened. Soon some suspected members within their ranks. Before long various candidates for high priest had assembled supporters from the rabble and were throwing stones at one another across the street. The priesthood became so fractious and leaderless that some temple priests would send their servants to the villages of poorer priests, snatching away the tithes from their very threshing floors. And the poorest among them died for want.

Judea was beginning to careen out of control. Until now the procuratorship of Felix had been as secure as the Fortress of Antonia because he was the brother of Pallas, the unrivaled freedman of Claudius and lover of Agrippina. Now Nero was emperor and the haughty Pallas was gone. Why did Felix continue to survive? Perhaps because Seneca and Burrus did not think anyone else could do better under the circumstances.

· · · · · · · · ·

I HAVEN'T GIVEN YOU A COMPLETE PICTURE of Paul's previous two years in Ephesus. I told you what he did in the Asian capital, but the story might have been disjointed had I reported that his days and nights were also filled with receiving reports and delegations from the various churches he had founded, each seeking guidance on how to cope with this setback or that troubling question.

Of these, none was more perplexing nor frustrating than the situation in Corinth, the site of Paul's greatest success before his journey to Ephesus. Midway during his stay in Ephesus a visitor had brought him news that too many Corinthian church members had lapsed into their old pagan ways of greed, idolatry, drunkenness and sexual immorality. Yet they were still attending worship services and calling themselves Christians. Paul responded with a harsh, but brief letter (of which no copy remains) warning them that such practices could have no place in the church. The news was especially troubling to Paul because in the organizational plan within his mind, Corinth was the Christian bastion in Greece. He could not hope to go on to Rome and Spain if this link in the chain of churches and communications that now stretched from Jerusalem to Antioch to Ephesus was not strong and healthy.

Paul was still awaiting a reply when some travelers from the house of a woman named Chloe (a house church, I presume) reported that the congregations in Corinth were also breaking up into cliques. Some of it had to do with wealth and poverty. The meals following church services had dissolved into dinner parties which often found the well-to-do dining amidst plenty at one table while their less fortunate brethren made do with scant pickings at the next table.

Worse, said Chloe's messengers, were their growing differences over who should lead the churches. Some members had been besmitten with the polished preaching style of the Alexandrian Apollos, who had been in their midst only recently. Because Peter was a known and revered name, some had decided that his ties to the original church in Jerusalem made him their logical leader. Others were calling themselves the Party of Christ because they would not be led by a flawed mortal. The memory of Paul and his place as their founder seemed to be receding in his absence. Why? Because their image of the apostle was not that of an imposing figure or spellbinding speaker. In fact, the more they thought about it, Paul's boldness as a leader was only in his letters. The man they remembered in person was, in fact, rather unimposing, and, to some, even a dissapointment.

This kind of turmoil occupied Paul's mind constantly in Ephesus even as he spent mornings in the tentmaking shop of Aquila and Priscilla and afternoons in the Hall of Tyannus. Not long after the report from Chloe's church members, he was surprised when there suddenly appeared a three-man delegation claiming to represent all the churches of Corinth. They might have found Paul lacking in charisma, but they certainly didn't hesitate to consult him with a long list of questions that were troubling them. The questions ranged from how to conduct services to how to live amidst idol worship to whether they should settle their differences in civil law courts and thus accept the judgment of heathens. In addition to general questions like these, they cited issues involving specific members. One young man, for instance, had married his widowed step-mother. It seemed indecent. Was it?

Paul decided it was time to send the three men back with a letter covering all these subjects that could be read to all the house churches. So one day, as a professional short-hand expert scrawled furiously, Paul paced back and forth dictating, his mind ablaze. He began by plunging into the subject of factions within the church.

> What I mean is that each one of you says, 'I belong to Paul,' or 'I belong to Apollos' or 'I belong to Cephas' [Peter] or 'I belong to Christ.' Is Christ divided? Was Paul crucified for you? Or were you baptized in the name of Paul? I am thankful that I baptized none of you [and here he mentions a few whom he actually did baptize]. For Christ did not send me to baptize, but to preach the gospel, and not with eloquent wisdom, lest the cross of Christ be emptied of its power.[29]

For it is not words about the power of the cross that redeem men, but the power of God, Paul said.

> For it is written, 'I will destroy the wisdom of the wise, and the cleverness of the clever I will thwart.'

> Where is the wise man? Where is the scribe? Where is the debater of the age? Has not God made foolish the wisdom of the world? For since, in the wisdom of God, it pleased God through the folly of what we preach to save those who believe. For Jews demand signs and Greeks seek wisdom, but we preach Christ crucified, a stumbling block to the Jews and folly to the Gentiles. But to those who are called, both Jews and Greeks, Christ [is the] power of God and the wisdom of God. For the foolishness of God is wiser than men, and the weakness of God is stronger than men.[30]

Paul then turned to the unflattering remarks he had heard about his own lack of luster as a speaker and leader.

> When I came to you, brethren, I did not come proclaiming to you the
> testimony of God in lofty words or wisdom. For I decided to know
> nothing among you except Jesus Christ and him crucified. And I was
> with you in weakness and in much fear and trembling; and my speech
> and my message were not in plausible words of wisdom, but in
> demonstration of the Spirit and power, that your faith might not rest
> in the wisdom of men but in the power of God.[31]

At the time he first came to Corinth, Paul added, the people were not yet spiritual people but men of the flesh — just "babes in Christ."

> I fed you with milk, not solid food, for you were not ready for it. And
> even yet you are not ready, for you are still of the flesh. For while there
> is jealousy and strife among you, are you not of the flesh and behaving
> like ordinary men? For when one says, "I belong to Paul," and another,
> "I belong to Apollos," are you not merely men?
>
> What then is Apollos? What is Paul? Servants through whom you be-
> lieved, as the Lord assigned to each. I planted. Apollos watered, but
> God gave the growth.[32]

Next, Paul addressed the reports of immorality among specific people in the
church. The man who married his step-mother should be "removed from
among you." As for associating with immoral people, Paul reminded the
Corinthians that his earlier letter of warnings was not directed just at robbers,
idolaters and the like from the outside, but those within as well. For:

> ...you are not to associate with anyone who bears the name of brother if
> he is guilty of immorality or greed or is an idolater, reviler, drunkard
> or robber — not even to eat with such a one. For what have I to do with
> judging outsiders? Is it not those inside the church whom you are to
> judge? God judges those outside. Drive out the wicked person from
> among you.[33]

This led Paul to address the question of whether to take disputes among the
brethren to the civil law courts. The apostle's letter shows that he never intended to impose new legislation on anyone or pose as a Moses-like lawgiver.
Christianity was not a matter of rules and laws, much less subject to those of
nonbelievers.

> To have lawsuits at all with one another is a defeat for you. Why not

rather suffer wrong? Why not rather be defrauded? But you yourselves
even wrong and defraud, and that even with your own brethren.

Do you not know that the unrighteous will not inherit the kingdom
of God? Do not be deceived. Neither the immoral, nor idolaters, nor
adulterers, nor homosexuals, nor thieves, nor the greedy, nor drunk-
ards, nor revilers, nor robbers will inherit the kingdom of God. And
such were some of you. But you were washed [with baptism.] You were
sanctified. You were justified in the name of the Lord Jesus Christ and
the Spirit of our God. [34]

Paul now continued to address the specific list of questions brought to him.
Should a man bother to marry considering that the end of the world is at hand?
It is better to remain single like himself, was the reply. But because of the temptation of immorality, each man should have his own wife and each woman her
own husband. And if only one spouse is a believer, let him not divorce, for that
would make their children unclean, "but as it is they are holy."

Should a circumcised Christian attempt to remove the marks of it? "Let
everyone lead the life which the Lord has assigned to him," Paul replied, because neither state "counts for anything [compared to] keeping the commandments of God." The same applies to slaves, he said. "Were you a slave when
called [to Christ]? Never mind. But if you can gain your freedom, avail yourself
of the opportunity. For he who was called in the Lord is a freedman of the Lord.
Likewise, he who was free when called is a slave of Christ."

The purchase and consumption of meat that had been sacrificed to idols perplexed the house churches of Corinth as it does churches everywhere today.
Paul took the occasion to transform a relatively simple question about food
into an answer about one's duty to God. On one hand, Paul observed that eating meat sacrificed to idols did not matter in the sense that "We are no worse off
[in the sight of God] if we do not eat and no better off if we do." On the other
hand, "this liberty of yours" to eat such foods could be "a stumbling block to
the weak," he added.

For if anyone sees you, a man of knowledge, at a table in an idol's temple,
might he not be encouraged, if his conscience is weak, to eat food offered
to idols? And so by your knowledge, this weak man is destroyed – the
brother for whom Christ died. Thus, sinning against your brethren and
wounding their conscience when it is weak, you sin against Christ. [35]

The best exercise of a right is sometimes not to use it, Paul concluded. In his
own case, his usefulness to the Holy Spirit had depended upon his decision to

forgo such inherent rights as having a home, a wife, security, respect and peace. Instead, he had freely chosen homeless wandering, loneliness, peril and even shame.

Paul now turned to the many questions that had been asked about proper conduct in Christian worship. How should women dress? Paul's churches had already departed radically from Judaism in that women were warmly admitted as equals and served in every office, including deacon. But when asked this specific question about dress, he reverted to his upbringing in the synagogue.

> Any man who prays or prophesies with his head covered dishonors his head, but any woman who prays or prophesies with her head unveiled dishonors her head — it is the same as if her head were shaven. For if a woman will not veil herself, then she should cut off her hair, But if it is disgraceful for a woman to be shorn or shaven, let her wear a veil. [36]

Even so, Paul did not attempt to issue an order regarding the obligations of women at worship. He appealed to each church's sense of propriety, adding that he was more interested in bringing people together than creating new divisions among them.

But he did express strong feelings about the Lord's Supper. This was in response to reports that the sacrament had degenerated into so many dinner parties of various cliques.

> When you meet together, it is not the Lord's Supper that you eat. For in eating, each one goes ahead with his own meal, and one is hungry and another is drunk. What! Do you not have houses to eat and drink in? Or do you despise the church of God and humiliate those who have nothing? What shall I say to you? Shall I commend you in this? No I will not.

> For I received from the Lord what I also delivered to you, that the Lord Jesus on the night when he was betrayed took bread, and when he had given thanks, he broke it, and said, "This is my body which is for you. Do this is remembrance of me." For as often as you eat this bread and drink the cup, you proclaim the Lord's death until he comes.

> Whoever, therefore, eats the bread or drinks the cup of the Lord in an unworthy manner will be guilty of profaning the body and blood of the Lord. Let a man examine himself, and so eat of the bread and drink of the cup. For anyone who eats and drinks without discerning the body eats and drinks judgment upon himself. [37]

Church members also asked Paul's opinion about the practice of speaking in tongues during worship services. To many, this ability was a gift to be used. To some Christians it was all too reminiscent of the way the frenzied followers of Diogenes and other cult gods babble in the streets at festival times. Others simply felt that it disrupted the service or showed disrespect to God.

Paul offered two replies on separate levels. In a practical sense, he said, those who speak in tongues possess a skill. Just as a body has many parts, the body of the church is served by apostles, prophets, healers, administrators, those who speak in tongues and those who interpret them. "I want you all to speak in tongues, but even more to prophesy," said Paul. But those who do should take care to be accompanied by someone who can interpret their meaning.

> If even lifeless instruments, such as the flute or the harp, do not give distinct notes, how will anyone know what is played? And if the bugle gives an indistinct sound, who will get ready for battle? So with yourselves; if you in tongue utter speech that is not intelligible, how will anyone know what is said?[38]

But Paul also saw the question about tongues as an avenue to instruct on a higher plane. Yes, speaking in tongues is one of the qualities that some Christians have, he said, but far more important than this are qualities that anyone can practice: faith, hope and love.

> If I speak in the tongues of men and of angels, but have not love, I am a noisy gong or a clanging cymbal. And if I have prophetic powers, and understand all mysteries and knowledge, and if I have all faith, so as to remove mountains, but have not love, I am nothing. If I give away all I have, and deliver my body to be burned, but have not love, I am nothing.[39]

Finally, Paul addressed the questions of death and the hereafter that had been posed. What happens when people die? Do they rise up in their present bodies? When will the end of the world come? Reminding them of what he had told the Corinthians in his first sermons to them, he wrote:

> ...I preached to you the gospel, which you received, in which you stand, by which you are saved, if you hold it fast — unless you believed in vain.

> For I delivered to you as of first importance what I also received, that Christ died for our sins in accordance with the scriptures, that he was buried, that he was raised on the third day in accordance with the

scriptures, and that he appeared to Cephas [Peter], then to the 12. Then he appeared to more than 500 brethren at one time, most of whom are still alive, though some have fallen asleep. Then he appeared to James, then to all the apostles.

Last of all, as to one untimely born, he appeared also to me. For I am the least of the apostles, unfit to be called an apostle, because I persecuted the church of God. But by the grace of God I am what I am, and his grace toward me was not in vain. On the contrary, I worked harder than any of them, though it was not I, but the grace of God which is with me. Whether then it was I or they, so we preach and so you believe.

Now if Christ is preached as raised from the dead, how can some of you say that there is no resurrection of the dead? But if there is no resurrection of the dead, then Christ has not been raised; if Christ has not been raised, then our preaching is in vain and your faith is in vain. We are even found to be misrepresenting God, because we testified of God that he raised Christ, whom he did not raise if it is true that the dead are not raised. If Christ had not been raised, your faith is futile and you are still in your sins. Then those who have fallen asleep in Christ have perished. If in this life we who are in Christ have only hope, we are of all men most to be pitied.[40]

Now Paul repeated some specific questions that had been raised about death and the hereafter. "How are the dead raised? With what kind of body do they come?"

You foolish men! What you sow does not come to life unless it dies. And what you sow is not the body which is to be, but a bare kernel, perhaps of wheat or some other grain. But God gives it a body as he has chosen, and to each kind of seed its own body. For not all flesh is alike, but there is one kind for men, another for animals, another for birds, and another for fish. There are celestial bodies and there are terrestrial bodies, but the glory of the celestial is one and the glory of the terrestrial is another. There is one glory for the sun and another glory for the moon and another glory of the stars, for star differs from star in glory.

So it is with resurrection of the dead, What is sown is perishable, what is raised is imperishable. It is sown in dishonor, it is raised in glory. It is sown in weakness, it is raised in power. It is sown a physical body, it is raised a spiritual body.

Thus it is written, "The first man Adam became a living being"; the last Adam became a life-giving spirit. But it is not the spiritual which is first but the physical, and then the spiritual. The first man was from the earth, a man of dust; the second man is from heaven.

As was the man of dust, so are those who are of the dust; and as is the man of heaven, so are those who are of heaven. Just as we have become the image of the man of dust, we shall also bear an image if the man in heaven. I tell you this, brethren: flesh and blood cannot inherit the kingdom of God, nor does the perishable inherit the imperishable.

Lo! I tell you a mystery. We shall not all sleep, but we shall all be changed, in a moment, in a twinkling of an eye, at the last trumpet. For the trumpet will sound, and the dead will be raised imperishable, and we shall be changed, For this perishable nature must put on the imperishable, and this mortal nature must put on immortality.[41]

When this happens, Paul wrote:

> "Death is swallowed up in victory.
> "Oh death, where is thy victory?
> "Oh death, where is thy sting?"

The sting of death is sin, and the power of sin is the law. But thanks be to God, who gives us the victory through our Lord Jesus Christ.

Therefore, my beloved brethren, be steadfast, immovable, always abounding in the work of the Lord, knowing that in the Lord your labor is not in vain.[42]

With this lengthy letter, signed himself after appending a closing paragraph in his own hand, Paul hoped to bring reconciliation among the Corinthians — and between them and himself. In fact, just before the close he had expressed his hope of coming there the next spring after going first to the churches of Macedonia. One of his purposes, he said, would be to take up a collection that might ease the pangs of hunger that the Syrian crop failures had wrought among the Jewish-Christians in Jerusalem. So confident was he of the reconciliation that he urged the Corinthians to "put something aside and store it up" each week "so that contributions need not be made when I come."

But several days had passed and stretched into weeks, all without any word from the Greek metropolis. Eventually, Paul learned to his shock and amazement that the letter — at least great parts of it — had been taken as an insult. An insult? A letter about love and hope and salvation? How could this be? Paul asked himself over and over. He felt the emptiness of a man losing his family.

I would only guess that the Corinthians took umbrage at the fire of Paul's initial words. After all, he did call them "foolish" several times. He likened them to "babes in Christ." But I think mainly they saw so much there that they considered unrealistic and too demanding of them when immorality flourished everywhere around their small band. Expel the wicked from their churches? Who would be the judge? Avoid civil law courts? How could they not defend their rights and property if falsely accused? How could anyone hope to attain the same standards of a man who by his own proclamation forsook family and personal comfort to wander as a lonely and often unwelcome missionary? As if this wasn't enough, there were even reports that the Corinthians took it as an insult that Paul had allowed the Philippians to give him money for living expenses while at the same time refusing theirs!

At any rate, Paul was distraught enough to drop everything, swallow his pride, and take a ship to Corinth, as I reported to you in the previous chapter. But the trip was all too brief. Rather than enter a dialogue that might have allowed him to turn the tide, Paul faced a sullen, icy group that really didn't want to argue with him about anything. He returned to Ephesus dejected. In fact, he later described himself as being "so utterly, unbearably crushed that we [I] despaired of life itself."

All this was rolling through Paul's mind in Ephesus that previous summer even as he managed to preach sermons of hope to new converts, helped ban books on magic and stood up to the opposition of the trade guilds that served the temple of Artemis. Even as the pressure on him to leave the city mounted after the near riot of the guilds, (some even alleged that he was detained there in prison for public safety reasons), Paul's greatest fear was not of mobs, but of being deserted by his churches in Corinth.

At last Paul decided to risk all, not on another visit that might only turn out unpleasant again for both parties, but on a single letter. He would dispatch his faithful assistant Titus to take it personally to Corinth and see that it was read to all the churches there. After giving Titus lead time, Paul would journey 150 miles up the Asian coast to Alexander Troas. There, in the main port for tourists visiting the nearby ruins of Troy, Paul would wait until Titus returned with a report on his mission. If it was favorable, they would go on to both Macedonia and Corinth. If the cause was lost, Paul would visit the Phillipian and Thessalonian churches of Macedonia briefly, then set sail for Cæsarea.

Well, have you ever faced a situation in your life when you thought someone dear — perhaps a wayward brother or son — was all but lost and that you had nothing left to lose by removing the shield from your most vulnerable emotions? Paul's second appeal to the Corinthians was such a letter.

It begins by appealing to them personally "by the meekness and gentleness of Christ" to consider his message. I don't wish to seem to be frightening you with letters, he says in reference to the previous one. In fact, Paul says he is well aware that people say behind his back, "His letters are weighty and strong, but his bodily presence is weak and speech of no account." But they may yet find out how bold he can be face to face!

I don't want to compare myself boastfully to others you hold in esteem, said Paul, but "we were the first to come all the way upon you with the gospel of Christ." One who works on behalf of the Lord should boast only of the Lord. But then, as if goading himself on, he asks that the Corinthians "bear with me in a little foolishness," for he feels that it was he who betrothed them as a bride to Christ and he worries that they have been deceived by those who preach a different gospel. Yes, perhaps his manner of speaking is unskilled, but "I am not in knowledge."

Were they upset because he had accepted no living expenses from them while he preached the gospel there? What a strange expression of envy! "When I was with you and in want," he pointed out, "I did not burden anyone, for my needs were supplied by the brethren who came from Macedonia." Moreover, children are not supposed to lay up money for their parents, but parents for children, and he is ready to give all of his personal capital for the churches of Corinth.

Not only would he continue not to burden them, but "as the truth of Christ is in me, I shall not be silenced in the regions of Achaia," Paul declared. And one reason is so that he will not be undermined by "false apostles, deceitful workmen disguising themselves as apostles of Christ."

Paul asks the Corinthians not to think him foolish while he "boasts a little."

> For you gladly bear fools, being wise yourselves! For you bear it if a man makes slaves of you or preys upon you or takes advantage of you or puts on airs, or strikes you in the face.

> ...But whatever anyone dares to boast of — I am speaking like a fool — I also dare boast of that. Are they Hebrews? So am I. Are they Israelites? So am I. Are they descendants of Abraham? So am I. Are they servants of Christ? I am a better one (I am talking like a madman) — with far greater labors, far more imprisonments, with countless beatings, and often near death. Five times I have received at the hands of the Jews the 40 lashes less one. Three times I have been beaten with rods. Once I was stoned. Three times I have been shipwrecked; a night and a day I have been adrift at sea. On frequent journeys [I have been] in danger from rivers, danger from robbers, danger from my own people, danger from Gentiles, danger in the city, danger in the wilderness, danger at

sea, danger from false brethren, in toil and hardship through many a sleepless night, in hunger and thirst, often without food, in cold and exposure. And apart from other things, there is the daily pressure upon me of my anxiety for all the churches. Who is weak [that] I am not weak? Who is made to fall and I am not indignant?[43]

Paul takes his readers all the way back to the early days in Damascus when he was lowered in a basket to escape the local authorities. Then, again apologizing for boasting, he turns to

...visions and revelations of the Lord. I know a man in Christ who 14 years ago was caught up to the third heaven — whether in the body or out of the body I do not know — God knows. And I know that the man who was caught up into Paradise — whether in the body or out of the body, God knows — and he heard things that cannot be told, which man may not utter. On behalf of this man I will boast, but on my own behalf I will not boast, except of my weaknesses.[44]

One of them, Paul adds, is that God, "to keep me at being too elated by the abundance of revelations," afflicted him with a "thorn" in the flesh.

Three times I besought the Lord about this, that it should leave me; but he said to me, "My grace is sufficient for you, for my power is made perfect in your weakness." I will all the more gladly boast of my weaknesses, that the power of Christ will rest upon me. For the sake of Christ then, I am content with weaknesses, insults, hardships, persecutions, and calamities. For when I am weak, then I am strong.[45]

Paul now declares that he is about to come to the Corinthians a third time. There may be quarreling, jealousy, anger and the like, and he may have to mourn over those who have not repented of their sins, but he is coming nonetheless. And he warns the wayward among them that "I will not spare them — since you desire proof that Christ is speaking in me. He is not weak in dealing with you, but is powerful in you."

Paul's letter closes with prayers for love and peace, but he has clearly declared that he will make his stand in Corinth and not retreat.

It was now late summer when Paul said good-bye to Aquila, Priscilla and all the new Christians who now filled the Asian capital of Ephesus. Paul was still in such suspense at the outcome of this letter that he did not even plan any missionary work in Alexander Troas. Besides, the time there would be too short, with Titus meeting him almost upon his own arrival.

Troas was only two days by sea — three if one hit rough weather — from the Corinthian port city of Cenchreæ. A week should have been enough for Titus to go from Cenchreæ to Corinth, deliver the letter, have it read to all the congregations and observe their reactions. But Titus didn't come. As each agonizing day passed, Paul could only conclude that he and his letter had been repudiated. Clearly, someone in Corinth must have had it in for him personally.

In time Paul gave up and took a ship across the Ægean to Philippi in Macedonia. He had been there only a few days, re-greeting his many church friends, when who should come striding up but a smiling, jubilant Titus. His effort had taken longer than expected, but the Christians of Corinth had accepted Paul's message! Unknown to Paul and Titus when they were in Ephesus, the churches in Corinth had fallen under the sway of someone [probably an elder whose name is not now known] who had fomented a revolt against the apostle. It took some personal preaching by Titus over several days, but the congregations had been persuaded to remove the ringleader and were now enthusiastically on Paul's side again. In fact, they were asking how soon he could come to them because they could hardly wait!

This must have marked the highest point in Paul's life and mission. One of his largest churches had nearly succumbed to worldliness, had nearly sunk back to the level of the many "religions" with their demonic idols, mercenary priesthoods and intoxicating rituals. But it had survived to live on a higher plane, and Paul could not wait to express his elation. He sat down quickly and wrote another letter to the Corinthians that was intended to he comforting and healing.

He began by citing his own suspense and despair in Troas, but noting now that the effect was "to make us rely not on ourselves but on God, who raises the dead." And now that he has delivered Paul from "so deadly a peril," that "we have set our hope that he will deliver us again.

Paul acknowledges that perhaps his previous words had seemed harsh, but he points out, "I wrote you out of much affliction and anguish of the heart and with many tears, not to cause you pain but to let you know the abundant love that I have for you." The letter, added Paul, hadn't been written because the Corinthians had done wrong or because he had suffered wrong, but "in order that your zeal for us might be revealed to you in the sight of God."

As for the one who led the revolt against him, "the punishment by the majority is enough" and Paul now asks that they "turn to forgive and comfort him" lest he be "overwhelmed with excessive sorrow." He adds that "anyone whom you forgive, I also forgive."

Paul ends the letter by referring again to his most immediate purpose in visiting them: the collection of funds for the hard-pressed Christian church in Jerusalem. Even before he appears for a tearful reconciliation, he wants to have the matter of fund raising taken care of in advance. Besides, they wouldn't want to be outdone by the Macedonians, would they?

> ...for I know your readiness, of which I boast about you to the people of Macedonia, saying that Achaia [the province] has been ready since last year; and your zeal has stirred up most of them. But I am sending the brethren [Titus and two companions] so that our boasting about you may not prove vain in this case, so that you may be ready as I said you would be. Lest if some Macedonians come with me and find that you are not ready, as I said you would be, we [would] be humiliated — to say nothing of you — for being so confident. So I thought it necessary to urge the brethren to go on to you before me, and arrange in advance for this gift you have promised, so that it may be ready not as an exaction, but as a willing gift.[46]

Why did Paul spend so much of this missionary trip and attach so much importance to collecting money (and probably food staples) for their brethren nearly 900 miles away? The first and most practical reason was that the Jerusalem Christians were in genuine need. Just as in the times of Pontius Pilate, the Jewish temple priesthood had to contend with a violent procurator (Felix), a violent Zealot group, rebellious native Syrians, the stealthy Sacarii, a plague of wild-eyed religious reformers and a new king (Agrippa II) of unproven allegiances. The very existence of the temple itself could be threatened, and the ruling Sadducees could not even be sure of where the challenge might come. And, as before, when similar conditions existed, the high priest would look nervously at the newly-emerging Christians. At the very least, he would see that they were shown no favors and certainly no distributions of alms from the Chamber of Secrets.

The collection was also seen by Paul as a way to remind the Gentile churches of their Judeo-Christian heritage in Jerusalem. To the Judeans, it would provide reassurance that they were venerated. And if in the process they also came to appreciate the fact that more churches had been founded among the Gentiles by Paul than by all the Jewish-Christian apostles combined, well, then so be it.

Finally, Paul was looking well beyond a visit to Jerusalem. His mind was already on Rome and beyond. Although Paul did not say so directly in any letters I have read, he certainly knew that the Christian church in Rome was built principally on its ties to the Jewish-Christian community in Jerusalem. Visiting the Roman Christians would certainly be less difficult if he arrived with the blessing of the church they looked to first for guidance. Perhaps taking the collection personally to Jerusalem could help. So might a vow to bow to Jewish customs while in Jerusalem. For as Paul had said in that emotional letter to the Corinthians,

...whatever anyone dares to boast of...I also dare to boast of that.
Are they Hebrews? So am I.
Are they Israelites? So am I.
Are they descendants of Abraham? So am I.
Are they servants of Christ? I am a better one...[47]

As the year ended during Paul's three-month stay in Corinth, his reconciliation with the churches there was so complete that he could turn to writing the longest and perhaps most important letter of his missionary life. It was addressed to the Christian churches in Rome, and it was an attempt to introduce himself properly into their presence.

For God is my witness, whom I serve with my spirit in the gospel of his Son, that without ceasing I mention you always in my prayers, asking that somehow by God's will I may now at last succeed in coming to you. For I long to see you, that I may impart to you some spiritual gift to strengthen you, that is that we may be mutually encouraged by each other's faith, both yours and mine. I want you to know, brethren, that I have often intended to come to you (but thus far have been prevented) in order that I may reap some harvest among you as well as among the rest of the Gentiles. I am under obligation both to Greeks and to barbarians, both to the wise and the foolish: so I am eager to preach the gospel to you who are in Rome.[48]

· · · · · · · · ·

A. D. 5 8 — 5 9

These years saw the emperor Nero's attention absorbed by his mistresses, mother,
the theater and games. There was no particular order to them because all were intertwined and created tensions that
affected the others. I will begin with the "arts" and theater, largely because they
had already begun to captivate the young man prior to the opening of this period, in which he turned twenty.

This fact might well puzzle those who have read elsewhere that this was also
about the time that all actors and mimes were banished from Rome. Actually,
this edict (poorly-enforced as it turned out) came in response to the Senate's
alarm at the gangs of unemployed young "actors" that had rampaged the city
(but no more so than the masked Nero and his own rowdies). When it came to
the display of artistic talents, the emperor was in awe and envy of anyone who
could captivate an audience on stage.

Indeed, Nero had scarcely assumed the throne when he sent for Terpnus,
perhaps the greatest lyre master that day, and had him play night after night at
dinner. Soon the youth had begun to practice the lyre himself while at the
same time observing various exercises that such artists use to cultivate their
voices. A friend or servant might find him lying on his back holding a leaden
plate to his chest as he breathed deep to strengthen his lungs. He would also
purge himself with a syringe, deny himself all foods said to injure the voice and
induce vomiting should he eat them. Although his voice hadn't reached
booming proportions, he soon longed deeply to appear on stage. Intimate
friends quickly came to recognize what he had in mind when he often quoted
the Greek proverb, "Hidden music counts for nothing."

Nero's ardor was just as great when it came to chariot races and games in the

Circus. At the beginning of his reign, callers might find their adolescent emperor playing with ivory chariots on a board as they addressed him. Whenever the races were held, everyone could count on Nero being there. So passionate was his enthusiasm that one of his first acts as emperor was to increase the prizes and number of races. It soon became common for drivers to race all day long and into the night. And Nero became such a devotee of the Green team that he allowed his Prætorians to be used as laborers in expanding its stables. Charioteers of all kinds soon began to deem themselves a favored class because they felt so secure in the emperor's esteem. They even became almost as menacing as the "actor" gangs as they tore all over the outskirts of Rome in their two-horse chariots upsetting pushcarts and injuring bystanders without fear of punishment.

Being a spectator was unendurable to Nero. He wanted to be a driver. No emperor had ever allowed himself to appear in public in such a way, be it a stage or racetrack. Seneca and Burrus tried at first to compromise: they rebuilt an enclosure in the Vatican valley, across the Tiber northwest of the city, that the young Gaius Caligula had used to accommodate his yen for chariot driving. There, in this replica of the Circus Maximus (but hardly its seating capacity), the young man could drive his horses away from the public eye. But before long Nero, of course, had happily invited his crowd of young dandies to observe him in the stands and certainly didn't shoo away the admiring commoners who scaled the walls of the circus and applauded wildly when they saw who was plying one their favorite pastimes. It wasn't long before Nero treated slaves and a few friends to "trial exhibition" in his own gardens. This led to a similar "private performance" in the empty Circus Maximus, with a freedman dropping the napkin in the starting position usually occupied by the magistrates of Rome.

Clearly all this pent-up ambition had to have an outlet. Nero may not have offficially debuted in public as a singer or driver, but his dress and manner already affected it. His hair was often done in rising waves from front to top as in the vulgar manner of the charioteer. Just as frequently he would be in Greek clothing, or a "pseudo-Greek" concoction consisting of a flowered mini-tunic with a frilly muslin collar. If ostensibly dressing "Roman," it might be with an amply flowing toga below the waist and a tunic above it, adorned by a garish scarf around the neck. Some Roman males may have lounged about at home in such outfits during holidays, but only women dared wear any such things in public. Whatever Nero's dress of the day, his appearance and speech invariably signaled that he was more preoccupied with the theatrical and equestrian arts than the governance of 70 million people.

Seneca and Burrus have been accused of nurturing this bent. After all, say their critics, the emperor's mental absence from important affairs prolonged their own influence. Perhaps, but it also rekindled the fire in Nero's mother. Agrippina, though reduced to the status of dowager-in-waiting, began using her all-too-brief audiences to carp at her son for his foppish ways.

Nero had three other women competing for his attentions as well. The least of them was his meek wife, Octavia, whom the court had come to regard as somewhat akin to a piece of palace furniture. The second was Acte, the lovely but low-bred mistress who continued to sleep in the emperor's chambers. The third and newest in the emperor's life was Poppæa Sabina. Born of an illustrious family, Poppæa was considered the most beautiful woman of her day – and in possession of a clever and shrewd mind to go along with it. Her father's only mistake had been to fall in with the hated Sejanus during the reign of Tiberius. But despite the public ridicule that followed, the family remained one of the wealthiest in Rome. Outwardly, Poppæa seemed respectable and reserved – almost mysterious – in her few public outings. But inwardly, one can only conclude that she used her beauty in a scheming and unloving way that led up the ladder of political power.

Poppæa was already married to a knight and the mother of a infant son when she succumbed to the wily charms of one Marcus Salvius Otho. One of Rome's most extravagant dandies, Otho was also one of Nero's closest chums in everything from tavern tripping to street crime. More than once, when he would argue a point with the emperor, Otho would say, "Why it's as certain as I'll one day be Cæsar!" Nero, who might have bound anyone else for such a remark, would simply laugh and retort, "I shall not even see you consul."

Just how close they were became evident when Otho persuaded Poppæa (or she him) to divorce her husband and marry him. Before long Otho was praising her charms and graces to anyone within earshot. Sometimes he would even leave the emperor's dinner table early because he had to go to his wife, "who in one person embodies all the beauty and nobility that ever one man could want."

One should not share such thoughts with an emperor, because before long Otho had been prevailed upon to share his treasure with his royal friend. Soon Poppæa would be seeing less of Otho and more of Nero. And all the while she played her new lover like a lyre. First she was flirtatious, pretending that only his irresistible good looks had made her succumb. But after she had snared her prize she became distant and haughty. If Nero would beg her stay with him another night, she would insist that she had to flee to her husband. "Now there is a man of character," she would say, "whereas you, Nero, are kept down because you keep a mistress who is but a servant. What a dreary, menial association!"

As the besmitten Nero reached out for ways to keep Poppæa, Otho receded from the emperor's company – even official receptions. Then one day a palace freedman informed him that he had been named governor of Lusitania in western Spain. He soon departed without his wife (but would, as if to make good on his boast, return one day as emperor).

Poppæa was now left with all her bets placed on one man. Although Nero showered her with gifts that exceeded anything her own wealth had ever provided, Poppæa managed to display a permanent pout. As she saw it, her prospects of marrying the emperor were thwarted, not by Octavia's presence, but because Octavia was stoutly defended by the emperor's mother. So Nero became subject to a constant stream of nagging. He was under his "guardian's thumb," Poppæa would whine. He was master of neither himself nor the empire. "Otherwise, why the postponement of our marriage?" she would ask. "I suppose my looks and glorious ancestors aren't enough. Or do you distrust my ability to bear children? Or is it the sincerity of my love?

"No," she would wail as skillfully manufactured tears began to flow," I think you are afraid that, if we are married, I might tell you frankly how the Senate is downtrodden and the public enraged by your mother's arrogance and greed. If Agrippina can only tolerate daughters-in-law who hate her son, let me be Otho's wife again! Oh to go anywhere in the world where I can merely hear about the emperor's humiliation rather than witness it here! How can you tolerate this danger we live in?"

Word of these performances naturally reached Agrippina soon enough. An intense assault was being waged on her last avenue to power, even though it was only the shy and bewildered empress, Octavia. Agrippina, long since stripped of her military escort, now "Augusta," in name only, had no weapons with which to fight back.

But one. Agrippina was still one of the most comely women in Rome. She had often used Cupid's arrow as efficaciously as a commander uses a brigade of archers. She used her sexual weapons on the Senator Marcus Æmilius Lucius Lepidus to help lift her back into Roman society after an impoverished exile by Caligula. She had used them to mesmerize and marry Claudius. She had used them to make Pallas an ally and the richest freedman in Rome. She tried them — and perhaps succeeded — on Seneca when she needed his influence. Now they were needed again — in this case to win influence over another emperor.

Her son.

I will begin this sordid tale by telling you what at least two court observers of the time have written: that Nero had yet another concubine at the time who closely resembled Agrippina. And when he fondled her or displayed her charms to others, he would joke that he enjoyed having intercourse with his "mother."

I mention this because it is not known who was the more guilty in the liaison that was next observed. Agrippina was now seen more with her son and she was dressed differently on these occasions — no less than as a seductress. Soon the two were seen together in a litter trading embraces and lover's kisses. One observer states that it became Agrippina's habit to wait until midday "the time when food and drink were beginning to raise Nero's temperature," when "she would appear before her inebriated son all decked out and ready for incest."

Seneca and Burrus were certainly not pleased with the intensity of Poppæa's "campaign" for wedlock, but they were even more alarmed by Agrippina's behavior. Assuming that another woman would be able to make Nero see the light, they prevailed on Acte. The ex-slave, considered fair and level-headed, was instructed to impress on the emperor how much she feared for his reputation. Did he know that his mother was boasting publicly of her intimacy with her son? Had he considered that the army would never tolerate an emperor guilty of incest?

Poppæa was hardly deaf to these reports as well. But it appears that she also saw them as an opportunity for her to goad the emperor to stand up like a man. Did this not prove that it was time to get rid of Agrippina? If so, why not play upon this new-found intimacy and trust to find a way to take her off?

As luck would have it for both parties, Agrippina had already laid plans to visit her country mansions in Tusculum and Antium, and a relieved Nero saw her off eagerly with fond farewell kisses as she departed. Meanwhile, he would use the interim to find a way to do the deed.

At first he contemplated the virtues of poison. But that was rejected because an "accidental" death while at the emperor's table would hardly be deemed plausible considering that Brittanicus had died in similar circumstances. Besides, since watching that shocking episode, Agrippina had reportedly strengthened her constitution by regularly taking preventive antidotes.

Stabbing was another consideration, but it was deemed too chancy because the schemers had no one reliable to attempt the job. Finally, a novel idea was advanced by Anicetus, an ex-slave who now commanded the naval fleet at Misenum. Anicetus had been Nero's original boyhood tutor until displaced by Seneca and he had always loathed Agrippina. Anicetus recalled that he had once seen a ship that had been built to break apart for a stage play. He suggested that a ship could be constructed with a section in the center — right under the royal cabin — that could break loose at sea and either crush or drown the occupants. After all, he said, who would think to blame a human conspiracy for the wiles of wind and water? Moreover, the emperor would deflect any accusations by honoring the departed Augusta with a temple and many other tokens of his undying fealty.

The plan no doubt seemed preposterous at first, but with the passage of time and the absence of anything better, the more acclimated to it Nero seemed to become. The time of year was "natural" because Nero was accustomed to attending the festival of Minerva at Baiæ near the naval fleet on the Bay of Neapolis. This year the week-long festivities would begin on March 19.

Nero issued his mother a warm and flowery invitation to join him there. To his intimates, astonished at this abrupt change of affairs (after all, they had been chided to shun her), the emperor would simply chortle that "One must humor one's mother." At the same time, Agrippina eagerly prepared to join him. As an old friend later recalled, "Women are just naturally inclined to believe welcome news."

Upon her arrival in Baiæ, Nero met Agrippina on shore and welcomed her with outstretched hands and embraces. He then conducted her to Bauli, the name of a sumptuous villa that overlooked the shore near Cape Misenum across the beautiful blue bay from Baiæ. Misenum then as now was home of the Roman naval fleet. And as the ships in the harbor closest to the villa swayed silently in the windless, starry night, one — a smaller barge with ornamental carvings on the bow — stood out as exquisite compared to the more lumbering, utilitarian warships alongside it. Upon learning that the smart new vessel was hers, Agrippina took it as a supreme compliment because she had been accustomed to traveling in the unadorned warships.

Her serene confidence was broken momentarily when an informant rushed up and motioned for her attention. He whispered breathlessly that the Augusta should be on the alert for a plot of some unspecified sort involving the ship she was now admiring. Instantly wary, Agrippina bided time by requesting that she be taken by sedan chair to the evening's banquet around the Cape in Baiæ.

Once there, her fears were soon dissolved by Nero's lavish attentions. He gave her the place of honor next to himself, and for many languid hours they talked of their life together and times still to be enjoyed. Nero was both the affectionate son and emperor-confidant. When he finally saw her off, he gazed into her eyes and clung to her under the full moon. Then he kissed her breasts and she departed up the gangplank.

The only flaws in the plan were the still seas and windless weather. Agrippina boarded her special ship, accompanied only by two close friends, and went into her well-appointed quarters astern near the tiller. One of them, Crepereius Gallus, stood not far from the tiller talking happily about how her mistress had re-established her influence with a remorseful son. The other, Acerronia, bent over Agrippina, massaging her feet as her mistress reclined on a couch. Once the ship had glided to a midway point in the bay, the captain gave a silent signal. Suddenly an onslaught of heavy lead weights, that had been secretly suspended above the all-too-slender ceiling of the cabin, came crashing in on the three women. Crepereius was brained by falling ceiling beams and died instantly. Aprippina and Acerronia were saved because the beams were stopped by the back of the couch.

The ship was supposed to sink as well, but did not immediately. The problem for sailors in on the plot was that they were outnumbered by those who weren't. When the plotters tried throwing their weight to one side in order to capsize the ship, the others naturally rushed to the other side to prevent it. Still, the ship began slipping gently below the water line. When Acerronia found herself thrashing about in the bay, she cried out (I suppose assuming that Agrippina was with her) "Help! Save the emperor's mother!" With that two of the conspirators rushed over and struck her dead with poles and oars. But Agrippina had managed to muffle her terror, just as when she had seen Brittinacus poisoned in front of her eyes. Although she had lost the use of one shoulder where a falling object had struck her, Agrippina managed to swim sidestroke in the still bay until she came to some moored fishing boats. From there she was taken to her guest villa on Cape Misenum.

Back in her bed at last, the exhausted Agrippina finally had time to reflect on what had happened. She realized that the informer was right and that the ship had been rigged to collapse at sea. But examining her remaining strengths and routes of escape, she concluded that she had only one: to profess ignorance of the whole matter. So she dispatched an ex-slave, Agerinus, to inform her son that, by divine mercy and his lucky star she had survived a serious accident. The messenger was also instructed to insist that Nero should not take the trouble to visit her because what she needed now was plenty of rest.

Nero, meanwhile, had been half-crazed with anguish as he paced alone awaiting the outcome. When finally informed that the matter had been bungled, he concluded that its instigator would be all too obvious to Agrippina. "She may arm her slaves," he fretted to attendants. "She may even whip up the army or gain access to the Senate and accuse me of wounding her and killing her friends. What can I do to save myself?"

Whenever the young emperor was unable to solve a problem, his path inevitably led to Seneca and Burrus. I can only presume that neither was a party to the plot (perhaps because they couldn't be trusted to keep it from Agrippina), but in any event they were awakened in their suites and brought to their distraught ruler. For a long time they heard the light-haired, red-bearded youth's ruminations in silence, neither one wanting to commit to a course that might bring himself down as well. Finally, they must have been convinced that matters were coming to a head so fast that it was now a matter of Nero striking before Agrippina did. Seneca ended the suspense by turning to Burrus and asking if the Prætorian Guard could be ordered to kill her. Burrus replied that the Guard was devoted to the whole imperial house and to the memory of Agrippina's father Germanicus. He doubted seriously that it would commit violence against his offspring.

By this time the three had been joined by Anicetus, the fleet commander. He spoke up at that point and said that because the whole scheme had been his to begin with, it was his obligation to see it through. The two imperial advisors nodded with great relief. Then Nero, mustering his last ounce of pluck, cried out, "This is the first day of my reign!" He ordered Anicetus to go quickly, shouting after him to "Take men who obey orders scrupulously."

Just minutes after Anicetus and his men had departed, in rushed Agrippina's messenger to assure that she was well and loyal to her son. Her response to the calamity was so different from what Nero had anticipated that he was momentarily struck dumb. But realizing that his own "delegation" was so irretrievably committed, he perceived an advantage at the same time. The emperor quickly produced a sword, dropped it at the freedman's feet, and shouted to his guards that he had just thwarted an attempt on his life. "Arrest and bind this man!" he called out. Already his mind was manufacturing the story that his mother's agent had plotted against his life and that she had committed suicide out of shame.

Meanwhile, word of Agrippina's shipboard disaster had spread all around the towns that stretched along the Bay of Neapolis. Not knowing what had become of her and her companions, people ran out onto the beach or climbed aboard fishing boats and drifted about in the calm waters in search of survivors. The whole shore echoed with prayers, wails and the din of ignorant inquiries and speculative answers.

When news came that Agrippina was safe, one could hear a chorus of rejoicing ripple along the beaches as word spread from group to group. But then just as quickly, menacing bands of soldiers broke through the crowds and ordered them home. The reason is that the fate of Agrippina — great granddaughter of Augustus, daughter of Germanicus, wife of Claudius, mother of Nero — had already been sealed. Anicetus, accompanied only by a naval captain and lieutenant, had wasted no time in brushing past the servants in her villa on Cape Misenum. Barging into her bedroom, lit only with a single dim lamp, the three marines found Agrippina alone with a maid.

Soon even the maid melted into the darkness.

"Are you leaving me, too?" Agrippina shouted in scorn from her bed.

She turned next to the three shadows in the doorway. "If you have come to visit me," she called out, "you can report that I am better. But if you are assassins, I know my son is not responsible."

Perhaps ten years before, when Agrippina had asked her astrologers about Nero, they had answered that he would become emperor but kill his mother. At the time she was in the midst of risking all to marry Claudius and advance her son above Brittanicus. "Let them kill me, provided that he becomes emperor!" she had answered defiantly.

Now the assailants closed around Agrippina's bed in silence. First the captain hit her over the head with a truncheon. Then, just as the lieutenant was drawing his sword to finish her off, she threw aside her blanket and exposed her abdomen. "Strike here," she cried out, "for this is what bore Nero!"

But the three naval officers were not as deft with swords as Prætorians. It took many thrusts and twists before Agrippina finally expired in a blood-soaked pile of pillows and bedsheets.

For the next week or so, the emperor remained at Baiæ in a very convincing state of numbness. His genuine state of speechless shock displayed both an outward sign of grief and an inward state of disbelief that so daring a deed had actually been done. And he anguished over how it would be received. Would the armies of Germany revolt on learning the fate of the great commander Germanicus' daughter? Would the Senate believe the ship "accident"? Would it tolerate a divorce of the deified Claudius' daughter Octavia after it had barely stifled its rage at the poisoning of his son Brittanicus?

Nero had taken no chances on a funeral in which throngs of mourners might erupt into an angry mob. Agrippina, her body reclining on a couch, was quickly cremated in back of the mansion in which she had died. In the first days afterward, Nero remained distracted and distraught. At night he claimed to see his mother's ghost, along with the whips and blazing torches of the Furies. By day he was driven nearly mad by the martial trumpets that signalled the official mourning by wailing constantly from towns around the Bay of Neapolis. But as days passed, no reaction at all had come from Germany or from Rome. Hope and confidence slowly returned to the emperor, beginning, perhaps, when Burrus prevailed on the colonels and captains of the Guard to come to him with congratulatory handclasps for having escaped from the menace of his mother's evil conspiracies. Nero's friends crowded into the temples to offer thanks for his deliverance, and soon, sacrifices were being offered by the magistrates of all the towns in Campania.

Why hadn't the Senate responded as well? Nero learned eventually that the Arval Priesthood, an elite body of senators and noblemen, had met for one of its regular ceremonies on March 28, a week after Agrippina's demise. Ordinarily the Brethren, as they are also called, routinely begin by offering sacrifices to the emperor and the imperial family. On this occasion, they had curiously failed to do so. But word now reached Nero that the reason was simply that they did not know how to word their incantations. They sought the emperor's guidance.

By April 5 the Arval Priesthood had met again and sacrificed to Nero. Their guidance had come in the form of a letter to the Senate, written of course by Seneca in the emperor's name, explaining what had happened. Agerinus, a confidential ex-slave of Agrippina, had been caught with a sword with which he had intended to murder the emperor in his very bed chamber. Once discovered, Agrippina had acknowledged her guilt by taking her own life.

But she was guilty of other crimes as well, the letter continued. She had been responsible for most of the scandals and murders during the latter years of Claudius. And as Nero had tried to assume his destiny, she had wanted to be co-ruler – to receive oaths of allegiance from the Guard and to subject the Senate to the same humiliation. She had opposed gratuities to soldiers and civilians alike. She had even tried to break into the Senate house and deliver verdicts to foreign envoys. "I can hardly believe that I am safe from her now," the emperor's letter continued. "Nor do I derive any pleasure from the fact."

The Senate obligingly expressed its relief and made appropriate shows of jubilation at the emperor's newly-gained safety. Still, Nero worried on. Would the *people* of Rome welcome him back? But in time he was brought around by the fawning of nearly every courtesan who had traveled with him to Campania. Agrippina was detested in Rome, they assured. The emperor's popularity was now soaring. Go to Rome and see for yourself, they insisted.

So he did, with a long train of sycophants preceding him and exhorting crowds along the way. When the emperor would gaze from his carriage along the road he saw families lining the streets, some sitting in tiers of wooden parade seats as though attending a triumph. And as he entered Rome he was greeted by senators, their wives and children lined up along the carriage path according to sex and age. Puffed with pride, Nero could barely keep the grim look of mourning as he proceeded to the Jupiter Capitoline and paid his vows to the god.

Soon the city was enveloped with thanksgivings at every shrine. Agrippina's birthday was included among ill-omened dates. Because she had met her end at the Festival of Minerva in Baiæ, the Senate decreed that the Curia was to house a gold statue of Nero and Minerva standing side by side.

The truth, Nero was beginning to grasp at last, is whatever an emperor proclaims it to be.

And where was Poppæa? "How quickly will Octavia be divorced and ourselves wed?" she must have been asking already. But one can also imagine Burrus and Seneca imploring the emperor to make her bide her time. After all, they would say, the Senate is not likely to see Octavia, the daughter of a deified emperor, pushed aside so quickly. Besides, Nero himself had come to realize that the Senate's acquiescence to "the deed" was in fact begrudging at best. No one believed that Agrippina would have sent a single elderly ex-slave, brandishing a large sword, past a cohort of Guards and into the emperor's bedroom. At best they blamed the concoction on Seneca. In addition, Nero would have heard by now that Publius Thrasea Pætus, one of the Senate's most respected leaders, had stalked out of the chamber in the midst of its plaudits to the emperor.

Once outside the Curia, Thrasea seemed to care not a whit who heard his feelings on Nero. "If I were the only one who he was going to put to death," he would tell friends, "I could easily pardon the rest who load him with flatteries. But since he will dispose of us all sooner or later, why should one degrade oneself to no purpose and then perish like a slave anyway? As for me, men will talk of me hereafter. They will talk of the others only to record the fact that they were put to death.

"Nero can kill me but he cannot harm me," he added (a phrase that would be echoed often by brave men in darker days to come). Indeed, Thrasea may have even gotten wind of a rumor that Nero was planning to murder his enemies in the Senate. One source says that Nero had talked of it, but had been dissuaded by Seneca. "No matter how many you may slay, you cannot kill your successor," was the advice that reportedly put an end to the notion.

If the emperor needed other evidence that not all the applause was sincere upon his return, he could have donned one of his wigs at night and slunk into the streets. Had he done so, he would realize that not all of Agrippina's statues had been thrown down and crushed. One of them, for instance, had been rescued and propped on a wall with garment thrown over it so as to make the head appear veiled. Around the neck had been affixed an inscription: "I am abashed and thou art unashamed."

Someone else had hung a leather bag from one of Nero's statues as if to remind him that the penalty for parricide was to be sewn up in it with a cock, an ape or wild dog and thrown into the Tiber to drown.

In the Forum, someone had left a baby boy to which was fastened a tag saying: "I will not rear you up, lest you slay your mother."

In latrines and on walls everywhere, a prowling Nero could have found newly-scrawled graffiti, such as this:

> Orestes and Alemeon, both their mothers slew,
> What Nero does is therefore nothing new.

Or this one:

> Sprung from Æneas, pious, wise and great,
> Who says our Nero is degenerate?
> Safe through the flames one bore his sire. The other,
> To save himself, took off his loving mother.[49]

Nero, however, always seemed to ignore or endure the criticism of street people. Might it be because it was they who attended the theater and determined the fate of singers and lyre players? For it was the theater that now preoccupied the mind of the newly-liberated artist-emperor.

How could Nero get away with the unthinkable – to ascend the stage as a common performer? His own strategy was to assure that it would not be so shockingly uncommon to see members of high-born families singing, dancing and reciting poetry in public. This would explain why Rome erupted in a profusion of games and theatrical spectacles soon after Nero's return. It started when the emperor prevailed on certain impoverished members of the ancient nobility to perform in the public theater. It didn't matter so much what they did, but that they were seen – all in exchange for sizable fees that allowed them to maintain their styles of living.

At about the same time, he proclaimed the Youth Games, or Neronian Games, which were held obstensibly to mark the first ceremonial shaving of the imperial beard. For several days, in as many as six theaters at once, eminent men and women were pressed into joining professional players. Some performed in the hunting theater, others in the Circus or in a stage orchestra. It was not uncommon to see patrician men playing parts with effeminate gestures and songs while their women danced in indecent dress. Some played the flute and danced in pantomimes or drove horses. Others who were too old or ill to do anything else were compelled to sing in choruses. When some of the patrician players were so ashamed that they put on masks to avoid recognition, Nero ordered the masks removed. Thus, one could hear a Macedonian in the crowd cry out, "Look there is a descendent of Philip" riding an elephant or a Sicilian pointing out the heir to one of the province's leading families fighting as a gladiator.

Goading them all on with lavish prizes was the young man in the royal box. Performers were given horses, slaves, gold, silver and all manner of costly jewelry as prizes. During a performance the emperor would often turn to the crowd and throw tiny brightly covered balls into their outstretched hands. Those who seized the little balls would return them for the expensive prize described inside. As for Nero's first shave, he placed the hairs in a small golden globe and offered it to Jupiter Capitolinus.

But what I described was just the half of it. At just about the same time Nero was inaugurating the Youth Games, he directed the erection of a new neighborhood of taverns and makeshift places for assignations in the grove of trees that had been planted around the lake that Augustus had constructed to display naval games. Its purpose was to sell every form of vice imaginable. And to encourage the process, Nero's agents were on hand distributing free coins, which disreputable people were happy to have and spend. Respectable people were ordered to go there and to spend the money they were given.

During all of this, the sensible ones among the participants – those who were prætors and ministers and magistrates by day – were both amazed and depressed at the extent of the money being spent. They grieved because they

feared it would bankrupt the country and compel Nero to embark on confiscations and other evil deeds in order to continue at this pace.

I doubt that any of them knew at the time that their predictions were already
proving true. For instance, just after his return to Rome and before the Youth
Games had been launched, Nero paid a visit to his aging, bed-ridden Aunt
Domitia. At one point the old woman stroked his soft red beard and said fondly,
"As soon as I receive this [meaning the shaved hairs signifying his entry into
manhood] I shall gladly die." Turning to those around him, Nero said aloud as if
in jest, "Well, then I'll just take it off at once!"

But it proved to be no joke. He ordered Domitia's doctors to give her an over-
dose of physic. Before her corpse was cold he had seized her considerable properties and confiscated her will.

Now as I have said, the emperor's sole objective with all this theatrical ca-
cophony was simply to launch himself on an artistic career in a way that would
not see him hooted down or run out of office for betraying his patrician heritage. Indeed, just as Caligula had fancied himself competing with this and that
god for supremacy, I would venture to say that Nero saw himself conquering all
other lyre players, then moving on to best all comers at singing, poetry, acting,
chariot driving, wrestling and who knows what else.

Just when the emperor first performed for the public is subject to two accounts involving two locations. The first came in Rome during the Neronian
Youth Games. And why not, after all that expense? On the final night the
crowd quieted quickly when they first glimpsed Cæsar striding upon the stage
wearing the garb of a lyre player. "My lords," he intoned, "of your kindness give
me ear." Awkwardly, and very nervously, he sang and played a piece called
"Attis" and then "The Bacchantes," neither of which was familiar to the audience because they had been written by the emperor himself. Beside him stood
Burrus and Seneca, prompting him like schoolmasters at a child's recital.

According to most accounts, the emperor wasn't such a bad poet, though the
fact that only a few of his verses remain preserved in books indicates that they
weren't exactly Homeric. But his voice was weak and husky, so that nervous
giggles and guffaws began to spread from row to row. But unknown to those in
the forward seats was the fact that the rear tiers had been commandeered by an
army — literally. To support his debut, Burrus had mustered a few hundred
Prætorians in civilian garb. Before long, at every pause in the performance they
would unleash a storm of applause while menacing all around them to join in.
By the time the songs had ended there were shouts of "Glorious Cæsar! Our
Apollo! Our Augustus! None surpasses thee, O Cæsar."

After the performance, a glowing Nero capped his debut by entertaining his
retinue with a feast aboard boats as they cruised along the lake that had been
the site of Augustus' naval battles. His first public effort had won him the crown

for lyre playing. Left unmentioned was the fact that all other lyre payers had been barred on the assumption that they were unworthy of being victors.

In the light of day, Nero began to conclude that although he had now broken through the barriers to a stage career, there remained something about the crowds in Rome that was, well, less than gratifying. While appreciative of his talents, they lacked the sophistication to fully understand a great performer. After all, the arts were developed and refined in Greece, and surely it followed that no true performer could realize fulfillment unless he could rhapsodize a Greek audience.

So it was soon back to Campania, where Neapolis was one of the most Greek cities in all of Italy. It was for this reason that some accounts cite Neapolis as the "true" debut of Nero as singer and poet. Here, by "popular demand," he sponsored a smaller version of the Neronian Games but with more performances by the star attraction. In Neapolis Nero was applauded night after night as he sang and played. In fact, it is reliably reported that on the final night the theater shook with earthquake tremors. Yet everyone sat at rapt attention until the emperor had concluded his performance. It was only after the audience dispersed that the theater collapsed completely.

Just as Nero had called on troops for support in the Roman theater, he soon found himself attracted to a large contingent of sailors from Alexandria who had just flocked to Neapolis from a recently-arrived fleet. What caught his ear was their enchanting rhythmic applause. Not content with their numbers, the emperor had his aides "recruit" some 5,000 young commoners from Neapolis, who were divided into three groups to learn the Alexandrian style of applause. The first was called the "bees" because they were able to produce a sound like a swarm of bees. The second, named the "roof tiles," made a hollow, resonant sound by cupping their hands like barrel tiles. The third, the "bricks," were so named for clapping in a way that produced the "clack" of two bricks being slapped together. All were selected for their thick hair and fine apparel. And their enthusiasm for Nero's singing was sustained by paying their leaders 400,000 sesterces for each performance.

But this was a pittance to what the emperor spent to keep Poppæa pacified. For instance, the mules that drew her carriage were each shorn with gilded shoes that probably cost 400,000 sesterces per animal. It is also said that Nero kept for her a stable of some 500 asses. Those that had foaled were milked daily so that Poppæa might bathe in their milk to preserve the loveliness of her skin.

. . . .

JEWISH TURMOIL WAS BOTH A BANE AND A BLESSING to Felix the procurator. Yes, conflict was incessant and one never knew what hour of the day or night troops might have to be deployed in the name of peacekeeping. But this constant agitation among factions also meant that one or the other was willing to pay to have the trouble settled (in its favor, of course) by a wise and impartial third party.

The thorniest problems came when *both* factions paid for the procurator's skillful mediation services and both expected to prevail.

Such was the case in the very city that housed the Roman government in Judea. At this particular time, the age-old animosities that continued to smolder among Jews and their Hellenistic neighbors, quite apart from anything to do with the quality of Roman justice, had managed to center themselves in Cæsarea. Jews there claimed pre-eminence because over a hundred years before, Herod the Great had built a city of marble from a crude village with a makeshift harbor. True enough, the local Syrians admitted, but Cæsarea was once called Strato's Tower (for an ancient lighthouse that stood on the shore) and at the time there was not a single Jewish inhabitant.

You may recall the riots that had broken out in Cæsarea immediately following the death of King Herod Agrippa I. Now, almost 20 years later, the two factions had managed to confine their old animosities to taunting one another on the streets or contesting in games of strength at festivals. But lately, and on more than one occasion, the enmity had erupted in episodes of rock throwing in which several people were seriously injured.

The Jews were generally more populous and wealthy and invariably managed to retain the upper hand, but the great majority of troops under Felix's command were Syrian Gentiles from Cæsarea and nearby Sebaste. As would later be alleged, the Syrians "counseled" with Felix and fattened his purse as a token of thanks. The next time a gang of Jewish rowdies started tossing rocks, Felix marched his troops in their midst and ordered them to desist. When a few bricks came flying in his direction, he ordered the soldiers to slay as many as they could. For good measure, the incensed troops went trampling through the homes of Jewish citizens and made off with a considerable amount of riches. It stopped only after a hastily-assembled group of Jewish leaders, representing the more moderate and mature among their numbers, went out and mollified Felix with their pleas and presents.

That was supposed to be the end of it, but younger, more hot-tempered Jewish men weren't about to give up the cause because a few soft old men told them to. They took to the streets, caves and roadsides, vowing to wipe out the Syrian population of Cæsarea if they had to. And soon the silent steel of the Sicarii penetrated the military capital as it had Jerusalem.

. . . .

PAUL SAW HIS FORTHCOMING JOURNEY to Jerusalem as a time of reconciliation and regeneration before moving on to Rome and Spain. Indeed, as the delegation of churchmen prepared to sail from the Corinthian port of Cenchreæ, a deaconess named Phœbe was already departing from the port that faced the other side of the isthmus to deliver the letter Paul had written to the Christians in Rome.

But this peace of mind was not shared by all of his fellow travelers, nor certainly by any of the churches they were leaving behind. Just as Paul and his churchmen were about to sail from Cenchreæ they had discovered a planned attempt on Paul's life by the Jewish elders of Corinth. If Jews could become so riled in an otherwise peaceful city, how might the temple priests and elders react in a Jewish city constantly wracked with outer conflict and internal division? Disciples on both sides of the Ægean were saddened on a personal level as well. Paul was already showing the signs of old age. If he were truly headed for Rome and beyond, chances were they would never see him again.

Paul would not be deterred, however. He directed the other delegates to sail across the Bay of Samathrace for their planned destination of Troas. Then he, Luke and probably Timothy booked a hasty passage on another ship headed up the coast to Macedonia. Paul's breach with the Corinthian churches had already caused him to miss his goal of reaching Jerusalem by the Passover on April 7. Now he was determined to arrive in time for the Festival of Pentecost, which followed a few weeks later.

After a five-day absence, Paul and Luke reunited in Alexander Troas with their fellow churchmen. Including Paul, who may have personally represented the churches in Corinth, there were nine in all, drawn from three of the four Roman provinces in the area. There were Sopater from Macedonia and Aristarchus and Secundus of Thessalonica; Gaius represented Derbe and the hard-working Timothy his home town of Lystra. From the many churches up and down the coast of Asia came Tychicus and Trophimus. In addition, I would suppose that Luke, the diarist, also served as delegate from his native Philippi.

Why so many to bring a gift? Their numbers would serve to ward off robbers in a dangerous land. But the size of a visiting delegation also added to its respect — and Jerusalem was a city accustomed to receiving many groups of luminaries who came to pay the temple tribute. Equally important, I think, is that these were the leaders of their respective churches. They had worked hard to raise the money and had wanted to travel as pilgrims to the birthplace of The Way. And they all wanted to cling to Paul for as long as they could.

The nine men stayed in Troas a week as they made preparations for passage to Cæsarea. They also worked to bolster the small Christian church there. Luke records that on their last night there, a Saturday, Paul spoke at a communal fellowship meal being held in one of the three-story tenements that clustered around the small harbor. In fact, Paul, being Paul, was still speaking at midnight. A young man named Eutychus, who had perched on one of the broad, open window sills, nodded off after, I suspect, finishing a skinful of wine while listening. Soon he was in such deep sleep that he rolled right off his ledge and plunged into the courtyard three stories below.

When they heard the sickening thud, everyone rushed down and those first to Eutychus declared him dead. But Paul wasn't far behind. He wrapped the lad in his arms and reassured everyone that he was still breathing. Paul revived him, and as soon as Eutychus had been carried off to his home to recover, Paul went back upstairs, finished his sermon and led everyone in the Lord's Supper.

As dawn broke, Paul was still sitting in the upstairs room talking to a few members of the Troas church when his companions came for him to board their ship for its first stop, Assos. But no, Paul couldn't tear himself away just yet. A few months before he had visited Troas all too briefly on his way to reconcile with the Corinthian church, and now he wanted to make up for lost time. Despite having no sleep, this tireless missionary had decided he would stay with the Troans a while longer. He'd then walk the 25 miles to Assos and meet his shipmates there.

When they finally sailed off with Paul, it was 35 miles south to Mitylene on the island of Lesbos, then 60 miles to Chios, 70 to Samos and another 30 or so to Miletus, each leg involving an overnight as the local crews loaded and unloaded their cargo. Miletus is a great city in itself, perhaps unfairly overshadowed by Ephesus. Blessed with four harbors and rolling pastures, it is a place where herders of sheep meet craftsmen who produce the famous fabric, *Milesia vellera*. It is also a city of culture and of many philosophers. But the importance of Miletus to Paul at the time was that it lay just 20 miles from Ephesus. Paul wanted to visit his churches again but probably risked danger if he went overland and was seen in town again by anyone connected with the Temple of Artemis. Besides, if he had scarcely been able to tear himself away from a few churchmen in Troas, he might be smothered in the embrace of the many in Ephesus and never make it in time for the Pentecost Festival.

So Paul sent a message asking the leading Ephesian Christians to meet him in Miletus. If this was a man who was physically unimpressive or lacked oratory skills, one would scarcely know it, for the Ephesian elders came in haste at the chance to see him.

Perhaps it was on the long walk from Troas to Assos when he realized that his arrival in Jerusalem would produce confrontation rather than reconciliation, because the Paul who spoke to his friends at the harbor in Miletus was more somber than the one who had sailed from Macedonia. Paul began by recounting how he had faced hardships and heartaches in preaching the gospel in the provinces.

> And now, behold. I am going to Jerusalem, bound in the Spirit, not
> knowing what shall befall me there; except that the Holy Spirit testi-

fies to me in every city that imprisonment and afflictions await me. But I do not account my life of any value nor as precious to myself, if only I may accomplish my course and the ministry which I received from the Lord Jesus, to testify the gospel of the grace of God.

And, now, behold, I know that all you among whom I have gone about preaching the kingdom will see my face no more. Therefore I testify to you this day that I am innocent of the blood of all, for I did not shrink from declaring to you the whole counsel of God. Take heed to yourselves and to all the flock, in which the Holy Spirit has made you guardians, to feed the church of the Lord which he obtained with his own blood.

I know that after my departure fierce wolves will come in among you, not sparing the flock; and from among your own selves will arise men speaking perverse things to draw the disciples after them. Therefore be alert, remembering that for three years I did not cease night or day to admonish everyone with tears.

And now I commend you to God and to the word of his grace, which is able to build you up and to give you the inheritance among all those who are sanctified. I coveted no one's silver or gold or apparel. You yourselves know that these hands have ministered to my necessities, and to those who were with me. In all things I have shown you that by so toiling one must help the weak, remembering the words of the Lord Jesus that "It is more blessed to give than to receive."[50]

With that it was time to go aboard ship. Paul then knelt and prayed with the Ephesians. Everyone was in tears, Luke writes, "because of the word he had spoken and [because] they should see his face no more."

From Miletus it was a day-long 80-mile run south to Cos by the crisp northerlies of spring, then a pass by Rhodes, with the parts of the earthquake-toppled Colossus of Rhodes still strewn about the harbor. The pilgrims now headed west to Patara in Lycia near the southwestern corner of Asia Minor, and a major center of the cult of Apollo. There they transferred to a large merchantman that was carrying cargo down to Phœnecia.

This time they were in for a four-day, 400-mile open sea voyage. One can imagine schools of leaping dolphins leading the ship as it plunged into the deep blue waters. Their midpoint would have been Cyprus, where, passing the capital of Paphos on their left, with its gleaming temple of Aphrodite, Paul doubtless wondered if the proconsul Sergius Paulus had remained a Christian.

And what of Barnabas? Was he still establishing Christian communities on the island?

After another day's run, they could sight the busy harbor of Tyre, one of the original Phœnician cities. Tyre was a major cargo loading port for the western provinces, and the churchmen stayed seven days there. Whereas the stop in Miletus had brought out the elders from Ephesus, word of Paul's landing in Tyre drew a flock of Christian men, wives and children from all over the area. The meeting was all the more emotional because these were residents of the region and they confirmed that Judea was in turmoil and begged Paul not to go. When Paul and his company insisted they must head on south, their new friends escorted them out of town and to the docks, praying and weeping all the way.

After a single overnight in Ptolemais and another outpouring of Christians to greet them, the delegation again boarded ship for a final 35-mile run and put in at the exquisite marble-covered harbor of Cæsarea. Paul's companions were already on edge to be in a strange new land, and now they could also sense the grim tension of its residents as well. Jew and Hellene had clashed often in the streets and their tempers were now held in check only by the fact that Cæsarea was policed by more Roman troops by far than anywhere in Judea. Yet, neither side was at all mollified at having been under the capricious thumb of Felix, the Roman procurator, for seven tumultuous years.

Paul's party, however, slipped into the market throngs with no apparent incident. There they were taken in by none other than Philip, the same member of Stephen's original seven who had established many — perhaps most — of the Hellenistic churches that now flourished up and down the Judean-Phœnician seacoast. Philip had settled in Cæsarea with his four unmarried daughters, all of whom were credited with the gift of prophesy. The newcomers must have gained new reassurance and strength as Philip told them of seeing first-hand the resurrected Jesus, of traveling with Peter, and perhaps of his early conversion of an Ethiopian official that led to the establishment of churches in that land over 20 years ago.

During their stay with Philip the delegates were surprised when a well-known Christian prophet asked to see them. His name was Agabus, and he had just come down from Jerusalem. His objective (had he been sent by the Jewish Christians there?) was to see Paul. After the briefest of greetings, Agabus grabbed the belt from Paul's outer cloak and proceeded to tie his own hands and feet with it in the fashion of the old Hebrew prophets.

"Thus says the Holy Spirit," he admonished. "This is how the Jews at Jerusalem will bind the man who owns this girdle and deliver him into the hands of the Gentiles."

Agabus had so frightened everyone that for the first time members of Paul's own delegation broke down in tears, urging him as well not to go.

"What are you doing, weeping and breaking my heart like this?" Paul answered. Their concern and sincerity touched him deeply, but he was also piqued because it was as if they still didn't comprehend his mission. "I am ready not only to be imprisoned, but even to die at Jerusalem for the name of the Lord Jesus," he declared.

And what about the gifts that dozens of churches had collected? No, he could not be dissuaded now. And so, the delegates showed their own resolve by joining him to the man. In fact, so did several Christians from Cæsarea. At Joppa, more than halfway on the two-day trek, they stayed with a long-time Christian who had immigrated from Cyprus. At that point the Cæsarean Christians turned back and the nine men faced the last 20 miles alone.

As they approached the walls of the holy city, most of Paul's companions were no doubt awed by the glistening of the temple bronze and the stout city walls that Herod and his sons had had put up to defy all comers. For Paul, this was his fifth visit and his first in eight years. It also became known that he had a married sister living in Jerusalem, though for how long I can't say.

Luke writes that "the brethren received us gladly" upon their arrival. Perhaps Paul arranged to stay that night in the home of his sister. But a longer reunion could wait, because on the very next day Paul had arranged a meeting with James and all the Jewish Christian Elders. There he introduced his associates and made a formal presentation of the funds that had been raised, which were gratefully received. Encouraged to bring the elders up to date, Paul gave an impressive account of his missionary work in Antioch and the western provinces. James, in turn, gave his own progress report, pointing with equal pride to the many churches that had sprung up throughout Judea, Samaria and Galilee. No doubt he took pains to point out that it was only after much pain and trauma that the Jewish Christians had been able to effect a tacit co-existence with the temple authorities.

And so, it was only a matter of time before the conversation turned to the one fear that James and his elders had about Paul's visit — that it might, as it had before, result in disrupting this fragile existence. Despite all the letters and "agreements" that had taken place between the Jewish and Gentile wings of the church, Paul's liberal ways were still subject to, shall we say, "misunderstanding" among Jewish Christians. And now Paul was in a different land than where he had formed his churches.

James and his disciples were grateful for the gift but worried as to whether it implied an obligation they couldn't honor.

After skirting diplomatically about the issue, one of the elders advanced an idea. "You see, brother, how many thousands among the Jews here have believed [in Jesus]," he said. "They are all zealous for the Law, and they have been told that you teach all the Jews who are among the Gentiles to forsake Moses, telling them not to circumcise their children or observe the customs. What then is to be done?"

His idea was this: "We now have four men among us who have vowed to undergo the Jewish purification ceremony. Why not join them? Purify yourself as well and pay their expenses. That way all will know that what they have been told about you is untrue and that you are in observance of the Law."

Well, Paul had never *rejected* Jewish customs for those who wished to observe them (*"Are they Hebrews, so am I! Are they Israelites, so am I!"*). The commitment meant abstaining from wine for seven days, shaving his head, burning his shorn hair on the altar and offering a formal sacrifice to mark the end of the period. The referred-to "expenses" entailed buying five lambs and ten pigeons for the final sacrifice. Paul was determined to hold together the Jewish and Gentile components of Christianity. He had no doubt been purified before and doing so again was a small price to pay for peace.

For six days Paul, with shaven head, appeared in the temple with his fellow initiates without incident.

On the final day his luck ran out. Some Jewish pilgrims from Ephesus happened to see Paul in the temple. Why, wasn't this the same rabble rouser who had tried to lead the synagogue astray in Ephesus? Indeed, this was the same man they had seen earlier in the market walking with Trophimus, a fellow Ephesian they knew to be a leading Gentile Christian. What was going on here? Had this Paul shaved that Gentile's head and smuggled him into the temple for some sacrilegious purpose?

The Ephesian Jews didn't wait to ask questions. They rushed up to Paul and tried to grab him while the apostle recoiled. "Men of Israel, Help!" they called out to the crowd. "This man is teaching men everywhere against the Law and this place. He has also brought Greeks into the temple and he has defiled this holy place!"

A few moments later Roman sentries overlooking the temple courtyards from the walls of the adjacent Fortress of Antonia puzzled as they saw a mob of angry men surging from the spacious Court of the Gentiles towards the inner precincts. A short, balding man was being held against a wall and the others were rushing toward him as if to tear him limb from limb.

Well, moments like this were why the Romans maintained extra riot control details during festivals. Within a few moments the gates to the temple had been pushed shut and a riot squad led by a tribune named Claudius Lysias descended the long stairs from their barracks. Petrified by the sight of armed soldiers brandishing swords and pushing them away with heavy shields, the Ephesian Jews melted away, leaving a bloodied and tattered Paul trembling in their midst.

"Arrest this man," the tribune commanded, and Paul was quickly bound in chains. Almost as an afterthought the tribune turned to the crowd and asked what it was he had done. But the uproar was so deafening that he couldn't make any sense of the men shouting and shaking their fists. Actually, Lysias later said he thought Paul might have been the so-called Egyptian "prophet" who had led 4,000 men into the wilderness several months before. But all he knew for sure at the time was that his men had better pick up their prisoner like a piece of lumber and spirit him off to the barracks before the crowd regained its courage and overwhelmed them all.

When they had reached the steps leading back up to the Fortress Antonia, Paul turned to the tribune. "May I say something to you," he asked in Greek.

"You know Greek?" replied Lysias. "Are you not that Egyptian who stirred up that revolt recently?"

His prisoner answered: "I am a Jew from Tarsus in Cilicia — a citizen of no mean city. I beg you, let me speak to the people."

The tribune shrugged and ordered Paul set upright. Maybe he would learn at last what this was all about. So Paul climbed several steps so that he looked out on the men in the courtyard. And when he motioned with his hand, there was a great hush. Speaking in Hebrew, Paul began to tell them the story of his life: how he had been raised in Tarsus, was taught Jewish Law at the feet of the great Gamaliel, and had come to persecute the followers of the crucified Jesus. He told of his role in the persecution of Stephen and his encounter with the voice of Jesus on the road to Damascus.

Paul then began to explain how Jesus was God's own son and how the Holy Spirit had sent him to the Gentiles. But this wasn't a crowd in the mood to stand in the hot sun and hear a long story in the first place, and now they began to add up the obvious: this polluter of the Law was also proclaiming someone as the Messiah and promoting him to Gentiles as well. Soon the muttering had changed to shouts of derision. "Away with this fellow," one voice called out. "He shouldn't be allowed to live!" Others began echoing the cry until soon they were waving their garments in the air and kicking up dust as a symbol of rejection.

Before the scene got any uglier the tribune hastened Paul up to the fortress barracks overlooking the temple. When the heavy door had been shut and secured, Lysias gave an order for Paul to be examined by the usual scourging to find out why he had agitated such a large crowd. They had stripped his already-bloody clothes to his scarred waist and tied him up with thongs when Paul looked up at a centurion standing by

"Is it lawful for you to scourge a man who is a Roman citizen, and uncondemned?" he asked.

When the tribune heard it he walked over and squared himself before Paul. "You're a Roman citizen?" he asked.

"Yes."

"My citizenship cost me a large sum," the tribune mused to no one in particular. "But I was *born* a citizen," Paul replied.

So those who had been waiting to examine Paul were dismissed. The prisoner was unbound but detained for the night. By the next morning Lysias had determined the real reason for all the commotion. He had Paul taken to the meeting place of the Jewish Sanhedrin, which gathered in a large, long hall off the Court of the Israelites in the temple. There Paul found himself confronting a mixture of Saduccees, who included virtually all of the leading priests, and the Pharisees, who made up the remainder. By this time, all had been able to inquire about Paul and form some impressions. Some older members by then would have remembered him as the hot-headed young temple official who had gone off to bring back members of the fledgling Way and wound up joining them. He had since corrupted perhaps hundreds of Jews by imploring them to abandon the Law and follow a false messiah. Had he himself begun eating "the other thing" and ignoring the Sabbath? Was he himself even still a Jew? If not, what was he doing in the temple attempting to undergo the purification ceremony? And who were those other shaved heads with him?

The tribune Lysias ordered Paul to rise and explain himself to the body.

The meeting did not begin well. "Brethren," Paul began as an introduction, "I have lived before God in all good conscience before this day."

No sooner had these opening words passed when an imposing fellow shouted "Blasphemy!" and ordered the man nearest Paul to strike him in the mouth.

Stunned, Paul shot back at the leader: "You whitewashed wall [referring to what Jews used to cover privies and mud sheds]. "Are you sitting to judge me according to the Law, and yet contrary to the Law you order me struck?"

Someone whispered to Paul that the council was accustomed to being addressed as "Elders of Israel" and that the man he had just insulted was the high priest Ananias. "Would you revile God's high priest?" another member asked aloud.

Paul became somewhat contrite, but without changing the salutation. "I did not know, brethren, that he is the high priest," he said. "For it is written, 'You shall not speak evil of a ruler of your people.'"

But Paul could see how on edge his "judges" were, and I believe at this point he resorted to a tactic that was somewhat diversionary and certainly divisive. It was easy to spot the Pharisees in the room with their amulets, tassels and long robes. Realizing that there were as many Pharisees in the room as there were Saduccees, he said: "Brethren, I am a Pharisee, a son of Pharisees. It is with respect to the hope and the resurrection of the dead that I am on trial here!"

Well, this was like driving an ax into a sliver of firewood, because the Sadducces believe that death is death and Pharisees believe that the dead rise to become spirits. In an instant the members were arguing among themselves. One of the

Pharisees managed to quiet things down long enough to say, "We find nothing wrong in this man! So what if a spirit or an angel spoke to him?"

With that the room again was full of shouting, jostling and even beard pulling. Lysias the tribune watched with bemusement at first; but then fearful that some of them might turn on Paul, he shouted towards the entrance for some of his men to rush in and take the prisoner away.

So it was back to the barracks again while Lysias pondered what to do. After all, he was only a *chiliarch*, the commander of a thousand men. This was beginning to look like a matter for higher authorities.

Paul pondered his fate as well. And Luke was to write later that during the night, "The Lord stood by him and said, 'Take courage, for as you have testified about me at Jerusalem, so you must bear witness also at Rome.'"

But that same night Paul's fate was also being discussed by another group. The writings don't indicate whether the instigators were the Sanhedrin itself or some of the crowd that had attacked Paul in the temple courtyard two days before. In any event, about 40 revengeful men took an oath not to eat or drink until they killed Paul. My own view is that the Sanhedrin maintained at its disposal a clandestine band of zealous youths who could be counted on to "take care of" certain temple business that the Romans wouldn't sanction. The irony is that Paul himself may well have belonged to a similar group long ago when called upon to root out a new upstart movement called The Way. In any event, the council sent a representative to the barracks the next morning to tell the tribune that the elders of Israel were prepared to resume hearing Paul's case in an orderly fashion later that same day.

But the real plan was to seize and kill him before he ever reached the council room.

During the same morning, the sister whose name no one seems to recall, and whom Paul had not seen for at least eight years before his recent arrival, intervened to save his life. Somehow she caught wind of the plot, and sometime during the interim before Paul was to be escorted out from the barracks, she ordered her young son to hasten there and warn his uncle.

Before long the tribune Lysias was confronted by one of his centurions who had a local boy in tow. "Paul the prisoner asked me to bring this young man to you, as he has something to say."

The tribune took the lad by the hand into an unoccupied room and asked him, "What is it you have to tell me?"

"The Jews have agreed to ask you to bring Paul to the council today, as though they were going to inquire somewhat more closely about him," said the boy anxiously. "But do not yield to them, for more than 40 of them lie in ambush, having bound themselves by an oath neither to eat nor drink until they have killed him. And now they are ready, waiting for the promise from you."

None of this surprised Lysias. He thanked the boy and sent him home after having promised to tell no one. Then he calmly called in two of his centurions and said: "At the third hour of the night I want 200 soldiers with 70 horsemen and 200 spearmen prepared to go as far as Cæsarea. I also want mounts for Paul to ride. And I want him brought safely to Felix, the governor."

Then Lysias sat down and wrote a letter to Felix describing the situation. Before signing off, he added his own opinion: "I found that he was accused about questions of their law, but charged with nothing deserving death or imprisonment. And when it was disclosed to me that there would be a plot against the man, I sent him to you at once, ordering his accusers also to state before you what they have against him."

Paul and his escort departed in the dead of night. The size of the guard sent to arm one politically unimportant pauper gives an indication of two things: how dangerous it was to be outside the walls of Jerusalem and how much this "Gentile" brand of Christianity agitated the Jews in their heartland. About 30 miles north at Antipatris and presumably out of danger from any followers from Jerusalem, the soldiers turned back and left the horsemen to deliver Paul to Felix.

With the prisoner safely standing before him in silence, Felix read the letter from Lysias and asked Paul what province he came from. When Paul told him Cilicia, Felix promised to hear his case "when your accusers arrive." Meanwhile, he was to be kept in the maximum security dungeon of Herod's castle.

The accusers did not disappoint. The Sanhedrin must have obtained a lawyer and set off for Cæsarea with all haste, because five days later Felix was seated in his judgment seat with Paul standing at one side and a delegation of distinguished Jewish elders on the other. Speaking for the latter was one Tertullus, an advocate who was trained in Roman rhetoric and more apt to sway a Roman procurator.

Tertullus, after praising the "most excellent Felix" for the "peace" and "reforms" he had "brought the nation," asked for his help in punishing the "pestilent fellow" before them. Paul was cited as a "ringleader of the sect of the Nazerines" and "an agitator among all the Jews throughout the world." He had even tried to profane the temple before he was seized.

Here is Luke's summary of what Paul said in turn:

> "Realizing that for many years you have been judge over this nation, I cheerfully make my defense. As you may ascertain, it was not more than 12 days since I went up to worship at Jerusalem; and they did not find me disputing with anyone or stirring up a crowd either in the temple or the synagogues or in the city. Neither can they prove to you what they now bring against me.

But this I admit to you: that according to The Way, which they call a sect, I worship the God of our fathers, believing everything laid down by or written by the prophets, having a hope in God which these themselves accept, that there will be a resurrection of both the just and the unjust. So I always take pains to have a clear conscience toward God and toward men.

Now after some years I came to bring my nation alms and offerings. As I was doing this, they found me purified in the temple, without any crowd or tumult. But some Jews from Asia – they ought to be here before you to make this accusation if they have anything against me. Or else let these men themselves say what wrongdoing they found when I stood before the council except this one thing which I cried out while standing among them, "With respect to the resurrection of the dead I am on trial before you this day."[51]

Felix himself was far from ignorant of the Way and the many Christian communities that now flourished throughout Syria. You may remember too that he was married to the Jewess Drusilla, the youngest daughter of Herod Agrippa I, and then only about 19. Felix knew something of Jewish-Christian politics.

The Jews pressed for a decision, but Felix put them off. "When Lysias the tribune comes down, I will decide your case," he said, dismissing them. Turning to Paul, he gave orders that he be kept in minimal custody, with rights to be visited by his friends and have food brought to him. This was a blessing because Luke and the others had also come down from Jerusalem, the latter probably beginning to wonder when they would be able to make their way back to their homes in the provinces.

Lysias later came and added his first-hand account of what happened, but Felix continued to postpone a decision. Several days later Felix's wife Drusilla joined him and together they dabbled at more interrogations without giving indication of when they might decide the case. Eventually autumn turned, the north winds began to blow and Paul's church friends from the proivinces – his constant source of moral support – simply had to take the last sailing vessels available. Finally there were just Luke, Timothy and certainly the comfort of Cesarean Christians like Philip and his daughters. From time to time Felix would summon Paul, have a pleasant enough conversation, then return him to his quarters.

Why? I agree with those who believe that although Felix was not about to release an innocent man to the Jews, he was hoping that Paul's churches might raise a purse for his freedom just as they had for their brethren in Jerusalem.

But Paul also knew that if simply discharged alone into the streets of Judea, the Jews would kill him.

Felix had his own case to consider. The same Jewish elders were petitioning Rome to recall the procurator on charges of orchestrating the Jewish-Syrian riots in Cæsarea. Releasing Paul would only inflame them.

Thus, Felix would toy with Paul for nearly two years until he himself was forced to go to Rome.

Paul thought of ways *he* might be freed from Cæsarea while at the same time being "forced" to go to Rome. It was the only way out. But more importantly, the fulfillment of his mission demanded it.

. . . .

A. D. 6 0 — 6 1

What could a budding musician do once the Neronian Youth Games were over? If he happens to be emperor he proclaims a new series of Greek-style stage competitions, to be held once every five years. To a nobility that had just been compelled to do all sorts of demeaning stage acts just a few months before, the decree touched off a new round of complaints that Roman morals were headed for an all-time low.

Objectors cited that for many years in the days of the venerated Republic, public entertainment was offered on temporary stages, and spectators had even been made to stand (because seats would only turn them into idlers). Now, as one senator railed, "This imported laxity makes everything potentially corrupting and corruptible flow into the capital so that our young men are demoralized into shirkers, gymnasts and perverts. And the crowds!" he thundered. "Debauchees are emboldened to practice by night the lusts they have only imagined by day!"

But the crowds, and even some patricians, were with Nero. Their view went something like this: "All throughout the Republic, ballet dancers were imported from Etruria and chariot drivers from Thurii. And ever since the annexation of Greece the numbers of performances and shows had increased steadily. Once every five years isn't a great number of days. And such an occasion should be seen as one of gaiety rather than debauchery. As for theaters, it's much more economical to construct a permanent one than to build and demolish every year. Besides, if the state pays for the shows, as Nero has promised, the wealthy won't be constantly hectored to become sponsors.

So the Nero faction easily carried the weight of public opinion. And when the first of the Greek competitions opened, Nero also used the occasion to dedicate a lavish new public bath and gymnasium (featuring a school of music) near the Pantheon. At the dedication the emperor celebrated by distributing rubbing oil to all the senators and knights present. The games went on, Nero again winning the first prize for lyre playing (no one else challenged him). Then, wearing the garb of the music guild, he proudly entered the gymnasium to be enrolled on a scroll honoring contest winners.

Nero, of course, continued his lavish living. He fished with a golden net, never wore the same garment twice, and played at dice for 400,000 sesterces a point. In one extravagant eccentricity, he took it upon himself to bathe in the source of the same Marcian Aqueduct that we have today. To what end, I do not know, because the public was outraged that he would pollute the sacred waters. But the gods got even with him when he soon came down with a serious malady.

Nero recovered soon enough, but other mounting concerns became much more time-consuming and worrisome than he had ever encountered. His mode of living (and the military campaigns I will soon mention) had by then drained off most of the 2.2 billion sesterces that Claudius had left the treasury. The result was an embarrassing currency devaluation — the first in imperial times. The *as,* originally a pound of copper centuries ago, was further reduced to a quarter ounce. The previous reduction had been 147 years before, when it had been reduced from one ounce to a half. At the same time, the *denarius* was lowered to 90 percent of its silver content. The *aureus* went from $\frac{1}{40}$th pound of gold to $\frac{1}{45}$th. The immediate result was that people paid more in real terms for merchandise, but relatively less to their creditors.

The second cause, as I indicated, was two long-running military misadventures. Although I have spared you the details in discussing them in recent years, the fact is that neither Armenia nor Britain had ever been brought fully into the Roman orbit despite what you may have read about Senate celebrations and proclamations.

Armenia was like a large-but-meatless soup bone. Most self-respecting dogs would pass it by on the street; but when there are two dogs named Rome and Parthia they will snarl over the bone until one of them backs off. Until now, the story of kingless Armenia seems to invoke another dog analogy. In one season Rome would enter unopposed, lift its leg on a few leading cities to mark its territory, then grow weary and depart. The next season would be the turn of the Parthian dog — and so forth.

But this year was different. Cnæus Domitius Corbulo and his forces were determined to put an end to the costly and embarrassing stalemate. With his largest army to date, Corbulo demolished the Armenian capital of Artaxata. He had begun to besiege the heavily-fortified city of Tigranocerta when a deputation came out and announced that its gates were open with the population awaiting his mercy. These and smaller victories took place with no opposition from the Parthians, who were waging war on another border at the time.

Corbulo was prepared to occupy Armenia for as long as it took to re-assert Roman dominance, but winter was coming on, water was scarce and his exhausted troops were existing almost exclusively on meat. So he must have had mixed emotions when his scouts brought word that Tigranes v and his entourage were in sight to the west. I should explain here that Corbulo and pro-Romans in Armenia had long urged Nero to send the country a king. Tigranes was Nero's choice, a young member of the royal family in neighboring Cappadocia. But Corbulo, the hard-bitten soldier, quickly realized he was also in the company of another in the long line of puffy, white-skinned aristocrats who had languished too long on Roman couches.

Well, orders are orders — including one that young Tigranes had brought for *him*. Quadratus, the governor of Syria, had died, and Corbulo was to replace him. So Corbulo was probably not too displeased at trading these barren, snow-swept hills for the relative refinement of Antioch. He left Tigranes with a guard of a thousand Roman regulars, three auxiliary infantry battalions, two cavalry regiments and an alliance of border kings who had sworn to prevent the Parthians from bothering Armenia. But with Tigranes, Corbulo probably knew at the same time that Rome had not laid the foundation for a lasting and honorable peace with Parthia.

In quite the opposite direction, the people of Britain had no other diversions than to hate Rome. Since the day Claudius had left their shores on his way back to a triumph, Britons of all tribes, religions and locations had nothing but contempt for Roman colonizers. The bridges, buildings and baths of "advanced civilization" meant nothing to them — and they sneered at hearing that the Roman emperor wore a Greek tunic and played music all day. The problem was that they were such a polyglot of tribes, religions and small towns that the Romans were always able to keep their leaders distracted or divided.

In this year two things happened to change Rome's weak grasp on the island. The first was that the small merchant class — Rome's only real source of support — was hit with a financial crisis that left it reeling. Claudius, in an attempt to win loyalty, had "loaned" leading Britons a good deal of money, which they assumed to be bribes for their allegiance. But now that Nero was scouring the empire for money, the terms were re-defined. No, said Nero's procurator, the Roman outlays were intended all along to be loans to help stimulate commerce in the region. Now the sums were to be paid back. Yes, new loans could be negotiated, but only at whopping interest rates.

The second rallying point was the emergence of a new leader — a woman. And it came about in the most ironic way. Perhaps the only staunch ally Rome ever had in Britain was Prasutagus, king of the Iceni in the eastern part of the island.

So desirous was he of Roman peace and protection that he had even made the emperor his co-heir with his two daughters. This official blanket of protection was sorely needed because Camulodunum, the largest town in the region, had also been made a settlement area for military veterans. As in many such towns, neighborhoods strained with the tensions between natives and newcomers. And outside of town, natives were under unrelenting pressure to cede ancestral lands to Romans for scandously low prices.

The Roman army could always be counted on to preserve this delicate co-existence, but this changed a year or so before the time of this chapter because the Romans sent a new governor, the ambitious and impatient Gaius Suetonius Paulinus. Jealous at the attention Corbulo had been receiving for his victories in Armenia, and regarding himself as Corbulo's peer in military prowess, Suetonius decided to gain greater glory for Rome by subduing the region of Mona in the extreme western part of the island.

In truth, all his men found upon their "invasion" from the sea were a beach full of Druid witches brandishing torches and shouting curses at them. Their greatest conquest was in destroying a grove of altars on which the Druids offered the blood of victims and consulted with their gods by using human entrails.

But while Suetonius was thus occupied, the blood of thousands to the east was being spilled. In his absence, the Romans who lived in Iceni — both civilians and ex-soldiers — took it upon themselves to plunder the lands held by King Prasutagus. The king had been killed by his own slaves, who then flogged his wife Boudicca, raped their two daughters and ransacked the household. The plundering then spread to the hereditary estates of the king's relatives and chiefs.

So this was the protection loyal Britons could expect from Rome? The minds of the Iceni now burned hotter than the timbers of their homes. They were soon joined by the neighboring Trinobantes clans, once their rivals, but no more. And all of their fury was focused on the Roman community at Camulodunum. The settlers, despite having driven most of the natives from their homes and building a temple to an alien conqueror, the dead emperor Claudius, had never bothered to fortify Camulodunum with walls.

One day, for no apparent cause, the statue of Victory in the Claudian temple fell and crashed. Before long, delirious women surrounded it, chanting of Roman destruction ahead. Reports spread of unexplained wailings in the empty theater, a blood-red color in the sea and shapes like human corpses left in the ebb tide. In Suetonius' absence, the local Romans were frightened enough to ask for help from the imperial agent Catus Decianus. All this yielded was a gaggle of 200 poorly-armed men. With only a local garrison to add to the total, the Romans of Camulodunum were reduced to a desperate last line of defense: relying on the traditional sanctuary of an imperial temple that the rebels detested.

It did not work. A horde of Iceni, Trinobantes and others stormed in one day and in a few hours tore to shreds everything in the city that was Roman. The few remaining garrison defenders barricaded themselves in the temple of Claudius, but after two days' siege it fell by storm. By then word of the attack had been received by the Ninth Roman Division, but the voracious Britons ran out to intercept the troops on the road to Camulodunum and wiped out every man like locusts on a wheatfield.

The insatiable Britons had now killed nearly 70,000 Romans and they were headed west, destroying everything Roman in sight. Often they marched right past Roman fortifications, focusing always on private estates, where the riches were easiest to grab. They took no prisoners because they knew not the tradition of civilized nations of exchanging captives. In any event, they would not have been deterred from hanging, burning and crucifying in revenge for their own losses at Rome's hand. Spare the women? Not a chance! They hung up naked the noblest among them, cut off their breasts and sewed them to their mouths so as to make their victims appear to be eating them. Then they impaled the women on sharp skewers running the length of their bodies.

Suetonius was now alerted and headed east. He had but 10,000 men. But rather than reserve them for a decisive battle, he exacted revenge as he went, slaughtering any one of any age or sex who stood in his way lest they be able to attack him from the rear once he had left. First, it was Londinium, not large enough for a Roman settlement, but considered an important center of local trade. Next in his path was Verulamium. Anyone who wanted to join his auxiliaries was taken in. All others were killed.

When the first of the British horde came into sight, Suetonius had no thought of parley. His provisions were already running low and he resolved to have at it instantly. He chose a position in a narrow gorge with a wood behind him. Before him was open country with no cover for ambushes.

Suetonius concentrated his regular troops in close order with the light-armed auxiliaries at their flanks in order to form three fighting divisions. He was fortunate to have positioned his men in clusters because when he saw the numbers of Britons who appeared before him, he realized that even if he had stretched his men from end to end he could not have begun to reach the flanks of the Britons. So vast were their numbers that estimates from observers ranged from 120,000 to 200,000. The Britons were so sure this would be the final blow against Rome that they had brought their wives and children in carts to witness the spectacle.

Then Suetonius got his first glimpse at who was leading them — a very tall, fierce-looking woman. A great mass of the tawny hair fell to her hips. She wore a tunic of many colors over which a thick mantle was fastened with a brooch. Around her neck was a large golden necklace.

When Suetonius first saw her she was driving a chariot with two girls in it and shouting to her assembled troops as she wove among them. She was Boudicca, the widow of Prasutagus, the Icenian king. The girls were the daughters who had been raped by Romans.

Now Suetonius watched as Boudicca mounted an earthen tribunal that had been hastily constructed for her. Grasping a spear and raising it in front of her armies, she exhorted them in a harsh and loud voice. "You have learned by special experience how different freedom is from slavery," she said.

> Now that you have tried both, you have learned how great a mistake you made in preferring an imported despotism to your ancestral mode of life, and you have come to realize how much better is poverty with no master than wealth with slavery. For what treatment is there of the most shameful and grievous sort that we have not suffered since these men made their appearance in Britain? Have we not been robbed entirely of most of our possessions, while on those that remain we pay taxes? Besides pasturing and tilling for them all our other possessions, do we not pay a yearly tribute for our very bodies? How much better it would be to have been sold to masters once and for all than to have to ransom ourselves every year! How much better to have been slain and to have perished than to go about with a tax on our heads! But even dying is not free of cost with them; nay, you know what fees we deposit even for our dead![52]

But now, Boudicca noted to a tremendous shout, the entire nation has come together to throw out the invaders. "Have no fear whatever of the Romans," she added,

> for they are superior to us neither in numbers nor in bravery. And here is the proof: they have protected themselves with helmets, breastplates and greaves and yet have further erected palisades, walls and trenches to make sure of suffering no harm by an incursion of their enemies. For they are influenced by fear when they adopt this kind of fighting. Indeed, we enjoy such a surplus of bravery that we regard our tents as safer than their walls and our shields as better protection than their suits of mail. When overpowered, the Britons can elude them, whereas the Romans are too burdened with heavy armor to pursue or flee. They require shade and covering. They require kneaded bread and wine and oil. For us, any grass or root serves as bread, the juice of any plant as oil, any water as wine, any tree as a house. We swim the rivers naked, whereas they don't get across easily

even with boats. So let us go against them boldly! Let us show them that they are hares and foxes trying to rule over dogs and wolves.[53]

With that Boudicca raised the fold of her dress and a hare escaped. And since it ran on the auspicious side, the whole multitude shouted with gusto. Then Boudicca, raising her hand heavenward, offered a prayer to Andraste, goddess of the Britons. Once more she vilified her foes.

> I supplicate and pray thee for victory...against men insolent, unjust, insatiable, impious — if indeed we ought to term these people men who bathe in warm water, eat artificial dainties, drink unmixed wine, anoint themselves with myrrh, sleep on soft couches with boys for bedfellows and are slaves to a lyre player — and a poor one, too. Wherefore may this Mistress Domitia-Nero reign no longer over me or over you men; let the wench sing and lord it over Romans, for they surely deserve to be the slaves of such a woman for having submitted to her for so long. But for us, Mistress, be thou alone ever our leader.[54]

Suetonius calmly urged his men to disregard "the clamors and empty threats of the natives" — and their numbers as well. "In their ranks are more women than fighting men," he said. "When they see the arms and courage of the conquerors who have routed them so often, they will break immediately. Even when a force contains many divisions, few among them win battles. What special glory for your small numbers to win the renown of a whole army!"

But Suetonius didn't have to exhort his men long. All had friends or family who had perished — some horribly — at the hands of the rebels. All knew that if they didn't muster every ounce of discipline they had been taught, all faced the chance of "looking on as our entrails are cut from our bodies, or spitted on red-hot skewers or being melted in boiling water — in a word, to suffer as though we had been thrown to lawless and impious wild beasts. Let us therefore, " he said, "either conquer them or die on the spot."

Suetonius raised the signal for battle and the two forces approached each other, the Britons shouting and singing songs of courage. The Romans advanced in silence, almost as if creeping. Then they were walking at a brisk pace. Now they charged behind their shields at full speed. Now they clashed and clanged head-on with the first ranks and broke right through them. Now they were in the midst of the Briton horde, fighting in tight clusters. Everywhere there was a confusing jumble: cavalry opposing infantry, missile throwers against bowmen, chariots rushing infantry. The chariots of the Britons would charge into a knot of Roman infantrymen, scattering them like so many wine jars. But after the impact the drivers, without any breastplates, would be cut down or pierced with arrows.

The screams and sounds of metal clashing on metal continued all day, with the Roman divisions moving as if in three concentric circles spinning here and there. As the sun began to sink lower, most of the Romans were still upright, with the vast majority of bodies at their feet Britons. The Romans also realized that more and more Britons were trying to retreat, but were being slowed by or caught up in the jumble of wagons that had formed a perimeter at the rear.

Then word spread among both sides that Boudicca had died. The first version was that she was struck down, which emboldened the Britons to rally in her name. But soon it became known that she had seen defeat at hand and poisoned herself. With that, the last flickers of hope died among the Britons and they scattered for their homes and hollows. There they would face equal calamities, for in their enthusiasm for war they had neglected to sow their crops and winter was now coming on.

For the Roman army it was a day to recall the triumphs of Julius Cæsar. Ten thousand tightly-knit men had killed more than 80,000 of their foe in one day. They had lost 400 men, not counting the many who were wounded and maimed.

But some calamities awaited the victors as well. Suetonious, rather than being hailed in a triumph, soon faced the unpleasant arrival of a new imperial agent from Rome. Nero's personal deputy wasted no time in reporting that Suetonius had probably been lucky in battle and now should be replaced as governor by someone who might be of kinder disposition to the battle survivors and populace of Britain.

When Suetonius protested by sending a letter with his own version, Nero responded by dispatching an "investigator": a freedman with a large entourage of courtesan-sightseers who took their time lumbering from banquet to banquet in Gaul and Germany. When the haughty dandy from Rome finally arrived, the embittered soldiers ridiculed him. Even the natives sneered at how so awesome a general could be intimidated by an ex-slave. In the end, Suetonius was allowed to stay as governor, but his career came to an ignoble end when he was later sacked for not bringing "hostilities" in Britain to an end soon enough.

In Rome itself Nero and the Senate found themselves engulfed in a local calamity that probably concerned them more than the ones in Armenia and Britain. The city prefect, Lusius Pedanius Secundus, was respected for the way he administered Rome's 16 precincts. Thus, people were shocked to learn that Pedanius was murdered in bed by one of his slaves. One story was that he had set a price on the man's freedom but had refused to make good on the bargain. Another version is that the two were in competition for a lover.

Whatever the cause, what consumed public debate was an ancient law stating that when a man is slain by his slave, all other slaves in the same household must be killed in return. Pedanius had 400 — an awesome retribution for even the sternest of slaveowners.

Soon a large, riotous crowd of protesters had gathered and converged on the Senate house. A debate was in progress on whether to amend or rescind the old law. The most powerful speech for those who opposed any leniency was made by Gaius Cassius Longinus. Stating that he had never before opposed relaxation of other ancient laws, he could not help but do so in this case.

> A man who has held the consulship has been deliberately murdered by a slave in his own home. None of his fellow slaves prevented or betrayed the murder...

> Pretend, if you like, that we are deciding a policy for the first time. Do you believe that a slave can have planned to kill his master without letting fall a single rash or menacing word? Or even if we assume he kept his secret – and obtained a weapon unnoticed – could he have passed the watch, opened a bedroom door, carried in a light and committed the murder without anyone knowing? There are many advance notifications of crimes. If slaves give them away, we can live securely. Or if we must die, we can at least be sure the guilty will be punished...

> Our ancestors distrusted their slaves. Yet slaves were then born on the same estates, in the same houses, as their masters, who had treated them kindly from birth. But nowadays our huge households are international. They include every alien religion, or none at all. The only way to keep down this scum is by intimidation.

> Innocent people will die, you say. Yes, and when in a defeated army every tenth man is flogged to death, the brave have to draw lots with the others. Exemplary punishment always contains an element of injustice. But individual wrongs are outweighed by the advantage of the community.[55]

As Cassius spoke, the crowds milled outside, shouting for mercy to be shown the many women and children, if nothing else. Yet, not one senator dared to speak or vote against Cassius. When the crowd began to pick up stones and bar the order from being carried out, Nero ordered troops to line the entire route by which the 400 slaves would be taken to their execution. That night the order was carried out to the last woman and child.

. . . .

THE USUAL TENSIONS IN JUDEA were aggravated at this time by its unsettled role in the Roman-Parthian battle of attrition for Armenia. Would Rome finally subdue the wretched place or would the Syrian governor soon be conscripting Samaritan and Galilean boys as front-line sacrifices to Parthian bowmen in an all-out war? Would Syrian corn and wheat supplies be carried off as army provisions, leaving famine and inflation in Jerusalem? Would the garrison at Cæsarea be depleted for the big war, leaving the rest at risk to police their tempestuous Jewish and Syrian townsmen?

But what among these could match the inner turmoil going on within the apostle Paul after nearly two years in a Cæsarean jail? Was his mission doomed to dissipate in the dark emptiness of captivity?

Felix had departed as well, and Christians wondered what to make of it. The procurator had been recalled to Rome. A deputation of leading Jews from Cæsarea had petitioned the emperor to censure the procurator for helping Syrians in town raid their homes and loot their property in the previous year. The evidence against Felix was so strong that the emperor probably would have banished him. Moreover, the Jews were probably able to win a nod of favor from Poppæa, who was known to have been attracted to the Jewish religion, as were several women among the nobility. Instead, Felix was quietly replaced, and word is that it was because he was a brother of the powerful Pallas, who had treated the boy Nero kindly when he oversaw financial affairs in the reign of Claudius.

Mid-summer saw the arrival of a new procurator. Porcius Festus seemed to be more eager to ease Jewish-Hellene tensions if for no other reason that they eroded the strength and stability of a province that was essential to containing Parthia. After just three days inspecting his new quarters at Cæsarea, Festus hastened on to Jerusalem to see how he might improve relations with the temple authorities.

One of the many causes of instability in Jerusalem arose from the fact that the position of high priest had changed hands among so many quarreling factions. Ironically, there had been fewer changeovers before the reign of Herod Agrippa I when the Romans had asserted control of appointments. Now, in the past ten years under Agrippa II's control there had been six different high priests. This not only encouraged factionalism, but created situations where new high priests were constantly testing the limits of their authority under Rome.

Well, the elders certainly weren't going to ask that Romans rather than Jews appoint high priests, but they could ask for help in stopping the spread of splinter groups. After all, the high priest Jonathan had been killed only a few years before by a Sicarii and the murderer had never been brought to justice. How could one be sure it hadn't been committed by an overzealous Christian — maybe even by one of Paul's Gentile converts? Festus, they said, could help restore stability by having the prisoner Paul sent up from Cæsarea so that they could judge him properly.

Festus had already heard about the failed ambush of Paul and feared another attempt on the road to Jerusalem. No, he said, "Paul is being kept in Cæsarea. Since I plan to return there shortly myself, let the men of authority among you go down with me; and if there is anything wrong about the man, let them accuse him."

Festus returned in around ten days, and another deputation of Jewish elders was not far behind. The very next day Festus was in his judgment seat, with the accusing advocate on one side and the chained prisoner on the other. But to the procurator's surprise, no new evidence was introduced to substantiate the charge of defiling the temple. The advocate did enter a new accusation: that in championing a Messiah, Paul had challenged the emperor's authority, but even this seemed like an afterthought. As far as Festus could make out, the Jews were arguing that the sage Jesus, who died some thirty years before, was indeed dead, while Paul was arguing that he was alive.

Paul rose to his own defense. "Neither against the laws of the Jews nor against the temple, nor against Cæsar have I offended at all," he said.

But Festus, still hopeful of doing the Jews a favor, asked Paul: "Do you wish to go up to Jerusalem, and there be tried on these charges before me?"

Said Paul: "I am standing before Cæsar's tribunal, where I ought to be tried. To the Jews I have done no wrong, as you know very well. If then I am a wrongdoer and have committed anything for which I deserve to die, I do not seek to escape death. But if there is nothing in their charges against me, no one can give me up to them. I appeal to Cæsar."

Festus recessed briefly and gathered his councilors about him. I can imaging them saying: "Procurator, if he is freed now, the elders will hate you, and may even find a way to kill him. If you go to all the trouble of trying him in Jerusalem and then finding him not guilty, even greater passions will be inflamed and many more could be killed."

Festus returned to his judgment chair and addressed Paul. "You have appealed to Cæsar, and to Cæsar you will go."

Going to Cæsar meant going under an armed escort, so Paul must have felt great relief on many fronts. The endless dark days in a dank jail would soon be behind him. He would be under protection from temple vigilantes. He would be free to continue his mission in the capital of the empire.

If Paul found his "trial" in Cæsarea all too brief and undramatic after so many months of preparation, he would soon have the opportunity to make his points again. Although Rome governed lower Judea directly, Agrippa II remained king of a region stretching north from the Lake of Gennesaret. Paying a welcome visit to the new procurator was just as important to him as it had been to the temple authorities, so Agrippa and his queen arrived in Cæsarea just a few days after Paul's hearing had concluded.

For Agrippa, now 32, it was more than just a protocol visit, for the following reason. He had stayed aloof from the previous procurator because Felix was married to his younger sister Drusilla, who couldn't stand the sight of Agrippa or his queen. No one has recorded exactly why, but one can guess. The "queen" I keep referring to was none other than his (and Drusilla's) sister Bernice. Once married to a wealthy commoner, then concubine to her Uncle Herod the King of Chalcis, Bernice had finally married properly to King Polemo of Cilicia, who had even agreed to undergo circumcision and live by the Law. But poor Polemo. Not long after he had endured one painful process, he was afflicted with another when the beautiful Bernice ran off to the court of her brother and became his partner in rule and in incest.

Since Agrippa was in charge of naming high priests, I'm sure Festus wanted all the information he could get about affairs within the temple hierarchy. But he would also welcome the king and queen's insights on another matter. The procurator was in the process of writing a letter to the emperor's secretary for provincial affairs about a religious prisoner named Paul and perhaps the two might help him frame the charges to be presented at trial.

"Why, yes," said Agrippa, "I would like to hear the man myself."

"Then tomorrow you shall hear him," said Festus.

The next day, perhaps even Paul might have been taken aback when he was led from the dinginess of his small cell to the large assembly hall. Therein had been gathered Agrippa, the bejeweled Bernice, their entire entourage and all the notables of Cæsarea. Paul might also have spotted a few Christians, among them the faithful Luke.

Festus stood along with the chained and tattered man before him. "King Agrippa and all who are present," he said, "you see this man about whom the whole Jewish people petitioned me, both at Jerusalem and here, shouting that he ought not to live any longer. But I found that he had done nothing definite to write my lord about him. Therefore I have brought him before you, and especially before you, King Agrippa, that after we have examined him, I may have something to write. For it seems to me unreasonable, in sending a prisoner, not to indicate the charges against him."

I suspect that Paul instantly recognized the setting to be something not unlike what he envisioned when he addressed the emperor himself in Rome. It would not only be a defense, but also a chance to tame the lion and wolf as well. Extending his hand in a slow sweeping gesture, Paul began by saying how much he welcomed the king's presence "because you are especially familiar with all customs and controversies among the Jews." Stating that his own history and "manner of life" is "known by all Jews," and that he, a Pharisee, was on trial for none other than believing the messianic promise that God had long made to the twelve tribes of Israel. For,

> Why is it thought incredible by any of you that God raises the dead? I myself [in his youth] was convinced that I ought to do many things in opposing the name of Jesus of Nazareth. And I did do in Jerusalem. I not only shut up many of the saints in prison, by authority from the chief priests, but when they were put to death I cast my vote against them. And I punished them often in all the synagogues and tried to make them blaspheme, And in raging fury against them, I persecuted them even to foreign cities.

> Thus I journeyed to Damascus with the authority and commission of the chief priests. At midday, O king, I saw on the way a light from heaven, brighter than the sun, shining round me and those who journeyed with me. And when we had all fallen to the ground, I heard a voice saying to me in the Hebrew language, "Saul, Saul, why do you persecute me...?"

> And I said: "Who are you, lord?" And the Lord said, "I am Jesus whom you are persecuting. But rise and stand upon your feet; for I have appeared to you for this purpose, to appoint you to serve and bear witness to the things in which you have seen me and those in which I will appear to you, delivering you from the people and from the Gentiles — to whom I send you, to open their eyes, that they may turn the darkness into light and from the power of Satan to God, that they may receive forgiveness of sins and a place among those who are sanctified by faith in me."[56]

"And it is for this reason that the Jews seized me in the temple and tried to kill me," said Paul. "To this day I have had no help but what comes from God. And so I stand here testifying both to small and great, saying nothing but what the prophets and Moses said would come to pass: that the Christ must suffer, and that by being the first to rise from the dead he would proclaim light both to the people and to the Gentiles."

Festus interrupted. "Paul, Paul, you are mad," he sighed loudly. "Your great learning is making you mad."

"I am *not* mad, most excellent Festus," Paul retorted. "I am speaking the sober truth. For the king knows about these things, and to him I speak freely; for I am persuaded that none of these things has escaped his notice, for this was not done in a corner. King Agrippa, do you believe the prophets? I know that you believe."

Agrippa laughed nervously. He could see where this might lead. "You think to make me a Christian in such a short time?"

"Whether short or long," answered Paul, "I would to God that not only you but also all who hear me this day might become such as I am – except for these chains."

Doubtless Paul had planned a longer expository, but suddenly Agrippa and Bernice rose, which meant that their entire retinue did as well. And as Agrippa strode off into a corridor with Festus, he could be heard saying, "This man is doing nothing to deserve death or punishment. He could have been set free had he not appealed to Cæsar."

This was the last public interrogation Paul would have to face in Cæsarea. By now it was late September and the northwest winds were already swirling. While they brought relief from the sweltering nights in the fortress dungeon, the winds were also signaling the last days in which passenger ships could sail north and west. Indeed, the Romans were busy trying to locate a merchant-man headed for Italy that also had enough capacity left to accommodate a centurion, a few of his soldiers, Paul and several other prisoners. Paul had also received permission to be accompanied by Luke and the tireless Aristarchus, who had helped bring the church collection from Macedonia, and who had refused to return as long as Paul was imprisoned.

Open seas shipping in the Mediterranean generally ceases for the winter around mid-November. It was now a few days past Yom Kippur (October 5) and the delay, I suspect, may have been caused by the inability to find a cargo ship owner who was willing to risk a round trip voyage that late. Finally, the best that the procurator's agents were able to find was a ship returning to its home port of Adramyttium, which lay a little southeast of Troas in Asia. Once the party from Cæsarea arrived there they would have to find another boat for Italy.

The man in charge of the prisoners was a centurion named Julius. That he was a decent fellow was demonstrated the first night when the ship pulled into Sidon, some 50 miles to the north. There, Julius allowed Paul and his companions to go ashore and greet a group of Christians who had caught wind of his arrival.

From Sidon they lumbered north against difficult crosswinds, passing to the east of Cyprus, then hugged the coast of Cilicia and Pamphylia before reaching the Lycian post of Myra in south central Asia Minor. Myra, being a major destination between Alexandria and Syria, had in its harbor a large grain ship from Alexandria. Usually, the owner of a leviathan like this is content to make one round trip per sailing season, but I think this ambitious merchant was trying to squeeze out one last run and take advantage of the higher prices fetched in the midst of winter. In any case, the ship was headed directly to Italy, and Julius the centurion decided to gamble that this would be the last time he would have to bother transferring such a large and cumbersome party.

So off they sailed, 276 passengers and a heavy load of wheat, combating a stiff northwesterly wind and waves that kept the giant ship rolling. For a while they were able to reduce the headwinds by creeping along the southern coast of Crete; but at the midway point of the island, just off the city of Lasea, the coastline angled to the northwest and the winds came howling in again. At that point the captain managed to maneuver the big vessel into a small harbor called Fair Havens.

Paul had already known high seas and shipwreck. Now he sought out the owner and captain. "Sirs," he said," I perceive that the voyage will be with injury and much loss, not only of the cargo and the ship, but of our lives."

Doubtless the word of this experienced traveler carried some weight, but the captain and owner worried that trying to winter in this particular harbor would also be dangerous. Besides, the winds had now abated some, so they set off hoping to reach Phœnix, some 60 miles further west along the shore of Crete. The harbor there faced the southeast, the most sheltered direction from the winter winds. It meant laying over for perhaps four months and incurring some unplanned expenses, but at least they'd arrive intact the next spring.

For several hours the ship even enjoyed a gentle southerly wind. But no sooner had it turned the corner of Cape Matala, the sharpest promontory on the Cretan coast, when it was slammed on the starboard side by a violent northeaster that swept down from the mountains. The unrelenting winds blew the huge ship out to sea. The captain tried desperately to slow its course by turning the bow into the wind, but to no avail. It even took hours to bring up the small harbor rowboat that had been towed behind the stern.

Their fear now was in being blown *too* quickly across the Mediterranean and crashing into any number of rocky outcrops that dotted their path. So the captain lowered the sail and let the ship drift. When the winds were just as severe the next day, the crew began dumping cargo overboard. The third day they cast out all the ship's tackle they could spare to further lighten their weight.

Now came a barrage of rain as well. A storm of such proportions lashed away at them that the passengers saw neither sun nor moon for day after day. After more than a week the galley fire had been doused and the bread was soggy, but most of the bedraggled passengers had ceased to care about eating anyway. They had all but given up hope of being saved from the raging seas.

It was about this time that the oldest of the prisoners began to assume a greater role in the ship's destiny. Paul, says Luke, sternly reminded the captain and owner that they should have listened to him on Crete. But having said that, Paul began going around urging everyone to take heart. "There will be no loss of life among you, but only of the ship," he assured. "For this very night there stood by me an angel of the God to whom I belong and whom I worship, and he said, 'Do not be afraid, Paul, You must stand before Cæsar. And lo, God has granted you all those who sail with you.' So take heart, men, for I have faith in God that it will be exactly as I have been told. But we shall have to run onto some island" [in order to be rescued].

The storm had now shown them nothing but high winds and gray skies for 14 days. They had been drifting in what they thought to be the widest, deepest part of the Mediterranean. But some of the sailors began to sense that they were approaching land, so they took out their remaining lead-weighted line and began taking soundings. One hundred twenty feet quickly became 90 — then less. Fearing they would smash into rocky shoals in the darkness, the crew quickly cast four anchors from the stern. Then they counted the hours and minutes to daylight as the waves beat against the stern.

At one point Paul noticed some sailors quietly lowering the longboat. As they started to scramble aboard, they explained that they also had to lay out anchors from the bow. But Paul was sure this was but a ruse for them to escape from the ship. He also saw the danger of it. Not only were the passengers seasick and weak, they would hardly know how to handle a ship in fair weather, much less a storm. Paul quickly sought out Julius. "Unless these men stay in the ship," he warned, "you cannot be saved." The centurion ordered them out of the boat; then he commanded his soldiers to cut away the ropes of the small boat and let it go.

As lighter skies signaled the coming of dawn, Paul was up and about, urging people to eat. "It will give you strength," he said, "since not a hair is to perish from the head of any of you." And as he urged them, he also took bread and offered thanks to God. And after they had all eaten, they further lightened the ship by throwing overboard all of the remaining wheat.

Daylight revealed a small bay not too far from where they'd anchored. Luckily, it also had a sand beach. The captain ordered the foresail raised. Then he had the anchors cast off in hopes of being able to run the ship up on the beach. But about halfway into the bay the ship ran into a shoal or reef and the bowsprit stuck fast in it. Water began to rush over the tilted bow. Surf waves crashed against the stern and its timbers began to break up. The soldiers dragged up the prisoners and drew their swords, preparing to kill them lest they escape. But Julius the centurion had come to see how important Paul was to their survival. He couldn't spare Paul and kill the rest, even if the escape of any of them meant his own death. Julius shouted at his men to sheath their swords. He ordered everyone on deck who could swim to jump overboard and make for the beach. When they were clear of the ship, he handed the others planks and pieces of the ship, then lowered them down so that they could float their way to shore.

The first gasping, salt-stained survivors to the beach found a crowd of local people had already gathered there in the rain and wind. Some island people help eke out their existence by selling shipwrecked survivors into slavery. But these natives, almost all simple fishermen, "showed us unusual kindness," wrote Luke, "for they kindled a fire and welcomed us all."

Paul and his shipmates quickly learned that they had drifted some 600 miles west from Crete. They had washed up on Melita, an island 50 miles south of Sicily and part of the province by that name. The reason why it has the Greek name for "honey" is for the fine nectar that swarms of black bees make from the many herbs growing on its rocky slopes.

Paul made an impression on the islanders from his first moments on their soil. He had gathered a bundle of sticks and was putting them on the fire when a viper jumped out (from the sudden heat, I assume) and fastened itself on Paul's hand. The natives gasped, because they thought it a sign that the stranger must be a murderer. Even though he had escaped death in the sea, the gods must have chosen the viper to exact their justice. But Paul simply shook the snake into the fire. And after not swelling up or falling down dead, as they swore he would, the people changed their minds and decided he must be a god himself.

As soon as he could, Julius the centurion marched his charges some six miles into the interior to the chief town, which is also named Melita. Although they were officially confined to some sort of government facility, Paul and his companions seem to have had considerable freedom (Julius may have reasoned that an island 18 miles long is enough protection against escape during winter). On one occasion during the mild winter, Luke reports that they spent three days as the guest of Publius, the island's chief magistrate.

"It happened that the father of Publius lay sick with fever and dysentery," Luke noted. "Paul visited him and prayed. And putting his hands on him, he healed him. And when this had taken place, the rest of the people on the island with diseases also came and were cured," says Luke (who contributed his own medical skills as well, I would think).

During those quiet winter months, Paul would finally have had some moments alone to plan what he would say to the authorities in Rome and how he would go about contacting the Christian and Jewish communities. But what he would tell both Christian and Jew had not changed from what he had already stated in the letter he had sent from Corinth two years before. The lengthy, powerful *Letter to the Romans* (which churches in many places have since copied) embodied the length and breadth of his beliefs after nearly 30 years of proclaiming the gospel.

God, Paul had written the Romans, has always revealed himself to man through his external creations and wonders. An upright life can come only through reconciliation with God. But that reconciliation had been made difficult in a world that had become brutal, treacherous and malicious. Those who have made it so were without excuse, for although they knew God, they did not honor him as God or give thanks to him, but they became futile in their thinking and their senseless minds were darkened. Claiming to be wise, they became fools, and exchanged the glory of the immortal God for images resembling mortal men or animals or reptiles.

Therefore, God gave them up in the lusts of their hearts to impurity, and to the dishonoring of their bodies among themselves, because they exchanged the truth about God for a lie and worshipped and served the creature rather than the Creator, who is blessed forever! Amen.[57]

The Jewish world was guilty in its own way, Paul wrote. It was obstinate, smug and impenitent, relying on observance of its special laws and condemning the rest of mankind as sinners – even when the accusers themselves were breaking the Law.

What then? Are we Jews any better off? No, not at all, for I have already charged that all men, both Jews and Greeks, are under the power of sin.[58]

Thus, Jews and Greeks are both in dire need of righteousness and without the visible means of attaining it.

But now the righteousness of God has been manifested apart from law, although the law and the prophets bear witness to it: the righteousness of God through faith in Jesus Christ for all who believe. For there is no distinction; since all have sinned and fall short of the glory of God, they are justified by his grace as a gift, through the redemption which is in Christ Jesus, whom God has put forward as an expiation by his blood, to be received by faith. This was to show God's righteousness, because in his divine forbearance he had passed over former sins; it was to prove at the present time that he himself is righteous and that he justifies him who has faith in Jesus.[59]

It is only through our faith and God's grace that we become reconciled, Paul continued.

Since we are justified by faith, we have peace with God through our Lord Jesus Christ. Through him we have obtained access to this grace in which we stand, and we rejoice in our sufferings, knowing that suffering produces endurance, and endurance produces character, and character produces hope, and hope does not disappoint us, because God's love has been poured into our hearts through the Holy Spirit which has been given to us.[60]

Does this reconciliation mean that we can continue to live in sin?

By no means! How can we who died to sin still live in it? Do you not know that all of us who have been baptized into Christ Jesus were baptized into his death? We were buried therefore with him by baptism into death, so that as Christ was raised from the dead by the glory of the Father, we too might walk in newness of life.

For if we have been united with him in a death like his, we shall certainly be reunited with him in a resurrection like his. We know that our old self was crucified with him so that the sinful body might be destroyed, and we might no longer be enslaved to sin...

Let not sin therefore reign in your mortal bodies, to make you obey its passions. Do not yield your members to sin as instruments of wickedness, but yield yourselves to God as men who have been brought from death to life, and your members to God as instruments of righteousness. For sin will have no dominion over you, since you are not under law but under grace. [61]

If God is for us, who is against us? Paul asked the Romans in his letter. If he gave up his own son for us all, will he not also give us all things with him?

No, in all these things we are more than conquerors through him who loved us. For I am sure that neither death, nor life, nor angels, nor principalities, nor things present, nor things to come, nor powers, nor height, nor depth, nor anything else in all creation, will be able to separate us from the love of God in Christ Jesus our Lord. [62]

It probably won't surprise you to learn that, within three months, Paul, Luke and Aristarchus had also established a small Christian community in Melita. Now it was the first week of March and the first southerly winds had made all of the stranded travelers eager to go. Fortunately, another Alexandrian cargo ship had been wintering in the same harbor. Its name was *The Twin Brothers* (meaning Castor and Pollux), and their carved likeliness jutted from under the bowsprit. The day before it set sail, the new Christians of Melita came down to the dock with many gifts and "put on board whatever we needed," Luke reported.

Soon the winds had become favorable. After about 75 miles, *The Twin Brothers* put in at the Greek-Silician city of Syracuse for three days. Another 75 miles further north, they called at Rhegium at the tip of the Italian boot. From there more favorable southerly winds drove them 220 miles in two days to the Bay of Neapolis. Since Puteoli is the port for all Alexandrian grain ships, I can imagine *The Twin Brothers* gliding slowly through the blue waters as it passed the ruins of Tiberius' villa atop Capri and saw the promontory of Misenum where Agrippina breathed her last. One might even imagine Seneca, sitting on the balcony of his villa at Neapolis, glimpsing *The Twin Brothers* when writing of his delight at watching the sun glisten off the grain ships that sail in from Alexandria.

It must have been an equal delight for Paul to learn that there were Christians in Puteoli. As Julius busied himself housing his soldiers and charges, Paul and his friends were given permission to stay in the homes of local Christians. During the week they remained in Puteoli, one of the two younger men probably hastened to Rome with news of the apostle's arrival. Later, as Julius and his party traveled north to Rome on the Appian Way, they were still some 40 miles from the city at the Market of Appius when they were hailed by a group of Christians. Walking out to greet Paul involved a two-day journey, no less, for people who had to leave their jobs as servants and tradesmen. Then, when still 24 miles from Rome at a place called The Three Taverns, their ranks were swelled as another group of Christians greeted them. More came as they entered the outskirts of the city and walked by the towering tombs of patricians that lined the ancient street.

Among those who met him, Paul must have been most gratified to greet a young man who had come all the way from Philippi in Macedonia. His name was Epaphroditus. Luke, you will recall, was an elder of the church in Philippi. When he had written them that Paul would soon sail from Cæsarea, the faithful churchmen there had resolved not only to send money for his needs, but also to assign him a volunteer who could serve as his go-between with the churches while in confinement. Epaphroditus, as he had lingered over the winter in a strange and bewildering city, must have wondered if the man he was supposed to meet had vanished into thin air. Now they were walking side by side trading the news of many months.

On that day, Paul must have even forgotten that he was a prisoner about to be tried for his life. As Luke reported, "He thanked God and took courage."

. . . .

A. D. 6 2 — 6 3

T he emperor of Rome was now a man and the unchallenged master of his realm. To be seen listening to the advice of a boyhood tutor or the chidings of an aging soldier was not only unseemly, but perhaps even subject to dangerous misinterpretation by foreign ambassadors or their kings. Yes, men like Seneca and Burrus kept a storehouse of administrative detail in their heads, and allowing them to conduct affairs did leave an artist with more time to refine his skills, but sometimes their mien was simply too heavy to tolerate. If one's reign truly had only begun on the day the infernal Agrippina had disappeared, then perhaps it was time to sweep away the remaining vestiges of a bygone era.

Besides, there were others eager to serve.

And besides again, Burrus was looking like death warmed over. For over a year the Prætorian prefect had complained of a lump in his throat that seemed to grow daily to the point where he was barely able to force down food. Yet he had lost none of his well-known bluntness. An oft-told story by courtesans is that Nero, just after becoming emperor, had asked his advisor a second time for his opinion on something under debate. Burrus, with a stern look, retorted: "When I have once spoken about anything, don't ask me again." Burrus had also been the greatest obstacle to Nero in his quest to divorce Octavia and marry Poppæa. His blunt advice: "If you *must* divorce her, then give her back her dowry (meaning the imperium the heiress of Claudius would have exercised had she not been compelled to marry the upstart son of Agrippina).

But Burrus soon passed from the scene. Some say the tumor alone did it, but others insist that Nero helped. The emperor, they say, brought his own doctor to Burrus' bedside and insisted that his throat be painted with a wondrous new balm, which was, of course, a poison.

If you still remember Sejanus you will recognize him in another man named Tigellinus. When Burrus died, leadership of the Prætorian Guard was divided among two co-commanders. The first was Fænius Rufus, a man who had risen throughout the ranks on his merits – the latest one being that he had managed the corn supply without taking any personal profit. His colleague in the critical Prætorian post was Gaius Ofonius Tigellinus, whose rise was enabled by being one of Nero's chief informants and an eager participant in his private palace debaucheries. "I have no divided allegiance like Burrus," he would assure the emperor often. "My only thought is your safety."

Seneca, without the careful delineation of power that he had honed with Burrus over several years, soon found the ship of state being rowed to confusing cadences. Lest the lesson of Burrus be lost on him, word soon spread that the financial secretary, Pallas, who had retired to his country estates a few years before to enjoy his old age, had been murdered by the emperor's Guardsmen. The only explanation: imperial finances were deteriorating rapidly and the old man's 400 million sesterces were simply too irresistible.

The estate of Pallas was probably matched by that of Seneca. Moreover, the latter had been under constant attack, both by envious patricians (his gardens were said to outdo the emperor's for splendor) and by debtors who were squeezed by his steep interest rates. There was also constant carping about how the learned tutor slurred his pompous protégé behind his back. "He openly disparages the emperor's amusements, underestimates him as a charioteer and makes fun of his singing," they would hiss. Or, one might hear: "How long must merit at Rome wait to be conferred by Seneca's word alone? Nero is a boy no longer and ought to discharge his tutor!"

By this time Seneca was not spending much time in Nero's company. One day he requested an audience during the emperor's morning reception. It was quickly granted – and judging from the smooth colloquy that ensued, I suspect that Nero was well versed on what to expect and how to respond.

Began Seneca: "It is nearly 14 years, Cæsar, since I became associated with your young rising fortunes and eight since you became emperor. During that time you have showered on me such distinctions and riches that, if only I could retire to enjoy them unpretentiously, my prosperity would be complete.

"May I quote illustrious precedents drawn from your rank and not mine?" continued Seneca. "Your great-great-grandfather Augustus allowed Marcus Agrippa to withdraw to Mytilene and allowed Gaius Mæcenas the equivalent of retirement at Rome itself. The one his partner in wars, the other the bearer of many anxious burdens at Rome, they were greatly rewarded for great services. I have had no claim on your generosity except my learning. Though acquired outside the glare of public life, it has brought me the wonderful recompense and distinction of having assisted in your early education.

"But you have also bestowed on me measureless favors and boundless wealth. Accordingly, I often ask myself: Why is it I, son of a provincial knight, who am accounted a national leader? Why has my unknown name come to glitter among ancient and glorious pedigrees? Where is my old self, that was content with so little? Laying out fine gardens? Inspecting grand estates? Wallowing in my vast revenues? I can only find one excuse. It was not for me to obstruct your munificence."

Now Seneca attempted to execute a clever amalgam of sycophancy and syllogism. "We have both filled the measure — you of what an emperor can give a friend, and I, of what a friend may receive from his emperor. Anything more will breed envy. Your greatness is far above all such mortal things. But I am not. So I crave your help. If, in the field or on a journey, I were tired, I should want a stick. In life's journey, I need just such a support.

"For I am old and cannot do the lightest work," continued Seneca as Nero's court eavesdropped. "I am no longer equal to the burden of my wealth. Order your agents to take over my property and incorporate it in yours. I do not suggest plunging myself into poverty, but [rather] giving up the things that are too brilliant and dazzle me. The time now spent on gardens and mansions shall be devoted to the mind. You have abundant strength. For years the supreme power has been familiar to you. We older friends may ask for our rest. This, too, will add to your glory — that you have raised to the heights men content with lower positions."

The emperor appeared to be surprised at the request. "My first debt to you is that I am able to make an impromptu reply to your premeditated speech," he said. "For it was you who taught me to improvise as well as to make prepared orations.

"True," said Nero, "my great-great-grandfather Augustus did permit Agrippa and Mæcenas to rest after their labors. But he did so after he himself was old and had already given them all the property and prestige that he could. Besides, Augustus didn't deprive either man the rewards they had earned from in the wars and other crises of his youthful years. If my life had been warlike, you, too, would have fought for me. But instead you gave what our situation demanded — wisdom, advice, philosophy — to support me as a boy and youth. Your gifts to me will endure as long as life itself. My gifts to you may seem expensive, but many people far less deserving than you have had more. I omit, from shame, to mention certain ex-slaves who flaunt greater wealth. I am even ashamed that you, my dearest friend, are not the richest of all men."

It seemed at first that Nero was not about to let Seneca go. "My reign is only beginning," he said at one point, and "you are still vigorous and fit for state affairs and their rewards." Besides, he said, "If you return my gifts and desert your emperor, it is not your unpretentiousness and desire for retirement that will be on everyone's lips, but *my* meanness and *your* dread of my brutality."

But all these expressions were apparently for the court's consumption. Having said them, Nero sighed theatrically and assumed a sad pose. "Well then, my old friend, if youth's slippery paths lead me astray, be at hand to call me back!" Then he embraced and kissed Seneca. The tutor expressed his gratitude and departed.

Seneca soon resigned himself to losing the argument about giving up the excess trappings of wealth. But as soon as he could he ceased holding receptions, dismissed his entourage and retreated to his country villas to devote the rest of his life to writing and studying. Invitations to visit Rome were met with regrets that his health would not permit it. The real reason was that Seneca had witnessed what had befallen others who had been in the effusive public embrace of the emperor. Now he, too, knew the constant wariness that comes with the knowledge that excessive flattery is often followed by treachery.

The time that Nero had once spent with men like Burrus, Pallas and Seneca was now filled by the presence of Tigellinus. Thus, it should be no surprise that in no more time that it had taken Sejanus to inflame the fears of Tiberius, Tigellinus was soon whispering to Nero about this and that threat to his safety.

The first such attempt did not go well. A young prætor, Antistius Sosianus, had written some verses satirizing the emperor and then read them aloud at a large dinner party. One of the guests was the father-in-law of Tigellinus, who had just been made a senator, and he accused Antistius under the old treason law that had been in abeyance since the days of Caligula. The dinner party host insisted he had heard no such verses from Antistius, but enough witnesses were produced to prompt one of the consuls to move that Antistius lose his prætor-ship and be executed according to ancient law.

The motion might have carried had not Publius Clodius Thrasea Pætus spoken. This was the same Thrasea who had stalked out of the Curia three years before when his colleagues were in the midst of heaping praise on Nero for surviving his mother's "attempt" to assassinate him. This time Thrasea praised Nero and vigorously blamed Antistius for his lack of good taste. But with such an excellent, munificent emperor, he said, the Senate was under no compulsion to inflict the maximum penalty. Besides, Antistius' position as a judge shielded him from personal harm for his actions. Instead, he urged, let Antistius lose his property to the state and be sent to an island where every prolongation of his guilty life would intensify his personal misery. At the same time, it would remind everyone of the emperor's infinite mercy.

So Thrasea's proposal carried. When the consuls reported the action to Nero more as a "recommendation" than a decree, he was angered at first. Eventually he cooled and sent the Senate a reply that I will summarize: Antistius, unprovoked, had grossly abused the emperor. The Senate had been asked to punish him and should have fixed a retribution befitting the enormity of the crime. Yet, the Senate might have acquitted him as well, Nero acknowledged. Thus, the emperor would not "amend" their leniency. They were free to do as they saw fit.

Thrasea's motion was left to stand. But Thrasea could not ward off the other charges of treason that followed, because as the financial condition of the country began to deteriorate, the emperor became more uneasy and Tigellinus became more active in finding threats to the "national security" I will not weight you down with every instance, but I will offer one to give you a sense of the fear that Tigellinus was fomenting within Nero. You may recall that just a few years before, people had stirred up stories that Rubellius Plautus, a Julian and distant relative of the emperor, was a possible rallying point for Nero's opponents. Although already living a simple, harmless life outside Rome, Plautus was ordered to confine himself and his family to their estates in Asia so as to quiet down any talk of rebellion.

Well, Tigellinus revived it. His distance from Rome now allowed rumors to circulate unchallenged that Asia has already risen behind Plautus. In fact, some even had Plautus on his way to Corbulo in Syria, whereupon the governor's mighty armies would march on Rome and proclaim this Julian patrician emperor.

In the midst of all this rubbish — or because of it — Tigellinus was preparing to send a cohort of Guardsmen to Asia to dispatch Plautus. The victim's father-in-law caught wind of it and quickly sent off an ex-slave of Plautus on the fastest ship possible with a message. "Escape while there is a way out," it urged. "Sympathy for your great name will make decent men back you and brave men help you out. Meanwhile, disdain no possible support. Sixty soldiers have been sent. If you can repulse them, much can happen — even a war can develop — before Nero receives the news and sends another force. In short, either you save yourself by this action or at least a bold end is as good as a timid one."

Plautus, however, never rose to the occasion. Perhaps he realized that to raise an army would deplete whatever assets he could leave his family. And because he loved his family dearly, he doubtless assumed that they would receive more lenient treatment if he went obediently.

When the squad of killers arrived at his home, they found him stripped for exercise. And there he was slain as he was. When the victim's head was brought to Nero, the emperor looked it over and said to himself: "Nero, how could such a long-nosed man have frightened you?"

The last vestige of Nero's former life was now his wife Octavia. The obstacles were no longer powerful defenders, but the fact that she led a chaste life and was much adored by the public. So Nero resorted to writing the Senate, which had just dutifully expressed great joy at his having managed to escape from the Plautus menace in Asia. In a rambling discourse about his solicitude for the national interests, he deemed it important to have an heir. Alas, his wife was barren. Hence, unless the conscript fathers disapproved, he was planning to divorce her.

Well of course they didn't disapprove. But the people did. They were starting to make a ruckus in the streets. So Poppæa thought to help her cause by prevailing on a servant in Octavia's household to accuse her of adultery with a slave, a flute player from Alexandria. Octavia's maids were tortured and some were induced by the pain to make confessions. But Pythias, the attendant closest to Octavia, bore all her tortures with contempt. When Tigellinus himself confronted her on the rack to urge her confession, Pythias spat in his face. "My mistresses's privy parts are cleaner than your mouth!" she fumed.

But Octavia was divorced and sent away, as you have expected all along. At first there was a show of leaving her with some dignity. Nero's intention was to give her Burrus' house in Rome and some of Rubellius Plautus' country estates. Then he thought better of it and ordered her banished to Campania under a military escort. Soon the commoners in the streets heard about it and within an hour statues of the emperor were toppling all over town to protest the fate of their beloved Octavia. In another few hours an angry mob had overwhelmed guards at the palace and invaded living quarters, knocking over more statues and destroying drapes and furniture. Only after reinforcements were rushed in from the Prætorian barracks was the crowd driven back outside with clubs and swords.

Nero was so shocked at the display that he sent word that he would remarry Octavia if that is what would please Rome. With that they overturned Poppæa's statues and carried Octavia's about on their shoulders, setting them about in various temples and forums. Even the emperor was acclaimed again.

But not by Poppæa. She was as furious at Nero as with the display of mass violence. She chose to convince him with tears, however. Falling at his feet, she cried: "Now that things have reached this sorry state, it is not marriage I'm fighting for, but my life. It's in danger every day from Octavia's dependents and slaves! They pretend to be the people of Rome! They commit outrages in peacetime that could hardly happen even in war! Their real target is the emperor — and all they lack at this point is a leader. If these disorders continue, one will surely be found. Octavia may be in Campania, but even her distant nod causes riots!

"What have I done wrong?" wailed Poppæa. "Whom have I injured? Is all this because I am going to give an authentic heir to the house of the Cæsars? Would Rome prefer an Egyptian flute-player's child? If you think it best, take back your empress voluntarily — don't be *coerced* into doing so. Otherwise, protect yourself! Punish severely. Because once the mob loses hope of keeping Nero through Octavia, it will find her another husband."

As much as Poppæa's entreaties infuriated him, they also terrified him. But better *reasons* were needed to disown Octavia. Accusing her of relations with a flute player hadn't yielded anything convincing — nor was the crime great enough even if true. No, what was needed were charges of adultery with someone who had the power to cause a real rebellion. Nero found his mind wandering back to Misenum and his mother's "accident" at the hands of Anicetus, the helpful fleet commander. This time no violence would be needed, no collapsing boat, no swords. All Anicetus would have to do is confess adultery with Octavia. Great rewards would be his — and an agreed-upon place of retirement free of all worries.

The alternative of course would be death.

Before long, Anicetus appeared before a "council of state," which had been assembled from among various senators and friends of Nero. There Anicetus made a dramatic confession of a scandalous affair with Octavia, then slipped away to a new villa in Sardinia (where it's said he lived out a long and happy life). Nero published an edict reporting to the people that Octavia had tried to win over the fleet by seducing its commander. For this she had been confined on the infamous island of Pandateria.

No one could stop Nero, but no exiled woman ever received more sympathy or prayers from the Roman people. They had lamented the banishment of the elder Agrippina by Tiberius and that of Julia Livilla by Claudius, but both had been mature women with at least some happy memories to look back on. Octavia was barely 20. She had seen her father and brother poisoned. No sooner had she been married than she had been discarded by her husband, first for a slave, then for a scheming shrew who strutted about the palace.

Octavia had been on her island no more than a few days when the dreaded order came for her to die. She protested that she was no longer Nero's wife, but his sister. She asked for Nero's mercy. The response was to have her bound tightly, then open her veins. However, her terror retarded the flow of blood and made the messy process take too long for the soldiers. So Octavia was carried into a hot vapor bath where, after a few minutes she suffocated. Then her head was cut off and taken to Rome for Poppæa to inspect.

Others who had opposed the divorce were soon killed off as well, but my hand grows too tired to write about them all. Suffice it to say that Poppæa was married to Nero. And less than a year later there were wild cheers to the announcement that she had borne the emperor a daughter. Moreover, the great event had taken place at Nero's own birthplace, the small beach resort town of Antium some 30 miles south of Rome. Hundreds of courtesans and the entire Senate (save only Thrasea, who was forbidden) had journeyed in their carriages to be on hand, and Nero's joy was outdone only by their displays of celebration. Mother and daughter were given the name Augusta. Thanksgivings were offered to the gods. A new Temple of Fertility was ordered to be built. Golden statues of the Two Fortunes of Antium were to be placed on the throne of Capitoline Jupiter and Antium was to have circus games in honor of the Claudian and Domitian houses.

In less than four months the baby was dead. Now came yet more inventive forms of sycophancy. The infant was declared a goddess and voted a shrine, a priesthood and a place on the gods' ceremonial couch. The emperor's mourning was as profound as had been his earlier delight.

Both events, however, had helped dim the public memory of Octavia. But just about this time she came creeping back into Rome's collective conscience. Someone – a very skilled writer – had authored a play titled *Octavia*. And now secret copies were making their way around Rome's finest homes.

Whoever wrote it knew the characters intimately. What made reading the play so deliciously dangerous was knowing that the author was surely aware that to be identified meant certain death, for every word in it rang out with loathsome rebuke to Nero and Poppæa. I will show you by quoting just the opening scene. It begins as the sorrowful Octavia sits combing her hair in her palace bedroom, knowing that Nero will stop at nothing to divorce her. Her maid enters and sees tears in her eyes.

> *Maid*: Your lot is hard, but God in mercy yet will give
> A brighter morrow to your darkness.
> Will you not try to win your husband's love
> By gentleness and service?
>
> *Octavia*: 'Twere easier to appease
> A lion's wrath, a tiger's rage,
> Than my imperious husband's heart.
> All sons of noble blood
> He hates, all gods and men
> He scorns alike; he knows not how to use
> His own good fortune and the place he won
> By his vile parent's crimes;
> For which – though he repudiate
> The gift of empire so bestowed
> By that fell mother [Agrippina], though he has rewarded
> Her gift with death – yet after death
> That woman till the end of time
> Must bear that epitaph.

Nurse: Nay, check those angry words,
Speak not so rashly, child.

Octavia: Ah, were these torments such as could be borne,
And were my patience strong enough to bear them,
Nothing but death could end my misery.
My mother and my father were slain,
My brother lost — now bowed beneath this weight
Of grief and bitterness and woe, I live
Under my husband's hate, my servant's scorn.
No day is joy to me, no hour not filled
With terror — not the fear of death alone,
But violent death. Oh Gods, let me not suffer
A criminal's death, and I will gladly die.[63]

Lest anyone think that the part of a meek woman since deceased is harmless prattle to an emperor, one need read only a few lines from a scene in which the emperor himself appears. This is a conversation with his tutor Seneca after the emperor has ordered a Guardsman to bring him the decapitated head of Plautus after it was returned from Asia.

Guard: It shall be done without delay.
I'll to the camp myself.

Seneca: Is that just treatment for one so near to you?

Nero: Let him be just who has no need to fear.

Seneca: The best antidote to fear is clemency.

Nero: A king's best work is to put enemies down.

Seneca: Good fathers of the state preserve their sons.

Nero: Soft-hearted graybeards should be teaching children.

Seneca: Headstrong young men should be sent to school.

Nero: Young men are old enough to know their minds.

Seneca: May yours ever be pleasing to the gods.

Nero: I, who make gods, would be a fool to fear them.

Seneca: The more your power, the greater your fear should be.

Nero: I, thanks to Fortune, may do anything.

Seneca: Fortune is fickle. Never trust her favors.

Nero: A man's a fool who does not know his strength.

Seneca: Justice, not strength, is what a good man knows.

Nero: Men spur humility.

Seneca: They stamp on tyrants.

Nero: Steel is the emperor's guard.

Seneca: Trust is better.[64]

The more a Roman pored over *Octavia,* the more he would have to conclude that only one man could have written it. And only one man would have had the courage to risk his life for the chance to warn the emperor one last time where he was headed. It was Seneca himself.

. . . .

I TOLD YOU EARLIER THAT THE SYRIAN GOVERNOR Corbulo knew instinctively that Rome's attempt to set the Tigranes on the throne of Armenia was not the final solution. One who would readily agree was King Vologeses I of Parthia. His brother Tiridates had been summarily rejected by the Romans. And equally insulting, Tigranes, the Romanized Cappadocian, had no sooner arrived in his strange new domain when he decided to march out and ravage Adiabene, one of Parthia's client kingdoms and buffers to Roman Syria.

The Parthian king was a cautious man by nature. Until now Vologeses had respected the long-standing truce with Rome. Even when Rome had rampaged through Armenia he had reacted with restraint (no doubt reaffirmed by the fact that he was also occupied in putting down a rebellion by the Hycranians on his eastern border).

But this was too much, and his grandees agreed. Client kings on all borders were demanding to know that if Parthia had let the Romans attack Adiabene, what was to stop them from being the next victims? King Monobazus of war-torn Adiabene put the matter bluntly to Vologeses in a letter. "Armenia is gone and the borderlands are following," he wrote. "If Parthia won't help us, we must give in to Rome and make the best of it. "Passivity does not preserve great empires," Monobazus continued. "It requires fighting with warriors and weapons. When stakes are highest, might makes right."

By this time Vologeses needed no further persuading. He called a council of his satraps and client kings. To demonstrate at the outset that the issue of war with Rome was no longer debatable, he sat his brother Tiridates next to himself and placed the royal diadem of Armenia on his head. The Romans have broken the peace, he stated. "I admit I should have preferred to rely on inheritance and tradition to retain what my ancestors won. But if I have delayed mistakenly, my prowess henceforth will make amends." The war on the eastern border would have to wait — or even be lost if necessary. Parthian honor depended first on standing up to Rome and retaining Armenia.

When Corbulo's agents reported these events to him in Antioch, he quickly authorized the expedition of two divisions to shore up Tigranes in Armenia. But he also gave his commanders secret orders not to march with all due haste — for two reasons. First, Corbulo had no confidence that the Rome-softened, Cappadocian "king" of Armenia would deploy reinforcements wisely in a land he knew little about. So Corbulo sent a dispatch to Nero asking that the Armenian campaign be led by a seasoned general (perhaps even having himself in mind). Second, Corbulo feared that the Parthians would not just defend Armenia, but would launch an all-out invasion of Syria. Specifically, Corbulo posted his remaining divisions at strategic points along the Euphrates River, which forms the most natural border between Rome and Parthia. The Euphrates was also an army's primary source of fresh water in an arid land. So when the river outposts were secure, his troops made forays to the various natural springs that the Parthians might visit on a march westward. All were filled with sand.

Tigranes was determined to make his stand against the Parthians in Tigranocerta, about 150 miles east of Corbulo's fortifications on the Euphrates. The city was powerfully garrisoned and well provisioned. A force of Parthians and Adiabenians soon showed up and began to besiege the walls, but the defenders quickly realized their attackers' lack of experience in siege warfare. The Parthians unleashed great numbers of arrows, but few landed near their mark. They brought up ladders and siege engines, but these were easily thrown back. In a short period the Parthians and their allies were spent.

Corbulo might have pressed for the kill, but instead he sent Vologeses, some 35 miles behind the war zone, an almost conciliatory letter. You have chosen to fight against friendly allies, he reminded the king. Either Vologeses must end the siege or Corbulo himself would begin invading Parthian territory.

Vologeses knew that the siege had not gone well. Tigranes was well-supplied while the Parthian's own cavalry suffered from lack of fodder and water. And quite unexpectedly, a swarm of locusts had ruined crops that his men had hoped to depend on. So Vologeses answered with a conciliatory letter of his own. He would send an embassy to the emperor reaffirming the claim to Armenia and his intention to conclude a stable peace. Meanwhile, the siege would be lifted as an expression of his good intentions as long as Corbulo saw to it that the Romans departed Tigranocerta as well.

The interregnum suited Corbulo. Maybe the emperor and his envoys could agree on a suitable peace. If not, time would at least buy the eastern forces the arrival of a skilled soldier who could direct an Armenian campaign properly.

But things went badly in Rome. The envoys of Vologeses postured that their king had shown munificent mercy in not routing the Romans from Tigranocerta. The Roman Senate had all but declared its version of the affair a victory almost deserving of a triumph. The envoys were sent home.

Corbulo soon got a general to lead an Armenian campaign, but he quickly regretted his request. Lucius Cæsennius Pætus was immediately assigned roughly half of all the Roman forces in the region. Although Corbulo was already a legend in Rome for his past military exploits, Pætus seemed to be oblivious to them. He asked bluntly why there had been no killing or plundering of the Parthians at Tigranocerta. He announced that *he* intended to impose, not merely a puppet king on the Armenians, but Roman law, government and taxes as well. Immediately he marched his men toward a direct confrontation with Vologeses.

Pætus did this despite sinister omens. A Roman soldier will trudge to any orders, but his step will become lively if he knows that augurs or astrologers have determined that the stars or the gods or even some chicken entrails have deemed the action a success. In this case, when Pætus' divisions first crossed the bridge over the Euphrates, the horse carrying the consular insignia took fright for no apparent reason and bolted to the rear. Then, just when the winter camp had been completed and a bull was about to be sacrificed, the animal kicked up and escaped outside the ramparts. Worse, some soldiers' javelins mysteriously caught fire – a particularly ominous portent considering that the Parthians base most of their fighting strength on missiles.

But Pætus disdained all the omens. His goal was to recover and reinforce Tigranocerta before Vologeses got to it. His troops captured a few small forts along the way and seized some loot (resulting in some dispatches to the Senate that read like major victories). But in his haste, Pætus outran his supply lines and arrived dependent solely on diminishing stores of rapidly-spoiling corn. Winter was coming on.

Parthia's strategy had been to occupy Tigranocerta with one army and invade Syria with another. As the latter force marched towards Syria, it found the Euphrates defended by forts with tall turrets and ships that plied the river. On both the Romans had built heavy engines with catapults that could hurl stones at far greater distances than the Parthian bowmen could shoot their arrows. The effect was so devastating that the Parthians quickly abandoned any thoughts of an assault on Syria. Now they turned all of their troops, not on the walls of Tiganocerta but on the winter camp that Pætus had just established at the base of the Taurus mountains.

Pætus' men dug the usual series of trenches and ramparts around the winter camp. After that, the general's staff urged him to draw his forces in to defend a tight perimeter, but the general was determined to best Corbulo's reputation by displaying his daring and independence. So he ordered his men out of the camp. He deployed the infantry along one route that the Parthians could be expected to travel and the cavalry along another possible route. But he also dispatched a letter to Corbulo urgently asking for reinforcements from Syria.

When Corbulo received the letter, he did not hurry. "The graver the peril, the more glorious the rescue," he quipped to an aide. He merely ordered that 2,600 infantry and cavalrymen to stand by for marching orders.

Pætus' winter camp amounted to less than two brigades. Now it had been split in two parts. Vologeses had better reconnaissance. He sent a small decoy force to occupy the Roman cavalry, then hit its infantry with everything he had. Romans fell by the hundreds before showers of firebrands. Some surviving infantrymen staggered off into the wilderness. Others fled back to the winter camp with exaggerated tales of wild, bearded Orientals and their cruelty. Pætus himself was reported to be paralyzed with shock at what was unfolding all around him. All he could do was send a courier running off in the night with one more letter begging Corbulo to hasten in order to save the Roman eagles, standards and whatever remained of the shattered army.

By then Corbulo was quite prepared. Setting off with well-armed troops and camels laden with corn and flour, he soon began to encounter Romans straggling in the desert from the Parthian onslaught. Rather than having them killed for desertion (as he would with his own men), Corbulo formed them into new units and told them their fate would depend on returning to fight and seeking Pætus' forgiveness. His own troops he bolstered with speeches about past glories and hopes of more. "Our worthwhile objectives," he said, "are not Armenian towns, but a Roman camp consisting of two brigades. Any of you soldiers can win from the emperor's own hand the glorious wreath for saving a citizen's life. But how infinitely more honorable it will be if this army can win it corporately for saving a force as large as itself!" His words inspired unanimous enthusiasm, especially because the brothers and relatives of many soldiers were under danger. So they marched at top speed – night and day.

King Vologeses tried to end it by intensifying his siege of the Roman winter camp, but was chary of penetrating its uncertain terrain of earthen walls and trenches. The Romans were quite willing to wait for Corbulo. Meanwhile, Pætus hedged his bets by writing another letter to Vologeses. "Even if you have the means to overwhelm us here," it said in essence, "peace is still the better option. For you have brought the whole strength of your kingdom here against just two Roman brigades. Look beyond the immediate situation and realize that if you prevail now, Rome has the power to draw armies from all over the world and devastate Parthia."

Vologeses replied vaguely that his decision would await the arrival of his brothers (Pacorus, the king of Media Atropane on his eastern border, and Tiridates, the king-designate of Armenia) to the battle scene. At the same time, he reminded Pætus that the fate of the Roman army was in the hands of Parthians – not their so-called commander.

But things were growing too desperate in the Roman camp in Armenia for much more waiting. Winter gales were howling and the hungry men were shivering in their tents. Pætus finally sent a messenger to Vologeses requesting a personal meeting. When Vologeses agreed to send only his cavalry commander, the Roman swallowed his pride and acquiesced. Pætus used the occasion for a long monologue on how Armenia had bowed to Rome since its conquest by Lucullus and Pompey a hundred years before. The Parthian remained impassive, insisting that Roman suzerainty had been but in name only. Whenever the Romans had left Armenia, its people's customs and loyalties had returned to the Parthian fold.

Eventually, the two faced the question of whether they were destined to depart again with no common perception of who ruled Parthia. What happened next is unrecorded, but one of the two gave ground, and you can take your own measure of which one it was.

The next day, Monobazus, the Parthian client king of Adiabene, was brought in to witness an agreement. The siege would be raised. All Roman troops would be evacuated from Armenia. All of their forts and provisions would be ceded to the Parthians. Vologeses would then send another deputation to the emperor to discuss the future of Armenia.

On the following morning the Parthians entered the winter camp and then watched from their mounts as the weary Romans complied with an order to fling their weapons and their dead in a great heap. Once the unarmed Romans left their fortifications and found themselves on the road, they encountered a long line of Armenians who pushed them about, tearing off this man's clothing, grabbing a pack from that one or shouting to another as they recognized a kinsman marching with the Romans as a slave. Soon the soldiers were staggering along alone in the steppe, with their dull eyes fixed on their ragged feet as they trudged westward over the icy road. The hungrier they became, the more they recalled how Pætus had ordered their remaining grain burned to avoid capture. The extra rations could have meant the difference between endurance and evacuation, because on the day the survivors left their camp, Corbulo had marched to within three days of rescuing it.

In one day, the fearful Pætus marched his already downtrodden men 40 miles — about twice the normal pace — in his effort to link up with Corbulo. This hardly reduced his disgrace, however, because it required abandoning all of the wounded along the way. When Corbulo and his troops finally met them at the Euphrates, there was no ceremony or even display of standards — only the tears of Corbulo's men as they encountered fellow soldiers who were so exhausted and humiliated they could scarcely mumble a greeting.

The generals held a short and awkward conversation. "My work is wasted!" Corbulo seethed. "The Parthians could have been routed and the war ended!"

"Nothing is ended," retorted Pætus. "Let us simply turn our eagles around and jointly invade Armenia. Vologeses is gone."

"I have no such orders from the emperor," Corbulo shot back. "As it was, I left my province only from anxiety at your army. Now my men are exhausted from racing to meet you. Besides, Parthian plans are unpredictable. Let's just hope that their cavalry isn't already galloping just behind you!"

Pætus wintered in Cappadocia, which was well: he wouldn't have been welcome in Antioch. Meanwhile, Corbulo and Vologeses used the time to exchange letters and work out another settlement. Corbulo would demolish all of the fortifications he had built up along the Euphrates River. Vologeses would evacuate all of his garrisons from Armenia.

But Pætus had been busy with his own correspondence. In fact, he had sent regular dispatches to Rome dating from the first days that he had erected the winter camp. When the Senate had read that Pætus' men were occupying Armenia without opposition, they had declared a victory and erected commemorative arches over the center of Capitoline Hill. And now no one removed them or rescinded the victory proclamation — quite as if ignoring what happened would make it go away.

The emperor learned otherwise the next spring when a Parthian delegation arrived with a letter from Vologeses. "I will not reiterate my repeated claim to Armenia," the king wrote, "since the gods have already handed the country to the Parthians — and not without Roman ignominy." In allowing Pætus to go free when he could have destroyed the Roman brigades, the king contended that he had demonstrated his clemency. As Nero and his generals fumed, Vologeses added that his brother Tiridates would have been willing to come to Rome to receive his crown in person had not some unspecified religious obligations prevented him at this time.

Nero held a war council with his generals on the same day. What a strange breed, these oriental kings, they agreed. This one claims total victory and wants us to confirm it by crowning his brother ourselves! All this was hardly consistent with the reassuring reports that had come from Pætus. The council decided to interrogate a Roman staff officer who had escorted the Parthian delegation to Rome. The officer, who had served with Pætus, replied as delicately as he could that there were, alas, no Roman soldiers remaining in Armenia — or any part of Parthia for that matter.

Well, what was it to be, a humiliating peace or another hazardous, costly war? Since insulting a nation's army seldom evokes a moderated response, the generals voted to a man for war and Nero agreed. But this time there would be only one general and it would be Corbulo.

To make sure Corbulo's attention would remain on one objective, Gaius Cestius Gallus was made governor of Syria. Corbulo was given sweeping military powers, unmatched in the hundred years that passed since Pompey himself marched east. Instructions were sent to all governors and client kings in the region to obey Corbulo's orders.

Meanwhile, Pætus arrived back in Rome. Perhaps he expected a new and greater assignment, but most observers thought he was unwittingly walking into the jaws of death. They were surprised when Nero simply relieved Pætus of further command and issued him a pardon. The emperor told the general he had done so immediately "because prolonged suspense (as to his fate) would damage so timid a person's health."

I could tell you how many brigades Corbulo summoned and where they came from, but the nub of it is this: the Romans had a skilled organizer who equipped and trained them so well that Parthian spies were genuinely fearful of the force they now saw marching their way. As one writer noted, "When Corbulo amassed his troops at the Euphrates this time, there was no need for an impassioned speech to arouse them. His words had the authoritative ring of a military man, which a soldier finds superior to eloquence."

Well before Corbulo met Vologeses, the Romans rooted out and demolished the homes of all Armenian chiefs in their path who had rebelled against them in recent years. By the time Vologeses' brother Tiridates loomed near with the first Parthian troops, they were concerned enough to request a meeting with Corbulo. To put themselves at the best advantage, the Parthians asked that it be held at the site of the demolished fort that Pætus' men had given up.

One might think that the Roman would insist on a more neutral place, but Corbulo quickly agreed, for reasons you will see. In fact, he even ordered Pætus' son, a colonel on his staff, to take a detachment and bury the remains of the disastrous battle as the new talks were going on.

Corbulo quickly attained the upper hand simply by displaying courage and clemency. First he ordered two of his senior-most staff officers to enter the Parthian camp unarmed as a guarantee that no treachery was planned. Later, when he and Tiridates approached each other — each with an escort of 20 cavalry — and the Parthian dismounted first, Corbulo quickly did so as well rather than appearing to receive the other on a higher plane. Corbulo then endured a long speech about the nobility and conquests of the Parthian royal family, but at the end of it his patience was rewarded. Tiridates said he would personally go to Rome and pay the emperor homage — provided that there would be no further challenge to a Parthian royal prince occupying the throne of Armenia.

Corbulo agreed, but had one condition himself. It was met the next day when both armies paraded with their national ensigns in splendid array. On a raised dais that the Romans had erected the night before was a chair on which was placed a statue of Nero. Flanking the chair were statues of several Roman gods, and behind them the Roman standards and eagles. When the customary sacrifices had been made, Tiridates advanced, took the diadem of Armenian rule from his head and laid it at the feet of Nero's statue. With the reminders of the defeated winter camp being buried just a few yards away, the contrasting spectacle of a Parthian prince declaring himself a prisoner to Rome was as inspiring to the average Roman soldier as a bloody massacre.

Having extracted what he wanted from Tiridates, Corbulo now devoted his remaining time to winning the prince's allegiance by entertaining him lavishly and instructing him in Roman traditions. For the real key to lasting peace, he believed, was to make Tiridates *desire* Rome's friendship. Tiridates asked for time to prepare for the long journey to Rome, but he prepared a petition for Nero and gave his daughter as hostage to deliver it in person.

This was the way Rome was supposed to govern.

. . . .

ONLY IN EXCEPTIONAL YEARS HAD THE LAND of the Jews ever resembled a model Roman state. At this time, suffocating taxes, a corrupt system of justice and the interminable Jewish-Hellene squabbles had already sparked high levels of sedition. Now, during some three years of confrontation with Parthia, the common farmer and wage earner in Syria felt the squeeze of tougher tax collections and greater requisitions of farm produce for military provisions. The going was especially difficult for poor families whose sons were taken off to fight as Corbulo's auxiliaries.

Did the Jewish king help alleviate the people's suffering? No. Herod Agrippa II chose this period in which to expand and glorify his base of operations, the young city of Cæsarea Philippi (the capital of the former tetrarchy under Philip). His rationale was that it was the Jews' duty to honor Nero with a city (it's new name: Neronia) as they had Tiberius. After that Agrippa went on to build a splendid new theater at Berytus (a Phœnician-Greek city) and brought to it the finest statues from all over his realm. One could argue that little of this affected common men, but then Agrippa did so when he gave the residents of this "foreign" city a largess of corn and oil, all shipped from Galilee. And for this they hated him.

At this point the fragile bond of toleration between the Jewish Christians and the temple sects began to fray. Paul's arrest in the temple and his "escape" into Roman hands had certainly put his sponsors, the Jerusalem Christians, under hostile stares. Now two things happened that the Christians could not withstand. First, Festus died unexpectedly, leaving Judea temporarily without a procurator. Then Herod Agrippa saw fit to depose the high priest Joseph, who was probably a Pharisee. The new high priest was Ananus, whose father had held the same position when Jesus was tried and crucified. But whereas the father was known as a "fortunate man" who had served long "with dignity," the son was described (by Josephus) as "a bold man in his temper and very rigid." Unlike the Pharisees, who were known as rather gentle judges, Ananus was, Josephus adds, "also of a sect of the Sadducees who are very rigid in judging offenders."

In his first few days in office Ananus decided it was time to confront — and even eliminate if necessary — the leader of the Jerusalem Christians. That this man was James the Just, the brother of Jesus, was both ironic and ignorant, for it would be difficult to find a more pious Jew. As a writer of the times described him,

> He drank no wine or intoxicating liquor and ate no animal food. No razor came near his head. He did not smear himself with oil and took no baths. He alone was permitted to enter the Holy Place, for his garments were not of wool but of linen. He used to enter the Sanctuary alone, and was often found on his knees beseeching forgiveness for the people, so that his knees grew hard like a camel's from his continually bending them in worship of God and beseeching forgiveness for the people. Because of his unsurpassable righteousness he was called the Righteous...and "Bulwark of the People"...[65]

If the temple authorities were looking for evidence of James' sedition, it could not be found in his preachings or writings. Indeed, because James did not travel to the Jewish Christian churches as Paul did among the Gentiles, one of his sermons was recorded at about this time and circulated widely among them. His writings on living the proper Christian life drew deeply from prophets, psalms and proverbs of ancient Jewry. Would any devout Pharisee quarrel with the following?

> Cleanse your hands, you sinners, and purify your hearts, you double-minded. Be afflicted and mourn and weep. Let your laughter be turned to sorrow and your joy to gloom. Humble yourself before God and he will exalt you.[66]

Or might the prophet Jeremiah have said these words?

> Come now, you rich; weep and wail at the miseries which are coming upon you. Your wealth is rotten and your garments are food for moths. Your gold and silver are corroded clean through with rust; and their rust is proof of how worthless they are. It is a rust which will eat into your very flesh like fire.[67]

If he had inquired, the high priest Ananus would even have learned that James believed more in the traditional Jewish definition of salvation than did Paul. Whereas Paul preached that salvation was available to all through God's grace if they but believed, James preached:

> What does it profit, my brethren, if a man says he has faith but has not works? Can his faith save him? If a brother or sister is ill-clad and in lack of daily food, and one of you says to them, "Go in peace! Be warmed and filled!" without giving them the things needed for the body, what does it profit? So, faith by itself, if it has no works, is dead.

> But someone may well say, "Have you faith?" My answer is, "I have works. Show me your faith apart from your works, and I will show you my faith by means of my works." You say that you believe that there is one God; you do well. Even the demons also believe — and shudder. Do you want to be shown, you foolish fellow, that faith without works is barren? Was not Abraham our father justified by works when he offered his his son Isaac upon the altar? You see that faith was active along with his works, and faith was completed by works, and the scripture was fulfilled which says, "Abraham believed in God, and it was reckoned to him as righteousness, for he was called the friend of God." You see that a man is justified by works and not by faith alone.[68]

In fairness to James and Paul, one should add here that their views on salvation were probably not as sharply contrasting as the above would seem to indicate. When Paul preached that salvation was a gift of God that could not be earned, he said often that if a person sheds his slavery to sin though God's grace, his subsequent acts and deeds can do no other but to reflect his new slavery to Jesus.

> For we are his workmanship, created in Christ Jesus for good works, which God prepared beforehand, that we should walk in them.[69]

Either view, however, would probably not have assuaged Ananus. What made him foment was the repeated references in James' sermons to the end of the world and the day of judgment.

> Make firm your hearts for the coming of the Lord is at hand. Brothers, do not complain against each other, that you may not be judged. Behold, the judge stands at the door![70]

Just who was this "judge at the door"? As always, the message led to Jesus, and that is what Ananus found so irritating and intolerable. And he had any number of reasons for acting at this time. Putting up with an unpredictable splinter sect was a luxury at a time when the Parthians might come thundering down on the temple at any time. But of even more immediate concern was that Passover was again approaching. More Jewish Christians than ever would be pouring into Jerusalem and one heard talk of organized pro-Jesus demonstrations.

Now James himself was hardly a brigand or renegade, but sometimes movements grow beyond the ability of their founders to control them. This was on the mind of Ananus when he summoned the Sanhedrin into session at the beginning of the Passover festival. The decision was to summon James for an overtly friendly "consultation." When the Christian leader appeared before the council, Ananus told him in essence: "Many people have come to believe that Jesus was the Messiah and many have done so because of you. Would you, the brother of Jesus, be good enough to restrain the people and acquaint them with the facts about Jesus so that they are disabused of this notion? We vouch that you are a righteous man and that everyone will accept what you say. So please mount the temple parapet, where you can be easily seen, where your words will be audible to all, and make it clear to the crowd that they must not go astray as regards Jesus."

Soon thereafter the elderly James found himself being half led, half pushed up the long stairs to one of the stone porticos that overlooked the teeming, pushing Passover throng in the courtyard below. When the criers had shouted for attention and the crowd quieted down, Ananus announced his purpose.

Turning to James, he said: "Righteous one, whose word we are all obliged to accept, the people are going astray after Jesus, who was crucified. So, tell us, what is meant when you tell people about 'the door of Jesus'?'"

James took a deep breath and replied as loudly as he could: "Why do you question me about the Son of Man? I tell you, he is sitting in heaven at the right hand of the Great Power, and he will come on the clouds of heaven!"

These words generated a great uproar in the crowd below, and shouts of "Hosanna to the Son of David" went up. The elders realized that they had miscalculated, so they did what they had agreed on in such a case. Suddenly the crowd saw James being lifted up by several men and hurled to the stone pavement in the midst of their feet. Although he was elderly and frail, James did not die from the initial fall. The report I have already quoted states that he struggled to his knees as if trying to pray and said,

> "I beseech thee, Lord God and Father, forgive them for they know not what they are doing." While they pelted him with stones, one of the descendants of Rechab the son of Rachabim, the priestly family to which Jeremiah the prophet bore witness, called out "Stop! What are you doing? The Righteous One is praying for you!" Then one of them, a fuller, took the club which he used to beat out the clothes, and brought it down on the head of the Righteous One. Such was his martyrdom...[71]

Ananus certainly hadn't acted with unanimous support. Many leading citizens were outraged. Herod Agrippa soon received letters protesting that the high priest had no such right. Another letter went by sea to Alexandria, where the new Roman procurator, Albinus, was preparing to make his way north to take up residence. Upon arriving in Cæsarea, Albinus sent off an angry letter saying that Ananus had no right either to convene the Sanhedrin or put men to death without his approval. The king, probably after consulting Albinus, withdrew the high priesthood from Ananus after he had been in office only three months.

I must, however, disabuse you of any notions that Albinus might have brought a higher moral standard to the procuratorship. On the contrary, he helped sow the seeds of Jerusalem's destruction because he actually made private agreements among the leaders of robbers and of merchants who charged scandalous prices in a period of shortages. Thus, nothing was stolen or sold but what Albinus did not receive a portion of the proceeds. And when thieves were put in jail, their relatives could buy their way out for a price.

Now the procurator, did, I might add, make attempts to snuff out the Sicarii. The daggermen were everywhere in Jerusalem during the Passover festival and many had been thrown in jail awaiting trial. But during the height of the festival, the Sicarii had also kidnapped Eleazer, chief scribe to the temple. They sent the high priest a message that they would return the scribe if he would persuade Albinus to free ten Sicarii who had already been arrested for murder. Albinus, who also received lavish gifts from the temple authorities, agreed to do so for, I presume, yet another payment. But the effect was calamitous, for the Sicarii now contrived to kidnap all the temple executives they could catch in hopes that the authorities would release even more of their confederates from jail. Soon, as Josephus reports, "as they had again become no small number; they grew bold and were a great affliction to the whole country."

Albinus' stay lasted only two years. When he learned that Gessius Florus was coming to succeed him, he sought to "settle accounts" as follows. He took all the imprisoned murderers and others whom he deemed serious offenders and had them all put to death at once. All those who remained in jail for robbery and lesser crimes he dismissed if they would pay him money. After a suitable interval, he simply emptied the prisons of all who remained – namely, the deranged and destitute.

Then one more thing happened. Albinus' departure just happened to coincide with the completion of the temple construction – more than 80 years after Herod the Great began it. The celebrations were muted by the fact that 18,000 temple workers now had no wages. They might risk traveling 100 miles north to work on the new city of Neronia, or if they were lucky they might be one of the relatively few chosen for a make-work project to begin paving parts of Jerusalem with white stone slabs.

But most were left to fend for themselves. They roamed the cities and countryside, joined by the aimless convicts Albinus had freed. All of southern Syria was rife with unemployment, hunger and crime. And whether one was a beggar or brigand might depend on what day it was.

. . . .

IF JULIUS THE CENTURION needed any further proof that this Paul was a special person, it became evident enough when dozens of Christians turned out on the Appian Way to escort him into Rome. Indeed, the "prisoner" seemed to be celebrating a triumph rather than going to trial. Thus, when Julius turned over Paul to the governor of the Foreign Camp, located on the fringe of the Prætorian Guard barracks just outside the city's northeastern wall, it must have been accompanied by a glowing report of his conduct and a warm parting embrace. This explains why Paul was eventually given the right to live in his own rented apartment with only a single guard to remind anyone who cared that there dwelled therein a person under house arrest.

Only Paul's heritage and unswerving missionary habit would explain why, when still surrounded by Christian well-wishers, he would excuse himself so that he could call together the Jewish elders of Rome. There, still bound to his lone soldier by a single long chain, he asked them for an opportunity to explain his mission in the synagogue. He recalled his arrest in the temple and his subsequent appeal to Cæsar "though I had no charge to bring against any nation.

"It is for this reason I have asked to see you and speak with you, since it is because of the hope of Israel that I am bound with this chain," Paul told them.

The elders must have seemed puzzled at first. "We have received no letter from Judea about you," they said, "and none of the brethren coming here has reported or spoken any evil about you. But we would like to hear what your views are, for we do know much about this sect, yet know that it is disparaged everywhere."

Paul, the prisoner, could not preach in the synagogue as he was accustomed. Rather, the elders did him the courtesy of calling "in great numbers" at his own lodgings. There they listened literally all day long as Paul explained his life and why he was now a "slave" of Jesus, the risen Messiah.

Some of the elders were convinced, but as usual the great majority were not. And it was at that point that Paul despaired of further arguments and hurled a charge that had so often riled synagogue congregations. "The Holy Spirit," he said, "was right in saying to your fathers through Isaiah the prophet":

> Go to the people and say,
> You shall indeed hear but never understand,
> and you shall indeed see but never perceive.
> For this people's heart has grown dull,
> and their ears are heavy of hearing,
> and their eyes they have closed;
> lest they should perceive with their eyes
> and hear with their ears,
> and understand with their heart,
> and turn to me to heal them.[72]

Finally the elders rose to depart. But Paul could not resist one more statement that surely cut their bonds forever. "Let it be known to you then that this salvation of God has been sent to the Gentiles," he said. "They will listen."

It was as if he and Barnabas were again shaking the dust off their feet at the Jewish elders of Pisidian Antioch so many years ago.

If Paul had any further contact with the Jewish community after that, there is no record of it. There is abundant evidence that he taught Roman Gentile Christians while also keeping up a busy correspondence with the churches abroad. The early months in Rome show every indication of a highly active – even exhuberant – apostle. One might have expected that all of the men who had accompanied him to Jersualem would have departed after so many months away from their homes and families, yet Paul's letters not long after his arrival mention the continued presence of Aristarchus, Luke, Timothy and Tychicus from this party. Others with Paul in Rome were Epaphroditis of Philippi, one Jesus (called Justus), Demas of Thessolonica, a runaway slave named Oneimus and Mark – the same cousin of Barnabas who had accompanied Paul on his first missionary trip in Cyprus.

Probably the first letter Paul dictated upon his arrival was to the church of Philippi that had so generously provided him with a rented apartment, a stipend and an all-purpose assistant. That this freed him to preach was clear enough in his effusive letter to the Philippians. "I want you to know," he wrote,

> that what has happened to me has really served to advance the gospel, so that it has become known throughout the whole Prætorian Guard and to all the rest that my imprisonment is for Christ. And most of the brethren have been made confident in the Lord because of my imprisonment, and are much more bold to speak the word of God without fear.[73]

Paul's message to the Philippians on living a Christian life was doubtless the same that he preached to the Romans who came to visit his apartment at this time.

> ...let your manner of life be worthy of the gospel of Christ so that whether I come and see you or am absent, I may hear of you that you stand firm in one spirit, with one mind striving side by side for the faith of the gospel.

> ...Do nothing from selfishness or conceit, but in humility count others better than yourselves. Let each of you look not only to his own interests, but also to the interests of others. Have this mind among yourselves, which you have in Christ Jesus, who, though he was in the form of God, did not count equality with God a thing to be grasped, but emptied himself, taking the form of a servant, being born in the likeness of men. And being found in human form he humbled himself and became obedient unto death, even death on a cross. Therefore, God has highly exalted him and bestowed on him the name which is above every name, that at the name of Jesus every knee should bow...

...Do all things without grumbling and questioning, that you may be blameless and innocent, children of God without blemish in the midst of a crooked and perverse generation, among whom you shine as lights in the world, holding fast the word of life, so that in the day of Christ I may be proud that I did not run in vain or labor in vain. Even if I am to be poured as a libation upon the sacrificial offering of your faith, I am glad to rejoice with you all. Likewise, you should be glad to rejoice with me.[74]

To his new Roman friends, Paul's teachings on how to live the proper Christian life would have differed little from those he had already penned years before in the letter he had written to them from Corinth.

For by the grace given to me, I bid every one among you not to think of himself more highly than he ought to think, but to think with sober judgment, each according to the measure of faith which God has assigned him.

For as in one body we have many members, and all the members do not have the same function; so we, through many, are one body in Christ, and individually members one of another. Having gifts that differ according to the grace given to us, let us use them: if prophecy, in proportion to our faith; if service, in our serving; he who teaches, in his teaching; he who exhorts, in his exhortation; he who contributes, in liberality; he who gives aid, with zeal; he who does acts of mercy, with cheerfulness.

Let love be genuine. Hate what is evil. Hold fast to what is good. Love one another with brotherly affection. Outdo one another in showing honor. Never flag in zeal. Be aglow with the Spirit. Serve the Lord. Rejoice in your hope. Be patient in tribulation. Be constant in prayer. Contribute to the need of the saints. Practice hospitality.

Bless those who persecute you. Bless and do not curse them. Rejoice with those who rejoice. Weep with those who weep. Live in harmony with one another. Do not be haughty, but associate with the lowly. Never be conceited. Repay no one evil for evil, but take thought for what is noble in the sight of all. If possible, so far as it depends upon you, live peaceably with all. Beloved, never avenge yourselves, but leave it in the wrath of God; for it is written: 'Vengeance is mine, I will repay,' says the Lord. No, 'if your enemy is hungry, feed him. If he is thirsty, give him a drink; for by so doing you will heap burning coals

upon his head.' [cause him to be remorseful]. Do not be overcome by
evil, but overcome evil with good.

> Let every person be subject to the governing authorities. For there is
> no authority except from God, and those that exist have been institut-
> ed by God. Therefore, he who resists the authorities resists what God
> has appointed, and those who resist will incur judgment. For rulers
> are not a terror to good conduct, but to bad. Would you have no fear of
> him who is in authority? Then do what is good and you will receive his
> approval, for he is God's servant for your good... [75]

Pay taxes that are due and honor to whom it is due, Paul continued. And observe the ten commandments. "Love does no wrong to a neighbor; therefore
love is the fulfilling of all the law."

Paul was also kept busy mediating specific problems that arose among the
Gentile churches abroad. For instance, The Christians of Colossæ, some 130
miles east of Ephesus, had sent their chief elder, Epaphras, all the way to Rome
to seek Paul's counsel about a problem he faced. It is a special tribute to Paul to
note that he had not even founded this Gentile church. Along with churches in
Hierapolis and Laodicea that lay along the valley of the Lycus River, it had been
founded by those who had first heard Paul in Ephesus.

What drove Epaphras across the Adriatic to see Paul was a religious dispute that
had split the church at Colossæ. Some of its members were well-educated Greeks
who held the view that there was a vast gulf between God in his goodness and
man, with his physical limitations. But by leading lives of self-denial, reflection
and other virtues, man could, they believed, rise at last to complete fellowship
with God. These people accepted the gospel because they saw Jesus as one of the
intermediaries of higher learning who could help them on their journey to
God's embrace. In time, these church members, with their fasts, vigils and holy
days, began to deem themselves a higher class of Christians. They had also begun
to lay down regulations as to food, drink and other aspects of daily living, so that
one of their best-known slogans was "Touch not. Taste not. Handle not." What
these people seemed to disdain most about Christianity was its very simplicity.

Paul's worst fear — and here it was confronting him — must have been that the
Gentile churches he had worked so hard to open to all classes and callings
might be captured by a new sort of stifling, exacting, Pharisaic rulemakers. And
in his letter to the Colossians he rose to the challenge. Jesus, he wrote, was *not*
one of several intermediaries to God, but the embodiment of God and all his
wisdom. In Jesus, he said, *all* fullness dwells.

He is the image of the invisible God, begotten before all creation, because by him all things were created, in heaven and upon earth, the things which are visible and the things which are invisible, whether thrones or lordships or powers or authorities. All things were created through him and for him. He is before all things and in him all things cohere. He is the head of the body, that is, of the church. He is the beginning, the firstborn from the dead, that he might be supreme in all things. For in him, God in all his fullness was pleased to take up his abode, and through him to reconcile all things to himself, when he had made peace through the blood of the cross. This was done for all things, whether on earth or in the heavens. And you, who were once estranged and hostile in your minds, in the midst of evil deeds, he has now reconciled in the body of his flesh, through his death, in order to present you before him consecrated, unblemished, irreproachable, if only you remain grounded and established in the faith, not shifting from the hope of the gospel which you have heard, which has been proclaimed to every creature under heaven, of which I, Paul, have been made a servant.[76]

The questions brought to Paul in Rome weren't always of cosmic consequences, but his answers sometimes were. Another case confronting the apostle involved one of his co-workers. Onesimus was a slave who had run away from his home in Laodicea. His master was a Christian named Philemon. Paul had become greatly attached to the youth and took a great interest in his future. But he also knew that there could be no future or security for a runaway, so he convinced Onesimus to go back and start life anew.

But convincing Philemon was another matter. Even the most lenient of masters usually believes in the sternest of measures against a runaway lest others be tempted to do the same. Paul himself risked censure in appealing to Philemon. He wrote a carefully-worded letter asking him to receive the young man kindly — not as a slave but as a brother Christian. If Onesimus had stolen anything from Philemon, Paul promised to make restitution himself. Paul makes it clear that he could — and would prefer to — retain the young man in Rome, for his present position as a prisoner and possible martyr for the faith has enhanced his authority in the eyes of believers. But he would rather have Onesimus voluntarily pardoned and sent back to Rome so he could continue to serve him in Philemon's place.

Finally, Paul further made sure that Philemon alone would not to be the sole judge of the matter. He addressed the letter to his wife and the church elders as well. He even referred to Onesimus warmly in his letter to the Colossians, whose church was only ii miles east of Laodicea.

After several busy weeks in Rome, it was time to send out some of his closest workers with the letters to the Philippians, Colossians and Philemon (and the church of Laodicea) and another letter to the churches of Ephesus. Tychicus, Paul's fellow envoy to the Jewish Christians in Jerusalem, would take the slave Onesimus and go to Laodicea, then journey on to Colossæ. The letter to the churches of Philippi would be delivered, much to their surprise, by Epaphroditus, the same lad they had only recently sent to see to Paul's personal needs.

What happened is that Epaphroditus had fallen seriously ill during Paul's first weeks in Rome, one of our many influenza epidemics, I suppose. Although in danger of dying, he had managed to pull through, and now Paul thought it best that he be sent home to recover fully. At the same time, he wanted to spare Epaphroditus the awkwardness of being accosted on the streets of Philippi and asked why he wasn't at Paul's side. Thus, the apostle went at great lengths to explain how hard the young man had worked for him – even risking his life in the process. "But God had mercy on him," Paul wrote, "and not only on him but on me, lest I have sorrow upon sorrow. I am the more eager to send him, therefore, that you may rejoice at seeing him again, and that I may be less anxious."

Paul resumes his good cheer in the closing, extending greetings from "all the saints" [Christians] in Rome – especially those of Cæsar's household."

The latter reference raises a profound question. In addition to ministering to the Christians of Rome, did Paul attempt to win over the leaders of Roman society? I have no doubt that the centurion Julius and the other guards probably told all their fellow soldiers and tavern chums about their harrowing shipwreck on Melita and how the Christian prisoner from Cæsarea had bolstered their courage. But there is an important distinction here: this is not the same as Paul reaching out to show Roman nobles The Way.

Did he? Paul's confinement would have made it difficult. Great men do not enjoy being jostled in crowded, smelly streets just so they can sit in the cramped dwellings of the humble and learn at their feet. That's why they held morning receptions in their own perfumed atria. Nonetheless I am strongly inclined to believe that Paul tried. There are persistent stories in Rome that Paul contacted Seneca and that the emperor's "tutor" (he was so much more!) responded favorably. I have even been shown copies of several letters that would seem to confirm the theory. The shortcoming here is that the correspondence lacks substance – most of it merely reflecting Paul's attempts to arrange meetings with Seneca and the latter's thanks for Paul's having enclosed a book or a writing of some sort. The letters further fail to confirm whether any such meetings actually took place.

Still, I find the hypothesis intriguing – even compelling. After all, did not Paul seize the chance to appear before everyone from the proconsuls Paulus in Cyprus and Gallio in Corinth to the procurator Festus and king Agrippa in Cæsarea? Was he not unfailingly confident that he could somehow unlock the hardest of hearts with the gospel? Why did he see Rome as the culmination of his mission?

Was it not as much to confront the highest imperial officials as it was to comfort Roman Christians? Such logic points to the likelihood that in Seneca, Paul saw a sensitive and sympathetic philosopher, a tutor who might read his works to a receptive young emperor, and a powerful official who might also help Paul secure a hearing before Nero himself rather than some obscure prætor in his stead.

The letters that purport to be from Seneca seem a curious mixture of polite encouragement and evasive procrastination. Again, logic would indicate that Paul's appeals for a dialogue came just as Seneca's star was descending. The Roman knew, perhaps unlike Paul, that the emperor had long since shut out all "tutoring" and that a rising artist and charioteer had scant time to hear an old man expound for hours on the immortality of a Jewish prophet and his new sect.

Whatever the case, Paul seems to have gained no satisfaction as to the date of his impending trial. True, Roman law prohibits any citizen from being held without trial for more than two years. But the mechanism at the time for appealing such injustices was either deficient or dependent on the lubrication of bribes to make the gears of justice turn. And Paul's case may well have been complicated by the shipwreck on Melita. One can imagine Luke or Timothy sitting on a hard bench for two hours in the office of the secretariat for foreign affairs for the fifteenth time, only to be reminded by a sleepy bureaucrat that Paul's papers had been lost at sea and that officials in Cæsarea had not yet supplied him with copies. After all, Festus had died and the new procurator may have had only rudimentary information about Paul's case.

As his confinement neared the two-year mark, Paul seems to have become resolved to enduring his fate, be it as a martyr for the faith or as an acquitted missionary ready to launch a new chapter in his life as he embarked on the road to Spain. In any event, Paul wrote the church at Philippi that he hoped to have the courage "to honor Christ in my body," whether in life or death.

> Yet which I shall choose I cannot tell, I am hard pressed between the two. My desire is to depart and be with Christ, for that is far better. But to remain in the flesh is more necessary on your account. Convinced of this, I know that I shall remain and continue with you all, for your progress and joy in the faith, so that in me you may have ample cause to glory in Christ Jesus because of my coming to you again.[77]

One wonders how Paul greeted the news that James the Just had been martyred in Jerusalem and the Jewish Christian church decimated. Had Paul's well-meant collection for the church been ill-starred? Was he in some indirect way responsible? Would the church of Peter and James endure?

. . . .

. . . .

LETTER FROM ROME — JULY, A. D. 80

Greetings to my dear brother Eumenes, his family, and all the workers of The
Pergamum Publishers.

I regret that my letter of last month was so brief — and not very cheerful. All I
can say is that I had my hands full every waking moment and could only stop long
enough to apprise you of the fire and why you had received no shipment.

The irony is that our letters must have crossed in the seas, for yours is so full of
good news from Pergamum. The best of it is that you are already experimenting
with various parchment sizes for the new codex process and that the parchment
makers guild has received the idea so well. I am also glad to learn that the travel
book on Rome and the smaller one on the Temple of Jupiter Capitoline have attracted such interest.

You had better sell the books fast, however, because we will soon need entirely
new ones about this city, which seems not so "eternal" after all. I am making bad
jokes, so I will get to the sad point. The fire I described so briefly last month turned
out to be almost on a level with the one that took out ten of Rome's precincts during
Nero's day. This one was not as widespread, but what made it so deadly was the
plague that followed.

I will first address the things that I'm sure concern you the most. The fire swept
through a goodly portion of the Argiletum and did not spare the Street of Book-

sellers. I would say that about one-third of our inventory was destroyed — including, I'm afraid, all of the scrolls in the scriptorium that dealt with the new Flavian Amphitheater. All 30 were piled up on the same shelf and all perished together — a stupidity I shall never repeat.

Alas, it isn't as if the remaining book inventory is exactly intact, either. If this were a glassworks we could toss out the charred or melted inventory and polish up what was left. But our inventory is books, and much of what's left has burn marks around the edges or smells like smoke. I am just hoping that buyers will understand.

Why didn't I rescue more? Because my purse doesn't match that of the Sosius Brothers and their ilk. When the firefighters came, they went straight to the Sosius bookstore because they knew they could get the highest fee. By the time they got down to our end of the street, much of the water in their engines was already used up and the brigade leader (I should say brigand leader) wanted 4,000 sesterces before his men would pump a drop. I offered 1,000 right then (which is all I could muster) and 1,000 in a week. He glared at me in silence and for a moment I thought we wouldn't get a thing. He disappeared and after a couple of long minutes a bunch of haggard men came back, pulling one of the sorriest old fire engines I ever saw. Its water level was already so low that you could hear the pistons sucking air as they pumped.

We got enough to put out the flames that destroyed the books in the first floor showroom. I didn't let the so-called firefighters upstairs into the scriptorium because heaven knows how much damage they would have done. Instead, a few of us passed buckets up. Then we stood guard all night with the few buckets of water and sand that they left us, hoping that the wind wouldn't change and send the fire roaring back through the Argiletum.

What I'm trying to say, Eumenes, was that this was more serious than the first reports you received — including my own. The fire burned one part of Rome or another for three days and three nights. The skin on my badly-burned left arm is just now starting to grow back (at least I hope it will) and I am still unable to inhale deeply without starting a painful coughing fit. But maybe the most dramatic way to *make my point is that the fire destroyed the famous Pantheon (you'd better sell out those books, too!), the Baths of Agrippa, the Theater of Balbus, the stage area in Pompey's Theater, the Temple of Neptune, the Temple of Serapis, the Temple of Isis, and — so soon after its magnificent restoration by Vespasian — the Temple of Jupiter Capitoline and many of its surrounding buildings.*

And more books were lost than just ours, dear cousin. Would you believe the Octavian Library, with all those rare volumes that I myself spent so many hours handling and copying? And finally, you won't be hearing about the exploits of the Green and Blue anytime soon. The fire ravaged the grandstands on both lengths of the Circus Maximus.

I still find it hard to accept its happening so soon after the tragedy that Mount Vesuvius rolled down on the people of Pompeii and Herculaneum. In fact, Titus was still in Campania supervising repairs when he got word of the tragedy in Rome. His leadership and generosity were noble indeed. He opened his own gardens and all the buildings in the Field of Mars to the homeless. As the rebuilding of temples has begun, the emperor has emptied the palace of his own statues and artwork to help restore their glory.

But even all the gold and palaces of the greatest emperor are no match when a plague strikes — and this is what crippled Rome in the weeks that followed. Nothing is so cruel and frustrating as seeing people drop over from a cause they can't see or fight. Yet, they say that on some days 10,000 persons have died of it. Why do plagues seem to follow great fires and natural disasters? Why do they seem to strike hardest at those who live in the poorest, most crowded conditions? Does something get into the water supply? Do fires stir up some mysterious vapors? Do dead bodies give off some disease?

If it had to do with breathing smoke, I surely would have succumbed by now. However, the plague has subsided and I am now starting to regard myself as one of the more fortunate. My apartment house in the Subura was untouched and for over a month now I have two whole burned-out families sleeping everywhere in my love-

ly living room and dining area. And if you must know, a few occupy the bookstore as well, which is another reason for all the production delays. All of them are of good cheer during this adversity and share what they have, for, yes Eumenes, they are Christians. And just now when I told them whom I was writing, they asked me to send you God's blessings!

Added to the many ironies that seem to occupy this letter is that so soon after all this disruption and misery, Romans have been enthralled by a new wonder. I'm referring, as you might guess, to the opening at long last of the Flavian Amphitheater, or more popularly, The Hunting Place. This monstrosity isn't entirely finished, but Titus has already held ten straight days of shows. They say he will give 100 consecutive days of games before they finish for the year.

That there would be enough beasts or men in all the realm to do so is difficult to fathom based on what has gone on so far. I will start by explaining that a stream flows through the base of the Flavian Amphitheater — the same one that was once dammed up to create the lake at Nero's Golden House. Just before the opening, this body of water was covered over with a platform of planks. On the first day no fewer than 400 wild animals were slain, with even women taking part in dispatching them. People are still talking about a raging battle between four elephants, but during the day men also fought in single and group combat, with about 40 men being dragged off dead before it was over.

The second day featured horse races. Then the next day the wooden floor was removed and the whole arena flooded with the waters of the dammed-up stream that had once provided Nero with his lake. Suddenly the crowd was treated to the sight of manned ships floating through the main entrance. Some 3,000 armed men fought a vigorous sea battle, followed by an infantry battle between the "Athenians" and the "Syracusans." In this case the Athenians landed on an artificial island and assaulted a wall that had been constructed around a Syracusan monument. Then there followed a novel entertainment in which horses, bulls and other large animals were put afloat in the water to see how they managed to swim and fight at the same time.

Meanwhile, at any given time during these days Titus would rise and scatter into the audience little wooden balls that would set the people scrambling. Each ball had on it a symbol of a useful prize they could redeem — perhaps a silver vessel, a horse, a slave or pack animal.

Once the naval displays were over, Titus ordered the stream to the amphitheater diverted again so that the vast labyrinth of underground chambers could be utilized for future shows.

I know your tongue must be hanging out by now and you are saying, "If I couldn't go, did my cousin Attalos?" Yes, Attalos went. I regarded it as part of my duty in writing the book on the amphitheater. But I reasoned that since any one of 70,000 persons could sit in the audience, a writer might gain a unique perspective by seeing what took place below the arena floor. This was not difficult to arrange, for you must understand that probably one-third of all the men who live here in the Subura have either taken part in some phase of the construction project over the last ten years or are currently working on its maintenance. The White Crane, my favorite tavern, is but three furlongs from the amphitheater; and if you go there any time after sundown you'll find a crowd who just came from working there. One of them is a burly Gaul named Curtius, a fellow freedman who built the system of pulleys and levers that makes platforms of men and animals rise from the holding areas to the arena floor. In fact, the wily Curtius made the system so intricate that only he can oversee its operation!

I bought Curtius some wine and told him I wanted to extol his achievements in our book. So it was that on the fifth day of the shows, I walked to work with him about two hours before the games were to begin. Rather than go through the spectator entrances, we went to the rear of the gladiatorial school, where everyone seemed to know Curtius. Just inside the outer wall you can descend into the underground tunnel that takes gladiators on a gradual incline right onto the arena floor. So, as we approached the light at the end of the tunnel, I imagined myself wearing a helmet and holding a sword and shield.

And suddenly there we were, standing at the large entrance, looking up into the four tiers of seats that encircle the arena. I'm sure you would have shouted for them to bring on a few tigers. I admit my own reaction was of frozen terror at knowing what took place there. The seats were empty, but clusters of workers were going about their business quietly. On the arena floor crews of stage equipment handlers were struggling to set in place the statue of a pharaoh, for the morning's theme was to be an animal hunt in the hills around the Upper Nile. So as I looked about I beheld the fallen columns of an Egyptian temple, steep hills, giant boulders and several palm trees — all of it built by the carpenters of the amphitheater and stored below.

Yet the most fascinating thing of all was getting to see the unfurling of the velarium. I think I wrote you before about this canopy that protects spectators from the sun. Rather than a single "tent," as you might imagine, it consists of a hundred or more long, thin pieces of canvas. So intricate is the whole operation of raising and lowering these "sails" that it requires a special unit of 100 men from the fleet to come up from Misenum each time the games are held.

We happened to walk in just as they were at work, and I could quickly see why only sailors could do the job. Protruding from the top of the amphitheater all around its circumference are large timbers, almost like the masts of ships. From these are suspended a spider-like network of ropes, which are drawn taut by pulling on them from ground level and fastening them to large winches. The marines fasten the ends of the rolled-up pieces of canvas canopy to the vertical timbers and then allow the rolls to unravel downward atop their rope supports. At that point the most nimble of the sailors climbs out to the central ring at the end and ties all the pieces of canvas together. This leaves a perfect circular gap in the center, through which the wind can pass.

There are two main entrances to the floor of the arena. There is the one for gladiators that we arrived by, then another for the unfortunate. Located at the opposite end, it is called the Libitinarian gate (yes, after the god of funerals), and is used to cart off dead beasts and gladiators.

But there are many smaller entrances around the perimeter as well, and here is where my friend Curtius comes in. Each of these small gates is connected inside to a platform which is raised and lowered to bring forth animals.

Going into the lower regions of the amphitheater was quite another experience — more like what I imagine a visit to Hades would be like. It is hardly what one would put in a tourist book, but I will complete my report to you nonetheless. The first thing that strikes one beyond all else is the overpowering and unforgettable stench of men and animals: sweat, urine, shit, hay, rotting meat and death. The next thing is the terrifying mixture of animal sounds. It is frightfully dark in there and the passageways twist about so narrowly that my constant fear of suddenly walking into an escaped lion at the next turn was scarcely calmed by Curtius' assurance that all are safely caged. It is also wet and dank. The drainage from the naval battles isn't complete and the wetness may never go away because the underground stream continues to seep through here and there.

Curtius could sense my discomfort and seemed bent on diverting my attention by lecturing me about the huge pulleys, winches and gears used to work the elevators. But in truth I listened to only half of it, for my eyes kept going to the cages of all these unfortunate creatures that had been captured and brought to this place for the amusement of man, the most bloodthirsty animal of all. At one point, as Curtius was showing off some piece of equipment, I kept staring at a giant bear who was pinned inside a cage so small that he could scarcely have stood upright. Flies crawled all over his matted hair, yet he had not even enough room to swat them. I could not think of the glory or excitement humans would feel at what would soon take place. All I could think of was that bear. I actually prayed for him and all the animals and men who would lose their lives that day. I know you are already squirming at what a fool your cousin is, but I even prayed that they might comfort themselves with visions of running freely through the cool, green forests and mountains that they were snatched away from.

In time one could hear the sound above us building above to thunderous proportions. Curtius, who had already begun to supervise the loading of cages onto the elevators, said he could tell from the increased noise level that it was time for me to go up and grab a seat, for the amphitheater would be full again as it had been every day of the games. I asked instead that he merely lead me again to the end of the gladiatorial walkway so I could see what the place looked like with a full crowd. Soon I stood among a few of the workers who were loitering about and I felt that same sickness in the pit of my stomach as I looked above me. In the tier nearest the arena I could see the well-dressed personages of knights as they began emerging through the 14 entranceways reserved for each of their 14 orders. Just to my left was the red-cushioned pavilion reserved for the emperor and his party. It was still empty, but I faced it and tried to imagine myself forcing out the words: "Hail Cæsar. Those who are about to die salute you!"

At first I couldn't equate the loud roar I heard with the fact that the amphitheater was still only half full. Then I realized that most of it came from the sound of the wind rushing through the "sails" of the velarium. People have told me that this can be greater than the roar of a full crowd. But Curtius says there is still a more awesome sound — that the roar of a dozen lions is so chilling as to render a crowd silent and becalm the velarium.

I walked quickly back down the gladiatorial entrance. I knew that in Rome the gladiators don't fight until the afternoon show, but all I could think of was that a gang of them might come clattering right at me in the tunnel and sweep me along with them just for the hell of it.

Yes, Eumenes, my step was as quick as I could make it the rest of the way. Outside, I could hear the crowd noise swelling as I walked back to the White Crane and ordered extra wine with my meal. But I could hardly taste either food or wine for the stench that remained in my nostrils.

No, little of this was in the books that burned up, nor will it be when we do the new ones. So why do I write about subterranean smells and the like? Well, you always want to know what I'm doing, and that's what I did. But maybe I report such things also to make you think about the nature of the world we live in and what other courses might be open to us while we still have hope of distinguishing man from beast. So as well might the manuscript that accompanies this letter. This is the final installment of the book I have been writing. I again entreat it to your safekeeping — especially this time because neither the scriptorium nor my apartment makes a fitting storage place with so many lodgers afoot and other disruptions taking place. This time I will refrain from begging you not to read it. Yea, I urge you to do so because it may open more insights to your cousin and the times he has lived in.

Diodoros is still with me — my rock in troubled times — and sends you fond greetings even though I know his presence in Pergamum made you uncomfortable.

Farewell, my cousin, and may at least one half of the Pergamum Publishers continue to prosper.

—— Attalos

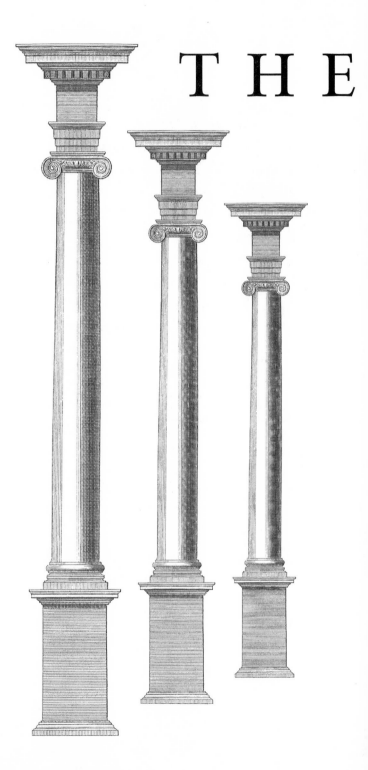

THE

REAPING

BOOK III

C orruption and crumbling morals per-
vaded the empire. Could "good" people
find shelter from it only in Christianity,
or in the punctilious practice of Judaism?
To say so would be to exclude the infl-
uence of many teachers, sages and philosophers. Admittedly, their influence
was minimized by the fact that they tended to live spare lives of solitude. At
most they might lead only a small circle of students. Nevertheless, many
proved to be the ballast that kept whole nations from sinking when they lost
their way in terrible storms.

I have decided to balance this story by telling of one philosopher who lived
through the treacherous, tumultuous years that I am about to describe, when
the Roman world probably came closer to destroying itself than at any other
time in history. And as you watch this conflagration unfold, keep in mind that
there were a few men who stood above the kings and conspirators and who remained reservoirs of reason when it was so desperately needed.

Apollonius of Tyana was such a man. As you will see, his insights and prophesies were to influence the three emperors of this period. However, I have also included Apollonius because I am fascinated by the fact that he was born around
the same time as Paul and in a city not far from Tarsus. As did Paul, he studied
briefly in Tarsus as a boy, then lived in Syrian Antioch for awhile and traveled
through Asia Minor.

Apollonius was born of a wealthy family in Tyana. They say the child was not
only beautiful to behold, but very early showed an astonishing ability to learn
his letters. At 14, after going to study in Tarsus and finding the city too raucous
and his teacher too Epicurean, he persuaded his father to send him to the quieter town of Ægæ to study in its Temple of Asclepius. There he could observe

the healing that took place while also studying Plato, Chrysippus and other philosophers.

But the special passion of Apollonius was Pythagoras. Imagining himself, like the ancient philosopher-poet from Samos, as driven by a higher spirit than pleasures of the flesh, Apollonius had decided by age 16 that he would live by different rules than other men. When asked when he began this departure, he answered: "At the point at which physicians begin; for the first thing they do is purge the bowels of their patients. Thus they prevent some from being ill at all, and heal others." So Apollonius thereafter rejected all forms of flesh because it was unclean and "made the mind gross." Wine he acknowledged to be clean because it was yielded by a carefully domesticated plant; but he rejected this, too, because it "endangers the mental balance" and "darkens the ether inside, which is the soul." Henceforth, said Apollonius, he would eat only bread, dried fruits and vegetables.

Nor would he dress the same as others. He took to walking without shoes and clad himself only in linen, declining to wear any animal product. He let his hair grow long and dwelled in whatever temple he happened to be studying in the course of his travels.

Some might think that such a demeanor would repulse those who dressed and acted otherwise. But as Apollonius continued to live at the temple of Asclepius for two more years, studying and assisting in the cure of patients, his reputation grew such that people flocked to see him from all over Cilicia.

Mostly, he was known for his common sense. A biographer reports of a wealthy young wastrel who beseeched the temple god to cure him of his dropsy, which had been brought on by gluttonous eating and drinking. Although the patient refused to relax his appetites, he would constantly offer sacrifices to Asclepius and pray for a cure. The young man grumbled that he received no attention from the god. But one night Asclepius came to him in a dream and said "You might do better to consult Apollonius."

The next day he confronted the younger Apollonius and asked, "What on earth is there in your wisdom that I can profit by?"

"Well, I can advise you of what, under the circumstances, will be most valuable to you," said Apollonius.

"By Zeus," thundered the impatient patient, "I want the health which Asclepius promises but never delivers!"

"Hush," said Apollonius, "for he gives it to those who desire it. But you do things that irritate and aggravate your disease – you wallow in luxury and accumulated viands upon your worn-out and water-logged stomach. It's as if you are choking your water with a flood of mud."

It was not exactly medical terminology, but it was this clear imagery that made the man understand and begin his road to recovery.

Apollonius also had the gift of prophecy as early as his days at Ægæ in Cilicia. The governor of the province at the time was known as a bully and a pervert. Not long after he heard of the handsome lad who lived at the temple of Asclepius, he journeyed there from Tarsus under the pretense of being sick and needing the god's help. Finding Apollonius walking alone, the governor asked if he would intervene with the god on his behalf.

"What recommendation does any good man need?" replied Apollonius. "For the gods love men of virtue and welcome them without any introductions."

"Because the god has invited you, Apollonius, to be his guest, but so far has not invited me," said the governor.

"Nay," was the reply, "tis only my humble merits, as far as a young man can display good qualities, which have been my passport to the favor of Asclepius. If you really care for righteousness, go boldly to the god and tender what prayer you will."

"By Zeus, I will," said the older man, "if you will allow me to address you with a prayer first."

"Why to me?"

"Ah, a prayer that can only be made to the beautiful, which is that they may grant to others participation in their beauty and not deny their charms," he said with a wink and a vile leer.

Apollonius stared him down. "You are mad, you scum," he said coldly.

This enflamed the other. Now he threatened to have the lad's head cut off.

"Ha!" said Apollonius. "It is true that a head will roll — and it will be next Thursday!"

With that he walked off. I can verify that on the day Apollonius had mentioned, the governor was captured on a highway by Roman soldiers and executed for having conspired with the king of Cappadocia against the interests of Rome.

By the time Apollonius was 20 he had made some other important decisions for himself as well. First, he vowed never to wed or have any connection with women. Second, he determined to go to the farthest extremities of the earth in his study of religions and philosophies. And third, he vowed that for the first five years of these journeys he would not speak. Why? Because holding his tongue, a biographer related, "would allow his eyes and mind to take note of very many things that...would be stored in his memory." And the memory, said Apollonius, is one's most treasured possession.

Armed with these resolutions, he spent his whole life traveling. He went to Antioch and lived in the temple of Apollo in the infamous Grove of Daphne. He learned from Arabs how to understand the prophesies of birds. He journeyed to Babylonia, was the king's honored guest and interpreted dreams with the Magi. He crossed the mighty Caucasus and watched the nomads along the Cophen River hunt lions and leopards. He saw herds of elephants along the

Indus River and worshipped at shrines established by Alexander's armies centuries before. He met with Brahmans at the Temple of the Sun in Taxila. He traversed the length of India to the Ganges, where he stayed with the sages and learned their wisdom. Then he went through all of Egypt and Libya, observing their religions and customs.

Wherever he was, Apollonius would begin his day with devotions to the sun, as Pythagoras would have it. When praying to the god of any temple, he would simply say, "O ye gods, grant unto me that which I deserve." The rest of the day, as Damis, a diarist who accompanied him, records it,

> If he were in a Greek city, he would call the priests together and talk wisely about the gods, and would correct them if they had departed from the traditional forms. If, however, the rites were barbarous and peculiar, then he would find out who had founded them and on what occasion they were established. And having learnt the sort of cult it was, he would make suggestions, in case he could think of any improvement upon them. Then he would go in quest of his followers and bid them ask any questions they liked. For he said it was the duty of philosophers of his school to converse at the earliest dawn with the gods, and during the rest of the day to discuss human affairs in friendly intercourse.[1]

In all things Apollonius urged common sense and moderation. For instance, when in Babylonia, the king was so pleased with their friendship that he offered Apollonius any ten requests if only he would name them. Apollonius asked only that he be provided with bread and dried fruits instead of the rich viands of the king's banquet. When the same king insisted that his guest stay in lavish palace quarters, Apollonius engaged him as follows. "Supposing, O king, that you came to my city of Tyana and I invited you to live where I live, would you care to do so?"

"Why no," said the king, "unless I were offered a house that was big enough to accommodate my escort, bodyguard and myself in a handsome manner."

"Then," said Apollonius, "I may use the same argument with you. Let me therefore be entertained by some private person who has the same means as myself, and I will visit you as often as you like."

Wherever he went, Apollonius inveighed against the sacrifice of animals, for he revered them all and was said to be able to communicate with many. Once when he had agreed to join the Babylonian king in sacrificing to the sun, he was caught unawares when the king's servants brought out a magnificent white horse of the Nisæan breed. The steed was adorned with all the trappings of a triumph, and the king's priests prepared to sacrifice it. Apollonius could only reply: "Please, O king, go on with your sacrifice in your own way, but permit me to sacrifice in mine." With that he took up a handful of frankincense and said: "O Sun, send me as far over the earth as is my pleasure and thine, and may I make the acquaintance of good men, but never hear anything of bad, nor they of me." And with that he threw the frankincense into the fire and watched the smoke as it curled upwards. Then he said: "Now O king, go on with your sacrifice in accordance with your traditions, for my traditions are such as you see."

In the first year of this chapter, Apollonius had returned from his long sojourn in Babylonia, India and Egypt and now desired to reacquaint himself with Greece. It was an exhilarating time to visit because the next Olympic Games were approaching and festivals and competitions were being held all over Attica and the Peloponnesus. It was also exciting for the band of students who by now accompanied Apollonius wherever he went. They sailed into the Athenian port of Piræus in the height of autumn and in the midst of the festivals that accompanied the celebration of the Eleusian mysteries. Philosophy students were everywhere, some stripped and enjoying the heat, others studying books and some rehearsing speeches or engaging in competitive debate. So well was Apollonius known to them by reputation that when they learned that he was on his way from the seaport to the Acropolis, most of the youths stopped what they were doing and fell in step with him.

Soon everyone in Athens knew that Apollonius was a man who taught philosophy and how worship of the gods was to be conducted — even if it challenged their accepted ways. In succeeding weeks, for instance, when the Athenians were enjoying their festival of Dionysus, Apollonius saw them flocking to the theater and assumed they were going to listen to the traditional processional and rhythmic hymns. But when he heard them dancing lascivious jigs to a pipe that played the sacred epic of Orpheus, he sternly rebuked them. "You are dancing away the reputations of those who lost their lives winning victory at Salamis," he admonished. "If this were a military dance I would say, 'Bravo, soldiers, for you are training yourself for war and I will join you.' But yours is a soft and effeminate dance. And what do you mean by your saffron robes and your purple and scarlet raiment? For surely your victorious ancestors never dressed themselves up this way. No one here bears a helmet, but disguises themselves as female harlequins! What can one say therefore of your national trophies? They are no longer monuments to the shame of the Persians, but to your own shame because you have degenerated so much from those who set them up. Nay, I see you turning to the wind and letting it billow up your skirts so you can pretend you are ships. But surely you might at least have some respect for the winds that were your allies and once blew mightily to protect you. You have turned Boreas, the most masculine of all winds, into a woman."

Apollonius attacked their sport as well. Athenians would flock to theaters to watch human slaughter, for the show promoters would pay large sums for convicted adulterers, burglars, kidnappers and similar rabble, then pit them against each other in mortal combat. When he was invited to attend, Apollonius refused to enter a place he called "so impure and reeking with gore."

"I am surprised that the goddess [Athena] has not already quit the Acropolis when you shed such blood under her eyes," he said. "For I suspect that presently, when you are conducting the Pan-Athenaic procession, you will no longer be content with bulls, but will be sacrificing whole herds of men to your goddess."

The days that Apollonius had spent in the temples of Asceplius also served him well in his encounters with the afflicted. Damis, who was constantly at his side, cites a case that arose when the philosopher was spending his morning lecturing and discoursing with his own party and the many local students who thronged to be at his side. At one point when they were discussing the proper use of libations in temple rites, there appeared in his audience a young dandy who had so evil a reputation for licentiousness that his conduct had been the subject of coarse street songs. As Apollonius was instructing how to pour a libation for the gods over the handles of the cup (because men are least likely to drink from that part), the youth burst out with loud and coarse laughter. After one or two similar outbreaks, Apollonius looked over at him and said, "It is not yourself who perpetrates this insult, but a demon who drives you on without your knowing it."

Indeed, the youth would laugh at things when no one else laughed. He would burst out crying or talk to himself for no particular reason. So Apollonius, recorded his biographer, got up and fixed his stare on the youth. Very soon the demon within him began to utter in fear and agony much like a torture victim on the rack. The ghost swore he would leave the young man alone and never take possession of anyone again. But Apollonius addressed him with anger as a master might a bad dog or rascally slave. He again ordered the devil to quit the young man and then give a visible sign that he had done so.

"I will throw down yonder statue," said the demon. Just then the lad pointed to one of the images in the portico behind them. The statue began swaying gently, then fell down. The students were aghast with amazement, then clapped their hands as if having seen the cleverest of magic acts on stage. With that the young man rubbed his eyes as if he had been asleep. And as he looked toward the sunlight he assumed a modest demeanor. Gone were his babbling and his spasmodic motions. That day he gave up his dainty dress and the rest of his sybaritic ways. He fell in love with the austere life of the philosopher, donned their cloak and modeled his life upon that of Apollonius.

So did many other aspiring youths. Before long Apollonius would lead a brave band of them to the capital of the empire and to the den of a beast more ferocious than any he had encountered in his far-flung adventures.

. . . .

THE SPRING OF THE FIRST YEAR in this period found Nero more impatient than ever to display his skills as an artist and charioteer. Although he had continued giving some performances in his private gardens in Rome, the small audiences never justified the enormity of the talent expended, in his view. Yet, he couldn't muster the courage to venture onto a more public stage in Rome. But Neapolis was another matter, and it is there that the emperor spent much of the spring playing to a theater packed with notables from all over Campania.

At the same time, a grander scheme was hatching in Nero's mind. He would travel to Athens, Corinth, Olympia and all over Greece to vie for the glorious and long-revered wreaths of its Games. The emperor actually began making plans for it while still in Campania, but when he consulted various augurs and seers about it, they said that the signs weren't propitious at the time. Some say that the people of Rome feared Nero would put an end to the free corn dole in order to help finance his trip, but who am I to say that this would influence the augurs? In any event, Nero announced that for the peoples' sake, he would postpone the trip to Greece. But in the meantime he should not have to suffer cultural deprivation. What followed were a series of feasts in public places as if the whole city were his own home. I will describe only one of them, which occurred at the artificial lake of Augustus and Marcus Agrippa. On one day after exhibiting a wild beast hunt, Nero immediately had water piped into the theater and produced a sea fight. Then the water was let out again for a gladiatorial combat. Then the lake was flooded once more for a costly public banquet, all supervised by the Prætorian prefect Tigellinus.

Now the arrangements for this "floating banquet" were as follows. In the center of the lake were floated dozens of the great wooden casks that ships and taverns use to store wine. On top of these they fastened planks. Nero, Tigellinus and the rest of the imperial party occupied the center, where they sat on purple rugs and soft cushions. The platform was towed about by other vessels, with gold and ivory fittings. The rowers were degenerates, sorted according to age and vice. The lakeside was rung with taverns and brothels, and at night it blazed with lights and echoed with singing and shouting. Inside the brothels were all sorts of high-ranking ladies, and outside them naked prostitutes postured lewdly at all who passed by. For as one observer wrote, the revelers would

> ...enter the brothels and without hindrance have intercourse with any
> of the women who were seated there, among whom were the most
> beautiful and distinguished in the city, both slaves and free, courtesans
> and virgins and married women; and these were not merely of the
> common people, but also of the very noblest families, both girls and

grown women. Every man had the privilege of enjoying whichever one he wished, as the women were not allowed to refuse anyone.

Consequently, indiscriminate rabble as the throng was, they not only drank greedily but also wantoned riotously. And now a slave would debauch his mistress in the presence of his master, and now a gladiator would debauch a girl of noble family before the eyes of her father. The pushing and fighting and general uproar that took place, both on the part of those who were actually going in and on the part of those who were standing round outside, were disgraceful. Many men met their death in these encounters, and many women, too, some of the latter being suffocated and some being seized and carried off.[2]

Nero himself showed that he was already corrupted by every type of lust. And just in case anyone at all had a lingering doubt, it would have been dispelled a few days later when the emperor went through a formal wedding ceremony with one of a gang of male perverts called Pythagoras. In the presence of witnesses, the emperor put on the bridal veil, gave a dowry, was married and performed in the nuptial bed with his new "mate" as the "wedding" party looked on.

· · · · · · · · ·

ROME'S REVELRIES came to an abrupt halt in July. For on the nineteenth day of that month, the entire city was swept up in a fire that raged for six days and proved to be the worst in its history. To this day you can see sooty scars on public buildings or go to Ostia and see the rotting piles of charred wood and rubble that were barged down from Rome to clear the way for new construction.

And to this day as well, you can always start an argument in a tavern by claiming either that Nero did or did not start the fire himself.

I will give you a sampling of both versions. One side argues that Nero coveted the lands around the Subura (in and about where the Amphitheater stands today) so that he could build a sprawling new "Golden House" on land big enough for a lake and gardens. So to begin what he might have termed this "municipal land clearance," he sent out agents who pretended to be roving rowdies, using their night torches to set fire to a few buildings each in several parts of the city. The people were soon at their wits end at not being able to find the cause of the fires. Those who ran to help friends in one section would have to run back because they learned their own homes were now burning. Soon there were reports that fire-fighting companies would not act unless paid outrageous fees. When the panicked home dwellers ran to the aqueducts with their own empty pails, they found only trickles and spurts of water because the homes of the rich had siphoned off so much of the flow. Then came the plundering of burning homes by soldiers and others who were supposedly sent to help.

And watching all this from a porch atop his palace on the Palatine — so the story goes — was the emperor himself. He was dressed in the Greek lyre player's garb and could be heard singing a song he had written himself entitled "The Capture of Troy."

The other version says that this is but fancy embroidery. Nero at the time had been visiting his ancestral home of Antium, some 25 miles to the southwest. The fire, they say, started in the Circus Maximus where it adjoins the Palatine and Cælian hills. It broke out in shops selling oil and other flammable goods. Fanned by a high wind, the conflagration quickly swept the whole length of the Circus. After rampaging over level spaces, it quickly climbed the hills and whirled through the public shrines and homes of the wealthy. Then it returned below, fanning itself through the narrow winding streets of the Subura and surrounding neighborhoods where it seemed almost to be chasing the helpless people as they fled screaming in its path.

Nero, says this version, happened to be returning from his ancestral home of Antium that night and actually reached the city just as the fire was beginning to engulf the Domus Transitoria, the mansion he had built to link the Palatine to the Gardens of Mæcenas on Esquiline Hill. He watched, strumming his lyre, as the flames ravaged the Palatine, including the family palaces of his Julio-Claudian ancestors.

Regardless of the cause or the intent, the fire had consumed all but four of Rome's 14 precincts by the time it spent itself. Three precincts were leveled to the ground. The calamity had no parallel since the destruction of Rome by the Gaul invasions, which had begun exactly on the same date 418 years before. Gone were most of Palatine Hill, the Theater of Taurus, most of the Circus Maximus. Gone were ancient temples and monuments: Servius Tullius' temple of the Moon, the temple vowed by Romulus to Jupiter the Stayer, Numa's sacred residence, Vesta's shrine of Roman household gods, the temples dedicated after the Gallic and Punic wars. But even these losses could not equal what was lost in so many homes of nobles: Greek artistic masterpieces, statues of ancestors and the authentic records of family genealogies.

The fire was so devastating that those who remained alive were said to worry more about whether the city itself would survive than about their own possessions. By the sixth day, some survivors were already camped out in temples and public monuments, where they clung to their few remaining possessions. Others hovered about the city walls or in fields on the outskirts. But Nero was not indifferent to them. He threw open the Field of Mars as well as his own gardens for relief of the homeless. Some of them were allowed to live in its public buildings and for others he built temporary accommodations. Food was brought from Ostia and the price of corn slashed sharply. Nero then began clearing housing sites at his own expense before turning them over to their owners. His engineers directed that rubble was to be collected and picked up by empty corn ships returning down the Tiber and dumped into the marshes around Ostia.

The fire caused some good because it prompted many meetings that led to improvements in city planning and regulations for better public safety. Once reconstruction began, it would be on streets that were made broader and straighter. Heights of houses were to be limited and each was to be equipped with firefighting equipment. All multi-family dwellings were to be built around courtyards and their frontages to be protected by colonnades. No two dwellings could have a common wall. Moreover, a fixed portion of every building had to be untimbered, fireproof stone. The public aqueducts were to be posted with guards to prevent illegal tapping for private uses. Despite steps such as these, Nero could not escape the gossip and derision of Romans that he had been directly responsible for the fire. The prominence and propriety given to the construction of his new Golden House was a daily reminder. Some half-joked that it was so large it would probably stretch all the way to the ancient Etruscan city of Veii some 12 miles outside the city walls. Thus, this graffiti about town:

> All Rome's become one house. To Veii fly,
> Unless it stretch to Veii, bye and bye.

One could also read this on walls:

> While Nero sweetly struck his lyre
> Apollo strung his bow.
> Our prince is now the god of fire,
> The other god our foe. [3]

Many priestly supplications were made to various gods and oracles to ascertain the cause or the divine reason behind the fire. The Sibylline books were consulted and prayers addressed to Vulcan, Ceres, Juno and other gods. Ritual banquets and cleansing rites were held. But nothing seemed to dull the enmity that people felt toward Nero. It was perhaps as long as a year after the fire that he tried to put an end to the persistent suspicions about his own motives. The emperor made it known that the real cause of the fire had been the mysterious Christians. He even referred to them as a "deadly superstition."

Why Christians? Why not blame it on a group of Egyptian astrologers or a gang of unemployed actors or even sabateurs from some hostile foreign power? The best answer is: why *not* Christians? They were a growing group and one that, like the Jews, remained apart from the rest of society. Their "secret" religious practices made outsiders uneasy and — as today — gave rise to rumors among the ignorant that they held orgies and practiced cannibalism in some secret ritual handed down by their founder that involved drinking blood and eating a body. This same strange "sect" was hated in some families because it had pitted husband against wife, son against father and slave against master.

After the fire had subsided, more than one Roman would swear he had heard a Christian leader preach of a coming day in which the world would be dissolved by flames. And — worst of all for the Christians — what a strange coincidence it was that the fire had spared all of Trastevere, which lies west of the Tiber, and much of the Aventine Hill, which lies just across from it. How interestesting that these were the very places that contained most of the Christian population! And how strange that when one walked these streets one could sense a marked indifference to the civil mourning that all other Romans were displaying at the loss of so many sacred temples and venerated shrines.

It isn't clear how many arrests were made at this time (for hundreds more would be held and tried in the next two years). But it was enough at the time to make the emperor's point. When hunting games were given in the theater, it was thought clever to dress Christians in the skins and make them quarry along with the wild animals. It was also at this time that Christians and other condemned persons were first used to dramatize scenes in stage tragedies. Thus, real "actors" were used when Hercules was burned on a mount or when Adonis was torn to pieces by wild boars or when Icarus was thrown down from the heavens.

The emperor himself seemed to enjoy being in the midst of it. The Circus Maximus was still too destroyed for public use, so Nero increasingly opened his own private circus and surrounding gardens that lay west of the Tiber some four miles from his palace on the Palatine. In both the circus and the gardens Nero reminded one and all who had started the fire. Christians were swabbed with pitch, fastened to poles, and made into human torches to help light the gardens at night or be displayed as exhibits in the circus. And in both cases, the emperor was often present, mingling with the crowd in the gardens or driving about the circus dressed as a charioteer.

But the spectacle soon sickened even the most hostile Roman. As one observer wrote: "Despite their guilt as Christians and the ruthless punishment it deserved, the victims were pitied. For it was felt they were being sacrificed to one man's brutality rather than to the national interest."

. . . .

WITH THE NEED TO REBUILD THE CAPITAL and showpiece of the world as quickly as possible (lest client states sense a weakness and rebel), the demand for money was intensified. With Nero also building the world's most ridiculously lavish palace at the same time, the demand for money became ravenous beyond even that of Caligula's final days. Now add to this one more project. For reasons known only to himself, Nero deemed it important at this time to order the digging of a 160-mile-long canal. The whole purpose seems to be that the emperor was weary of traveling by land from Rome to Neapolis and Misenum. Just north of Misenum, the naval port, was the popular Lake Avernus. Nero's plan called for the canal to Ostia to be wide enough to allow ships with five banks of oars to pass one another. To execute the project, Nero issued an edict that prisoners from all over the empire be transported to Italy. Even those convicted of capital crimes were to be spared so that they could serve until the canal was completed.

With all these wants and needs, one can easily see why the Roman world was now ransacked for funds. It began in Rome itself, where temples were emptied of their treasuries and the gold that had been dedicated for triumphs and vows. Provinces were ruined – the privileged and poor alike. Not only were the treasuries of foreign temples scoured, but their statues taken as well. Perhaps the most prominent among them, as I will later describe, was the enormously wealthy temple in Jerusalem.

So intense was the search for funds to rebuild Rome (and the imperial palace) that Nero was even eager to grasp at the claims made by a lunatic who somehow managed to worm his way into an imperial audience. Cæsellius Bassus, a Carthaginian, breathlessly told the emperor about the discovery on his property of a deep cave that contained masses of unworked bullion, enormous ingots just lying about like so many toppled columns. All these, he gushed, had been hidden there by the Phœnician Dido after she had fled from Troy and founded Carthage nearly 1,300 years before. She had stored the treasure there in case too much wealth would corrupt her young nation or prompt war by envious Numidian kings.

So wide-eyed (and desperate) was Nero that he didn't even pause long enough to send inspectors or verify the man's credentials. In fact, he even exaggerated the size of the hoard. Warships with the best rowers were commissioned to fetch it. Preparations were already underway for the second series of Neronian Games, and underlings crowed about the good fortune of their emperor in discovering a timely means of financing them. "Earth," they beamed, "is now producing not only her accustomed crops, not only gold mixed with other substances—she is teeming with a new kind of fertility!" Nero, in fact, didn't even wait for results. He began drawing on this certain largesse for free distributions to the people to commemorate the Games.

Soon the imperial "expeditionary force" landed at Carthage and began digging up the property of Bassus. They dug and dug with no sign of any gold. Then they decided to confront Bassus. Well, said Bassus, he hadn't actually seen the gold. He had seen it in a vision. But his interrogators needn't worry because he had had such visions before and they had all come true.

Needless to say, the demented Bassus did not live long enough to have another vision. But even though the state confiscated all of his property, it was small recompense for the cost of all those men and ships.

Now the search for real money became even more frantic. This, of course, brought about more forced suicides and confiscations of estates, but the law itself became more onerous as well. Nero, for instance, caused the Senate to amend the law that required one-half of a freedman's estate to go directly to the emperor. The amount now became five-sixths if the deceased bore the name of any family of which Nero was "connected" — a term that could be stretched to include almost any family. Yet it hardly mattered, for the same new law stipulated that in the case of a deceased who was "ungrateful" (did not bequeath the emperor five-sixths) his entire estate would go to the state treasury. There were penalties as well for any lawyer who had helped to write such a will.

Well, as with Caligula, it is only a matter of time before patient and patriotic people are moved to action by disgust and exasperation. It was in the winter of the second year of this period — some six months after the fire — that a plot to dispose of Nero began to coalesce. This one had so many participants ranging from nobles to Prætorians to women that I will simply accept Nero's own count of 51. They hated Nero, and their rallying point (although not the instigator) was Gaius Calpurnius Piso. His aristocratic Calpurnian house was honorably linked to many noble families and he himself had gained a great reputation for his eloquent defenses in court and his generosity to friends and strangers alike. That Piso was also somewhat superficial and ostentatious was rationalized as qualities that could serve him well as an emperor.

I will cite only a few of the conspirators to give you some indication of their diversity. The knight Antonius Natalis was a confidant of both Piso and Nero, making his position the most precarious of all. Lucan, the rising poet, hated Nero on a purely personal basis: the emperor had the gall to vie with Lucan in competitions, then forbid him to publish or perform again in public. Plautius Lateranus, a distinguished senator and consul-designate, had no personal quarrel with Nero: he simply hated the emperor and was willing to risk his life for patriotic reasons. In contrast, Quintianus was a notorious degenerate who wanted revenge for having been insulted by Nero in a poem. An indispensable conspirator was Fænius Rufus, the man who had been serving as co-commander of the Prætorian Guard with the hated Tigellinus. He was weary of being tormented by Tigellinus — especially the persistent allegation that he had been Agrippina's lover. And he had at least three tribunes who were willing to cast their lots with him.

Seneca, too, was listed among the plotters. But was he really one of them? It seems that Piso tried to contact the tutor-in-self-exile to enlist his help, but received only an oblique reply. But this, as we shall see, proved to be enough evidence for one who now coveted the properties Seneca had once tried so hard to relinquish.

Fortified by having the Prætorian commander in their cause, the discussion now turned to the location and timing of the deed. Fortunately, the Neronian Games were almost upon them and the emperor's beloved Circus Maximus was being restored in time to host them. Although Nero rarely left the seclusion of his palace and gardens at this time, he wouldn't miss a chance to attend the Circus and display himself in public.

The method would be this: the Senator Plautius Lateranus, a large and physically strong man, also known for living beyond his means, would prostrate himself before the seated emperor, ostensibly petitioning for financial assistance. Then he would suddenly grab Nero and pull him to the ground. In the same instant, the military men and a few other skilled swordsmen would rush in to dispatch the emperor. Piso, meanwhile, was to wait at the temple of Ceres, from which Fænius Rufus and his cohort of conspirators would take him to the Prætorian camp to be proclaimed emperor.

The secret was amazingly well kept considering the number of plotters. But it took only one crack in the wall to make it crumble. Flavius Scævinus, a senator, had stoutly insisted that he would be the most eager among those sworn to rush upon Nero with their swords drawn. As a silent reminder to his conspirators, he had taken to wearing an ancient dagger that had been stored in the temple of Safety (a family heirloom, he said). Then he returned home and began to act in a way that seemed peculiar to his freedman Milichus. First, he had his will amended. Next, he gave the blunt old dagger to Milichus and asked him to sharpen it. Then Scævinus gave a dinner party, quite more luxurious than usual, at which he freed his favorite slaves and gave others presents of money – all with what seemed like a strange air of superficial gaiety. Finally, before retiring, he asked Milichus to prepare him some bandages and styptics for wounds.

Who knows how the ex-slave reasoned as he did, but he tallied all these peculiarities in his mind and concluded that his master was up to something sinister against none other than the emperor. Perhaps with visions of rich rewards for his discovery, Milichus left at daybreak for the Servilian Gardens, where Nero was residing during the palace construction. After being denied access for many minutes, the anxious freedman finally was led to an ex-slave of Nero's to whom he displayed the dagger and told the story. Soon he was telling Nero himself.

That same morning Scævinus was arrested by soldiers and brought before the emperor. The senator remained composed. "The weapon you refer to is a venerated heirloom kept in my bedroom," he said coolly. "This ex-slave has stolen it. As to my will, I have often entered new clauses without particularly noting the date. I have often given slaves their freedom and gifts of money. In this case it may have seemed more generous than usual, but my creditors have been pressing me of late and I feared I might lose the slaves anyway. As for the last night's banquet, my table has always been generous, even though I acknowledge that it may seem too much so to those who would like me to lead a more austere life. Finally, I never ordered any bandages for wounds. This man's allegations are so unconvincing that he simply added this charge on his own."

Scævinus went on to describe the ex-slave as an infamous rascal. Milichus had been all but sunk by the senator's calm, confident manner when he remembered that Scævinus had spent a good deal of the previous day in intense, hushed conversation with Nero's good friend, the knight Natalis. What was that discussion all about?

So now Natalis was summoned. Both he and Scævinus were interrogated separately about their conversation. When their descriptions failed to coincide, both were put in chains.

The next step was to get at the truth through torture. But when Natalis was taken to the torture room and saw what lay in store for him, he broke down and became the accuser. He named Piso first, then — curiously — Seneca. Some say that Natalis had been Piso's go-between in his attempt to enlist Seneca. It is also possible that Natalis sought to conciliate Nero by naming someone he knew the emperor would want to destroy — both for his property and his seditious verse. In any case, it wasn't long before a dozen or more conspirators had been rounded up and broken down.

By now Nero was wild with fear, still unsure of how many his assailants numbered. That same day his personal guard was redoubled and all Rome was virtually put in custody, with armed soldiers patrolling the city walls and stationed along public squares. At the same time, line after line of chained men were marched to Nero's gardens to face fierce interrogation by the emperor and the ever-present Tigellinus. Curiously, no one had yet implicated Fænius Rufus, the Guard commander; so to insulate himself, I suppose, he became one of the harshest interrogators. In fact, at one point when Nero was boring in on an accused suspect, one of the tribunes who had been in on the plot fixed his gaze on Fænius and made a sign as if to ask whether he should draw his sword and kill Nero on the spot. Fænius walked over and stared the officer down just as his hand was moving to the hilt.

At about the same time, Piso, still at his home and uncaptured, was urged by his closest supporters to go to the Guard's camp and test the attitude of the troops — or mount the platform in the Forum and try the civilians. "If your fellow conspirators rally around you, outsiders will follow," they argued. "Otherwise, you, too will be put in chains and go to a degrading death. How much finer to die for the good of your country, calling for men to defend its freedom!"

But Piso remained unconvinced. That same day he shut himself in his house and screwed up his courage, waiting for the Guardsmen. Nero, suspicious that the older soldiers would favor a man of such stature, selected a cohort of new recruits to hasten to Piso's home. But by the time they got there, Piso had opened his veins and died. He had also loaded his will with repulsive flattery of Nero because he loved his wife and hoped it would earn her clemency.

Next on Nero's list was the consul-designate Plautius Lateranus. So swift was his removal that he was not even allowed to embrace his children. Hurried off to the place reserved for slave's executions, he was dispatched by one of the Guard colonels who had been his co-conspirator just the day before. But he died with his lips sealed.

I will spare you the gory and monotonous parade of those who followed – except for one, Lucius Annæus Seneca. One account has it that Nero so ardently wanted the death of his tutor and minister that he had actually bribed one of Seneca's servants to poison him. But Seneca had thwarted all such efforts by seeing no visitors and existing on dried fruit and water from a stream. This, in fact, could verify the testimony now given by Nero's accused friend Natalis. He said that he had been sent to visit Seneca and complain because the philosopher had refused to receive Piso on grounds of having a "muscular" ailment that confined him. Seneca had added, said Natalis, that a conversation with Piso would benefit neither, but that his own welfare depended on Piso's.

Seneca couldn't have been too ill, because on this day he had been traveling from Campania and had just arrived at one of his villas, some four miles from Rome. Towards the evening, as Seneca and his wife Paulina dined with two guests, a colonel of the Guard arrived and surrounded the villa with troops. The tribune said he had come to ask a question on behalf of the emperor. Would Seneca admit, as Natalis had claimed, that he had spoken words to the effect that his welfare was linked to that of Piso?

Answered Seneca: "Natalis was sent to me to protest, on Piso's behalf, because I would not let him visit me. I excused myself on grounds of health and love of quiet. I could have had no reason to value any private person's welfare above my own. Nor am I a flatterer. Nero knows this exceptionally well. He has had more frankness than servility from Seneca."

The officer returned to Rome and reported these words to Nero, who was flanked by Poppæa and Tigellinus. Asked if Seneca was preparing for suicide, the officer said he saw no signs of it – nor any fear or sadness in Seneca's words. So now he was ordered to return and notify Seneca of the death sentence.

Unknown to both parties was that Gavius Silvanus, the tribune sent to Seneca's home, had been one of the conspirators. Instead of returning directly to the villa the way he had come, he led his men on a detour that took him to the Prætorian headquarters. There he sought out his commander and supposed ally, Fænius Rufus, and asked if he should obey the emperor's orders.

"Obey," said the stony Fænius.

It was now late at night when the soldiers returned. Silvanus, unable to face Seneca himself, sent a junior staff officer inside to announce what must be done. Appearing unperturbed, Seneca asked if he could retrieve his will. The officer refused. Seneca turned to his friends. "Being forbidden to show my gratitude for your friendship," he said, "I leave you my one remaining possession, and my best: the pattern of my life. If you remember it, your devoted friendship will be rewarded by a reputation for virtuous accomplishments."

When his friends began to weep, Seneca checked their tears and sought to revive their courage. Where had their philosophy gone? he asked. Where was their resolution against impending misfortunes which they had devised over so many years? Were they really unaware that Nero was cruel? After murdering his mother and brother, it only remained for him to kill his teacher, Seneca added with the obvious intent that his words be reported back.

With that Seneca embraced his wife very tenderly, all the while entreating her to set a limit on her time of mourning and to take consolation in contemplating his well-spent life.

But Paulina insisted on dying with her husband, and she turned to the officer, asking for the executioner's stroke. Seneca, to my own surprise if no one else's, said he would not oppose her brave decision. "Solace in life was what I commended to you," he said, "but if you prefer death and glory, I will not begrudge your setting so fine an example. We can die with equal fortitude, but yours will be the nobler end."

With that the two went to their bedroom. With one incision of the blade on each, Seneca and Paulina cut their arms and lay down to die.

Before long it became evident that Seneca's aged body, so lean from austere living, was releasing the blood too slowly. So he severed the veins in his ankles and behind his knees. Now exhausted and wracked with pain, he was afraid of weakening his wife's quiet resolve by betraying his agony or losing his composure at the sight of her own suffering. So he asked her to go to another bedroom.

Still, Seneca's death was slow and lingering. He called in some secretaries, made sure they had made plans to protect his library from Nero, then painfully dictated a dissertation. By this time his physician, also an old friend, had arrived, and Seneca asked him for a poison such as is used to execute state criminals in Athens. But even after drinking it, it had no effect, because his limbs were already cold and numbed to its action. Finally, he was placed in a bath of warm water, where he drank some more and playfully sprinkled some of it on his slaves, saying that this was his "libation to Jupiter." When even this failed, he was carried into a vapor bath, where he suffocated.

I do not know what the dissertation was that Seneca dictated in his final moments, but it would have been suitable enough had it been the passage I found in one of the last of his published Epistles:

It is not the number of days that makes a life long, but the full employment of them upon the main end and purpose of life, which is the perfecting of the mind, in making a man the absolute master of himself. I reckon the matter of age among external things. The main point is to live and die with honor. Every man that lives is upon the way and must go through his journey without stopping until he comes to the end. And wheresoever it ends, if it end well, it is a perfect life... Take away from life the power of death and it is a slavery.[4]

As Seneca breathed his last, his slaves were already struggling to bind up his wife's wounds. Nero, it seems, had given orders to avert Paulina's suicide to avoid increasing his reputation for wanton cruelty. Much is confusion here, because I cannot believe that once Paulina opened her veins, the officer would have traveled four miles back and forth to ask what the emperor thought about it. One can only assume that the junior officer neglected to tell his superior outside the villa what she had done until some time later. Or perhaps servants took it upon themselves to rescue the comatose Paulina once her husband removed himself from the room. In any event, several anxious servants bandaged her arms and managed to stop the bleeding. Paulina lived on for a few years, honorably loyal to her husband's memory. But she retained a pallid countenance that reflected her inability to recover fully from all the blood she had lost.

Now Nero's insatiable need for money was matched by reckless revenge. Rather than relate each killing ad nauseum, I will present you with an assortment so that you can see the character of the charges and the lack thereof in the man who brought them.

I cite Junius Torquatus, a distant descendant of Augustus, for the remarkably unique logic of the charges against him. Because Torquatus had squandered his wealth foolishly, it followed that he must be covetous of the goods of others, so the prosecution charged. And if he was covetous, this must surely imperil the one who possessed the greatest wealth of all.

Then came those who were in Seneca's orbit. Annæus Junius Gallio (the same proconsul who had heard Paul's case in Corinth), was denounced as a public enemy because he was Seneca's brother. The poet Lucan was doubly unfortunate because his prose irritated the emperor and because his father, Annæus Mela, was another brother of Seneca's from Cordova. Now, at the tender age of 26, Lucan was forced to open his veins. When he felt the loss of blood numbing his feet and hands, the young poet recited some verses he had written about a dying soldier. His epitaph (did he write it?) read:

> Cordova bore me, Nero slew. My lyre
> The duel sang of son-in-law and sire.

Not mine the long-drawn period's delays
Of crawling verses, mine the short sharp phrase.
If thou wouldst shine, dart with the lightning's flight:
A style is striking only if it smite.[5]

I will close the circle on the conspiracy by reporting that it was not the lot of the Prætorian Fænius Rufus to remain unscathed. For weeks, conspirators had withstood his blistering courtroom accusations in silence, I suppose, because they may have feared that his Guards had the power to prolong their torture or menace their families. But it was finally Scævinus, Nero's prize catch, who could not restrain himself. During his trial, when Fænius pressed him for details of the plot, Scævinus sneered and retorted hotly that the commander himself shouldn't have to ask because he already knew more about the plot than anyone. Words failed Fænius for a fatal few seconds. And as he stammered in obvious terror, Nero ordered the largest soldier in the court to seize Fænius and bind him.

When Fænius was exposed, so were the tribunes who had cast their lot with him. They went meekly, except for a tough colonel named Subrius Flavus, who not only admitted his guilt but said he gloried in it. When pressed by Nero as to why he would violate his oath to protect the emperor, his exact words were these: "Because I detested you. I was as loyal as any of your soldiers as long as you deserved affection. I began detesting you when you murdered your mother and wife and became an actor, charioteer and incendiary!" Except for Seneca, perhaps, Nero had never been spoken to in this way, and the words were a shock to his ears.

As the next summer approached, Rome was still a junkyard of charred, skeletal buildings, stacks of bricks and roof tiles piled beside rebuilding sites, families making do in public parks full of makeshift tents and a nobility wracked by purges, taxes and corruption. On top of this, the fire had been followed by a full-blown plague that struck down people of all classes. No miasma was discernible in the air or water, yet houses were full of corpses, the streets clogged with never ending funeral processions and the skyline broken by spires of black smoke curling up from burning pyres.

But somehow the city managed to assume a festive mask for visitors as the second of the five-yearly Neronian Games opened. Knowing that the emperor was now determined to appear on stage anywhere he chose, the Senate politely tried to avoid scandal by offering him, in advance, the first prize for song and a special crown for his "eloquence" (even though it wasn't an official category of competition). But Nero declared there was no need for favoritism. He would compete on equal terms and rely on the conscience of the judges to award him his just due.

First, he recited a poem on stage. But when the crowd shouted that he should display "all his accomplishments" (their exact words), Nero made a second appearance as a lyre player, throughout which he was the soul of propriety. So that he would not lose points from the judges, he used only his robe to wipe away perspiration while performing. He allowed no moisture from his mouth or nose to be visible. At the conclusion, he awaited the judges' verdict on bended knee and with a gesture of humility to the audience. As he knelt, the theater crowd cheered in measured, rhythmical cadences. The emperor may have been a national disgrace to the Senate (and to visitors from foreign lands), but the Roman rabble seemed to love the show they were getting. When those who weren't familiar with the clapping technique broke the desired rhythm, many were cuffed by the Guardsmen who roamed the theater aisles.

It was not long after the Games that Nero's wife died. Poppæa was said to have prayed often that she might die before she passed her prime, and Nero accommodated her – albeit unintentionally. Poppæa was pregnant, and it seems that one night her husband came home drunk and probably foul-tempered. Soon afterward he either kicked his wife in the stomach or jumped on it. Since he had always professed to love his wife, everyone took his disconsolation as sincere. Rather than having Poppæa cremated in the Roman fashion, Nero had her body stuffed with spices and embalmed in the manner of foreign potentates. Then she was placed in the Mausoleum of Augustus where her widower could visit her.

Nero missed Poppæa so greatly after her death that upon learning of a woman who resembled her, he sent for her and kept her in his household.

. . . .

WHAT OF THE ROMAN CHRISTIANS at this time? Just how many were arrested after the fire and how many died in Nero's gardens? Did Christians continue to meet in their house churches? Did they continue coming to Paul? Did Paul comfort the flock and confront the authorities?

The information available today about these two years is sparse and subject to varied versions. Now if you are a Christian in, say, Corinth or Antioch, the lack of precise details about events just over 15 years ago must seem incredible and maybe irritating as well. But it is quite understandable to a Christian living in Rome, as I will try to explain.

The Great Fire was devastating beyond anything that great cities like Corinth or Antioch ever experienced in their long histories. Thousands died in the blaze itself and thousands more perished in the plague that followed. Jails and dungeons were no less afflicted, and records of prisoners and trials went up in flames in no less proportion than sacred scrolls in temples. The fact that predominently Christian neighborhoods were among the least touched does not mean that some Christians did not suffer loss of life and property. Moreover, Christians were made to suffer an especially inhumane persecution directed only at them.

But even those who escaped that hideous display now lived amidst a wave of trea-son trials that followed the "Piso conspiracy." It had everyone in Rome cowering under a cloud of suspicion as informers cupped their ears to even the most inno-cent of conversations in hopes it would yield them a percentage of some victim's estate. Those who were snared by this madness were jailed and/or sent off as slaves to construct the 160-mile canal that would allow a delusional monarch to be rowed from Rome to Misenum rather than brought by carriage. Is it then any wonder that most Christians had either vanished in the chaos or wished to be-have as though they had? I mean this literally, because this is when many Chris-tians started frequenting the catacombs, that growing labyrinth of tunnels that were being bored through the travertine rock on the city's southern outskirts.

Still, I have not even mentioned the most devastating turn of events for Christians. Until the Great Fire, they were little understood by the authorities and simply regarded as a sect of Judaism. This meant that they were one of the *religiones licitæ* and thus to be officially tolerated. When Nero singled out Chris-tians as the sole cause of the fire, Christians by fiat became a *religione illicitæ* – one of the few superstitions or cults banned by the state for its seditious or sinister practices. Officially, Christians were to be as loathed as, say, the Celtic Druids, with their witches and gory human sacrifices. Legally, it meant that Paul, for ex-ample, could no longer defend himself by proving that he had broken no Roman laws. Now, an advocate need only prove to a prætor that the defendant was a Christian and that was proof enough of guilt.

I do hasten to add, however, that no official decree (to my knowledge) went out declaring Christianity *religione illicitæ*; but the stigma was nearly the same. If the governor of a province happened to despise Christians, he would have little trouble in depriving them of life and property, just as the police in a Roman precinct might be easily prevailed upon to arrest a Christian on some com-plaint of his neighbors.

One might compare the practical applications of *religione illicitæ* to the edict Nero issued in the same year that taverns must limit their food service to veg-etables. Well, as one knows, you can find sausage-flavored mushrooms at this place or even whole plates of viands at the next one down the road – and you'll even see prætors and quæstors downing them heartily. But if some tavern poi-sons a few wealthy patrons with rancid meat, you'll see the authorities sudden-ly hauling shopkeepers to court in droves. The law is there if they want to use it.

Paul continued to exist amidst this peril and confusion. I can find no one who says that he perished in the fire or the plague that followed. Some say that he was acquitted of his charges – or was simply released after being confined for two years without trial – and went on to visit the churches in Asia or Achaia. Perhaps so, but the story believed by Christians in Rome is that Paul remained here for all or most of the time following his first arrival from Melita.

This view would seem to be supported by a letter that Paul wrote to Timothy who was probably at his home in Derbe at the time. For the first time in any of Paul's letters from Rome, this one is filled with the grim air of approaching finality. "At my first defense, no one took my part," he writes. "But the Lord stood by me and gave me the strength to proclaim the word fully, that all the Gentiles might hear it. So I was rescued from the lion's mouth."

But now the others had gone: Demas having forsaken him for "the present world" and gone back to Thessalonica, but others like Crescens, Titus and Tychicus because Paul himself sent them back to the churches on various missions. Only Luke remains with him. And now, he tells Timothy,

> ...I am already on the point of being sacrificed. The time of my departure has come. I have fought the good fight. I have finished the race. I have kept the faith. Henceforth there is laid up for me a crown of righteousness, which the Lord, the righteous judge, will award to me on that day — and not only to me but also to all who have loved his appearing.[6]

Paul devotes most of the letter to expressing his love for Timothy, whom he regards as a son, and to the need for holding steadfast to the mission being entrusted to him.

> You then, my son, be strong in the grace that is in Christ Jesus. And what you have heard from me before many witnesses, entrust to faithful men who will be able to teach others also. Take your share of suffering as a good soldier of Jesus Christ.[7]

Paul exhorts Timothy not to become entangled in "stupid, senseless controversies" over points of theology because "it will lead people into more and more ungodliness, and their talk will eat its way like gangrene." Finally, he urges Timothy to learn from the suffering that Paul himself endured during their times together in places like Antioch, Iconium and Lystra, "yet from which the Lord rescued me." Indeed, he adds,

> ...all who desire to live a godly life in Christ Jesus will be persecuted, while evil men and impostors will go on from bad to worse, deceivers and deceived. But as for you, continue in what you have learned and have firmly believed, knowing from whom you learned it and how from childhood you have been acquainted with the sacred writings which are able to instruct you for salvation through faith in Christ Jesus.

...I charge you in the presence of God and Christ Jesus who is to judge
the living and the dead, and by his appearing and his kingdom: preach
the word; be urgent in season and out of season. Convince, rebuke and
exhort. Be unfailing in patience and in teaching. For the time is coming when people will not endure sound teaching, but having itching
ears they will accumulate for themselves teachers who suit their own
likings, and will turn away from listening to the truth and wander
into myths. As for you, always be steady. Endure suffering. Do the
work of an evangelist. Fulfill your ministry.[8]

Again, the tradition and the letter to Timothy indicate that Paul continued to
live under custody in Rome during this two-year period. Had he been condemned and in jail, conditions would have been so severe that having access to
a transcriber like Luke, or even his own writing instruments, would be very unlikely. Rather, I would guess that Paul's reference to having endured a "first defense" may have been a preliminary hearing – perhaps a perfunctory proceeding so that the prætor's office could say that Paul's case had been heard more or
less within the two-year limit on holding an accused without trial. But the fact
that Paul was not acquitted is obvious by his continued confinement in fetters.
And the likelihood that he did not expect imminent resolution of his fate is indicated by the fact that he ends the letter by asking Timothy to come to Rome
"soon" and bring him some books and parchments he had left behind on his
earlier travels.

No, Paul did not die in the first persecutions after the fire. To be dispatched so
quickly was probably the lot of slaves and foreigners. Because Paul was a Roman
citizen, and because his case was already lodged somewhere in the bureaucracy,
his life was prolonged by the confusion and delay that followed the fire.

At some point during this time, the apostle Peter arrived in Rome. As I stated
before, it may be that he had visited the city before. But this time he was resolved to stay and to stand by the Christians of Rome in their hour of need. He
would not deny Jesus this time, even if it cost him his life.

. . . .

COMPARED TO THE NEW PROCURATOR of Judea, who arrived at the beginning of
this period, the corrupt Albinus had been "a most excellent man," the Jews
would joke ruefully. For while the latter made his bargains with thieves in private, Gessius Florus acted in a pompous manner. "It was as though he had been
sent as an executioner to punish condemned malefactors," the historian Josephus wrote. "Nor could any one outdo him in disguising the truth, nor con-
trive more subtle ways of deceit." Whereas Albinus had ruined individual men,

Florus despoiled whole cities and ruined entire toparchies to the extent that a great many Jews of prominence now fled their own country and took up residence in foreign lands.

During all this, Cestius Gallus, now the governor of Syria, never saw fit to send an embassy to investigate the claims of Florus' cruelty. In fact, when Cestius came down to the Passover in the second April of this period and stayed in Herod's palace, an enormous throng flocked into the public square outside and implored the governor to grant them relief from the miseries brought on them by Florus. But as the two Romans stood side by side at the portico above, Florus could be seen laughing as Cestius pointed out something in the crowd as if enjoying a private joke. When Cestius finally quieted the throng below, he assured them jovially that he would see to it that Florus treated them "in a more gentle manner." The next day he set off for Antioch.

Everyone assumed that Florus would mend many of his ways for fear that a delegation would be sent to Cæsar accusing him. But Florus must have reasoned in a different way. If he could incite a rebellion among the Jews and bring in Roman troops to smother it, his own evil deeds would be overlooked in the process.

Yet another episode in Cæsarea can serve to illustrate the manipulative mind of Florus. At about the time he began to reside there, the city's Hellenistic population had at long last gotten the upper hand over their Jewish neighbors. They accomplished this, not by battle, but simply by successfully petitioning the emperor to be allowed to take over control of the municipal government.

As you can imagine, this did nothing to quiet the tensions that existed between the two contentious cultures of Cæsarea, and all it took was a small flame to set passions ablazing again. The kindling was one of the major synagogues in town, which happened to adjoin an empty plot owned by a Greek. The Jewish congregation was already crowded and wanted to expand their facilities. They had already offered the landowner many times the property's fair value, but he, in what could only be a deliberate affront to the Jews, began erecting some stores and workshops on the land. As the walls began to go up, it was obvious that the Greek owner had designed them capriciously. Such a narrow passage — or what was practically an alleyway — was left between the shops and the synagogue that the large Jewish congregation would scarcely be able to elbow their way to and from the main entrance.

In a few days a group of incensed young Jews served notice they were going to tear down the project. But when Florus got wind of it and threatened them against using force, the synagogue elders stepped in to avoid trouble. With an offer of eight talents, they persuaded the procurator to halt the work. But Florus, once accepting the money, left for a trip to Sebaste, which was about eight miles away. He hadn't "stopped" the project, he said. He merely meant that the Jews were free to try whatever solution they wanted while he was gone.

On the next Sabbath as the first of the Jewish worshippers wound through the ugly, narrow passageway that now constituted the only path to their synagogue, they encountered a Greek Cæsarean on the portico outside the main door. The Greek was hunched over an earthen pot that he had placed upside down before the doorway. On this makeshift "altar" he was butchering a small bird. The Jews quickly recognized this as the sacrificial rite for cleansing a leper — meaning by this sign that the Jews were a leprous people and should be quarantined.

As usual, the young men among the Jews wanted to tear the Hellene to shreds as well as any other Greek who showed his face. The older men struggled to restrain them. As you can imagine, the Greek prankster had several friends hiding nearby, waiting for the Jews to strike the first blow. Hearing angry shouts and not being able to see what was happening to their friend, the gang of young Greeks burst out of hiding and once again, clubs and fists were flailing in all directions. When a small group of Roman soldiers tried to break up the melee, they were simply swallowed up in it.

When the Jewish elders realized that no imemdiate end was in sight and that the synagogue itself was now threatened, they grabbed the Torah and other sacred books from the Ark inside and fled to the outskirts of the city. After sequestering the books in another building not far from Sebaste, they continued on to that city in a desperate search for Florus. Finally locating him as the guest in the home of a prominent citizen, the Jews found themselves in the company of a man not happy to be suddenly aroused from his leisure. However, the desperate elders pressed their case. Couldn't his excellency do something to punish the mischievous Greeks for polluting their meeting house? Especially in light of the eight talents they had already given him?

But Florus responded only with more cruel contempt. He cut off the pleas of the elders and ordered them arrested on charges of violating Roman law by taking the sacred books out of Cæsarea without official permission.

Such was the justice of Florus. Later, as he turned his attentions to a far greater source of ill gain — the temple treasury in Jerusalem — he would touch off an uprising that did not stop until the entire Jewish nation had spent its people and wealth in a frenzied, suicidal struggle to disgorge the Roman oppressor.

. . . .

A. D.   6 6

As the year began, the emperor would re-mark that he, at long last, was beginning to feel as though he were being "housed as a human being." His new palace, now called "The Golden House," had, by hav-ing first priority on all men and materials during the post-fire restoration, reached a state of completion sufficient to occupy the imperial court.

It was never to be fully furnished during Nero's lifetime, but he could already claim that it was the largest dwelling ever built. Nor did any one "home" ever occupy so much land within a large city. Within the roughly 300 acres that Nero had appropriated for himself out of the fire-ravaged north and central section of the city were grounds containing a lake surrounded by miniature buildings representing various cities. Situated about this centerpiece were a mixture of woods, tilled fields, pastures and vineyards, through which roamed great num-bers of wild and domestic animals.

Also roaming through this tract was the Golden House itself, whose triple colonnades stretched over a mile. One entered in a vestibule high enough to contain a colossal statue of the emperor 120 feet high. In the rest of the house, all surfaces were overlain with gold and adorned with jewels and mother-of-pearl. Some dining rooms had ceilings of ivory whose individual panels could be opened so that pipes could send out sprays of perfume or showers of flower petals on the guests below. The main banquet hall was circular and constantly revolved day and night like the heavens. The baths supplied both sea water and sulfur water.

Fortunately, Rome now had at least one showplace at a time when the streets were otherwise a jumble of piled up roof tiles and half-restored temples. This was important, because the imperial court had already known for a few months that the Parthian Tiridates, younger brother of King Vologeses, was headed for Rome with a royal entourage to pay Nero the obeisance that conditioned his return to the throne of Armenia. Could the capital of the civilized world expect to provide anything less than a splendorous reception to the brother of the second most powerful monarch in the empire?

· · · · · · · · ·

IN JUDEA, THE PROCURATOR FLORUS continued to behave so scandalously, so outrageously against the Jews that one can only conclude that he was acting on the clear instructions of Nero and/or his financial advisors. I would surmise that Florus was trying to goad the Jews into "forcing" him to pillage Rome's last and largest source of ready funds — the temple treasury in Jerusalem. In any event, Florus did indeed march his troops to Jerusalem early in the year and announce that he had been sent by Cæsar to remove 17 talents of its sacred treasure. Before long, Jews from all walks of life were running towards the temple from every direction, beseeching Florus to desist. The more spirited among them openly spat curses at the procurator. A few sneering young men carried a large basket about, sarcastically begging the people for coins so that Florus might be sated and go away. But all this did was cause the procurator to close himself inside Herod's palace while he sent to Cæsarea for more reinforcements.

The next day Florus brought out his tribunal chair and sat upon it, ordering all the high priests and men of power to come before him. First, he asked them to round up the "criminals" who had taunted him the day before and either punish them or bring the men to him for judgment. The Jewish leaders insisted that the populace was peacefully disposed. They begged forgiveness for any youths who had spoken rashly in the heat of the moment.

Now Florus was more provoked than ever. Suddenly he turned to his soldiers and ordered them to plunder the Upper Marketplace and slay anyone who opposed them. To the greedy soldiers, this command meant not only plundering merchant stalls, but barging into houses and killing their inhabitants. Women and children were butchered in their bedrooms and kitchens. Beggars and old people were cut down in the streets. Others were dragged before Florus, who had some flogged and some even crucified. When the bloody day was over, it is estimated than Florus and his men had slaughtered more than 3,600 men, women and children. Now this was hardly the first time Romans had killed unarmed civilians, but never before had men of the equestrian order — by birth Jews, but also men of Roman dignity — been whipped and nailed to crosses as well.

Florus' cruelty is further confirmed by the fact that all this had happened under the eyes of Bernice, the Jewish queen. Herod Agrippa had gone to

Alexandria to congratulate the prefect Alexander on having been appointed by Nero. Bernice had gone to Jerusalem from their home in Cæsarea Philippi to fulfill a vow she had made to God (for deliverance from some illness) and was in another part of the enormous palace watching in horror as Florus' men began their butchery. At once she went to Florus with her guards and horsemen. There, barefoot and with shaven head, as required for her vow of prayer, she begged Florus to cease, but he showed absolutely no deference to her nobility. In fact it is said that the rampaging soldiers would have killed the queen as well had she not fled back inside the palace walls, where she spent the night surrounded by her guards.

The next morning families of the dead were out in the Upper Marketplace bewailing their losses. But others were shouting against Florus and were beginning to amass in strength when the leading priests and elders rushed to them. They rent their garments and fell down before the angry mob, begging them to leave off lest they provoke Florus into something even more savage. Eventually the crowd quieted down and complied out of deference to their elders.

But now it was Florus who was troubled. He was actually hoping for another outburst and it hadn't come. Now he would have to find another pretext for violence. His reinforcements had already departed Cæsarea for Jerusalem. So he again sent for the leading Jews. When they again assured him of no further trouble, Florus answered that the only way to persuade Rome that there would be no further demonstrations was to go out beyond the city walls and meet the soldiers who were ascending the hills from Cæsarea. They should give the men a salute of friendship and plead their case for clemency.

The elders began assembling the multitude to explain to them what must be done. While they were doing so, the procurator sent a dispatch by horseman ordering the centurions of his cohorts not to return the salute of the Jews when they appeared. Further, if the Jews should say anything disadvantageous to Florus, the soldiers were to attack them all.

The leading priests, of course, had told the people to salute the Romans very civilly when they encountered them on the road. And because some of the more rebellious young men still insisted that any such signs of servility were worthless, the temple leaders had every available priest bring out the holy vessels and ornamental garments that they used for sacred rites. Accompanying them were the harpers and singers of hymns with their various instruments. As all of the priests fell down before the large crowd that was about to depart the gates, the high priests, still in their rented garments, begged them not to say anything that would cause the Romans to carry off these sacred treasures. "For if you salute them civilly," they said, "all reason will be cut off from Florus to begin a war. Thus, you will gain [back] your country and freedom from all other sufferings."

But what happened next was just as Florus had planned. The Jews waited quietly for the soldiers as they approached outside the city gates. They saluted politely. The centurions and their soldiers gave no response. A few of the young and seditious muttered oaths against Florus. The soldiers, awaiting such words as their signal, took out their clubs and were soon bludgeoning everyone in their path. Then they galloped after all those who fled, chopping at people and trampling them as they ran toward the city gates for protection. As the huge crowd struggled to get inside the narrow gates to escape the terror of hooves and clubs, they themselves trampled one another to death – some so badly that it is said they could not even be distinguished by their families who came to carry them off to funerals.

This was just what Florus wanted, because now, with the crowd overrun by soldiers at one end of the city, he rushed out of Herod's palace with his small guard and headed for the Fortress of Antonia. From there he could presumably gain access to the temple, which adjoined it by a common wall. But hundreds of people were standing on their rooftops overlooking the scene and quickly realized his intent. They hurled stones and darts on the procurator and his guard, forcing them to retreat back into the palace. Meanwhile, a large number of young men climbed to the temple cloisters and knocked them down so that the Romans could no longer use the Fortress to gain access to the temple and its treasury.

Florus was thwarted for the time being, so he called the Sanhedrin before him the next morning and exacted their pledge to undertake no more sedition. Then he departed for Cæsarea, leaving the Jewish leaders with a band of soldiers to protect them should any part of the citizenry decide to rebel. But the procurator was no sooner in Cæsarea than he sent the governor Cestius a letter accusing the Jews of revolting against Rome.

By this time the Jewish leaders knew Florus well enough to anticipate just such an attempt, so they sent their own letter to Cestius defending their case. Queen Bernice wrote as well with the same accusations.

Cestius, after reading both accounts, decided that before taking any action he should send his own representative to Jerusalem to make his own investigation. The man picked was a tribune named Neopolitanus. It so happened that King Herod Agrippa was returning by ship from his trip to Alexandria, so Neopolitanus arranged to meet him at the port city of Jamnia and make the trip into Jerusalem together.

Agrippa had received letters, too, but he was of a mind to disbelieve the worst of the claims against Florus and dissuade the people from avenging themselves. Indeed, when the Jewish leaders welcomed the king and Neopolitanus on the road as a sign of respect, they didn't argue when Agrippa reminded them of all the possessions they would lose if they breached the peace with Rome. But as they approached the city walls, people spotted the royal party and began to flock outside with tears and lamentations. They begged for the king's help. They cried out to Neapolitanus of the miseries they had suffered at the hands of Florus. When the two men came inside the city, they soon saw the devastation of the Upper Marketplace and the plundered houses. And they extracted a promise from Neopolitanus that he would walk around the city, accompanied by a single servant, to see for himself what had taken place. They were loyal to the Romans, they said, with the sole exception of the barbaric Florus. And Neopolitanus, after calling the multitude together at the temple, earnestly exhorted them to keep the peace.

Once the tribune had departed for Antioch to make his report, the people asked King Agrippa for permission to send ambassadors to Nero against Florus. If they remained silent, they said, they could expect to be accused of being the instigators of war. But with Parthia now on friendly terms, Agrippa saw Rome as already all too willing to risk an all-out war with the Jews. Gathering a crowd into a large gallery of the temple, he delivered a long, impassioned speech imploring them to acknowledge the undeniable superiority of Rome and do their best to live within the present system. This appeal, he said, was being made because "some are earnest to go to war because they are young and without experience of the miseries it brings, and because some are for it out of unreasonable expectation of regaining their liberty, or...because they think they may gain what belongs to those who are too weak to resist them."

Agrippa told the young rebels that they could still retain their present viewpoint after he had finished speaking. Yet he felt an obligation to point out flaws in their reasoning. For:

> ...If you aim at avenging yourselves on those that have done you injury, why do you pretend this to be a war for recovering your liberty? And if you think all servitude intolerable, to what purpose are you making a complaint [against Florus] to your governors? For if they treated you in moderation, it would still be an unworthy thing to be in servitude.

> Consider now the several cases that may be supposed, how little occasion there is for your going to war. Your first occasion is the accusations you have to make against your procurators. Nor here you ought to be submissive to those in authority and not give them any provocation; but when you reproach men greatly for small offenses, you excite those whom you reproach to be your adversaries; for this will only make them leave off hurting you privately...and to lay what you have waste openly. Now nothing so much damps the force of strokes as

bearing them with patience; and the quietness of those who are injured diverts the injurious persons from afflicting.[9]

But even assuming that Roman administrators are injurious to you, Agrippa said, it is still not *all* Romans who are responsible. It is not Cæsar who has caused the injury, for a person in the west cannot see what happens in the east. So it is absurd to make war with a great many for the sake of one person. "Nay, such crimes as we complain of may soon be corrected, for the same procurator will not continue forever."

As for waging war to recover one's liberty, said the king, "you ought to have labored more earnestly in the old days that you might never have lost it," At that time, a struggle for freedom might have been just. But now, "the slave that has once been brought into subjugation and then runs away is rather a refractory slave than a lover of liberty."

Agrippa then dwelt on the impossibility of a successful insurrection. The Greeks who had beaten back the Persians, their Parthian successors with their vast lands to the east, the venerable Egyptians with all their kingly dynasties, the mighty Macedonians, whose armies Alexander had led conquering even to India, the wild and fierce Britons, all had fallen under the disciplined armies of Rome and all were now content to live under Roman law. "Has not your army even been beaten by neighboring nations?" the king asked the subdued crowd. "Are not the Illyrians, who inhabit a country stretching to Dalmatia and the Danube, governed by barely two legions?" And look at the Gauls, he said.

Need he speak more of Roman power, asked Agrippa, when the mighty Parthians to the east are on the verge of sending hostages to Italy to proclaim their allegiance to Nero? "When almost all people under the sun submit to the Romans, will you be the only people who make war against them?"

Finally, the king struck at the soul of the rebellion.

What remains, therefore, is this, that you have recourse to Divine assistance. But this is already on the side of the Romans. For it is impossible that so vast an empire should be settled without God's providence.

Reflect upon it: how impossible it is for your zealous observations of your religious customs to be here preserved, which are hard to be observed even when you fight with those whom you are able to conquer. How can you then most of all hope for God's assistance, when forced to transgress his law, you will make him turn his face from you?

And if you do observe the custom of the Sabbath day and cannot do anything thereon, you will easily be taken, as were your forefathers by

Pompey, who was busiest in his siege on those [Sabbath] days in which the Jews rested.

Then Agrippa delivered this final appeal:

> Now all men that go to war do it either as depending on Divine or human assistance. But since your going to war will cut off both those assistances, those who are for going to war choose evident destruction. What hinders you from slaying your children and wives with your own hands and burning this most excellent native city of yours?[10]

For going to war, he added, will force the Romans to:

> use you as an example to other nations, burn your holy city and utterly destroy your whole nation. For those of you who shall survive the war will not be able to find a place whither to flee, since all men have Romans for their lords already or are afraid they will soon after. Indeed, the danger concerns not just those Jews who dwell here, but those of them who dwell in other cities. For there is no people upon the habitable earth which have not some portion of you among them whom your enemies will slay. And so, every city which has Jews will be filled with slaughter for the sake of a few men, and they who slay them will be pardoned. So consider how wicked a thing it is to take up arms against those who are so kind to you. Have pity, if not on your own children and wives, then upon this metropolis and its sacred walls. Spare the temple and preserve this holy house with this holy furniture for yourselves. For if the Romans get you under their power, they will no longer abstain from them...[11]

By the time the king had finished his long appeal, both he and his sister were in tears, and many of the people as well. Most still cried out that while they would not fight against Rome, they would continue to demand justice from Florus. But Agrippa reminded them that they had already declared war on Rome in the sense that they had not paid the tribute the procurator had demanded. They had also demolished the temple cloisters where they had joined the Fortress of Antonia—a union more symbolic than just two buildings.

The king's words were not lost. Immediately the people began rebuilding the temple cloisters. At the same time, members of the Sanhedrin sent out into the surrounding cities and painstakingly collected 40 talents of tribute to Rome. Agrippa oversaw the appointment of a delegation of Jewish leaders to take the money to Florus; then he and Bernice departed for their home in Cæsarea Philippi.

Sedition, however, managed to seep to the surface like boiling lava through a fissure. In one instance, some of the boldest Sicarii headed for Masada, the steep fortress some 40 miles to the south that Herod the Great had carved from an Idumean mountaintop. Using their stealth and surprise at night, they overcame the small Roman garrison there and killed them all.

Meanwhile, within Jerusalem, the upper hand was gotten by Eleazar, son of the high priest Ananias – the same Eleazar who had been kidnapped and ransomed by the Sicarii at Passover time a few years before. Having since become governor of the temple and in charge of its daily administration, he suddenly declared that the temple priests were no longer to receive sacrifices for Cæsar or any other foreigners.

The leading priests and citizens begged the seditionists not to reject the sacrifices of foreigners. They called one more mass meeting, held in the temple Court of the Priests. There they argued that the temple had been built mainly by the sacrifices and contributions of foreign nations. Whether it be Cæsar or any foreign individual, such an act would only invite enmity and the eventual destruction of Judea itself.

But not one of the "innovators," as they were called, would listen. And all around them one could see preparations being made for war.

The point of no return had come at last.

. . . .

IN ADDITION TO HIS INSATIABLE NEED FOR MONEY, Nero had one chief ambition. He wanted to take an artist's sojourn to Greece and to stay as long as he wished without having to worry about trouble at home or abroad. Achieving the latter meant pacifying the Parthians on his eastern front. The former meant employing the worst traditions of Tiberius and Caligula to methodically destroy all persons, families, factions or philosophies that might possibly challenge, or perhaps even inconvenience, the freedmen who would govern in his absence.

And so, once more Rome became an alleyway of fear as informers scurried about like rats after the backdoor dumpings of tavern keepers. And in the frenzy, many great Romans – senators, scholars, generals – were denied the chance to give their lives in public service, but were instead needlessly sacrificed in hopes of warding off the fears of a single man. Others have listed their names elsewhere and to do so here would only produce a sickening monotony. Instead, I will cite the cases of the only two men among all these victims who dared defy the emperor's terrible power – and how even they could not succeed at it.

The first, Gaius Petronius Arbiter, was the epitome of the charming gadabout who seems to show up at all the right parties, then occupy center stage even

though the host can't remember inviting him. Out of all this came his entertaining book, *The Satyricon,* which was about (what else?) a charming but aimless
young traveler who managed to be entertained in some of Italy's finest estates.
Eventually, Petronius succeeded at his craft so well that he was admitted into
the small circle of Nero's intimates (which at one point gained him the governorship of Bithynia and a consulship). His unofficial title in court was "Arbiter
of Taste," meaning that no food or fashion was truly in vogue unless Petronius
declared it so.

Well, all this attention made for a jealous rival in the ever-watchful Tigellinus. Before long the Prætorian commander was reminding Nero that Petronius had been a fast friend of Flavius Scævinus, the late senator whose ex-slave
had first revealed the conspiracy of Calpurnius Piso. Various slaves were bribed
to support the story that Petronius had been part of the plot (the number had
since widened considerably from the original 51 instigators).

At the time, both Nero and Petronius happened to be staying in Campania
but at different villas. When Petronius received the arrest notice, he didn't even
consider the possibility of a trial. He severed his own veins. Then, as friends
came to call, he bound the vessels up again and engaged them in conversation –
never about weighty philosophy, always about a frivolous poem or the latest
gossip. Petronius then appeared at dinner, imbibing and chatting. In the course
of it he dozed off into death so naturally that his guests assumed for quite
awhile that he had simply had a bit too much to drink.

What made Petronius such a different victim was that, having no family, he
could afford to leave a will that neither left his possessions to the emperor nor
flattered him. Indeed, this one offered a detailed list of Nero's vices. Each male
and female bedfellow was named, along with their favorite debaucheries. Then
copies were made and dispatched to friends for their amusement.

But the power of an emperor reaches even into the grave. When the astonished Nero read the will, he wondered who had filled Petronius with such a
complete census of lust and lewdity. This led him to Silia, a senator's wife and
imperial playmate who apparently knew all of Nero's obscenities from personal
experience. She was also a personal friend of Petronius. Silia was exiled, but that
wasn't enough. Tigellinus arranged for the ex-slave of a prætor to testify that
his patron had taken part in the "listing." And so the prætor forfeited his life
without being able to summon Petronius to testify that it was all a posthumous
prank gone wrong.

Next, I offer a man who better embodied all those of noble spirit and great
achievement who were so wantonly sacrificed. You have already read of
Clodius Thrasea Pætus, who on so many occasions stood alone in upholding
ancient Senate traditions by standing up to Nero. Thrasea, as you will recall,
once walked out of the Senate when it was voting to praise the emperor for ex-

tinguishing the "threat" posed by his mother, Agrippina. The elderly patrician later gave equal offense by refusing to join other nobles in parading about the stage, even though he had once sung in a Greek tragedy presented in his native city. When Poppæa died, Thrasea had deliberately stayed away from the funeral, where divine honors were voted her.

Indeed, Thrasea had gained a reputation as the conscience of all Rome. But in the past three years he had demonstrated his feelings towards the emperor simply by staying away from the Senate altogether. And although a member of the Board of Fifteen for Religious Ceremonies, he absented himself from taking the new year vows and sacrificing for the emperor's welfare.

Thrasea was an obvious target for any informer who wanted to build a case, and eventually one came along who had a personal grudge against Thrasea as well. Cossutianus Capito hadn't forgotten the time when he was tax collector for Cilicia and a local delegation came to Rome to ask that he be tried for extortion. Thrasea had helped their case. Now Capito was eager to make a case that Thrasea's absences from public life constituted a crime against the state. "It is no less than succession," he charged. "If many more have the same impudence, it is the same as war." Addressing the emperor's empty chair in the Senate, Capito continued:

As this faction-loving country once talked of [Julius] Cæsar versus Cato, so now, Nero, it talks of you versus Thrasea. And he has his followers – or his courtiers, rather. They do not yet imitate his treasonable voting. But they copy his grim and gloomy manner and expression. They rebuke your amusements. He is the one man to whom your safety is immaterial, your talents unadmired. He dislikes the emperor to be happy. But even your unhappiness, your bereavements, do not appease him. Disbelief in Poppæa's divinity shows the same spirit as refusing allegiance to the acts of the divine Augustus and the divine Julius. Thrasea rejects religion, abrogates law.

In every province and army the official Gazette is read with special care – to see what Thrasea has refused to do. If his principles are better, let us adopt them. Otherwise, let us deprive these revolutionaries of their chief and champion.[12]

All this took place just before the long-awaited arrival of the Parthian Tiridates to receive the diadem of Armenia from Nero. When the emperor let it be known that Thrasea's presence at the gala ceremonies would be forbidden, the senator wrote to Nero asking the nature of the charges against him and insisting that he would clear himself if given an opportunity. Nero, hoping that

Thrasea would make a humiliating apology that would diminish his stature, announced that the Senate would convene in a few days to discuss his case.

When Thrasea consulted friends on whether he should attempt to defend himself, the advice was mixed. "We know you will stand firm," some said. "Everything you say will only enhance your renown. Nero might be miraculously moved. But if his brutality persists, at least posterity will distinguish a whole end from the silent, spiritless deaths we have been seeing."

Other friends urged Thrasea to wait at home, forecasting only jeers and insults if he attended the Senate. Some, they added, might even attempt physical violence, and fear makes even decent men follow their lead. "To make Nero ashamed of his misdeeds is a vain hope," another said. "Much more real is the danger of his cruelty to your wife and daughter and other dear ones."

One of those present, a young man who was serving as tribune of the people, proposed to veto any condemnation decree by the Senate, but Thrasea would have none of it. "My time is finished," he said. "I must not abandon my long-standing, unremitting way of life. But you are just starting your official career. Your future is uncompromised, so you must consider carefully beforehand what political cause you intend to adopt in such times."

The next morning, the approach to the Senate house was guarded by Prætorians in civil clothes, displaying their swords. Troops were arrayed around in the principal forums and law courts. And it was under menacing glares that senators entered the building.

The emperor was present, but a quæstor read his opening address because Nero had a case of flu and couldn't risk harming his singing voice. Without mentioning any names, he rebuked "members" for neglecting their official duties and setting a slovenly example for the knights. No wonder, he said, that senators from distant provinces stayed away when many ex-consuls and priests in Rome showed greater devotion to the embellishment of their gardens.

With that the accusers took over. Senators, they said, had allowed themselves to be ridiculed with impunity. Said one: "I insist that a former consul should attend the Senate, that a priest take the national vows and that a citizen swear the oath of allegiance. Or has Thrasea renounced our ancestral customs and rites in favor of open treachery and hostility?"

Well, it went on and on in this vein. When it was over Thrasea had been condemned as well as two other senators and various relatives. The two chief accusers received 5 million sesterces each while a third received 1,200,000 — all to be paid from estates of the condemned. It was a scenario to which senators had long since grown numb and even perhaps indifferent. All they knew was that their feelings became as acute as the prick of a knife point when they saw the Guardsmen with their hands on the hilts of their weapons.

That evening the consuls sent their quæstor to Thrasea's home. They found him in his garden in the company of several distinguished men and women. Thrasea himself was conversing calmly with a Cynic professor, and one could overhear them discussing the nature of the soul and the dichotomy of the spirit and body. When the Senate's decision was announced formally, shouts of protests split the calm night air and people began weeping. But Thrasea urged everyone to leave rapidly and avoid the perils of association with a doomed man. His wife, Arria, swore she would share his fate, but Thrasea persuaded her that she must remain alive as the only source of support for their daughter.

Thrasea walked to the colonnade where the quæstor joined him. Actually, Thrasea smiled broadly when the quæstor told him that his politically active son-in-law had been banned from Italy. The senator had assumed that the young man would be executed for his affiliation. Then Thrasea went into his bedroom, opened his veins and sprinkled some of his blood on the ground. "This is a libation to Jupiter the Liberator," he said, calling to the quæstor. "Look, young man! For you have been born into an age when examples of fortitude may be a useful support!"

. . . .

ROME PUT ON A HAPPY FACE for Tiridates. The Parthian, of course, had taken pains to assure that his arrival would look anything like a vassal come to pay respects to his patron. Since crossing the Euphrates, the Armenian king-to-be, in the fullness of youthful strength and countenance, had proceeded across the Roman empire with a retinue that seemed to contain half of Parthia's royalty and possessions. Three thousand horsemen followed him and an equal number to handle the royal baggage. Cities were gaily decorated and the people jammed the rooftops to watch the party pass through, the handsome Tiridates on horseback and his wife wearing a golden helmet that shielded her face according to Parthian custom. Whatever they wanted was theirs. Nor were they in any hurry: the Roman Senate had already agreed to pay 800,000 sesterces from the public treasury for each day the Parthians traveled.

After several months the procession wound down through northern Italy and came to Neapolis where Nero met them. On first approaching the emperor, Tiridates compromised on the question of whether he would first give up the dagger at his hip: he had it nailed shut in the scabbard. Yet he knelt on the ground and with arms crossed called Nero master and did obeisance.

Nero took an instant liking to the king, who was probably about his own age. During the first days they relaxed at Puteoli, where Nero gave a costly gladiatorial exhibition in which Tiridates was said to have impressed his hosts by shooting arrows from his elevated seat and killing two wild bulls. Soon afterwards the party went up to Rome, which had been decorated with lights and garlands, where Nero would crown Tiridates with the royal diadem of Armenia.

Scarcely had dawn arrived on the ceremonial day when the Forum was already so crowded that one could not even see the rooftops for the people sitting on them. First to enter was Nero. Wearing triumphal dress and accompanied by the Senate and Prætorian Guard, he ascended the temporary open air rostra and seated himself on a chair of state. Next, Tiridates and his retinue passed between lines of heavily armed Roman troops drawn up on either side. The Parthian stood at the base of the rostra and did obeisance to the emperor as he had done in Neapolis.

As he did so, such a great roar went up that Tiridates stood in what seemed like numb terror, not knowing if his life were at stake. But quickly recovering, he faced Nero and said (as I myself watched from a perch atop the Tabularium): "Master, I am the descendant of Arsaces, brother of the kings of Vologeses and Pacorus, and thy slave. And I have come to thee, my god, to worship thee as I do Mithras. The destiny thou spinnest for me shall be mine, for thou art my fortune and my fate."

Replied Nero: "Well hast thou done to come hither in person, that meeting me face to face thou mightest enjoy my grace. For what neither thy father left thee nor thy brothers gave and preserved for thee, this I do grant thee, that both thou and they may understand that I have power to take away kingdoms and bestow them."

With that the emperor beckoned the Parthian to ascend the rostra and sit beneath his feet. Then he placed the diadem upon his head – again evoking a tremendous shout.

The large imperial party then proceeded to the theater where entertainments now became the order of the day. The entire interior of the theater had been gilded, as had all the surrounding statuary. Overhead, the curtains that kept out the sun showed an embroidered figure of Nero driving a chariot, with golden stars gleaming all about him.

Next came a lavish banquet at which Nero publicly sang to the lyre. Later he drove a chariot, clad in the costume of the Green Team and wearing a charioteer's helmet. These displays, however, surprised and disgusted Tiridates. At one point he turned to general Corbulo at his side and asked how he could put up with such a master.

Yet, by keeping quiet and playing the role of the dutiful client king, Tiridates left Rome with more than its own governors could amass during a lifetime in the provinces. His gifts alone were said to be worth over 200 million sesterces. He also received permission to rebuild the torn capital of Artaxata (to be called Neronia) and prevailed on the emperor to assign him many of Rome's most prized artisans to do so. Nero did all this, I am convinced, because he wanted a stable peace on his eastern borders so that he could undertake his life-long dream of sojourning in Greece without worry. Even if the already unpredictable, fractious denizens of Syria tore themselves to pieces, at least Parthia would not be running in to take advantage of it.

. . . .

IF LIFE WAS DIFFICULT for independent-minded senators, it was impossible for anyone else who brought new religions or philosophies to the capital city at this time. But Apollonius seemed oblivious to all such concerns. After traversing Attica and the Peloponnesus, he had gone to Crete and decided that from there he would like to visit Rome. During this sojourn Apollonius had acquired a retinue of 34 students who seemed determined to follow him anywhere.

But as they were still a few miles from the city walls, the travelers learned two pieces of disturbing news. The first was that Musonius of Babylon, a philosopher known as second only to Apollonius, had been languishing near death in a Roman prison for no other crime than being a sage. The second alarm they heard personally when the group encountered the Roman philosopher, a polished orator whom Apollonius had known by reputation. This man was already in retreat from his home city and pled fervently with the travelers not to proceed further. Indeed, the whole time he addressed the group Philolaus kept looking over his shoulder as if someone were watching. "A whole band of philosophers won't even get past the sentries Nero has watching the gates," he warned in a half-whisper.

"And what of Nero these days, O Philolaus?" asked Apollonius cheerfully.

The philosopher rolled his eyes. "He drives a chariot in public. And he comes forward on the boards of Roman theaters and sings songs. He lives with gladiators and himself fights as one."

"Well, then," replied Apollonius with a smile, "do you think that there can be any better spectacle for men of education than to see an emperor thus demeaning himself? For if in Plato's opinion man is the sport of gods, what a theme we have here provided for philosophers by an emperor who makes himself the sport of man and sets himself to delight the common herd with the spectacle of his own shame?"

"Yes, by Zeus – if you could do it safely," said Philolaus. "But if you are going to be taken up and lose your life, and if Nero is going to devour you alive before you see anything of what he does, your visit will cost you more dearly than it ever cost Ulysses to visit the Cyclops in his home. He lost many of his comrades because they yielded to the temptation of beholding so cruel a monster."

Apollonius could feel the nervous whispers of the students around him. "So you think this ruler is less blinded than the Cyclops if he commits such crimes?"

"Let him do what he likes," was Philolaus' answer. "But you should at least save your companions."

He said these last words in a loud voice and with tears in his eyes. And Damis, the oldest among the followers, took Apollonius aside and warned that the younger men of his party were showing signs of being unnerved by the terrors Philolaus had described.

But Apollonius' face lit up with a beaming smile and he answered Damis boldly: "Of all the blessings given to me by the gods – often without my praying for them at all – this one is the greatest that I have ever enjoyed. For chance has thrown my way a touchstone to test these young men as to which of them are philosophers and which prefer some other line of conduct."

His assessment proved accurate. By the day's end the knock-kneed among them began reporting to Apollonius that they were ill or had run out of provisions for the journey or that they were homesick or had been deterred by prophetic dreams. The result was that the band was soon reduced from 34 to eight.

Now the sage assembled those who were left and said to them: "I shall not scold those who have abandoned us, but I shall rather praise you for being men like myself. I shall not think a man a coward because he has disappeared for dread of Nero. But anyone who rises superior to such fear I will hail as a philosopher, and I will teach him all I know. I think we ought first to pray to the gods who have suggested these different courses to you and to them. And then we ought to solicit their direction and guidance, for we have not any succor to rely upon apart from the gods. We must then march forward to the city which is the mistress of so much of the inhabited world, But how can anybody go forward unless the gods are leading them? The more so because a tyranny has been established in this city, so harsh and cruel that it does not profit men to be wise."

Yet, that was not a reason to halt in their tracks, he said. "Let not anyone think it foolish to venture along a path from which many philosophers are fleeing, for I don't esteem any human agency so formidable that any wise man can be terrified of it. Secondly, I would not urge you upon the pursuit of bravery unless it were attended by danger."

Apollonius was beginning to steady and embolden the youths he addressed. Now he shared with them his own strengths. "I have traversed more of the earth than any man has yet visited," he reminded them. "I have seen hosts of Arabian and Indian wild beasts. But as to this wild beast, which many call a tyrant, I know not how many heads he has, nor whether he has crooked talons and jagged teeth. In any case, whereas you can sometimes tame and alter the character of wild animals that inhabit the mountains and forests, this one is only roused to greater cruelty than before by those who stroke him so that he devours all alike. In any case, there is no animal that devours its own mother, yet Nero is gorged by his quarry."

But Nero was not to be feared, Apollonius reassured his charges. If anyone forsakes philosophy because it is not safe to thwart the emperor's evil temper, "let him know that the quality of inspiring fear really belongs to those who are devoted to temperance and wisdom, because they are sure of divine succor."

With that, the philosopher's companion Damis records that the students reminded themselves of Homer: that when warriors are knit together by reason, they become as it were a single plume and helmet and a single shield. "For it seems to me that this very sentiment found its application in regard to these heroes," he wrote. "For they were welded together and encouraged by the words of Apollonius to die in behalf of their philosophy, and...to show themselves superior to those who had run away."

The band of nine men approached the gates of Rome. The sentries scrutinized their dress but asked no questions, perhaps thinking them beggars rather than philosophers. The group put up at an inn not far from the gates and were taking supper when they were approached by a tipsy fellow who announced himself as an entertainer. Indeed, it seems that he had been somehow commissioned by the emperor himself – or said he was – to go around to the taverns singing Nero's songs. He said he had the right to arrest anyone who refused to pay him for his music.

Well, the besotted bard seemed convincing enough. He carried a harp which he said he had bought from Nero himself for two minas and which he would not sell to anyone who was not fit to contend for the prize at Delphi. He proceeded to perform a short hymn composed by Nero, then proceeded to drawl out the rondos that Nero habitually murdered by his writhings and modulations.

The travelers were clearly indifferent to the performance, which soon had the piqued performer accusing them of being enemies of Nero's divine voice and majesty. But the philosophers held fast, politely dismissing the man with a few coins.

The group went to bed and thought no more of the drunken fool. But he must have been part of the network of petty informers, because it wasn't long before daybreak that they had a visit from no less than Telesinus, one of Rome's two consuls for the year.

"What is the dress you wear?" he asked Apollonius politely.

"A pure garment made from no dead matter," was the answer.

"And what is your wisdom?"

"An inspiration that teaches men how to pray and sacrifice to the gods," replied Apollonius.

"And is there anyone, my philosopher, who does not know this already?"

"Many," said the sage. "If there is here and there a man who understands these matters, he will be very much improved by hearing from a man wiser than himself, who, what he knows, he knows for certainty."

Now Telesinus was a man disposed to the study of worship and religion, and he suddenly realized he was talking to a man he had known only by reputation. Since Apollonius had not volunteered his name, the consul didn't ask for it because he was the first to understand the fearful conditions that existed in Rome. So he continued the conversation about religion.

"What do you pray for when you reach the altars?" he asked.

"For my part," replied Apollonius, "I pray that justice may prevail, that the laws may not be broken, that the wise may continue to be poor, but that others may be rich as long as they are so without fraud."

"When you ask for so much, do you think that you will receive it?" asked Telesinus.

"Yes, by Zeus," said the philosopher, "because I string together all my petitions in a single prayer. It goes like this: 'O ye gods, bestow on me whatever is due. If therefore I am of the number of worthy men, I shall obtain more than I have asked. But if the gods shall rank me among the wicked, then they will send me the opposite of what I ask, And I shall not blame the gods, because for my demerit I am judged worthy of evil.'"

Telesinus was so struck by the words of Apollonius that he granted him permission to visit all the temples of Rome. "And their priests will receive written instructions from me to adopt the reforms you suggest," he said.

"And had you not written?" Apollonius wondered aloud. "Would they not admit me?"

"No, by Zeus," said the consul, "for that is my office and prerogative."

"I am glad that so generous a man holds such a high office," Apollonius replied, "but I would like you to know one thing about me. I like to live in such temples as are not too closely shut up, and none of the gods object to my presence, for they invite me to share their habitation."

"I wish that as much could be said of us Romans," Telesinus said, taking his leave.

So Apollonius lived in the temples of Rome, changing his place of residence often. And when he was criticized for doing so, he retorted that "Neither do the gods live all their time in heaven, but take journeys to places like Ethiopia and Olympus and Athos. So I think it a pity that while gods go roaming among the nations, men should not be able to visit all gods alike. After all, though masters incur no reproaches for neglecting slaves, slaves who do not devote themselves wholly to their masters would be destroyed by them as cursed wretches."

In time, Apollonius held many discourses about religion as he taught in the temples. His conversations weren't opposed because he held them in public and addressed himself to all men alike. If they included some of the high and mighty, so be it – he had not sought their favor. In contrast, another philosopher, a man named Demetrius whom Apollonius had known in Corinth, came to Rome and began lashing out against Nero. He exercised a particular zeal in going to the gymnasium of Nero and haranguing the senators and knights who bathed there, declaring that they enfeebled and polluted themselves. One day he appeared there when Nero was singing in the tavern that adjoined the gymnasium, naked except for a girdle around the waist. Fortunately, Nero was in good voice that day and good-naturedly overlooked the harangue taking place in the adjoining gymnasium. But the ever-present Tigellinus, who had been given the power of life and death, had Demetrius snatched up and hauled out of Rome on threat of death if he ever returned.

By this time Tigellinus had become aware of Apollonius and planted informers during his discussions in hopes he might trap the other philosopher in similarly dangerous rhetoric. But Apollonius mystified his predator. He showed no disposition to ridicule the government. Nor did he display any of the anxiety usually shown by those who are on guard against some danger. He continued to discuss topics of philosophy in simple terms, and prominent men like Telesinus attended his discussions with no fear even though the study of philosophy had been determined a perilous exercise.

The Prætorian commander's spies were present during one such discussion when there came an eclipse of the sun followed by an unusual clap of thunder. At that point Apollonius looked heavenward and said to the assembled: "There shall be some great event and there shall not be." Three days after the eclipse Nero had been at an outdoor dinner party when a lightning bolt split his table in two. He was spared, and Tigellinus became in awe of Apollonius' prophesy. Soon afterward the city was afflicted with another of its many flu epidemics – one that left the emperor hoarse and unable to sing. This sent many to the temples asking the pardon of the gods for so afflicting them. But Apollonius was overheard by agents of Tigellinus making a remark to the effect that the gods could be forgiven if the disease they had brought had silenced the voice of a buffoon.

This was enough for the Prætorian commander. Apollonius was arrested and charged with impiety against the emperor. An accuser – an advocate – was hired to press charges. The lawyer began by striding back and forth in the courtroom, brandishing a scroll like a sword, declaring that inside were enough provable charges to doom the stranger in the white linen robe. It so happened that during a brief recess when the advocate had left the room, Tigellinus unfurled the scroll and found it completely blank. Now I suspect that the busy lawyer had been through so many such trials against low-ranking enemies of the state that he found preparation a needless formality. But to Tigellinus this was but further evidence that Apollonius possessed demonic powers. He had cast a spell that erased all the evidence! With that the Prætorian cut short the trial and took his intended victim into a secret proceeding reserved for more serious cases.

First, Tigellinus ordered everyone else to leave the room. Then he plied Apollonius with questions. The philosopher patiently supplied such facts as his name, his country of origin and how he sought wisdom in order to gain knowledge of the gods and human affairs.

"And what about demons?" asked Tigellinus. "And the apparitions of specters? How, O Apollonius, do you exorcise them?"

"In the same way as I should murderers and impious men," was the answer aimed at the cruel Tigellinus himself.

Indeed, I suspect that Tigellinus was haunted by his role of executioner or perhaps felt his own life at peril from his unpredictable patron. He bore in with questions about the will of the gods and the fate of men. "Could you prophesy if I asked you to?" he asked.

"How can I, being no prophet?" Apollonius responded.

"And yet," said the other, "they say it is you who predicted that some great event would come to pass and not come to pass."

"Quite so," said the sage. "But you must not put this down to any prophetic gift, but rather than to the wisdom which God reveals to wise men."

"Why are you not afraid of Nero?" the emperor's gatekeeper asked bluntly.

"Because the same God who allows him to seem formidable has also granted me to feel no fear."

"And what do you think about Nero?" asked Tigellinus.

"Much better than you do," he replied. "For you think it is dignified for him to sing, but I think it is dignified for him to keep silent."

Tigellinus remained silent for a long time. His puzzlement showed. "You may go," he said at last, "but you must give sureties for your person."

Answered Apollonius: "And who can give surety for a body that no one can bind?"

Tigellinus was now convinced that this was a wit above that of ordinary men – maybe even a god in disguise. "You may go wherever you choose," he said at last, "for you are too powerful to be controlled by me."

Apollonius continued to teach in the temples, but his compatriot Musonius, who lay confined in the dungeons of Nero, was much on his mind. Apollonius, using two of his students as go-betweens, sent a note to the prison. "I would fain come to you, to share your conversations and lodgings, in the hope of being some use to you," he wrote, "unless you are disinclined to believe that Hercules once released Theseus from hell. Write what you would like me to do."

Musonius sent back the following: "For your solicitude on my behalf, I shall never do anything but commend you. But he who has strength of mind to defend himself and has proved that he has done no wrong, is a true man."

Replied Apollonius in another letter: "Socrates of Athens, because he refused to be released by his own friends, went before the tribunal and was put to death."

Then, finally, this from Musonius: "Socrates was put to death because he would not take the trouble to defend himself. But I will defend myself. Farewell."

It was now September and Nero was ready to depart for Greece. But just before leaving he issued a proclamation that no one could teach philosophy in public within the walls of Rome. So Apollonius and his band of eight set off for Spain and the furthest western extremities of the empire. As Damis noted: "He wanted to see the famed pillars of Hercules and behold the ebb and flow of the ocean."

. . . .

WHEN NERO EMBARKED ON HIS GRAND TOUR of Greece, as it was called, Tigellinus was at his side. Left in complete charge of Rome was the freedman Helius, whose orders were to eradicate any sign of trouble with no less cruelty and finality than his master would have displayed in person. As one writer put it:

> Thus the Roman empire was at that time a slave to two emperors at once, Nero and Helius. And I am unable to say which was the worse. The only point of difference was that the descendant of Augustus was emulating lyre players and tragedians, whereas the ex-slave of Claudius was emulating the Cæsars.[13]

All this was required so that the mind of the emperor would be free from distractions as he concentrated on establishing himself as the greatest artist and athlete in all history. Anyone with lingering doubts had only the imperial retinue to observe for himself. Their sheer numbers were large enough to conquer a nation, but instead of weapons they carried lyres and plectra, masks and buskins.

Once away from Rome, Nero dressed more as he thought a Greek and a performing artist should be seen. Now he let his hair grow long and hang down his neck. But in front his blond hair was arranged in tiers of curls. By day he might be seen in a short, flowered, ungirdled tunic adorned with a muslin neck-cloth. Dinner often saw him wearing the kind of bright-colored silk gown that a man would sport in Rome only during the Saturnalia or some equally frivolous occasion.

Because Nero also knew the Greeks to be more "reasonable" about sexual practices than the suffocating patricians of Rome, he was eager to oblige on that front as well. Wherever he went, his "Sabina" was now at his side. Sabina, as most Romans know, was an adolescent boy by the name of Sporus who caught Nero's eye because he resembled the late, lamented Poppæa Sabina, whom the emperor had managed to kill by kicking her in the stomach while pregnant. Because he looked so much like her, Sporus or Sabina – take your choice – was made into a eunuch. Once taken to Greece, Sporus (the name I will use from here on) was brought into the light of day, traveling with his own entourage and wardrobe wagons. Not long after their arrival Nero and Sporos were solemnly married in a lavish ceremony in which the bride was given away by Tigellinus. Greek cities everywhere held celebrations to mark the marriage, uttering prayers for the union that even included one that healthy children might be born to them. From then on Nero had two constant bedfellows at once: the pervert Pythagoras, whom he had "married" during the Neronian games, and Sporos, now addressed as "queen" or "Lady Sporus."

One couldn't, of course, avoid imperial business altogether. Upon arrival in Corinth, Nero was eager to demonstrate his power to the Greeks and put them in a good mood besides. The vehicle he chose was a formal ceremony announcing that he would cut a canal through the Isthmus of Corinth to improve travel between the Ionian and Ægean seas by eliminating the need to sail around Cape Malea. At a signal from a trumpet, the emperor himself was the first to break ground with a mattock and carry off a basket of earth on his shoulders. (But after the loss of who knows how many slave lives, the work was stopped in a year or so after advancing no more than four stadia. Nero ordered the halt after some men of science showed him that the force of onrushing waters from the two seas would obliterate the island of Ægina.)

When crushing all possible resistance could not be achieved from Rome, Nero did so while on tour. His greatest fears outside the orbit of Rome were the power of three formidable generals. The first two were brothers, Scribonius Rufus and Scribonius Proculus, who commanded Upper and Lower Germany respectively and represented a powerful portion of the total Roman military strength. Both received messages ordering them to commit suicide, and both otherwise fearsome combatants obliged without so much as a peep.

Then came the turn of the great Corbulo, who had enjoyed powers second to Pompey in subduing the Parthians on the eastern front. Corbulo's situation was more intricate because his son-in-law Vinicianus had been implicated in plotting a revolt in central Italy in early summer. In any event, Corbulo was commanded to report to Nero's party in Greece. I would surmise that he thought he was again going to be put in charge of the Syrian legions in order to quash the spreading Jewish rebellion. Instead, upon arriving he was ordered to take his own life.

"I deserved it!" are the words Corbulo first exclaimed, according to those present. Left unexplained is whether he meant it literally because of having supported his son-in law or because he was angry with himself for coming unarmed to Nero when he could have led the armies of the East to Greece and destroyed the unarmed emperor with ease.

Now Nero's best generals were gone. And in Judea he needed one.

. . . .

ALTHOUGH ROME RETAINED an outward semblance of order after Nero departed for Greece, the soul of Jerusalem was as rent as if it had been the veil that hung before the Holy of Holies. In July, when Eleazar and his young Zealot rebels turned a deaf ear to the impassioned plea by King Agrippa, the temple elders and city fathers decided that they had no choice but to ask for help in preserving the temple – and themselves. They sent ambassadors both to Florus and Agrippa, asking them to send armies quickly so as to save the city before it was too late.

The upshot was only more chaos and misery. Florus gave no answer at all, being content to wait for the Jews to dissolve themselves in internal warfare. Agrippa, however, quickly dispatched 3,000 horsemen. They arrived just as Eleazar and his men were in the process of seizing the upper city and temple. Now, buttressed by the king's soldiers, the priests and townspeople fought back and after seven days of furious hand-to-hand fighting, they regained the upper city.

At this point a Jewish tradition again turned the tide for the Zealots. It was now late July, which marked the Festival of Xylophory in which everyone in the city brings wood for the temple altar so that its fire can continue unextinguished. Eleazar and his men made sure that only unarmed pilgrims entered the broad temple courtyard. But the surrounding upper city became its usual confused jumble of people at festival time, and the seditionists were quick to take advantage of it. As the first day wore on, several Sicarii, or secret daggermen, had slipped into the surging crowds in the upper city. Soon many of the king's soldiers and leading citizens had been stabbed to death. In the confusion and hubbub, ordinary people fled for their lives and seditionists stormed in behind them to regain control of the upper city. Within an hour flames were shooting from the house of the high priest Ananias and the palace of Herod and Bernice. The marauders next invaded the place where archives and commercial records were deposited; and as debtors cheered, they burned hundreds of deeds and contracts. Some of the priests and recordkeepers who had not been able to flee now scurried below and hid themselves in the palace vaults. Others shut themselves up in the upper palace.

The seditionists stopped for the day. But the very next morning they began an assault on the adjacent Fortress of Antonia. After two days they had captured and killed most of the Roman garrison that Florus had left behind. Having set the citadel on fire, the rebels next marched on the upper palace, where Agrippa's soldiers were sequestered. For many days the rebels tried to assault the palace, but were repulsed from the turrets and breastworks above by the defenders.

The rebels had grown resigned to waiting and starving out the defenders when a new development changed the struggle. As so often happens, the original leader of a revolt finds his position usurped by a bolder, more radical rival, and exactly this now took place. Judas, who was called the Galilean, had been a famous brigand in older days, and his son Manahem was known for being just as ferocious. When Manahem and his roving outlaws realized the struggle going on inside Jerusalem, they hastened south of the capital to the Fortress of Masada, gathering other robbers as they went. Once inside the mountain citadel, they broke into the formidable armory that had been there since the days of Herod the Great. Then Manahem returned north with a fully-armed band of brigands, hailing himself as the new king of Jerusalem, and took control over the seditionist forces by brute strength.

Manahem's first bold move as rebel leader was to storm the palace of Herod the Great, which held the Jewish leaders who had fled from the upper city as well as what remained of Agrippa's "rescue force" and the former Roman garrison. When it appeared that the defenders were about to be dislodged, they pled to Manahem that they might surrender and go free. This he granted to the Jews and king's soldiers, but not the Roman guardsmen who were with them. These fled into yet a higher tower (called Mariamme) as the rebels chased and killed those who could not run fast enough.

If there was any doubt now as to who commanded the seditionists, it was removed the next day when the high priest Ananias, father of the Zealot Eleazar, was caught hiding in an aqueduct. I don't know if Eleazar sought mercy from Manahem (for father and son were already estranged by his sedition) but it would have been useless anyway. The high priest was killed by a rebel mob as soon as he was paraded in the streets. But this senseless act made Eleazar and the more traditional among his men lament that they now had a leader in Manahem who was every bit as barbaric to his own people as had been Florus.

Manahem, mind you, had also proclaimed himself king of the Jews. That same day he declared that he would adorn himself with a purple robe and lead a procession of his fully-armored men into the temple for what promised to be some sort of pompous coronation ceremony.

Now he was leading into Eleazar's strength, for the Zealot had been the temple governor and knew its rooms and corridors well. When Manahem and his entourage passed by a certain place (I am not certain where) they were ambushed by Eleazar and his strongest men. Soon the whole multitude was thrashing away at Manahem and his soldiers. Many were killed as they fled and some escaped to Masada. Manahem and some of his captains ran away to a village called Ophla. But they were caught, subjected to the worst tortures, and killed.

Eleazar may have been more reasonable than Manahem, but he was certainly no lamb. When Metilius, the ranking officer of the besieged Romans, heard that Manahem had been overthrown, he sent Eleazar a message offering to give up all his arms if the Jews would but send his men on their way home to Cæsarea. The Jews sent a delegation of four men, who offered the Romans the security of their right hands. The soldiers then marched out and piled up their swords and shields. With that Eleazar's men let out a roar and fell upon the astonished Romans, barbarously slashing away in total breach of their pledge. All but the officer, Metilius, were cut down in a minute or two. He was spared only after promising that he would turn Jew and become circumcised.

The more moderate among the Jews were now in extreme distress at the lawlessness that had fallen over their city, because they feared what would happen to Jewish communities everywhere when word of the massacre spread. In fact, it had already begun, ironically, at roughly the same hour on the same day. At Cæsarea, in about one hour's time, some 20,000 Jews were slaughtered and the city all but emptied of its Jewish inhabitants.

Now the cycle of revenge and retribution spun out of control. When news spread of the massacre at Cæsarea, Jews in cities where they dominated the population rose up and killed their Syrian neighbors. Soon every city in Syria was divided into two armies. Yet, the dividing lines weren't always simple. In some cases, Jewish businessmen and religious leaders would side with the Syrians because they feared the ferocity and plunder of the Jewish rebels. And everywhere greed undergirded everything as homes and temples were pillaged for their riches.

Of the turmoils that erupted in virtually every Jewish community, I will specifically mention only the worst of them — Egyptian Alexandria with its half million Jews. At one point the Hellenist leaders called a meeting of their people in a theater to discuss sending an embassy beseeching Nero to rescind the rights of equality that Claudius had given the Jews there over 20 years before. When the Jews heard about it several of their boldest barged into the theater, I suppose to harass the Greeks. When they saw the Jews approaching they shouted "spies" and set upon them, killing some. Now a larger mob of Jews rushed into the theater with lamps, threatening to burn it down with everyone in it unless the city's governor, Tiberius Alexander, restrained the Greeks' passions.

Alexander himself arrived soon enough and entreated them to be quiet and not provoke the two Roman legions that were stationed outside the city. But some of the hotter Jewish youths made sport of the governor's pleas and convinced him that they would not subside unless they were taught a lesson. Coincidentally, the two regular legions had been joined by some 5,000 other Roman troops who had arrived at their camp from Libya for some sort of military exercises. Alexander ordered them all to set upon the Delta, the part of the city where the Jewish people lived, and kill and plunder as they saw fit. When some Jews gathered arms and rushed out at them, the ferocity of the soldiers only increased. They did not stop until more than 50,000 Jews lay dead in heaps. Only then did Alexander order the men to retire. But by that time it was difficult to restrain the rest of the population, which had joined in the massacre.

In Antioch, the governor Cestius, hearing that the Jews were everywhere in arms, marched out with Agrippa at his side with a force that included the entire 12th legion and parts of others. The march eastward led them first to Zebulon in Galilee, just across the border from Ptolemais. This they found deserted, the population having fled to the mountains. But "all sorts of good things" remained, writes Josephus, and these Cestius gave to his soldiers for plunder. Then "they set fire to the city, although it was of admirable beauty, and had its houses built like those in Tyre, Sidon and Berytus."

Cestius and his troops left one of his generals to pacify Galilee and then marched his own greater force – including King Agrippa and his own military force – down the Judean coast. When they came to Joppa and found that the citizens had made no provision for fighting, they slew them all (about 8,400), plundered the city and left it in flames. Gallus, the Roman general in Galilee, now marched his men down the center of Palestine, killing populations and burning their cities as he deemed necessary to restore peace.

The two armies met in Cæsarea and moved on to Jerusalem, pitching their camp at Gabao, about six miles from the walls of the city. Now this was in August during the Feast of Tabernacles and Jerusalem was already crowded with pilgrims. But when the Jews saw the Roman armies approaching, they dropped what they were doing and took to arms, gaining courage from their great numbers. It was the Sabbath day, and Cestius had hoped to gain some advantage from it, but the tremendous shouts going up within the city walls showed him that the rage of the Jews had overcome their desire for religious rites. Few in the crowd had received any military training, nor had anyone organized them into brigades. Yet, the emotions of the multitude simply propelled them out of the city gates with such force that they actually pierced the ranks of the Romans and slaughtered many. I should point out that a great part of Cestius' army were recruits who had not been tested in battle. The Romans scattered, and when the Jews counted the dead bodies left behind, they numbered 515. The Jews themselves counted their losses at 22. Most of the Jews withdrew back into the city, but some bands chased the Romans, who were making for their camp, and captured many of the animals that carried their weapons of war.

For once it was the Romans who were in real danger, because in addition to facing the walled bastion that was Jerusalem, they had all around them Jewish refugees and robbers camped about on mountainsides and poised for action. King Agrippa took all this into account and persuaded Cestius that now might be a good time to send the Jews an embassy. The governor's message complimented them for their show of strength and said that this represented an opportunity to admit the Romans into Jerusalem if each side guaranteed the other's safety. For Cestius was prepared to offer his right hand and a guarantee of forgiveness if they would but lay down their arms. Behind this was King Agrippa's conviction that the more sober elements of the Jews would sue for peace and thus split from the militant seditionists.

But both sides miscalculated. Agrippa proved wrong because the envoys had no sooner been admitted into Jerusalem when they were pounced on and killed before saying a word. This the seditionists had done to guarantee that none of the Jews would be tempted to cease fighting in return for their security. Yet the seditionist leaders were not prepared for the wrath that erupted from the rest of the populace. Obviously, the common people, if I may call them such, must have hoped privately that the Romans would have been able to arrange a settlement that would end the killing. Now, in a rage, they rose up and chased the seditionists into the inner city, where they barricaded themselves inside the temple.

Cestius did not know this. He bided his time for another three days, using it in part to ride into neighboring villages and seize their corn. Then as the month turned to September, the governor moved his men to within a furlong or two from the city and set camp on Mount Scopus, which overlooked the king's palace and almost the whole city besides. Then, after using his siege engines to set parts of the city aflame with fiery missiles, he marched his troops inside the outer city walls and pitched camp against the royal palace. The Jews expected Cestius to begin an immediate assault on the temple walls, but again he halted and waited.

When the remaining priests and elders saw the Romans wavering, they sent word that they were ready to open the temple gates if Cestius would again guarantee peace. But while the governor wondered aloud if this was more treachery, the rebel leaders found out what was afoot and hurled one of the leading citizens over the wall in a show of defiance. Then, as Cestius watched, they heaved large rocks at the already lifeless body.

After this, Cestius spent five days trying to besiege the city. Thousands of fiery darts were flung over the walls. More than once the Romans used their famed tortoise shell tactic (called a *testudo*) in which some men stand in a cluster with shields raised while others dig to undermine the base of the city walls. They tried scaling the walls as well, but each time they were beaten back with considerable casualties.

It is said that with a little longer siege, Jerusalem would have fallen. It is also alleged that Cestius still did not realize how many people on the ramparts were praying that he would succeed and offer them a chance to repent (when their own leaders would not do the same). But one day Cestius unceremoniously ordered his troops to pull camp and leave. The task at hand was simply too risky.

Yet, the governor could not even look forward to an orderly departure. The more emboldened of the rebels poured out of the city and harassed the Romans' rear, stealing their baggage and animals. And whenever the weary soldiers crossed narrow valleys they were pelted with stones and darts from hundreds of taunting Jews on the hillsides. Cestius managed to return to his original camp at Gabao, six miles from the city. There they stayed for two nights, but the crowds of Jewish harrassers were growing so large around them as to begin resembling an army. The governor, realizing that to camp there any longer was a danger, ordered his pack animals all killed except for those that carried darts. Then he ordered his men to close ranks, carry only their weapons and march rapidly to the town of Bethoron, another 14 miles to the northwest on the way to Cæsarea.

The hostile crowds pressed on them from the moment they broke camp. Every time the Roman columns had to file through narrow passes, they lost more men. Cestius' misfortune was aggravated by his own cavalry. Horses can make a steep climb if led slowly and surefootedly. But now the troops were mostly descending at a rapid pace, with the horses being constantly excited by the shouting of enemies and the blows of incoming stones and arrows. The result was that the horses often tumbled down steep hills – sometimes with the men who were leading them. Moreover, parts of columns were now attacked and killed as they wound through the passes, unable at times to see the soldiers in front of them. All of this increased the sense of confinement and pending doom. One could hear mournful cries from men in utmost despair, as if they now were the ones under siege.

That night after the Romans bivouacked in the hills of Bethoron, Cestius realized his situation was desperate, for the marauding Jews had filled all the hilltops around them, waiting for daylight. Quietly, he selected 400 of his best soldiers and placed them at the strongest of his fortifications at the makeshift camp. They were ordered to place their flags all about the camp so that when the Jews saw them fluttering in the dawn's light they would assume that the entire army was still there. Then Cestius took the rest of the forces with him and set out on a silent march hoping to get at least four miles away and down into the safer coastal plain before they were noticed.

Daylight was just upon them when the Jews began to perceive that the camp

was strangely silent. They quickly rushed the 400 defenders and easily overcame them, slaying all. They tried to catch the fleeing Cestius; but when they
realized they could not, the Jewish troops – if the rebels could now be called an
organized fighting force – returned to the camp and retraced the Roman
route of the previous day, retrieving a wealth of discarded siege engines, carts,
animals, and supplies along the way. They also took toll of the Roman dead,
which were 5,300 footmen and 380 horsemen. The defeat had ended on the
eighth day of the Jewish month of Marchesvan, or probably October 23 in the
12th year of Nero's reign.

Even the most moderate of Jewish leaders now knew that there was no turning back. But rather than being emboldened by the victory, as Josephus reports,
"many of the most eminent of the Jews swam away from the city, as from a ship
when it was going to sink." Cestius sent an appeal to Nero, who was by then in
Achaia, that he was in great distress and needed a larger army to put down the
Jews. As the Jews had once said when they petitioned him much earlier, the
governor charged that Florus had been the cause of it all.

There was no Corbulo to call on for heroics – Nero had seen to that. Instead
the command went to a career soldier who was as squatty, rough-hewn and
prone to earthy jokes as Corbulo had been tall, regal and aloof. Raised in a non-
descript village in the Sabine country, the new commander had begun his military career in Thrace as a tribune of the troops and had risen on the strength of
his practical soldiering skills to command legions in Germany and Britain
under Claudius. His name was Titus Flavius Vespasian. He was already about 60
and, some said, his best campaigns were behind him. Perhaps so, answered Vespasian's defenders, but he came with a rare and valuable resource – a son, Titus,
whose military skills were as respected as his loyalty to his father.

. . . .

SOMETIME AFTER THE GREAT FIRE and before Nero's departure for Greece, the
apostle Peter came to Rome, determined to lead and comfort the Christians
there, both Jewish and Gentile, no matter what the cost to himself. He was now
about 60 and apparently still retained his full head of hair and rough, muscular
features. I say this because the few frescoes one sees in Christian catacombs and
mausoleums are remarkably consistent despite the often-crude talents of their
artists. Peter is seen as a stocky, muscular man with thick curly hair and beard.
Paul is invariably portrayed as slight and somewhat stooped, with balding head,
thin face and long straight beard.

There is some irony in Peter's decision to come to Rome at this time. He had
probably been driven out of Jerusalem four years before when James was murdered, then spent the remaining years among the churches of Antioch and

eastern Asia Minor. Now, perhaps as soon as he arrived in Rome, Peter read the imperial edict with the rest of us that Nero would soon sojourn in Greece.

Might this absence have given Peter or Paul a freer hand to spread the gospel in Rome? This is doubtful because it also meant that there would now be no restraints on the corrupt freedman Helius, who remained behind as de facto emperor. Unlike Nero, whose passion for arts and athletics left him scant time for governance, Helius' sole charge was to keep order in his master's absence.

Equally bad, the same *religio illicita* that now marked Christians in Rome would soon be exported abroad. Indeed, as local authorities tried to anticipate threats to the emperor's safety and pleasure that might flare up within their borders, Christians could expect to be rounded up with all other suspected seditionists and criminal elements, then used as animal bait in the games or herded off to haul pots of earth in some public works project.

Exactly this was beginning to happen when Peter decided to interrupt his preaching and write a letter to the churches of Asia Minor. No doubt his Greek was adequate for conversation, but not for writing. Yet, the letter received by the churches of Asia Minor was in perfect Greek. Why? Because Peter arrived in Rome accompanied by a man who was both a Roman citizen and facile writer in Greek. He was none other than Silvanus, the man I wrote about as Silas (the shortened version of the same name) who, some 25 years before, had undertaken the first missionary journey to Asia Minor with Paul after Barnabas had decided to go his separate way. It would also be Silvanus, who knew both apostles so well, who would deliver Peter's letter to the churches they had founded in Pontus, Galatia, Cappadocia, Asia and Bithynia.

Peter urged them to hold to their faith despite impending personal peril. By God's great mercy, he wrote,

> ...we have been born anew to a living hope through the resurrection of Jesus Christ from the dead, and to an inheritance which is imperishable, undefiled and unfading, kept in heaven for you, who by God's power are guarded through faith for a salvation ready to be revealed in the last time. In this you rejoice, though now for a little while you may have to suffer various trials, so that the genuineness of your faith, more precious than gold...may redound to praise and glory and honor in the revelation of Jesus Christ.[14]

As God loves you, love one another, Peter urged.

> You know that you were ransomed from the futile ways you inherited from your fathers, not with perishable things but with the precious blood of Christ, like that of a lamb without blemish or spot. He

was destined before the foundation of the world but was made manifest at the end of the times for your sake. Through him you have confidence in God, who raised him from the dead and gave him glory so that your faith and hope are in God.

Having purified your souls by your obedience to the truth for a sincere love of the brethren, love one another earnestly from the heart. You have been born anew, not of perishable seed but of imperishable, through the living and abiding word of God. For

> "All flesh is like grass
> and all its glory is like the flower of grass.
> The grass withers, and the flower falls,
> but the word of the Lord abides forever."[15]

Peter admonished the Christians of Asia Minor to abstain from the passions that "wage war" in their souls to retaliate against ruthless reprisals.

Maintain good conduct among the Gentiles, so that in case they speak against you as wrongdoers, they may see your good deeds and glorify God on the day of visitation.

Be subject for the Lord's sake to every human institution, whether it be to the emperor as supreme or to governors sent by him to punish those who do wrong and praise those who do right. For it is God's will that by doing right you should put to silence the ignorance of foolish men. Live as free men, but without using your freedom as a pretext for evil, but live as servants of God. Honor all men. Love the brotherhood. Fear God. Honor the emperor.[16]

Again, Peter urges the churches to stand fast in the midst of their coming ordeal.

The end of things is at hand: therefore keep sane and sober for your prayers. Above all, hold unfailing your love for one another, since love covers a multitude of sins. Practice hospitality ungrudgingly to one another. As each has received a gift, employ it for one another, as good stewards of God's varied grace...

Beloved, do not be surprised at the fiery ordeal which comes upon you to prove you, as though something strange is happening to you. But rejoice so far as you share Christ's sufferings, that you may rejoice and be glad when his glory is revealed. If you are reproached for the name of Christ, you are blessed, because the spirit of glory and of God rests upon you. But let none of you suffer as a murderer or a thief or wrongdoer or a mischief maker. Yet, if one suffers as a Christian, let him not be ashamed, but under that name let him glorify God. For the time has come for judgment to begin with the household of God. And if it begins with us, what will be the end of those who do not obey the gospel of God?[17]

This was the last written communication from Peter. Most likely he had been under surveillance by agents of Helius from the day of his arrival. Having jotted down enough to prove that he was openly espousing one of the *religiones illicitæ,* they seized Peter on the street and carted him off to prison — by almost all accounts, the Mamertine Prison. This would surely explain why he had no recourse to a writing tablet and was allowed no communication with anyone except prisoners and guards, for the Mamertine is a gruesome place not deserved even by a mad dog. Any Roman knows it, and like me, feels his pace quicken even as he passes by the outside on the way to the Forum. And they share in silence the chilling knowledge that for centuries no man has ever emerged alive from this pit of filth and starvation except to be led to a public execution.

. . . .

As winter settled on Jerusalem, the Jews found themselves for the first time in anyone's memory without the sight of Roman sentries standing watch over the temple courtyards or the sounds of hooves and Latin shouts as cohorts clopped in from Cæsarea. Yet they knew it was but an eerie calm before a storm, and so they went about busily organizing themselves for the dreaded return of Cestius – or worse, of Nero's new general Vespasian and who knew how many battle-tough legions.

But creating order and assigning leaders was no easier than it had been when the Romans were camped outside the city walls the previous year. Chosen to govern all affairs within the city were two men: Joseph, the son of Gorion, and the high priest Ananus, the same iron-willed youth who had seen to the murder of the Christian leader, James, five years before. But the two rulers of Jerusalem still had to reckon all along with the bitter and intractable Eleazar. I refer here to the son of the slain high priest who had been temple administrator and the one who had suddenly forbidden all sacrifices by foreigners. You may recall that he had become the seditionist leader until the bandit Manahem and his gang raided the arsenal at Masada and used it to seize control over the rebel cause. Now, having ambushed and killed Manahem, Eleazar and his men kept for themselves all the arms and equipment that Manahem's faction had plundered over the months. Eleazar had expected this show of power to get him named leader of Jerusalem, but the others had been too fearful of what one called his "tyrannical temper" to comply.

So, while Eleazar subverted their actions and tried to win allies by bribery, the "elected" leadership went about choosing generals for all of the various Jewish regions. There were seven governor-generals in all. To acquaint you with how they went about preparing their regions for war, I will cite only the case of Josephus, a young priest who was put in charge of Galilee. I single him out for one simple reason: only Josephus among them has taken pains to write a detailed first-hand account of the entire Jewish War (although, naturally enough, it centers on the places and events he personally witnessed).

Since this Josephus was both a leading figure and chronicler of the events I shall soon relate, it is proper for you to know something more of his background. Josephus seemed bent upon a priestly life almost from birth. By his own description, he was born in Jerusalem, the son of Matthias, a leading priest and the latest in a long line of priestly families under the Hasmonean kings. By Josephus' own pretentious account, he had become so learned by age 14 that the leading dignitaries of the city had already begun seeking his advice. At age 16 he immersed himself, successively, in the lives and learning of Judaism's three major schools of thought: the Pharisees, Sadducees and Essenes. But during that same period be began attaching himself increasingly to one Bannus, a monk-philosopher who lived in the Judean desert and wore clothes of bark and leaves and ate only vegetation. But by age 19, Josephus was back in Rome and beginning his public career as a priest.

At age 26 he had perhaps his most formative experience of all. He was named as part of an embassy that the Jewish elders sent to Rome. The purpose was to help plead the case of some men, whom Josephus describes as pious æsthetic priests who the procurator Felix had sent off in chains to be judged before the emperor. No, in case you're wondering, Paul of Tarsus was not one of them, because the elders would have been pleading against and not for him. Josephus says only that the charges by Felix were "small and trifling."

But Josephus did encounter another trial very much in common with Paul. Midway in its journey, and in the open sea, the immense grain ship that bore them was swamped in a mighty storm. Writes Josephus:

> We that were in it, being about 600 in number, swam for our lives all the night. Upon the first appearance of the day, and upon our sight of a ship of Cyrene, I and some others, 80 in all – for God's providence prevented the rest – were taken up in another ship.

> And when I had thus escaped and had come to...Puteoli, I became acquainted with Aliturius, an actor of plays, and much beloved by Nero, and a Jew by birth. Through his interest I became known to Poppæa, Cæsar's wife, and took care as soon as possible, to entreat her to procure that the priests might be set at liberty. And when, besides this favor, I had obtained many presents from Poppæa, I returned home again.[18]

Josephus adds that the greatest impression he took away from the long journey was that of Rome's insurmountable power. Acknowledging that talk of re-volt was already in the air in Jerusalem, he took pains to persuade his country-men "that they were inferior to the Romans not only in martial skill, but also in good fortune," and that to rebel rashly would "bring on the dangers of the most terrible mischiefs upon their country, upon their families and upon themselves."

How much of this was brilliant foresight, or simply for the consumption of his Roman patron when he wrote it some 20 years later, I will leave to your judgment; but within six years Josephus had emerged to become one of the seven generals chosen to lead the rebellion. He has explained that when the rabble-rouser Manahem had come to Jerusalem after looting the arsenal at Masada, he (Josephus) "retired to the inner court of the temple" and did not emerge until Manahem had been ambushed and killed by Eleazar and his men. At that point Josephus rejoined the other leading priests. He is very candid about their confused state of mind.

> But no small fear seized upon us when we saw the people in arms,
> while we ourselves knew not what we should do, and were not able to
> restrain the seditious. However, as danger was directly upon us, we
> pretended that we were of the same opinion with them, but openly
> advised them to be quiet for the present and let the enemy go away,
> still hoping that Gessius Florus would not be long ere he came, and
> with great forces so put an end to these seditious proceedings.[19]

But the procurator Florus and the Syrian governor Cestius had instead come and gone, leaving the issue unresolved and leaving the Jews with no recourse but to prepare for a Roman storm. And now at the age of 33, Josephus ruled a "kingdom" that covered over 600 square miles and contained perhaps 600,000 persons. From his explanation, I judge Galilee to be one of the more desirable places on earth in peacetime,

> ...for the soil is universally rich and fruitful, and full of the plantations of
> trees of all sorts, inasmuch that it invites even the most slothful to
> take pains in its cultivation, by its fruitfulness. Accordingly, it is all cul-
> tivated by its inhabitants and no part of it lies idle. Moreover, the cities
> here are very thick, and the very villages there are everywhere so full
> of people, by the richness of their soil, that the very least of them con-
> tain about 15,000 inhabitants. [20]

When Josephus first entered Galilee, his primary concern was to build the good will of the area's leaders. So he chose 70 of the most prudent men (as had

Moses) to be rulers over all affairs and to hear all cases involving life or death. Then he appointed seven judges in each city to hear lesser cases involving individual disputes. Josephus himself concentrated on building the defenses against the expected Roman onslaught. He built walls around 15 chief cities and even around the caves that are found in some areas around the Lake of Gennesaret. At the same time he raised an army that included over 60,000 footmen, several hundred horsemen, a mercenary force of 4,500 and his own personal guard of 600. These were equipped with old weapons that had been donated or captured from all over the land.

But Josephus worried less about the condition of weapons and more about the remarkable discipline with which Roman soldiers obeyed orders. Except for the mercenaries, his own ragtag recruits were not only untrained, but quick to argue with each other and even their superiors. Josephus now hurled all his efforts into organizing and teaching. Using the Romans themselves as his model, he assigned the soldiers to captains of tens, centurions of hundreds, tribunes of thousands and commanders for greater numbers. The men first learned to send signals to one another and recall soldiers by the sounds of trumpets. At the same time, they practiced how to expand an army's wing, then how to wheel about in order to assist another wing that was getting the worst of it.

Finally, Josephus lectured on the importance of becoming fit enough to contest those whose strength and courage had enabled themselves to conquer the habitable earth. And he implored them to give up robbery, vice and other evils so that they would face only enemies in their path to victory and not the wrath of God.

Although the raw but rugged Galileans made rapid progress, the process of governing was always a trial. A constant thorn in Josephus' side was one John of Gischala, a man he describes as a "knavish and cunning" vagabond. When Josephus arrived in Galilee, John was known only as a marauder who led a gang of about 400 men in a life of plundering Romans, Jews and Syrians alike. But John, it seems, was also ambitious to lead more men than this. Displaying a sizable cache of money, he persuaded the young general that he would use it to rebuild the walls of his native Gischala if he were made commander of the forces there.

Once established in Gischala, John had a shrewd scheme that went beyond rebuilding walls. Since the area was a major producer of olive oil for export, he sent agents throughout the Jewish cities of Syria persuading citizens that they should buy only oil produced by Jews and not of foreigners. Thus he was able to sell oil at twice the price that Jews had paid before, and in the process built an immense sum of money. This he used to persuade leading citizens of Galilee that they should overthrow Josephus and install him as governor general. He also increased the intensity of robberies in the countryside, then went about campaigning among the populace with promises that the plundering would end if only he were put in charge!

At the same time, John spread rumors that Josephus was in collusion with the Romans. Whether by design or not, one of the travelers who passed under the noses of John's highwaymen one day was Ptolemy, the chief steward of Agrippa and Bernice. By the time the robbers had relieved Ptolemy and his entourage of their baggage train, they had found themselves with some six hundred pieces of gold, several silver cups and place settings, and an untold number of royal garments. The booty was so great that the brigands reconsidered what might be their fate if King Agrippa set his soldiers upon them, and so they decided to seek out Josephus and deliver the goods to him.

They found the general staying in the town of Tarícheæ as he supervised fortification of its walls. The governor duly scolded them for their treachery, and having other duties to attend to just then, left the royal plunder with a leading elder of Tarícheæ for safekeeping until it could be sent back to the king.

Well, the robbers, still smarting from their unwelcome reception by Josephus, began spreading word in neighboring towns that the governor himself had betrayed the Jewish cause by returning to the allies of Rome a wealth of property that could have been converted to instruments of war. All night long the clamor spread, so that by the next morning, thousands of armed men converged on the hippodrome at Tarícheæ, chanting that Josephus the traitor be displaced at once. Others demanded that he be burned, and before long the riled-up mob left the hippodrome and jostled its way to the house where Josephus was staying — still asleep, as a matter of fact. When the shouting of the approaching mob reached the ears of Josephus' personal guardsmen, all melted away in fear except for four, who awakened the young governor.

By the time the crowd appeared in the street in front of Josephus' house, they were startled when the governor himself jumped out at them from the front door. His clothes were rent and ashes were sprinkled on his head. His hands were behind him and his sword was hanging around his neck.

After recovering from their shock, some of the more zealous among them began to reproach Josephus. Those who thought his government too taxing shouted for him to produce the king's riches so they could share in it. Others demanded he confess that he was in league with the Romans. For they assumed that he was dressed in such a pitiable condition because he was ready to confess to everything in order to beg their pardon.

But Jospehus' humble posture was merely the cutting edge of a stratagem, which was to set his critics arguing amongst themselves. When he raised his hands for silence, they assumed he was ready to confess all. But when he had their attention, he said: "I neither intended to send this money back to Agrippa nor to gain it myself. For I never did esteem one who is your enemy to be your friend. Nor did I look upon your disadvantage to be my advantage. No, people of Tariche æ, I saw that your city stood in greater need than others for fortifications and that you needed money to build a wall. I was also afraid that people of other cities should lay a plot to seize upon these spoils. So therefore, I intended to retain this money so that I might build you a wall.

"But if this does not please you," added Josephus, "I will produce for you what was brought me and leave you to plunder it."

As he expected, the people of Tariche æ loudly commended him, while those who had run down from Tiberias and other surrounding cities began to call him harsh names, for they would rather take home some loot than build walls for Tariche æ. Soon the two groups had begun quarreling. But Josephus, knowing that his 40,000 or so new friends from Tariche æ outnumbered all the others by far, again raised his hand for attention. This time he singled out the people who had rushed down from Tiberias — the largest group next to those of Tariche æ. He reiterated that it was his intent to build walls around Tariche æ. But if that bothered them, said Josephus, he would use the money to increase the security of other cities as well if they would but agree to whose specific benefit it should be used.

By this time most of the once-angry multitude had gone away so that there were but 2,000 or so remaining in a general state of turmoil. At that point Josephus employed a second stratagem: he climbed atop the roof of his host's house, and again signaling to them, said, "You shout in such a confused noise that I cannot tell what it is you want of me. If you would but elect a few of your number to represent you, they may come into the house and talk with me about it."

When the elected delegates appeared on the portico, Josephus bid them enter with a bow and ushered them into the most private part of the house, whereupon he closed the door so that no one might hear what went on. What the delegates found were the four guards who had remained loyal to their governor. The guards set upon them with whips and scourged them so severely that even their inner parts were raw and bloody.

Meanwhile, the remaining crowd had relaxed its ire, assuming that a long discourse was underway with regard to disposition of the king's property. Suddenly the doors were flung open and the "ambassadors" were flung out upon the crowd in such a bloody state that the frightened mob threw down their arms and ran away in terror.

Such was the ingenuity of Josephus. He seems also to have had that "good fortune" he attributed to the Romans, because his thwarting of the designs of John had a rippling effect. Leaders of other cities who had been threatened by the robber-merchant of Gischala to the point of overturning the Jerusalem-appointed government now rushed to the governor's support. Josephus took advantage of the changing tide to declare that all those who did not renounce John within five days would have their homes and families burned. Thus, 3,000 of John's followers left him immediately and deposited their arms with Josephus.

All this reduced Josephus' opposition to just two centers of power in Galilee. The first was Gischala, to which John himself retreated and made his personal bastion. The second was Tiberias, the city beside the Lake of Gennesaret that had been built just 50 years before and named for the Roman emperor. The Tiberians decided to revolt on a day when their commander had just sent out nearly all of his soldiers to the countryside to gather corn to sustain them for the upcoming campaign. It was also the Sabbath.

When Josephus learned of the revolt, he resorted to yet another of his "stratagems," as he called them. As the Tiberians made ready for a possible land assault by Josephus, the inventive governor remained in Tiracheæ. There he had his troops commandeer every fishing or pleasure boat they could find moored in or about the city's harbor. They numbered about 230 in all, including some of the smallest, most decrepit vessels ever summoned to serve in a "navy." In most boats he stationed no more than four soldiers each. Some carried no soldiers at all, being towed behind the other boats with thin lines.

Josephus now sailed the entire wobbly, makeshift fleet south towards Tiberias. When still a considerale distance offshore of the city, Josephus ordered the boats to drift. His intent was that the Tiberians might spot a great many ships on the horizon but not be able to tell how large they were nor many attackers they held. Josephus himself could be seen in the largest ship, but those on shore would not know that it contained but seven men.

When the defenders of Tiberias squinted out at the sunrise to the east, they were astonished at the sight that confronted them in the early morning mist. They lowered their standards and signaled that Josephus should enter the port unopposed lest he be provoked into destroying the entire city.

Now Josephus entered the harbor and lectured the Tiberians boldly. What a waste, he said, that the only respite before the Roman onslaught had been squandered in internal bickering. How dare they shut the gates against him who had been responsible for rebuilding their walls! Still showing an indignant mood, the young governor ordered that ten of the most important men of Tiberias and 50 members of the local senate be delivered to him so as to give security for the loyalty of the city. All were immediately boarded on the boats he had brought from Taricheæ and their captains given orders to transport them back there for safekeeping.

Such was the ingenuity of Josephus. But I will relate one more story to show that, despite all the charges of treason muttered against him, he was indeed committed to the cause of solidifying the Jews in their defense of the Romans. As the leading men of Tiberias were being put to sea for their trip to Taricheæ, the people on shore began to lament loudly that none of this would have happened had it not been for the instigations of one Clitus, who was among the hostages. They feared that all would be slain for the cause of one man. Now Josephus, who claims that it was never his intent to slay anyone who might be useful in the cause against the Romans, ordered one of his chief guards to go out to the vessel and cut off both the hands of Clitus in retribution for his role in the affair. But Levius, the guard, was afraid to go because there were actually more Tiberians in that group of boats than there were loyalist soldiers. Josephus became so agitated at this lack of courage that he started rowing a boat from shore strenuously, determined to hack off the man's hands himself. The Tiberian Clitus was so alarmed at the fury of Josephus' rowing that he called out to the governor, offering to cut off one of his hands if he were spared the other. When the frustrated Josephus nodded – for the seas were becoming rough and the boat of Clitus would be difficult to board – Clitus without hesitation drew his sword and with his right hand delivered a blow that severed his left arm at the wrist.

Meanwhile, in Jerusalem, preparations for war against the Romans also proceeded at an uneven pace. The new leadership frequently sent out its hastily-trained forces against the foreign populations of Judea. But all too often, Jews in those cities were forced to side with their more numerous Hellenistic neighbors, which meant that they too perished at the hands of the attacking force from Jerusalem.

One place all Jews could agree on attacking was Ascalon. Just 50 miles to the southwest as the crow flies, or 70 miles if one counts the tortuous downhill passes that troops must negotiate, Ascalon was an almost wholly Roman settlement, and its very presence had rankled Jewish leaders since the days of Herod the Great. Armed mostly with energy and hatred, the hardiest of the Jewish rebels almost raced down to the coastal plain where stood the strongly fortified city.

At the time Ascalon was garrisoned by one Roman cohort of footmen and fewer than 100 horsemen, a minimal outpost linked only by signal to the military barracks at Cæsarea, some 80 miles up the coast. Its commander was a young captain named Antonius, and it was he, the unsuspecting but willing custodian of Roman military tradition, who first taught the Jews that victory in war takes more than numbers and zeal. Antonius met them by stationing his horsemen outside the city walls. The attackers were poorly equipped, and, as Josephus says, "full of rage when what they needed was sober counsel." The horsemen fought off the first wave patiently, then suddenly charged right past the bewildered attackers. Then, on the sound of a trumpet, the under-sized cavalry wheeled an about-face and drove the attackers backwards. Now it was the Jews who were the defenders, with their backs pressed against the city walls and being cut to pieces for lack of anywhere to run. With arrows also raining down on them from the Roman soldiers inside the walls, the dismayed Jews would scatter on the flat coastal plain only to be chased and cut down by the horsemen.

The systematic slaughter repeated itself – chase, round up, force back, press against the walls, chase into the plain – until night fell and the pursuers could no longer see their quarry. When it was over, two Jewish generals and 10,000 men had perished beneath the walls of Ascalon.

Still, their wrathful zeal was undiminished. Several days later and well before their wounds had healed, the Jews of Jerusalem brought down even more men. But this time Antonius and his men had set traps all along the hilly crevices the Jews would pass through. As soon as the traps unleashed landslides of rocks, the Romans ambushed the dazed marchers. Another 8,000 Jews were hacked to death or knocked off the narrow footpaths by rock slides and arrows before the rest limped back to Jerusalem.

Yet, by now the very zeal of the Jews had a chilling effect on the Romans. Vespasian knew that men like Antonius in remote outposts could not be expected to display Olympian heroics forever. Reports like his only enervated Vespasian to pack up and move all the more quickly. He dispatched his son Titus to Alexandria to march back with the Roman fifth and tenth legions, two of the most illustrious in her history. Vespasian, who had been with Nero in Attica, would march the 15th legion from Antioch. But attached to this were 18 cohorts – five from the camp at Cæsarea and others from various Roman garrisons – and typically with a thousand or so footmen each. Now add to these the auxiliaries of archers, horsemen and footmen from several client kings. When all these converged with the forces of Titus at Ptolemais on the Syrian coast, the fighting men numbered some 60,000 in all. This still does not count vast numbers of servants, who continued to serve their masters into battle and who often were adept with weapons as well.

As Josephus knew well from the day he assumed command, the Romans' first target would be the first Jewish soil they would have to cross on their march to Jerusalem. This, of course, was Galilee. Shortly before the Romans arrived, Josephus had attempted to strengthen his position and test the mettle of his battle troops by storming the Roman-Hellenistic city of Sepphoris, which lay some 25 miles southwest of Tiberias. The people of Sepphoris were already undermining the Jewish cause by riding out of their walls and plundering the outlying farms and stealing livestock; so Josephus was determined to lay the city waste before Vespasian could save it. But such was not the outcome. A lone Roman tribune and some 7,000 auxiliaries were able to withstand the Jewish assault.

Thus, I cannot imagine that the seditionist cause in Galilee was basking in self-confidence when it became known that Vespasian himself had embarked from Ptolemais and was on his way. In fact, almost as soon as the seemingly end-less train of men, horses and seige engines could be seen winding through the mountains and passes, many Galileans became overpowered with a sense of fear and hopelessness. As the march advanced closer to their towns, thousands repented of their rebellion and fled before ever having a chance to defend them-selves. In fact, when the general came to Gadara, the first city in his path, "he found it destitute of any men grown up and fit for war."

Poor Gadara. Vespasian, ordinarily a good-natured man with a quick wit, was grimly determined that the first city he encountered would be made to pay for the slaughter of the Roman garrison in Jerusalem and the humiliating retreat of Cestius to Cæsarea. He slew every woman and child in Gadara. He then set fire to it and all the surrounding villages. Those who weren't slain were taken as slaves.

Terror was now everywhere, abetted by the actions of Josephus himself. The Jewish general had been in a small town near Sepphoris when Vespasian's force first showed. He had immediately gone to Tiberias, judging it the most secure of Galilean cities. But when the Tiberians saw him enter their gates they quick-ly concluded that Josephus would not have fled his first post had he not de-spaired of the war.

In truth, this was exactly what Josephus felt, but he claims not to have shown it outwardly. He was prepared to die in the defense, he wrote, but not if the eld-ers in Jerusalem had perchance decided instead to repent. So he dispatched a letter to Jerusalem reporting unemotionally on the extent of the Roman forces. If the Jewish leaders wished to come to terms, he wrote, they should tell him immediately. If they were resolved upon war, they must send him an army sufficient to fight the Romans.

While Josephus was awaiting a reply, Vespasian decided to assault Jotapata. His intelligence reports had identified it as the most strongly fortified city and the one with the most defenders. If he could demolish Jotapata with one bold stroke, he reasoned, the lesser cities of Galilee might just dissolve in fear.

The Romans had delayed their march to Jotapata for some four days while their engineers planed off the top of a steep road that made it difficult to trans-port such a large train of men, carriages and animals. The road work was still in progress on May 21 when Josephus hastened from Tiberias to Jotapata. Al-though their leader's arrival raised the spirits of the defenders there, it had the same effect on Vespasian as well. When told that Josephus, the general of all Galilee, was now in the city he planned to assault, the Roman counted it as a blessing and ordered his battle preparations hastened. In fact, he had auxiliaries march immediately to the city and surround it lest his good fortune be thwart-ed by Josephus escaping.

Within two days Vespasian's force had set up camp within a mile of Jotapata and were ready for battle after a well-rested night. Until then the Jews inside had been too petrified to venture outside the walls, even for firewood. Now, as they saw the Romans methodically begin preparations for a siege, they realized that they could either die from fear or die in brave battle. Suddenly the gates opened and erupted with a ferocious charge of Jewish footmen. The Romans, recalled Josephus, "had skill as well as strength; the other had only courage, which armed them and made them fight furiously."

The hand-to-hand combat lasted all day and ended only when darkness made it impossible to see one's foe. By Josephus' count, the Jews had killed 13 Romans and "wounded a great many." The Jews suffered 17 dead and more than 600 wounded.

The same desperate scene repeated itself the next day. It went on for four more days as well until both sides stopped due to sheer exhaustion. It was at this point that Vespasian decided to return to his original plan: the slow, systematic siege.

Now nearly all of Jotapata is built on a steep precipice that surrounds three sides. Only at the north side does the mountain descend more gradually toward a plain. This side Josephus had encompassed with a high wall. Vespasian met with his counselors and resolved on their advice to raise a bank against the north wall. So they had cut down all the trees on the mountains adjoining the city and collected a vast amount of stones as well. Then, covering the soldiers with a shield against the darts that were constantly hurled from above, they began piling up the debris alongside the wall. At the same time, they kept the Jews all along the ramparts busy dodging the rocks and fiery missiles that were being hurled inside by no fewer than 160 Roman siege engines.

But this was not a one-sided affair. By night, small raiding parties would sneak out from the city to burn the timbers that supported the makeshift siege tower or to pull down the large iron-plated roofs that shielded the workers. Meanwhile, Jewish workmen were building the north wall still higher. To protect them against Roman darts, they stretched the thick hides of newly-killed oxen between upright pikes. Thus, as the Romans raised their tower, the walls of Jotapata became higher by 35 feet.

All this caused Vespasian to summon his counselors again. This time the agreed-upon stratagem was that, while the Romans could probably take the city by armed force, they could do so with greater certainty if they simply waited until the defenders were weakened by starvation. So they simply ceased the fighting and waited in silence, hoping that the number of deserters would increase as well.

Inside, the defenders took stock. Corn they had aplenty. But water was another matter. The city lacked a spring-fed fountain, relying traditionally on rain water. And the approaching summer was the season with the least of it.

They decided to ration water, but in time the stark reality that a man could have only so much per day to slake his thirst made him think all the more about it. The Romans knew of their plight, and would taunt those on the ramparts by lining up their water carriers and allowing the men to withdraw their liberal measures.

Josephus was not to be outdone by games of the mind. One morning the Romans squinted up at the battlements and saw that the Jews had flung garments along the ramparts for as far as the eye could see. The clothes were hung out as on laundry day, all dripping with much of the precious water they had left.

After this taunt the Romans resumed their attack – and it was welcomed by the Jews. For as Josephus explained it, "As they despaired of either themselves or their city being able to escape, they preferred death in battle before one by hunger and thirst."

Soon Josephus perceived that the city couldn't hold out much longer. He faced an excruciating dilemma. Meeting with the city elders, he said that there was little else he personally could do improve their lot. But if he could escape, he could rally other cities in Galilee to come to their rescue and defeat the Romans. This reasoning may have been sound, but it only fanned the feelings of despair. As Josephus' own diaries state (with himself described in the third person):

> Yet did not this plea move the people, but inflamed them to hang about him. Accordingly, both the children and the old men, and the women with their infants, came mourning to him and fell down before him. And all of them caught hold of his feet, and held him fast, and besought him, with great lamentations, that he would take his share with them in their fortune. And I think they did this, not that they envied his deliverance, but that they hoped for their own; for they could not think they should suffer any great misfortune provided that Josephus would but stay with them.[21]

Josephus says that he was touched by these entreaties, but that he knew, too, that if he tried to escape, his own people would probably arrest or kill him. So he announced to the Jews of Jotapata, "Now is the time to begin to fight in earnest, when there is no hope of deliverance left." And to show them what he meant, Josephus himself led a party of raiders that rushed out from the main gate and ran to the edge of the Roman camp where they pulled down several tents and set fire to other parts. From that day forward the daring and bravery of the Jews was relentless. They learned that when they made these disruptive raids, the Romans, laden with their heavy armor, could not pursue them very far.

But so mighty is Rome that even passion can be manipulated to the conqueror's advantage. Vespasian calmly rebuffed the angry cries of his troops for revenge. "Nothing is more courageous than despair," he counseled. And when the Jews saw that their purposes failed, it would be like a fire being quenched for lack of more fuel. Instead, Vespasian chose to wear down and decimate the raiders by having Arabian archers and Syrian slingers pepper them with a hail of missiles flung from a safe distance.

When the general's earthen bank had advanced against the walls to his liking, he gave the defenders their first look at a battering ram. As thick and long as the mast of a ship, the instrument was carved like the head of a ram and capped with a thick head of iron. Above the ram, which swung from leather straps, was a roof covered with animal hides, so that the men who swung it back and forth were protected from the hail of darts and rocks from above.

The ram was now fixed in place. From its very first stroke, as Josephus reports, "the wall was shaken, and a terrible clamor was raised by the people within the city, as if they were already taken."

The ingenious Josephus countered this by having the people fill large sacks of chaff. These they lowered down the wall by ropes to the place where the ram was battering back and forth. Thus, every time the ram struck, its impact was muffled by the overstuffed sacks and its damage greatly minimized.

Now the Romans countered. They invented a long contrivance on poles on whose ends they fastened knives. Now they could jab the pole at the ropes that held the sacks of chaff and cut them down.

Thus, the ram continued with its former efficiency, and soon the extended wall that Josephus' men had hastily built could be seen to ripple with each blow as it prepared to give way. So the Jews resolved to make what was perhaps their boldest sally ever. They rushed out in the dead of night with fire, bitumen and pitch. When they broke through the few guards around the battering ram, they smeared it with pitch and set it afire. Now as it began to burn through, a strong and brave youth hoisted a huge stone atop the north wall. Then he climbed along side it and stood in full view. Several Roman darts struck him at once, but he managed to push the boulder down directly on the fiery ram, breaking it in two. Then, as he was about to die from his wounds, the youth hurled himself on top of the ram's head.

But the Romans, as they say, have good fortune. When Vespasian had left camp to investigate the ruckus at the walls, a dart hit him in the heel. It had been flung from some distance and lacked enough force to penetrate deeply. But soldiers saw their commander fall. They saw his blood on the ground beside him, and word spread that he was seriously wounded or even dead. Now Roman discipline was abandoned to Roman rage as soldiers clamored for a full-scale assault. Far worse for the Jews inside the walls was that another battering ram was soon wheeled into the place of the burned one, and once again the sickening sounds of impending doom reverberated throughout Jotapata. Moreover, the Romans took the largest of their siege engines and trained them en masse against the same crumbling wall. Before long the huge stones that they hurled had carried off pinnacles of walls and broken off the corners of the towers. As Josephus adds:

> One may learn the force of the engines by what happened this very night; for as one of those who stood around Josephus was near the wall, his head was carried away by such a stone so that his skull was flung as far as three furlongs. And in the daytime, a woman who was with child had her belly so violently struck, as she had just come out of her house, that the infant was carried to a distance of half a furlong, so great was the force of the engine. The noise of the instruments themselves was very terrible...as was the noise of bodies when they were dashed against the wall.[22]

The defenders fought on through the night, the streets now running with blood from bodies that were being piled up all around. The noise from the missiles and the battering ram made everyone all the more wretched because the mountains behind them would send back an echo with each blow. The cries of the stricken and their mourners would resound with an eerie echo as well.

Then, just around daybreak, the north wall began crumbling from the ram's hundreds of blows.

The remaining morning was strangely silent. This was because Vespasian knew he had to grant his troops a respite to eat and lick their wounds. And he had to organize for the invasion that would soon pour through the breach.

Vespasian's first action was to place a ring of horsemen and archers around the walls so that there would be no escaping once the city was taken. Next, the veteran general ordered his bravest horsemen to get off their horses, to don heavy armor and stand with poles and ladders at the base of the embankment where the wall had been breached. His best footmen were then brought into position to be ready to ascend the ladders and hurl themselves into the opening where the upper part of the wall had fallen in. Also brought into position were hundreds of archers, who would keep the defenders pinned down with a hail of darts.

As Josephus saw these preparations unfolding below him, he ordered that all the women be shut up in their houses (not just for the personal safety, but because he didn't want the resolve of his men weakened by female wailings of despair when they saw the Roman onslaught). Calling his men together, the Jewish governor general told them to cover their ears as soon as the Roman trumpeters gave the signal to charge, for neither did he want them to quake at the terrible roar that would go up from the invaders. And he told the men to kneel down and cover themselves with their shields when the Romans first charged. For this would allow them protection until the first wave of arrows was expended. Then, only when they saw the Romans beginning to lay their instruments for ascending the walls, they should then rise up and in one ferocious rage rush into a life or death battle with the enemy.

Soon the trumpets blew, and Josephus' men did just as they were told. After a rain of darts so thick that they seemed to block the light, the defenders rushed out and began to topple the first of the ladders that had been placed against the wall. The combat went on for a few hours, but the Jews at last began to sag because the Romans had the luxury of suspending their assault so they could replace tired men with fresh ones. They also climbed with shields braced together, as though it were a wall of steel advancing at the Jews.

It seemed that the Romans would finally break through, but at that point Josephus had one more "stratagem" to employ. He gave orders to pour scalding oil down on those who were still on the ladders. The Jews had boiled a great quantity of it, and poured it over the walls when it was still hissing from the heat of the fire. Now the Romans screamed and tumbled down, one on top of another, in horrible pain. Being encased in helmets and heavy breastplates, the boiling, unctuous fat trickled through their bodies from head to foot, causing them to writhe on the ground in the greatest agony.

At the same time, Josephus' men poured boiling fenugreek (an oriental herb used in making curry) upon the boards of the ladders. The means of ascent now became so slippery that the men furthest along the ladders fell upon those beneath them. Others plunged into the earthen embankment below, where many were killed by arrows from Jewish archers above.

The Romans were furious and clamored for more Jewish blood, but Vespasian prudently called off the assault for the day, for evening was already coming on. The Jews had suffered only six killed, although some 300 were wounded.

They now had some time to catch their breath, but not for a good reason. Vespasian had decided on a new tactic: raising the earthen banks still higher. He also began erecting three towers, each 50 feet high, and with iron plates on all sides. Once put into place atop the banks, the towers would actually look down inside the walls of Jotapata and allow archers and slingers inside them to bombard the defenders continually.

This is exactly what happened. But it was not by a mighty Roman onslaught that Jotapata was finally taken, but by thieves who crept in during the still of night. For it was approaching the 47th day of the siege when a deserter came to Vespasian and told him that the people of the city were much less numerous and more exhausted than he had assumed. The deserter said that even the guards at a particular watchtower by the breached wall were so fatigued that they usually lapsed into sleep sometime after midnight. If the Romans used stealth, he said, they could kill the watchmen in their sleep and take the city before the rest of the people awoke the next morning.

The Roman commander hesitated, fearing a trick. So far the Jews of Jotapata had been unfailingly loyal to one another. Vespasian remembered one man in particular who had been captured and tortured by fire in hopes of getting some insights into Josephus' defenses and tactics. The man had never uttered a word of betrayal. And even when the Romans crucified him in front of the wall, he had died in silence with a smile on his lips.

But then the general thought again. How much could he lose by investigating the theory? So he ordered that the deserter be kept in custody, then killed if his advice proved to be a sham.

Late the same night a small band of elite Roman troops quietly dropped down on the city from the towers that had just been erected on the earthen bank. Titus, ever the most daring and valiant of the Roman commanders, was first over the wall, followed by two of his best tribunes and some members of the 15th legion. They found the watchmen sleeping, as predicted, and quickly cut their throats. Now they entered the city stealthily. The Roman cohort, if their small numbers could be called as much, crept through dark, narrow streets all the way to the citadel, which was in the most elevated part of the city. Now they waited until most of the Roman army slipped over the wall in the still darkness and hastened on cat feet to meet them.

By dawn the Romans had already made progress downhill, entering homes quietly and butchering people in their sleep. Even when they aroused whole neighborhoods and engaged in armed combat, much of the populace elsewhere in the city still failed to understand what was happening inside their walls. Soon, the Romans abandoned all pretense of stealth. Now when the rising sun would ordinarily have families of Jotapata baking bread and stretching themselves on their rooftops, they faced an armed and angry Roman mob, chasing down helpless victims in narrow streets and hacking to death anyone it could catch; for the Romans were full of revenge against those who had poured out the hot oil and the wild-eyed raiders who had rushed out from the walls to ambush them. When the elders and guardsmen around Josephus grouped together briefly, the discussion was not how to defend themselves, but of how to escape and/or when to kill themselves. Some did so on the spot.

That day, on June 16, the Romans killed everyone they could find in the town — about 40,000 in all. Vespasian also resolved to destroy everything in Jotapata and level the fortifications. But before doing so the Romans spent the next two days methodically searching for anyone who might still be hiding in basements and cisterns – or even in the piles of dead bodies that lay rotting all around in the blistering summer heat. Most of all, they wanted Josephus. He held the key to the subjugation of all Galilee. Where was he?

In the midst of the final slaughter, the young governor general was, he writes, "assisted by a certain supernatural providence." He, along with about 40 of the city's leaders, had descended into a deep pit in a quiet part of the city. Off to the side of it was a large den that could not be seen by anyone above ground. Quite conveniently, Josephus reports, the den was already equipped "with provisions enough to satisfy them for not a few days."

Two days passed. Late each night Josephus would clamber up the sides and look about for some way of escaping, but all avenues were tightly guarded by the Romans. On the third day Josephus was betrayed by a woman who was interrogated by the Romans (further evidence, I think, that many of Jotapata's elite had long provided themselves with a place of refuge). Vespasian immediately dispatched two tribunes, who called down into the pit for Josephus to come out. They promised their hands as security if he did so.

But Josephus couldn't be persuaded, knowing that Vespasian must be well aware of how the rebels of Jerusalem had treated a Roman embassy after promising their safety. This time Vespasian sent down into the pit a single tribune named Nicanor, whom Josephus had known and respected in the days before the rebellion. Nicanor talked in a mild and gentle tone, reminding Josephus that Romans had a tradition of showing respect and hospitality to foes whose courage they admired. He vowed solemnly that Vespasian wanted to see Josephus – not to punish him, but to preserve a man of such courage. Vespasian, he said, would never pretend friendship and display perfidy.

At this point, Josephus (always appearing to be the detached historian in his writings), says he began to recall many dreams and prophesies that had come to him at night and wondered if God were beckoning him to some purpose that he should follow.

> Now Josephus was able to give shrewd conjectures about the interpretation of such dreams as have been ambiguously delivered by God. Moreover, he was not unacquainted with the prophecies contained in the sacred books, being a priest himself.

So he put up a secret prayer to God:

> "Since it pleaseth thee, who has created the Jewish nation, to depress the same; and since all good fortune has gone over to the Romans, and since thou hast made a choice of this soul of mine to foretell what is to come to pass hereafter, I willingly give them my hands and am con-

tent to live. And I [state] openly that I do not go over to the Romans as
a deserter of the Jews, but as a minister from thee."[23]

So Josephus announced he would accept Nicanor's invitation. Now it was his
own confederates with whom he had to contend. They were incensed to a man.
"Josephus," one of them thundered, "are you so fond of life that you can bear to
see the light of day in a state of slavery? If so, you have a false reputation for manhood and for wisdom! Yes, the Romans may have good fortune, but it is up to us
to take care that the glory of our forefathers not be tarnished."

Another drew his sword and made ready to hand it to Josephus. "We will lend
you our right hand and our sword," he said. "And if you will die willingly, you
will die as a general of the Jews. But if you die unwillingly, it will be as a traitor to
them." And with that several of them thrust their swords at him in a show of
what would happen if he tried to abscond in Nicanor's company.

Josephus reacted by assuming the role of philosopher-priest. He rose to his
full height and delivered a formal oration. Could anyone pretend that he was
not the same courageous warrior he had been a few days ago? Yes, it is brave to
die in war. But how courageous would it to be to die at one's own hand when
one's conquerors stand ready to spare him? "If they would spare their enemy,
how much more ought we to have mercy upon ourselves!"

Indeed, said Josephus the philosopher, if a person is a coward who will not die
when he is obliged to, is it not an equal coward who will die when he is not
obliged to? It is a most unmanly act to kill oneself just as would be a ship's captain who would deliberately sink his own vessel because he feared a storm.

And now from Josephus the priest:

> Self-murder is a crime most remote from the common nature of all
> animals, and an instance of impiety against God our creator. Do you
> not think that God is very angry when a man does injury to what he
> hath bestowed on him? For from him it is that we have received our
> being, and we ought to leave it to his disposal to take that being away
> from us.[24]

When his colleages would still have none of it, Josephus became the advocate
and defender of Roman law. "Our law," he argued, " justly ordains that slaves
which run away from their master should be punished, even though the masters they run away from may have been wicked. So, shall we endeavor to run
away from God, who is the best of all masters, and not think ourselves guilty of
impiety?"

No, concluded Josephus the priest. If one has a mind to die, "it is good to die by
the hand of those who have conquered us. Should the Romans prove treacher-

ous with their offer, I shall die cheerfully and carry away with me the sense of their perfidiousness as a consolation greater than victory itself."

A remarkable extemporaneous dissertation for one trapped in a cave by allies and foes alike. But the Jewish leaders would have none of it. Finally shouting Josephus down, they rushed at him from all angles with drawn swords. They were to a man committed to die and they were irritated that their own general would delay it any longer. "However, in this extreme distress, he was not destitute of his usual sagacity," Josephus the historian writes of Josephus the general. "Trusting himself to the providence of God, he put his life at risk" as follows:

"Men," he cried out, "since you have resolved to die, let us commit our mutual deaths to determination by lot. He whom the lot falls to first, let him be killed by whom has the second lot so that fortune will make its progress through us all. This way, no one will perish by his own hand; for it would be unfair to the rest if somebody should repent and save himself."

The proposal seemed just. They drew lots, Josephus included. As the Roman tribune Nicanor watched from the entrance to the den, the man who drew the first lot, bared his neck to the next, and so forth, each supposing that their general would be one of the next to die with them. The rest I had better relate in Josephus' own words:

> Yet was he [Josephus] and another left to the last, whether we may say
> it happened so by chance or whether by the providence of God. And as
> he was very desirous neither to be condemned by the lot, nor — if he
> had been left to the last — to imbrue his right hand in the blood of his
> countrymen, he persuaded the man who was next to last to entrust
> his fidelity to him, and to live as well as himself.[25]

What happened to the man who was next to last I cannot say. But Josephus, at least, was then led by Nicanor through the Roman camp as crowds of soldiers strained to get a look at the Jewish general who had bedeviled them for nearly two months. Now, as the haggard Josephus stood in the tent of Vespasian, a throng of soldiers outside shouted for his immediate execution. But inside the tent, Titus delivered an ardent appeal to his father, citing Josephus' bravery, and now, his almost regal calm under such adversity. Vespasian replied simply that the governor of Galilee would be bound and held under close guard until such time as he could be sent to Nero for disposal.

Josephus had been silent until this time. Now he spoke up firmly. He said that he had something important to say to the Roman general that was for his ears alone.

Vespasian hesitated suspiciously, then ordered all senior staff officers except Titus and two commanders to withdraw from the tent.

The remaining men sat quietly and curiously facing their captive. "Vespasian," said Josephus without a trace of supplication, "do you think no more than that you have taken Josephus captive? In truth, I come to you as a messenger of greater tidings.

"You intend to send me to Nero? Why? Thou, O Vespasian, will be Cæsar and emperor. And so, too, will thy son.

"Bind me now still faster," said Josephus, "but keep me for thyself, For thou, O Cæsar, are not only lord over me, but will be over the land and the sea and all mankind. And for saying such things, I certainly deserve to be kept in closer custody in order to be all the more severely punished should I prove rash in stating that all this has been prophesied to me by God."

Well, Vespasian was outwardly a modest and uncomplicated man, even given to jokes at his own expense. Perhaps he felt awkward at hearing these words in the presence of others, but deep inside he had already felt that God had inexplicably destined him to become emperor even though he was content with a general's life. So he had Josephus imprisoned without further commitment, yet began making discreet inquiries as to the accuracy of the young general's previous predictions. For instance, Josephus had been known to have told intimates that Jotapata would be captured on the 47th day of the siege and that he would be captured alive by the Romans. Vespasian heard all this and began to believe that Josephus, albeit a strange messenger to him from a Jewish God, had been correct in foretelling his own future. So, while he kept Josephus under close watch, he gave him gifts of clothing and jewelry and "treated him in a very obliging manner" with "Titus joining his interest in the honors that were done him."

. . . .

IN ROME, as spring gave way to the humid, languid summer, the mood seemed equally torpid. With much of officialdom in Greece with Nero, those who were not seemed relieved to escape to their country villas. But for everyone who remained, fear and suspicion were as stifling as the heat.

This is difficult to explain to an outsider, but I will try. It is as if, during the persecutions that preceded Nero's departure to Greece, all of the ingenuity in inventing believable charges against senators and anyone else who might be considered an imperial threat had been used up. Yet, the freedman Helius, I suppose in his assumed obligation to keep up the prosecutorial pace in order to satisfy his master that he was diligent in his task, began inventing charges so wild as to cause the most dutiful of his lackey-advocates to say, "Eh, how's that again?"

Rather than bore you to death with their farcicality, here is one example to give you a taste. Helius used Nero's absence to take off one of Rome's foremost senators, Sulpicius Camerinus, together with his grown son. The charge was that his family name had included the name of Pythicus, which it had received as an honor for oratory in some Greek games perhaps centuries before. Continuing to use this name, it was now charged, showed irreverence for the title Pythicus that was awarded to Nero for some of his artistic victories in Pythia.

When the senators and knights weren't being picked apart, Helius swatted at philosophers and out-of-favor religious orders to keep up his pace and keep the jails full.

And this brings me to the Mamertine prison.

How ironic it is that only a minute's walk from where the Via Sacra ends at the door of Rome's most venerated institutions, the Senate house, squats a small, mean, stone building that seems oddly misplaced on such a prominent street, for it deserves to be hidden in the shadows of Rome's history. But the Mamertine prison nonetheless is a Roman tradition in its own right. It was erected many centuries ago as a fortification around a large cistern, which probably lay atop one of Rome's many underground streams or natural springs. Thus, the walls of its soot-colored travertine rock are round. Inside the outer parts of the building, which serve as barracks for guards, the walls of the old cistern measure perhaps no more than 30 feet in diameter.

Long ago the deep cistern was partially filled in to build a small prison with two tiers. The top was a crude foyer and guard station. The bottom layer was more like a grotto, with no more than six or seven feet from floor to rocky ceiling. All that separated the two levels was a small stairway and a bored hole in the top floor perhaps three feet in diameter.

In the early days of the Republic the building, known then as the Tullianum, was not so much a prison (for Rome kept no long-term prisoners), as an execution place. Some enemies of Rome — often defeated but defiant foreign rulers — were simply cast into the hole and into utter darkness until they succumbed to starvation, fetid air and all loss of hope.

The Tullianum was also the place where condemned men were held briefly before execution. Perhaps once or twice a year before a triumph or certain festival, the public might see the ugly wooden doors creak open long enough to admit a few dozen brawny bare-chested slaves who had been marched there from the public slave barracks north of the old city walls. The men would enter the hole by means of narrow, slippery stairs. Then the victims would be pushed down one at a time — always foreigners at first, for it was unlawful then to kill a Roman inside the pomerium, or sacred boundary of the city. As the victim gagged in the foul darkness and struggled to collect his wits, the burly executioners would rush out from the shadows, grab their prey and hold him fast while one of them wrapped his hands around the man's neck and snapped it in two.

Their assignment now completed in the slippery dank cistern, the slave crew would simply leave the dead to rot away, perhaps to have their remains pushed out into the underground sewer system several months later when the next group arrived to do its duty. And I can add, sadly, that in subsequent years, even prominent Romans sometimes perished in a similar manner. For instance, we all think of Cicero as a lawyer and orator; yet it was in his term as consul, 113 years before Nero, that he sent the senator Cataline and several co-conspirators to the same grim place to be strangled in exactly the way I have just described.

The Tullianum languished as but an embarrassing historical memento for many years after it became more common to house prisoners in another, larger building, the Lautimæ, that sat alongside it at the foot of Capitoline Hill. But by Nero's time the ugly little coop, now known more commonly as the Mamertine, was in use again as a holding place for prisoners from the overcrowded Lautimæ. Those not yet destined for execution were housed in the small upper room, which has a window opening to the neighboring guards' quarters.

The tradition is strong that agents of Helius watched and recorded Peter's preachings and miracles of healing from the time he first performed them in the public squares of the Subura. If this led to any formal charges, they have never been discovered, but Helius could have picked from any number of possibilities. Peter could have been cited for teaching philosophy publicly, for being a leader of a *religio illicitia* or for being a dangerous Jewish rabble rouser during a time when the Jews of Rome were trying desperately to be inconspicuous.

In any case, the tradition among Christians today is very strong that Peter simply disappeared from view one day and was taken to the Mamertine prison. Whether he stayed in this horrid place for days or weeks I cannot say, for how can anyone know exactly what happens when a loved one is suddenly snatched up, taken off to an unknown place and allowed no contact? How can one even investigate when to do so is to invite one's own disappearance?

Still, I have come to trust accounts that are reported faithfully by many persons of different backgrounds and neighborhoods. The stories I am about to relate fit this standard. They also involve miracles, which, I must confess, make me nervous as a historian. Why is it that I find it much more readily acceptable to believe in a miracle that happened before I was alive rather than during my lifetime? Yet, these stories are so strongly believed among Roman Christians today and depictions of them are so pervasive in their sarcophagi and places of worship that I feel compelled to relate them to you here.

First, it is said that the prisoners in the Mamertine were parched for thirst, and that Peter touched a rod to a place in the old cistern wall, causing a spring to gush forth. I can only report to those who have not been to Rome that if you went to a Christian necropolis or into the new catacombs that line the Via

Appia, you would see many artistic representations of Peter making the water flow as grateful prisoners and guards looked on.

The second account is that Peter preached the gospel and made believers of two of his guards, then baptized them with water from the same underground spring. We know their names as Processus and Martinianus. We know that both have since died, that they were entombed on the the Via Aurelia, and that Christians today venerate their tombs.

Thirdly, I relate to you a story that you will have to accept or reject on faith because I cannot imagine how there would be witnesses to verify it. Peter's guards, it is said, were prepared for him to leave the Mamertine free. "Nero is in Greece and has forgotten all about you," they reportedly told him. So, late one night after leading a liturgy, the account continues, Peter strode out the dingy prison doorway and made for the city walls. Perhaps at first he thought himself directed by the Holy Spirit, as he had that night over 20 years before when he was arrested for preaching in the temple at Jerusalem. But as Peter was about to pass through the gate of the city, he saw Christ coming towards him.

Peter fell down in astonishment and asked: "Lord, where are you going?"

Jesus replied: "I am going to be crucified once again."

Then Peter repeated himself: "Lord, you will be crucified *again?*"

And Christ replied: "Yes I will be crucified again."

"Then, Lord," answered Peter, "I am returning to follow you."

No sooner had Peter turned around than Jesus vanished. After weeping and collecting his thoughts, Peter understood that the words were meant for his own martyrdom, that the Lord would suffer with him as he suffers with all those who live and die in his name. And so, Peter, bursting with new strength, returned to the prison glorifying God and singing praises to the risen Christ.

It is also a strong tradition that on June 29 – the day since marked by Christians – that Peter was taken from the Mamertine. He was probably crowded into a mule-driven cart and hauled northward on the road that borders the Tiber. After a mile or so the grim calvacade would cross the Neronian bridge from the 14th district of Rome and proceed along the Aurelian consular road into the Vatican area.

No one knows where the name "Vatican" comes from. For centuries it was simply an outlying suburb full of marshes, vineyards and banks of clay that were used for brick manufacturing. It was here that the mother of Caligula built large gardens, and where the young emperor began building the private racetrack we now know as the Circus of Caligula and Nero. Official games now took up some 80 days per year, and with the Circus Maximus still undergoing reconstruction, the Vatican Circus was now their focal point. And the condemned people in the cart would be needed to enliven the spectacle.

The Circus, by the way, was an exact replica of the one in the city center: 590

meters long and 95 wide. At its center or spina was a huge Egyptian obelisk that Caligula had loaded onto the world's largest cargo ship, sent to Ostia, dragged some 20 miles by teams of oxen, then set upright in his private circus. And it sems to be there, at the base of the giant obelisk, that Peter was taken to be crucified. It is said that Peter asked only one thing of his executioners: "I beg you crucify me in this way – head down – and no other way." And he explained that he was not worthy to be executed as had his lord and master.

I suspect that his request was granted without hesitation, for executing a prisoner upside down would only add to the theatrics of the spectacle. As any well-read Roman knows, crucifixions of criminals or conquered peoples are done in a variety of positions so as to demonstrate to the living populace the many ways that rebels can pay for abusing the government of Rome.

So Peter suffered as had his Lord, hanging naked on the cross, his heels and hands nailed. Finally, if the guards were in a merciful mood, one of them might crush the victim's thighs with a few mighty hammer blows. Now with no means of support, the victim's body would thrust forward and suffocate because the lungs had no means of taking in air.

I doubt that many Christians were there to see Peter die. Chances are it was only Romans who witnessed their fellow humans writhing on crosses as a diversion to the main spectacle of races and animal hunts.

I wrote earlier that close attention should be paid to oral traditions repeated by many and diverse peoples. By these accounts one should pay attention to the many Christian sarcophagi and mausoleum frescoes that depict Peter and Paul facing death together in Rome. But common opinion is that they did not and that all these sculptures and paintings simply reflect an understandable desire to associate the deceased with both apostles.

Paul indeed was caught in the same wave of repression unleashed by Nero's nervous custodians of Rome, but I believe he was probably seized where soldiers would know where to find him – the same insulæ he rented under house arrest from the day he arrived in Rome. Again, there is strong tradition. Christians say that Paul was led south, beyond the sacred pomerium (the boundaries within which no foreigner might be buried) on the road to Ostia. Three miles further, just before reaching the village of Ardea, stood a lovely grove of Eucalyptus trees. There in a small clearing stood a beheading block that was to be the last destination of Paul, the tireless traveler for the cause of Christ.

I would like to think of him still preaching to his guard, as one of them unsheathed his sword with trembling hands, that he, too, could know the grace of Jesus Christ if he would but ask for it.

· · · · · · · · ·

By now Nero had been absent from Rome for longer than any other emperor save Tiberius. But this was a trivial detail if indeed he ever thought about it, for the Grand Tour had seen a glorious flowering of his multicolored talents and the culmination of his destiny. The emperor had led his bulky entourage everywhere that games were held — all save Athens and Sparta, which various omens and prophesies had cautioned him against visiting. By November the emperor had won 1,808 prizes in athletic and dramatic contests. The judges had acclaimed him Pythian Victor, Olympian Victor, Universal Victor, Victor of the Grand Tour and so on. Whatever the event, his proclamation of acceptance invariably ran something like: "Nero Cæsar wins the contest and crowns the Roman people and the inhabited world that is his own."

Sometimes it required ingenuity — and sometimes even a spell of temporary blindness — for the judges to figure how to award the first prize to Nero. On one occasion during the Olympic Games, the emperor was driving a team of ten horses when he was knocked out of his chariot. His servants rushed from the sidelines, pushed him back into it and handed him the reins, but he was too dazed to continue. Nonetheless, the judges awarded him first prize (perhaps on grounds that he would have won had not some flaw in the track caused his fall). In any case, the judges' decision proved prudent (for them at least) because the emperor awarded them with a gift of a million sesterces.

All those about him were constantly sunny in the presence of such a winner — especially the senators who attended him. Nero, like Caligula, hated the Senate as an institution and enjoyed using its members in servile roles. His freedmen constantly scrutinized their faces, gestures and shouts at the games for any sign that they were not blissfully happy to be in the emperor's company. Thus, they were usually to be seen listening reverently to his performances and leading the wild applause as he accepted his prize. Once when one of them appeared to be frowning as he conversed with the emperor, Nero ordered him dismissed and refused to see him ever again.

"But where shall I go?" the puzzled man asked the freedman who scheduled the emperor's appointments. "To the deuce!" said the freedman with an angry wave.

But the private thoughts of most Romans were quite otherwise. One of them, writing years later, offered this description of the "Grand Tour":

> How could one endure...an emperor, an Augustus, named on the program among the contestants, training his voice, practicing various songs, wearing long hair on his head while the chin was smooth-shaven, throwing a toga over his shoulder in the races, walking about with one or two attendants, looking askance at his opponents, and constantly uttering taunting remarks at them, standing in dread of

the directors of the games...and lavishing money on them all secretly to avoid being brought to book and scourged?

And all this he did, though by winning the contests of the lyre players and tragedians and heralds he would make certain his defeat in the contest of the Cæsars. What harsher proscription could there ever be...what stranger victory than one for which he received the crown of the wild olive, hay, parsley or pine and lost the political crown? Yet, why should one lament these acts of his, seeing that he also elevated himself on high-soled buskins only to fall from the throne, and in putting on a mask threw off the dignity of his sovereignty to beg in the guise of a runaway slave, to be led about as a blind man, to be heavy with child, to be in labor, to be a madman or to wander as an outcast...?

The masks that he wore were sometimes made to resemble the characters he was portraying and sometimes bore his own likeness. But the women's masks were all fashioned after the features of Sabina [Poppæa] so that, although dead, she might still take part in the spectacle. All the situations that ordinary actors simulate in their acting he, too, would portray in speech or action or in submitting to the action of others. The only exception was that golden chains were used to bind him, for apparently it was thought improper for a Roman emperor to be bound in iron shackles.

All this behavior, nevertheless, was witnessed, endured and approved, not only by the crowd in general, but also by the soldiers.[26]

Greek audiences also appeared happy and grateful, for they often received lavish gifts, which of course made them clamor for even more performances. But the truth is that the privilege of seeing the emperor perform or of receiving a gift from his bounty invariably meant that the Greeks themselves were fleeced to pay for it. One critic goes as far as to complain that Nero "devastated the whole of Greece precisely as if he had been sent out to wage war." As in Italy, he commanded the survivors of executed freedmen to leave him half their property. Later he took away the entire property of those who were executed and banished all their children with a single decree. Executions became so common that the same critic as above writes that "dispatch bearers hurried back and forth [from the camp of Nero and Tigellinus to various guardsmen] bearing no other communications than 'Put this man to death' or 'So and so is dead...'"

After taking off so much of their money and leading men, Nero still found a way to evoke applause as the Grand Tour wound down. On November 28, in an oration delivered in the stadium at Corinth, he suddenly declared all of Greece free of Roman taxation.

> It is an unexpected gift, Hellenes...which I grant you, one so great that you were incapable of requesting it. All Hellenes who inhabit Achæa and the land until now called the Peloponnese receive...exemption from tribute, which not even in your most fortunate days did you all enjoy, for you were subjects either of foreigners or of one another.

> Would that I were making this gift while Hellas was still at its height, so that more people might enjoy this boon! For this, indeed, I have a grudge against time, for squandering in advance the fullness of my boon. Yet even now it is not out of pity but out of good will that I bestow this benefaction upon you, requiring your gods, whose care for me both on land and sea I have never found to fail, for affording me an opportunity to bestow so great a benefaction.

> For to cities other rulers, too, have granted freedom, but Nero alone to an entire province![27]

Perhaps the emperor knew then that his tour would soon end. Helius had been writing him urgent letters begging him to return to an increasingly restless Rome. Then, in early December, Helius decided to underscore the urgency of his plea by sailing to Greece in the fastest ship available. Within seven days he was in the emperor's presence, begging him to return to save his throne. It was not so much that Rome itself was in an uproar, but the provinces were a different matter. Britain and the two Germanys were rife with angry outbreaks. And rumors were incessant that the commanders of several legionary forces were nervous that they might be the next to follow Corbulo and the Scribonius brothers to their deaths. And what about Vespasian with all those legions in Syria? He was being heard from all too little.

Nero seemed quite unperturbed about all this. Yet, winter was coming on and the Games were dwindling. Perhaps it would be convenient, after all, to display his crowns to the people at home and treat them again to the talents that won so many laurels for Rome.

Or so he thought.

. . . .

. . . .

A fter the fall of Jotapata, Vespasian might well have marched his men straight to Jerusalem for a final battle to shatter the Jewish rebellion. That he waited nearly a year before making the 90-mile trip from Galilee was due to three factors. First, Vespasian was a deliberate, orderly tactician who felt safer in assuring that all armed threats north of Jerusalem – no matter how trivial – had been minimized before engaging in his principal task. Second, although no remaining center of resistance was large enough to deter the Roman advance, even though some of them – such as Gamala and Taricheæ – were full of valorous defenders who made the attackers pay dearly for every stone in the walls they destroyed. Third, Vespasian himself knew he could afford to take his time so that the defenders of Jerusalem could consume their own strength in an orgy of deceit and rivalry.

After the annihilation of Jotapata, Vespasian divided his men into winter camps at Ptomelais, Cæsarea and Scythopolis, from which smaller forces were sent out to pacify the surrounding areas. During all these maneuvers it became apparent that most of the survivors from the demolished cities were escaping still further down the coast to Joppa, which had been desolate since the Syrian governor Cestius had destroyed it the previous year. So Vespasian sent out a small expedition to make sure the renegades would not re-create another center of rebellion.

Joppa's defenses had become nothing but rubble, but the new occupants had anticipated that the Romans might come snooping around. So they had built a makeshift fleet of ships and planned to use Joppa as a base for pirating cargo ships that plied the Syrian coast. Thus, when the Romans showed themselves, the defenders simply boarded their boats and sailed beyond the range of darts, determined to spend whatever time it took until the Romans gave up and went away.

The problem is that the shore around Joppa has no natural protections. When the winds blow from the north and west, they beat relentlessly on the rocky shore. Just before the next sunrise a violent unseasonable wind blew up and the "mariners" found that their new abode was less reliable than the fortified cities they had fled. The ships either were dashed against one another or driven against the rocks on shore. Boats overturned, men thrashed about towards land, and when they finally were able to grasp onto a rock on shore they were run through by Roman swordsmen standing above them. Others simply elected to kill themselves by their own swords rather than face the agony of drowning. In all, 2,400 were killed in this way and the Romans again leveled the city before leaving.

A somewhat similar scene was repeated in Taricheæ – the city on Lake Gennesaret where Josephus had once spent King Agrippa's stolen gold to fortify with high walls. Like Tiberias, Taricheæ sits where the side of a mountain slopes gradually eastward to the Lake of Gennesaret. Like the refugees in Joppa, the leaders of Taricheæ had provided that, should the city fall, they could escape into the lake on a fleet of boats. After a long and arduous battle in which most of the defenders were slain, the survivors remembered their escape plan and fled to the lake, pushing their boats out from the shore and scrambling inside as the Romans hacked at them from behind.

The lake itself is 20 miles long and six miles wide, so the escapees from Taricheæ thought they had gained freedom. But it wasn't long before the Romans had commandeered their own boats and were rowing after them. The difference was that the pursuing boats were occupied by archers and slingers, whereas the best the Taricheæns could do was throw stones back at them. Once they had killed or wounded enough Jews with darts, the Romans pulled alongside and boarded with drawn swords. Those who jumped overboard had their heads and limbs hacked off in the water. When it was over some 6,500 Taricheæns had been killed on the lake alone (and many more in the land battle). As Josephus writes:

> One might then see the lake all bloody and full of dead bodies, for not one of them escaped. A terrible stink, and a very sad sight there was on the following days over that country. As for the shores, they were full of shipwrecks and of dead bodies, And as the dead bodies were inflamed by the sun and putrefied, they corrupted the air, inasmuch that the misery was not only the object of commiseration to the Jews, but to those that hated them, and had been the authors of that misery.[28]

This is the same lake that Josephus had described earlier as having been blessed by the Creator.

> Its waters are sweet, and very agreeable for drinking, for they are finer than the thick waters of other fens. The lake is also pure, and on every side ends directly at the shores and at the sand. It is also of a temperate nature when you draw it up, and of a more gentle nature than river or fountain water, and yet always cooler than what one would expect in so diffuse a place as this.

And the surrounding countryside Josephus had depicted:

> ...as wonderful as well as its beauty. Its soil is so fruitful that all sorts of trees can grow upon it...for the temper of the air is so well mixed that it agrees very well with those several sorts, particularly walnuts, which require the coldest air, flourish there in vast plenty. There are palm trees also, which grow best in hot air. Fig trees also and olives grow near them, which yet require an air that is more temperate. One may well call this place the ambition of nature, where it forces those plants that are naturally enemies to one another to agree together. It is a happy contention of the seasons, as if every one of them laid claim to this country.[29]

But the disparate forces of humankind behaved in no such harmony. As the Roman purge wore on, it seemed that all the most zealous, contentious, corrupt, and desperate men of the resistance scurried into a common sewer. I refer, of course, to the holy city of Jerusalem. It was inevitably there that Judaism as a nation would take its final stand against Roman authority.

Into the gates of the capital came John of Gischala and his band of brigands. The once mortal enemy of Josephus had taken control over his native city of Gischala, ordinarily the home of peaceful farmers and herdsmen. When Titus and his men arrived at the gates and invited everyone to surrender or die in battle, John called down from the wall that it was the Sabbath, and that he would deliver an answer the next day if only the Romans would allow them to observe the Jewish day of rest. Since Titus could see no harm in giving the Jews another day to deplete their food and water supplies, he withdrew his men to a base camp they had established out of sight.

That night John and his men opened the southern gate and left in haste for Jerusalem, followed by some 9,000 women and children. But about three miles down the road, John turned to the straggling multitude and said they must now fend for themselves. And as the women and children lamented and called to the men not to leave them to the revenge of Roman pursuers, John and his gang galloped off for Jerusalem.

The next day the Romans caught up with the "escaped stragglers" and slew some 6,000 in revenge for John's perfidy. But by then John and his men had already been greeted as heroes as they rode through the gates of Jerusalem. People inside crowded around them, eager for reports on the war in Galilee. John dwelt not on defeats and escapes, however. He said that his men had come to strengthen the defense of Jerusalem, because this, after all, was the best place in which to defeat the Romans. He reported the Roman condition as weak and predicted that many more contingents from Galilee would soon arrive to bolster Jerusalem for its final victory. After all, reassured John, if the Romans had encountered such great stress in taking the small fortifications of Galilee, how could they hope to surmount the most formidable walls in the world? The only way, he joked, would be if the Romans suddenly sprouted wings!

Almost at the very time John entered Jerusalem, Titus and Vespasian changed tactics, sending word to the remaining towns that they would offer sanctuary for surrender. This invariably forced the issue in each city, causing most people to flock to the Romans for protection and the diehard rebels to head for Jerusalem. Yet, the results were what neither the defectors of Galilee nor defenders in Jerusalem expected. By this I mean, first, that the Galileans who surrendered were simply left to roam and forage. The Romans did nothing for them while at the same time laying first claim on all available food supplies. This forced people to coalesce in roving roadside gangs that robbed and plundered anyone in their path. When these grew to such size to attract reprisals by Roman garrisons, the most desperate of the gang leaders fled to Jerusalem for protection. So now the capital was teeming, not with the valiant heroes John had promised the populace, but with the worst elements from all over Judea and Galilee. And once they were inside the walls of Jerusalem, these disheveled and disorganized bands not only helped themselves to supplies that were needed for the war effort, but "omitted no kind of barbarity," writes Josephus.

> For they did not measure their courage by their rapines and plunderings only, but proceeded as far as murdering men. And this not in the night time or privately...but they did it openly in the day time, and began with the most eminent men of the city. This caused a terrible consternation among the people, and everyone contented himself with taking care of his own safety, as they would do if the city had been taken in war.[30]

The most rapacious of all the troublemakers were the Zealots. It was they who controlled the temple and they who now elevated tensions to a new level.

They arrested some of the city's leading men, including one Antipas, who had been in charge of the public treasury. Worried that the populace would soon form a mob and demand their release, a dozen or so leading Zealots stole into the prison and cut the throats of their victims. Then they went about the city announcing that the dead elders had been caught in a conspiracy to surrender to the Romans.

When no one revolted, the Zealots decided they would make their seizure of the temple official by appointing their own ruling priests. Disregarding the families who had supplied high priests for generations, they gave offices to what Josephus calls "certain unknown and ignoble persons...that they might have their assistance in their wicked undertakings."

Indeed, they even cast lots for the position of high priest. The "winner" was a bumpkin named Phannias, who came from a tiny backwater village. Until he saw his mates casting lots and asked to get in on the fun, Phannias had not even known what a high priest was! Now, as the lucky winner, he was outfitted with the sacred garments as though the chief actor in a comedy. Soon Phannias the high priest had gotten into the spirit of the day, strutting about the inner temple courtyards giving orders with a grave face as his companions guffawed and swilled wine from sacred vessels. The same crew ate off ritualistic plates and threw them in a corner when they were dirty.

Some people could bear this no more and decided that they cared no longer about the risks of speaking out because life in these conditions was not worth living. One was Symeon, son of the famous rabbi Gamaliel, and president of the Sanhedrin in the days of normalcy. Another was Ananus, who was perhaps the most esteemed of the high priests who had managed to survive in Jerusalem. One day Ananus could be seen going among the crowds in the marketplaces, reproaching the people for their sloth in doing nothing against the Zealots. It was obvious that Ananus no longer cared whether he was observed or not. Soon he was surrounded by a large, curious crowd who clearly wanted to hear more. Ananus obliged by mounting some steps and announcing to them that he despaired of living.

> For to what purpose is there to live among a people so insensitive to their calamities and [who have] no notion remaining of any remedy for the miseries that are upon them? For when you are seized upon, you bear it! And when you are beaten you are silent! And when the people are murdered, nobody dares so much as to even groan openly! O bitter tyranny that we are under!
>
> But why do I complain of tyrants? Was it not you, in your sufferance of them, that have nourished them? Was it not you who overlooked

those who first of all got together? For they were then but a few, and by your silence have grown to be many.[31]

"Now that the tyrants have seized the temple — the strongest place in the whole city — what now will you do?" Ananus asked. "Have things plunged to such a low state where the Jews must wait for the Romans to take pity on them? Even if fortune dictates that we must bear having the lords of the inhabitable earth rule over us, is it right to bear tyrants of our own nationality as well?"

Romans, lamented Ananus, had at least traditionally respected ancient Jewish customs by keeping a distance from the inner temple precincts. But those who now occupy them "walk about in the midst of the holy places at the very time their hands are still warm with the slaughter of their own countrymen." How ironic, he said with scorn to the murmuring crowd, that "one may hereafter find the Romans to be the supporters of our laws and those among ourselves the subverters of them!"

With this exhortation Ananus was able to rouse the crowd to vow vengeance against the Zealots in the temple. The difficulty was that Ananus didn't have an immediate plan and knew that the youth and daring of his adversaries would be difficult to overcome for ordinary citizens not skilled in fighting.

The Zealots, of course, heard about what had been said in the speech to the crowd in the lower city. The seditionists were more frightened than Ananus or any of the others anticipated, because they were greatly outnumbered and feared the unpredictable frenzy of an angry mob.

Their fear was justified. Ananus selected commanders from among the bravest of the populace, and when the "army" they had mobilized first appeared below the temple walls, hurling javelins from a harmless distance, the Zealots tried to crush their spirits by rushing out at them with the finest gleaming weapons that had been taken from Herod the Great's fortress at Masada. To their surprise, the people held their own ground. After a few hours of hand-to-hand combat, the Zealots were driven back beyond the first temple walls and into the inner courtyard. This further inflamed the people, because whereas their families took the wounded to their homes and treated them, the Zealots dragged their casualties into the holiest places of the temple and defiled it with their blood.

Ananus chose not to challenge the Zealots further that day because he decided as high priest that his side, too, would defile the inner precincts if they warred there with their foes. So he chose a continuous, rotating guard of 6,000 volunteers to keep the Zealots penned in their now-smaller temple quarters as they met to plan their next move.

Ever since his arrival, John of Gischala had been waiting for an opportunity to thrust himself into the leadership of Jerusalem. But John was patient and Vespasian was still nowhere in sight, so he began by appearing as an interested and helpful participant in the meetings of Ananus and his advisors. John knew that he and his men from Gischala were not powerful enough alone to wrest control from the Zealots, so he plotted to rise within their leadership by plying them with useful information known only to him. Thus, in the evenings after Ananus and his advisors had gone home, John would sneak past the guards who watched the temple walls and report to the waiting Zealots all that he heard. Meanwhile, he cultivated the greatest of friendships and trust with Ananus himself.

John, in fact, was such an excessive flatterer of the high priest that Ananus and his advisors eventually suspected him of betraying their secrets. One day at such a meeting the group asked John to swear an oath that he was not in league with their enemies. He did so readily, adding his own vow that he would fight to the death on the people's side.

Soon afterward, John embarked on his next ploy. He went to the Zealots and told them he had just returned from a meeting in which Ananus and the city leaders had agreed to send Vespasian a message to the effect that, if he would come quickly, they would open the gates to him. He said that Ananus, as self-appointed high priest, had proclaimed the following day a religious fast, meaning that people would come to the temple on the pretext of prayer and then take it by storm once inside. Just for good measure, John added that Ananus had singled out Eleazor and Zacharias, the two most ruthless Zealot leaders, for especially barbarous punishment.

Ananus, of course, had said none of this, but the frightened Zealots were now asking their new confidant what to do. John's answer was that they needed help from a foreign army. But with Vespasian coming so soon, the reinforcements would have to be already nearby. Who else but the neighboring Idumeans? They were practically Jews anyway, having once spawned none other than Herod the Great. Now you may recall that these were the same neighbors who had opened their country to the Babylonians 600 years before so that they could rush in after them and plunder the stricken Jews. But all that was forgotten as the Zealots quickly drafted a letter appealing for help. Ananus, they charged, was about to hand over the metropolis to Vespasian and only a few brave patriots stood ready to defend it.

I am guessing that when the Arabs read the letter they quickly realized that they had three interesting options. If they entered Jerusalem and didn't like the situation they found, they could raid the wealthiest Jewish homes and depart with whatever they could cart off. They could also wait until the Romans came, have a hand in forcing defeat from within, and gain reward from Vespasian. Or, if the flattering letter was correct and the addition of the noble and valiant Idumean forces made the Jews the stronger force, they'd get their reward from the victorious Jews.

Whatever their frame of mind, the appeal was enough to rally Idumean warriors in a mad rush to arms as if, says Josephus, "they were going to a feast." Soon 20,000 armed Idumean warriors — much to the astonishment of Ananus — were thronging outside the gates of Jerusalem, demanding to be let in. What to do? Jesus, the eldest of the priests next to Ananus, went to the ramparts and called down to them: "It is true that many troubles indeed have fallen upon this city," he said, "yet none of them has given me more cause to wonder at her fortune as right now, when you have come to assist wicked men. For if you would examine them one by one, each of them would be found to have deserved 10,000 deaths. They are murderers and robbers who have profaned this most sacred temple and who can now be seen drinking themselves drunk in the sanctuary and expending the spoils of those whom they have slaughtered upon their unsatiable bellies. When the men of this city look down on you with your finest armament," shouted Jesus, "what can we call this procedure of yours but the sport of fortune? "

Jesus went on to deny that the people had sent Vespasian an offer. "We cannot but admire these wretches [the Zealots] in devising such lies against us," he said, "for they knew there was no other way to bring wrath against men who are so naturally desirous of liberty, than a lie that we were ready to betray that liberty." Jesus assured the Idumeans that he, Ananus and the others "having once made war upon the Romans and fought with them, now prefer death with reputation before living in captivity under them."

Jesus even invited the Idumeans to send in a delegation of leaders to inspect the damage done by the Zealots and to sit in judgment of their crimes. "But if you are unwilling to take our part in the indignation we have against these men," he said, "then I propose that you leave us alone and neither contribute to our calamities or abide with these plotters against their metropolis." Until the Idumeans made up their minds, concluded the priest, "do not wonder why the gates are shut against you while you bear so many arms."

Crowds are seldom in a mood to assimilate intricate reason, and this one hardly paid attention to the priest. All the Idumeans knew was that they had dropped what they were doing and rushed to Jerusalem — and for what? To be left outside the walls with no food or warmth as night came on? One of their commanders, Simon, asked for quiet, then shouted that he simply had no choice but to conclude that those who wouldn't open the gates to those who wished to defend Jerusalem must in fact be the same faction that had offered the Romans their surrender. Concluded Simon: "We shall abide before these walls in our armor until either the Romans grow weary waiting for you or you become friends to liberty and repent of what you have done against it."

Now the city was besieged from above and from without. Nor did the rage of the Idumean footmen subside. As I said, they hadn't been prepared to camp in this place, and now a storm began to rage over the land that only worsened their conditions. This was, as Josephus describes,

> ...a prodigious storm in the night, with the utmost violence, and very strong winds, with the largest showers of rain, with continued lightning, terrible thundering and amazing concussions and bellowings of the earth that it was as if it were an earthquake. These things were a manifest indication that some destruction was coming upon men, when the system of the world was put in this disorder, and anyone would guess that these wonders foreshadowed some grand calamities that were coming.[32]

The Idumeans thought God was angry at them for taking up arms. Ananus and his party thought that God was acting as their general, allowing them to conquer without fighting. But both proved wrong. As the Idumeans shivered beneath their makeshift roofs of locked shields, the inventive Zealots devised a way to use the noise of nature to good advantage. Amidst the loud thunder they slipped out of the upper temple, overpowered the few guards that had huddled about it, and darted off in the night shadows to the main gate. There, as expected, they also found people shut tight in their houses and the watchtower guards in disarray from the storm. The Zealots had brought saws from their armory, and in the darkness they began to cut the bars of the gate. By this time the Idumeans were lined up ready, one by one, to squeeze through the small opening made by the saws.

Once the angry Arabs streamed inside, they were ready to chop everyone in the city to bits. But cooler heads prevailed for the moment. The Zealots persuaded them to congregate in the upper city where they attacked the remaining guards and set up their own watch over the temple. Now, after resting briefly and no doubt helping themselves to the Zealots' storehouse of temple wine, they burst forth in a wild frenzy of hate.

By then some of the people had realized that a hostile force was in their midst and began rushing out of their houses as well. Many, assuming that they had only the Zealots to contend with, fought back boldly and defiantly. But at the sight of so many irate Idumæan troops as well, they were soon overwhelmed.

> The Zealots also joined in the shouts raised by the Idumeans. And the storm itself rendered their cry more terrible, Nor did the Idumæans spare anybody, for as they are naturally a most barbarous and bloody nation, and had been distressed by the tempest, they made use of their

weapons against those who had shut the gates against them and acted in the same manner as to those that supplicated for their lives as to those who had fought them. Now there was neither any place for flight nor any hope of preservation, but as they were driven one upon another in heaps, so they were slain.[33]

As the first daylight appeared, some 8,500 bodies were counted in the outer temple alone. Yet the Idumeans were still not satiated. They now plundered every house and butchered everyone inside. Among them were Ananus and the leading priests, who were first upbraided for their discourtesy in not opening the gates. The killers, said, Josephus, proceeded to cast away dead bodies without burial. "I should not be mistaken," he added, "if I said that the death of Ananus was the beginning of the destruction of the city, the overthrow of her wall, and the ruin of her affairs."

A new type of governance now began in Jerusalem. The bloodletting went on to the extent that 12,000 more were killed. Many of the leading citizens were arrested and invited to go over to the Zealots and Idumeans, but all refused. Their stubbornness "brought upon them terrible torments," writes Josephus, "for they were so scourged and tortured that at last they considered it a favor to be slain."

Eventually the new rulers grew arm-weary from all the killing or perhaps decided that merely bringing about the death of men wasn't enough. If they could hold "tribunals" and judge the accused guilty of various crimes, they could gain legal authority to divide up the property of the "traitors" as well. To give this show some legitimacy, they called together 70 ordinary citizens to serve as judges, assuming all the time that these frightened wretches would be cowed into voting as their new masters wanted.

I don't know how many rump trials actually took place, but it wasn't long before the tribunal found itself considering the case of one Zacharias, who was one of the richest and most respected men in Jerusalem. The charges were that he had been part of the plot to betray the city to Vespasian. There was no proof that Zacharias was part of any such doings, but the defendant could see that anything he could say mattered naught and that his life wasn't worth a mina (the smallest Jewish coin). So Zacharias stood up, waved off the accusation with a few words of bitter sarcasm and launched instead into a fierce, biting indictment of his accusers. He recited all the Jewish laws they had broken and the low state to which they had brought the great city.

Now the Zealots were in a turmoil. They had their hands on the hilts of their swords and would have run him through right there were it not for the fact that they had determined to make a show of impartiality. They decided to calm down and wait for the jury of 70 to convene in private and return with a "suitable" verdict.

After a considerable time, the 70 judges filed back into the large courtroom and with solemn, ashen faces announced that Zacharias was acquitted. They had chosen to die rather than have his death on their consciences.

The Zealots sat in silent disbelief for a few eerie moments. Then, without a sound two of their boldest members rushed at Zacharias from their benches with drawn swords and hacked him down as he stood in proud defiance. Other Zealots were ready to deliver the same fate to the 70 judges, but the leaders decided to herd them out of the building while beating them with the flat parts of their swords. Then they were kicked down the court steps and sent stumbling into the crowd milling outside as messengers to the rest that they were no better than naughty slaves.

Some Idumean leaders had seen all this. In fact, after several days in the city, their commanders began to realize that their first perceptions of the situation in Jerusalem simply had not been accurate. They had watched the Zealot leaders get sloppy drunk and brag about all the tricks they had played on the rest of the citizenry. They observed the tortures and sham trials. They had failed to see any evidence that anyone had offered to hand Vespasian the city. Moreover, the Romans were reported to be still many miles away and showing no signs of preparing to march. So, one day the Idumeans surprised the Zealots by announcing that they were leaving. And perhaps because they felt guilt at the disaster they had helped bring about, the Idumeans bulled their way into the prisons and led their 2,000 occupants outside the gates under their protection as the Zealots looked on helplessly.

And what of the Zealots now? Initially, the people grew somewhat bolder, as if testing their outnumbered overlords. But the Zealot leaders quickly adopted an even more insolent attitude. Their Arab rescuers of several days ago were now depicted as witless barbarians who had only hindered the Jewish cause. Before others could regroup, the Zealots had resumed their trials, with even more speedy convictions of those who headed the most illustrious and wealthy families who still remained.

Vespasian's camp was not oblivious to all this, for his intelligence scouts slipped in among the departing Idumeans and got an earful. The general's advisors unanimously urged that they march quickly and descend upon the Jews lest they might reunite again. But the ever-practical Vespasian opposed them all. If the Romans began the siege just then, he said, the Jews would indeed unite just as they feared. But if the Romans continued to tarry, they could count on having fewer enemies. After all, the Jews were not then engaged in making armor, building walls or recruiting auxiliaries. Rather, they were in the process of destroying themselves with their own hands.

The general then turned to his younger, ambitious aides. "If any one of you imagines that the glory of a victory gained without fighting is insipid," he said, "let him know that a glorious success, quietly obtained, is more profitable than the dangers of battle. For we ought to esteem those who succeed through temperance no less glorious than those who have gained great reputation by their actions in war."

Indeed, every day a greater number of Jews managed to escape the walls of Jerusalem. How could this be, you may wonder, when the Zealots guarded the gates and killed those who challenged them? It was so because by now the Zealots had deduced that to harbor traitors in their midst would only detract from their defenses. It would be better to let such people purchase their freedom for a steep price. Thus, rich people who were willing to forfeit everything they possessed were allowed to leave, while the poor were slain if they tried to escape.

At about this time John of Gischala had finished his "preparations." With his own band of men from Gischala and all the former Zealots he had won over by perfidy, he appeared before the decimated Zealot leaders and proclaimed himself leader of Jerusalem. I should say leader of the Jews, because John had been thinking in grander terms than the cutthroats and highwaymen he sought to replace. John proclaimed a new Jewish monarchy with himself as king.

· · · · · · · · ·

As I MENTIONED EARLIER, the commanders of the Roman provincial legions — and indeed the subjects they were pledged to keep in check — were roiling with discontent against a man who, more than even his cruelties, they simply found an embarrassment to the dignity of the empire. Yet, in early March, when Nero yielded to his freedman's pleas and returned to Rome, the emperor seemed blissfully oblivious to anything other than the constant outpouring of adulation that surrounded him. The return was a theatrical event in itself worthy of a conqueror's most lavish triumph. In a revival of an ancient tradition in which the Greeks honored the winners of their games, a portion of the city wall was torn down and a section of the gates broken in.

First through the breach were men bearing the crowns won by the emperor. Then came those bearing on the end of spears wooden panels upon which were inscribed the name of the games, the kind of contest and a statement that it was won by Nero Cæsar, first among Romans from the beginning of the world. Next came the victor himself, seated in the same revered carriage that Augustus had used to celebrate his triumphs.

Nero was clad in a vestment of purple covered with spangles of gold. His head was crowned with a garland of wild olive and his hand held the Pythian laurel. The imperial train, also comprised of the soldiers and senators who had been to Greece, passed through the Circus and the Forum, then ascended to the Temple of Jupiter Capitoline. From there it proceeded north to the Golden House.

The city was all decked out with garlands, ablaze with lights and reeking with incense. And throughout the procession, the senators led an unending chorus that shouted "Hail, Olympian Victor! Hail Pythian Victor! Augustus! Augustus! Hail to Nero, our Hercules! Hail to Nero, our Apollo! The only Victor of the Grand Tour, the only one from the beginning of time! Blessed are they that hear thee!"

When he had finished these ceremonies, Nero announced a series of horse races. All of his crowns for chariot racing that he had won in Greece were then carried back to the Circus in the Vatican and placed around the obelisk that stood at its center. Then he appeared as a charioteer. During the ceremonies, a wealthy Lydian ran up to him and offered to pay 1 million sesterces if he would but play the lyre for them. Nero disdained the money, but said that he would indeed play the lyre that day in the theater. Later, on Nero's orders, Tigellinus went around to the Lydian in private and reproached him for his affront. He extracted 1 million sesterces as the price for not putting the man to death.

Once the festivities had ended, Nero and his courtesans went down to Neapolis to spend the rest of the spring. As always, it was so much more Hellene than Rome and far more appreciative of his artistry. But, as I said, the people in the other provinces were not. At just about the same time that the royal entourage was winding its way to Neapolis, Gaius Julius Vindex, the governor of Gaul, became the first to publicly announce that he had had enough of an emperor who pranced about in high heels and sapped his subjects with outrageous taxes. Vindex was from a Gaul from Acquitania, descended from a long line of royalty and a father who had become a Roman senator. He was powerful in body, of shrewd intelligence and had a burning desire to lead his people in a great undertaking.

Vindex called together the leaders of the Gauls and delivered a long and detailed tirade against Nero — the first such public utterance anyone could remember. Nero must fall, he charged, "because he has despoiled the whole Roman world, because he has destroyed the flower of their senate, because he debauched and then killed his mother and now does not even preserve the semblance of sovereignty." Said Vindex:

> Many murders, robberies and outrages, it is true, have often been committed by others, But as far as the other deeds committed by Nero, how could one find words fittingly to describe them?

> I have seen this man — if man he is who has married Sporus and been given in marriage to Pythagoras — in the circle of the theater, sometimes holding the lyre and dressed in loose tunic and buskins, and again wearing high-soled shoes and mask. I have seen him in chains,

hustled about as a miscreant, heavy with child, eye in the travail of childbirth — in short imitating all the situations of mythology by what he said and did.

Will anyone, then, style such a person emperor and the Augustus? Never! Let no one abuse these sacred titles. They were held by Augustus and Claudius, whereas this fellow might most properly be termed Thyestes, Œdipus, Alcmeon or Orestes, for these are the characters he represents on the stage. Therefore, I urge you to rise against him...and liberate the entire world![34]

Vindex finished to lusty shouts of approval. What made his words so refreshing and appealing was that he did not seek any office for himself. Rather, he proposed the name of Servius Sulpicius Galba, a distinguished Roman patrician who was then serving as governor of Spain. All the more remarkable was that the philosopher Apollonius, then in Spain, had already forecast that the austere, dignified Galba — the very antithesis of Nero — would be proclaimed emperor. And as he was preparing to leave for Sicily, Apollonius had said to one of Galba's chief allies in Spain: "Take care to remember Vindex."

As Galba was contemplating the meaning of all this, Nero himself received a dispatch about Vindex in Neapolis just as the royal party was finishing lunch while at the same time watching a wrestling match. The emperor showed no visible reaction to its contents. In fact, he left his couch and vied with one of the contestants so that he could try out a new wrestling hold.

The next day Nero wrote the Senate, apologizing for not coming to Rome but complaining that he had a sore throat and needed to devote some care to his voice because he had been hoping to go there and sing for them. Besides, he had important business to tend to in Neapolis. He had just overseen the erection of a lavish shrine to the memory of Poppæa Sabina and must now plunge himself into the dedication ceremonies.

Actually, Nero seemed to be delighted at the news about Vindex. He had increasingly viewed the ambitious Gaul as an irritant and now at last had a solid reason to replace him and seize his property in the bargain. After sending orders to Rufus, the governor of Germany, to go to Gaul and remove the troublemaker, the emperor returned to more important pastimes.

Rufus, it turned out, held the emperor in the same esteem as Vindex. After all, his able predecessor had been ordered to fall on his sword simply because he had proven inconveniently competent at his post. But what happened next between two men of similar purpose is one of the great tragedies of Roman military history. Rufus brought his forces to the city of Vesontio in Gaul as if ready to besiege it. Vindex marshaled reinforcements and marched toward the city to help the defenders. Both generals sent messages back and forth inquiring as to each other's intentions. Then finally they held a personal meeting at which they realized that both loathed the emperor.

Now the bizarre happened. While still at their secret out-of-the-way meeting, Vindex – with Rufus' consent, I'm sure – gave orders to an aide to continue marching his men to Vesontio at a leisurely pace. There the two forces would link up in what would be the first opposition army to Nero.

But for some unexplained reason, no notice was sent to the Roman forces that were now encamped about the city. When the Romans saw the Gauls approaching directly at them, they grabbed their swords and shields and rushed out to battle. The confused Gauls were hacked down by the hundreds before they could regroup and try to make sense of what had happened. Vindex was so grief-stricken at the fate of his men that he committed suicide as a sacrifice to them.

Rufus, I think, was of a similar mind, but now his own troops demanded that he take up Vindex' cause. Rufus might have done so, because he was a large, energetic man and witnessed his men throwing down statues of Nero and hailing him by the titles of Cæsar and Augustus. But he steadfastly told them that it was up to the people and Senate of Rome. And it may have been just as well, because on April 2 Galba in Spain declared himself emperor and sent an appeal east for support from the armies of Britain, Germany and Gaul. Within a few weeks he received it.

When word reached Nero of Rufus' "treason" in Gaul, eight days passed before he gave the Senate any reply or direction. All that anyone could tell was that the emperor was still thinking grandly, because he talked of embarking on a Grand Military Tour in which he would journey to Syria, the Caucuses and Alexandria to show that he was mightier than even Alexander the Great.

In any event, Nero finally went up to Rome, no doubt wondering what to expect. On the way he spied a roadside monument showing a Roman horseman dragging a Gallic soldier by the hair, and he raised his hands to heaven with a joyous look because he thought it a good omen for launching another campaign in Gaul. But once in Rome he neither addressed the Senate nor issued any orders for combating his foes in the provinces. Indeed, when a delegation of anxious, stony-faced senators finally called on him at the Golden House, the emperor spent the alloted time showing them some new, unusual water organs and prattling on about how he intended to demonstrate them in the theater.

Rome and Nero now learned that Galba had revolted and was preparing to march toward Italy. The emperor's first reaction was to faint and spend the next 24 hours in bed, unable to utter a word. When he did arise, he rent his clothing and beat his brow, declaring that it was all over with him. When his old nurse tried to comfort him by recalling that other princes had survived similar set-backs, he moaned that he would be the only one to lose supreme power while he still lived.

Still, Nero would revive his spirits from time to time. If someone reported good news from the provinces – perhaps the prospect of this or that general remaining loyal – he would respond by giving a lavish feast at which he would ridicule the leaders of the revolt in verses he set to music. Meanwhile, more schemes were hatched but thankfully abandoned: massacring all men in the city of Gallic birth, poisoning the entire Senate at a banquet, setting fire to the city after first letting all the wild beasts loose.

The closest that the emperor's wild schemes came to anything was an attempt to marshal a military campaign to confront the invaders on their way to Rome. Nero began by mobilizing everyone at the Golden House – that is, such drastic measures as selecting wagons to carry his musical instruments and having his concubines equipped with Amazonian axes and shields. But when his order for military enlistment went out about the city, no one came forth. So he ordered all masters to send a certain percentage of their slaves and all classes to contribute a part of their incomes. He also demanded that the government mint new silver and gold coins.

But all this only increased the seething resentment against him. If any one event made the public bile pour out upon the streets, it may have been the arrival of a large Egyptian grain ship at Ostia. Rome was in the midst of a severe corn shortage, and when news traveled that a great cargo ship was on the horizon, spirits rose. But they sank even lower when the ship tied up in the harbor: its entire supply consisted of sand for the court wrestling arena and other bric-a-brac for the Golden House.

The unrest now turned to open taunts and jeers. On one statue of Nero someone hung a sign in Greek that said: "Now you have a *real* contest and you must at last lose." To the neck of another statue a sack was tied, inscribed with the words: "I have done what I could, but you have earned this sack." And this graffiti on a wall: "By your singing you have stirred up even the Gauls."

Before that Nero had continued to go to the theater and even act on its stage. In fact, I can't resist reporting that the last piece he sang in public was "Œdipus in Exile." It ended with the line: "Wife, father, mother drive me to my death."

It was now June 8. The emperor was at dinner when he received word that virtually all the armies to the north and west were now in revolt. He tore the dispatches to pieces, upended the table in a fit of rage and dashed to the ground his two favorite drinking cups, which were carved with scenes from Homer's poems. He lurched outside and went over to the Servilian Gardens where he exhorted the tribunes and centurions of the Guard to prepare to take him to Ostia. Then he ordered some trusted freedmen to rush there in advance and prepare a fleet for him. But most of them gave evasive responses as they melted away into the darkness, and one even shouted a line from Homer's Æneid over his shoulder:

Is it, then, such a dreadful thing to die?

Now the emperor was left with a few servants and freedmen. He mumbled and his mind wandered. He talked in one minute of going to Parthia as a supplicant to the king. The next minute it would be about entreating the Senate to give him the prefecture of Egypt. Finally, he wondered that if he went to the Senate with a heartfelt apology, perhaps it would simply allow him to go peacefully to Egypt, where he could earn his living as a lyre player. He kept mumbling that he needed time to make a plan, and since he was probably drinking himself into senselessness anyway, his servants convinced him to go to bed and make his plan on the morrow. Before he was led to his bedchamber, Nero took care to take a small box of poison that had been prepared by Locusta, the same old alchemist who had served to take off Brittanicus and other imperial nuisances over the years.

While Nero had dined, the consuls of Rome had received the same dispatches from the provinces. The new guarantee of unanimous revolt among the military had finally stiffened the spine of the Senate enough to gather in special session that night and declare Galba emperor. The Prætorian Guard was persuaded as well. Eventually, the Roman people would be going wild with delight, many even wearing liberty caps to signify that they had been set free from slavery. But not that night, because they weren't sure where the deposed emperor was nor what he might be planning.

Nero arose sometime around midnight and found the household eerily still. His chamberlains were gone. He opened the door and called out for some Guards, but none responded. He then went about the hallways, calling out to friends and trying various doors. But all were locked. Nero rushed back to his bed chamber to fetch the box of poison he had left on the bedside table. It was gone. He shouted again for a Guardsman — or anyone — whose skillful sword might deliver him death, but none came. "Have I neither friend nor foe?" he wailed at last.

Actually, Nero did have at least three loyal friends who were presumably sleeping or at least away from his desperate shouts in the dead of night. The next morning found him in the company of Phaon, one of his freedmen, Epaphroditus, his private secretary, and Sporus, his eunuch-wife, or whatever you choose to call him-her. The plan now was for Nero to retire to Phaon's own villa, in the northern suburbs near the fourth milestone. But as the road led out nearby the

Prætorian camp, Nero needed to travel in disguise. Barefooted and in his tunic, he put on a faded cloak, covered his face with a handkerchief and mounted a worn-out horse. A nasty late spring squall was beginning to kick up, which would keep most people off the streets. But Nero shuddered as they passed by the Prætorian camp and heard a shout go up for Galba. And then they heard someone inside the wall say, "Is there anything new in the city about Nero?"

It was raining hard now. The four wet stragglers had passed the camp and had just turned a corner when Nero's horse started at the smell of a corpse lying on the road. As Nero steadied himself by gripping the bridle with both hands, his faced was exposed and a man on the roadside recognized him instantly. The observer was a retired guardsman, and as he saw the rider's face, his hand went up with an automatic reflex to salute the emperor.

Now the party couldn't be sure if or when pursuers might be on their trail. Their pace quickened. As they turned into a by-path leading to Phaon's villa in the early morning, they dismounted and set the horses loose. Nero, told to sneak in so that slaves and servants wouldn't notice, made his way amid some thick bushes and brambles that lined the back wall of the house. Nero had great difficulty negotiating the prickly thicket until someone threw down a cloak over the bushes so he could tread on it.

Phaon urged him to go crouch inside a nearby pit that had been used to dig sand, but Nero refused to "hide underground," as he put it, while he was still alive. So, while the others tried to clear the way for him to enter the house without being detected, Nero sat in the bushes, picking the thorns and twigs from his torn cloak. Adjacent to the bushes was a small fishpond of green slimy water, into which he dipped his hand for a drink. "This is Nero's distilled water," he muttered, referring to how drinking water was always boiled first, then cooled with ice.

Still signaling for quiet, Phaon opened the back door and bid Nero crawl on all fours into the hallway, and then into the first vacant room. There a cloak had been placed over an old saggy couch, and Nero slumped on it bemoaning his fate. "What an artist the world is losing," he wept and wailed repeatedly.

It was now obvious that there would be no further plan, no retaliation, no escape. Nero's companions could talk only of the indignities that would be visited on his body if he did not take steps quickly to prevent them. Refusing some coarse bread that was offered him, Nero asked his companions to dig a grave, collect any marble that could be found for a marker, bring some water for washing his body and wood for a fire to burn it.

His decision was reinforced shortly thereafter when one of Phaon's couriers brought a letter from the Senate. It announced that Nero had been pronounced a public enemy and was now being sought so that he could be punished in the "ancient tradition."

It would seem to me that Nero, having declared so many public enemies himself, would know exactly what this "ancient tradition" entailed. However, he reportedly asked Phaon to describe it to him. The freedman replied that the criminal was stripped naked, fastened by the neck to a forked stake and then beaten to death with rods.

Nero sobbed softly. He picked up two daggers he had brought with him and pressed their points to his chest. Then he put them down, pleading that the fated hour had not yet come. Rather, he turned to the boy Sporus and begged him to begin a widow's wailing. Then, changing his mind again, he beseeched anyone from his party to help him take his life at once. Now he reproached himself for his cowardice. "To live despoiled, disgraced," be mumbled, "does not become Nero, does not become him. One should be resolute at such times. Come now, rouse thyself."

What did rouse him finally was the sound of horsemen who had come with orders to take him alive. "Ah, the trampling of swift-footed studs in my ear," he said, quoting *The Iliad* in a quavering voice. Then he drove a dagger into his throat. Epaphroditus quickly reached over and closed his hand over Nero's to give the blow added force.

He was all but gone when a centurion rushed in. The guardsman placed a cloth to the wound as if to be aiding him, but Nero merely gasped, "Too late." He died with his eyes so set and staring that all who saw him shuddered with horror.

Phaon reported Nero's last request to the Senate — that his head not be removed and that his body be buried with no further mutilation. The Senate, in its last acquiescence to Nero, agreed and provided a minimal funeral service for the cost of 200,000 sesterces. He was laid out in a white, gold-embroidered robe and his body buried in the family tomb of the Domitii on the summit of the Pincian Hill, which is visible from the Campus Martius. Nero's death had come on June 9. He had lived 30 years and five months, of which he ruled the world for 13 years and 10 months.

Thus, so pitifully ended the Age of Augustus with the last of his descendants.

. . . .

VESPASIAN PLAYED A MINIMAL ROLE in this drama, due mostly to his distant location. But his reaction to events had a profound effect on the way the Jewish war was conducted and, ultimately, of course, on how the Roman world was ruled.

Until that spring Vespasian had methodically eliminated pockets of resistance north of Jerusalem. Perhaps the strongest was Gadara, the principal city of Perea, which lay a few miles northeast of Jerusalem. Like the capital, it had been occupied by a seditionist minority, and the leading men had sent a secret appeal to Vespasian to rescue them. When the seditionists had seen the Romans approaching, they slew a few of the richest men on suspicion of having betrayed them, but then they fled the city into the mountains. Vespasian sent Placidus to hunt them down with 5,000 horsemen and 3,000 footmen.

At about this time Vespasian decided to accelerate the elimination of resistance forces and to completely encircle the city of Jerusalem. He had three strong reasons. First, those who fled from Gadara mostly headed south along the river Jordan and as far as the Lake of Asphaltitis, the great saltwater body whose northern tip stretches just east of Jerusalem.

Second, the beginning of the year had seen the Sicarii take over the massive fortress of Masada, which towered over the lake at a point 30 miles south of the capital. Now Masada is a forbidding fortress considered unassailable even to the Romans, but it also lacked provisions. So the Sicarii began making nocturnal raids in which they could descend on nearby cities and carry back their provisions. In the small city of En-gadi, for instance, they had slain some 700 people, carried off everything from their houses and even harvested the fruits and grains they had been raising. Now it was one thing for Jews to destroy one another within the confines of Jerusalem, but it was quite another when they terrorized the unarmed friends of Rome and seized supplies that the Army had counted on.

Third, Vespasian had by now learned of Galba's revolt and claim to the throne. I have no doubt that the burly general found the effeminate Nero as disgusting as had his slain comrades, Corbulo and the two commanders of Germany. He certainly had nothing against Galba, who had already served twice as consul of Rome in addition to his being a respected governor general. Without committing himself, Vespasian's instincts told him that regardless of who emerged as emperor, it was time to tidy up his theater of war so as to present the victor with a clear-cut decision on Jerusalem: destroy it or seek a negotiated peace. Moreover, if Rome was to be ensnared in civil war, Vespasian could at least assure the empire that the eastern provinces were safe.

Thus, the Roman troops conducted a sweep all around Jerusalem. The tribune Placidus and his troops tracked the survivors of Gadara to a small walled village called Bethennabris. There they killed nearly everyone inside and then chased the rest to the banks of the Jordan, where the current was too swift for them to cross. The Romans then chased them all the way down the banks of the Jordan to where it emptied into the Lake of Asphaltitis. It was said that at some points along the river, one could actually cross it by stepping on the piles of dead bodies that lay in it. Even then, the Romans boarded small boats at the northern shore of the lake and hacked down all of the other stragglers who had floated into the lake for safety.

Having now subdued all the Jewish cities to the north and west, the Roman forces wheeled around and put themselves between Jerusalem and Masada to the south. The Sicarii still held Masada, but they had to live on the provisions already stored up, for it was now impossible to get up and down the mountain without paying a severe penalty.

The holy city was now ready for siege. Vespasian went up to Cæsarea for a respite and it was there he learned that Nero was dead and that Galba was on his way from Spain to succeed him as emperor.

It was also at that time that Vespasian's fate took a decisive turn, for he resolved — as part of his effort to see a peaceful, united eastern front — to meet with Gaius Licinius Mucianus, the powerful, wealthy Roman who had become governor of Syria while he was away on his campaigns.

. . . .

THIS BOOK WOULD BE A GOOD DEAL LONGER if I had described all the omens, auguries and portents that heralded the arrivals and exits of emperors. Every priest and soothsayer can claim to have made some such prediction, yet it seems there is some law requiring that they be recorded only after several years, because I have yet to find anyone who can say he witnessed one as it happened.

So I'll give you but a sampling. When Livia first married Augustus an eagle flew by and dropped in her lap a white hen holding a sprig of laurel in its beak. Livia decided to rear the hen (which hatched a great brood of chicks) and plant the sprig of laurel. A great grove of laurel sprang up and thereafter the Cæsars always had worn sprigs from the same laurel grove in their triumphs.

But lo, dear reader, we learn now that in Nero's last year he quaked upon discovering that the whole grove died from the roots up as well as all the hens. The day before his death Nero's dinner table was cleaved by lightning, and the day after his death another bolt struck the Mausoleum of Augustus, toppling all the heads from all the family statues at once and dashing the scepter from Augustus' hand!

And Fate, we are to believe, had selected Galba all along. Fate must have been patient, since it had to wait until his seventy-third year for him to become emperor. Nonetheless, the omens of his ascendancy seem to have begun when, as a small boy brought to a palace reception, Augustus pinched his cheek and said, "You shall have a nibble at this power of mine." And Tiberius, we learn, when told that Galba would be emperor, but at a very old age, said, "Well, then let him live, since that would not concern me." Indeed, Galba's very grandfather was busy with a sacrifice when an eagle snatched the intestines from his hand and carried them back to an oak full of acorns, meaning, said the diviners, that great power would come to the family, but very late. To this he said, "Very likely, when a mule has a foal!"

So it is said that when Galba was considering the plea of Vindex to declare for the throne, one of the events that determined his decision was when aides told him that a camp mule had foaled. Ah, but he was also encouraged when a dispatch informed him that a ship from Alexandria had glided mysteriously into a nearby harbor loaded with arms – and all without a captain or crew. This, said one historian, "removed all doubt in any one's mind that the war was just and holy and undertaken with the approval of the gods."

I rather suspect Galba's decision had a lot to do with the fact that his aides intercepted a message from Nero ordering Galba's aide-de-camp to kill him. Moreover, Galba must have wondered about his omens just after declaring himself emperor. He learned that Vindex, his most ardent ally, had slain himself after a military disaster. He then had a visit from Rufus, who departed with a stony frown after being told that he and his army of Upper Germany would have no special favors for their brave rebellion. Galba also must have known that he would make a mortal enemy of Nymphidius, the prefect of Nero's Prætorian Guard. When Nymphidius inquired by letter what special rewards that he and the guardsmen might expect for abandoning the emperor, Galba replied that, to the contrary, it was his intent to discharge many of them!

For this solemn, austere man was determined to break the grip that the Prætorians had held on the throne of the Roman Empire for over 50 years. After a lifetime of rendering rigidly faithful service as a general in Germany under Caligula, as a close advisor to Claudius, and as proconsul of the difficult African province, Galba had retired to a quiet life, only to be called to Spain by Nero and serve eight tedious years. I use the word "tedious" because the same man who had properly impressed the emperor Gaius in Upper Germany by running alongside his chariot for 20 miles in partial armor, had wizened with age by the time Nero ordered him to Spain. He took utterly no initiatives in governance on the belief that he could not incur the emperor's jealousy for doing nothing.

Now Galba saw his mission as restoring dignity, frugality and honesty to the government of Rome. His biggest shortcoming was that he was almost too solemn, too traditional – a Tiberius with moral values, if you will. This was a man who believed so much in eternal love that he never remarried after his wife died at an early age – despite being courted (some say hounded) by the single-minded Agrippina right after she was widowed at the death of Nero's natural father, Domitius. Galba was also a traditionalist to the extent of maintaining an old, forgotten Roman custom: he required that his freedmen and slaves appear before him twice a day, greeting him in the morning and bidding him farewell at evening, one by one.

Galba accepted the title of Cæsar only when a delegation of senators arrived to offer it formerly. He then departed on a slow march, for he was old and often ill, bringing with him much of a legion from Spain. It was August before the calvacade arrived in Rome, and the citizenry's first impressions of the new emperor were not very favorable.

There was the basic matter of appearance, for one thing. Galba was, while of average height, very bald and with a severely hooked nose. His hands and feet were so distorted by gout that he could not wear shoes or hold a book for very long. The flesh on his right side, perhaps from some old wound, hung down to the extent that it had to be held in with a bandage.

All that aside, there was the matter of frugality. To common folk, who benefited from Nero's extravagance, Galba's acts were seen as miserly and unusually severe. Even before he arrived, they had heard tales from Spain, such as the one when he had a dishonest moneylender's hands cut off and hung from his trading counter. Then there was the soldier who was accused of selling some of the wheat from his rations at a neighborhood market. Galba gave orders to the entire army that when the man began to lack food he should receive aid from no one. He didn't, and starved to death.

The Romans also buzzed about the time when the people of a Spanish town had given the governor a golden crown weighing 15 pounds from their temple of Jupiter. Galba was said to have melted it down, and discovering it three ounces shy of the stated 15 pounds, sent the city an invoice for the difference. I daresay the crown might well have been rightly owed as payment for taxes in arrears, but Romans were more willing to believe otherwise after seeing some of the same mean spiritedness in their own city. On one occasion the newly-arrived emperor rescinded an order of Nero's that had made regular soldiers out of some men who had been mere rowers. When the men gathered to protest and insist they remain under the eagle and standards, Galba ordered the a cavalry unit to charge into their midst. Then he had had them rounded up and their ranks decimated.

What unnerved people more than anything were all the strange, foreign soldiers loitering around. They included not only the legionaires from Spain, but parts of special detachments from Germany, Britain and Illyricum that had been recalled with the idea that they would be sent to crush Vindex in Gaul. But as it turned out, Galba needed them all against the Prætorians.

What was already a clash-in-the-making began when Nero's personal guard of German mercenaries asked to be allowed to protect the new emperor. They were refused—and then sent back to their homeland. Next, it was the Prætorian camp in a flutter, because the Prætorian prefect Nymphidius was under extreme pressure from his men. In the grand tradition of paying off the guardsmen whenever they supplied or took off an emperor, Nymphidius had been assuring them all along that he would somehow pry loose Galba's purse once the old skinflint arrived in Rome. But Galba would not budge. "I am accustomed to levy soldiers, not to buy them," he snorted. Nymphidius, rather than being killed by his own mutinous men, had no choice but to lead them in revolt. But Galba was ready with his more numerous legions from Europe. Before they restored order, some 7,000 Prætorians (about half their strength) had been slain and their power presumably broken.

Thus exited Nymphidius and some other threats. Galba also pleased the patricians by exterminating most of the "scum" as he called them, who had infested the Golden House. Made to march in chains through the streets to their executions were such characters as Helius, the freedman who had terrorized the city in Nero's absence, and Lucusta, the sorceress whose poisons had killed steadily since Nero first employed them against young Brittanicus. And yet, Galba's justice was annoyingly uneven. Tigellinus, who had taken part in more of Nero's debaucheries than anyone, was allowed to go free by an edict that even rebuked the people for their "cruelty" in demanding his head.

Also unsettling was that Galba's three closest advisors were hardly paragons of Roman nobility. Titus Vinius, one of the generals from Spain and now a consul, was fast becoming known for coveting any property not yet his own. Cornelius Laco, who had been Galba's judicial assistant, was now Prefect of the Prætorian Guard and already beginning to behave with intolerable hautiness. Both lived with Galba in the palace and scarcely left his side. "To these brigands, each with his different vice, he so entrusted and handed himself over as their tool, so that his conduct was far from consistent," observed one reporter of the times. And as he became weakened by advancing age and relinquished even more day-to-day powers, Galba increasingly became the butt of jokes

As you might imagine, with Rome in such a state it would not take much to embolden a provincial army to become unsettled as well. This time the first move of defiance came not from Gaul, but from the armies of Germany. This time the general Rufus was their victim instead of hero. Incensed at finally realizing that Rufus would not be able to wrest from Galba any bonuses or favors, they revolted and put at their head Aulus Vitellius, who had just arrived as Galba's governor of Lower Germany. This hard-drinking, corpulent politician (some might say an older version of Nero) was the son of the same Lucius Vitellius who had once served Tiberius as governor of Syria and as sycophant senator-confidant to Claudius. Whether or not he welcomed the cheers of his men as he was hoisted along with their standards, he was their leader and he would be ill-advised to oppose them.

. . . .

WITH PETER AND PAUL GONE, there was every reason to believe that the Christians might either be stamped out or dissolve of their own accord. Certainly it was not a year in which one could expect Christian boldness. To proclaim The

Way in Judea was to risk being seen as an impediment to the Zealot cause against the Romans. In the rest of Syria a Christian message would likely be brushed aside by Hellenes who were trying their utmost to display oneness with their Roman governors. Greece and Asia were still in a torpor after Nero's Grand Tour, and as far as most people understood, Christianity was still a banned religion. In Rome, even the death of Nero brought only a brief sigh of relief. Who could know what the rigidly aristocratic and traditional Galba thought about Christians or the recent persecutions? The city remained as tense as it had been when Tiberius had been reported dead – then not.

Some Christian house churches continued to meet in Rome, but only those that were small and/or cohesive enough to trust each member completely. Increasingly, many Christians found it safer to meet and pray together inside the labyrinth of underground necropoli that had only recently begun to be carved out of the soft tufa rock underlying the open land that lay just outside the city walls.

These underground tunnels did not originate because of any special Christian causes, but simply because no Roman may legally inter their dead inside the city walls and because land around the perimeter was becoming too expensive for individual families. Thus, enterprising landowners began hiring the guild of fusatores (excavators) to create more affordable space underground.

When first begun, the underground necropoli were called "cœmeteria," or sleeping places. But after a large excavation along the Appian Way was dubbed the "Catacombs," all others have been since referred to by the same generic name. Today, these catacombs are said to extend a dozen or so miles altogether. In the year of which I write they already made up two or so miles of labyrinths and the excavators worked continually to lengthen them.

To go inside a catacomb usually begins simply by walking into a hillside and then descending gradually. You must take an oil lamp, but during the daytime you may also be guided by weak shafts of light from bores that the fusatores created to remove rubble to the ground level.

Once your eyes are accustomed to the dark, your most powerful impression will be what a cosmopolitan place Rome is! Along the great highways we see the tombs of the great Roman patrician families, but along these narrow corridors one finds the graves of tanners and traders and bakers and seamen from every place in the world. One mostly encounters rectangular niches into which bodies are deposited and then covered over with marble or terra cotta slabs giving the deceased's name. But one can also find many whole chambers, or cryptia, decorated with stuccoes or expressive paintings in richly contrasting colors and lit (during family visits) with large candelabra. Alas, I cannot say that the artistry is exquisite because those who labor in the catacombs face certain handicaps. The light is poor, of course, and the rock is porous, meaning that it does not resist dampness well nor permit precise carving. It also tolerates only one coating (usually of lime and volcanic dust). But mostly it is obvious that very few of the living have had funds with which to hire a trained artist. They have made do with their own funereal art.

It is not difficult to pick out the Christian tombs because the headstones almost always contain recognizable symbols, carved crudely by the hands of loved ones. As must be true of Christian graves elsewhere, the ones in Rome employ such symbols as a fish (Christ), ship's anchor (salvation), the lamb (also salvation), the peacock (immortality), the fish and basket of loaves (for the Lord's Supper) and the dove (the soul). One also finds crude frescoes of Peter and Paul, but more often the symbol of the sword is used to mean Paul (by his beheading) while Peter is revered by a cock (referring to the time when he wept bitterly as he heard the cock crow to begin the day of Jesus' crucifixion).

I do not mean to convey by describing all these subterranean activities that Christians were wholly secretive or cowardly. While it is true that few would dare, for example, to preach in a marketplace or even volunteer one's name to a stranger, the faith burned brightly in the souls of hundreds and many found ways to keep their light from being buried under a bushel. One such illustration was the way in which the graves of Peter and Paul came to be established and venerated.

I have not been able to discover who it was who came forward to take responsibility for the burial of Peter's body — only that it took a special act of courage at this time of persecution. What I can confirm to all who live beyond Rome is the location of Peter's grave: right next to where he was crucified. In the Trionfale section of the Vatican, the Circus of Caligula and Nero spreads out along the bottom of a hillside. Neither emperor ever finished it in marble, and now its base of travertine and upper story of rotting wood project a gray, eerie gloominess, its Egyptian obelisk peering out atop the walls almost as if to ask where the crowds have gone.

The Circus is situated from west to east. Running the length of its northern side are the basalt paving stones of the Via Cornelia. Across the road the hillside begins its gradual rise, with a large stairway leading to another road at the top. It is at the foot of this once-unused hillside that one now finds a growing necropolis. Most of the graves are simple and poor, with no markers. What seems strange at first glance is that many of them are clustered around — and on the hillside above — a slightly larger grave. In front, at street level, is a low wall not quite waist high. In the middle is a simple unmarked grave covered by terra cotta tiles. In the back is a plaster wall.

So far I have merely given you the architectural dimensions of a million graves. This one is distinctive, however, because the back wall is covered with graffiti: Christian symbols, greetings from visitors in many languages and invocations to Peter. Running the length of the low wall in front is a narrow drainage ditch to prevent rainwater from rushing down the hill and flooding the area. In the ditch are coins from all nations and eras. Yet, no one seems to have dared loot the grave of these offerings.

Is this the grave of Peter? All I can tell you is that when one stops pilgrims and asks, the answer always comes back: "Well, of course!" To this one can add that no one in Rome or any other city has ever claimed that Peter is buried anywhere else.

The same is true of Paul. South of the city proper, where the Tiber swings Southeast and practically meets the road to Ostia, there had already existed a large necropolis that served the polyglot of foreign-born families who occupied the Trastavere neighborhood across the river. It is along an unpretentious side path in that necropolis, lined with the tombs of pagans and Christians alike, where one will find the simple grave of Paul. It is covered with a thin marble slab through which are bored two square openings and one round hole of different dimensions. They allow pilgrims to lower objects of devotion, such as thuribles of francinsence or pieces of cloth, so as to be blessed by touching the holy tomb below. Atop the marble slab is an inscription that looks as if it might have been scrawled in haste by someone who did not want to remain for long under the watch of Roman soldiers standing nearby. Indeed, he seems to left before finishing. The inscription says simply in Latin,

PAULO
APOSTOLOMART[YRI]

. . . .

By January a visitor might have judged Rome to be at peace with its new emperor. Except for the always unruly Lower Germany and its curious infatuation with Governor-General Vitellius, legions from Spain to Syria had all declared for Galba. Indeed, Vespasian had just sent his son Titus off solely to express the loyalty of his four legions.

Yet, the emperor's support was as thin as it was broad – both in and out of Rome. Galba himself knew it and determined the reason to be that he was old and had no heir. So, during his morning reception on January 10 he surprised everyone there by bringing forth one Piso Licinianus, a handsome 31-year-old nobleman, and announcing him as his adopted heir. "Once the news of your adoption has spread," he said, holding Piso's hand on the dais, "I shall cease to be charged with my advanced age, which is now the only fault they find with me."

Galba was correct that the public perception of his feebleness sapped his prestige and power. He was wrong, however, that choosing an heir would win him the hearts of Rome. The first to agree with that assessment would have been 37-year-old Marcus Salvius Otho, former governor of neighboring Lusitania and a man who many saw as Galba's ablest ally. That *he* wasn't chosen was a shock and affront to Otho. The Prætorians, realizing that the selection of Piso, a man of impeccable character, would dash all hopes of bonuses, wasted no time in making secret overtures to Otho. Nor did others who felt slighted by Galba's stern governance and stingy spending. Galba, for instance, made a report to the Senate charging that Nero had given away some 2.2 billion sesterces of the public treasury to cronies, mistresses, chariot drivers and the like. He now decreed that the recipients must return it, save 10 percent, and commissioned 50 knights to set about collecting it. Since nearly all of the recipients were wastrels in the first place, you can imagine the turmoil that erupted in trying to reclaim the money.

On January 15 Otho was attending the emperor's morning reception when one of his freedmen arrived and said, loudly enough for others to hear, that the "architects" had arrived to show him a house he was planning to buy. With this – the prearranged signal that all was ready – Otho made his apologies and hastened out a back door of the palace. From there he hurried down the wide steps that led to the Forum and across to the Golden Milestone at which all Roman military roads meet. There, two dozen soldiers of the Guard waited for him with a covered litter used for women. As the party sped its way north to the camp, it was joined in well-timed stages by more and more soldiers running alongside with drawn swords. When the now noisy, blustery juggernaut of soldiers and their prize cargo approached the barracks gates, it was already obvious to the tribune who let them in that the plot already had too much momentum to oppose. Once inside, others were ready with a rallying cry as Otho was rushed upon the march platform and proclaimed emperor. As one of them later summed up the prevailing attitude: "Few dared to undertake so foul a crime, many wished it done and everybody condoned it."

By the time Galba learned that Otho had hatched some sort of plot, he sent his newly-adopted son outside to address the palace Guards. This time Piso curtly promised the hated bonuses, but he couldn't resist adding that the money would be gained more honorably by defending a sitting emperor than staining their hands with his blood to commit murder for an undeserving aspirant. A courier sped off to the Prætorian camp with the same appeal, but by then it was too late. The newly-crowned Otho had already gone off to the Senate to announce that he had been swept away by the Guards and "commanded" to take the throne.

By now night was coming on. Word was spreading among the populace and two spectacles were unfolding. In one "arena," it seemed that half of Rome was flocking to the imperial palace, professing concern for the emperor's safety. In truth, it seemed more like a crowd heading into a theater in anticipation of exciting entertainment. "Where is Galba? Show us Galba!" the mob chanted outside the gates. "Death to Otho!"

Galba, sequestered with his advisors, was torn between two strong opinions. The consul Titus Vinius urged him to remain within the palace and block all the doors. "This will give time for the disloyal to repent and the loyal to unite their forces," he urged. "Crimes profit by haste, good counsels by delay."

Others counseled immediate action before the conspirators (of unknown strength at the time) could expand their numbers. "Why give Otho time to set his camp in order and start practicing at how to be an emperor?" they argued. "Why shut up this house as if we are anxious to endure a siege?"

Galba, believing that Otho's supporters were small in number, decided to go down to the Forum rostra and rally the people to his cause. Servants helped the old man strap on a breastplate and hoisted him into a litter.

In the second "arena," Otho had returned to the Prætorian barracks and now sat again on the platform in a makeshift throne. Surrounding him were uneasy soldiers, who constantly shouted over their shoulders, "Don't let any officers near you! Don't trust any officers!" Meanwhile, as groups of soldiers straggled in from their day's duty around town, their comrades would rush up and make them swear allegiance to Otho, who, trying to look imperial, would nod and smile back from the platform.

But now word came that Galba, Piso, the consul Vinius and a bodyguard were headed for the Forum. It was now or never for Otho. He gave a rousing call to action, cursing Galba's "strictness" and complaining that the emperor's fortune alone "could provide you the largess which he daily casts into your teeth but never pays into your pocket!" As the soldiers cheered, Otho gave orders to open the arsenal. The men roared even louder. They immediately seized the arms in such haste that all distinctions of military service were neglected. No tribunes or centurions tried to organize them, so that each man was his own leader and motivator. And in such cases, the brazen always step in front of the thoughtful.

As Otho's new guardians rushed towards the Forum, a throng of people had already begun to line the roads and rooftops to watch what looked like great entertainment in the making. Now they scattered in fear as the Prætorians came rushing down the sacred avenues. Neither the sight of the Capitol nor the sanctity of the temples towering above them could diminish their lust for blood.

And now they were upon Galba and his guard. The emperor's thought of rallying the people ended abruptly when the standard bearer of his private guard tore off the effigy of the emperor that he carried and flung it to the ground with a defiant smirk. The people fled in terror. Galba's bearers dropped their litter with a clumsy crash and disappeared into the night. Soldiers stood with drawn swords to prod anyone who dared linger. The Forum that had been a din of voices just minutes before was filled with such an eerie silence that one could hear the leaves rustle in the night air.

The next sounds were from the old man. Struggling to his feet as rapidly as his gouty knees would permit, he asked what harm he had caused anyone. He implored the men surrounding him for a few days' respite to pay the troops their largess. Some say he also stretched out his neck and bade them, "Come, strike, if it serves the country's need."

Nothing he could have said would have mattered. In the ninth month and 13th day of Galba's reign, a common soldier pierced his throat with a sword thrust, then whacked off his head. Others quickly did the same to the arms and legs so that only the torso with its breastplate was left.

Next a soldier approached the consul Vinius, who looked in shock at the outrage, and brought him to the ground with a blow behind his knees. Then with no further word he ran him through with his sword.

The young Piso managed to break away and run for his life. But he was tracked down an hour or so later hiding inside the Temple of Vesta. He was dragged out and butchered on the temple steps.

Now it was a triumphant strut for Otho back to the camp in the winter moonlight. The heads of the murdered victims were fixed on poles and carried along with the standards and the eagle of the legion. Those who had done the deed vied with each other in displaying their bloody hands as proof, I suppose, of the extra bounty they deserved. Indeed, the public records would later show that some 120 petitions were received seeking rewards for distinguished service that day.

What happened upon their arrival at the Prætorian camp confirmed, of course, that all of Rome had been Otho's worshipful supporter from the day he returned from Spain. Senators raced ahead of the soldiers, overtaking the bloody entourage so they could be first to fall at the new emperor's feet when he arrived. Senators and knights covered his hands with kisses and praise in inverse proportion to their sincerity.

Better that they had kissed the asses of the Prætorians, because the common Guardsmen now ruled more supremely than ever. Galba had nearly brought them back to the level of a household bodyguard. Now they were more independent than ever, choosing their own prefects and punishing officers who had upheld their oaths by defending Galba.

Soon Rome was to learn just why it was that Galba had not made Otho his heir. It is true that Otho had been an acceptable governor and general in the western provinces. It was knowledge of his previous years in Rome that had repelled Galba. This was the same patrician-born Otho who was so wild in boyhood that his father had him flogged. This was the Otho who later prowled the streets in the young Nero's gang of thugs, sharing in the emperor's sexual soirees. It was he who had first married the lustfully legendary Poppæa and traded her back and forth with Nero until the besmitten emperor claimed her for himself and sent the husband off to Lusitania. This was the same immoral Otho who was immortalized in this couplet:

> You ask why Otho's banished? Know the cause
> Comes not within the scope of vulgar laws.
> Against all rules of fashionable life
> The rogue had dared to sleep with his own wife.[35]

Galba knew, too, that Otho's lifestyle was so grand beyond his means that he often complained in half-jest that unless he became emperor he would have to die either in battle or at the hands of his creditors in the Forum. With Otho as emperor, Galba reasoned, the public treasury would be no safer than with Nero.

That Otho regarded himself as Nero's heir rather than Galba's successor was evident from his first day as emperor. In sending notices of his ascension to the governors and legion commanders, he used the surname Nero. The first grant Otho signed as emperor was for 50 million sesterces to finish work on the Golden House. Nero's statues re-appeared in the city and the boy-eunuch Sporous was brought back to the Golden House as Otho's pet.

From his first day on the throne, Otho lived under the same cloud of impending invasion that his predecessor faced. During the time that Otho was still plotting against Galba, a legion from Lower Germany, led by the general Fabius Valens, had ridden into the city of Cologne and declared all of Upper Germany for the governor Aulus Vitellius. So swept up in the enthusiasm were the Roman troops on that day that many handed over their savings, medals and handsome silver ornaments to the cause. The leaders of Cologne picked up on cue (which was easy with a menacing cavalry staring down at them) by making pledges of money and provisions. Within a few days all other legions of both Germanys had taken up the same cry, and the many officers who opposed them could only look on quietly.

Why did all this happen so quickly? It's almost the same story as the Prætorians in Rome. The legionaries had expected rewards from Galba that never materialized. There were also scores to be settled in some of the provincial towns and perhaps booty to be taken as well. But an equal factor, I think, is simply that they were tired of being cooped up in the cold hinterland for too long while rival legionaries were getting rich elsewhere. They longed to flex their military muscles and didn't especially care whether it be at the expense of provincials or fellow Romans.

That the figure of Aulus Vitellius would inspire so much gusto is the biggest surprise of all. I mentioned briefly that he was the son of Lucius Vitellius, the senator and twice consul — the same man who had governed Syria for Tiberius and who had been a fawning friend and counselor to both Gaius and Claudius. It was the father who was first to "recognize" Gaius as a god, because when paying the emperor a call on his return from Syria he came to the palace with veiled head and prostrated himself. In Claudius' reign, when the appalling Messalina was in her zenith, Lucius Vitellius begged the queen to grant him the highest possible favor by allowing him to take off one of her shoes. Then he took her right slipper and constantly carried it under his toga, from which he would take it out and kiss it rapturously in her presence.

Aulus Vitellius was born the year after Augustus' death, making him 17 years older than Otho. Although his mother was known as one of Rome's finest ladies, her son spent most of his early years on Capri, to which his father had accompanied Tiberius. It is even said that he became one of the depraved emperor's "little fish." True or not, people in later years continued to snicker the nickname Spintriæ behind his back.

Vitellius had held public positions both in Rome and abroad, but was never considered a military man. How he got sent to rule Germany remains unclear, though the most popular account is that it stemmed from the fact that both Vitellius and the consul Titus Vinius were big supporters of the Blue faction at the races. Vitellius, badly in debt, begged Vinius to ask Galba for the rich governorship of Lower Germany; and since Vinius had Galba's ear, that was that. But some say that Galba acted more from contempt than favor, reasoning that a man of such indolence would pose the least threat to him. I say this because at the time Galba had been heard to say, "No men are less to be feared than those who think of nothing but eating" and that "perhaps Vitellius' bottomless gullet can be filled by the resources of the province." Indeed, gluttony was his most outstanding trait. By now a jowly, overstuffed 54, Vitellius usually began his first banquet at noon, was woozy and wobbly by mid-afternoon, then napped in his tent so that he would be alert enough to repeat the sequence the same evening.

As for his military prowess, a contemporary writes, "He was ignorant of soldiering, incapable of forethought, knew nothing of marching order or scouting, or how far operations should be pressed forward or protracted. He always had to ask someone else."

Yet, his was an army that seemed happy to run itself in his name, thanks to two ambitious generals. Fabius Valens was an older career soldier who had been raised in poverty and who now was developing a taste for the finer things that could be gained either by bribing or plundering the towns along his marches. His counterpart was Alienus Cæcina, a handsome youth with a statuesque build who easily inspired admiration among his men. Once, in his first command, Cæcina had been convicted of misappropriating public funds. He had insisted all along that it had been done on Galba's orders. Now he was eager to erase the black mark from the public's memory and Galba from his.

Within just two weeks Valens could claim 40,000 men in Lower Germany and Cæcina another 30,000 in Upper Germany. But this was just the core. Both columns were reinforced by German auxiliaries, and the strategy was for Cæcina to take his men direct to alpine Italy via the Pennine Pass while Valens was to wind south through Gaul, winning the province to his side — or destroying it.

The outcome for Valens was uncertain at first. Upon reaching Divodurum, one of the northernmost towns in Gaul, the leading citizens rushed out and greeted the troops with presents and supplications. But something happened that no one has yet explained properly. Before their own commanders realized it, the soldiers had seized their arms in a mad frenzy and began massacring all within their reach. Something like 4,000 people had fallen by the time the officers could call off their men.

Such an episode might well have brought all of Gaul to arms. Instead, word of it spread stark terror everywhere. Afterward, it was relatively easy for Valens to engage in a new form of money-raising he had developed. Before entering a town, a Roman officer would arrive with word to the magistrates that the city might be spared upon assembling a certain amount of money commensurate with its size. Once the bribe was delivered to the general in private, he would assemble his men, preach to them on the virtues of mercy, then bestow on them perhaps 300 sesterces apiece to drive home his point. It helped his cause that the townspeople were often at the feet of the troops, with small children begging for mercy and magistrates praying for their deliverance. All this didn't stop the army from commandeering provisions and auxiliaries as well, so Valens' army swelled with but few losses along the way.

As reports of the march filtered back, all of Rome was in a panic. Yes, there was the understandable fear of bloodshed, but equal was the agony of knowing that both factions were headed by men who rivaled only each other in their immorality, indolence and extravagance. And for this people openly deplored their fate. As one man wailed, "Are we now supposed to go into temples and pray for Otho or Vitellius? It would be wicked to offer vows for the success of either in a war of which we can only be sure that the winner will prove the worse."

But the worse perversity for the moment was that of the Prætorian Guards. People hated Otho for having bought his office from them and for the insolent way they swaggered about town, helped themselves to things in markets and wrested endless amounts of money from the emperor himself.

All this was happening at the same time another Prætorian "tradition" was getting out of hand. I refer to a growing practice in which centurions would collect fees from soldiers who wanted to be excused from this or that duty. This led both to unprecedented absenteeism and discord. For instance, a soldier who might win a tidy windfall at dice might be assigned to miserable tasks until he at last coughed up most of his cache to his centurion. As "patron" of the Prætorians — or as their client, I rather think — Otho had little choice but to be a spectator to their avarice and arrogance.

One can see both vices at work in a single incident. To set the stage, I should first explain that Otho had ordered that a contingent of marines from Ostia be given some surplus armaments from the Prætorian camp to take back to their garrison by barge. They arrived in Rome on an evening when the emperor hap-

pened to be entertaining a large number of senators and nobles at a palace dinner. When the marines arrived at the Prætorian barracks with their empty wagons, it was already quite late. Since it was quiet all about, most of the guardsmen
already having drunk themselves into sleep or sluggishness, the tribune on
duty decided that it would be a good idea to take advantage of the lull by opening the arsenal for the marines and loading up their wagons.

But some of the guardsmen who observed it began to scratch their heads. Who
were these "marines" from Ostia with swords at their sides? Why had they taken
weapons from the arsenal? Where did their wagons go? Was this a plot? Had the
Prætorian officers put them up to it? Before long men were being roused from
their barracks beds and being told to strap on their armor. "Some senators have
bribed a garrison from Ostia to assassinate Otho," they shouted, "They've raided
the arsenal and they're headed for the palace. We've got to hurry!"

So off they went on horses, half of them drunk, half rubbing sleep from their
eyes. Once at the palace gates, they shouted and brandished their swords,
threatening the guards inside to let them in or else. In the dining room, Otho
and his dozens of startled guests froze in fear. Was this some ruse cooked up by
Otho to destroy the Senate? Should they fly in all directions or stay and be arrested? They looked to Otho for some indication and found that his face
showed as much terror as anyone's. After a moment's hesitation, the emperor
ordered the Prefects of the Guards to go to the gates and appease the troops'
anger. Then he told his guests to leave immediately. Soon official signets and in-
signias were being flung on the floor as notables scurried past their bewildered
attendants and ran for back doors of the palace.

And not a moment too soon. Just then the Prætorians stormed the gates and
invaded the banquet hall, flashing their steel and demanding to see Otho. Soldiers pressed against their palace counterparts, threatening to kill all tribunes,
then the whole Senate. At long last, Otho, who had been sheltered in a corner,
emerged in their midst and, tossing aside all imperial dignity, climbed atop a
couch and shouted for attention. Only by crying copious tears and invoking the
gods with prayers did he succeed in getting the incensed Prætorians to back off
and return to their barracks.

That night patricians – including many old gentlemen and their wives –
roamed the cold, narrow streets, afraid to return to their homes, some eventually rapping on the doors of friends for shelter as the night wore on. The next
day Rome was like a captured city. Houses were shut, streets almost deserted.
People were somber, but perhaps no more so than the sobered soldiers who
now sulked in their camp. That afternoon they were called into formation by
companies and scolded by their prefects. Then, as if to underscore the insecuri-
ty of even prefects, each man was given 5,000 sesterces. Afterwards, they were
surprised when Otho himself appeared and mounted the platform.

"Fellow soldiers," he said in a soothing tone, "I have not come to fan the fire of your affection for me, or to instill courage into your hearts, because in both these qualities you are more than rich. No, I have come to ask you to moderate your valor and to set some bounds to your devotion to me." Otho talked of the importance of self-discipline and of following orders. "What more could Vitellius have hoped for than to find us in the state of mutiny and dissension as was exhibited last night?" he asked gently, like a father looking down on naughty boys who had plucked some muffins from the kitchen.

The Prætorians were cowed for the moment, especially because Otho had singled out only two of them for punishment. But fear and suspense continued to brood over Rome. The emperor's strategy for survival was two-pronged. First, he attempted to woo all the senators, knights and influential freedmen within the orbit of Rome so as to tighten its solidarity against the invader. Second: while plucking up the courage of his compatriots, he corresponded constantly with the invader himself in hopes that bloodshed could be averted by some sort of accommodation. It began by offering Vitellius money, or an influential position, or any retreat he would care to select in which to lead a life of luxury. At first the letters were couched in flattery, but soon they hardened into coarse insults, each accusing the other (and without lying!) of lechery and various crimes. Before long the letters had ceased. Indeed, the general Fabius Valens was now writing openly to the tribunes of the Prætorian Guards and City Garrison extolling his own strength and accusing them of swearing for Otho after they had declared for Vitellius in the name of the Roman army.

Thus, Otho's plans now turned to battle itself. The biggest lesson he had learned from his mentor, he said, was that Nero had waited too long to react while his enemies advanced. Cæcina had already crossed the Alps into Italy. It was time to invade Gaul by sea, stop Valens and double back on the entrapped Cæcina.

Foremost in the fighting force he had assembled was a legion of marines – one built around the same core of men who had been decimated by Galba after petitioning to become a regular unit of the army. It was they who would take the force by ship to Narbonese Gaul. Marching as well was the legion Galba had brought from Spain, various cohorts of the Prætorian Guard and City Garrison and no fewer than 2,000 gladiators. Accompanying them was a glittering array of knights, leading freedmen and adventuresome youths. Unfortunately, most of the knights had never learned to fight, even though some shored up their spirits with fine horses and glittering armor. His commander, the Guard Prefect, Licinius Proculus, had never been tested in warfare. In fact, Otho was relying principally on being joined in northern Italy by four legions from Dalmatia and Pannonia. Each had already sent 2,000 men on an accelerated march with orders to reach the Po River and hold it against the advancing Vitellian general, Cæcina.

Otho and his force marched out from the Campus Martius on March 14 after a glittering ceremony in which senators vied to compare him with Cæsar Augustus. Until such time as the reinforcements arrived from Pannonia and Dalmatia, they could expect to face a hard-bitten, ill-tempered army of professional soldiers three times their size.

. . . .

THANKFULLY FOR THE JEWS barricaded inside Jerusalem, the new year had come with no further Roman advances in Judea. With both Titus and the Jewish king Agrippa off to pay their respects to Galba, the calm and pragmatic Vespasian now awaited any directions that might result from the encounter. In addition, Vespasian again saw no need to deploy his troops against Jerusalem at a time when the Jews seemed to be destroying themselves by slow poison.

I had said earlier that the Romans had wiped out all the Jewish defenses around Jerusalem except for the mountain fortress of Masada. While this was true at the time, there were also small bands of survivors who had been driven into the rugged mountains south of Jerusalem. Many had been robbers and seditionists all along. Others were plain farmers and tradesmen who had managed to scurry for their lives as their cities were destroyed in the Roman onslaught. Within a few months these desperate and disparate holdouts had coalesced around a single leader, Simon of Gerasa. And as is so often the case with rebels and outcasts, they wind up being led by a man who demonstrates the most courage and physical strength.

This Simon and his followers lived in the mountain caves. Because the Romans had made it very difficult to raid the low-lying cities for their foodstocks, these brigands eked out their existence by exacting tribute from the smaller villages that dotted the mountainsides. They also went about enlisting slaves in their cause by "guaranteeing" their freedom. Eventually Simon assembled such an "army" that they were able to reclaim many lowland cities. Eventually they amassed 20,000 men under arms and resolved to conquer all of Idumea. And after that they boasted of even bringing down Jerusalem. Simon accomplished his aims in Idumea largely through treachery. Thus, by enlisting one of the defending generals of Hebron to betray his cause, the ancient Idumean city surrendered and admitted its new masters almost without bloodshed.

That is, without bloodshed to Simon and his men. As the Jewish historian Josephus describes it:

> Beside the want of provisions that he [Simon] was in, he was of a barbarous disposition and bore great anger at this nation. Thus, it came to pass that Idumea was greatly depopulated; and as one may see a woods despoiled of their leaves by locusts...so was there nothing left behind

Simon's army but a desert. Some places they burnt down, some they
utterly demolished, and whatever grew in the country, they either
trod it down or fell upon it. And by their marches they made the
ground that was cultivated harder and more intractable than that
which was barren. In short, there was no sign remaining of those
places that had been laid waste that ever they had a being.[36]

The Zealots who ruled Jerusalem were well aware of this threat to themselves (as was Vespasian's reconnaissance, of course). Since they could not rush
out from the walls and attack Simon (for fear that the remaining populace
would gain control inside) the Zealots resolved to send out a small party under
stealth and capture Simon as he rode through the mountain passes.

This may have been the Zealots' most misguided act, because their ambush
yielded not Simon, but his wife. When the raiding party returned to the city
with her, they rejoiced as if they had captured Simon himself. But instead of
this making a simpering supplicant of him, Simon erupted with a wild anger.
Whereas he might not have deemed his army ready yet for an assault on
Jerusalem for several weeks, he now brought his full force around the walls
and roared that unless they set his wife free he would breach the walls and destroy every living thing in the city. As if to signal that those inside had not
much time to make up their minds, Simon's men began catching and slaughtering people who had ventured out from the walls to trade or gather herbs
or sticks.

The Zealots, who had gained their own name with their passion, had never
seen such furious rage. They quickly decided that the best course of action was
to set Simon's wife free if they could extract a promise that his men would depart. Simon did so, but only long enough to finish gathering provisions for the
assault on Jerusalem that they had been planning all along. In the process of
doing so they drove so many Idumeans to desperation that they had nowhere
to go but to the walls of Jerusalem and beg for refuge at its gates.

What a terrible predicament for so many ordinary, honest people! The survivors of plundered Idumean cities were forced to beg a savage, self-appointed
king for admittance so that they could flee an equally treacherous, self-appointed king.

Within Jerusalem, John of Gischala, who held the temple and much of the
city, had sunk to unprecedented depths as he whiled away the days in the sacred precincts. As always, his closest confederates were his fellow Galileans, and
their leader gave license to their wildest imaginations. As Josephus reports:

> He permitted them to do all the things that any of them desired to do,
> while their inclination to plunder was insatiable, as was their zeal in

searching the houses of the rich. As for the murdering of men and abusing of the women, it was sport to them.

They also devoured what spoils they had taken, together with their blood, and indulged themselves in feminine wantonness without any disturbance. They decked their hair and put on women's garments and were besmeared over with ointments. And that they might appear very comely, they had paints under their eyes and imitated not only the ornaments, but also the lusts of women....

And thus did they saunter up and down the city, as in a brothel house, and defiled it entirely with their impure actions. Nay, while their faces looked like the faces of women, they killed with their right hands. And when their gait was effeminate, they presently attacked men...and drew their swords from under their finely dyed cloaks and ran everybody through that they alighted upon.[37]

So outrageous was their depravity that even the newly-admitted Idumeans, no strangers themselves to cruel exploitation, refused John their allegiance. And just about this time many of his own army rose up against him – but not for the purest of reasons. At the time, John had been living in the palace of Herod and had acquired many of the trappings of a king. Jealous of his riches, his soldiers stormed the palace and drove John and what remained of the Zealot force across the city so that all they now occupied was the temple. For the majority of townspeople to dislodge John and his men from their stronghold would take a mighty effort, for the Zealots held commanding heights and could wreak damage by hurling their arsenal of darts below.

At about this time word came that Simon of Gerasa was about to arrive at the city walls with a force that now numbered some 40,000. The high priests and populace found themselves facing as crucial a decision as the Zealots did when they decided to kidnap Simon's wife. Should they admit Simon as savior and defender of Jerusalem in order to rid it of the vermin that now infested the temple?

In this case a terrible dilemma led to a terrible decision. The leading citizens and priests met. After much anguish they determined to admit Simon. Perhaps the most critical aspect of their decision was that they simply didn't know what the unstable John and his men might do. They feared that he might at any time burn down the entire city for the sheer perverse pleasure of it. Simon, they reasoned, might be more inclined to respect their homes and personal property.

So the priests entreated Simon to come save their city. They strew the streets with flowers and offered supplications as the outsiders entered the gates. But no sooner had Simon marched in than he began behaving like a haughty despot whose subjects warranted a watchful eye. He and his men did attempt to undermine the walls of the temple, but within days grew tired of the methodical discipline required and the casualties who fell to the darts from above.

Just before Simon entered Jerusalem, Titus, Herod Agrippa and their small entourage arrived in Corinth on their way to Rome. There they learned that Galba had been hacked into pieces in the Forum, that Otho was emperor and that Vitellius was already opposing him. Agrippa, foreseeing no personal threat to himself from either rival, quickly resolved to press on to Rome and pay his respects to Otho. But instinct told Titus to hold back. Counseling with the few advisors who accompanied him, he reasoned that he would earn scant gratitude for paying homage intended for another sovereign. Yet, if he returned to Judea he would no doubt offend whoever emerged victorious among Otho and Vitellius. But then, to return would also offer his father time to contemplate declaring for the throne himself. And in that case, it wouldn't really matter which one of the rivals he had offended.

. . . .

BEFORE RETURNING TO SYRIA, Titus stopped off at the island of Paphos, on which sits the ancient Temple of Venus and its equally-famous oracle. After inspecting the temple treasures, which have been presented by many kings through the centuries, he consulted the oracle about his forthcoming voyage. Learning that the seas would be calm and that no obstacles stood in his way, Titus began to put covert questions about his own fortunes. After responding in a general way that agreed with his ambitions, the oracle granted a private interview and, as he said later, "revealed the future" to him. It was this more than anything that sent Titus back to his father in Cæsarea with boundless confidence that fortune would grant him success.

"Success" by now was understood by all in the Vespasian camp to mean much more than crushing Jerusalem. Ever since word had reached his troops about Otho's rise and Vitellius' rebellion, the camps had been rife with the mutterings of restless men. As they saw it, either the Prætorians or the armies of Germany were about to win favor and fortune with a Roman ruler, and there was not one legion among them which was more skilled in war nor led by a better man than the three legions of Judea. Add these to the four legions maintained by the governor Mucianus in Antioch and there was no force in the world that could stand up to them!

Vespasian, of course, heard this daily. He had heard, too, the prophesies of the Jewish general Josephus and of several soothsayers consistently reinforce his own inner intuition that he, the product of plodding, hard-working Flavian peasant-soldiers was the best hope for Rome to succeed the utterly exhausted Augustan line. But again he waited.

One reason was that Vespasian now realized the need to reconcile with Mucianus, his nominal superior as governor of Syria. When Vespasian was first named to head the Jewish campaign, he encountered the same natural chain-of-command problems that Corbulo had faced with Syrian governors years earlier in his war on Parthia. Who should send formal deputations to enemies? Who controls orders to advance or retreat? Who corresponds with the emperor about the war's progress? Things of this sort. But now the fear of Otho — or the danger that Rome had fallen into the hands of another Nero — was enough to make both men realize the advantage of forming a common cause.

For this they could thank Titus, who had found Mucianus personable and accommodating even when his father had not. On the surface, both older men were opposites. Vespasian was the plain speaking soldier who dressed like his troops, marched at the head of a column, chose each night's camp and spent most of the evening plotting the next day's strategy. Mucianus dressed according to his grandeur as one of Rome's most plutocratic patricians, best orators and most polished administrators. Some said the two would have made a splendid emperor if they could combine their qualities. It was enough, however, that they soon agreed to overlook their differences and combine their seven legions and strong naval fleets. That the whole is often greater than all its parts was shown by the fact that the two even assigned tribunes and centurions to each other's units based on their individual strengths for the tasks required. And in so doing, they also infused Mucianus' troops, which had had no experience in battle, with men from Vespasian's who were steeled by years of combat.

Yet, Vespasian and Mucanius continued to bide their time. In fact, they sent word of their support to Otho. The eastern leaders reasoned that because either the new emperor or Vitellius would best the other, the Roman military would probably be weakened in the process. They also agreed that to launch a civil war from the east would take extraordinary preparation. All other Roman civil wars had begun in Italy and spread outward. In this case, the acquiescence of the Armenians and Parthians would have to be secured first, then all of the eastern Roman lands from Syria down through Egypt united and synchronized like gears on a water wheel. But if this could be accomplished, Mucianus and Vespasian were confident of the outcome because their ultimate strength was in their foe's weakness.

. . . .

ALL SOLDIERS FEAR BATTLE, but a Roman soldier gains both comfort and resolve in knowing that he is fighting a stranger with alien customs on the latter's own soil. This makes killing easier and enervates one at the prospect of plunder, sport with the losers' women and the added gain from seizing property and selling prisoners into slavery.

But in a civil war, these "conditions of engagement" are abandoned, leaving only confusion and uncertainty in their place. The foe looks alike, dresses the same and uses similar tactics. One's blade might pierce the neck of an old comrade from some bygone campaign, or perhaps even one's own brother. I mention the above because all of it preyed on the minds of soldiers in both the Othonian and Vitellian troops as they marched towards each other in northern Italy in late March. The tensions were reflected most dangerously in the way that infantrymen questioned routine decisions by their junior officers and how centurions and tribunes suspected the motives of their generals, who in turn behaved like rivals for spoils and the favor of their supreme commander. At the core of it, both forces saw their leaders as nothing more than hedonistic opportunists whose loftiest visions were probably no more than the number of dinner courses they might dazzle guests with at the Golden House.

This inner turmoil can only explain the behavior of Otho's troops as they marched through northern Italy. This was their own land. The fields were full; and at first whole families went out to line the roads to greet their new emperor and his troops. But not after the first day or so. Italian townspeople found that they were subjected to the same ravage and plunder that Romans reserved for hostile foreign nations. Indeed, Cæcina decided to use his foe's crass insensitivity to advantage. As if he had abruptly left his own greed and profligacy in the mountains, Cæcina became the soul of benevolence as he led his Vitellians into northern Italy. He also wanted no distractions until his men reached their objective: the fortified Po River town of Cremona, which would serve as his primary base in northern Italy.

Some 20 miles west of Cromona, Cæcina's force had come upon 3,000 Othonians ensconced at Placentia, a smaller but equally well-fortified city. After an all-day assault in which his superior manpower had failed to dislodge them, Cæcina brooded again about never regaining his lost prestige as he led his men on toward Cremona. Also preying on his mind was that Valens and the remainder of the Vitellian forces had reached the Po behind them and would probably link up soon — all of which Cæcina viewed gloomily because it meant that the glory of future victories would be diluted.

Just then he brightened when an advance patrol reported that a large force of about 15,000 Othonians were approaching on the same road. Cæcina, now about 12 miles west of Cremona, halted his own columns and carefully concealed his best troops in a thick wood that overlooked the road. He then ordered his cavalry to ride briskly toward the advancing Othonians and provoke the oncoming enemy into an engagement — but only long enough to gallop off on a retreat that would lead the pursuers right through the ambush.

All during this whole campaign one army's plans would be betrayed to another's, and this was no different. Alerted to Cæcina's plan, the Othonians formed three columns — one to march on the main road and one column each on higher grounds flanking it. Just before reaching the ambush point, the Othonians ground to a stop. Cæcina's men were so pent-up in the long wait for their prey that they jumped out from behind their rocks and trees, chasing after the retreating foe. In a few minutes it was Vitellians who were the prey, because they had now run headlong down a road that was occupied on high ground by two of the advancing Othonian columns.

Then came one of those inexplicable lapses that change wars and keep old soldiers in taverns arguing for years afterward. The Othonian general, Suetonius Paulinus, was somewhere amid the winding columns and may not have known the Vitellians were exposed. No attack order came. Suetonius later said his men were fatigued. Later critics called him overly cautious — one who took so long to clear fields and fill ditches that he forgot to do battle. Yet, this was the same Suetonius Paulinus who decisively led 10,000 men to victory over Boudicca and her 150,000 Britons. I merely note that Suetonius was later welcomed into the Vitellian fold. Might he already be giving them a reason?

This delay of several minutes gave the Vitellians time to realize their plight and take cover in the surrounding vineyards. The vines were thick and prevented Otho's cavalry from chasing the men down. Behind the vineyards was a wood where the Vitellians regrouped, joined in successive waves by various auxiliary forces that had been kept in check as fresh reinforcements for their own "ambush."

The confusing skirmish ensued for the rest of the day, with heavy losses on both sides. But the difference was that enough time lapsed for Valens to arrive the next day at Cæcina's camp and nearly triple the size of the Vitellian force. Now the scales were dramatically tipped.

Now that Cæcina and Valens had combined forces and seemed poised for battle, Otho held a council to decide whether to fight or delay the war. The case for delay was led, fittingly enough, by Suetonius Paulinus. "The barbarians of Gaul and Germany will soon be in turmoil unless their Roman legions return," he argued. "Moreover, the Vitellians cannot remain long in Italy anyway because they have no means of obtaining grain. And once the hot muggy summer months come, the German troops won't be able to stand the change in climate."

"But our troops," said Paulinus, "can call on rich and reliable resources. On our sides are fresh armies from Pannonia, Dalmatia and the East. We have the Senate and people of Rome and vast resources of all the cities south of the Po.

And in a civil war a vast quantity of money is stronger than the sword."

Otho himself was instinctively for immediate action and he was quickly cheered on by the other generals. In order to check any further opposition, they resorted to effusive flattery, predicting that the gods and Otho's divinely inspired policies would carry the day.

It carried the argument, at any rate, with only one concession. All agreed that it was best for Otho himself to retire to nearby Brixellum, away from the immediate battle, so that he could continue running affairs of the empire while the battle raged. But this in itself was a fateful decision. Not only did Otho depart with a considerable number of Guards and cavalry, but with him the spirit of his troops. They trusted only Otho himself and immediately began to carp at the decisions made by his unproven generals.

The Othonians had to march further to engage the enemy than they had planned. After covering nearly 16 miles, the tired and footsore legions finally encountered the Vitellians near a small settlement called Bedriacum, located about 20 miles east of Cremona.

It was not an ideal battlefield at all, being encumbered by trees and vines. All thoughts of a disciplined, classic cavalry engagement had to be forgotten. Nor could one mount an effective javelin attack. Instead, the scene became a blur of Romans hacking with their short swords and axes at the helmets and breastplates of other Romans.

The only place that gave rise to a classic military confrontation was on an open field that lay between the road and the river. There, the Vitellian 21st Legion, which had a proud tradition since the days of Augustus, prevailed over a spirited First Adiutrix, which had only seen its first combat a few days before. Down on the river, some open boats containing Otho's gladiators appeared, including baggage as well. When the German auxiliaries saw them coming, they let out a roar, rushed to the banks and began cutting the wobbly occupants to pieces as they tried to land.

After several hours of the most furious hand-to-hand combat in Roman history, the larger Vitellian forces began to prevail. Some of the Othonian generals and tribunes fled in disorder. Quickly their troops did as well. The roads were already heaped with dead, for there is no profit in keeping captives in a civil war. When the Othonians regrouped in their various camps, some of them turned on their generals, assailing them as deserters and sparing them no abuse.

The entire Vitellian army bivouacked five miles from Bedriacum, and on the next day their hopes were fulfilled when the Othonians sent a deputation. At first there was stiffness between both parties, but as a witness reported,

> Soon both victors and vanquished burst into tears, and with sorrowful satisfaction cursed their fate of civil war. Sitting in the same tents, they

nursed wounded brothers or other relatives. Their hopes of recompense were doubtful. All that was certain was bereavement and grief, for no one was so fortunate as to mourn no loss.[38]

Otho awaited news of the battle with firm and patient resolve. As I have noted before, the same man known as a dissipate and deviate in the confines of Rome always had a sterling reputation as a soldier in the field. Now word began to reach him that all was not well at Bedriacum. Yet, the officers of the Guards and Garrison who surrounded him genuinely spoiled for the chance to return with him to "risk everything and suffer everything," as one of them insisted. Some near him clasped at his knees as others farther away stretched out their arms in supplication. As the officers made their appeals to continue the fight, the soldiers watching now cheered, now groaned, depending on whether Otho's expression softened or hardened at hearing them. Indeed, the arrival of the first legionary reinforcements from the province of Mœsia (800 miles to the east) shored up their courage.

Although Otho listened thoughtfully and seemed to maintain good cheer throughout, he was not convinced as to continuing the war. At last he stood before his advisors and said this:

> Am I to expose all your splendid courage and valor to further risks? That would, I think, be too great a price to pay for my life. Your high hopes of succeeding, if I were minded to live, will only swell the glory of my death. We have learned to know each other, Fortune and I. Do not merely count [a life's worth in] length of time. Self-control is all the harder when a man knows that his fortune cannot last. It was Vitellius who began the civil war. He initiated our contest for the throne. But one battle is enough. This is the precedent that I will set: let posterity judge Otho by it.

> Others may have held the scepter longer, but no man can ever have laid it down so bravely. Am I the man to allow the flower of Rome in all these famous armies to be mown down once again and lost to the country? Let me take with me the consciousness that you would have died for me. But you must stay and live. I must no longer interfere with your chance of pardon, nor you with my resolve.[39]

With that Otho addressed each man according to rank and urged them all to hurry away so as not to risk their chances with the Vitellians by showing hesitation. He even helped his secretaries arrange for carriages and boats for each of them. He then destroyed all correspondence he had that referred adversely to

Vitellius.

Outside, the uninformed had been alarmed at the number of officers preparing to leave camp and threatened to kill them as deserters. So Otho went out and rebuked the ringleaders, then stayed to receive the tearful good-byes of those departing. As day deepened into night, two daggers were brought to him, and after examining them both for sharpness, he put one under his pillow. The next morning the emperor's steward heard a groan inside the tent and rushed inside. Otho apparently awoke, held the dagger with the blade fixed upward on the bed, and leaned his chest into it. He was already dead when the attendant reached him.

The date was April 16. And so did Otho become known best for the first and last things he did during these very long three months: the atrocious murder of Galba and the noble way he ended his life in order to spare Rome countless other deaths. To this day no one can explain how a man could have sunk to such depths as Nero's malevolent young companion and to the heights of nobility that he achieved on his last day on earth.

In Rome itself, there was no sign of panic. The festival of Ceres was in progress, and when it was reported in the theater that Otho had ended his life and that the City Prefect, Flavius Sabinus, made all the troops in Rome swear allegiance to Vitellius, the audience dutifully cheered the new emperor. By the end of the day, busts of Galba had reappeared, and garlands had been placed in a mound on the place where he was slain.

Three months would pass, however, before Vitellius appeared at the gates of Rome. He had remained in Gaul during the battles, and now was met there by the victorious generals. Lavish praise had to be bestowed on Valens and Cæcina, and justice had to be meted out to the defeated Othonians (most of it satisfied by executing a few centurions). The victorious army's return was also slowed by its own pillaging and the need to stop bands of abandoned Othonians from doing even more of it. Italy, which had already been exhausted from provisioning the war, was now picked clean of whatever people had left. And the people themselves joined in, some of them buying uniforms from soldiers so they could charge off and settle old scores with enemies and rival towns.

Then there was the necessary stop at Bedriacum to show the emperor the now-famous battlefield. As Valens and Cæcina escorted an impervious Vitellius about, an observer recalled:

> Forty days after the battle, it was a disgusting and horrible sight: mangled bodies, mutilated limbs, rotting carcasses of men and horses, the ground foul with clotted blood. Trees and crops all trampled down: the countryside a miserable waste. No less heartless was the stretch of road which the people of Cremona had strewn with laurel-leaves and

roses, erecting altars [to Vitellius] and sacrificing victims as if in honor of an oriental despot.[40]

A final reason for the slow march to Rome was Vitellius himself. As one wag explained, "This was because he could not advance a step without first eating everything in his path. Rome and Italy were scoured for dainties to tickle his palate and leading provincials were ruined by having to provide for the feasts." And it is no surprise that the Vitellian entourage reflected the tastes and priorities of its leader. "Disorder and drunkenness were universal," said one observer.

It was finally on July 15 when the new emperor arrived at the gates of the Eternal City to take his place in the pantheon with men such as Julius Cæsar and Octavian Augustus. But to arrive in the splendor that Romans expected would be difficult in this case. Vitellius had accumulated an ungainly gaggle of 60,000 troops and an even greater number of soldiers' servants, camp-followers, friends, low-bred entertainers and others who had attached themselves along the way. The confusion was more muddled by the number of senators and knights who had come out to greet the party, each with his own retinue. The soldiers straggled in disarray, slowed by sellers of snacks and souvenirs. Men urinated along the roadside, harlots beckoned to the carriages and relatives of soldiers picked their way through the mass asking when this or that company of men would pass by.

Vitellius, realizing that some attempt to assume order was needed before entering the city gates, called a halt to his clumsy cavalcade at the seventh milestone. It was his intention to spruce up and feed the wandering camp enough so as to last out the procession and not overwhelm the city's food purveyors. The only problem was that great numbers of townspeople were already walking about in the midst of the dismounted travelers. Among them were some young pranksters who would sneak up behind a distracted soldier and cut away his belt. Then one of their chums would walk up and say, "Hey, soldier, have you got your sword on?" After too many such episodes and many guffaws from the crowd, some soldiers decided that this wasn't the "triumph" they had expected, so out came their swords and people were killed. Only after they had accidentally killed a father who had come out to greet his long-absent son did they quiet down and resume the march.

When the massive caravan resumed, the new emperor entered the gates in civilian dress, walking on foot at the head of his column. After the endless parade of eagles, standards and white uniforms, Vitellius gave a grandiloquent eulogy to himself in which he extolled his industry and self-discipline. The unknowing crowd applauded wildly, then chanted that he must (though he had thus far refused it) accept the title of *Augustus.*

In the weeks that followed, Vitellius Augustus spent his days languishing in the Curia, where he seemed to tolerate debate as long as it was confined to public policy. Valens and Cæcina spent theirs running the government, amassing their own ill-gotten fortunes and spending most of it competing to see whose wealth and retinue could surpass his rival's. As for the average Roman's impression of the regime, it might be summed up, "soldiers, soldiers, soldiers." They seemed to be everywhere – too many foreign-speaking Gauls and Germans and even too many Italian provincials who dressed and acted as though they had spent too much time in the woods.

It was almost humorous at first. As soon as the triumphal march had ended, most of the soldiers from other lands hastened away to get a better look at the famous Forum – especially the spot where Galba had fallen. In their rush they created a fearsome site with their long coats of animal skin and long pikes. Worse, because they weren't used to picking their way through crowds, they would simply bowl over anyone in their way. And because they weren't accustomed to slick, greasy pavements, their feet often slipped out from under them, much to the laughter of Romans.

More than anything, it was simply their day-to-day presence that became oppressive. The barracks were severely overcrowded, and those who weren't fortunate enough to find shelter in private homes were forced to camp among the public colonnades and temples. Many of the foreign auxiliaries settled along the Tiber, where the summer heat and foul air soon began to take its toll on their health. Everywhere soldiers ceased to observe roll call, to go on guard, or keep themselves in training. Most gave themselves over to sloth and debauchery, their only source of funds the bribes that Valens and Cæcina proffered in exchange for their allegiance.

Vitellius contributed to the situation by granting every demand of the soldiers. This he did because it was cheaper than paying the bonuses he had long promised and now lacked funds for. Indeed, Vitellius had by late fall managed to spend some 900 million sesterces in public funds, some of it for the most outlandish banquets in Roman history. His most conspicuous building project was new stables for chariot drivers and his most common expense was for shows of gladiators and wild beasts. He had even held a lavish "funeral" for Nero in the Campus Martius. Victims were killed and burnt in public, the torch being applied by none other than the Augustales, members of the sacred college that Tiberius had founded to honor the Julian family.

Oh, yes, cruelty had become part of Vitellius' daily routine as well. Inflicting torture on one's suspected enemies was now a sport – especially when it came to the creditors who had pressed him as a civilian. One of them, while in the act of saluting him, was sent off to be executed, only to be recalled immediately before the guards had dragged him too far. Then, as all around the emperor were praising his mercy, he gave orders to have the man killed in his presence because "it would be a feast for my eyes." Another, a knight, cried out as he was being taken off to execution: "You are my heir!" Vitellius compelled him to produce his will. Reading that the man had actually named one of his freedmen as co-heir, he ordered the freedman brought to him at once so that both men could be killed.

. . . .

EVEN WITH THE BEST POST SYSTEM in the world, it still takes two weeks (or more with pirates or bad weather) for a message to travel from Judea to Rome. Were there some magic means to communicate instantly between such vast distances, Vitellius might never have entered Rome because he would have known that Vespasian was already in the process of withdrawing the allegiance his troops had sworn after the battle of Cremona.

In truth, when Vespasian had asked his legions to salute Vitellius, his tone was tepid and the troops' reaction was a mixture of silence and slurred words. By July their general heard Vitellius slandered every day and himself championed. The troops' arguments ran something like this: Vitellius was much Vespasian's inferior as a military man. The Vitellian legions were a moral disgrace and hardly deserved to be considered the flower of Rome when the nine strong and disciplined legions of the east were the epitome of military professionalism. The Vitellian family may have had some luster, but the emperor, with but one infant son, could not hope to serve Rome more ably than a distinguished general with two grown and able sons.

But it seemed that the more they flattered and cajoled him, the more obstinate Vespasian became – and in the process, I believe, showed his superior wisdom and maturity. For Vespasian knew that unlike the Vitellians, his own legions had no experience in civil war; and whereas the commanders of the defeated armies were rich in their zeal for revenge, they were poor in resources. He considered, too, that while he could at age 60 claim to have already lived a long and full life, a decision to contest Vitellius would risk losing his two sons in the fullness of their manhood. Indeed, as Vespasian would sometimes bark at his eager young aides, "You simply don't understand that when one covets a throne there is no middle way between the zenith of success and headlong ruin."

But what did prey on Vespasian's mind the most was something that had nothing to do with his own fortunes. Each day, a visitor or military messenger would add more disquieting news from Rome than the day before: aimless soldiers clogging the city streets, imperial indifference, contagious corruption, impending bankruptcy – and, Vespasian feared – the prospect that the empire might be wracked by another series of power struggles among whomever could commandeer a couple of legions and make the most extravagant promises to their men.

The moment of decision was probably forced on Vespasian when he came to Berytus to meet the governor Mucianus, who had traveled down from Antioch. It was clear that the governor, his one-time partner in caution, had now come to convince the man he now admired greatly that the time had come to change course. In a carefully-staged public reception that left Vespasian no more room than a wrestlers' pit to struggle with his conscience, Mucianus turned to the general and said:

> Everybody who plans some great exploit is bound to consider whether his project serves both the public interest and his own reputation, and whether it is easily practicable, or at any rate, not impossible. He must also weigh the advice which he gets. Are those who offer it ready to run the risk themselves? And if fortune favors the supreme undertaking, who gains the supreme glory? I, myself, Vespasian, call you to the throne....

> You need not be afraid that I may seem to flatter you. It is more of an insult than a compliment to be chosen to succeed Vitellius. It is not against the powerful intellect of the deified Augustus that we are rising in revolt; not against the cautious prudence of the old Tiberius; nor even against a long-established imperial family like that of Gaius, Claudius or Nero. You even gave way to Galba's ancient lineage. To remain inactive any longer, to leave your country to ruin and pollution, would appear [to be] sheer sloth and cowardice, even if such slavery were as safe for you as it would be dishonorable.

> The time is long past when you could appear to be unambitous: the throne is now your only refuge.[41]

As for himself, Mucianus vowed that he would always be second to Vespasian. "I shall have such honor as you grant me," he said. "But of the risk and dangers, we will share the burden equally" (meaning that Mucianus was ready to lead the Syrian legions into Rome).

It was probably at the conclusion of this stirring appeal that Vespasian changed his mind and was never to look back. On the same day, Mucianus administered the oath of allegiance to the legion commanders of Syria, then announced the decision to the public in the splendid theater Herod Agrippa I had built for the people of Berytus nearly 30 years before. At the same time, he "confided" to the people that he had learned of a plan by Vitellius to transfer the Syrian legions to the inhospitable climes of Germany and force Syria, in turn, to quarter Germany's ill-mannered barbarians. That alone sent them home chanting "Victory to Vespasian."

Once the decision was behind them, Vespasian and Mucianus put the following events into motion:

They quickly secured the support of virtually every client state in the region. Of greatest concern was Herod Agrippa II, who was notified in Rome and managed to slip out by ship unknown to Vitellius. As for the powerful Parthians, it was enough that they agreed not to make trouble.

A dispatch was sent to Tiberius Alexander, governor of Alexandria, asking for his support. The governor responded boldly, administering the oath to his two legions on the same day.

New troops were conscripted and veterans recalled. Some towns were assigned specific arms manufacturing tasks, with Vespasian himself often inspecting their progress. New gold and silver was coined at Antioch, but Mucianus himself became the war effort's single largest financier, issuing loans to the army at high interest rates.

Vespasian gave his troops a small "donation" and announced that no more would be forthcoming. As one observer reported: "He had set his face with an admirable firmness against largess to the soldiers, and his army was the better for it."

By early October, everything seemed to be going Vespasian's way. At a war council several weeks before, a debate had ensued as to whether to invade Italy immediately or simply to seal off the Alps from northern reinforcements and wait until the full Flavian force arrived from Syria. Vespasian himself was inclined to the latter view, but the officers were roused when one Antonius Primus, a relative newcomer to the cause, made a passionate speech for striking at once. The Vitellians' victory "has not served to inspirit or enervate them," he declared with a loud voice and flashing eyes. "The men are not held in readiness in camp but are loitering in towns all over Italy. If we give them time to train for war they will regain their energy, then draw more strength from Germany and Britain."

The final decision combined both views. Vespasian himself would proceed to Egypt, inspecting the readiness of its legions and making arrangements so that the grain supply could be systematically withheld from Rome, which needed some 8,000 tons a week to feed its million people. In fact, he believed the odds were good that Rome could be brought to its knees without bloodshed simply by choking off its food supply.

At the same time, the newly-promoted general Antonius Primus would set out westward with two legions in hopes of securing others stationed on his way to Italy. Mucianus would follow with another force. Their ultimate objective was to land on both coasts of Italy and drive a wedge between Rome and its provinces to the north.

Indeed, the first weeks went almost precisely as anticipated. The three legions of Mœsia – the ones that had still been rushing towards Bedriacum when Otho's troops were fleeing – quickly came over to Vespasian. Then came the armies of Pannonia, Dalmatia and Illyricum so that virtually all the armies east of Italy were now in the Vespasian camp.

Vitellius ignored the first reports, but soon he had no choice but to order Valens and Cæcina to mobilize for war. Cæcina, despite having grown slack with wealth and self-indulgence, managed to start off first after a ceremony of warm embraces and accolades from Vitellius. Accompanied by most of eight legions and detachments from three legions that had come from Britain, Cæcina's orders were to return to the Po and re-occupy Cremona – their base of operations after the Battle of Bedriacum that spring.

Unknown to either Vitellius or the Flavian command at the time is that both forces would converge on Cremonia. Vespasian had ordered Antonius Primus to halt near the Italian border and wait for Mucianus, but the general of their advance legions was bent on an ambitious course. Antonius Primus was a curious sort: In Nero's time he had been stripped of his senatorial rank and exiled for forging a will. Yet, by sheer determination and intrigue he had regained enough stature in time to secure command of the Seventh Legion from Galba. Described as "a man of great physical energy," this war was his chance to be one of the first men in Rome if he could attain feats of glory.

And so, when Antonius led his two legions westward through Illyricum and into Italy, he couldn't help but covet the city of Verona, which lay just 100 more miles to the west. News of its destruction would not only humiliate Vitellius, but add luster to his own career.

However, by the time Antonius' legions had traveled this added distance, they had both outrun their supply lines and alerted the Vitellians. Cæcina and his far greater force took position just east of Verona and easily resisted the first parries of the advancing Flavians. It was at this point that Cæcina unwittingly forced Antonius even further into Italy – but to the latter's lucky advantage. Agents of the Flavians had already courted the Vitellian general with promises of a powerful position in Rome if he would come over to their side. Indeed, Cæcina had sent "private" dispatches to Antonius to discuss a specific time and strategy for it. But this didn't fit the Flavian general's own strategy for personal glory. Rather than treating the dispatches in confidence, the Flavian general had them read aloud to his soldiers because they did wonders for their courage. No doubt Cæcina learned of it and knew that word might soon drift back to his own men.

His escape from this mess came when he received word that the fleet at the naval port of Ravenna had gone over to Vespasian. So Cæcina, seizing on a time when most of his men were out on detail and the camp rather empty, sounded the call to assembly and delivered an oration to the few who were rounded up. He painted a ferocious portrait of the Flavian army and noted that they had support of all the powerful eastern armies. He reminded his men that they had now been deprived of maritime support at a time when they were already short on supplies. He had it on good authority that Spain and Gaul would soon declare against Vitellius; and everybody knew, of course, that the Germans were as about as faithful as harlots at an orgy. Under the circumstances, he, their leader, had boldly decided that their future lay in swearing allegiance to Vespasian.

That evening, when all the Vitellian soldiers returned from their various duties, the statues of Vitellius were gone. Soon one could hear a buzz throughout camp, gradually building to an uproar. What? Had the pride of the Vitellian armies sunk so low that they should allow themselves to be shackled without a battle? *They* should yield to the former armies of Otho, whom they had already routed just a few months ago? Eight legions were to follow the lead of one lousy fleet made up mostly of Dalmatians and Pannonians anyway? No! Cæcina alone would not be able to rob the troops of their emperor!

Within minutes a mob swooped down on Cæcina and clapped him in irons. After that they tore down their camp and marched back to Cremona to join the two legions that Cæcina had already sent ahead from Rome to occupy and fortify the city.

Antonius was fortunate indeed. Would he now come to his senses and await reinforcements? No. He told his men that because the Vitellians were now leaderless, it was time to oust them from Cremona before they had further chance to strengthen the walls. He added that Fabius Valens was doubtless well on his way from Rome with his armies and would hasten his pace when informed of Cæcina's treachery.

The truth about Valens is that when Vitellius had summoned him in Rome, he had been recovering from a serious illness. His march through Italy had been at tortoise speed, given this and the fact that the train was bogged down with harlots, eunuchs, banqueting paraphernalia and other trappings of Vitellian Rome.

Antonius marched his whole force from Verona to Bedriacum, already the graveyard of so many Roman soldiers, and struck camp there. The next day around II A.M. he took about 4,000 cavalrymen and soldiers on the road further west to Cremona — ostensibly to forage for supplies, but in truth to whet their appetites for plunder — when they saw a detachment of Vitellian cavalry riding towards them. The most eager of Antonius' horsemen whooped and immediately rode into their midst. They had their foe in fast retreat when they came to the rise of a hill. There, every Flavian heart must have dropped in his stomach, because coming at them just over the rise was a much larger Vitellian force.

Now it was Antonius' cavalry turning tail and galloping back into the midst of their infantrymen with the Vitallians behind them slashing at everything in sight. Most of the Flavians found themselves running for their lives across a rickety narrow bridge and up a steep river bank. Antonius stood near the bridge as one of his standard bearers ran toward it, his eyes blinded by terror. Antonius speared the man with his lance, grabbed the standard and turned to face the enemy. This rallied about a hundred of his troopers, who made a stand together. Meanwhile, the Flavians on the steep riverbank were now out of cavalry range. They regrouped and returned, all of them aided by the fact that the leaderless Vitellian charge had been reckless and disordered. Soon they had the enemy in retreat, and those who had fled to the hills returned to help their comrades count prisoners, pillage the dead and capture horses.

Antonius had not intended to follow up his advantage, though they were now only four or five miles from Cremona. But at this point his full force of fresh troops came up the road from Bedriacum to meet them. Having wound their way through so many corpses and other reeking remains of slaughter, the newcomers were distraught because they thought the war might be over. At least, they demanded, Antonius should allow them to advance at once on Cremona and either receive it by submission or take it by storm. What was really on their minds, I believe, was that if they waited for daybreak, the generals would start negotiating terms and wind up with Cremona's wealth in their pockets, leaving the soldiers with nothing for their wounds and labors.

Soon mutiny was in the air, and to avert it Antonius went around among the companies, telling them why they should trust the planning and foresight of their generals. "The risks we face are obvious," he implored. "It is night. The enemy is behind walls. Are you going to begin storming the town when you can't possibly see where the ground is level and how high the walls are? How do you know whether to assault it with engines or showers of missiles, or with siege-works and mantlets? Are you going to break through the walls with swords and javelins? Why not wait one night until our siege engines arrive and carry the victory by force?"

With a rapid fire of questions like these did Antonius reduce an uproar to sullen muttering. But it was not to last long. The freshest of the troopers had been sent back to Bedriacum to bring back supplies and war equipment, and while the others waited, some of their scouts had captured some Cremonian stragglers and learned something staggering. Only four or five Vitellian legions were actually inside Cremona. Another six legions had been camped at Hostilia, a smaller city some 45 miles east of Cremona. Once they were alerted, they would surely rush to the rescue of Cremona in overwhelming numbers.

The Flavians had begun to form ranks to withstand any such assault. It was now about nine at night. The Vitellians inside the walls could have waited for reinforcements. Or even without them they could regain their strength with a night's food and sleep, then try to annihilate the Flavians, who would be weakened by then with cold and hunger. But, with Cæcina in chains, they had no general and no plan. I should add that it was also the time of a popular festival, and the city's population was swelled half again with people from all over Italy. The great majority backed Vitellius. Bolstered, perhaps, by their added supporters, the soldiers inside felt emboldened enough to throw caution to the winds. They rushed out from the walls in a furious, disorganized attack. From that point on the battle was a confused slaughter on both sides.

As fate would have it, the fighting took place during an eclipse of the moon, and it became so dark that one could barely see in front of him. Worse, both sides were dressed and armed alike. Standards were easily captured and trod upon. Even watchwords were quickly known and used by both sides.

This was the strangest of battles I have ever studied. One man reports that as the night wore on,

> ...one might have seen them sometimes fighting, sometimes standing and leaning on their spears or even sitting down. Now they would all shout the name of Vespasian, and on the other side that of Vitellius, and they would challenge each other in turn, indulging in abuse or praise of one leader or the other.
>
> One soldier might have a private conversation with an opponent: "Comrade, fellow citizen, what are we doing? Why are we fighting? Come over to my side!"
>
> "No, indeed! You come to my side!"
>
> But what is there surprising about this, considering that the women of the city in the course of the night brought food and drink to give the soldiers of Vitellius, only to find that after eating and drinking themselves, they passed the supplies on to their antagonists? One of them would call out the name of his adversary (for practically all knew one another) and would say: "Comrade, eat this. I give you, not a sword, but bread. Drink this that I hold out to you — not a shield, but a cup. Thus, whether you kill me or I you, we shall quit life more comfortably.[42]

Fortune had favored neither side, but eventually the full moon emerged from its eclipse in eerie fullness. It shone behind the Flavians and as such changed the battle's course. This was because the glow from the full moon magnified the shadows of their men so that the Vitellians took the shadow for substance and often caused their missiles to fall short. Moreover, the moon shone in full on the Viltellians and made them easier targets. At last Antonius was able to recognize his own men and firm up their ranks.

As dawn brightened the sky, a rumor spread (started by Antonius himself?) that Mucianus and his fresh legions from Syria would arrive at any moment. With that the Flavians fought all the harder and the Vitellian line became more ragged. With no general to lead them, the Vitellian ranks filled and thinned according to each soldier's own appetite for more war. But eventually the line disintegrated and broke. Vitellians scurried off along the main highway from Cremona with Flavians in headlong pursuit.

When the bulk of Antionus' troops returned at last from their chase and viewed the walls of Cremonia in the morning sunlight, they gaped at their challenge. In the previous summer's occupation, ramparts had been erected all around and the fortifications further strengthened. The Flavian troops had had no rest and scant food for over 24 hours. To storm the town now would be exhausting and perilous. To return to the camp at Bedriacum would involve an equally fatiguing march and undo their victory. Yet, if they tried to erect a camp in this place, it would be subject to a rain of missiles. When all was said and done, their thirst for plunder was greater than their thirst for water and rest.

A brief delay ensued while the Flavians scoured the carnage of the surrounding battlefield for pickaxes, mattocks and hooks and ladders. Then, holding these weapons under shields that were raised above their heads, they advanced in the well-known tortoise formation. But of course their opponents were Roman soldiers who knew what to expect: they rolled down huge masses of heavy stones. Whenever the tortoise withered under the barrage, the defenders thrust at it with lances and poles until the whole cover of shields was broken up. Then they mowed down the torn and bleeding soldiers below with another flurry of missiles.

You would think that would be the end of this tactic; but no, another tortoise would be formed. Then another tortoise would climb upon the extended shields of the men below until the highest men could reach out and grab the limbs or weapons of those in the ramparts. Eventually the Vitellians, frustrated at seeing so many of their missiles glide off the tortoise, sent their largest catapult crashing down upon them. In an instant it scattered and crushed the men beneath it. But a part of the great engine had been affixed by chains to the ramparts, and as it came thundering down, its heavy weight dragged the top of the ramparts down with it. Stones, timbers, men all came tumbling down atop the already crushed invaders in the throes of gruesome death. But even as the dust blinded and choked everyone, Flavian soldiers were beginning to pour through the gaping break in the wall that had been opened.

At this point the spirit of the Vitellians began ebbing quickly. Their officers became the least enthusiastic for continuing the battle because they reasoned that if the city became too demolished for plunder, they would lose all hope of pardon. The common soldiers, perhaps feeling more secure in their individual obscurity, either continued offering resistance or hid themselves in houses. Meanwhile the tribunes and centurions rushed to where Cæcina was being held in irons and begged his help in pleading their cause. When he haughtily turned away from them, they resorted to tears. At the same time the officers hung olive branches and ritual bands — the symbols of surrender — on the walls. Antonius gave the order to cease fighting, and minutes later a miserable column of soldiers shuffled out from the walls, their heads hung low.

What followed was an astonishing contrast. Cæcina, whom the Senate had earlier made consul, appeared majestically in full consular regalia, surrounded by his lictors. I believe he had done this to stand out from the crowd and assure that he would be taken directly to Antonius and granted asylum. But the sight of him so inflamed his own soldiers that they broke ranks and had to be restrained from rushing on him — all of which accomplished Cæcina's objective, I might add. He was quickly delivered to Antonius and later sent to Vespasian.

And what of the unfortunate people of Cremona? All eyes were on Antonius for a sign of what he would decide. It came when he went to the baths to wash off the stains of blood from the battle. Criticizing the temperature of the water as too tepid, his aides heard him say, "Well, it won't be long before it's hot."

That is all it took for the soldiers to begin torching the city.

> Without any respect for age or for authority, they added rape to murder and murder to rape. Aged men and decrepit old women, who were worthless as booty, were hustled off to make sport for them. Any grown girl or handsome youth who fell into their clutches was torn to pieces by the violence of rival rapists, leaving the plunderers themselves to cut each other's throats. Whoever carried off money or solid gold offerings in the temples was cut to pieces if he met others stronger than himself. Some, disdaining easy finds, hunted for hidden hoards and dug out buried treasure by flogging and torturing householders. They held torches in their hands and, having once secured their prize, would fling them wantonly into the empty houses and bare temples.[43]

One thing more. Antonius ordered that no citizen of Cremona was to be taken prisoner. This was both because there was revulsion among Romans against selling Italians into slavery and because Antonius probably wanted no witnesses to tell of his butchery. Thus, his soldiers killed everyone who could not come up with enough money to buy his release. When it was over, some 32,000 civilians were slain – citizens of Cremona and neighboring Italians alike who had thought they were coming to a festival.

As October turned to November, much more took place in the aftermath of the Battle of Cremonia.

Valens, who might have bolstered Cæcina at Cremona in time to turn the tide, halted abruptly when learning that the fleet at Ravenna rebelled. Upon hearing the results of Cremona, he and a few loyal supporters left the men and set sail for the province of Maritime Alps in Narbonese Gaul.

The armies of Spain, Britain and Gaul defected to Vespasian.

The people of Britain, Germany and Dacia began to rise up against Rome. It wouldn't have mattered who held the throne: with so many Roman occupiers now deployed in Italy, insurrection rushed in like a tide into an empty basin.

Vitellius, unwilling to believe the news from Cremona, sent a centurion to inspect the area himself and report back. When he confirmed all the unfavorable reports that had come to the emperor, Vitellius continued to scoff, suggesting his investigator had been bribed. "You want further evidence?" said the exasperated centurion. "Since you have no further use for me either dead or alive, I will give you evidence that you can believe." He then turned on his heels and committed suicide the moment he left the emperor's presence.

This act was enough to startle Vitellius into action. He soon dispatched 14 cohorts of Guardsmen, all of his remaining cavalry and a legion of marines to the Apennines, some 80 miles north of Rome, to form a wall against the expected Flavian advance. Even at this point Vitellius had reason to be hopeful. His brother Lucius had mustered an army in Campania, to the south, and the newly-dispatched force might actually outnumber the Flavians once Valens returned from Gaul with his newly-fortified troops.

It was just a few days later that a secretary delivered a message from Gaul. Valens and his top officers had been on a small ship when a gale drove it onto the Stœchades, a group of small islands just off Massilia in Narbonese Gaul. There they had been tracked down and executed.

Vitellius, already into his cups for the day, blubbered that it surely was not true. The secretary stood by, unmoved. "Would his lordship care to see for himself? Valens' head has been sent to the Prætorian barracks and can be brought to you for inspection if you wish."

The emperor got drunk in silence.

. . . .

December found Vespasian in Egypt. That a general and emperor-designate

would go to the furthest corner of the empire at this time rather than into its turbulent center is due to three factors. First, with so much of Rome and surrounding Italy already exhausted by revolution and war, Vespasian wanted more than
anything to take the capital without further bloodshed. Squeezing its supplies
of critical grains would surely cause his countrymen hunger and unrest, but
both would be better than death by siege engines and swords. And in order to be
successful at stopping the grain supply, Vespasian would also have to control
not just Egypt, but the crops along the African coast. That meant enlisting both
legions and merchants, and all this could best be directed from Alexandria.

Next, the empire's second largest city also deserved the newly-declared emperor's attention in its own right. It gave him a royal reception, and it was from
Alexandria that he began to receive emissaries from all over the realm. The
offers of assistance were gratifying indeed; for instance, the promise of 40,000
cavalry from Parthia. The men weren't needed, but what Vespasian did need
was evidence that Parthia remained an ally.

A third factor was that Vespasian had heard that the sage Apollonius was also
in Alexandria, and he sought his counsel on the eve of his ascendancy. Indeed,
Apollonius, accompanied by the philosophers Dion and Euphrates, had arrived
in the city sometime before Vespasian and had received a reception almost as enthusiastic. A biographer writes: "It is no exaggeration to say that, as he advanced
from the ship to the city, they gazed upon him as if he were a god, and made way
for him in the streets, as they would for priests carrying the sacraments."

When Vespasian arrived some days later, the magistrates and priests of Egypt
all met him at the gates. Although the schools of philosophers were also lined
up in attendance, Apollonius had remained conversing in one of the temples.
After giving a short acceptance speech, Vespasian turned to one of the magistrates and asked: "Is the man of Tyana living here?" When the reply was affirma-
tive, Vespasian asked, "Do you suppose he can be induced to give us an interview? For I am very much in want of him."

The philosopher Dion, who was in the crowd, shouted, "Yes, he will meet
you at the temple, for he said as much to me when I was on my way here."

"Well then," said the emperor (if I may now call him that), "let us go on at
once to offer our prayers to the gods and to meet so noble a man."

They did so. After Vespasian had sacrificed in the temple he was scheduled to
begin giving audiences to envoys from the cities of Egypt. But at that point he
asked that Apollonius be brought before him. And turning to the sage as if still
in the act of praying, Vespasian asked him: "Do you make me an emperor?"

"I have done so already," replied Apollonius, "for I have already offered a
prayer for a king who should be just and noble and temperate, endowed with
the wisdom of gray hairs and the father of legitimate sons. And surely in my
prayer I was asking from the gods for none other than thyself."

The dignitaries at the temple all murmured their approval. Responded the emperor: "What then, do you think of the reign of Nero?"

"Nero perhaps understood how to tune a lyre," said the sage, "but he disgraced the empire by letting the strings go too slack and then by drawing them too tight."

"Then," said Vespasian, "you would like a ruler to observe the mean?"

"Not I," answered Apollonius, "but God himself, who has defined equity as consisting in the mean."

With that Vespasian held up his hand and said: "O Zeus, may I hold sway over wise men, and wise men hold sway over me." And turning around to the Egyptians, he said, "You shall draw as liberally upon me as you do upon the Nile."

After Vespasian had dispensed with his interviews with ambassadors, he again sought out Apollonius and asked that he stroll with him to the nearby palace where he was lodged. The emperor rambled as he walked, opening his heart to the sage.

Perhaps some will think me foolish because I assume the reins of kingship in my 60th year. I will tell you my reasons for doing so in order that you may justify my actions to others. For I was never a slave of wealth that I know of, even in my youth. And in the matter of magistracies and honors in the gift of the Roman sovereign, I bore myself with so much soberness and moderation as to avoid being thought either overbearing, or on the other hand, craven and cowardly.

Nor did I cherish any but loyal feelings towards Nero. Inasmuch as he had received the crown, if not in strict accordance with the law, at any rate from an autocrat, I submitted to him for the sake of Claudius, and contrasted with him the wretch who had inherited the greatest of his possessions. And now when I see that even the disappearance from the scene of Nero has brought no change for the better in the fortunes of humanity, and that the throne has fallen into such dishonor as to be assigned to Vitellius, I boldly advance to take it myself. Firstly, I wish to endear myself to men and win their esteem. And secondly, the man I have to contend with is a mere drunkard. For Vitellius uses more ointment in his bath than I do water, and I believe that if you ran a sword through him more ointment would issue from the wound than blood. His continuous bouts of drinking have made him mad, as if he were at dice and...hazarding the empire while at play. And though he is the slave of his mistresses, he nevertheless insults married women and says that he likes to spice his amours with a little danger. His worst excesses I will not even mention in your presence.

May I then never submit meekly while the Romans are ruled by a man such as he. Let me rather ask the gods to guide me so that I may be true to myself. And this, Apollonius, is why I make fast my tether to yourself; for they say that you have the amplest insight into the will of the gods, and [this is]why I ask you to share my anxieties and aid me in plans on which rest the safety of sea and land.[44]

Apollonius stopped, raised his eyes to heaven, and with emotion intoned: "O Zeus of the Capitol [meaning the temple of Jupiter Optimus Maximus in Rome], for thou art he whom I know to be the arbiter of this issue, do thou preserve for this man and this man for thyself. For this man who stands before thee is destined to raise afresh unto thee the temple which only yesterday the hands of malefactors set on fire!"

Vespasian stared at him wide-eyed. The date was December 20. How could anyone know what happened the previous day in a place 1500 miles away?

"Yes," said Apollonius, "the facts will reveal themselves to you in time, so please ask nothing further of me about it." Since it was now afternoon and it was the philosopher's own rule (which he learned from the Indian Brahmins) to spend the rest of the daylight hours in quiet meditation, he left the emperor puzzled as to the prediction but content, at least, to believe that his future was assured by the heavens.

The next day Apollonius, Euphrates and Dion were invited to call on Vespasian again at the palace in the early hours before his morning reception. The emperor, having been on the previous day set at ease as to his worthiness to rule, now asked the men for advice on how he might govern wisely. The other two philosophers, no doubt feeling envious of the attention given their colleague, saw fit to deliver long, tedious sermons that left him ill at ease. Vespasian was wrong, they said, for concentrating on "setting Jewry to rights" when he should have been bringing down the far more dangerous Nero. Now, rather than again risk falling into the trap of excess power that was the ruin of all imperial rule, he should achieve the greatest "triumph" of all: bringing about the return of a democratic republic and then retiring gracefully.

There followed a long spell of uneasy silence. Then Apollonius spoke up. "It seems to me you are mistaken in trying to cancel a monarchical policy when it is already a foregone conclusion," he said to his companions icily. "You indulge a garrulity as childish as it is idle in such a crisis. If it were I, as a philosopher, that you were advising on how to go about doing what good I could in the world, that would be one thing. But you are pretending to advise a consul and a man accustomed to rule — moreover, one over whom ruin impends should he fall from power."

Apollonius offered an analogy. "Suppose we saw an athlete well endowed with courage and stature, and by his well-knit frame marked out as a winner in the Olympic contest. Suppose we approached him when he was already marching through Arcadia, and while encouraging him to face his rivals, yet insisted that in the event of winning the prize he must not allow himself to be proclaimed victor. Should we not be set down as imbeciles, mocking at another's labors?"

Here before you, said Apollonius, is a man "who yesterday accepted the crown offered by the cities herein the temples around us and whose rescripts are as brilliant as they are ungrudging. Do you bid him issue a proclamation today to the effect that he had assumed the reins of government in a fit of madness and now wishes to retire to private life?"

Vespasian, he said, should be "sent forward, with great encouragement, on the path leading to his goal. For myself, I care little about constitutions, seeing that my life is governed by the gods. But I do not like to see the human flock perish for want of a just and modest shepherd."

The emperor's peasant face broke into a wreath of smiles. "Apollonius," he said, "if you were the tenant of my breast, you could not more accurately report my most innermost thoughts. 'Tis yourself, then, that I will follow, for every word which falls from your lips I regard as inspired. Therefore, instruct me in all good duties of a king."

Apollonius began by saying that being a king is the one art that cannot be taught. But he went on to offer "some thoughts that are on my mind." I will not report them all, but among them were the following:

> Tremble before the very absoluteness of your prerogative, for so you will exercise it with the greater moderation.

> Let the law govern you as well as other men, O king, for you will be all the wiser as a legislator for so holding the laws in respect.

> Reverence the gods more than ever before, for you have received great blessings at their hands and have still great ones to pray for.

> You have two sons, both, they say, of generous disposition. Let your disciplining of them proceed to the extent of threatening not to bequeath them your throne unless they remain good men and honest. Otherwise they will be prone to regard it not as a reward of excellence, but so much as mere right of heritage.

> As for the pleasures that have made Rome their home...I would advise you, my sovereign, to use much discretion in suppressing them. For it

is not easy to convert an entire people suddenly to wisdom and temperance. You must feel your way and instill order and rhythm in their characters step by step, partly in the open, partly by secret correction.[45]

The two had many more discussions together in Alexandria — and not merely on the subject of governance. The emperor loved to hear Apollonius tell of the Indian Phraotes, the rivers of India and the animals that inhabit it. And he asked the sage continually what forecasts and revelations had been imparted to him by the gods on the future of the empire. He even asked that Apollonius accompany him to Rome, but the latter declined. He said he had not yet seen the whole of Egypt or conversed with the naked sages of the Upper Nile nor seen the source of the Nile itself.

"Bear me in your prayers," said Vespasian, as he prepared to return to Cæsarea.

"I will indeed," replied Apollonius, "if you continue to be a good sovereign and mindful of yourself."

. . . .

WITH EACH FLAVIAN ADVANCE, the leading men of Rome increasingly looked for guidance to Flavius Sabinus, the City Prefect and elder brother of Vespasian. Since his duties included command of the City Garrison, Sabinus would obviously be instrumental in preparing their way for Vespasian and his two sons to assume rule.

If so, you might ask, why would the present emperor have allowed Sabinus to live? One answer is that he was already quite elderly and had always been regarded as Vespasian's rather stern and distant older brother. Besides, Sabinus had never been prone to intrigue or violence. City prefects are traditionally seen as impartial managers of roads, aqueducts and public safety, and Sabinus filled the position admirably.

A larger reason at this particular time was that maintaining the good will of Sabinus might also afford Vitellius refuge or pardon should it be needed. Indeed, Vitellius had been receiving tempting letters from the Flavian camp for several weeks and he knew that Sabinus was well aware of them. The Flavians offered to install Vitellius in the Campanian villa of his choice and grant him safe sanctuary there for the rest of his life if he would surrender Rome without bloodshed and place his family in the hands of Vespasian. At one point Vitellius even held lengthy discussions as to the number of slaves he would require and the size of his annual purse. So close was he to accepting that he even summoned Flavius Sabinus to a private meeting to discuss the logistics of moving safely from Rome.

But the emperor's closest advisors scoffed at the possibility. Their views can be summarized as follows: "Once the conqueror took the city, what was there to make him honor his promise? Neither Vespasian's friends nor army will feel their safety assured until the rival claimant is dead. Look at Fabius Valens, executed upon his capture because he became too great a burden for those who seized him. Julius Cæsar did not let Pompey live. Did Augustus allow Antonius? Do you suppose that Vespasian has a loftier disposition? No! Think of your father's three consulships and all the honor your great house has won. Do not disgrace them. The troops — yes, now reduced in number — remain steadfast. If we are defeated in battle, we will die. If we surrender we will die. All that matters is whether we breathe our last amid mockery or whether it be bravely and with honor."

Vitellius nodded at their pleas, but his mind was obsessed with concern for his wife and the infant son who was his only heir. On December 18, hearing that more cohorts in Italy had deserted, the emperor decided to quit his throne. He put on somber raiment and left the palace, his small son carried in a litter. After tearful laments from his household staff, a Roman emperor, yesterday master of the world, was now passing through the streets of the city as a common citizen. True, emperors from Julius Cæsar to Galba had been cut down, but here for the first time in Roman history was an emperor simply quitting and leaving the world's most powerful empire leaderless.

Vitellius and his pitiful entourage reached the rostra of the Forum. There — reliable observers say he was drunk — the emperor mumbled that it was in the interests of peace and the country that he resign. He begged everyone to take pity on his brother, his wife and innocent child. Turning to the consul Cæcilius Simplex, who stood at his side, he unstrapped the dagger from his side and offered to surrender it as a symbol of his power over the life and death of his subjects.

The consul refused it. A crowd had assembled below, and it chanted "No! No! No!" Shouting the loudest were members of the emperor's German bodyguard, who feared their days in Rome would be over. Now I find all this ironic, because had the people in the crowd known the full extent of defections around the empire and Vespasian's overwhelming military strength, they would have understood the inevitability of Vitellius' decision. But because the emperor ignored or suppressed such news, people now used their false assumptions against the man who supplied them.

As the shouts of protest grew louder, Vitellius, confused, lumbered down the platform steps and said he was going to the Temple of Concord (a few yards away) to deposit his imperial regalia. From there he intended to go to his brother's house.

This brought an even greater uproar. The swelling throng shouted for him to return to the palace. No doubt directed by the German Guards, they began blocking every available road except for the one leading back to the palace. Not knowing what else to do, Vitellius and his family went back from whence they had come.

In the meantime, Flavius Sabinus soon found his house surrounded by a clamor of senators, knights and troops from the City Garrison. They had thought the end of Vitellius at hand. Now they feared that the sudden show of popular support for Vitellius – and the obstinacy of his German bodyguard – could turn the tide and sweep them away in the mindless revenge that would follow. They urged the old man to lead a fight while the Vitellians were still in disarray.

But nothing was done immediately. Later that day, Sabinus and an armed escort were marching through the Forum (quite likely on a mission to confront and persuade Vitellius) when they encountered a cohort of the German bodyguards. With no authority of any officer, the Guards suddenly attacked the smaller party. They were beside the Fundane Pool at the time, and the nearest refuge was Capitoline Hill, with its sacred Temple of Jupiter Optimus Maximus. So after getting the worst of the skirmish, Sabinus and his party ran up the hill and barricaded themselves in the Temple along with several hapless tourists who were there at the time.

For several hours the Guards milled about, swearing that no one would get out alive. But as day became night, the more lax their vigilance became. Finally, in the dead of night Sabinus was able to send for Vespasian's youngest son, Domitian. Also slipping through the guard was a courier to the Flavian generals, now camped 80 miles to the north, with an urgent message that Sabinus and his men were in great danger unless rescued. At daybreak, before the hostilities resumed, Sabinus sent a centurion to Vitellius himself with this message: why had the emperor violated an agreement that he himself had initiated? Why had he made an empty show of abdication and now endangered so many eminent men? Why had he unleashed a column of soldiers in a crowded part of the Forum, and why was he now menacing Rome's most sacred building? If Vitellius had suddenly decided to resist, why did he not take up arms against the Flavian legions in Italy rather than try to kill one youth and an old man?

Vitellius expressed alarm. It was evident to the centurion that the emperor had scant knowledge of the assault and no control over his soldiers. Instead, he complained wearily about their "overpowering impatience." All he could do was offer the messenger a way out of the building by a secret passage so that the Guards outside wouldn't kill him.

That morning a column of guardsmen marched at full speed through the Forum and up the hill until they reached the lowest gates of the fortress on the Capitol. To those within, it was evident that the Germans had no leader. Worse, the men had obviously worked themselves into a frenzy. I should point out here that the hill leading to the temple had a series of colonnades on the right side, covered by a roof. Because the attackers carried only swords, some of the men inside climbed out onto the roof atop the colonnades and hurled down stones and terra cotta tiles on them. The assailants retreated, but quickly they returned, brandishing torches, which they used to ignite the ancient, dry wood roof supports. Soon the blaze had spread to the giant wooden doors of the Capitol. As these were burning, Sabinus ordered everyone inside to tear down the sacred statues and build a barricade to replace the huge burning doors.

Again frustrated, the furious assailants (whose sacrilege can only be explained by the fact that the majority were barbarians), now ran around to the opposite, steeper side of the hill. Where once the hill and temple towered above all Rome, the many years of peace had seen houses erected around this part of the hill so that some of their rooftops were nearly level with the floor of the Capitol. The German Guards crawled out on the roofs and with their torches were able to reach the wooden parts of the temple. Soon the fire had spread to the ancient wooded gables supporting the roof.

And so, on December 19, the very day Apollonius had so informed Vespasian in far-off Egypt, the building which had been built by king Tarquinius Priscus during the Sabine war as a monument to the future greatness of Rome, and which most symbolized Rome's glory for over 500 years, was burnt to the ground at the hands of Rome's own troops. And they showed no shame whatever.

Inside, as the temple burned, "everybody gave orders and nobody obeyed them," writes one historian. When the Vitellian guardsmen finally burst inside, a few soldiers formed up to fight, but were quickly cut to pieces. Flavius Sabinus stood unarmed, offering no resistance. He was immediately surrounded, along with the counsel Quintius Atticus as the rest scurried for hiding places among the buildings in the temple compound. Young Domitian took refuge with the sacristan and, later wearing the linen mantle of an Isis worshipper, escaped among a group of tourists who had been trapped inside the temple since the day before.

Sabinus and Atticus were fettered and hastened to Vitellius at the palace as a mob of Rome's worst dregs followed in hopes of seeing more bloody sport. Rome's Saturnalia had begun just two days before, and in addition to the usual non-stop drinking, the lower classes were emboldened by the traditional reversal of master and servant roles during the festival week.

Inside the palace, the soldiers crowded around Vitellius and his two prisoners with a menacing air. Their attitude was that surely the emperor would want these men executed, just as surely as they, the Guards, would be suitably rewarded for all the personal risks they had taken to capture them.

Vitellius, painfully aware that he had little control over his soldiers, had the two bound men brought outside to the front palace steps, where he hoped that

the crowd below might be persuaded to support clemency. He was only partially right. When Vitellius pled for Atticus and the crowd seemed to be going
against it, the chained consul offered up one of the best examples of clever
thinking I have ever heard. He took full blame for setting fire to the Capitol,
hoping that the Vitellian soldiers would get the message that their "innocence"
would live only as long as Atticus himself did to verify it. By this ploy was Atticus spared, but this only turned all the odium and lust for blood on the old man
who stood next to him. Before Vitellius could even raise a hand, the mob raced
up the palace steps and stabbed Sabinus. His head was cut off and the trunk
dragged away to the Gemonian Steps. Thus was the brother of Vespasian rewarded for 35 continuous years of efficient public service.

At this time the Flavian forces in Italy had advanced to Ocriculum, less than
50 miles directly north of Rome. The two chief generals in camp were Antonius Primus, of whom you have read much, and Petillius Cerialis, a relative of
Vespasian and proven commander. The only Vitellian forces still active in the
field were in Campania. Led by the emperor's brother Lucius, they had managed to take the coastal city of Tarracina and were thought to be actually holding most of Campania. Should they gain strength and march on Rome, only
60 miles to the northeast, they could still rally enough men to defend the
throne of Vitellius.

Indeed, Lucius Vitellius had offered to bring up his battle-fresh troops, but
the offer arrived on one of the many days when the emperor was vacillating between abdication and war. At the time, the Flavians seemingly had been content to wait as well on the certain (they thought) collapse of Vitellius. Many
reasons have been advanced for their delay, including stories that Antonius
Primus was pondering an offer from Vitellius to make him consul in exchange
for treason. I find it more logical to believe that they were simply following Mucianus' orders to stay put until his army arrived from Syria, and that Mucianus
in turn was trying his best to heed Vespasian's wish that Rome not be subjected
to bloodshed if at all possible.

The plea from Sabinus arrived too late, of course. But the Flavian commander didn't know it, and it convinced him that Vitellius was not withering on the
vine. A detachment of 1,000 cavalry, led by Pettillius Cerialis, was quickly dispatched with orders to enter the city on the northeast and rescue their entrapped comrades. The size of the force sent again shows that the Flavians still
hoped to spare Rome a full-scale battle.

It was late at night and the cavalry unit had just passed the "Red Rocks," a
familiar outcrop along the road a few miles from the city, when they learned
that Sabinus was dead. Ahead of them, they could even see the glow of fire on
Capitoline Hill. Around them now were the outlying settlements, where it
seemed that everyone was up and about, mobilizing to defend Vitellius. When

the people realized that the horsemen were not their own, the Flavians found themselves being assailed in by staves and pitchforks in vineyards and narrow neighborhood streets that were totally strange to them. In a few minutes their ranks had been shattered and individual soldiers were galloping north in disarray.

Word of the "victory" soon reached Vitellius, and he used it as a pretext to send envoys to the Flavian headquarters in hopes of gaining a bloodless settlement. But neither the humiliated Cerialis nor the ambitious Antonius would have any of it. Nor would the death of Vespasian's brother permit any less than full retaliation. In a few days the Flavians broke camp for Rome, traveling in three columns, bent on entering the city from the northeast, north and west across the Tiber via the Mulvian Bridge. After a series of indecisive skirmishes outside the gates, the two forces regrouped for a decisive battle on the very Campus Martius where no doubt every soldier among them had trained and paraded at one time in his life.

I have already said that the Battle of Cremona was the strangest I have ever encountered. But I think that the battle *within* Rome was the most appalling, because it clearly showed the rot that had eroded the city and the depths to which the people within it had fallen. The Saturnalia was supposed to have ended; but in truth one would not have known it, because seldom has the horror of death been observed amidst such merriment.

> The people came out and watched the fighting, cheering and applauding now on one side, now the other, like spectators in a gladiatorial contest. Whenever one side gave ground and its soldiers hid in shops or some private house, [the spectators] clamored for them to be dragged out and slaughtered. In this way they got the greater part of plunder for themselves. For, while the soldiers were busy with the bloody work of massacre, the spoil fell to the crowd.

> The scene throughout the city was cruel and distorted. On the one side were fighting and wounded men, on the other baths and restaurants. Here lay heaps of bleeding dead, and close at hand were harlots and their ilk. All the vice and license of luxurious peace, and all the crime and horror of a captured town. You would have thought the city mad with fury and riotous with pleasure at the same time.
> Armies had fought in the city before this, twice when Sulla mastered Rome, once under Cinna — nor were there fewer horrors then. What was now so inhuman was peoples' indifference. Not for one minute did they interrupt their life of pleasure. The fighting was a new amusement for their holiday. Caring nothing for either party, they enjoyed

themselves in riotous dissipation and took pleasure in their country's disaster.[46]

Eventually the Flavians wore down their outnumbered foe. Fifty thousand Vitellians and plain citizens lay dead. Everywhere the city was now free of fighting except the Guards' camp just outside the Colline Gate. Here were clustered all the Germans and other soldiers whose murders and other dirty deeds on behalf of Vitellius had left them no alternative but to die fighting. They had nothing to gain but to postpone peace and make as many of the living as possible join them in death. When the camp gates were finally torn down, those remaining faced their foes in a body and fought, steeped in each other's blood, until the very last of them fell dead.

As soon as the city had been taken, Vitellius left the palace by a back way and was carried in a litter to his wife's family home on the Aventine. His intent was to stay hidden for the day, then escape by night to his brother's army in Campania. For reasons only Vitellius could tell us (perhaps the Flavians had learned of his location), he sneaked back to the nearly empty palace during the day. There he wandered the deserted halls like a latter day Nero, no doubt mumbling to himself and dragging a flagon of wine with one hand.

His assailants searched there, too, of course. Just before they arrived, Vitellius put on a ragged slave's tunic and hid in a small dark storeroom in which the palace doorkeeper had kept his watchdog. When the soldiers came ransacking everything in the usual way, they dragged the forlorn-looking fat man from his hiding place and asked him his name. He gave a false one; but being soon recognized, he asked to be imprisoned because he had some valuable information regarding the safety of Vespasian.

The soldiers would have none of it. They tied his hands behind his back and put a rope around his neck. They pulled and prodded Vitellius all the way through the Forum towards the Rostra where he had addressed the cheering crowds the previous July. Along his path, jeering people poked at him, hurled insults and covered him with garbage and feces. He was dragged up the Rostra, where his captors used the points of their swords to make him hold up his head as he watched them smashing his statues.

At one point a German soldier who was in the crowd shouted that he could not endure the sight. "I will help you the only way I can," he shouted. With that he leaped on the Rostra and stabbed his sword into Vitellius' ample stomach. Then he turned his sword on himself.

But Vitellius did not die of the wound immediately. As a soldier on the Rostra mocked him, he gasped meekly, "And yet, I was once your emperor." With that he was stabbed several more times and taken off to the Gemonian Steps. After more torture there, he was killed and his body thrown down. Its head was cut off and carried about the city on pikes, as seemed to be the growing custom for honoring deposed emperors in the capital of the civilized world.

The death of Vitellius ended the war but did not inaugurate peace. The Flavian victors remained under arms.

Lucius Vitellius and his forces in Campania surrendered and their commander was executed.

The defeated Vitellians were hunted throughout the city and butchered wherever found. Streets were strewn with corpses, which bred rats and the foulest air imaginable.

On the pretext of hunting for hidden enemies, no one's door was left unopened and no privacy uninspected. Resistance was an excuse for murder.

Slaves betrayed masters and greedy citizens their wealthy clients.

Antonius Primus, whom it is said removed enough money and slaves from the imperial palace to make one think he was plundering Cremona, was made consul by the Senate.

Domitian, the new emperor's 18-year-old son, could not yet be interested in matters of governance. He was too busy devoting himself to rape and affairs with married women.

. . . .

THE CHRISTIANS REMIND ME of the trees that grow in the public gardens of Rome. When one of them flourishes to the extent that its branches spread out across a road or over a courtyard wall, slaves of the prefecture will chop the whole tree back severely as if to warn it against ever growing again. But I have noticed that nature seems to tell such trees that they must now compensate by sending out new shoots and at a more vigorous rate than ever. It always amazes me to see so much new growth atop a trunk with so many severed limbs, but then I realize that what is visible to my eye is only the top of a broad, strong root system.

My perhaps inadequate analogy is simply a way of saying that it would be wrong to think of all Christians as mortally wounded because Peter and Paul were purged. Rome had been the trunk of the Christian tree only to the extent that Peter and Paul had both been there in their final years. The same analogy holds true for the Jewish Christians who had been centered in Jerusalem. The seizure of the temple by the Zealots and the rupture with Rome had felled the Jewish Christian trunk that had stood in Jerusalem; but new roots were put down in Pella, some 50 miles to the northeast, and old ones were deepened in places like Antioch and Cæserea.

And of course other roots had been long planted in other places – often in far-away lands beyond the reach of regular communications with what we who live in them smugly call the "centers" of the empire. For instance, while Paul traveled throughout the western provinces, the apostle Thomas left his footprints well beyond Rome's easternmost reaches. Almost from the day after he had personally inspected the nail wounds on the risen Jesus, Thomas had set out to evangelize Parthia, often with Jude at his side, and had never returned. One story Christians from the east tell often is that Thomas's mission had taken him through Parthia, to Bactria and eventually to the Arabian isle of Socotra, where he now pondered entering India. It was probably in the last years of Claudius (not that a Roman emperor had any sway over these people). It was also a period in which the Buddhists of India were winning many converts among the Zoroastrians of eastern Parthia and the latter were showing their displeasure by invading several Indian border provinces.

Bloodshed was rampant, and the tradition says that Thomas was fearful for his life and doubtful that anyone would want to hear about a new religion when two others were vying for supremacy. But one night Jesus appeared to Thomas in a bedside vision. "Fear not, Thomas," he said. "Go into India and preach the Word there, for my grace is with thee."

The next day, the story goes, Thomas hired himself as a servant to an Indian merchant and sailed with him to the city of Cranganore on the southwestern coast. There Thomas sought out the king of that land, named Gondophares, and entered into his service. He must have had the king's ear, because tradition continues that Thomas remained for years, converting several high-caste Hindu families, making some of the men priests and establishing seven houses of prayer. The area was somewhat isolated because it consisted of a flat coastal plain, hemmed in by steep mountains to the east. There, oblivious to the arguments over circumcision, dietary laws and other issues that divided western churches, the Indian church welcomed and tolerated all comers.

Thomas, the tradition continues, left this pleasant scene and embarked on the third leg of his life's journey: he went overland to China, where he built at least one house of prayer. Afterwards, he is said to have returned to India, settling in the eastern coastal city of Mylapore. According to a manuscript from Chaldea (where Thomas had once settled briefly) he built both a house of prayer and a house for himself, which the locals called the "house of the holy man."

The same source alleges that Thomas met his end not far from that house in Mylapore. It states that the treachery was brought about by leading Brahmins with the assent of the provincial king. Once resolved to do their deed, they waited for Thomas outside an empty tomb or mausoleum, where he often went to meditate.

> The envious Brahmins, who had been discredited before the king by the virtue of Thomas, went to kill him. Hearing that he was in the cave

near the Little Mount (which at the time of the apostle was called An-
tenodur), they stood near the slope of the mountain, where there was
a narrow opening to let in a little light, and looking through it they
found the apostle on his knees with his eyes closed, in a rapture so profound that he appeared to be dead. The Brahmins thrust a lance
through the opening and wounded him mortally. It is not proved
where exactly this place was, but all authorities are in accord in saying
that it was on the slope of a mountain. The wound was about half a
span deep. When [Thomas] sighed, all the murderers ran away and he
in his death agony got out of the cave and dragged himself down to the
Big Mount. And there he died.[47]

Thomas was buried at Mylapore, says the Chaldean report. The time would
have been equivalent to the 11th year of Nero's reign. One wonders if the apostle
at that time even knew who ruled distant Rome.

I wish I could report more about this bold and brave man. It is probably all to
obvious to state the following, but the reason why Peter and Paul, Rome and
Jerusalem occupy so many pages of early Christian history is simply that more
information about them is available where the author happens to live. As the
stories of Thomas indicate, there must be other disciples who traveled equally
great distances to, as Jesus said, "Go out and make disciples in my name" among
strangers in often hostile lands. I yearn to hear more, for instance, of the apostle
Simon, the one-time Zealot (at least at the time Jesus chose him as an apostle)
who has been tracked through Egypt, Libya, Carthage, Spain and then Britain.
By one report Simon got swallowed up in the vicious war that destroyed perhaps 200,000 Britons and Romans in the early years of Nero. But other reports
say that Simon fled from Britain and went on to Parthia, where he was martyred along with the apostle Jude. I have no evidence upon which to decide. I
can only note that the Tabularium in Rome has a record stating that in the last
year of Nero's reign the wife of Aulus Plautius, a Roman official in Britain, was
brought before a magistrate on charges of being a Christian. How did she come
to believe? Well, someone had to journey there to preach the word, and in the
absence of any claims, let us give Simon the benefit of the doubt until shown
otherwise.

As the story of Simon suggests, reports of many far-flung apostles tend to put
their deeds and deaths in conflicting places, and it is maddening to a historian to
be left with no other choice but to relate all the available stories and offer one's
readers no further assistance in deciding which versions to believe! The apostle
Andrew is another such example. Both Jewish and Gentile Christians in Rome
agree that the younger brother of Peter spent his earliest missionary years in
Parthia, many of them in the company of Bartholomew. But at some point

later some say he went to Scythia and spent several years bravely preaching the gospel to the pirates who ruled that part of the Black Sea and the wild, nomadic horsemen who prevailed along its blustery shores. I cannot verify this because I have yet to meet a Scythian in Rome and because Andrew himself has since been martyred.

But martyred where? Some say in Scythia. But there is also evidence that Andrew went on to Greece where he met his death in the city of Patræ, the port city on the western side of the Gulf of Corinth. It seems that Andrew's preaching had been instrumental in making the wife of the Roman proconsul Ægeates a devout Christian. So firmly did she refuse all his demands to recant that the exasperated proconsul ordered the apostle to renounce his faith before a public tribunal or face a severe scourging. Each man begged the other to recant, with Ægeates imploring Andrew not to lose his life and the apostle in turn beseeching the governor not to lose his soul.

At last Andrew was ordered to be put to torture. When he endured the rod in silence, the governor called for crucifixion — but of an unusual kind. The cross was to be in the shape of the letter X. In order to prolong Andrew's suffering — or perhaps to offer him still more time to repent — Andrew was not nailed but tied to the cross by ropes at his wrists and ankles. According to an account by a Roman named Flamion, the apostle hung in a public place for some two days, preaching as he hung in agony and piercing the hearts of the people who gathered before him. As the end drew near, the Roman recorded these words:

> Ye men that are here present, and women and children, old and young, bond and free, and all that will hear...take no heed of the vain deceit of this present life, but heed us rather who hang here for the Lord's sake and are about to depart out of this body. Renounce all lusts of this world, and condemn the worship of the abominable idols, and run unto the true worshipping of our God that lieth not, and make yourselves a temple pure and ready to receive the Word. Hasten to overtake my soul as it hastens toward heavenly things. In a word, despise all temporal things and establish your minds as men believing in Christ.[48]

Suddenly Ægeates himself despaired at what he had done and ordered his men to untie the ropes that bound his victim. But Andrew summoned all his strength and resisted them. "Oh, Jesus Christ," he shouted, "let not your adversary loose him that is hung upon thy grace. O Father, let not this small one humble any more him that hath known thy greatness."

With that he gave up the ghost as all about him wept and lamented. Flamion says it was the last day of November in the year of Galba, a year and six months after Peter and Paul met their martyrdom.

By the end of Galba's reign it is probable that all of the original apostles save Matthew and John had died martyr's deaths. These two and the many other disciples who had been living witnesses to at least some portions of Jesus' ministry were now becoming quite elderly. After all, if a disciple were age 25 at the crucifixion of Jesus, he would be approaching 65 in the year of the four emperors. If he had been 35, as old or slightly older than Jesus, he would by now be well into what the rest of us would call the ripeness of old age.

What a pity it would have been if all had gone to their reward without leaving a written account of what they witnessed; but much to the relief of historians, we now have one gospel, written by John Mark, and a later one by the apostle Matthew that I will mention in the last chapter.

I cannot say with absolute assurance that Mark's account is the first ever written – only that it is the first one to be circulated among the Christians of Rome and the western provinces. In any case, who would be better qualified to write such a history? As you may recall from an earlier chapter, Mark and his mother lived in a large house in Jerusalem with their cousin Barnabas as a frequent visitor. This is the house where Christians were meeting when Peter and John were arrested for preaching in the temple, and some say it is also the same house with the "upper room" where the apostles gathered after Jesus' crucifixion.

The young Mark had been especially valuable as a missionary because he seems to have spoken both Greek and Hebrew, having had a Jewish mother (hence the name John) and a Roman father (from whom came his second name Mark). Mark was always a favorite of Peter's and probably accompanied him to Babylon. Later, Mark reportedly struck out on his own to Alexandria, where he won many converts.

I would guess that Mark arrived in Alexandria around the fourth year of Nero. The story goes that he had broken the strap of his sandal during the journey and that the first thing he did after entering the city's eastern gate was to seek out a cobbler to mend it. When the cobbler took his awl to work on it, he accidentally pierced his hand and cried out, "*Heis ho Theos*" (God is one). Mark saw this as a sign that he might have a willing convert. He miraculously healed the man's wound and soon found that the cobbler was anxious to hear all that he said about Jesus and the new covenant. Before long, the man, whose name was Anianus, had taken Mark home with him to baptize his whole family.

Many more converts followed. Within several months so many people in Alexandria had been won over that Mark's renown began to put him at risk. Authorities had spread word that a Jew from Judea was preparing to incite a crowd to overthrow the city's pagan idols. Mark decided it was time to leave until matters had calmed down, so he ordained Anianus bishop, along with three priests and seven deacons, to watch over the congregation in his absence.

Exactly where Mark went immediately I cannot say (one tradition says

Venice). But certainly by the 12th year of Nero Mark had joined Peter and Paul in Rome, most likely as a translator and amanuensis to Peter. It was probably when the apostle faced the possibility of arrest and even death at any time that Mark began writing the gospel based on Peter's personal accounts. And in this account was a prophecy that was now about to unfold all around them. The prophecy, Mark records, came when Jesus and his disciples had returned from the temple on the first day of his fateful visit to Jerusalem. They had climbed the Mount of Olives opposite the temple in the late afternoon, and as they gazed down on its huge marble walls and glistening buildings, the disciples couldn't stop marveling about what splendid sights they had beheld. It was then that Jesus said to them, "Do you see these great buildings? There will not be left here one stone upon another that will not be thrown down!"

Peter, James and some others pressed him to tell more. "When will this be?" they asked. "And what will be the sign when these things are all to be accomplished?"

Instead of a simple answer, Jesus painted a much larger portrait of what was to come after his mission on earth was over:

> Many will come in my name, saying, "I am he!" and they will lead many astray. And when you hear of wars and rumors of wars, do not be alarmed. These must take place, but the end is not yet. For nation will rise against nation, and kingdom against kingdom. There will be earthquakes in various places; there will be famines, this is but the beginning of the sufferings.

> But take heed for yourselves, for they will deliver you up to councils and you will be beaten in synagogues and you will stand before governors and kings for my sake to bear testimony before them (for) the gospel must be preached to all nations.

> And when they bring you to trial and deliver you up, do not be anxious beforehand what you are to say, but say whatever is given you in that hour; for it is not you who speak, but the Holy Spirit. And brother will deliver brother up to death, and the father his child, and children will rise against parents and have them put to death, and you will be hated for my name's sake. But he who endures to the end will be saved.[49]

Sometime after Peter's martyrdom in Rome, perhaps even before, Mark returned to Alexandria and the church he had founded. To his delight, its numbers had multiplied to the point where they had organized a large communal compound in the suburban district of Baucalis, where cattle grazed by the seashore. While this community no doubt struck Alexandrians as strange and secretive, it seemed to exist peacefully enough. But there was something about the reappearance of John Mark, the founding patriarch, that again inflamed the local authorities – undoubtedly because the Jewish revolt in Jerusalem had given the Hellene majority in Alexandria an excuse to settle old scores with local Jews and any "splinter sects." Another irritant may have been Mark's gospel, which they could now read for themselves. In any event, word circulated that Mark was back and again intended to incite his Christians to topple all the statues of pagan deities they could find.

This was in the last year of Nero, almost a year after Peter and Paul had met martyrdom in Rome. The occasion was Easter, which fell on the same day as the festival of Serapis, honoring the consort of the Egyptian goddess Isis. A mob whipped itself up in the Serapion temple and then set out for Baucalis, where the Christians had begun celebrating Easter. Marching on the settlement, the hooligans seized Mark and carried him off to the road from which they had come. Mark by then was probably well over 50 and worn by years of travel. No one cared about that. They tied a rope around his neck, bound his hands, and had him dragged through the streets by horses. At nightfall, they grew weary of their prank and threw Mark into a jail, bloody and barely alive. The next morning they dragged him out again and made him suffer many hours of the same torture until he at last expired.

Mark's murderers had planned to cremate the torn and bloodied body, but a spring gale blew up so suddenly and brought such heavy torrents of rain with it that the mob quickly scattered. At nightfall some Christians from Baucalis crept into the street where the body lay and carried it off. A secret grave was dug beneath the altar of the house of prayer, and there the Christians buried another of the men who had witnessed the life of Jesus – scarcely a year after the Christians of Rome had buried Peter and Paul.

As I said, by the end of Galba's reign all the apostles, save one or two, had already gone to their deaths preaching the gospel. Whether Matthew was still alive I cannot say for sure because he may have perished not long after dictating his gospel in Antioch. But, yes, I can say that the apostle John was and is alive. He lives in Ephesus.

Who would be a better living legacy of all Jesus did and all that happened in those years? As I have said earlier, John was the younger brother of James and both were the sons of Zebedee, a Galilean fisherman so prosperous that he employed servants in his work, had a second home in Jerusalem, and with it connections to the priestly families there. John's mother was Solome, and probably the sister of Jesus' mother Mary. Moreover, John was often referred to as "the beloved disciple," or the "one Jesus loved." He was present at the transfiguration and sat at the right of Jesus at the last supper. He was present at his master's trial (perhaps due to his priestly connections) and stood at the foot of the cross, where the stricken Jesus told him to care for his mother, Mary. Afterward, John was Peter's tireless companion when preaching to the Jews by the temple gates.

John continued preaching in Judea for years, even after his brother James became the first apostle to meet martyrdom in the persecutions of King Herod Agrippa. It may have been then that he moved to Ephesus. But I think it was probably later, early in the reign of Nero, when the unscrupulous procurators began vexing the people beyond all endurance. Paul had already formed churches in Ephesus, and during his subsequent imprisonment in Cæsarea and Rome John would have been a welcome fortification to the faith. Ephesus would also be a more secure haven in which to honor his obligation to care for Mary.

If one assumes that Mary was perhaps 16 when she bore Jesus, she would have been just over 50 at the time of his crucifixion, around 65 at the time of Herod Agrippa's persecution and nearly 80 in the early years of Nero. Her husband Joseph had undoubtedly passed on many years before either of her probable departure dates for Ephesus. Although Mary was by then too old to have lived long in Ephesus under the wing of her kinsman, several Christians from Asia Minor say that the house where she lived is already visited by pilgrims as a shrine.

Meanwhile, John has become the patriarch, not only of the church of Ephesus, but of those in the seven major cities of Asia Minor. Having been one of the youngest apostles when he began his mission, John would have been about 70 in the year of Galba's short reign. Perhaps it is only fitting that the same God who allowed one brother as the first martyr among the apostles should allow another brother to live the longest.

. . . .

. . . .

T he Jerusalem that Titus and his four legions encountered in the early spring
contained somewhere between 600,000
and 1 million permanent residents, depending on how many had escaped or
died by then. But at this particular time the actual number of people within the
walls was probably nearer 3 million. The reason is that Titus came upon the city
just before the Passover Festival, and so devout were these Jewish visitors from
all over the world that they came to their religious center even in such dire
times as these.

The population during a typical Passover had been estimated by Romans at
2.95 million a few years back when the commander Cestius had requested additional troops to police the rebellious throngs at the time. When Nero had asked
how many were in the city at the time, Cestius had the priests count how many
sacrifices of paschal lambs were made at the altar. The actual count, reported
after the Festival ended, was roughly 256,500. Now since it was unlawful for a Jew
to sacrifice alone, and because the groups who shared a lamb usually ran from
ten to 20, Cestius estimated a conservative 13 per sacrifice and arrived at the
number 2,700,200. But since this number represented only those deemed pure
enough to sacrifice – it did not account for lepers, those with gonorrhea or
menstruating women – he added enough to make a total of 2.95 million. The
total was probably less in this especially troubled year, but certainly no fewer
than 2 million were on hand – and trapped inside – when Titus' legions encir-
cled the city.

Before I describe one of the largest and longest military struggles in human
history, it would be well that the reader have a fuller understanding of the

Roman invasion force that marched south to Jerusalem and of the geography and condition of this citadel of Jewish civilization.

The three legions that now plodded relentlessly uphill from Cæsarea and other wintering camps to the north had at first been culled of their most seasoned veterans by the four legions that left for Rome with Mucianus. But these in turn were soon bolstered by absorbing 2,000 troops that had been led from Egypt by no less than Tiberius Alexander, the governor and enthusiastic supporter of Vespasian. To these could be added several cohorts from the forts on the Euphrates and auxiliaries drawn from loyal kingdoms as distant as Macedonia. The most bloodthirsty of all were auxiliaries from the Syrian Hellenistic cities who had fought their Jewish neighbors so bitterly over the years.

As this force approached, the defenders who watched from the walls were dazzled as the armor and shields of 80,000 soldiers sprayed glistening beams of reflected sunlight in all directions. More impressive was the precision and discipline of such a large force. First in the long winding train came the auxiliaries, followed by the engineers who prepared roads and measured out the camps. Then came the commander's luggage, Titus himself with a select body, followed by the horsemen and the pikesmen. After all these came the engines of war, the tribunes of the cohorts and their elect bodies, the ensigns and their eagles, and then the trumpeters. But all these were only the beginning of the column, for they were followed by an endless parade of foot soldiers marching six abreast, then their baggage, and in curious Roman tradition, the force of mercenaries who had been hired to guard the rear.

The divided and desperate state of the people within those walls was not yet apparent to the Roman invaders. What first met their eyes was the same awesome spectacle that had left all pilgrims breathless for over 60 years. I refer to the huge white blocks of stone that had been fused into city walls and the almost blinding light that lit up the late afternoon landscape as the declining sun shone on the great plates of gold that covered the exterior of the temple at its highest places. So fiery was the reflection that it made men turn their eyes away just as if they had tried to look at the sun. As for its marble facing, one traveler wrote that "the temple appeared to strangers, when they were coming at it from a distance, like a mountain covered with snow; for as those parts of it that were not gilt, they were exceedingly white."

As Titus approached from the north, he faced, if you will, the short side of a roughly-hewn rectangle that stretched just over four miles to encompass the city. The northern approach also put the Romans at the strongest point of the city, for the natural elevation was high and was further fortified by a succession of three walls.

The newest and outermost wall extended along the city's entire northern border, ran for a mile or so along the western boundary, and connected to an ancient wall that protected its western flank. The northern wall is the one that Herod Agrippa I had feverishly attempted to build until halted by a suspicious emperor Claudius 27 years before. Agrippa's purpose had been to enclose the homes, gardens and natural springs of the rapidly-expanding "New City" to the north. The present defenders of Jerusalem had used the lull created by the Roman civil wars to justify Claudius' concerns: they built a wall 44 feet high that would be used to defy Roman authority.

The second, much older inner wall encompassed Herod's palace and Upper City to the west. As it turned northeast it joined the Fortress Antonia, which had garrisoned Roman troops and housed their arsenal until the rebels captured it. Parts of its north and eastern faces were at the same time the walls of the temple itself.

The wall continued along the eastern and southern perimeters, through what is called the Lower City. But at these points Jerusalem is defended primarily by the fact that the land just outside these walls plunges sharply into the Kidron Valley below.

Some of the towers along the inner wall to the north were fortresses within themselves. For instance, the tower of Hippicus, just north of Herod's palace, was 44 feet on each side and rose 52 feet. It included a reservoir 35 feet deep, over which was built a two-story house. The nearby Tower of Phasælis had a cloister atop it, covered by bulwarks and breastworks. Above this was built another tower full of private living and bathing rooms. It was also adorned with battlements and turrets so that the whole thing stood 157 feet high and was often compared to the famous Pharos lighthouse that once stood in the harbor at Alexandria.

As for the adjoining king's palace, Josephus writes:

> It was adorned with...large bed chambers that would contain beds for a hundred guests apiece, in which the variety of stones is not to be expressed, for a large quantity of those that were rare was collected together. Their roofs were also wonderful, both for the length of the beams and the splendor of their ornaments.

> The number of rooms was also very great, and the variety of the figures that were about them was prodigious; and the furniture was complete, and the greater part of the vessels in them was of silver and gold. There were besides many porticos, one beyond another, round about, and in each of those porticos curious pillars.

> Yet were all the courts that were exposed to the air everywhere green. There were several groves of trees and long walks through them, with

deep canals and cisterns, that in several parts were filled with brazen statues through which water ran out. There were many dove courts of tame pigeons about the canals. But indeed it is not possible to give a complete description of these palaces [because] the very remembrance of them is a torment to me.[50]

The temple I have previously described. From a military standpoint, I have already said that its eastern and northern walls connected to the city's existing defensive walls. The southern and western walls of the temple were made of massive stone blocks, and for the Romans, constituted a third, innermost military wall to be confronted eventually.

The defenders under arms numbered no more than 25,000. Until almost the very day that the Romans appeared from the hills below, Jerusalem had been wracked by the fighting of three factions. Simon of Geresa occupied Herod's palace. John of Gischala and his Zealots occupied the lower temple precincts. A splinter group of Zealots, headed by the tenacious Eleazar, had fled to the upper precincts of the temple. Thus, for weeks Eleazar's men reigned down missiles on John's Zealots, who constantly skirmished with Simon on their other flank. All during this incessant melee pilgrims and priests came and went to the temple despite the fact that its courtyards were constantly strewn with the corpses of those who had been felled by stones and darts from the warring factions.

The Passover Feast in April had only intensified the temple traffic and the number of killings as thousands of pious Jews from all over the empire came each day in order to be faithful to the ritual their forefathers had practiced for generations. To do so they had to brave the menacing scrutiny of Eleazar's guards, knowing that their sacrificial fees would probably wind up in some brigand's purse.

Meanwhile, the permanent residents of Jerusalem suffered the most. As Josephus writes:

> The people of the city were like a great body torn to pieces. The aged men and women were in such distress by their internal calamities that they wished for the Romans and earnestly hoped for an external war in order to secure delivery from their domestic miseries. The citizens were under a terrible consternation and fear...nor could such as had a mind flee away; for guards were set at all places, and the heads of robbers, although seditious against one another, yet did they agree in killing those who were for peace with the Romans or were even suspected of an inclination to desert them, as their common enemies. They agreed in nothing but this: to kill the innocent.[51]

One might assume that at first sight of the Romans, the three factions would have united instantly in common bond. They did so only to the extent that Eleazar made an uneasy truce with John and brought his 2,400 men back under Zealot command. Added to John's 6,000 men and 20 commanders, they controlled everything in and around the temple. Five hundred yards to the west, Herod's palace and the Upper City were controlled by Simon, who lived in the Tower of Phasælis that I have just described. Under Simon were 10,000 men and 50 commanders as well as 5,000 Idumeans, who paid them allegiance. While it is true that both Jewish factions were determined to fight the Romans, they never ceased skirmishing within the city – even to the point of designating an area between their camps as a mutually convenient spot in which to vent their hostilities.

Titus' expectation was that, in approaching a foe that was already sealed off, his legions would have ample time to establish camps, trenches and the usual security precautions. He also had heard reports about the populace being in disarray and ready to defect. Thus, it was without great precaution for his own safety that on the day after his legions struck camp outside Jerusalem, Titus and 600 horsemen rode out to inspect the city's perimeter and decide where they should position their siege engines. All seemed calm enough as the detachment approached the city from the main highway to the west, but when it turned north and rode through the gardens and olive groves that lay outside the northern gates, the Romans were shocked to see Jews suddenly leaping off the walls and rushing upon them with swords flailing. What ensued was a series of skirmishes with Titus himself at the center, now charging his horse through the disorganized Jewish attackers, then killing several with his sword. Eventually the Romans got the high ground and drove off their ferocious assailants, but this "greeting" convinced Titus that the defenders were probably more numerous than he had anticipated and that their zeal would not be easily overcome.

After a more careful and distant ride around the perimeter, Titus located his main camp to the west of the city about a thousand feet from the walls guarding Herod's palace. A secondary camp was set up northeast of the city on the Mount of Olives, where Jesus and his disciples had once looked down on the temple as they rested.

The objective Titus settled upon was a portion of the new third wall, north of Herod's palace, that had been left lower and narrower in the builders' haste because that part of the New City was less occupied than the others. Once breached, the Romans, reasoned, they could pierce the second wall in the Upper Market, gain access to the Fortress of Antonia, and from there ascend on the temple.

But many hours of tedious preparation came first. Titus began by uprooting all the gardens outside the walls and cutting down every tree that grew. Then the men set fire to all the suburbs around the walls. All of the timber and vegetation they could gather was used to start the piling up of crude embankments against the wall he intended to breach. To protect those who built the banks he stationed archers and engines that threw javelins, darts and stones. The engines were the army's finest, and could hurl a 60-pound stone for 400 yards. At first the massive stones inflicted great damage, but the Jews soon grew accustomed to hearing the fearsome noise and seeing the whiteness of the incoming missile as it reflected the sun's rays. Thus, they would post a single watchman on the ramparts who would yell, "The stone cometh!" Immediately everyone would drop on all fours by the wall as the stone crashed harmlessly in the streets. That is, they did until the Romans learned of the tactic. Afterwards the invaders took to blackening the stones in advance so that they could not be obvious in flight. Such are the innovations of modern siege warfare.

Once the Romans finished their banks, they were able to bring battering rams up to the wall. Now the pounding reverberations of many engines filled the air night and day. After many hours the walls remained intact, but so frightened by now were John and Simon that they vowed to ignore their differences for the duration and concentrate their ire on the attackers below. Some of their bravest men hurdled over the ramparts and landed on the wooden and metal roofs that had been erected over the rams and attacked the men underneath them. Dozens more ran about the ramparts, flinging torches on the wooden engines. At one point when it seems that the majority of Romans had retired to their camp, either out of weariness or perhaps to take a meal, the Jews poured out from their gates and descended on the few men who guarded the rams. An elite cohort from Alexandria was the first to realize what had happened and they rushed to the defense, sometimes killing, sometimes extinguishing a newly-lit fire under one of the engines. So furious was the fighting that Titus himself rode out with a cavalry unit and alone slew 12 of the attackers before they retreated back into the city.

Before long the Romans had added another type of "weapon" that did as much damage as their siege engines. As the building of the earthen embankments began, Titus had ordered the construction of three wooden, iron-plated towers, each over 80 feet tall. Once these were finished and put into place atop the banks, they allowed the Romans to hurl missiles down on the opposing ramparts without letup. Yet their height and iron sheeting were such as to render the Jewish darts ineffective. The result was that fewer defenders remained on the ramparts and no one now resisted the constant pounding of the rams. At the first breach in the wall's weakest point, the Romans poured through uncontested as the few remaining Jewish guards fled inside the second wall.

Thus, on April 22, just 15 days after their arrival, the Romans entered the outer city walls of Jerusalem and re-established their camp in the far northwest corner. Now they were in a position to contest simultaneously two key parts of the inner second wall: Simon's forces in Herod's Palace and John's commanding perch in the Fortress of Antonia and adjoining temple.

It may have been at this point that the most furious fighting of the campaign took place. The Jews by now had realized that their best successes had come when they could rush out from their gates and attack the Romans when they were in the open and not formed up. Once the Romans could regroup and push the Jews back against their walls, the latter invariably got the worst of it. But in the first furious rush the Jews could inflict great damage. Thus, for days, as Josephus writes,

> Neither side grew weary. Attacks and fightings upon the wall, and perpetual sallies out in bodies were there all day long. Nor were there any sort of warlike engagements that were not then put in use.

> When night itself had parted them they would lie in their armor, then begin to fight as soon as morning came. Nay, the night itself often passed without sleep on both sides.[52]

So eager were men on both sides for valor that they seemed to be in a contest as to who could perform the most stupendous deed. As Josephus notes, Jewish bravery seems to have stemmed from their awe and fear of Simon, who "at his own command they were ready to kill themselves with their own hands." The Romans in turn were inspired by the fact that Titus was everywhere among them; and as Josephus notes, "it appeared a terrible thing to them to grow weary while Cæsar was there." Besides, to have one's valor witnessed by Cæsar could win promotions and bonuses. Thus it was that a knight named Longinus leaped alone into a vast number of Jews. One man he struck in the mouth with a javelin; then as another man rushed toward him, he wrenched the dart from the fallen man and plunged it through the second man's side.

Feats like this were even endemic to entire cohorts. One of these units was the auxiliaries from Macedonia, which were full of tall, eager young men who weren't much past boyhood. Their leader, Antiochus Epiphanes, no doubt sure that he was the next Alexander, was full of swagger and actually harangued Titus about why he was taking so long to storm the city. Titus only smiled back and assured Antiochus that he would get his share of danger and glory when the time came. But as soon as Titus was out of sight, Antiochus and his men made a sudden assault on the wall with an intent to scale it. I think they were all convinced that they shared Alexander's famous good fortune, but the Jews on the ramparts didn't know any such thing. The young attackers found themselves in a hailstorm of heavy stones and darts. They fought bravely, and most survived, but they came limping back looking more like pincushions than warriors.

Indeed, death had become such a small matter to the men of both sides that it may have frightened even Titus — perhaps not as a soldier, but certainly as a commander. Gathering his men after one such battle, he counseled them that "inconsiderate violence" amounted to madness. True courage, he said, was "joined by good conduct." Henceforth, he made it clear that he would judge a "truly valiant man" as one who also took care not to be in a position of being harmed by his enemies.

It took the Roman engines only five more days to breach the second wall. This happened about a thousand feet north of Herod's palace where the wall meets the narrow streets in the Upper City populated by the many merchants of wool and other cloths. Now had Titus cleared a larger opening in the wall and laid waste everything directly on the other side, he would have encountered no risk; but this is one of many instances demonstrating that Titus consistently hoped to gain a bloodless surrender by showing restraint when he held an advantage. Thus, Titus entered the second wall with only a thousand armed men — all of them forbidden to kill anyone or set any buildings afire. He even promised that people's effects would be restored to them.

John and Simon perceived it as a sign of weakness that Titus knew he could not take the rest of the city. They also threatened death to anyone who said a word about surrender. Two things then happened. A large army of Simon rushed outside the wall and drove off the Romans who had been ordered to guard it until their comrades inside returned. Next, bands of Jewish soldiers burst forth from this house and that alleyway, ambushing the Romans as they wound their way through the narrow streets. As the disoriented Romans raced back and tried to funnel through the narrow breach in the wall, they would have been cut down had not Titus ordered his archers to stand in a solid row and fire at the attackers until everyone had gotten through to the other side.

The Jewish forces were jubilant, for they thought Titus would never again venture beyond the second wall. But the next day the Romans were back again, of course. For three days as they battered and charged, the Jews barred their entrance through the narrow breach by covering themselves with armor and literally stuffing themselves into the space. But on the fourth day they broke under the incessant pressure and fled as the wall behind them came tumbling down. This time Titus demolished it from one end to the other. Soon his legions had struck new camps at the foot of both Herod's Palace and the Fortress of Antonia.

By now Titus could see for himself conditions that existed inside the walls. While the men of both Simon and John seemed healthy enough, it was obvious who held the food supplies and who did not. Outside the soldiery, the masses of

Jerusalem were clearly suffering for want of nourishment. If the soldiers did not have enough to spare the populace, Titus reasoned, the time would come soon enough when they, too, had none.

So Titus decided to relax the siege for awhile and give the people of Jerusalem time to let their stomachs influence their thinking. It also happened to be time to distribute the soldiers their regular subsistence pay, and Titus decided to make a show of it. One bright sunny morning, as thousands of Jews watched from the temple and other high places, 80,000 soldiers polished their armor, adorned their horses and paraded in full dress. Josephus, who was there, recalled what a "very great consternation seized upon the hardiest of the Jews themselves" as they saw the heartiness of the men and their good order. Even the seditious, he opined, would have changed their minds at the sight "unless the crimes they had committed against the people had been so horrid" that they found death by war better than the retribution the victors would exact.

But four days came and went without even an offer to talk. Now Titus faced a crucial decision. The Jewish forces held the high ground. Titus did not want to destroy the temple, but he could not leave Jerusalem without removing the force that now occupied it. To assault the temple and its massive, almost seamless stone walls would be long and difficult. When the siege had begun almost a month before, the Jews had brought out the catapults they had captured from the Fortress of Antonia. But they were untrained and clumsy in hurling stones. By this time they had much improved their skills and — the Romans counted 340 such engines along the walls — were making it much more dangerous for the attackers to raise banks than it had been a few weeks before. Titus decided on one more attempt to negotiate.

After the Romans had paraded their troops about the walls, they were followed by a single man in his mid-thirties, sitting on a mule. He was Josephus, once the Jewish general in the defense of Galilee, then a deserter held in fetters. But the previous fall, at the intervention of Titus, Vespasian had cast off his chains and Josephus now accompanied the commander as advisor on Jewish affairs. Now the time had come to justify the reason for preserving him. And Josephus in turn had every reason to see Jerusalem preserved: his mother, wife and children were being held hostage inside.

Josephus moved about the perimeter cautiously on his mule until he could find a place that was out of the range of missiles, yet close enough for him to be heard. Then dismounting and shouting in their own tongue, he harangued and beseeched the men on the walls for over an hour.

There is a "fixed law" that causes both brute beasts and men to yield to those who are too strong for them, Josephus declared. Romans were mightier, as all the world could attest, and even those who were far stronger than the Jews had willingly submitted. How fortunate it was that this power was also one that respected Jewish worship and traditions. Besides, what could they hope to gain when most of the city was already taken from them? Even now, said Josephus, Cæsar was willing to offer his right hand in security if they surrendered. But if he was forced to take the city by other means, no one would be spared.

None of this mattered, however. As Josephus spoke, the air was full of jeers and jokes. Some even threw darts at him. At last the derision was too much to bear; Josephus raised his voice even louder and spoke with fire.

> O miserable creatures! Are you so unmindful of those that used to assist you that you will fight by your weapons and hands against Rome? When did we ever conquer any nation by such means? And when was it that God, who is creator of the Jewish people, did not avenge them that had been injured? Will you not turn again and look back and consider...how great a supporter you have profanely abused? Will you not recall the prodigious things done for your forefathers and this holy place, and how great enemies of yours were by him subdued under you?[53]

No, said Josephus, it was not Jewish might that had preserved them as a people, but the divine providence that came only when they had placed themselves in God's hands. Did they not remember their forefathers who had been in Egyptian bondage for 400 years? Did the Jews ever fight their way out of Egypt? No! Only when they committed themselves to God did he take them in his hands.

> Who is there who does not know that Egypt was overrun with all sorts of wild beasts and consumed by all sorts of distemper? Do you not remember how their land did not bring forth its fruit, how the Nile failed of water and how the ten plagues of Egypt followed one upon another? And do you remember how our fathers were then sent away under guard, without any bloodshed, and without running any dangers, because God conducted them as his special servants?[54]

Josephus spoke of how the Assyrians had left off their assault of Judea after they were afflicted with a loathsome distemper. He told of how the Jews were freed from slavery in Babylonia, not by any uprising, but because "God made Cyrus his gracious instrument in bringing it about." He cited many more cases and concluded, "To speak in general, we can produce no example wherein our fathers got any success by war or failed of success when they committed themselves to God."

The taunts from the wall were growing more bellicose, but Josephus was determined to give them his final appeal. Jerusalem's predicament was caused by robbers who profaned the temple and abused the people, he shouted. "Hardhearted wretches that you are, cast away all your arms and take pity of your country already going to ruin. Return from your wicked ways and have regard to the excellency of that city which you are going to betray — to that excellent temple with the donations of so many countries in it."

If nothing else, implored Josephus,

> ...have pity on your families and set before your children and wives and parents, who will be gradually consumed either by famine or by war. I am aware that this danger will extend to my mother, wife and to that family of mine...and perhaps you may imagine that it is on their account only that I make this appeal. But if that be all, kill them. Nay, take my own blood as a reward if it may procure your preservation. For I am ready to die should you return to a sound mind after my death.[55]

Titus could not fathom the exact words of Josephus, but he could understand the reaction on the wall above. He ceased to expect a peace deputation and he was not surprised by one. Indeed, every display of mercy, every proposal to leave off the violence was seen as Roman weakness. So this time Titus succumbed to another tactic, proposed by his officers, on the theory that the sight of it would demonstrate Roman power so convincingly that the Jews would finally surrender and spare many more lives.

The new tactic arose from the fact that, despite their increased isolation and the risks of getting caught, gnawing hunger still prompted many Jews to slip out of Jerusalem at night in search of anything edible in the steep valleys that surround the southern and eastern perimeters. Most were poor people who were deterred from deserting altogether by the certainty that John or Simon would kill their families inside if they did. Thus far Titus had chosen to overlook them. Now he dispatched regular cavalry patrols to scour the valleys and bring back anyone they could catch. In a given day they would snare over 500 Jews, and each day the soldiers would nail them to crosses that were rung about the perimeter of the temple wall. As Josephus witnessed: "Some they nailed one way, another after another way, to the crosses by way of jest, so that their multitude was so great that room was wanting for the crosses, and crosses wanting for the bodies."

Yet, there was no change in the Jews. Indeed, Simon and John merely pointed to the crosses as proof of what awaited all Jews within the walls. The Romans had not been idle, however, during the two weeks that armed clashes had been suspended. The Romans had now finished building four towers at various points along the temple wall and were now ready to resume the assault.

But the Jews had not been idle, either. As the Romans were building a tower against the face of the Fortress of Antonia, John's men had been busy burrowing underneath its foundation. Indeed, their tunnel had extended beyond the walls and under the base of the earthen banks and Roman siege tower that stood atop it. As in constructing a mine, they had buttressed the top of their tunnel with large timbers. Only in this case they had first covered the supports with pitch and bitumen. Now they were lit afire as the Jews scurried out of their tunnel. Before long, and after the Romans had climbed into their new tower, the inflamed mine supports burned through and gave way. Without any notice, the earthen embankment collapsed into the mine tunnel below and the giant tower toppled over in a heap of dust and smoke. And there it continued to burn, for the Romans could not control the source of the fire.

Elsewhere along the wall the Romans had installed siege engines on the other banks and the great stones now shook endlessly with their constant pounding. But just two days after demolishing the Roman siege tower, Simon and his men made a ferocious assault outside the temple, making the Romans fight for their lives while other Jews risked theirs setting the rams afire with great torches. Some were punctured by several darts each, yet did not give up their mission and die until the rams were ablaze. So frenzied was the attack that the Jews actually forced the Romans back to their camp, where for many minutes *they* became the ones defending their fortifications.

When the Jews finally retired, nearly all the towers and siege engines had been either badly burned or broken, and Titus was forced to call a meeting of his officers and re-assess their position at Jerusalem. Without towers and battering rams, the risk of heavy casualties was too great to assault the temple. With absolutely no more trees or vegetation available around Jerusalem, finding replacement materials meant journeying at least 20 miles and back. Yet, Titus despaired of keeping so large an army idle for so long, and he worried that it would also diminish the glory of the triumph he envisioned in Rome.

The answer was to build another wall. This one would be earthen. It would cover the entire four-mile perimeter of the remaining Jewish defense line and it would be broken by 13 Roman garrisons. Each garrison would maintain 24-hour-a-day patrols atop the entire earthen works so that absolutely no one could get in or out.

If siege engines could not conquer Jerusalem, famine could.

And one thing more. Anticipating that his fighting men would moan at the prospect of a protracted ditch digging exercise, Titus and his officers promoted the project among the troops as a stupendous display of Roman engineering prowess that would be remembered for centuries. The entire army was to build a four-mile wall in just three days. Each legion would be given a segment to complete. Rewards would be theirs if they bested their brother legions. Within each legion it became soldier versus soldier within a platoon, centurion against centurion, tribune versus tribune and so forth.

The wall was finished in three days. And as the Romans reclined in their camps full of praise and extra rations, Josephus records that "a deep silence...a kind of deadly night, seized upon the city." And "then did the famine widen its progress" as May turned to June and the scorching months of summer.

. . . .

During the earlier months of winter and early spring, Vespasian in Alexandria and Titus in Judea had more to show for their efforts than did the uneasy coalition that tried to rule Rome in their absence. It was enough that General Antonius Primus had to learn a new role as consul while fending off the ambitious Domitian. In theory, his position superseded that of the emperor's young son, who had been named prætor. Yet an uncertain Senate also had recognized the lad's special status by adding that his rank would be co-equal to that of consul. The presence of Mucianus would have made the problem of power a moot point, but he still hadn't arrived from Syria.

And so, problems festered. The Senate argued endlessly about whether postwar retributions should be taken against this friend of Vitellius or that informer of Nero. There was even quarreling as to who should be included in a delegation being formed to pay the Senate's respects to Vespasian in Alexandria. There was growing anguish over the spreading revolt in Germany and the fact that Roman fortifications there had been reduced to older men and raw recruits when the flower of the legions had gone down to fight in Italy. Ironically, Rome was now caught up in a serious grain shortage – ironic because it was Vespasian himself who caused it, thinking that he would be squeezing Vitellius into surrendering the city. Now his success had made victims of his own subjects.

When Mucianus finally arrived in early March, the ship at last had a captain – but at a price. The Senate returned to its fawning ways, as if it had just crowned a new emperor, and Mucianus himself seemed to expect it. In addition to accepting triumphal honors (which until then had been reserved for those who gain victories over foreign armies), Mucianus was liberal in telling the Senate, "It was I who had held the empire in the palm of my hand and gave it to Vespasian." Mucianus seemed to delight in staying in the many villas available to the emperor, but I must say that he also was decisive in assuming leadership in Vespasian's name. For instance, he quickly diminished the cult status that Antonius was gaining among his troops by moving his Seventh Legion to winter quarters in Pannonia. The best men in other units of Antonius were combed out and sent to the German front. You may also recall Otho's Prætorian Guards, who had been discharged by Vitellius after they lost to him at Bedriacum. For weeks they had menaced Rome with their demands that they be re-admitted to the Guard. Mucianus simply assented and quickly relieved the city of another threat. Domitian was cooled off, I suspect, by means of a letter to his father that no one else but Mucianus could risk writing. The dispatch documented the lad's excesses, ranging from the pilfering of other men's wives to his insistence on being given command of the troops in Germany. The terse reply from Vespasian in Alexandria was this: "I thank, you, my son, for permitting me to hold office and that you have not yet dethroned me." A popular story is that, upon reading this, a chastened Domitian sulked alone for weeks in a room of a country villa, using a sharpened stylus to spear flies for hours on end. Thus, when someone in town would ask, "Where is Domitian these days?" another would answer, "He's living alone without even a fly to keep him company." Yet, it was not any one man who kept Rome from governing effectively and regaining its tarnished luster during these months; it was more a matter of money. The treasury was severely depleted by Nero and the succeeding wars, and there was no quick way to replenish it. One glaring reminder was the ugly charred shell of the Temple Jupiter Optimus Maximus that glared down from atop Capitoline Hill. This had been the symbol of Rome's might; and now, when a native German chieftain was asked why he decided to join the revolt, he answered that the Roman Empire was finished. Why? Because its leaders could not even afford to rebuild their most sacred temple.

Vespasian's declining popularity in Egypt directly reflects his financial predicament. No doubt the most difficult decision the new emperor would ever make was this: if Rome were to continue as an empire, it would have to have the funds necessary to govern it. Vespasian and his advisors estimated that Rome needed 1.6 billion sesterces just to get back on an even footing. And in getting on with the unpleasant task, Egypt felt the impact quickly simply because that is where the emperor happened to be at the time. Thus, the Alexandrians, the first foreigners to acclaim this unregal-looking princeps with great hopes of gaining a largesse – or perhaps even the tax exemptions that Nero had granted Greece – were stunned to learn that there would be no bounty, nor even bonuses for the Roman legionaries who had sworn allegiance. In fact, Vespasian revived some small sales taxes that had been allowed to go unenforced. And imagine the outcry when Vespasian even sold off part of the palace grounds that had been maintained for the emperor's use (a prudent decision, given the fact that no princeps had visited Egypt for a hundred years). Thus, by the time the emperor departed, the Alexandrians had taken to calling him "Cybiosactes," the surname of a past king who had been scandalously stingy. The name translates roughly to "dealer in pieces of salt fish."

Vespasian's last action in Egypt was to respond to a dispatch from Rome saying that the city's corn supply had dwindled to about ten days' worth. Despite the fact that the ocean winds were still unpredictable, he sent off a large fleet of corn ships. No doubt he would have wished to join them. Instead, by April Vespasian was back in Cæsarea, hoping that Titus could have finished his destruction of Jerusalem and depart with his father for a triumphant entry to Rome. But as we have seen, such an event was not even in sight.

So, embarking on as direct a path as the swirling winds of early spring would permit, Vespasian and a small party sailed a merchantman from Cæsarea to Lycia and then proceeded by both land and sea to the eastern Italian port of Brundisium. There, just as their predecessors had journeyed from Rome to meet the family of Germanicus 44 years before, a delegation of senators and notables were on hand as he disembarked. Not among them was the young prætor-consul Domitian, who sent word to his father that he was ill.

Before the emperor had departed Cæsarea, Titus had begged him to be lenient with his younger brother. "Friendships can be extinguished by time, chance and misunderstandings," Titus had reportedly said, "but a man's own blood cannot be severed from him." Apparently Vespasian accepted this counsel, but I suspect Domitian was left to jab at many more flies with his stylus, because in the remainder of this year the focus shifted wholly to a very busy emperor and his attempts to pull Rome back from the edge of self-destruction.

Vespasian was swift in relieving internal dissension. He freed most of those who had been exiled or condemned by Nero and forbade all new indictments based on similar charges. The properties of Otho, Vitellius and other fallen foes he left their kinsmen. He replenished the ranks of senators and knights, which had been depleted by years of murder and purge. The courts, which were so clogged with lawsuits that many litigants could not hope to have their cases heard in their lifetimes, were stripped of all but the most important cases by selecting commissioners by lot to decide on their own the most routine disputes. He struck a blow against greedy advocates who prevail on a son to prosecute his wealthy father – this by inducing the Senate to vote that those who lend money to a young man who is still under the control of his father shall have no right to enforce payments resulting from lawsuits against the same. And in a blow against licentiousness, he pried from the Senate a law that any woman caught in a liaison with a slave shall herself be reduced to similar status.

However, rebuilding public works was the emperor's highest priority. He resumed work on a temple to the deified Claudius that had been begun by Agrippina but then destroyed by her son Nero. He began work on a new temple of Peace in the Forum as well as his grandest project of all, a new amphitheater on the grounds of the Golden House (which itself would soon be converted into a public bath). Numerous projects were launched to restore works that had fallen into sad states of disrepair. Whether it was a monument defaced during war or an aqueduct that had been allowed to sag, Vespasian ordered that, upon restoration, the names inscribed on them were to be those of the original builders and not his own. As for the many lots of ugly rubble that still remained from the great fire of six years before, the emperor ordered that anyone could seize and build upon them if the current owners failed to do so within a given date.

Of course the largest charred site of all was the temple atop the Capitoline, and to this Vespasian gave his utmost attention. First, the blackened timbers and tiles were carted to the wharves and barged to the marshes of Ostia, with the emperor himself carrying the first load to a cart. Then on June 21, a bright day of sunshine, the whole consecrated area of the temple was decorated with chaplets and garlands. In marched soldiers — all chosen for having names of good omen — carrying branches of trees deemed to be equally propitious. Then came the Vestal Virgins, who cleansed it all by sprinkling fresh water from a spring or river. The Pontiff Maximus further purified the site by a solemn sacrifice of a pig, sheep and ox, then prayed to Jupiter, Juno and Minerva, the guardian deities of the empire, to shine their divine grace on the temple to be built there.

After the purification rite, an assemblage of nobles dragged a huge cornerstone into place. Gifts of gold and silver were thrown into the foundation trenches and over them were placed blocks of virgin ore, unscathed by any furnace, just as they had come from the womb of the earth.

Vespasian himself had led the stone laying, and now he took charge of restoring the 3,000 bronze tablets that had been destroyed in the blaze. These were the most priceless and ancient records of the empire, containing the decrees of the Senate from the city's foundation on such matters as alliances, treaties and honors to individuals.

Yes, all these projects cost a great deal of money, and Vespasian was no less aggressive in obtaining it at home than he had been in Egypt. To do what needed to be done, he felt justified in openly selling positions ranging from stewardships to governorships. On several occasions he used treasury money to corner certain markets on commodities, then releasing them at a profit. One of his most unpopular acts was to rescind the exemption from taxes that Nero had so munificently (and thoughtlessly) granted to the Greek states of Achaia, Lycia, Rhodes and Samos. But even more unpopular in Rome was the nuisance of many small taxes never before imposed, many of which are with us today. For instance, we can thank Vespasian for the toilet tax. Romans love to relate the old story of when Titus, a few years later, complained to his father about this odium. Vespasian held up a piece of money to his son's nose and asked if he found its odor offensive.

"No," said Titus.

"Well, good, because it comes from urine," said his father with a wide grin.

All this was not for personal gain, however. One time Vespasian was told by a deputation from a large city that they would like his permission to honor him with a colossal statue of his likeness. The emperor held out his palm, saying, "Here is its base," meaning that he preferred having an equivalent amount of money for the treasury.

Indeed, none of the money seems to have gone into his own coffers. What need would he have of it? Vespasian's own living style was nearly as Spartan as his days as a general in the field. He rose before dawn and had usually completed his correspondence in time for a morning reception. His afternoons were typically spent in the Senate or courts, then at bath. He entertained often and was a cordial and gracious host. While he did not skimp on things like banquets, neither his personal dress nor behavior was lavish. And he detested foppery to the same degree than Nero loved it. Thus, when a young military officer, reeking with perfumes, came to thank him for having given him a commission, Vespasian drew back his head in disgust. "I would rather you had smelled of garlic," he said, and revoked the appointment.

I suppose the greatest change in Rome was that Vespasian tolerated debate and withstood personal criticism. "He bore frank talk from his friends, the quips of pleaders and the impudence of philosophers with the greatest patience," writes one biographer. His "deaf ear" extended to Mucianus, who continued living like a potentate, and to the usual rumors as to potential rivals. When friends repeatedly warned the emperor to "keep an eye" on an ambitious senator named Mettius Pompusianus, Vespasian made him consul-elect on the belief that the man would now be mindful of the favor.

Allow me to add one more incident that describes Vespasian. During one of his morning receptions a man approached him, all a-tremble, to beg his forgiveness. Perhaps you will recall how, during Nero's "Olympic" stage performances in Greece, the emperor's freedmen scrutinized the dignitaries in the audience to spot those who weren't applauding wildly enough. You may recall as well that one of them, who had been detected in a state of some discomfort amidst his otherwise elated colleagues, had been escorted outside and told to "Go to the deuce." That man was Vespasian. Now the same freedman sought relief from his mortification — and no doubt a favor or two.

Nero would have had the man killed, but Vespasian's sense of unflagging humor usually took the edge off his temper. "Well now," he said, "now it's *your* turn to go to the deuce, isn't it?" And with that the man was dismissed with a theatric good-bye wave.

. . . .

As summer baked the temple in Jerusalem, John of Gischala lived well when he was not fighting Romans. Many days he engaged in melting down the gold that abounded within the temple. This included many of the sacred utensils, caldrons, dishes – even the gold pouring vessels that had been sent as gifts from Augustus and Livia. Most eagerly he seized upon the many gifts of foreigners, telling his accomplices that it was proper for them to use Divine elements because they were fighting for the Divinity against the heathen.

But in the narrow streets of Jerusalem, the summer heat was less stifling than the hunger. And even hunger was less smothering than the scrutiny the common family felt from the men of John and Simon. Houses were searched continually. If the men found corn, the householder was tortured for having denied he had any. But if the ransackers found none, their torments were even worse because they assumed that food was being cleverly concealed. When people were able to eat what they had, they didn't even bother to grind corn, but shut themselves up in their houses and ate it whole. And if they baked bread, they snatched it from the oven half-done and ate it quickly in fear that the aroma might alert those who prowled outside. Yet, when the soldiers saw that a house was shut up at midday, they took it as a sign that those inside had gotten some food. In such cases,

> ...they ran in and took pieces of what they were eating almost up out of their very throats. The old men, who held their food fast, were beaten. If the women hid what they had within their hands, their hair was torn for so doing. Nor was any commiseration shown either to the aged or infants. They would lift up children from the ground as they hung upon the morsels they had gotten and shook them upon the floor. But still they were more barbarously cruel to those who had prevented their coming in and had managed to swallow what they [the soldiers] were about to seize upon, as if they had been unjustly deprived of their right.

> They also invented terrible methods of torments to discover where any food was, and they were these: to stop up the passages of the privy parts of the miserable wretches and drive sharp stakes up their fundamentals...in order to make them confess that they had but one loaf of bread or a handful of barley.[56]

In many ways it was worse to be rich than poor. Those who still had material possessions were more apt to be taken directly before tribunals of Simon and John and accused of laying treacherous plots to deliver the city to the Romans. But far easier to convict were those accused of trying to desert. And so, as Josephus observes, "He who was utterly despoiled by Simon was sent back again to John; and of those who had been plundered by John, Simon got what remained."

There may have been more truth to these accusations simply because desertion remained a possible salvation. With the new siege dike, Jews could not forage for food and return, but they could still slip over the earthen mounds and deliver themselves to a sympathetic (or bribed) Roman guard, because at this time Titus continued to receive common citizens and allow them to leave Jerusalem for any area they chose.

At this time there may have been more gold in Jerusalem than food, so that a man intending to escape would often swallow a few gold pieces and hope to retrieve them from his stool afterwards so that he could pay his way into safety. This tactic worked well enough for a few weeks, but about this time the Roman soldiers began to get wind of it. Now when a Jew escaped he ran the risk of being butchered alive by Roman guards in search of gold. Even worse, some of the Roman forces had begun prowling about the depths of the Kidron Valley. Whenever the Jews would fling the body of another famine victim over the east wall, the human vultures below would quickly cut it apart in hopes that the entrails would yield gold or jewels.

When Titus heard about the wicked practice he assumed they were some of his auxiliaries, no doubt barbaric Syrians or Idumeans, and he threatened to charge the guilty himself on his horse and kill them at once. But at learning that the practice was widespread and also involved many Roman soldiers, he summoned all his commanders and ordered that any man caught doing so in the future would be killed without a hearing. But such is the allure of gold that some continued the practice in spite of the danger to them.

How much toll did famine take on the people of Jerusalem? In case you might be thinking this was merely an affliction of life's less fortunate, I am able to give you a good indication to the contrary. At the eastern, or Essene gate, there was a man named Manneus whose position was to collect a public stipend for having to transport a corpse outside the city limits, as long required by law. By the end of June he alone had collected fees for removing 115,880 dead bodies. Yet everyone agrees that many more were stacked in the attics of large houses or hurled into the Valley of Kidron. Those of the leading citizens who had deserted to Titus agreed that the number who had perished by this time was no fewer than 600,000.

By mid-July the Romans had finished raising banks again at the Tower of Antonia. To find materials for this painstaking task, detachments of soldiers had traveled with oxen and wagons 20 miles out from Jerusalem all directions. Now, no tree remained standing anywhere within that distance. Suburbs that had once been adorned with pleasant gardens and groves were now a desolate desert, so that any foreigner who had once seen Jerusalem in its splendor could hardly believe his eyes if he came upon it now.

The Roman earth banks were once again in place, and both sides knew that the decisive moment of the war had arrived. All understood that if the Romans took Antonia, they would have access to the entire temple complex – and they would occupy higher ground because the old Roman citadel looked directly into the Court of Gentiles. But both sides knew as well that if the Jews could somehow destroy the towers and rebuilt siege engines, the Roman soldiers alone could not surmount the wall and would be forced to retire for lack of any more building materials.

However, the Jews had lately been wanting in that task. They seemed to lack the great zeal and ferocity that had so often overcome Roman order and discipline. Yes, they had sallied out often against the siege engines with their torches, but they often seemed more listless, their movements mechanical. It is true that this lack of success was partly because the Romans now had more men guarding the engines and archers were positioned permanently to slow down any raiding party that ran out from the city. But the decisive factor had to be famine, and a tell-tale sign of it was that the bellies of the Jews had become swollen and distended.

For two days the rams battered against the walls of Antonia without effect. At that point the Romans took drastic action: they employed brigades of men to undermine the foundation stones of the fortress despite a constant rain of stones and darts all around them. As some men held shields aloft in an improvised tortoise formation, others would be crouched below digging or prying at the giant stones with crowbars. Although many men fell from the darts and stones, the Romans eventually succeeded in dislodging four large foundation blocks. Yet by the time they retired for the night, King Herod's already battered and undermined tower remained upright.

In the middle of the windless, starry night, Roman soldiers bolted from their cots when they heard a tremendous crash in the direction of the Fortress of Antonia. Grabbing their armor as they rushed to the camp perimeter, they saw a great cloud of dust and mound of rubble. The Tower of Antonia still stood, but the much-battered wall connecting it to another corner of the old Roman citadel had apparently been so underlain with tunnels from John's "surprise" of the previous month that it had finally toppled without further help.

Trumpeters blared as Roman soldiers formed up ranks, expecting this night to plunge through the opening and take the temple at last. But when they marched to the wall, and when the dust clouds cleared enough for them to see, they squinted in the moonlight and saw before them another wall. John and his men, while fighting Romans and famine, had also managed to build a second wall connecting the gap left when the first wall fell. Titus and his men looked in disbelief.

The Romans went to bed dejected. In the light of the next day they took a closer survey of the new wall and determined that, given its hasty construction, it probably was not as thick or sturdy as the first one. And because the stones from the first wall now lay in front, it would not be as high to scale. It might succumb to the rams.

And yet...Titus was feeling his men's frustration and fatigue at the many weeks of building, battering and digging. The time for a more dramatic solution had come at last, and those who had begged for a chance to show their valor would now have it.

Titus gathered men from every legion and gave them a rare oration. He began by calling it an "exhortation" and he quickly let them know it was about going over the wall they now faced. God himself had shown Romans the way to victory by making the first wall collapse, declared the young commander. Yet so far, it was "unbecoming" that men who were trained to conquer and rule had been too often outshone by the "pure courage" of their opponents. Yes, he said, "we can wait until famine and fortune work their will, but we also have it in our power now...to gain all that we desire!"

Titus forthrightly acknowledged that the first ones over the wall would undoubtedly die, but to a soldier death in battle was preferable to death by another means. A man who dies in combat is commended and finds immortality, while those who die in peace from some distemper find their souls condemned to the grave along with their bodies.

> For what man of virtue is there who does not know that those souls which are severed from their fleshly bodies by the sword are received by the ether, that purest of elements, and joined to that company which are placed among the stars, that they become...propitious heroes and show themselves as such to their posterity afterwards? But upon those souls that wear away with their distempered bodies comes a subterranean night to dissolve them to nothing [but] deep oblivion...

> Since fate has determined that death is to come of necessity upon all men, a sword is a better instrument for that purpose than any disease whatsoever. Why is it not then a very good thing for us to yield up that to the public benefit which we must yield to fate?[57]

But should a man survive the ordeal, Titus concluded, earthly rewards would be there as well.

> As for that person who first mounts the wall, I should blush for shame if I did not make him to be envied of others by the rewards I would bestow upon him. If such a one escapes with his life, he shall

have the command of others that are now but his equals [even though] it is still true that the greatest rewards will accrue to such as die in the attempt.[58]

Despite Cæsar's emotional exhortation, its conclusion drew no hurrahs – only a wall of petrified silence. At last Titus was rescued from his embarrassment when one man came forward. His name was Sabinus, a black-skinned, common foot soldier who served with the Syrian auxiliaries. He was already known for his courage in battle, yet one would not have expected it from his short and very lean stature.

"I will readily surrender myself up to thee, O Cæsar," he said, looking up at the thickly-muscled commander. "I will first ascend the wall and I heartily wish that my fortune will follow my courage."

Eleven others were stirred by Sabinus' declaration, and soon they marched up to the edge of the new wall with shields raised over their heads. As they climbed their ladders, some of the 12 were quickly knocked off by darts and large stones. Sabinus himself, who was first, had already been hit by a few darts himself by the time he fought his way over the wall. At first the men on the ramparts were astonished by the fury of his fighting. Many others gave way because they thought Sabinus was merely the first in a tidal wave of Romans.

Sabinus was actually chasing a crowd of Jewish soldiers through the Court of Gentiles when he was knocked to the ground by a large stone. He managed to get to one knee and wounded several attackers with his sword. But another gash disabled his right hand, and now all he could do was lie on the ground and try to cover himself with his shield. But he was soon pierced by many more darts and died.

When it was over, three of his companions had been dashed to pieces by stones inside the walls. The eight others were wounded while climbing and were rescued by the Romans below.

Why this futile exercise? Where were the troops who were supposed to rally behind Sabinus? In a way, Sabinus did stir the men to victory for this reason: after two days of sulking in their shame and cowardice, some of them at last could stand it no more. As night fell, a dozen men who had been on forward guard duty at the Roman banks were quietly joined by two cavalrymen, a trumpeter and a standard-bearer from the Fifth Legion. Waiting until about nine o'clock, when they expected the Jewish guards to be nodding off, they sneaked through the ruins and up to the base of the Tower Antonia. The Romans quietly climbed the wall and cut the throats of the three sleeping guards. Then they ordered the trumpeter to sound a charge while they themselves yelled as loudly as they could.

The sound, of course, woke up the rest of the guards on the wall. Thinking this the beginning of a massive invasion, they scrambled down into the broad temple courtyard. When Titus heard the trumpet signal, he ordered everyone into their armor immediately and rushed them to the site. But as they were mobilizing, the first men over the wall couldn't see well in the dark and hadn't realized that the opening of John's underground tunnels lay just below them. As the Jewish guards fled across the temple court, the Romans fell into the tunnel entrance, causing their quarry to turn about and become the pursuers. By this time Romans were pouring over the wall and Jewish reinforcements were coming from all parts of the city.

They met in the middle between the Tower of Antonia and the steps of the temple itself. And there took place the most furious hand-to-hand warfare of the campaign. The Jews would drive the bulk of the Romans back towards the tower, only to be themselves pushed back to the steps of the temple.

> Now during this struggle the positions of the men were undistinguished on both sides, and they fought at random, the men being intermixed with one another and confounded by means of the narrowness of the place.[59]

> The clashing of swords and shouts of men made a deafening sound as it reverberated about the stone walls of the great enclosure.

> Great slaughter was now made on both sides, and the combatants trod upon the bodies and armor of those that were dead, and dashed them to pieces. Accordingly, to which side the battle inclined, those that had the advantage exhorted one another while those who were beaten made great lamentation. But still there was no room for flight nor for pursuit but disorderly revolutions and retreats. Those who were in the first ranks were under the necessity of killing or being killed, without any way of escaping.[60]

The battle raged continuously until seven the next morning. Gradually, the zeal and courage that the Jews had somehow summoned from their starved bodies at the prospect of their temple being invaded proved too much for the Romans. The latter were forced back into the Fortress of Antonia, where they were at least content to savor their new advantage of looking down on the temple courtyard.

The Jews, with an awesome courage that overcame their gnawing stomachs, had won the night valiantly. But they had already lost the days to come, for the Romans, in truth, had waged the battle with only a part of their army. Fresh reinforcements could now be brought up, and the next battle chosen at their convenience.

Another short period of relative calm ensued. During the chaos of recent days, several Jewish notables and priestly families had managed to find their way into Roman hands, and Titus had sent them all off to the small city of Gophna with the promise that he would restore them to their possessions after the war. When John and Simon spread word that the Romans had killed all of the new deserters, Titus had them quickly recalled while on their journey and now paraded them about the walls of the temple for all to see. This was also the day (August 6) in which the Jews, for want of men or piety – or both – had ceased offering the daily sacrifice to God. And so, Titus, seeing this as a possible sign of desperate fatigue, decided to send Josephus out to them once again.

With tears and groans, Josephus told John and the others inside that Cæsar had beseeched them to save the temple from fire by moving his men to another place of his choosing to do their battle there. Would they do so?

John shouted back that the temple was in no danger because it was God's place and would be protected by him. To which Josephus retorted,

> To be sure you have kept this city wonderfully pure for God's sake! The temple continues entirely unpolluted! Nor have you been guilty of any impiety against him for whose assistance you hope! He still receives his accustomed sacrifices! Vile wretch that thou art! If anyone would deprive you of your daily food, you would esteem him to be your enemy. But you hope to have that God for your supporter in this war whom you have deprived of his everlasting worship![61]

Josephus again said that if John would yet repent, " I dare venture to promise that the Romans will still forgive you."

But again all Josephus received back was more torment. In fact, it was evident to the Romans in the background that John's men were more interested in luring Josephus closer to the walls so that they might kill him with darts or somehow get their hands on his neck, for they saw him as the worst Jewish traitor of all. But Josephus turned their reproach back against them:

> Indeed, I cannot deny I am worthy of worse treatment because...in opposition to fate, I...am endeavoring to force deliverance upon those whom God has condemned. Who is there who does not know that the writings of the ancient prophets contain in them...that oracle which is just now going to be fulfilled upon this miserable city? For they foretold that this city should be taken when somebody shall begin the slaughter of his own countrymen. And are not both the city and the

entire temple now full of the dead bodies of your countrymen? It is
therefore God himself who is bringing on this fire, to purge that city
and temple by means of the Romans and who will pluck up this city
which is so full of your pollutions![62]

Josephus was sobbing, and in such great distress that Titus himself now
stepped from the background. All about them in the outer courtyard were
heaps of bodies from the all-night battle before. After staring up at John for
some time, he held up his hand for silence and shouted, with Josephus interpreting his words, "Hasn't Rome given you permission to deny Gentiles your
sanctuary on pain of death – even if they be Romans? Have not Romans respected its sanctity?

"Why do you now trample upon dead bodies in this temple? Why do you pollute this holy house with the blood of both foreigners and Jews? I appeal to the
gods of my own country and to every god that ever had any regard for this
place. I also appeal to my own army and to those Jews that are now with me,
and even to yourselves, that I do not force you to defile this sanctuary. And if
you will not but change the place whereon you will fight, no Roman shall either come near your sanctuary or offer any affront to it."

But Titus, too, was rebuked and refused. And as if to leave no doubt about it,
John ordered that his largest catapults be positioned at the very gates of the
temple. So Titus resigned his men to raising more banks – this time against the
walls of the temple building that stood in the great outer courtyard.

Meanwhile, the famine all over the city below worsened almost beyond description. Now that it was impossible to gather wild herbs in the valley, some people were driven to searching the common sewers and old dunghills of cattle.
Gangs of desperate men staggered from house to house as if in a drunken daze,
sometimes searching the same one several times a day. People fell upon the
newly dead, thinking they might have hidden some food in their clothing. Many
had even taken to chewing anything, such as girdles and shoes and the very
leather on their shields. Even the very wisps of old hay became prized as food.

Josephus himself relates something so horrible I could not bear even to treat
it as a rumor except that he swears upon having several witnesses to confirm it.
It seems there was a certain wealthy woman from the village of Bethezob, who
had come to Jerusalem for the Passover and became trapped in the city with so
many others. She had long since forfeited her material possessions to a gang of
bullies, and now every time she found food, the same rapacious villains would
come and snatch it from her. I leave Josephus to tell the rest.

It had now become impossible for her in any way to find more food.
Yet the famine pierced through her very bowels and marrow, [so that]

her passion was fired to a degree beyond famine itself. Nor did she consult with anyone but with the passion and necessity she was in. She then attempted a most unnatural thing. Snatching up her son, who was a child sucking at her breast, she said, "O thou miserable infant! For whom am I to preserve thee in this war, this famine and this sedition? As to the war with the Romans, if they preserve our lives, we must be slaves. This famine also will destroy us, even before that slavery that comes upon us. Yet are these seditious rogues more terrible than both the other. Come on, be thou my food, and be thou a fury to these seditious varlets and a byword to the world, which is all that is now wanting to complete the calamities of the Jews."

As soon as she had said this, she slew her son and then roasted him. She ate one half of him and kept the other half concealed. Upon this the rogues came in presently, and, smelling the horrid scent of this food, they threatened that they could cut her throat immediately if she did not show them the food she had prepared. She replied that she had saved a very fine portion of it for them, and quickly uncovered what was left of her son.

Thereupon the men were seized with horror and revulsion. Then she said to them, "This is my son, and what hath been done was my own doing! Come, eat of this food, for I have eaten it myself! Do not pretend to be either more tender than a woman or more compassionate than a mother! But if you do be so scrupulous, and do abominate my sacrifice, then let the rest be reserved for me as well."

After that the men went off trembling, never having seen such a sight in their lives, and left the rest of the meat to the mother. Upon which the whole city was full of this horrid story. When everyone laid this miserable case before their own eyes, they trembled as if this unheard-of action could have been done by themselves as well.[63]

On August 28 Titus called a council of his legion commanders and tribunes. The temple siege had not gone well for the Romans. The rams had battered Herod's 14-foot-thick temple walls for six days with scarcely a shiver. Soldiers had tried to undermine the foundations of the massive north gate, but the gate held fast and many legionaries lay dead from the stones the Jews had flung constantly with their captured Roman catapults. Titus had even ordered an attack with ladders, but the Jews had flung his men back upon the hard pavement with many casualties. And now at this very moment, parts of the outer cloisters

—the colonnades that lined the square courtyard perimeter—had been set afire. In one case a daring Jewish raiding party had torched the northwest cloisters in hopes it would spread to the adjacent Tower of Antonia. But neither were Romans blameless: they, too, had fired other parts of the cloisters, and Titus himself, in frustration, had ordered the temple gates set ablaze after his men failed to dislodge the foundations. Then, a day later, he changed his mind and had the fire extinguished.

The reason for the war council was Titus' own torment over the temple. I have not mentioned yet that Titus had taken up with queen Bernice, the beautiful sister of Herod Agrippa II, and one can imagine that she had entreated him incessantly to save the temple. And yet he could not ignore that it was a military sanctuary as well. Titus must have been well aware that he had already caused excessive casualties to his own men—by mounting ladders, for instance—when it was likely that burning the whole temple would facilitate its capture more than all their siege engines combined. What should he do?

Some of the commanders were adamant that the Jews would never cease rebelling as long as the temple stood. It was both their symbol of nationhood and their citadel of defiance, and it deserved to be demolished as would any enemy stronghold under the rules of war, they argued.

"And yet," said Titus, "is it right that we should avenge ourselves on an inanimate object rather than the men themselves?" Consider as well, he added, that leaving the building intact would be a monument to Rome as part of the dominions it governs.

Alexander, the Egyptian governor, and Cerealis, the Fifth Legion commander who had been with Titus and Vespasian throughout their campaigns, agreed with the latter reasoning, and they carried the others. So Titus decided that early the next day the entire army would try to overwhelm the temple defenses and even bring up all their encampments on all sides of it if the struggle became protracted.

But the plan was never carried out as envisioned. Later that same afternoon, a detachment of Roman soldiers was attempting, as Titus had ordered, to put out a fire that burned along one of the cloisters when a band of Jewish soldiers ran out from the temple and attacked them. After a few of them were killed, the Romans began to get the best of their assailants and drove them all the way back to the temple steps. But so incensed were some of them that they gave no thought to Titus' wishes. One soldier climbed on another's back with a lit torch and was able to heave it through a golden window that was open above them. The window happened to be at the end of a corridor that led to several rooms that ran along the north wall. Soon one could see smoke and flames billowing out from the upper windows and the people inside in an obvious state of great agitation.

The rest is a blur of confusion and conflicting recollections. The Roman version is that Titus was in his tent resting before his planned attack on the morrow. When an officer came running to tell him that the temple was afire, he hurried out all the way into its outer courtyard to see if it could be stopped. Behind him came most of his commanders, and behind them, soldiers tying on their armor as they ran. No trumpets had sounded, no call to battle came, but at the sight of the flames, the soldiers let out a beastly roar and rushed forward. I grant that they might have thought that some of their comrades had already launched a surprise attack and that they were now needed to join in. However, it seems more probable that this was a surge of blind fury brought by their long weeks of frustration and the fact that the temple may have contained more gold, silver and jewels than any building on earth save the temple of Saturn in Rome (and maybe not even *that* considering the low state of the state treasury). Thus, a mass of men — "each one's passion his only commander," as Josephus notes — blindly stampeded past their starving enemies through the charred temple gates and into the small inner courtyards. Behind them, more Romans ran from their camps, often falling amid the hot and smoking ruins of the outer cloisters as they scrambled towards the temple. The Jews inside were too busy defending themselves to put out fires. Outside, Titus stood shouting for the men to quench the fire, but they swept by him with fires of their own burning in their eyes. In fact, they soon lit even more parts of the temple ablaze.

As they stormed inside, the Romans found many of the people too weak even to fight. These quickly had their throats cut. Many Jews had chosen to say their farewell to the world on the altar, which lay in the Court of Priests just to the left of the entrance to the sanctuary. Within the first few minutes the altar was already piled with bodies, and a great quantity of blood ran down from it all the way to the entrance steps.

Titus, seeing that he had no control over the men inside, raced in with a few of his officers and ran to the sanctuary steps, thinking they might still save it. Since the fire was already raging around the rooms that faced the outer wall, Titus commanded a centurion and some of his men to beat soldiers with their staves — if for no other reason than to command their attention so he could address them. And yet, writes Josephus, "their passions and hatred of the Jews was too hard even for the regard they had for Cæsar" and the fear of disobeying his command.

Plunder drove them most of all, of course. The men had heard often that every room was full of money and even the walls plated with gold. Plunder they did, but they were denied much of it by their own disorganized fervor. Even as Titus implored them to leave the sanctuary intact, other fires were being set all over the temple. Now the flames and smoke were spreading so wildly that Romans and Jews alike soon were pushing and shoving their way out of the temple. Among them was Titus himself, who just managed to run back through the front gates as the flaming support structure began to crash around him. All that now remained alive inside were a handful of brave priests. Those who didn't perish quickly climbed atop the sanctuary roof. As their last desperate measure they grabbed the spikes which were set in lead to deter birds as makeshift darts and hurled them down on the Romans below.

Outside the temple the slaughter was even worse, because the Jews who fled now had Romans at their backs and the advancing legions in the courtyard in front of them. Those slain either in the temple or in the outer courtyard exceeded 10,000. Another 6,000 Jews — mostly women and children — had managed to find a some relief among the surrounding cloisters; but as the Roman officers were in the process of deciding to spare them, the soldiers had already begun slaughtering most of them.

Below, a multitude had gathered from all over the city. What they could see at the top of their highest hill was a blaze so huge that it seemed as if the entire city were on fire. But what they could hear was more horrifying. Both the walls of the courtyard and the mountains to the east had an eerie way of echoing back great noises, and now the sound was like no other.

> The flame was carried a long way and made an echo, together with the groans of those that were being slain. Nor can one imagine anything greater or more terrible than this noise; for there was at once the shout of Roman legions, who were marching all together, and a sad clamor of the seditious, who were now surrounded with fire and sword. The people who were left were beaten back by the enemy...and made sad moans at the calamity they were under.

> The multitude that was in the city joined in this outcry with those who were upon the hill. Many of those who were worn away by the famine and their mouths almost closed, when they saw the fire of the holy house broke out into groans and outcries again.[64]

The next day, Titus took stock of the destruction and determined that nothing could be saved of the temple. That same day he ordered that fires be set to the remaining parts of the cloisters that still stood as well as those small parts of the temple that had not already burned down. Perhaps the most convincing argument that Titus had not wished to destroy the temple — and that the attack had not been planned — is the fact that the treasury chambers burnt down along with everything else. According to Josephus, the losses included "an immense quantity of money, an immense number of garments and other precious goods there reposited."

Thus was the great temple of Herod destroyed. The next day the Romans brought their ensigns to the temple and set them against the eastern wall. There they made sacrifices to their eagles and standards in a way that would convince any observer that the troops worshipped these more than gods themselves.

The same day Titus agreed to grant the security of John (who had managed to flee the temple) and Simon (who had been encamped in the Palace of Herod). That afternoon the two Jewish leaders were escorted through the pedestrian bridge that led to the western entrance of the temple courtyard. As they rose through the tunnel-like walkway they came immediately upon the imposing west wall and a platform that had been erected just in front of it. Seated thereon was a stern-looking Titus and his advisors.

Before the two Jewish generals uttered a word, they were made to endure a withering outburst from Titus that excoriated the Jews for constant rebellion and ingratitude from the days of Pompey to the present. It went on for several minutes, but I think the bitter core of it was this:

> It can be nothing but the kindness of Romans which has excited you against us; who in the first place have given you this land to possess; and in the next place have set over you kings of your own nation; and in the third place have preserved the laws of your forefathers...and have withal permitted you to live, either by yourselves or among others as it shall please you.
>
> And in what is our chief favor of all, we have given you leave to gather up that tribute which is paid to God [i.e. the annual temple taxes] with such other gifts as are dedicated to him. Nor have we called to account those who carried those donations...until at length you became richer than we ourselves! You made preparations for war against us with our own money. Yes, when you were in enjoyment of all these advantages, you turned your excessive plenty against those who gave it to you, and like merciless serpents have spewed out your poison against those who treated you kindly.[65]

Seeing them standing before him proudly in their full armor was almost too much for Titus. "Even now do you stand at this time in your armor," he thundered. "Even now you cannot bring yourselves so much as to pretend to be supplicants even in this, your utmost extremity." Yet Titus added that he would not "imitate your madness." If they would surrender at once, he told the rebel leaders, "I will grant you your lives and I will act like a master of the family. What cannot be healed shall be punished, and the rest I will preserve for my own use."

To this John and Simon answered that they could not accept, because they had sworn never to surrender to a Roman. But if they were granted permission to leave Jerusalem with their families, they would go to the desert and leave the city to him.

Titus glared down, sputtering, as if scarcely able to comprehend that the conquered were actually making demands on him. When he regained his composure, he dismissed them with this proclamation: that they should never again come to him as deserters, nor hope for any further security. For from this point on he would treat all to the rules of warfare and spare no one.

The next day Roman troops burned and plundered everything in the Lower City, including houses that had been stacked full of bodies of people who had died in the famine. They also burned the repository of Jewish archives and the Sanhedrin meeting house, which had been left standing atop the south cloister of the temple. All that now remained of the resistance were the Upper City and the adjoining Palace of Herod, the latter being as much fortress as it was residence.

One might think this task would take but a few days. It was to take the Romans another 30 days. For one thing, building up banks against the palace walls meant extending the search for materials to a 33-mile radius of Jerusalem. But even before the rams again began their ominous battering, the outcome was obvious: the Jewish nation was already obliterated for generations to come. Moreover, Titus' men were battle-fatigued and literally arm-weary from the drudgery of killing. I myself am weary of reporting about bloodshed and you, dear reader, have probably been sick to your stomach several times already. Yet, we have a problem: we cannot merely leave so many souls suspended in ether. So I will summarize what ensued.

When the Roman rams finally knocked a hole in the palace wall and poured forth, they found many Jews already dead by their own hands and others too weak from hunger to resist any longer. Even those in the great towers above also surrendered, causing Titus to exclaim, "It was none other than God who ejected the Jews out of these fortifications, for what could the hands of men or machines do to overthrow these towers?"

The Upper City was stormed and burned. But most often when the soldiers entered houses in search of plunder, "they found in them entire families of dead men, and the upper rooms full of corpses...of such as died in the famine," writes Josephus. "They stood in horror at such sights and went out without touching anything."

Some 2,000 persons were discovered hiding in subterranean caverns, together with as many corpses and a considerable treasure. John of Gischala was among them and sent word asking Cæsar's right hand of security. It was denied. Simon held out longer, but finally surfaced for want of food and was spotted wandering about in the streets of the Upper City. He was preserved for a certain purpose, as you shall see.

Despite the fact that much of the temple treasury disappeared in the fire, Titus learned that great quantities had been hidden, and several priests were willing to tell him where in exchange for their lives. Plunder from other caches and deserters was so enormous that gold sold for about half its usual price throughout Syria for several months.

One of Titus' secretaries, the freedman Fronto, was given the task of determining who should live or die. Some 40,000 persons – mostly those who had deserted prior to the temple destruction – were allowed freedom to live anywhere but Jerusalem. Fronto culled out 700 of the handsomest young men, to be reserved for the triumph in Rome. He marked 97,000 other adult males for slavery, some to be distributed to the provinces for gladiatorial and wild beast shows, but most to be sent to the mines of Egypt.

While Fronto was making his decisions, 11,000 prisoners died of famine because their Roman guards withheld food for no other reason than pure hatred.

In all, it is estimated that 1,100,000 Jews perished from famine, disease or battle. No one could argue with Josephus when he wrote that this "exceeded all the destructions that either men or God ever brought upon the world" at any one time or place.

Titus now ordered the entire city and temple demolished with only a few exceptions. He left the inner west wall of the city and its three strongest towers (Phasælus, Hippicus and Mariamne). This he did for the convenience of housing a Roman garrison, and at the same time, to show posterity how well-fortified a city he had conquered. But after the rest had been demolished, Josephus observed that "it was so thoroughly laid even with the ground by those who dug up to the foundation, that there was nothing left to make those who came thither believe it had ever been inhabited."

In his last act in Jerusalem, Titus assembled all of his legions and thanked them for their courage and devotion to him. Seated on a long platform, he then presided as a seemingly endless procession of men had their names read by their commanders for having performed this and that heroic deed. These the young princeps presented with golden crowns, golden ornaments around their necks, long spears of gold, and so forth. All were elevated to a higher rank. Then Titus sacrificed a large number of oxen and began a three-day feast. After it was over the legions were officially dispersed, two back to Egypt, several cohorts to the Euphrates River positions, two to accompany Titus and his captives to Cæsarea and the rest to their camps in various provinces to the west. Only the tenth legion was left at the battle site to guard what would become a mere desert garrison.

In Cæsarea, Titus celebrated his father's birthday by giving games at which 2,500 Jewish captives perished. Similar numbers died when Titus went on to visit

Berytus, Cæsarea Philippi and Antioch. Yet it is interesting that when the leaders of Antioch petitioned him to reject all the Jews from their city, he dismissed them coldly. "How could this be done," he replied, "when the country to which you would oblige them to retire has been destroyed and no other place will receive them?"

It would be two more years before the Romans could actually claim to have subdued the whole Jewish nation, for a thousand Sicarii still looked down defiantly from the mountaintop that Herod had leveled to build the fortress of Masada. Titus, in fact, marched right past it when he led his two legions on a farewell visit to Egypt as the year drew to a close. On the way they passed the forlorn scene of what had been Jerusalem. Titus claims to have despaired at seeing such a "melancholy site." Yet his father, at least, would have been soothed at learning that the tenth legion was busying itself uncovering a bonanza of gold and silver in the rubble.

The following spring Titus and his two legions, with their captives and booty, sailed from Alexandria to Rome, where the city was bedecked with flowers in expectation of seeing a joint triumph – a long-delayed one to celebrate the emperor's victories over his rivals and the other the son's stupendous exploits in war.

After Vespasian had spent hours walking in the tiresome procession, he would lament to everyone within earshot, "It serves me right for being such a fool as to want a triumph in my old age." But for the 30-year-old Titus it was a day of pure splendor. It was in the sun-streaked blue of a spring evening that everyone from miles around stood packed along roadsides or waved from windows and rooftops. Others sat in theaters, for the procession would wind through them as well in order to give everyone a chance to see the victors, their captives and the spoils from the distant and mysterious orient.

First the soldiers marched in procession. On the Palatine Hill, Vespasian and Titus came out crowned with laurel, clothed in their purple-rimmed togas. They proceeded as far as Octavian's Walk where they were met by the Senate and equestrian leaders. After Vespasian gave a short speech and both men sacrificed, with their heads covered by priestly shawls, the soldiers gave up great shouts of acclamation. Then they were all sent off to a banquet provided by the emperor.

Now it was time to display all that had come from Jerusalem. First came marchers carrying a variety of riches – silver, gold, ivory sculptures and jewels, giant purple wall hangings that had been embroidered in Babylonia, the golden table from the temple and the large golden menorah, or holder of seven candlesticks. The last of all the spoils was the temple ark, containing the Laws of the Jews. Later, Vespasian would build the Temple of Peace, which put these trophies on display for Romans and tourists to see for years to come.

Next came people dressed in purple garments interwoven with gold, each carrying the large image of a god made of costly materials. Then marched the male captives from Jerusalem, all of them adorned in fine dress as well. But the greatest delight of the crowd was reserved for the great platforms, each carried by 60 or more bearers, that depicted various scenes from the battles that Vespasian and Titus had fought throughout Judea. Some were three or four tiers tall. Some were built upon golden carpets. On this one the audience could see squadrons of enemies slain; on that one a stout wall battered by Roman siege engines; here an army pours through a breached wall; over there the replica of a temple actually burning with fire. Trade guilds throughout the city had put all their skills into the "walking platforms" and never was the result better. And I almost forgot: on the top of each exhibit stood the commander of the troops who had performed the deed depicted.

At the end of the procession trod Simon, son of Giorus, who had been led throughout by a rope over his head and exposed to the torments of the throng that pressed against him on the narrow parade path. Now came the last and most ritualistic part of the ceremony. The procession wound up to the steps of the Temple of Jupiter Capitoline, which was nearing full restoration. Here the crowds suddenly fell silent as an ancient Roman tradition unfolded. Simon was brought forward; and as he stood proudly, quietly erect, an executioner swung a heavy sword and lopped off his head.

The triumph had ended, as rules of Roman warfare had long dictated. As the crowd at the temple let up a mighty cheer, the throngs below knew what it meant, and their roar cascaded across the Forum below, to the 30,000 in the Theater of Marcellus, and even across the Tiber to Trastevere, the crowded section of narrow alleys and strange food smells where thousands of Jews still attempted to ply their ancient trades.

. . . .

EVERY JEW FROM SPAIN TO BABYLONIA was affected by the destruction of Jerusalem in two ways. To the extent that they lived in isolated quarters amidst suspicious and unfriendly Gentiles, they could now expect more visible expressions of enmity and more risk to their personal safety. Thus, each time some legionary swaggered out of a tavern just as a Jew happened to pass by, there was always the instant possibility of a cursing that sparks a fight that produces crowds and riots and killings.

The second thing that was common to all Jewish adult males is that they no longer paid annual tribute to the temple in Jerusalem. Instead, they were now taxed an equivalent sum to support the temple of Jupiter Capitoline in Rome. Gone forever, along with the pilgrimages to the festivals of Passover and Pentecost, was the proud reassurance of having a central secular storehouse of wealth that gave evidence to a powerful religion and a great people.

These changes were dramatic, to be sure, but beyond Judea the life of religious worship was changed little because the community synagogue, rabbi and elders remained the center of it. It was the Jews of Judea who now had to absorb these institutions themselves. With the obliteration of the temple and slaughter of so many eminent citizens, the Sanhedrin was no more and the influence of the priestly families crippled beyond repair. Even the Essene community at Qumran, a traditional refuge for priestly reflection, had been shattered and its buildings fired to the ground. The absence of temple ritual and its priests as a central authority placed these things in the hands of individual congregations and their rabbis, who were mostly Pharisees.

And as Jews re-established order among themselves, Jewish Christians were not a part of it. These Christians had fled Jerusalem well before the siege and now took pains to convince Roman soldiers that they were in no way a sect of Judaism. So it is no wonder that Christians would be barred from the synagogue, if for no other reason than the risk that they might even be agents of Rome.

In any case, a movement had already begun to preserve and purify Jewish traditions. Even as Titus and his legions were breaking camp to leave the wreckage of Jersusalem, a group of surviving scholars had taken up residence in Jamnia, just 30 miles west where the coastal plain begins. They included priests who had fled early from the procurator Florus, Pharisees who had escaped the tyranny of John and Simon, and those who had been pardoned by Titus and his freedman Fronto in the aftermath of battle.

Their focus now was the Torah. Together the scholars began a long, painstaking effort to decide what scriptures it should include. Moreover, many versions of the Law had been in circulation throughout the world and the men at Jamnia wanted to arrive at a single authorized canon. When this was accomplished it would then be translated into Greek for the Jews of the Diaspora. All this would take years.

The men of Jamnia labored under the scrutiny of the tenth legion, now garrisoned in the towers of Herod that rose above the rubble of Jerusalem. But the scholars enjoyed at least some peace of mind: their project had received the personal blessing of Vespasian and Titus thanks to one man – the turncoat Josephus. Still a young man and now consigned to the gardens of Titus' household, he would begin writing an account of the Jewish wars that would, unsurprisingly, extol the achievements of his Roman patron. After that Josephus would begin work on an extensive history of the Jewish people from the creation of mankind.

. . . .

BY THE TIME THE ROMANS had begun the siege of Jerusalem, it would seem that most of the Jewish Christians within the city had managed to flee it. Even as the battles raged, the Jewish Christian leaders of Judea had largely re-settled in Pella, which lies about 60 miles northeast of Jerusalem along the slopes that overlook the River Jordan and Samaria to the west. I am told their leader is Symeon, who has presided over the community ever since James, the brother of Jesus, was killed. Under Symeon's guidance, the Christian communities in Judea and Samaria have continued to grow in numbers — partly, I'm sure, because the synagogues have rejected Jewish Christians from their congregations.

This growth may also be due to the same reasons that have affected all Christians throughout the empire with the end of Nero, his persecutions, the civil war and the Jewish wars. With the peaceful reign of Vespasian have come at least five important changes, which I shall now cite.

First, Christians now have more freedom to meet in the open. I do not imply that Vespasian ever studied or encouraged Christianity. In fact, there were some who feared a return to the former era when the emperor banned astrologers from Rome; but I rather think this was because they tended to conflict with his own favorite star gazers and issue prophecies designed to enflame the ambitions of unscrupulous men. No, I mean only that Vespasian is naturally inclined to kindliness and is not disposed to disrupt those who do not deliberately demean or threaten the gods of Rome.

This freedom is also more possible because Christians are now seen by the average Roman citizen as more distinct from Jews than before the war on Jerusalem. As I said earlier, the Jews themselves contributed to this when the Christians departed Jerusalem before the siege. Jews saw it as confirmation of their long-held suspicions that their ties to Jesus were stronger than to the Torah, and the bonds were broken when the Christians did not remain to share in the city's defense. Jews even found it irritating that Christians continued to quote rabbinical scripture in their worship.

Christians in turn often viewed the destruction of the temple as God's punishment for rejecting the savior he had sent them. And when citizens throughout the empire harassed and made miserable their Jewish neighbors during the wars in Syria, Christians were quick to tell the persecutors that they were in no way associated with Judaism. Finally, I believe more people now proclaimed Jesus openly because they had come to believe that the risk of ridicule and even martyrdom was expected as part of being an active disciple.

The second change in Vespasian's reign flows from the first one. As it became possible for Christians to become more visible, new leaders rose by necessity to walk in the footsteps of the original apostles and evangelists. Thus, the Christian Titus, who learned at the feet of Paul, now heads the churches of Crete. Timothy, Paul's companion from Asia Minor to Rome, is now called "bishop" of Ephesus (although I am sure the apostle John would be if not for his advanced age). Similarly, in Athens the patriarch is none other than the Æropagite Dionysius, who became the first Christian convert after Paul's address to the Athenians in the Areopagus, or chief meeting place. In Alexandria, the patriarch is the same Anianus, the cobbler who mended the sandal of Mark and then became his first convert. And in Rome, the bishop and principal minister of the gospel is Linus, who was soon recognized as such after the death of Peter and Paul.

The various titles that we see associated with their names are very new to Christian communities. They certainly suggest a tendency towards a formal hierarchy of authority, which helps explain the third major change in Vespasian's reign, and that is the devolvement toward a uniform worship ritual. It was as if Christians had collectively come to the conclusion that if they were now deprived of Jesus and the apostles in the flesh, they must take their strength from common worship and a common effort to support evangelism beyond their immediate communities.

Ironically, the efforts of Christians to detach themselves from Judaism are belied by the fact that the heart of their worship service seems to follow that of any synagogue. That is, they begin by reading passages of Jewish Scripture that may have a bearing on their own people and problems. Yet they also read from the letters of Paul, Peter, the gospel according to Mark and other works (which, ironically, seem to be written more by Jewish Christians than not). The same can be said for the hymns and psalms that are said and sung at various intervals in the service. Some are of Christian authorship, but most are taken from rabbinical scripture.

Each service also includes several common prayers to God, and here I think the Christian is more apt to depart from the Jew. In the earliest years of the Christian house churches, I am told that a time was reserved in which people would pray in their own way at the same time. Some might be making esthetic utterances, as in a trance, or speaking in tongues, while others prayed aloud to ask God's blessing or offer him thanks. Some of this continues today, but prayer today is more apt to be led by the leader of the church as the others listen in silence. Then the leader may ask if others have special prayers to offer, at which time the congregation listens as he speaks. I should add that during the week, a Christian is expected to recite the Lord's Prayer, which was first told to them by Jesus.

> Our father, who art in heaven,
> Hallowed by thy name,
> Thy kingdom come.
> Thy will be done,
> On earth as it is in heaven.

Give us this day our daily bread;
And forgive us our debts,
As we also have forgiven our debtors;
And lead us not into temptation
But deliver us from evil.
For thine is the kingdom forever and ever. Amen.[66]

Baptism is something that may be part of a given service or may be reserved for special occasions. Again, this ritual seems to have been based on the Jewish rite of purification by water. Christians believe that by being immersed in "living" or "flowing" water, a person washes away sinful habits and begins a new life. But in another sense, the person being immersed shares in the crucifixion of Jesus and shares in his resurrection when he emerges from the water.

After all these things take place in a service, the head of the congregation, or perhaps an elder, will deliver a prepared oratory on some insights about the life of Jesus or how to lead a life of service to one's fellows. Yet the longest ritual of the service is what follows next: the Lord's Supper. Now in this we have a distinctly Christian tradition unless one wants to compare it to the meals that some of the trade guilds take together.

No persons may take part in the Lord's Supper unless they have declared themselves for Jesus and joined a particular congregation. The meal originates from the last night Jesus was with his disciples, when he took bread and said, "This is my body, which is broken for you." And after the meal he took some wine and said, "This cup is the new covenant in my blood. Do this, as often as you drink it, in remembrance of me."

This is a full meal today, and more than once Paul had to remind congregations that it was intended to fulfill a spiritual need and not merely one's stomach. Yet, I daresay that few churches today can say that they merely break bread and serve wine — and there are at least two good reasons why. Devout Christians are expected to fast on both Wednesdays and Fridays, and when Sunday comes around one often looks forward to a full meal, prepared by the women of the church, as much as one does a good sermon. In addition, the meal is often used to serve members who are poor or ill. In many churches it is the role of deacons to take part of the Sunday meal to the homes of members who can't attend.

The Lord's Supper typifies the fourth change in Christian churches that emerged in Vespasian's time: their growth as providers of care to the poor, the homeless, the elderly, widows, orphans and the afflicted. By this time, 40 years after the resurrection, the immediacy of the Parousia, or second coming of Jesus, had receded to the extent that few Christians were selling all their possessions and keeping watch for the final day of judgment. Yet, churches were sharing their resources like never before to reflect Jesus' love in acts of charity and compassion. Is a Christian traveler new to the city? Let him seek lodging in a Christian home. Is an old woman lonely? Let her seek comfort in a Christian congregation. After all, do we not still live in a world where rich men abandon enfeebled slaves and the most a poor widow can hope from an emperor is the bread dole? People once saw Christians only as a strange group that performed suspicious rituals and banded together in self-defense. Now one hears people in streets saying, even if begrudgingly, "Look how Christians love one another! Look how they care for each other!" They are amazed as well that a church may contain rich people, poor, women and slaves all behaving as equals. Indeed, where else would one find women leaders, as those who serve as church deacons? Where else would there be an Order of Widows that makes visits to the bedridden and helps to raise orphans?

Christians, of course, have always cared for one another; but in the grim days of Nero's persecutions, when whole families were shattered, their numbers did not necessarily grow. Now they *have,* and one result is that some churches have become too large and busy to be contained in private homes and villas. Even the Lord's Supper has created problems – and resentment – when some are served in the homeowner's inner dining room while others must eat outside in the courtyard at rough tables. And so, a few congregations in the provinces, where land is less dear, have actually built or acquired separate buildings for their churches. In crowded cities, such as Rome, I know of one church that now occupies several rooms on the ground floor of a large brick tenement.

Growth is what the apostles sought, of course, when they spread the gospel, but it has also brought a fifth change in recent years. The more the numbers, the greater propensity for debate, division, sects, false prophets and rivalries among competing personalities. Paul had written in his letter to the Romans that Gentile Christians were "a wild shoot grafted into the olive tree that is Israel." But without Paul or the other apostles to prune it when needed, the wild shoot grew in many directions after their passing. Thus, while most churches of Antioch consider themselves the fulfillment of Judaism, most of those in Asia Minor consider themselves a new religion. In Ephesus some church members have stirred up a tempest by proclaiming that, since they have already been granted eternal life by God's grace, they see no need to do good deeds or follow the Ten Commandments. Elsewhere in Asia, a few preachers state that because Jesus was a spiritual being to begin with, he did not actually "die" on the cross and was therefore not resurrected. So why should they be willing to be martyrs?

In some churches, members argue about who has the more direct genealogy to the family line of Jesus. In Antioch, the churches have been dazzled by the magic tricks of Menander, a disciple of Simon the Magus, (whom Peter tracked down in Rome and silenced). Now this successor again uses more magic as he claims to emulate the miracles of Jesus.

In Alexandria, a "Christian" named Cerinthus has attracted a following of fools by reciting tales of wonder that have been revealed to him by "angels." When Christ returns to his kingdom, he says, it will be on earth, and Jerusalem will be reborn as a paradise of carnal pleasures, including a thousand years of uninterrupted wedding festivities.

Much more formidable, however, is the onslaught of philosophical schools, each with its body of literature and erudite teachers. One can, for instance, find a fair number of Ebionites, who believe that Jesus was but a man, born of natural union, who elevated his ordinary circumstances merely by learning and growth of character. However, the most enduring "sect," if such it can be called, are the Gnostics, whom I have previously mentioned. Knowledge of God, they say, can be "earned" by study of many sources, of which Jesus is only one. To be sure, Jesus possessed a special knowledge, they say; but by learning his teachings, one can attain equality with him and even go on to loftier levels of excellence.

Some Christians bemoan the fact that leadership in each church is passing from the hands of several elder members to men with more authoritative titles such as pastor and presbyter and bishop. The common need to sort out and give guidance regarding cases like the above is one more reason why Paul himself foresaw the need in his last days when he told Timothy, as I think he would have any of these men:

> I charge you in the presence of God and of Christ Jesus who is to judge the living and the dead, and by his appearing and his kingdom: preach the word, be urgent in season and out of season, convince, rebuke and exhort. Be unfailing in patience and in teaching. For the time is coming when people will not endure sound teaching, but having itching ears they will accumulate for themselves teachers who suit their own likings, and will turn away from listening to the truth and wander into myths. As for you, always be steady, endure suffering, do the work of an evangelist, fulfill your ministry.[67]

The main reason why Paul believed that ordinary men could carry on Christ's mission successfully against so many distractions was that the message itself is uncomplicated: *salvation comes from God's grace to all who will simply believe in him, love him and love his neighbor.* Paul and the other apostles believed that this one bright beacon would be sufficient to keep a congregation on course provided that the pastor and presbyters kept a firm hand on the tiller.

The winds that could blow this ship off course were the words of those who preached that only this man possessed the Truth or only that philosophy spoke the mind of God, or that God blessed this or that bodily nourishment. And again, Paul's reasoning was simple and clear: even the wisest of men is but a foolish child to God. If knowledge of God were a great river and the wisest of all philosophers were to dip into it, he could retain no more than a cupful.

But unlike knowledge, we have been given something by God that is boundless, the power of love. For as Paul wrote to the quarreling Corinthians many years ago:

> If I speak in the tongues of men and of angels, but have not love, I am a noisy gong or a clanging cymbal. And if I have prophetic powers and understand all mysteries and all knowledge, and if I have all faith, so as to remove mountains, but have not love, I am nothing. If I give away all I have, and if I deliver my body to be burned, but have not love, I am nothing.

> Love is patient and kind. Love is not jealous or boastful. It is not arrogant or rude. Love does not insist on its own way. It is not irritable or resentful. It does not rejoice at wrong, but rejoices in the right. Love bears all things, believes all things, hopes all things, endures all things.

> Love never ends. As for prophecy, it will pass away. As for tongues, they will cease. As for knowledge, it will pass away. For our knowledge is imperfect and our prophecy is imperfect. But when the perfect comes, the imperfect shall pass away.

> When I was a child, I spoke like a child. I thought like a child. I reasoned like a child. When I became a man I gave up childish ways. For now we see in a mirror dimly, but then face to face. Now I know in part. Then I will understand fully, even as I have been fully understood. So faith, hope and love abide — these three.

> But the greatest of these is love.[68]

. . . .

LETTER FROM ROME — JULY, A.D. 81

My Dear Eumenes, Greetings

If the weather in Pergamum is as bright and cheerful as it is this day in Rome, I would have expected your letter to reflect a little more sunshine. But it seems to have come from a sour old man rather than from Pergamum's most prosperous book publisher! You asked once again why you have received no books on the Flavian Amphitheater. Well, I might ask again — as does our partner Literato — where are the promised anthologies of the letters of the Christians Paul, Peter, Luke, and so forth? Your argument that we have no proof of buyers for them is specious until we can at least put them on the shelves and find out.

And in the same vein, it is time for you to begin work on the large history of the Christians and Jews in the Roman empire that you have so far stored for me (along with, I am sure, the money I sent you to cover the production). Thanks to the enlightened Titus, Rome today is flowering with literary freedom, and the Street of Booksellers is full of new works and can look forward to more of them throughout our emperor's long life.

But I fear that none of these will be forthcoming unless we resolve an issue that you yourself have brought to a head in your letter. You ask if I am a Christian — as if whether I am or not will change the fact that we are blood relations and partners in business. You also ask it in a way that one might interrogate a youth who has run off to join a gang of brigands that lives in caves. I will give you your answer, but it is not so simple as being "here" today and "there" tomorrow. Rather than read this between talking to customers and copyists, wait until you have gone home, poured yourself a glass of your favorite Artemis red and seated yourself under one of those broad shade trees in your courtyard. Do me that one favor, will you please?

Very well, now. Let us begin by recalling the fact that while you have been free to prosper in Pergamum, the whim of a dictator made me the son of a slave in Alexandria. Like boys everywhere, I don't recall thinking seriously about the "order" of things in the real world until I was age 16 or 17. Until then I suppose my life was divided between studying to be a copyist in two languages and sneaking off to fish in the streams of the delta. When I began to observe people and events outside of my narrow existence, I wasn't mature enough to embrace a philosophy or religion. But I did question many things and begin to oppose others. For instance, in the temples I saw some priests worship snakes while others bowed to the divinity of cattle. One day on the river bank I saw a dozen slaves beating the reeds and bulrushes to trap ibises. And I knew why instantly: these beautiful white birds would be killed by the thousands in a temple in order to bring good luck to some wretch who paid the priests a profitable sum as his ancestors had done for centuries without really knowing why. It was about then that I realized the annual festival procession I had most enjoyed watching as a child was in honor of the birthday of the crocodile god — who might devour me if it were not properly appeased.

It wasn't long before I began to learn that even great men did not initiate momentous enterprises unless guided by the cleverly ambiguous prophecy of an oracle (which at least is human), or just as often according to the way entrails of a chicken happened to spill upon an altar. Then I realized the awful truth that these same men could snuff my life out like blowing on a lamp, or send whole columns of slaves like me marching off to the quarries for the rest of their lives.

At first, I saw none of this personally. I kept my nose in my tablets and scrolls. But when I was approaching manhood there was a slave girl about my age named

Herais who tended the well and the kitchen in the household next door. The grace of her body was exceeded only by the sweetness of her smile. You can be sure that I would often pop up when she went to the well or went for a walk to pick flowers for the dining tables, and she would listen with devoted attention as I attempted to captivate her with my nervous prattle.

Then one day she failed to appear at the usual time. It ruined my day. When a week went by with no sight of her I knew that it must be because she found me loathsome. But then I worried that she had taken sick. In a few more days I waited behind the house until I saw the large old woman who ran the kitchen step outside to cool off in the shade. I walked up and boldly asked her if I might see the girl Herais. The woman sized me up and I think recognized me as Herais' awkward and amorous friend. "She's gone off," the cook said brusquely and went back through the kitchen door.

Her words stabbed me like a dagger, but I soon realized that she had only been trying to protect me from reality. Not long afterwards the old gardener from the same household told me that the master of the house — a man in his fifties — had been using Herais as his bed toy since before she had even reached puberty. Now he had sent her off to his brother's estate on the Nile because she had become pregnant. I never saw her again, and I still wonder if the innocent countenance she showed me was the only touch of a loving courtship she would ever experience.

Oh, you don't want to hear such things, cousin, do you? Indeed, I have spared you the experiences of my past because I could not bear to see you so uncomfortable. But the question you have asked is the key that unlocks them from the strongbox that sits in the attic of my mind. Later in the same year that Herais disappeared I began working at the restored library in Alexandria. Jewish scholars were among the biggest users of books there, and I began to read many of their ancient works. Then suddenly no Jews came to the library and their works disappeared from our shelves. And why? Because one man in far-off Rome named Gaius Caligula decided that it was quite acceptable for all the Jews in Alexandria to be persecuted because they were late in praying for his success. I watched from a balcony atop the library as gangs of my fellow Greeks ran wild in the streets killing and looting the homes of a half million people who until then had been their peaceful neighbors.

Even then I still didn't know what I believed in — only that I was angry and knew what I did not believe. Certainly I didn't worship anything, yet I found myself reading Jewish books of worship because they often were the mirror of my own feelings. As the Jewish quarter burned, I would turn to a psalm by an ancient prophet named Habakkuk and read it aloud as if I were the rabbi Attalos weeping the bitter tears for everyone below:

> O Lord, how long shall I cry for help
> and you will not listen/
> Or cry to you, "Violence!"
> and you will not save.

Habakkuk even reminds the God of the Jews that he has promised to avenge them.

> O Lord, you have marked them [the evil ones]
> for judgment;
> And you, O Rock, have established them for punishment.
> Your eyes are too pure to behold evil
> and you cannot look on wrongdoing;
> Why do you then look on the treacherous
> and are silent when the wicked swallow
> those more righteous than they?

And then Habakkuk laments that his people have been left without protection.

> You have made people like the fish of the sea,
> like crawling things that have no ruler.[1]

Yes, this is how I continued to feel as I grew older. By the time I was 40 I had come to understand that there is even less protection or justice for the mighty. The most exciting day of my life up to that point was when I learned that I would be going to Rome to work under the freedman Pallas. Why? Because this exalted servant of Claudius and Nero had snapped his fingers one day and decided that it would be convenient to have some copyists from Alexandria to help him with his petitions and correspondence from Egypt. Yet I had been here but two years when the young Nero decided he had become wiser than his long-time advisors. Pallas was poisoned and his entire retinue re-distributed among other imperial favorites. I am lucky that my social status was beneath anyone's notice and my library skills of use to the quæstor in charge of the Tabularium. But I was no less bitter at how others could claim me like a barnyard animal.

Did you know that when I had finally saved enough to purchase manumission that I still regarded it as a grim duty? Picture the scene in a large courtroom. A few times each month, a panel of five senators and five equestrians sits idly gossiping among themselves as a magistrate parades what may be 100 persons by him one at a time. After establishing that a man's petition is legal, the magistrate asks his "jury" to pass judgment and the bored nobles turn from their chattering long enough to wave a hand in his direction. At this the magistrate taps the slave on the shoulder with a rod to symbolize his last beating at the hands of a master and bids him good luck.

Most of the candidates were dressed as for a festival day. Men wept with gratitude and offered praises to Jupiter, caressing their new freedman's caps as though they were silver urns. I stood there quietly and congratulated myself only to the extent that, at the age of 51, I had risen from a fifth-class resident of Rome to fourth class. I had paid good money, yet was still not trusted enough to join the military, could not become a magistrate and could not marry into a senatorial family. Nor did I smile even though I may have been the only one there who was not bound to a former master. All the others would remain his loyal client, paying obeisance at his morning reception for the rest of their lives and perhaps risking those lives to render him some special service.

I was liberated from a master, yet I still had found nothing worthy enough to serve of my own free will. My life was more burdensome because my years of learning had encumbered my mind with all the gods and men I had rejected.

But wait, you say? What about the greatest of Greek philosophers? What about the noble Apollonius, who still lives as an example of the virtuous life? These, too, I spat out, though certainly not so bitterly. You often refer to Socrates, so let us cite him as an example. He believed that virtue comes from knowledge. That is, if a man only knew the proper thing to do in any given situation, he would do it. If so, one can assume that Nero failed only for lack of better tutors. I rest my case.

Apollonius justifies only slightly more analysis. True, the sage of Tyana's exemplary personal traits have stood him well during his long and colorful life. He himself would agree that these tools were adopted so as to sharpen his senses and enhance his quest. So what was this mission? First, it was to understand the proper form of prayer, sacrifice and other forms of ritual at the various temples he frequented. And all this, in turn, was necessary so that Apollonius could acquire knowledge of the gods and their intentions.

And what did he learn about these gods? First, that there are many indeed: Apollonius has discovered through his great powers that there are "many gods in heaven and many in the sea, and many in the fountains and the streams, and many round about the earth, and some even under the earth," so that if you believe this, poor Eumenes, you had better pull your sheet tightly over your eyes at night because they are probably dancing above you and lying under the bed waiting out there in the dark for you to make your nightly privy call!

So, you see, Apollonius is first a prisoner of ritual and a slave to many gods and icons. And he, like that slave boy from Alexandria, is puppet to the whims of the mighty who live unseen in the "ether," as he says, and go about their own lives of lust, greed, jealousy and murder. If a mortal finds mercy among them, it is only because he may be lucky enough to find them in a good mood when he begs for it with the right offering of flesh and incense.

But wait: our famous sage is not only a slave to idols, but an eager purveyor of superstition. When I first read of his life, my heart was gladdened because Apollonius visited Egypt and did what I would have been killed for: he repudiated the priests in each temple he visited for their bloody sacrifices of bulls, geese and other animals. But it turned out that all Apollonius was merely saying was that his brand of superstition (which happened to be sacrificing of waxen images of animals) was better than theirs, for superstition accompanies him wherever he goes. Thus, the sage's biographer writes that when he was in Sparta and was contemplating a sail to Italy, he had a dream in which a very tall and beautiful woman embraced him and asked that he visit her first. She told Apollonius she was the nurse of Zeus, and he saw that she wore a wreath that "held everything that there is on the earth or sea." Now Apollonius says he pondered all this and concluded that he should go to Crete, which is regarded as the nurse of Zeus, because the god was born on that island. So off he went, his life course directed by a dream. The only difference between Apollonius and Tiberius in this regard is that the latter would have referred the matter to his astrologer before sailing.

But what, you may ask, of the sage's well-witnessed power of prophecy? What about his being in Egypt and telling Vespasian that the temple of Jupiter Capitoline had been fired the day before? I agree, dear cousin, that some men do have an unexplained gift to predict events. Are they perhaps given a peek inside the window of God's workshop? I only know that Apollonius has done it many times. Yet, let me tell you about the time Apollonius was sailing from Sicily to Greece with several followers. When their ship put into the island of Leucas on the Ionian Sea, the sage suddenly declared that it would be wise if his party changed to another ship in the harbor because the one they were on would soon sink. So everyone did, following their teacher like so many sheep. As they boarded the new ship, they saw their former craft depart and quickly sink like a stone soon after leaving the harbor — all of which Apollonius seemed to view with calm indifference.

He is said to have great powers of divination as well. Let me offer one such instance. Several years ago, when Ephesus was in the throes of a plague, the people invited Apollonius to become their physician in curing it. The sage arrived and ordered that all the citizens assemble in the theater. As his biographer reports:

> There [in the theater] he saw what seemed to be an old mendicant blinking his eyes as if blind. He carried a wallet with a crust of bread in it. He was clad in rags and was very squalid of countenance. Apollonius quickly arranged the Ephesians around him and said: "Pick up as many stones as you can and hurl them at the enemy of the gods."

> Now the Ephesians wondered what he meant, and were shocked at the idea of murdering a stranger so manifestly miserable, for he was begging and praying them to take mercy upon him. Nevertheless, Apollonius insisted that the Ephesians launch their stones on him and not let him go.[2]

Well, they did so, dear cousin, and the plague was miraculously cured, according to Apollonius' biographer. After all the stones had piled up so high around the fallen old man that no one could see beneath them, Apollonius ordered them to take the stones away. And there, O bedazzled citizens of Ephesus, lay the dead body of a mad dog as large as a lion!

Perhaps I could also tell you about the time when Apollonius broke up a wedding and exposed the bride as a vampire who was fattening up her handsome groom at the wedding feasts so that she could devour him later. But I know by now you are asking: Where does all this lead?

For me, the path has led to men who would not have allowed a condemned ship to sail. Nor would they have stoned a harmless old beggar. You see, what has driven

Apollonius onward was not just the perfection of worship ritual nor the gathering of knowledge from the gods, but the belief that men who attain that knowledge can themselves become gods. And all this is demolished quickly by Paul of Tarsus with a simple beam of sunshine. He taught that man can never attain complete knowledge because knowledge constantly changes or "passes away." Paul said that our confidence and trust should not be placed in knowledge of God, but in God himself.

Go back to that psalm of the Jewish prophet Habakkuk that I wrote earlier in this letter. Habakkuk upbraided God for not protecting his people and even for abandoning them. This was my own constant lamentation for so many years that I came to forget that the psalm has a different ending. For Habakkuk kept talking to God. He finally says:

> *I will stand at my watchpost*
> *and station myself on the rampart.*
> *I will keep watch to see what he will say to me,*
> *and what he will answer concerning my complaint.*
> *Then at last Habakkuk was answered:*
> *Write the vision:*
> *make it plain on tablets*
> *so that a runner may read.*
> *For there is still a vision for the appointed time;*
> *it speaks of the end, and does not lie.*
> *If it seems to tarry, wait for it;*
> *It will surely come. It will not delay.*
> *Look at the proud!*
> *Their spirit is not right in them,*
> *but the righteous live by their faith.*[3]

Eumenes, it was only six or seven years ago that I met Christians. Paul and

Peter were already dead, but what I read of their fragmented writings was more powerful than all the tomes of Homer or Plato or Seneca. What they require is that we trust God to take care of us rather than our ideas of God. In other words, God's love does not depend on the perfection of my ideas or knowledge. Therefore, the only way to gain salvation is through his grace. In the course of our lives, the only way we might truly know a measure of God is not by our knowledge, but to reflect to others the love he has for us.

Am I then a Christian? Well, once I accepted that we know God only by reflecting his love, I could not very well keep him in my dark closet. I became part of a group of Christians. So, yes, Eumenes, I am a Christian and have been one for quite some time.

Why haven't I told you before? I had hoped that the manuscript I sent you would fill you with questions and show you the light. But then I also feared that you could not bear the news of it. I use the word "bear" in the same way that Jesus used it with his disciples on the night before he died on the cross. He said, "I still have many things to say to you, but you cannot bear them now." He meant not that they would find his words unpleasant, but that they did not have the foundation to bear the weight of them, as a bridge must withstand an army marching over it.

However, you have brought this matter to a head and I will continue with the truth. I was already a Christian at the time Diodoros came with the money and manuscripts. So was Diodoros. I had hoped he would "grow" on you.

Why did I move to the Subura? Yes, it was partly to be nearer the Street of Booksellers and our shop, but it was also to be nearer to the house church where I worshipped. When I described in the manuscript a large apartment house that contained a Mitrhræum, I was describing the place where we worship. However, I have even used my own apartment for smaller gatherings.

I will tell you something of our patron "Literato" as well. He, too, is a Christian — a man of means whose house was used for a church until we outgrew it. Part of the money I have sent you has been his, but some of it has been my own savings from my share of the business.

Why did I want to build up your part of the business in Pergamum? The reasons I offered you in my letters were true enough, but there is more to it than trading expensive space in the Argelitum for the lower costs of Pergamum. I wanted to spend the rest of my life doing less work on tourism books and more in service to Christ and his church. You cannot deny that as you have performed the greater portion of the work, the greater share of earnings has been yours to keep.

At the same time, I admit that it has been increasingly difficult for me to be a Christian and publish books about temples, idols and blood sports. I realized this a year ago in the fire. I confess to you now that only some of the books on the Flavian Amphitheater went up in flames. A dozen more remain up in the second floor storage loft. I didn't send them to you because it bothered me that the writer we hired glorified in the gladiatorial blood and gore beyond measure. To be sure, this sells books, but I can tell you that in the first hundred days of shows, over 10,000 wild animals and 2,000 human beings died simply for the amusement of others. I feel as though reading such books will only cause rich men to build more such places and multiply the killings to the ends of the earth.

I'm sure you do not agree. And because I anticipate as much, I have already made a decision. It is my plan to curtail the shop in Rome so that it is devoted mostly to works of Christians. I will also reduce work in the scriptorium to the same extent. I plan to use some of the building as a school for children of all kinds, although many will be Christians. I refer to children of workmen, slaves and the like who at present have no opportunity to learn because they cannot read. It will even include young girls to the extent that they want to learn and I can persuade their parents of its sensibility. This I aim to do by telling them that the children will also be trained as apprentice copyists so that they can be hired out to publishers on the Street of Booksellers. I won't be lying because this might even come true in some cases.

And what of our partnership, dear cousin? Fortunately, you can afford the eccentricities of an elderly relative rattling about in your closet because you no longer need me as a business partner. I am prepared to send you all of our tourist book inventory from Rome, including the books on the Flavian Amphitheater. I would also encourage you to produce the book I wrote as well as the letters by the Christian apostles and the tract by Luke. The growth of churches continues throughout Asia Minor and I know you will find ready buyers for these books. If you cannot find it possible to display them, then I ask that you return to me two sets of the Christian materials just described via two separate ships. In such an event, it is our plan for Diodoros and some eager young church members to travel throughout the churches of Asia Minor at least once a year to distribute these works.

I pray that you will assist me in this plan. We will both be richer for it. I ask, too, that you find it in your heart to give my new life your blessing. Perhaps we can agree that your cousin's life is coming to an end with an ironic twist. I labored long so that I would be able to say I was no longer anyone's slave. Now I am a slave again and deeply grateful for it.

Farewell to all and God bless your family.

— Attalos

EPILOGUE

Titus, who became emperor in the fullness of his manhood and maturity, ruled but two years and two months. He was only 42 in September A.D. 81 when he succumbed to a deadly but undefined disease. Most ancient writers attributed it to a "distemper" of some sort brought on by taking the cold waters of a spa near his ancestral home. Others say his younger brother Domitian fed him a poisoned fish.

Whatever the cause, 30-year-old Domitian took the throne and soon undid the 12 years of stability and tolerance that had been the legacies of his father and brother. During his 15-year rule Domitian became one of Rome's most vicious tyrants, his outlandish ego perhaps best symbolized when he erected a new palace complex on the Palatine that was probably larger than even Nero's Golden House.

Among Domitian's many victims throughout the empire were both Christians and Jews. The latter were often seized for not paying what had been the former temple tax to the rebuilding of the Temple of Jupiter Capitoline. Christians were sometimes arrested for the same offense, which shows that many Roman officials continued to identify them as a Jewish sect.

However, both religions suffered even more because one of Domitian's primary tools for consolidating power was to strengthen the state religion and wipe out those who appeared to threaten it. Thus, Christians died by the thousands in purges and in gladiatorial shows. The Flavian Amphitheater (which was not called the Colosseum until the Middle Ages) claimed the most of all.

Many more persecutions took place in the second and third centuries, yet the movement spread as tenaciously as the sprouts of a pruned tree in a Roman garden. One way to document Christianity's growth in numbers and its frequent need to convene in secrecy is simply to visit the catacombs around Rome. In Nero's time these subterranean necropoli were just beginning and may have measured two miles in length. Today, excavations of now-famous catacombs such as San Sebastiano, San Callisto, Domitilla and Priscilla have so far revealed a combined 360 miles of corridors, tombs and grottos.

The frequency and intensity of persecutions had tapered off by A.D. 320 when the emperor Constantine declared Christianity an officially sanctioned religion (partly for his own political reasons). Within a few years, Rome, Jerusalem and the new Christian capital of Constantinople (today's Istanbul) bustled with the construction of Christian basilicas and monuments.

The work of the post-temple Jewish scholars culminated in A.D. 100 when the Synod of Jamnia formally decided which books were to be accepted by all Jews as Holy Writ. A uniform version of the text was translated and circulated to Jewish communities of the Diaspora. Although Jews were without a geographical center, their communities prospered and in time many even returned to Jerusalem to replant their roots.

By the year A.D. 132 Jerusalem had again become such a Jewish stronghold that its citizens once more defied Rome, re-establishing the high priesthood and minting their own coins. And again the Roman legions came marching up from Antioch and Cæsarea. The Jewish defenders held out for three years, finally being reduced to a resistance movement that fought on from caves in the desert around the Dead Sea.

In its aftermath, Jerusalem was turned into a Roman provincial town and given the name of Colonia Ælia Capitolina. On the temple hill the Romans built a sanctuary honoring Jupiter Capitolinus, and on the traditional site of Calvary they built a temple to Venus. The city was populated with Romans, Greeks and people from the east. Jews were forbidden to enter it on pain of death.

Apollonius of Tyana, whom I chose as an example of how philosophers influenced this period, continued his travels and quest for truth, indifferent to those who held power in Rome. Not long after the death of Titus he was arrested as a fomenter of sedition, but again awed Domitian's bureaucratic protectors with the power of his persona and was let go. According to his chief biographer, Philostratus, Apollonius may have lived to be as old as 100, dying in the reign of Nerva, who succeeded Domitian.

Some 200 years later, certain pagan scholars advanced Apollonius as the head of a new religion of sorts. They reasoned that his many miracles, prophecies and power over demons made him a worthy "competitor" to Jesus. Christian leaders dismissed him as a charlatan and magic worker.

The apostle John died in Ephesus around the year A.D. 100 after living to be about the same number of years. The reliable Eusebius, who was bishop of

Cæsarea in A.D. 316, states that John decided to write or dictate his gospel (the fourth and last) late in life in order to proclaim Christ's divinity and to supply information about his earlier ministry that the others had omitted. Eusebius adds that Domitian banished John to Patmos (an island just off Miletus) and that he returned to Ephesus after the emperor's assassination in A.D. 96. While on Patmos he wrote Revelation, the last book of the New Testament and one full of thunderous apocrypha about the evils of Rome.

Or did he? Eusebius himself notes that a prominent "John the Presbyter" also preached in Ephesus and that both Johns are buried there. Some scholars attribute Revelation to the second John, but I find it more inspiring to think of a righteous old apostle enduring on Patmos, defying an emperor's curse and spouting fiery encouragement to the seven churches of Asia. This sounds more like the "Son of Thunder" whom Jesus named for his fearless faith.

What happened to Luke remains a mystery. Absent any evidence, the most logical scenario is that he went back to his Greek home of Philippi, wrote the gospel of Luke, became an elder in his local church, and continued being a compassionate physician.

The earthly fates of Peter and Paul deserve some further comment as well. One of the many questions that cannot be answered with any certainty is: did Paul remain incarcerated in Rome until his death or was he acquitted and set free at one point? In Paul's first letter to Timothy, written from Rome during his darkest hours, he asks his faithful co-worker to come to his side and "bring the cloak that I left with Carpas at Troas, also the books and above all the parchments." This would indicate that Paul had left Rome at one point and returned to Asia Minor. If so, there is no atom of evidence to explain how or why he returned to the clutches of Nero's nervous henchmen and certain death. Given this historical fog, I chose to assume (yes, with nagging questions) that these personal items had been left behind when Paul sailed for Cæsarea in A.D. 58 and that the apostle never left Rome once he arrived there from Malta.

Equally perplexing is the whereabouts of Peter in the years just before his death. Many scholars believe that because the epistle Peter 1 refers once to one of his colleagues sending greetings from "Babylon," that this far-off city is the source of his letter. It's possible: maybe Peter did write from Babylon during A.D. 65, as Christians everywhere braced for a wave of persecutions, then left soon afterward to be at their epicenter in Rome. In any case, oral tradition — along with some evidence — is very strong that Peter was preaching in Rome after the great fire and died during the purge of imperial nuisances that took place in A.D. 67 after Nero had left for his tour of Greece.

You may also read some accounts by the Vatican — but find no direct evidence — that Peter came to Rome with his wife and at least one daughter, Petronilla, who was said to be lame throughout life. You may also read that he lived in Rome for seven years under the patronage of a wealthy senator named Pudente and that he preached in that part of the Subura that became the ancient parish of St. Pudente. There is a tradition as well that Peter's wife was crucified next to him.

The above, however, depends chiefly on the account by the Christian bishop Eusebius writing over 200 years later, and most scholars are wary of it because his own sources are several works that have since disappeared with time. Although I see no reason to doubt the good Eusebius, I omitted mention of these accounts in the narrative—a decision made primarily by not wanting to lard the book with the kind of scholarly squabbles that cause lay readers to nod off.

Regardless of when Peter came to Rome and who came with him, there is no doubt in my mind that the apostle (who probably never heard himself called "the first pope") was crucified in the Circus of Caligula and Nero and that the "Vatican" neighborhood in which he was entombed is the same Vatican we now know as the Holy See.

In about A.D. 150 an ornamental and protective structure with a roof and four white marble columns was erected around the plain tomb of Peter. The enclosure was called "The Trophy of Gaius," probably after a prominent churchman of the day. When the first St. Peter's was completed by the emperor Constantine in A.D. 326, the altar was placed directly over the roof of the Trophy of Gaius. In 1506, when the present St. Peter's replaced the aging basilica, the new altar was placed in the same spot. In 1939 Pope Pius XII ordered some probing excavations below St. Peter's as he sought to find suitable space for his own burial place. This led to an announcement in 1950 that the excavators had not only uncovered an entire street of the first century necropolis, but the "Trophy," the tomb below it, and part of the red wall behind the tomb.

Visiting the ancient necropolis beneath the Vatican is available to anyone who can advance a legitimate academic reason, provide ample advance notice and be ready to bend with the winds and whims of the Vatican bureaucracy. It is a stirring experience.

And what of Attalos the narrator and his cousin Eumenes? Since I invented them, I can report their fates with certainty.

The death of Titus and emergence of the sharply-contrasting Domitian quickly crumbled any resolve Eumenes had to co-exist with his cousin and his Christianity. As directed, he sent two identical packages by two separate ships containing the letters of the apostles and Luke's Book of Acts. One package was lost at sea after pirates bribed its captain to run his ship into one of the rocky Cyclades islands. The other arrived safely and was carefully copied dozens of times by the scribes of Attalos' scriptorium.

As for the large book manuscript, Eumenes trembled at the thought of its ever seeing the light of day. Not even wanting to risk being seen burning it, he put the sheets of Attalos' handwritten papyrus in an old brass linen box and hid them in a niche hollowed out in the stone wall above his scriptorium. It would only be until Domitian died or changed his ways, Eumenes told himself. And to prove his honorable intentions, he placed in the box the remaining sesterces that Attalos had allotted for the project.

In the spring of A.D. 83, a letter was brought to Eumenes in his scriptorium. It was obviously from Rome, but not in the hand of his cousin. It read:

To Eumenes, greetings.

It is my sad duty to inform you, my friend, that your cousin Attalos has disappeared from our midst and may be in prison — or perhaps worse.

As you may know, things have been "different" for Christians in Rome since the recent ascendancy of Domitian. All I can tell you for certain is that Attalos and a group of perhaps 30 other Christians were holding worship services at a tenement we call the Church of Clement. I was not present. Others say that the group was suddenly surrounded on all sides by soldiers of the City Garrison and that everyone inside was quickly taken away in chains. There seems to have been no resistance or bloodshed.

Friends and family members are trying their best to determine their whereabouts. We have inquired at the usual precinct prisons and even the Marmentine, but have not a trace of them. Nor have any of them turned up at the slave auctions. We are even asking some guards at the Flavian Amphitheater to make inquiries within their "holding" prisons, as a week of gladiatorial games are scheduled soon.

I know you will find this alarming and you may be sure that I will send news as soon as I receive it. Meanwhile, I am doing what I can to keep our scriptorium open, although some of the men here are uneasy about continuing to work here under the circumstances.

I offer you the peace of Jesus Christ and the assurance that he loves Attalos wherever he is at this moment.

— Farewell. Diodoros

Attalos was not seen on the streets of Rome again. Nor would anyone have recognized him as he was shoved onto the floor of the amphitheater with a dozen other Christians from the Church of Clement. The afternoon was already stifling and the floor around was strewn with patches of blood that work crews had covered with sand. Overhead, the ropes of the giant valerium groaned as the canvas sails shifted with the winds. Attalos, now dirty, thin and stooped, had been covered with a cloak crudely knit together from the hides of several animals. No one he knew was in the vast faceless crowd that rose above him. Nor would they have seen him anyway, because all eyes were on the two elevators that had suddenly disgorged six lions.

Now a mighty roar went up – not from the lions, but from a crowd that yelled with an excited frenzy that made the entire Amphitheater vibrate. As the animals squinted in the sunlight, they began to circle their quarry warily. It was then that the crowd saw the criminals below straighten their stance and clasp their hands together. They seemed to be singing.

It was Attalos who led them, with all the courage he had prayed for.

Ω

. . . .

APPENDICES

~ENDNOTES
~SUGGESTED READING
~MODERN NAMES & LOCATIONS *of* ANCIENT PLACES
~LIST *of* VISUALS
~ILLUSTRATIONS, MAPS & PHOTOGRAPHS

ENDNOTES

For complete references to the works cited in these endnotes, please see the *Suggested Reading* list on page 625.

PREFACE

1. The *Res Gestæ,* which appeared on the stele beside Augustus' mausoleum, was one of four public statements the efficient emperor prepared for publication at his death. The others were his will, the directions for his funeral and a lengthy statement of public accounts. The *Res Gestæ,* a statement of his achievements, is preserved in the pages of historians such as Tacitus and on public buildings, the most intact of these today being at the Temple of Augustus and Rome in Ankara, Turkey.

2. William Whiston, a Cambridge University professor who translated the works of Josephus in 1737, appended his own short dissertation entitled *Of the Jewish Weights and Coins.* According to Whiston, a Hebrew shekel was equal to about one Tyrian coin (the exchange medium of the temple in Jerusalem) and four Roman denarii, or very roughly about $4 in U.S. currency today. The half shekel, or bekah, which all Jewish adult males were required to contribute to the temple each year, would then have been worth about $2. A Jewish talent of silver was equivalent to about 3,000 shekels.

· · · · · · · · ·

BOOK I

1. Suetonius, p. 153.
2. Tacitus, *Annals,* p. 121.
3. *Acts,* 2:17–18.
4. Suetonius, p. 153.
5. Ibid, p. 145–46.
6. Ibid p. 170.
7. Josephus, *Wars of the Jews,* p. 785.
8. *Acts,* 26:16–18.
9. Philo, *Embassy to Gaius,* Vol. 10, p. 9–10.
10. Ibid, p. 13.
11. Philostratus, *Apollonius of Tyana,* Book 1, p. 17.
12. Bradford, *Paul the Traveller,* p. 90.
13. Ibid, p. 91.
14. *Romans,* 1:22–24.

~ ENDNOTES ~

· · · · · · · · ·

BOOK II

1. British Museum Papyrus No. 1911. Cited in *Roman Civilization*, p. 366–67.
2. *Roman Civilization*, p. 368. See also Josephus, *Antiquities of the Jews*, p. 578.
3. Josephus, *Antiquities*, p. 578.
4. Suetonius, p. 210.
5. Juvenal, *Satires*, VI, as quoted by Grant's *Twelve Cæsars*, p. 145.
6. *Acts*, 13:26–34.
7. Tacitus, *Annals*, p. 243–44.
8. Onesiphorus' description of Paul outside Iconium is taken from *The Acts of Paul*, written in A.D. 160 and translated by M.R. James in *The Apocryphal New Testament* (Oxford, 1924).
9. *Acts*, 15:6–11.
10. Ibid, 15: 16–18.
11. Ibid, 15:22–29 .
12. Ibid, 17:22–31.
13. Suetonius, p. 243–44.
14. 1 *Thessalonians*, 4:16–22.
15. Tacitus, *Annals*, p.280.
16. Seneca, *Apocolocyntosis*, p. 471–75.
17. Ibid, p. 481–83.
18. Seneca, *Morals*, p.278–79.
19. *Galatians*, 1:6–10.
20. Ibid, 3:1–5.
21. Ibid, 3:28–29.
22. Ibid, 5:16–24.
23. Seneca, *Morals*, p.123.
24. Ibid, p. 232.
25. Suetonius, p. 258.
26. Seneca, *Morals*, p. 357.
27. Ibid, p. 359.
28. Ibid, p. 98.
29. 1 *Corinthians*, 11:12–17.
30. Ibid, 1:20–25.
31. Ibid, 2:21–25.
32. Ibid, 3:2–6.
33. Ibid, 5:11–13.
34. Ibid, 6:7–9.
35. Ibid, 8:10–12.
36. Ibid, 10:4–6.

37. Ibid, 11:20—29.
38. Ibid, 11:7—8.
39. Ibid, 13:1—3.
40. Ibid, 15:1—11.
41 Ibid, 15:35—53.
42. Ibid 15:54—58.
43. 2 *Corinthians*, 2:21—29.
44. Ibid, 12:1—5.
45. Ibid, 12:8—10.
46. Ibid, 9:1—5.
47. Ibid, 11:22—23.
48. *Romans*, 1:8—14.
49. Suetonius, p. 269—69.
50. *Acts*, 20:22—35.
51. Ibid, 24:10—21.
52. Dio Cassius, Book 62, p. 85.
53. Ibid, p. 89—91.
54. Ibid, p. 93—95.
55. Tacitus, *Annals*, p. 333—34.
56. *Acts*, 26:9—18.
57. *Romans*, 1:21—25.
58. Ibid, 3:9.
59. Ibid, 3:21—26.
60. Ibid, 5:1—5.
61. Ibid, 6:2—14.
62. Ibid, 8:37—39.
63. Seneca, *Four Tragedies and Octavia*, p. 260—61.
64. Ibid, p. 274.
65. Eusebius, p. 59.
66. *James*, 4:8—10.
67. Ibid, 5:1—3.
68. Ibid, 2:14—26.
69. *Ephesians*, 2:10.
70. *James*, 5:8—9.
71. Eusebius, p. 59—60.
72. *Acts*, 28:26—27.
73. *Philippians*, 1:12—14.
74. Ibid, 1:27, 2:1—18.
75. *Romans*, 12:3—21, 13:1—4.
76. *Colossians*, 1:15—23.
77. *Philippians*, 1:22—26.

. . . .

BOOK III

1. Philostratus, *Life of Apollonius*, p. 45–47.
2. Tacitus, *Annals*, p. 362.
3. Suetonius, p.269.
4. Seneca, *Morals*, p. 346–47.
5. Cited in *Latin Literature*, p. 317.
6. 1 *Timothy*, 4:6–8.
7. Ibid, 2:1–3.
8. Ibid, 4:1–5.
9. Josephus, *Wars of the Jews*, p. 690.
10. Ibid, p. 692.
11. Ibid, p. 692.
12. Tacitus, *Annals*, p. 391.
13. Dio Cassius, Book 62, p. 157.
14. 1 *Peter*, 1:3–7.
15. Ibid, 1:18–25.
16. Ibid, 2:12–17.
17. Ibid, 4:7–18.
18. Josephus, *Life of Flavius Josephus*, p. 2.
19. Josephus, *Wars of the Jews*, p. 695.
20. Ibid, p. 713.
21. Ibid, p. 721.
22. Ibid, p. 724.
23. Ibid, p. 726 .
24. Ibid, p. 729.
25. Ibid, p. 730.
26. Dio Cassius, Book 62, p. 151–53.
27. Speech from an inscription in the town of Acræphiæ (modern Karditza), quoted in *Roman Civilization*, p. 394–95.
28. Josephus, *Wars*, p. 737.
29. Ibid, p. 737.
30. Ibid, p. 745.
31. Ibid, p. 747.
32. Ibid, p. 753.
33. Ibid, p. 754.
34. Dio Cassius, Book 63, p. 175.
35. Suetonius, p. 299.
36. Josephus, *Wars*, p. 765.
37. Ibid, p. 766.

38. Tacitus, *The Histories*, p. 84.
39. Ibid, p. 85.
40. Ibid, p.98.
41. Ibid, p. 101.
42. Dio Cassius, Book 64, pp. 241–43.
43. Tacitus, *Histories*, pp.136–37.
44. Philostratus, *Life of Apollonius*, p. 531.
45. Ibid, p. 553–57.
46. Tacitus, *Histories*, p. 168.
47. McBirnie, *Search for the Twelve Apostles*, p. 160 (quoting from the book, *The Traditions of the St. Thomas Christians*).
48. Lockyer, *All the Apostles of the Bible*, p.248.
49. *Matthew*, 24:5–8.
50. Josephus, *Wars*, p. 782.
51. Ibid, p. 788.
52. Ibid, p. 791.
53. Ibid, p. 794.
54. Ibid, p. 795.
55. Ibid, p. 797.
56. Ibid, p. 799.
57. Ibid, p. 810.
58. Ibid, p. 810.
59. Ibid, p. 811.
60. Ibid, p. 812.
61. Ibid, p. 813.
62. Ibid, p. 813.
63. Ibid, p. 818.
64. Ibid, p. 823.
65. Ibid, p. 826.
66. *Matthew*, 6:9–13.
67. *2 Timothy*, 4:1–5.
68. *1 Corinthians*, 13:4–13.
. . . .

LETTER FROM ROME, JULY, A.D. 81
1. *Habakkuk*, 1:2, 12–14.
2. Philostratus, *Life of Apollonius*, p. 365–67.
3. *Habakkuk*, 2:1–4.
. . . .

SUGGESTED READING

PRIMARY SOURCES

The primary sources for this book were ancients who lived during or not more than three centuries after the years A.D. 31-71. They are:

Dio Cassius. *Roman History, Books 56–60.* Trans. Earnest Cary. Cambridge, MA: Harvard University Press, 1994.

—————. *Roman History, Books 61–70.* Trans. Earnest Cary. Cambridge, MA: Harvard University Press, 1995.

Eusebius. *The History of the Church from Christ to Constantine.* Trans. G.A. Williamson. Ed. Andrew Louth. London: Penguin Books Ltd., 1989.

Holy Bible, Revised Standard Version. New York: Thomas Nelson & Sons, 1953.

Lucan. *Lucan.* Trans. J.D. Duff. Cambridge, MA. Cambridge, MA: Harvard University Press, 1986.

Petronius. *Satyricon.* Trans. Michael Heseltine and W.H.D. Rouse. Cambridge, MA: Harvard University Press, 1987. (The volume also contains Seneca's brief *Apocolocyntosis,* the satirical account of how the gods on Mount Olympus greeted the newly-deified Claudius.)

Philo. *The Embassy to Gaius* (Vol. X in the works of Philo). Trans. F.H. Colson. Cambridge, MA: Harvard University Press, 1991.

Philostratus, Flavius. *The Life of Apollonius of Tyana,* Vols. I and II. Trans. F.C. Conybeare. Cambridge, MA: Harvard University Press, 1989.

Pliny (The Younger). *Letters and Panegyricus* (Vol. I). Trans. Betty Radice. Ed. G.P. Goold. Cambridge, MA: Harvard University Press, 1989.

Seneca, Lucius Annæus. *Four Tragedies and Octavia.* Trans. E.F. Watling. Harmondsworth, Middlesex, England: Penguin Books Ltd., 1984.

Seneca, Lucius Annæus. *Morals.* Trans. and Ed. Sir Roger L'Estrange. New York: A.L. Burt Company Publishers, n.d.

Suetonius (Gaius Tranquillus). *The Lives of the Twelve Cæsars.* Trans. and ed. Joseph Gavorse. New York: Modern Library Inc., 1959.

Tacitus, Publius Cornelius. *The Annals of Imperial Rome.* Trans. Michael Grant. Harmondsworth, Middlesex, England: Penguin Books Ltd., 1956.

————. *The Histories.* Trans. W.H. Fyfe. Ed. D.S. Levene. Oxford: Oxford University Press, 1997.

Whiston, A.M., trans. and ed. *The Life and Works of Flavius Josephus.* (Complete works, with seven dissertations.) New York: Holt, Rinehart and Winston, 1977.

. . . .

MODERN RESOURCES
Aharoni, Yohanan and Michael Avi-Yonah, eds. *The Macmillan Bible Atlas.* New York: Macmillan Publishing Co. Inc., 1968.

Balsdon, J.P.V.D. *Romans and Aliens.* Chapel Hill, NC: The University of North Carolina Press, 1979.

Basso, Michele. *Guide to the Vatican Necropolis.* Rome: Fabbrica of St. Peter's, the Vatican, 1986.

Bradford, Ernle. *Paul the Traveller.* New York: Macmillan Publishing Company. Inc., 1976.

Boyle, Leonard. *A Short Guide to St. Clement's.* Rome: Collegio San Clemente, 1989.

Crowe, Jerome. *From Jerusalem to Antioch.* Collegeville, MN: The Liturgical Press, 1997.

Cwiekowski, Frederick J. *The Beginnings of the Church.* Mahwah, NJ: Paulist Press, 1988.

Durant, Will. *Cæsar and Christ.* New York: Simon and Schuster, 1944.

Earl, Donald. *The Age of Augustus.* New York: Crown Publishers, 1968.

Fasola, Umberto M., *Peter and Paul in Rome*. Rome: Vision Editrice, 1983.

Feldman, Louis H., *Jew & Gentile in the Ancient World*. Princeton, NJ: Princeton University Press, 1993.

Filson, Floyd V. *A New Testament History*. Philadelphia: The Westminster Press, 1964.

Freely, John. *Classical Turkey*. London: Penguin Books, 1991.

————. *Western Mediterranean Coast of Turkey*. Istanbul: Sev Matbaacilik ve Yayincilik A.S., 1997.

Goodspeed, J. Edgar. *Paul*. Nashville and New York: Abingdon Press, 1947.

Grant, Michæl. *Herod the Great*. New York: American Heritage Press, 1971.

————. *The Army of the Cæsars*. New York: Charles Scribner's Sons, 1974.

————, Ed. *Latin Literature*. Harmondsworth, Middlesex, England: Penguin Classics, 1958.

Holum, Kenneth G., et al. *King Herod's Dream: Cæsarea on the Sea*. New York: W.W. Norton & Co., 1988.

Hornblower, Simon and Anthony Spawforth, eds. *The Oxford Classical Dictionary*. Oxford: Oxford University Press, 1996.

Landels, J.G. *Engineering in the Ancient World*. Berkeley, CA: University of California Press, 1978.

Lewis, Naphtali. *Life in Egypt Under Roman Rule*. Oxford: Clarendon Press, 1983.

Lewis, Naphtali and Meyer Reinhold, eds. *Roman Civilization. Sourcebook 11: The Empire*. New York: Harper & Row, Publishers, 1955.

Locker, Herbert. *All the Apostles of the Bible*. Grand Rapids, MI: Zondervan Publishing House, 1972.

Marks, RCA. *Christianity in the Roman World*. New York: Charles Scriber's Sons, 1974.

Martini, Carl M. *The Testimony of St. Paul.* Trans. Susan Leslie. New York: Crossroads Publishing Company, 1981.

Mason, Steve. *Josephus and the New Testament.* Peabody, MA: Hendrickson Publishers Inc., 1992.

McBirnie, William Steuart. *The Search for the Twelve Apostles.* Wheaton, IL: Tyndale House Publishers Inc., 1973.

Pagels, Elaine. *The Gnostic Gospels.* New York: Random House, 1979.

Rowley, Harold H., Ed., et al. *New Atlas of the Bible.* Garden City, NY: Doubleday & Company Inc., 1969.

Wilson, A.N. *Paul: The Mind of the Apostle.* New York: W.W. Norton & Company, 1997.

. . . .

MODERN NAMES & LOCATIONS
OF ANCIENT PLACES IN THIS BOOK

Names not followed by parentheses are cities. Places described only as "sites"
today have neither permanent populations nor significant ruins.

1st Century Name ....Present Name and Location

Achaia (Roman province)...Greece
Adiabene (kingdom) ....NE Iraq–NW Iran
Adramyttium..Edremit, W Turkey
Ægæ ....Yumurtalik, SE Turkey
Alba Longa ....Castel Gandolfo, Central Italy
Alesia ....Alise-Ste. Reine, France
Alexandria ....Alexandria, N Egypt
Amphidpolis ....Amfipolis, NE Greece
Antalya ....Antalya, S Turkey
Antium..Anzio, W central Italy
Antioch (Syrian) ....Antakya, E Turkey
Albania (kingdom) ....Azerbaijan, N Iran
Alexander Troas...Ruins near Bozcaada, NW Turkey
Anthedon ....Ruins in central Greece
Apennines (mountains) ....N central Italy
Apollonia ....Apollonia, NE Greece
Arcadia (region) ....Central Peloponnesus, Greece
Ardea...Site W of Rome, Italy
Armenia (kingdom)...Armenia–NE Turkey
Artaxta ....Site near Yerevan, Armenia
Ascalon ....Ashquelon, SW Israel
Asphaltitis (lake)..Dead Sea, SE Israel-SW Jordan
Assos..Behramkale, W Turkey
Athens..Athens, Greece
Avernus (lake) ....Averno, SW Italy
Babylonia (region)..Central Iraq
Bactria ....Tajikistan-Uzbekistan
Baucalis...Site in or near Alexanrdia, Egypt

Delphi ....Ruins at Delfol, central Greece
Derbe ....Site near Karaman, S central Turkey
Divodurum ....Site in N France
Edessa (city-state) ....Urfa, SE Turkey
Edom (region) ....S Israel and Jordan
Engaddi..En Gedi, SE Israel
Ephesus ....Ruins near Kusadasi, W Turkey.
Eturia (region)..Tuscany - Lazio, N Italy
Euboea (island)..Evvoia, E Greece
Euphrates (river) ....Runs through Syria and Iraq
Fair Havens (harbor) ....S Crete
Fucine Lake ....Site N of Rome, Italy
Gabao..Site NW of Jerusalem, Israel
Gadara..Umm Qays, NW Jordan
Galilee (region)..N Israel
Gamala ....Site near E Israel-W Jordan border
Ganges (river) ....E India
Gangites (river)..Struma R.(?), NE Greece
Gaul (Roman province)...................Alpine Italy N through W France
Gaulanitis (region).....................................S Syria, N Jordan
Gaza (region) ....Gaza Strip, SW Israel
Gennesaret (lake)................................Sea of Galilee, N Israel
Geresa ....Jarash (W Jordan)
Gerizzim (mountain) ....At Jabal at Tur, Samaria, central Israel
Ginae ....Site in Samaria, Israel
Gischala ....Jish, NW Israel
Gophna..Site (?) N of Jerusalem, Israel
Herculaneum ....Ruins in W Italy
Herodium ....Tal Horodos, S Israel
Hostilia..Site E of Cremona, N Italy
Hyacrania..Al Mird, E of Jerusalem
Iberia (kingdom) ....Georgia
Iconium..Konya, S Turkey
Idumea (region) ....Southern Israel
Illyricum (Roman province) ....Nations along NE Adriatic Sea
India (region) ....India
Issus ....Site near Adana, SE Turkey
Jamnia ....Near Yavne, Israel
Japha..Site W of Nazareth, Israel
Jericho ....Ariha, E central Israel
Jerusalem ....Jerusalem, Israel

Pannonia (Roman province)..W Hungary and Serbia
Paphos..Paphos, SW Cyprus
Parthia (empire) ....E Syria to India
Patara ....Ruins near Kinik, S Turkey
Patræ ....Patrai, W central Greece
Peloponnese (region)..Peloponnesus, S Greece
Perea (region) ....W Jordan
Perga ....Site near Antalya, S central Turkey
Pergamum..Bergama, W Turkey
Persia (empire)...Iran
Philadelphia ....Amman, Jordan
Philippi...Site N of Amfipolis, Greece
Phœnix ....Site in SW Crete
Piræus ....Piræus, SE Greece
Pisidia (region) ....S central Turkey
Pisidian Antioch ....S central Turkey
Placentia ....Placenza, N central Italy
Pompeii ....Ruins in W Italy
Pontia (isle) ....Ponza, off W Italy
Ptolemais..Akko, NW Israel
Puteoli ....Puzzuoli, SW Italy
Ravenna ....Ravenna, NE Italy
Rhegium ....Reggio di Calabria, S Italy
Rhodes (city) ....Rhodes
Rhodes (island)...Rhodes, Greek isle S of Turkish coast
Salamis ....Salamis, eastern Cyprus
Samaria (region)..Central Israel
Samos (island)...Samos, Greek isle W of Turkish coast
Samothrace (island) ....Samothrace, NE Greece
Scythia (region) ....S Ukraine to Caspian Sea in Russia
Scythopolis, ...Bet Shean, E Israel
Sebaste ....Shomron, in Samarian Israel
Seleucia ....Samandagi, SE Turkey
Sepphoris ....Zippori, NW Israel
Sidon..Sidon, Lebanon
Socotra..Suqutra, off SE Yemen
Spain (Roman province) ....Spain and Portugal
Sparta (city-state) ....Sparti, S Greece
Syracuse ....Siracusa, Sicily, Italy
Syria (Roman province) ....S Turkey S to Egypt
Tarracina..Terracina, W Italy

LIST *of* VISUALS
The following is commentary on the sources and subjects of the *Illustrations,*
Maps & Photographs, beginning on p. 659.

ILLUSTRATIONS
The following illustrations were hand-rendered by artist Diana Nickels of Pear
Design, Lantana FL.

1A. Octavian Cæsar Augustus as the young princeps. Based on a bust at the
Museum of Fine Arts, Boston.

1B. Livia, early in her marriage to Octavian. Based on a bust at the Louvre,
Paris.

1C. The Mausoleum of Augustus as it may have appeared in the late first
century.

2A. Tiberius, well before his becoming emperor at age 56. Based on a bust at
the Royal Ontario Museum.

2B. Claudius, probably just after becoming emperor at age 51. Based on a bust
at Ny Carlsberg Glyptotek, Copenhagen.

2C. Gaius Caligula. Based on a bust at Ny Carlsberg Glyptotek, Copenhagen.

3A. Agrippina (The Younger, and mother of Nero). Based on a bust in the
British Museum.

3B. Nero, late in his reign. From a bust at the Louvre, Paris

3C. Seneca. From a bust in the Ufizzi Gallery, Florence.

4A. Galba. Based on a bust in the Capitoline Museum, Rome.

4B. Otho, based on a bust in the Ufizzi Gallery, Florence.

4C. Vitellius. Based on a bust in the Archeological Museum, Venice.

5A. Vespasian. Based on a bust in the Ufizzi Gallery, Florence.

5B. Titus. Based on a bust in the British Museum, London.

5C. Domitian. From a bust in the Communal Museum, Antiquarium,
Rome.

6A. The apostle Paul. A composite based on one New Testament description
and several frescoes in the catacombs of Rome.

6B. The apostle Peter. From a bust (circa. third or fourth century) in the
Museum of St. Sebastian, Rome.

. . . .

· · · · · · · · ·

· · · · · · · · ·

ILLUSTRATIONS,
MAPS &
PHOTOGRAPHS

IA

IB

IC

· IA) Octavian Cæsar Augustus · IB) Livia · IC) Mausoleum of Augustus

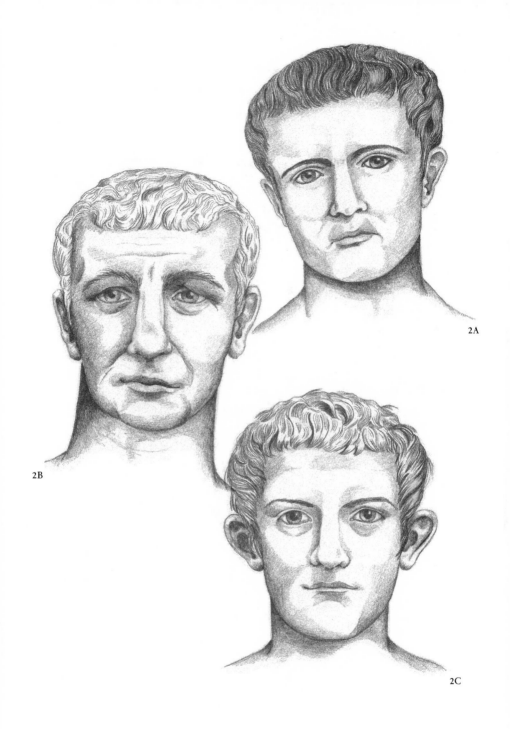

2A) Tiberius · 2B) Claudius · 2C) Gaius Caligula · 6 6 1

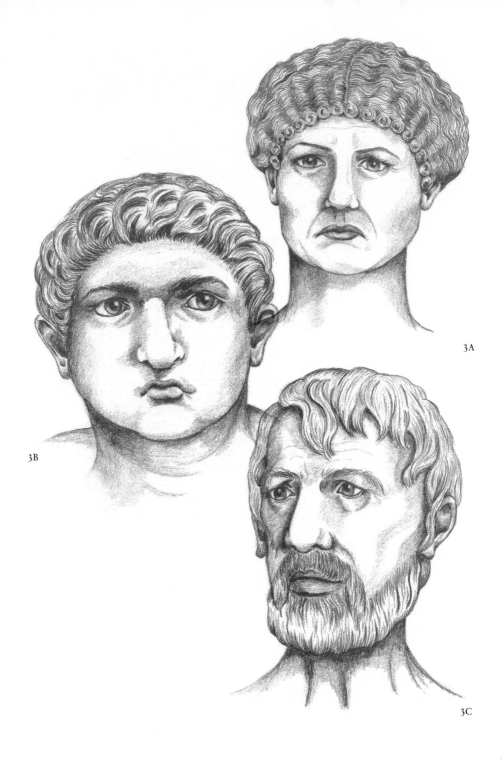

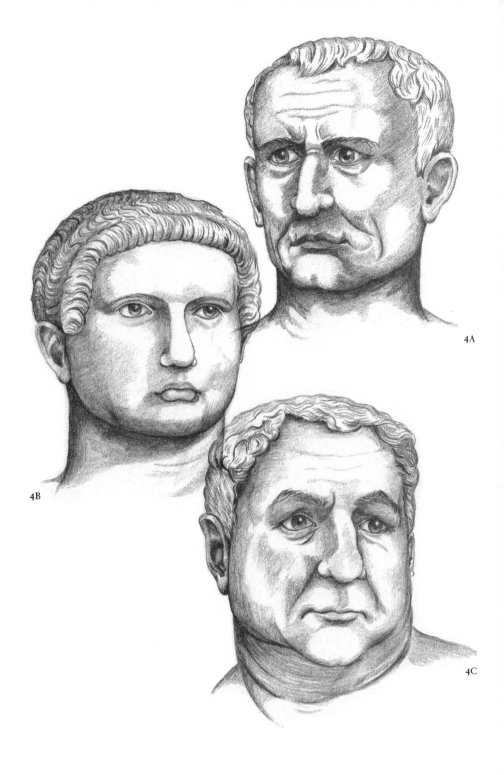

4A) Galba · 4B) Otho · 4C) Vitellius · 6 6 3

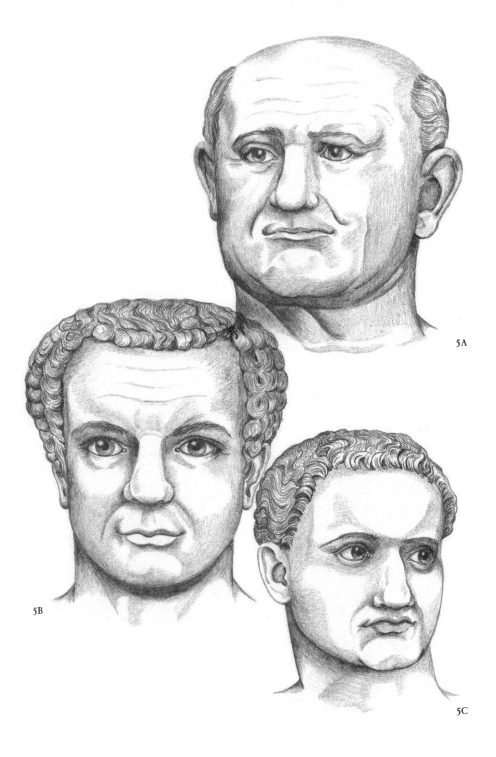

664 · 5A) Vespasian · 5B) Titus · 5C) Domitian

6A) Paul · 6B) Peter · 6 6 5

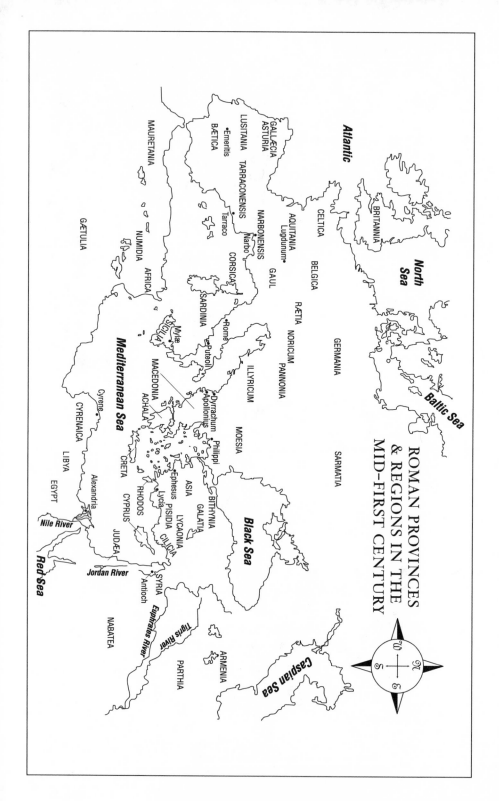

ROMAN PROVINCES
& REGIONS IN THE
MID-FIRST CENTURY

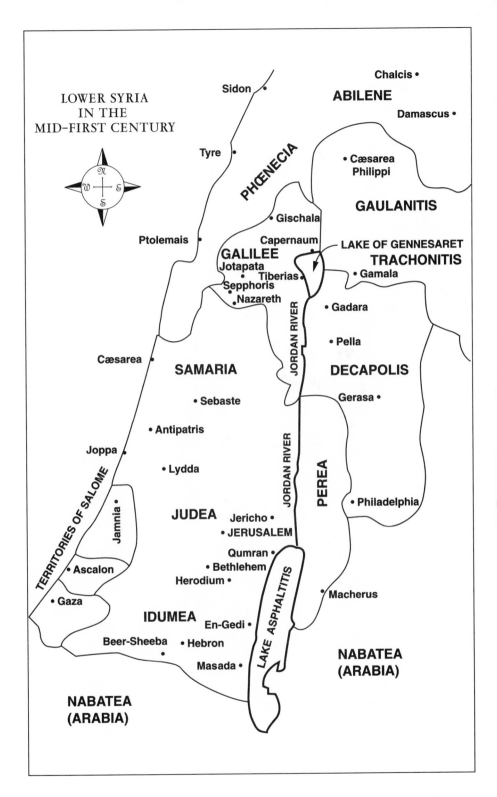

LOWER SYRIA
IN THE
MID-FIRST CENTURY

Chalcis •

Sidon

ABILENE

Damascus •

Tyre •

PHŒNECIA

• Cæsarea
Philippi

GAULANITIS

Ptolemais •

• Gischala

Capernaum

GALILEE

Jotapata •
Tiberias •
Sepphoris •
• Nazareth

JORDAN RIVER

LAKE OF GENNESARET

TRACHONITIS

• Gamala

• Gadara

• Pella

Cæsarea •

SAMARIA

DECAPOLIS

• Sebaste

Gerasa •

• Antipatris

Joppa •

• Lydda

JORDAN RIVER

PEREA

TERRITORIES OF SALOME

JUDEA

Jericho •
• **JERUSALEM**

Jamnia •

Qumran •
• Bethlehem
Herodium •

• Philadelphia

• Ascalon

LAKE ASPHALTITIS

• Macherus

• Gaza

IDUMEA

En-Gedi •

Beer-Sheeba •

• Hebron

Masada •

**NABATEA
(ARABIA)**

**NABATEA
(ARABIA)**

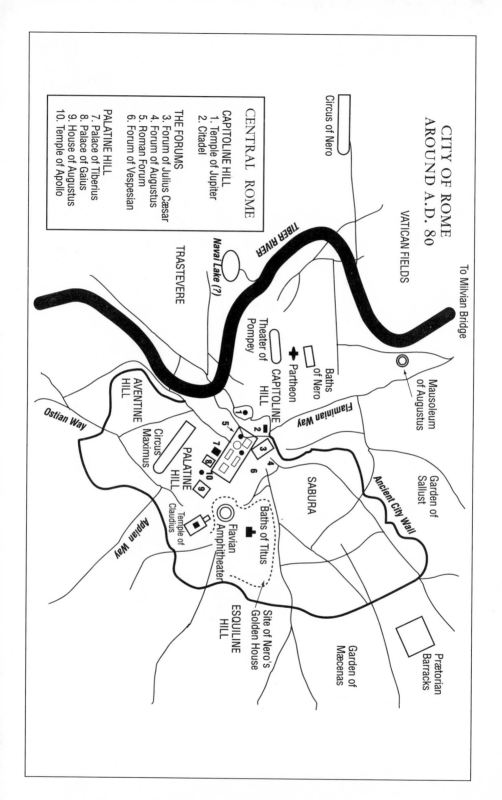

CITY OF ROME
AROUND A.D. 80

CENTRAL ROME

CAPITOLINE HILL
1. Temple of Jupiter
2. Citadel

THE FORUMS
3. Forum of Julius Cæsar
4. Forum of Augustus
5. Roman Forum
6. Forum of Vespesian

PALATINE HILL
7. Palace of Tiberius
8. Palace of Gaius
9. House of Augustus
10. Temple of Apollo

Circus of Nero

VATICAN FIELDS

To Milvian Bridge

TIBER RIVER

Naval Lake (?)

TRASTEVERE

Theater of Pompey

Pantheon

CAPITOLINE HILL

Baths of Nero

Mausoleum of Augustus

Flaminian Way

AVENTINE HILL

Ostian Way

Circus Maximus

PALATINE HILL

Temple of Claudius

Appian Way

Baths of Titus

Flavian Amphitheater

SABURA

Garden of Sallust

Ancient City Wall

Site of Nero's Golden House

ESQUILINE HILL

Garden of Macenas

Prætorian Barracks

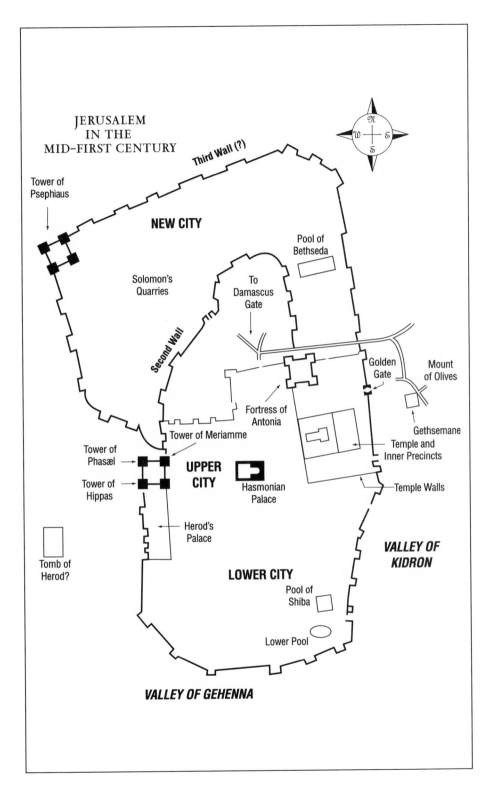

JERUSALEM
IN THE
MID-FIRST CENTURY

Third Wall (?)

Tower of
Psephiaus

NEW CITY

Pool of
Bethseda

Solomon's
Quarries

To
Damascus
Gate

Second Wall

Golden
Gate

Mount
of Olives

Fortress of
Antonia

Tower of Meriamme

Gethsemane

Tower of
Phasæl

UPPER
CITY

Hasmonian
Palace

Temple and
Inner Precincts

Tower of
Hippas

Temple Walls

Herod's
Palace

Tomb of
Herod?

LOWER CITY

VALLEY OF
KIDRON

Pool of
Shiba

Lower Pool

VALLEY OF GEHENNA

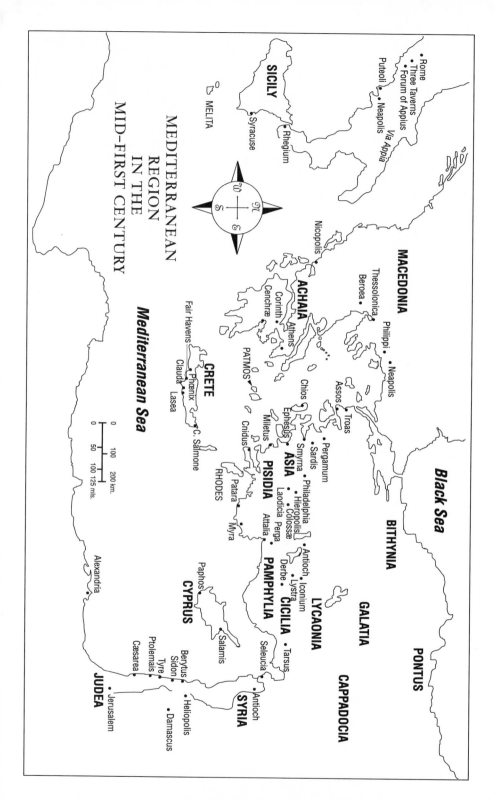

MEDITERRANEAN
REGION
IN THE
MID–FIRST CENTURY

Mediterranean Sea

Black Sea

SICILY

MELITA

Syracuse

Rhegium

Rome
Three Taverns
Forum of Appius

Puteoli

Neapolis

Via Appia

MACEDONIA

Nicopolis

Thessalonica

Beroea

Philippi

Neapolis

ACHAIA

Corinth

Cenchræ

Athens

PATMOS

Fair Havens

Phœnix

Clauda

Lasea

CRETE

C. Salmone

Chios

Assos

Troas

Ephesus

Miletus

Cnidus

RHODES

Patara

Myra

Smyrna

Sardis

Pergamum

ASIA

PISIDIA

Philadelphia

Hierapolis

Laodicia

Colossæ

Perga

Attalia

Antioch

Iconium

Lystra

Derbe

PAMPHYLIA

CICILIA

Tarsus

LYCAONIA

BITHYNIA

GALATIA

PONTUS

CAPPADOCIA

CYPRUS

Paphos

Salamis

Seleucia

Antioch

SYRIA

Heliopolis

Damascus

Berytus

Sidon

Tyre

Ptolemais

Cæsarea

JUDEA

Jerusalem

Alexandria

0   50   100   125 mls.

0   100   200 km.

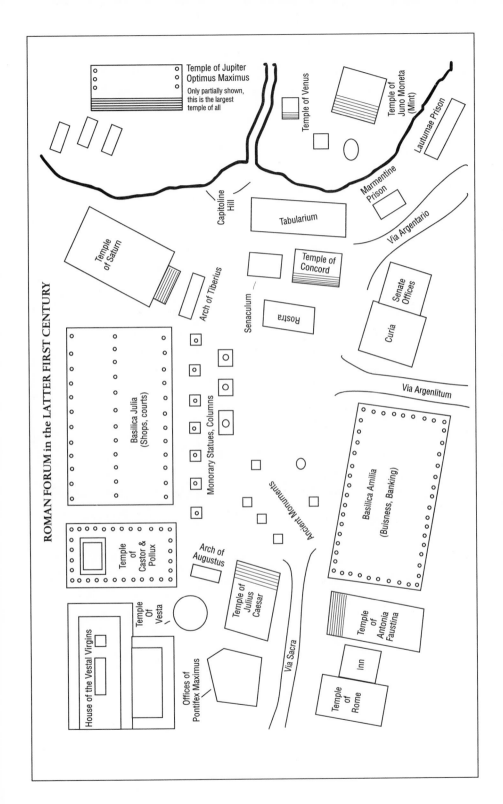

ROMAN FORUM in the LATTER FIRST CENTURY

Temple of Jupiter Optimus Maximus

Only partially shown, this is the largest temple of all

Temple of Venus

Temple of Juno Moneta (Mint)

Lautumae Prison

Marmentine Prison

Via Argentario

Capitoline Hill

Tabularium

Temple of Saturn

Arch of Tiberius

Temple of Concord

Senate Offices

Senaculum

Rostra

Curia

Via Argenlitum

Basilica Julia (Shops, courts)

Monorary Statues, Columns

Basilica Amilia (Buisness, Banking)

Temple of Castor & Pollux

Arch of Augustus

Ancient Monuments

Temple of Vesta

Temple of Julius Caesar

Temple of Antonia Faustina

House of the Vestal Virgins

Offices of Pontifex Maximus

Via Sacra

Inn

Temple of Rome

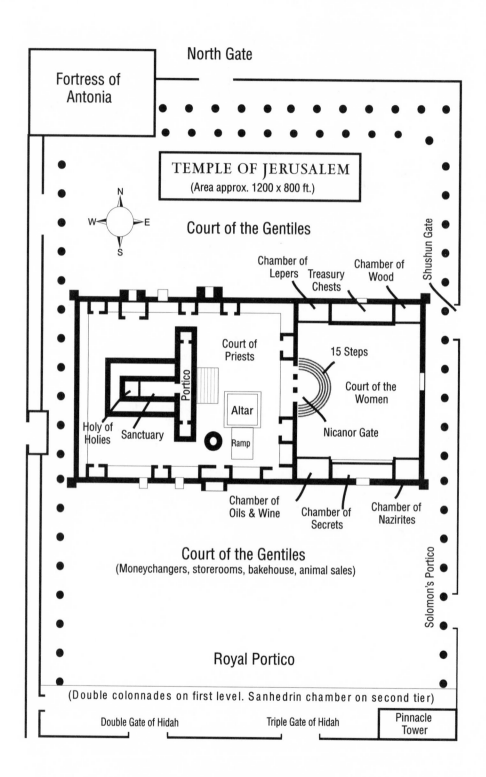

North Gate

Fortress of Antonia

TEMPLE OF JERUSALEM
(Area approx. 1200 x 800 ft.)

Court of the Gentiles

Chamber of Lepers

Treasury Chests

Chamber of Wood

Shushun Gate

Court of Priests

15 Steps

Court of the Women

Portico

Altar

Holy of Holies

Sanctuary

Ramp

Nicanor Gate

Chamber of Oils & Wine

Chamber of Secrets

Chamber of Nazirites

Court of the Gentiles
(Moneychangers, storerooms, bakehouse, animal sales)

Solomon's Portico

Royal Portico

(Double colonnades on first level. Sanhedrin chamber on second tier)

Double Gate of Hidah

Triple Gate of Hidah

Pinnacle Tower

672 · 13) The Temple at Jerusalem

14) Paul [from a fresco in the Roman Catacombs] · 6 7 3

15A) Athena · 15B) Artemis · 15C) Isis · 15D) Mithras sacrificing a bull

16A) The Temple at Jerusalem

16B) Herod's Palace

17) The Circus Maximus

18) The Flavian Amphitheater

678 · 19) Attalos?

ABOUT *the* AUTHOR...

WRITING AND REPORTING have been at the heart of Jim Snyder's life since he graduated from Northwestern University's Medill School of Journalism in 1958. While studying for his master's in political science at The George Washington University, he served as a Washington corespondent for several business magazines. Over the next 25 years he would write for more than 100 magazines ranging from business newsmagazines and medical journals to the Harvard Business Review and Parade magazine. More recently, he served as Chairman / CEO of a company that founded seven magazines and several related conferences.

DURING ALL THOSE YEARS, church, history and travel were always a big part of Jim Snyder's life. More recently, these interests have centered on the roots of the early Christian church, and this book is an attempt to shed light on them through the prisms of journalism and political science.

ORDER FORM *for* ADDITIONAL COPIES

BOOK INFO: All God's Children, by James D. Snyder
ISBN# 0-9675200-0-2 / LCCN# 99 096082
Pharoscan, Inc. / SAN# 253-0317

FAX ORDERS: **(419) 281-6883**

TELEPHONE ORDERS: **(800) 247-6553** Please have your credit card ready.

E-MAIL ORDERS: **order@bookmasters.com**

WEB ORDERS: **www.bookmasters.com**

QUANTITY: _____ copies of *All God's Children*

NAME: _____

ORGANIZATION: _____

ADDRESS: _____

CITY / STATE / ZIP CODE: _____

TELEPHONE: _____

EMAIL ADDRESS: _____

PAYMENT: ❏Cheque (must be a US bank) ❏Credit card

CREDIT CARD: ❏Visa ❏MasterCard ❏AMEX ❏Discover

NUMBER: _____

EXPIRATION: _____

AUTHORIZED SIGNATURE: _____

PRICE: $28.95 per book

US SHIPPING: $4 for first book / $2 for each additional copy

INTERNATL SHIPPING: $9 for first book / $5 for each additional copy

TOTAL COST (Price of Book x quantity + Shipping + Tax) _____
(Ohio and Florida residents please add sales tax)